Jack Higgins

Jack Higgins

The Eagle
Has Landed

Luciano's
Luck

CHANCELLOR
PRESS

The Eagle Has Landed first published in Great Britain
in 1975 by William Collins Sons & Co. Ltd.
Luciano's Luck first published in Great Britain
in 1981 by William Collins Sons & Co. Ltd.

This edition first published in Great Britain in 1984 by

Chancellor Press
59 Grosvenor Street
London, W.1.

ISBN 0 907486 57 6

Printed in Great Britain at The Pitman Press, Bath

Jack Higgins

Contents

The Eagle Has Landed
9

Luciano's Luck
393

Jack
Higgins

The Eagle
Has Landed

For my children, Sarah, Ruth, young Seán and little Hannah, who each in their separate ways have suffered and sweated through this one, but most of all for Amy who has learned to live with that significant little click each time she lifts the telephone for more than two years now . . .

AUTHOR'S NOTE

At precisely one o'clock on the morning of Saturday
6 November 1943, Heinrich Himmler, Reichsführer of the
SS and Chief of State Police, received a simple message.
The Eagle has landed. It mean that a small force of German
paratroops were at that moment safely in England and poised
to snatch the British Prime Minister, Winston Churchill,
from the Norfolk country house near the sea, where he was
spending a quiet weekend. This book is an attempt to recreate
the events surrounding that astonishing exploit. A least fifty
per cent of it is documented historical fact. The reader must
decide for himself how much of the rest is a matter of
speculation, or fiction . . .

Now the field of battle is a land of standing corpses; those determined to die will live; those who hope to escape with their lives will die.

Wu Ch'i

1

Someone was digging a grave in one corner of the cemetery as I went in through the lychgate. I remember that quite clearly because it seemed to set the scene for nearly everything that followed.

Five or six rooks lifted out of the beech trees at the west end of the church like bundles of black rags, calling angrily to each other as I threaded my way between the tombstones and approached the grave, turning up the collar of my trenchcoat against the driving rain.

Whoever was down there was talking to himself in a low voice. It was impossible to catch what he was saying. I moved to one side of the pile of fresh earth, dodging another spadeful, and peered in. 'Nasty morning for it.'

He looked up, resting on his spade, an old, old man in a cloth cap and shabby, mud-stained suit, a grain sack draped across his shoulders. His cheeks were sunken and hollow, covered with a grey stubble, and his eyes full of moisture and quite vacant.

I tried again. 'The rain,' I said.

Some kind of understanding dawned. He glanced up at the sombre sky and scratched his chin. 'Worse before it gets better, I'd say.'

'It must make it difficult for you,' I said. There was at least six inches of water swilling about in the bottom.

He poked at the far side of the grave with his spade and it split wide open, like something rotten bursting, earth showering down. 'Could be worse. They put so many in this little boneyard over the years, people aren't planted in earth any more. They're buried in human remains.'

He laughed, exposing toothless gums, then bent down, scrabbled in the earth at his feet and held up a finger-bone. 'See what I mean?'

The appeal, even for the professional writer, of life in all its infinite variety, definitely has its limits on occasion and I decided it was time to move on. 'I have got it right? This is a Catholic church?'

'All Romans here,' he said. 'Always have been.'

'Then maybe you can help me. I'm looking for a grave or perhaps even a monument inside the church. Gascoigne – Charles Gascoigne. A sea captain.'

'Never heard of him,' he said. 'And I've been sexton here forty-one years. When was he buried?'

'Around sixteen-eighty-five.'

His expression didn't alter. He said calmly, 'Ah, well then, before my time, you see. Father Vereker – now he might know something.'

'Will he be inside?'

'There or the presbytery. Other side of the trees behind the wall.'

At that moment, for some reason or other, the rookery in the beech trees above our heads erupted into life, dozens of rooks wheeling in the rain, filling the air with their clamour. The old man glanced up and hurled the finger-bone into the branches. And then he said a very strange thing.

'Noisy bastards!' he called. 'Get back to Leningrad.'

I'd been about to turn away, but paused, intrigued. 'Leningrad?' I said. 'What makes you say that?'

'That's where they come from. Starlings, too. They've been ringed in Leningrad and they turn up here in October. Too cold for them over there in the winter.'

'Is that so?' I said.

He had become quite animated now, took half a cigarette from behind his ear and stuck it in his mouth. 'Cold enough to freeze the balls off a brass monkey over there in the winter. A lot of Germans died at Leningrad during the war. Not shot or anything. Just froze to death.'

By now I was quite fascinated. I said, 'Who told you all that?'

'About the birds?' he said, and suddenly he changed completely, his face suffused by a kind of sly cunning. 'Why, Werner told me. He knew all about birds.'

'And who was Werner?'

'Werner?' He blinked several times, the vacant look appearing on his face again, though whether genuine or simulated it was impossible to tell. 'He was a good lad, Werner. A good lad. They shouldn't have done that to him.'

He leaned over his spade and started to dig again, dismissing me completely. I stayed there for a moment longer, but it was obvious that he had nothing more to say, so, reluctantly, because it had certainly sounded as if it might be a good story, I turned and worked my way through the tombstones to the main entrance.

I paused inside the porch. There was a notice-board on the wall in some sort of dark wood, the lettering in faded gold paint. *Church of St Mary and All the Saints, Studley Constable* across the top and, underneath, the times for Mass and Confession. At the bottom it said *Father Philip Vereker, S.J.*

The door was oak and very old, held together by iron bands, studded with bolts. The handle was a bronze lion's head with a large ring in its mouth and the ring had to be turned to one side before the door opened, which it did finally with a slight, eerie creaking.

I had expected darkness and gloom inside, but instead, found what was in effect a medieval cathedral in miniature, flooded with light and astonishingly spacious. The nave arcades were superb, great Norman pillars soaring up to an incredible wooden roof, richly carved with an assortment of figures, human and animal, which were really in quite remarkable condition. A row of round, clerestory windows on either side at roof level were responsible for a great deal of the light which had so surprised me.

There was a beautiful stone font and on the wall beside it, a painted board listed all the priests who had served over the years, starting with a Rafe de Courcey in 1132 and ending with Vereker again, who had taken over in 1943.

Beyond was a small, dark chapel, candles flickering in front of an image of the Virgin Mary that seemed to float there in the half-light. I walked past it and down the centre aisle between the pews. It was very quiet, only the ruby light of the sanctuary lamp, a fifteenth-century Christ high on his cross down by the altar, rain drumming against the high windows.

There was a scrape of a foot on stone behind me and a dry, firm voice said, 'Can I help you?'

I turned and found a priest standing in the entrance of the Lady Chapel, a tall gaunt man in a faded black cassock. He had iron-grey hair cropped close to the skull and the eyes were set deep in their sockets as if he had been recently ill, an impression heightened by the tightness of the skin across the cheekbones. It was a strange face. Soldier or scholar, this man could have been either, but that didn't surprise me, remembering from the notice board that he was a Jesuit. But it was also a face that lived with pain as a constant companion if I was any judge and, as he came forward, I saw that he leaned heavily on a blackthorn stick and dragged his left foot.

'Father Vereker?'

'That's right.'

'I was talking to the old man out there, the sexton.'

'Ah, yes, Laker Armsby.'

'If that's his name. He thought you might be able to help me.' I held out my hand. 'My name's Higgins, by the way. Jack Higgins. I'm a writer.'

He hesitated slightly before shaking hands, but only because he had to switch the blackthorn from his right hand to his left. Even so, there was a definite reserve, or so it seemed to me. 'And how can I help you, Mr Higgins?'

'I'm doing a series of articles for an American magazine,' I said. 'Historical stuff. I was over at St Margaret's at Cley, yesterday.'

'A beautiful church.' He sat down in the nearest pew. 'Forgive me, I tire rather easily these days.'

'There's a table tomb in the churchyard there,' I went on. 'Perhaps you know it? "To James Greeve . . ." '

He cut in on me instantly. '. . . who was assistant to Sir Cloudesley Shovel in burning ye ships in Ye Port of Tripoly in "Barbary, January fourteenth, sixteen seventy-six." ' He showed that he could smile. 'But that's a famous inscription in these parts.'

'According to my researches, when Greeve was Captain of the *Orange Tree* he had a mate called Charles Gascoigne who later became a captain in the navy. He died of an old wound in sixteen-eighty-three and it seems Greeve had him brought up to Cley to be buried.'

'I see,' he said politely, but without any particular interest. In fact, there was almost a hint of impatience in his voice.

'There's no trace of him in Cley churchyard,' I said, 'or in the parish records and I've tried the churches at Wiveton, Glandford and Blakeney with the same result.'

'And you think he might be here?'

'I was going through my notes again and remembered that he'd been raised a Catholic as a boy and it occurred to me that he might have been buried in the faith. I'm staying at the Blakeney Hotel and I was talking to one of the barmen there who told me there was a Catholic church here at Studley Constable. It's certainly an out-of-the-way little place. Took me a good hour to find it.'

'All to no purpose, I'm afraid.' He pushed himself up. 'I've been here at St Mary's for twenty-eight years now and I can assure you I've never come across any mention of this Charles Gascoigne and St Mary's was not Roman Catholic at the time in question anyway.'

'Yes, I was wondering what happened to Henry the Eighth and the Reformation in these parts.'

'St Mary's became Church of England like most English churches of the period,' he said. 'But at the end of the last century the building was reconsecrated in the Roman Catholic faith.'

'Isn't that rather unique?' I asked.

'Not really.' He made no further attempt to elaborate and his impatience was clear.

It had been very much my last chance and I suppose I allowed my disappointment to show, but in any case, I persisted.' Can you be absolutely sure about Gascoigne. What about church records for the period? There might be an entry in the burial register.'

'The local history of this area happens to be a personal interest of mine,' he said with a certain acidity. 'There is not a document connected with this church with which I am not completely familiar and I can assure you that nowhere is there any mention of a Charles Gascoigne. And now, if you'll excuse me. My lunch will be ready.'

As he moved forward, the blackthorn slipped and he stumbled and almost fell. I grabbed his elbow and managed to stand on his left foot. He didn't even wince.

I said, 'I'm sorry, that was damned clumsy of me.'

He smiled for the second time. 'Nothing to hurt, as it happens.' He rapped at the foot with the blackthorn. 'A confounded nuisance, but, as they say, I've learned to live with it.'

It was the kind of remark which required no comment and he obviously wasn't seeking one. We went down the aisle together, slowly because of his foot, and I said, 'A remarkably beautiful church.'

'Yes, we're rather proud of it.' He opened the door for me. 'I'm sorry I couldn't be of more help.'

'That's all right.' I said. 'Do you mind if I have a look around the churchyard while I'm here?'

'A hard man to convince, I see.' But there was no malice in the way he said it. 'Why not? We have some very interesting stones. I'd particularly recommend you to the section at the west end. Early eighteenth-century and obviously done by the same local mason who did similar work at Cley.'

This time he was the one who held out his hand. As I took it, he said, 'You know, I thought your name was familiar. Didn't you write a book on the Ulster troubles last year?'

'That's right,' I said. 'A nasty business.'

'War always is, Mr Higgins.' His face was bleak. 'Man at his most cruel. Good-day to you.'

He closed the door and I moved into the porch. A strange encounter. I lit a cigarette and stepped into the rain. The sexton had moved on and for the moment I had the churchyard to myself, except for the rooks, of course. *The rooks from Leningrad.* I wondered about that again, then pushed the thought resolutely from my mind. There was work to be done. Not that I had any great hope after talking to Father Vereker, of finding Charles Gascoigne's tomb, but the truth was there just wasn't anywhere else to look.

I worked my way through methodically, starting at the west end, noticing in my progress the headstones he'd mentioned.

They were certainly curious. Sculptured and etched with vivid and rather crude ornaments of bones, skulls, winged hourglasses and archangels. Interesting, but entirely the wrong period for Gascoigne.

It took me an hour and twenty minutes to cover the entire area and at the end of that time I knew I was beaten. For one thing, unlike most country churchyards these days, this one was kept in very decent order. Grass cut, bushes trimmed back, very little that was overgrown or partially hidden from view or that sort of thing.

So, no Charles Gasgoigne. I was standing by the newly-dug grave when I finally admitted defeat. The old sexton had covered it with a tarpaulin against the rain and one end had fallen in. I crouched down to pull it back into position and as I started to rise, noticed a strange thing.

A yard or two away, close in to the wall of the church at the base of the tower, there was a flat tombstone set in a mound of green grass. It was early eighteenth-century, an example of the local mason's work I've already mentioned. It had a superb skull and crossbones at its head and was dedicated to a wool merchant named Jeremiah Fuller, his wife and two children. Crouched down as I was, I became aware that there was another slab beneath it.

The Celt in me rises to the top easily and I was filled with a sudden irrational excitement as if conscious that I stood on the threshold of something. I knelt over the tombstone and tried to get my fingers to it, which proved to be rather difficult. But then, quite suddenly, it started to move.

'Come on, Gascoigne,' I said softly. 'Let's be having you.'

The slab slid to one side, tilting on the slope of the mound and all was revealed. I suppose it was one of the most astonishing moments of my life. It was a simple stone, with a German cross at the head – what most people would describe as an iron cross. The inscription beneath it was in German. It read *Hier ruhen Oberstleutnant Kurt Steiner und 13 Deutsche Fallschirmjäger gefallen am 6 November 1943.*

My German is indifferent at the best of times, mainly from lack of use, but it was good enough for this. *Here lies Lieutenant-*

Colonel Kurt Steiner and 13 German paratroopers, killed in action on the 6th November, 1943.

I crouched there in the rain, checking my translation carefully but no, I was right, and that didn't make any kind of sense. To start with, I happened to know, as I'd once written an article on the subject, that when the German Military Cemetery was opened at Cannock Chase in Staffordshire in 1967, the remains of the four thousand, nine hundred and twenty-five German servicemen who died in Britain during the First and Second World Wars were transferred there.

Killed in Action, the inscription said. No, it was quite absurd. An elaborate hoax on somebody's part. It had to be.

Any further thoughts on the subject were prevented by a sudden outraged cry. 'What in the hell do you think you're doing?'

Father Vereker was hobbling towards me through the tombstones, holding a large black umbrella over his head.

I called cheerfully, 'I think you'll find this interesting, Father. I've made a rather astonishing find.'

As he drew closer, I realized that something was wrong. Something was very wrong indeed, for his face was white with passion and he was shaking with rage. 'How dare you move that stone? Sacrilege – that's the only word for it.'

'All right,' I said. 'I'm sorry about that, but look what I've found underneath.'

'I don't give a damn what you've found underneath. Put it back at once.'

I was beginning to get annoyed myself. 'Don't be silly. Don't you realize what it says here? If you don't read German then allow me to tell you. "Here lies Lieutenant-Colonel Kurt Steiner and thirteen German paratroopers killed in action sixth November nineteen-forty-three." Now don't you find that absolutely bloody fascinating?'

'Not particularly.'

'You mean you've seen it before.'

'No, of course not.' There was something hunted about him now, an edge of desperation to his voice when he added, 'Now will you kindly replace the original stone?'

I didn't believe him, not for a moment. I said. 'Who was he, this Steiner? What was it all about?'

'I've already told you, I haven't the slightest idea,' he said, looking more hunted still.

And then I remembered something. 'You were here in nineteen-forty-three, weren't you? That's when you took over the parish. It says so on the board inside the church.'

He exploded, came apart at the seams. 'For the last time, will you replace that stone as you found it?'

'No,' I said. 'I'm afraid I can't do that.'

Strangely enough, he seemed to regain some kind of control of himself at that point. 'Very well,' he said calmly. 'Then you will oblige me by leaving at once.'

There seemed little point in arguing, considering the state of mind he was in, so I said briefly, 'All right, Father, if that's the way you want it.'

I had reached the path when he called, 'And don't come back. If you do I shall call the local police without the slightest hesitation.'

I went out through the lychgate, got into the Peugeot and drove away. His threats didn't worry me. I was too excited for that, too intrigued. Everything about Studley Constable was intriguing. It was one of those places that seem to turn up in North Norfolk and nowhere else. The kind of village that you find by accident one day and can never find again, so that you begin to question whether it ever existed in the first place.

Not that there was very much of it. The church, the old presbytery in its walled garden, fifteen or sixteen cottages of one kind or another scattered along the stream, the old mill with its massive water wheel, the village inn on the opposite side of the green, the Studley Arms.

I pulled into the side of the road beside the stream, lit a cigarette and gave the whole thing a little quiet thought. Father Vereker was lying. He'd seen that stone before, he knew its significance, of that I was convinced. It was rather ironic when one thought about it. I'd come to Studley Constable by chance in search of Charles Gascoigne. Instead I'd discovered something vastly more intriguing, a genuine mystery. But what was I going to do about it, that was the thing?

The solution presented itself to me almost instantly in the person of Laker Armsby, the sexton, who appeared from a narrow alley between two cottages. He was still splashed with mud, still had that old grain sack over his shoulders. He crossed the road and entered the Studley Arms and I got out of the Peugeot instantly and went after him.

According to the plate over the entrance, the licensee was one George Henry Wilde. I opened the door and found myself in a stone-flagged corridor with panelled walls. A door to the left stood ajar and there was a murmur of voices, a burst of laughter.

Inside, there was no bar, just a large, comfortable room with an open fire on a stone hearth, several high-backed benches, a couple of wooden tables. There were six or seven customers and none of them young. I'd have said that sixty was about the average age – a pattern that's distressingly common in such rural areas these days.

They were countrymen to the backbone, faces weathered by exposure, tweed caps, gumboots. Three played dominoes watched by two more, an old man sat by the fire playing a mouth-organ softly to himself. They all looked up to consider me with the kind of grave interest close-knit groups always have in strangers.

'Good afternoon,' I said.

Two or three nodded in a cheerful enough way, though one massively-built character with a black beard flecked with grey didn't look too friendly. Laker Armsby was sitting at a table on his own, rolling a cigarette between his fingers laboriously, a glass of ale in front of him. He put the cigarette in his mouth and I moved to his side and offered him a light. 'Hello, there.'

He glanced up blankly and then his face cleared. 'Oh, it's you again. Did you find Father Vereker then?'

I nodded. 'Will you have another drink?'

'I wouldn't say no.' He emptied his glass in a couple of swallows. 'A pint of brown ale would go down very nicely. Georgy!'

I turned and found a short, stocky man in shirt-sleeves standing behind me, presumably the landlord, George Wilde. He seemed about the same age range as the others and was a reasonable enough looking man except for one unusual feature. At some time in his life he'd been shot in the face at close quarters. I'd seen enough gunshot wounds in my time to be certain of that. In his case the bullet had scoured a furrow in his left cheek, obviously taking bone with it as well. His luck was good.

He smiled pleasantly. 'And you, sir?'

I told him I'd have a large vodka and tonic which brought amused looks from the farmers or whatever they were, but that didn't particularly worry me as it happens to be the only alcohol I can drink with any kind of pleasure. Laker Armsby's hand-rolled cigarettes hadn't lasted too long so I gave him one of mine which he accepted with alacrity. The drinks came and I pushed his ale across to him.

'How long did you say you'd been sexton up at St Mary's?'

'Forty-one years.'

He drained his pint glass. I said, 'Here, have another and tell me about Steiner.'

The mouth-organ stopped playing abruptly, all conversation died. Old Laker Armsby stared at me across the top of his glass, that look of sly cunning on his face again. 'Steiner?' he said. 'Why, Steiner was . . .'

George Wilde cut in, reached for the empty glass and ran a cloth over the table. 'Right, sir, time please.'

I looked at my watch. It was two-thirty. I said. 'You've got it wrong. Another half-hour till closing time.'

He picked up my glass of vodka and handed it to me. 'This is a free house, sir, and in a quiet little village like this we generally do as we please without anybody getting too upset about it. If I say I'm closing at two-thirty then two-thirty it is.' He smiled amiably. 'I'd drink up if I were you, sir.'

There was tension in the air that you could cut with a knife. They were all sitting looking at me, hard, flat faces, eyes like stones and the giant with the black beard moved across to the end of the table and leaned on it, glaring at me.

'You heard him,' he said in a low, dangerous voice. 'Now drink up like a good boy and go home, wherever that is.'

I didn't argue because the atmosphere was getting worse by the minute. I drank my vodka and tonic, taking a certain amount of time over it, though whether to prove something to them or myself I'm not certain, then I left.

Strange, but I wasn't angry, just fascinated by the whole incredible affair and by now, of course, I was too far in to draw back. I had to have some answers and it occurred to me that there was a rather obvious way of getting them.

I got into the Peugeot, turned over the bridge and drove up out of the village, passing the church and the presbytery, taking the road to Blakeney. A few hundred yards past the church, I turned the Peugeot into a cart track, left it there and walked back, taking a small Pentax camera with me from the glove compartment of the car.

I wasn't afraid. After all, on one famous occasion I'd been escorted from the Europa Hotel in Belfast to the airport by men with guns in their pockets who'd suggested I got the next plane out for the good of my health and didn't return. But I had and on several occasions; had even got a book out of it.

When I went back into the churchyard I found the stone to Steiner and his men exactly as I'd left it. I checked the inscription once again just to make sure I wasn't making a fool of myself, took several photos of it from different angles, then hurried to the church and went inside.

There was a curtain across the base of the tower and I went behind it. Choirboys' scarlet cottas and white surplices hung neatly on a rail, there was an old iron-bound trunk, several bell ropes trailed down through the gloom above and a board on the wall informed the world that on 22 July 1936, a peal of five thousand and fifty-eight changes of Bob Minor was rung at the church. I was interested to note that Laker Armsby was listed as one of the six bell-ringers involved.

Even more interesting was a line of holes cutting across the board which had at some time been filled in with plaster and stained. They continued into the masonry, for all the world like a machine-gun burst, but that was really too outrageous.

What I was after was the burial register and there was no sign of any kind of books or documents there. I went out through the curtain and almost instantly noticed the small door in the wall behind the font. It opened easily enough when I tried the handle and I stepped inside and found myself in what was very obviously the sacristy, a small, oak-panelled room. There was a rack containing a couple of cassocks, several surplices and copes, an oak cupboard and a large, old-fashioned desk.

I tried the cupboard first and struck oil at once. Every kind of ledger possible was in there, stacked neatly on one of the shelves. There were three burial registers and 1943 was in the second one. I leafed through the pages quickly, conscious at once of a feeling of enormous disappointment.

There were two deaths entered during November 1943 and they were both women. I hurriedly worked my way back to the beginning of the year, which didn't take very long, then closed the register and replaced it in the cupboard. So one very obvious avenue was closed to me. If Steiner, whoever he was, had been buried here, then he should have gone into the register. That was an incontrovertible point of English law. So what in the hell did it all mean?

I opened the sacristy door and stepped out, closing it behind me. There were two of them there from the pub. George Wilde and the man with the black beard whom I was disturbed to notice carried a double-barrelled shotgun.

Wilde said gently, 'I did advise you to move on, sir, you must admit that. Now why weren't you sensible?'

The man with the black beard said, 'What in the hell are you waiting for? Let's get this over with.'

He moved with astonishing speed for a man of such size and grabbed hold of the lapels of my trenchcoat. In the same moment the sacristy door opened behind me and Vereker stepped out. God knows where he'd come from, but I was distinctly pleased to see him.

'What on earth's going on here?' he demanded.

Blackbeard said, 'You just leave this to us, Father, we'll handle it.'

'You'll handle nothing, Arthur Seymour,' Vereker said. 'Now step back.'

Seymour stared at him flatly, still hanging on to me. I could have cut him down to size in several different ways, but there didn't seem a great deal of point.

Vereker said again, 'Seymour!' and there was really iron in his voice this time.

Seymour slowly released his grip and Vereker said, 'Don't come back again, Mr Higgins. It should be obvious to you by now that it wouldn't be in your best interests.'

'A good point.'

I didn't exactly expect a hue and cry, not after Vereker's intervention, but it hardly seemed politic to hang around, so I hurried back to the car at a jog trot. Further consideration of the whole mysterious affair could come later.

I turned into the cart track and found Laker Armsby sitting on the bonnet of the Peugeot rolling a cigarette. He stood up as I approached, 'Ah, there you are,' he said. 'You got away then?'

There was that same look of low cunning on his face again. I took out my cigarettes and offered him one. 'Do you want to know something?' I said. 'I don't think you're anything like as simple as you look.'

He grinned slyly and puffed out smoke in a cloud into the rain. 'How much?'

I knew what he meant instantly, but for the moment, played him along. 'What do you mean, how much?'

'Is it worth to you. To know about Steiner.'

He leaned back against the car looking at me, waiting, so I took out my wallet, extracted a five-pound note and held it up between my fingers. His eyes gleamed and he reached. I pulled back my hand.

'Oh, no. Let's have some answers first.'

'All right, mister. What do you want to know?'

'This Kurt Steiner – who was he?'

He grinned, the eyes furtive again, that sly, cunning smile on his lips. 'That's easy,' he said. 'He was the German lad who came here with his men to shoot Mr Churchill.'

I was so astonished that I simply stood there staring at him. He snatched the fiver from my hand, turned and cleared off at a shambling trot.

*

Some things in life are so enormous in their impact that they are almost impossible to take in, like a strange voice on the other end of a telephone telling you that someone you greatly loved has just died. Words become meaningless, the mind cuts itself off from reality for a little while, a necessary breathing space until one is ready to cope.

Which is roughly the state I found myself in after Laker Armsby's astonishing assertion. It wasn't just that it was so incredible. If there's one lesson I've learned in life it's that if you say a thing is impossible, it will probably happen next week. The truth is that the implications, if what Armsby had said was true, were so enormous that for the moment, my mind was incapable of handling the idea.

It was there. I was aware of its existence, but didn't consciously think about it. I went back to the Blakeney Hotel, packed my bags, paid my bill and started home, the first stop in a journey which, although I didn't realize it then, was to consume a year of my life. A year of hundreds of files, dozens of interviews, travelling half-way round the world. San Francisco, Singapore, the Argentine, Hamburg, Berlin, Warsaw and even – most ironic of all – the Falls Road in Belfast. Anywhere there seemed to be a clue, however slight, that would lead me to the truth and particularly, because he is somehow central to the whole affair, some knowledge, some understanding of the enigma that was Kurt Steiner.

2

In a sense a man called Otto Skorzeny started it all on Sunday 12 September 1943 by bringing off one of the most brilliantly audacious commando coups of the Second World War – thus proving once again to Adolf Hitler's entire satisfaction that he, as usual, had been right and the High Command of the Armed Forces wrong.

Hitler himself had suddenly wanted to know why the German Army did not have commando units like the English ones which had operated so successfully since the beginning of the war. To satisfy him, the High Command decided to form such a unit. Skorzeny, a young SS lieutenant, was kicking his heels in Berlin at the time after being invalided out of his regiment. He was promoted captain and made Chief of German Special Forces, none of which meant very much, which was exactly what the High Command intended.

Unfortunately for them, Skorzeny proved to be a brilliant soldier, uniquely gifted for the task in hand. And events were soon to give him a chance to prove it.

On 3 September 1943 Italy surrendered, Mussolini was deposed and Marshal Badoglio had him arrested and spirited away. Hitler insisted that his former ally be found and set free. It seemed an impossible task and even the great Erwin Rommel himself commented that he could see no good in the idea and hoped that it wouldn't be put on to his plate.

It wasn't, for Hitler gave it to Skorzeny personally who threw himself into the task with energy and determination and soon discovered that Mussolini was being held in the Sports Hotel on top of the ten-thousand-foot Gran Sasso in the Abruzzi, guarded by two hundred and fifty men.

Skorzeny landed by glider with fifty paratroopers, stormed the hotel and freed Mussolini. He was flown out in a tiny Stork spotter plane to Rome, then transhipped by Dornier to the Wolf's Lair,

Hitler's headquarters for the Eastern Front, which was situated at Rastenburg in a gloomy, damp and heavily-wooded part of East Prussia.

The feat earned Skorzeny a hatful of medals, including the Knight's Cross, and started him on a career that was to embrace countless similar daring exploits and make him a legend in his own time. The High Command, as suspicious of such irregular methods as senior officers the world over, remained unimpressed.

Not so the Führer. He was in his seventh heaven, transported with delight, danced as he had not danced since the fall of Paris and this mood was still with him on the evening of the Wednesday following Mussolini's arrival at Rastenburg, when he held a meeting in the conference hut to discuss events in Italy and the Duce's future role.

The map room was surprisingly pleasant, with pine walls and ceiling. There was a circular table at one end surrounded by eleven rush chairs, flowers in a vase in the centre. At the other end of the room was the long map table. The small group of men who stood beside it discussing the situation on the Italian front included Mussolini himself, Josef Goebbels, Reich Minister of Propaganda and Minister for Total War, Heinrich Himmler, Reichsführer of the SS, Chief of the State Police and of the State Secret Police, amongst other things, and Admiral Wilhelm Canaris, Chief of Military Intelligence, the Abwehr.

When Hitler entered the room they all stiffened to attention. He was in a jovial mood, eyes glittering, a slight fixed smile on his mouth, full of charm as only he could be on occasion. He descended on Mussolini and shook his hand warmly, holding it in both of his. 'You look better tonight, Duce. Decidedly better.'

To everyone else present the Italian dictator looked terrible. Tired and listless, little of his old fire left in him.

He managed a weak smile and the Führer clapped his hands. 'Well, gentlemen, and what should our next move be in Italy? What does the future hold? What in your opinion, Herr Reichsführer?'

Himmler removed his silver pince-nez and polished their lenses meticulously as he replied. 'Total victory, my Führer. What else? The presence of the Duce here with us now is ample proof of the brilliance with which you saved the situation after that traitor Badoglio signed an armistice.'

Hitler nodded, his face serious, and turned to Goebbels. 'And you, Josef?'

Goebbels' dark, mad eyes blazed with enthusiasm. 'I agree, my Führer. The liberation of the Duce had caused a great sensation at home and abroad. Friend and foe alike are full of admiration. We are able to celebrate a first-class moral victory, thanks to your inspired guidance.'

'And no thanks to my generals.' Hitler turned to Canaris, who was standing looking down at the map, a slight, ironic smile on his face. 'And you, Herr Admiral? You also think this a first-class moral victory?'

There are times when it pays to speak the truth, others when it does not. With Hitler it was always difficult to judge the occasion.

'My Führer, the Italian Battle Fleet now lies at anchor under the guns of the fortress of Malta. We have had to abandon Corsica and Sardinia and news is coming through that our old allies are already making arrangements to fight on the other side.'

Hitler had turned deathly pale, his eyes glittered, there was the faint damp of perspiration on his brow, but Canaris continued, 'As for the new Italian Socialist Republic as proclaimed by the Duce.' Here, he shrugged. 'Not a single neutral country so far, not even Spain, has agreed to set up diplomatic relations. I regret to say, my Führer, that in my opinion, they won't.'

'Your opinion?' Hitler exploded with fury. 'Your opinion? You're as bad as my generals and when I listen to them what happens? Failure everywhere.' He moved to Mussolini, who seemed rather alarmed, and placed an arm around his shoulders. 'Is the Duce here because of the High Command? No, he's here because I insisted that they set up a commando unit, because my intuition told me it was the right thing to do.'

Goebbels looked anxious, Himmler as calm and enigmatic as usual, but Canaris stood his ground. 'I implied no criticism of you personally, my Führer.'

Hitler had moved to the window and stood looking out, hands tightly clenched behind him. 'I have an instinct for these things and I knew how successful this kind of operation could be. A handful of brave men, daring all.' He swung round to face them. 'Without me there would have been no Gran Sasso because without me there would have been no Skorzeny.' He said that as if delivering Biblical writ. 'I don't wish to be too hard on you, Herr Admiral, but after all, what have you and your people at the Abwehr accomplished lately? It seems to me that all you can do is produce traitors like Dohnanyi.'

Hans von Dohnanyi, who had worked for the Abwehr, had been arrested for treason against the state in April.

Canaris was paler than ever now, on dangerous ground indeed. He said, 'My Führer, there was no intention on my part . . .'

Hitler ignored him and turned to Himmler. 'And you, Herr Reichsführer – what do you think?'

'I accept your concept totally, my Führer,' Himmler told him. 'Totally; but then, I'm also slightly prejudiced. Skorzeny, after all, is an SS officer. On the other hand, I would have thought the Gran Sasso affair to be exactly the kind of business the Brandenburgers were supposed to take care of.'

He was referring to the Brandenburg Division, a unique unit formed early in the war to perform special missions. Its activities were supposedly in the hands of Department Two of the Abwehr, which specialized in sabotage. In spite of Canaris's efforts, this elite force had, for the most part, been frittered away in hit-and-run operations behind the Russian lines which had achieved little.

'Exactly,' Hitler said. 'What have your precious Brandenburgers done? Nothing worth a moment's discussion.' He was working himself into a fury again now, and as always at such times, seemed able to draw on his prodigious memory to a remarkable degree.

'When it was originally formed, this Brandenburg unit, it was called the Company for Special Missions, and I remember hearing that von Hippel, its first commander, told them they'd be able to fetch the Devil from hell by the time he'd finished with them. I find that ironic, Herr Admiral, because as far as I can remember, they didn't bring me the Duce. I had to arrange for that myself.'

His voice had risen to a crescendo, the eyes sparked fire, the face was wet with perspiration. 'Nothing!' he shrieked. 'You have brought me nothing and yet men like that, with such facilities, you should have been capable of bringing me Churchill out of England.'

There was a moment of complete silence as Hitler glanced from face to face. 'Is that not so?'

Mussolini looked hunted, Goebbels nodded eagerly. It was Himmler who added fuel to the flames by saying quietly, 'Why not, my Führer? After all, anything is possible no matter how miraculous, as you have shown by bringing the Duce out of Gran Sasso.'

'Quite right.' Htler was calm again now. 'A wonderful opportunity to show us what the Abwehr is capable of, Herr Admiral.'

Canaris was stunned. 'My Führer, do I understand you to mean . . . ?'

'After all, an English commando unit attacked Rommel's headquarters in Africa,' Hitler said, 'and similar groups have raided the French coast on many occasions. Am I to believe that German boys are capable of less?' He patted Canaris on the shoulder and said affably, 'See to it, Herr Admiral. Get things moving. I'm sure you'll come up with something.' He turned to Himmler. 'You agree, Herr Reichsführer?'

'Certainly,' Himmler said without hesitation. 'A feasibility study at the very least – surely the Abwehr can manage that?'

He smiled slightly at Canaris who stood there, thunderstruck. He moistened dry lips and said in a hoarse voice. 'As you command, my Führer.'

Hitler put an arm around his shoulder. 'Good. I knew I could rely on you as always.' He stretched out his arm as if to pull them all forward and leaned over the map. 'And now, gentlemen – the Italian situation.'

*

Canaris and Himmler were returning to Berlin by Dornier that night. They left Rastenburg at the same time in separate cars for the nine-mile drive to the airfield. Canaris was fifteen minutes late and when he finally mounted the steps into the Dornier he was not in the best of moods. Himmler was already strapped into his seat and, after a moment's hesitation, Canaris joined him.

'Trouble?' Himmler asked as the plane bumped forward across the runway and turned into the wind.

'Burst tyre.' Canaris leaned back. 'Thanks very much, by the way. You were a great help back there.'

'Always happy to be of service.' Himmler told him.

They were airborne now, the engine note deepening as they climbed. 'M God, but he was really on form tonight,' Canaris said. 'Get Churchill. Have you ever heard anything so crazy?'

'Since Skorzeny got Mussolini out of Gran Sasso, the world will never be quite the same again. The Führer now believes miracles can actually take place and this will make life increasingly difficult for you and me, Herr Admiral.'

'Mussolini was one thing,' Canaris said. 'Without in any way detracting from Skorzeny's magnificent achievement, Winston Churchill would be something else again.'

'Oh, I don't know,' Himmler said. 'I've seen the enemy newsreels as you have. London one day – Manchester or Leeds the next. He walks the streets with that stupid cigar in his mouth talking to the people. I would say that of all the major world leaders, he is probably the least protected.'

'If you believe that, you'll believe anything,' Canaris said drily. 'Whatever else they are, the English aren't fools. MI five and six employ lots of very well-spoken young men who've been to Oxford or Cambridge and who'd put a bullet through your belly as soon as look at you. Anyway, take the old man himself. Probably carries a pistol in his coat pocket and I bet he's still a crackshot.'

An orderly brought them some coffee. Himmler said, 'So you don't intend to proceed in this affair?'

'You know what will happen as well as I do,' Canaris said. 'Today's Wednesday. He'll have forgotten the whole crazy idea by Friday.'

Himmler nodded slowly, sipping his coffee. 'Yes, I suppose you're right.'

Canaris stood up. 'Anyway, if you'll excuse me. I think I'll get a little sleep.'

He moved to another seat, covered himself with a blanket provided and made himself as comfortable as possible for the three-hour trip that lay ahead.

From the other side of the aisle Himmler watched him, eyes cold, fixed, staring. There was no expression on his face – none at all. He might have been a corpse lying there had it not been for the muscle that twitched constantly in his right cheek.

*

When Canaris reached the Abwehr offices at 74–76 Tirpitz Ufer in Berlin it was almost dawn. The driver who had picked him up at Tempelhof had brought the Admiral's two favourite dachshunds with him and when Canaris got out of the car, they scampered at his heels as he walked briskly past the sentries.

He went straight up to his office. Unbuttoning his naval greatcoat as he went, he handed it to the orderly who opened the door for him. 'Coffee,' the Admiral told him. 'Lots of coffee.' The orderly started to close the door and Canaris called him back. 'Do you know if Colonel Radl is in?'

'I believe he slept in his office last night, Herr Admiral.'

'Good, tell him I'd like to see him.'

The door closed. He was alone and suddenly tired and he slumped down in the chair behind the desk. Canaris's personal style was modest. The office was old-fashioned and relatively bare, with a worn carpet. There was a portrait of Franco on the wall with a dedication. On the desk was a marble paperweight with three bronze monkeys seeing, hearing and speaking no evil.

'That's me,' he said softly, tapping them on the head.

He took a deep breath to get a grip on himself: it was the very knife-edge of danger he walked in that insane world. There were things he suspected that even he should not have known. An attempt by two senior officers earlier that year to blow up Hitler's plane in flight from Smolensk to Rastenburg, for instance, and the constant threat of what might happen if von Dohnanyi and his friends cracked and talked.

The orderly appeared with a tray containing coffee pot, two cups and a small pot of real cream, something of a rarity in Berlin at that time. 'Leave it,' Canaris said. 'I'll see to it myself.'

The orderly withdrew and as Canaris poured the coffee, there was a knock at the door. The man who entered might have stepped straight off a parade ground, so immaculate was his uniform. A lieutenant-colonel of mountain troops with the ribbon for the Winter War, a silver wound badge and a Knight's Cross at his throat. Even the patch which covered his right eye had a regulation look about it, as did the black leather glove on his left hand.

'Ah, there you are, Max,' Canaris said. 'Join me for coffee and restore me to sanity. Each time I return from Rastenburg I feel increasingly that I need a keeper, or at least that someone does.'

Max Radl was thirty and looked ten or fifteen years older, depending on the day and weather. He had lost his right eye and left hand during the Winter War in 1941 and had worked for Canaris ever since being invalided home. He was at that time Head of Section Three, which was an office of Department Z, the Central Department of the Abwehr and directly under the Admiral's personal control. Section Three was a unit which was supposed to look after particularly difficult assignments and as such, Radl was authorized to poke his nose into any other Abwehr section that he wanted, an activity which made him considerably less than popular amongst his colleagues.

'As bad as that?'

'Worse,' Canaris told him. 'Mussolini was like a walking automaton, Goebbels hopped as usual from one foot to the other like some ten-year old schoolboy bursting for a pee.'

Radl winced, for it always made him feel decidedly uneasy when the Admiral spoke in that way of such powerful people. Although the offices were checked daily for microphones, one could never really be sure.

Canaris carried on, 'Himmler was his usual pleasant corpse-like self and as for the Führer . . .'

Radl cut in hastily. 'More coffee, Herr Admiral?'

Canaris sat down again. 'All he could talk about was Gran Sasso and what a bloody miracle the whole thing was and why didn't the Abwehr do something as spectacular.'

He jumped up, walked to the window and peered out through the curtains into the grey morning. 'You know what he suggests we do, Max? Get Churchill for him.'

Radl started violently. 'Good God, he can't be serious.'

'Who knows? One day, yes, another day, no. He didn't actually specify whether he wanted him alive or dead. This business with Mussolini has gone to his head. Now he seems to think anything is possible. Bring the Devil from Hell if necessary, was a phrase he quoted with some feeling.'

'And the others – how did they take it?' Radl asked.

'Goebbels was his usual amiable self, the Duce looked hunted. Himmler was the difficult one. Backed the Führer all the way. Said that the least we could do was look into it. A feasibility study, that was the phrase he used.'

'I see, sir.' Radl hesitated. 'You do think the Führer is serious?'

'Of course not.' Canaris went over to the army cot in the corner, turned back the blankets, sat down and started to unlace his shoes. 'He'll have forgotten it already. I know what he's like when he's in that kind of mood. Comes out with all sorts of rubbish.' He got into the cot and covered himself with the blanket. 'No, I'd say Himmler's the only worry. He's after my blood. He'll remind him about the whole miserable affair at some future date when it suits him, if only to make it look as if I don't do as I'm told.'

'So what do you want me to do?'

'Exactly what Himmler suggested. A feasibility study. A nice, long report that will look as if we've really been trying. For example, Churchill's in Canada at the moment, isn't he? Probably coming back by boat. You can always make it look as if you've seriously considered the possibility of having a U-boat in the right place at the right time. After all, as our Führer assured me personally not six hours ago, miracles do happen, but only under the right divine inspiration. Tell Krogel to wake me in one hour and a half.'

He pulled the blanket over his head and Radl turned off the light and went out. He wasn't at all happy as he made his way back to his office and not because of the ridiculous task he'd been given. That sort of thing was commonplace. In fact, he often referred to Section Three as the Department of Absurdities.

No, it was the way Canaris talked which worried him and as he was one of those individuals who liked to be scrupulously honest with himself, Radl was man enough to admit that he wasn't just worried about the Admiral. He was very much thinking of himself and his family.

Technically the Gestapo had no jurisdiction over men in uniform. On the other hand he had seen too many acquaintances simply disappear off the face of the earth to believe that. The infamous Night and Fog Decree in which various unfortunates were made to vanish into the mists of night in the most literal sense, was supposed to only apply to inhabitants of conquered territories, but as Radl was well aware, there were more than fifty thousand non-Jewish German citizens in concentration camps at that particular point in time. Since 1933, nearly two hundred thousand had died.

When he went into the office, Sergeant Hofer, his assistant, was going through the night mail which had just come in. He was a quiet, dark-haired man of forty-eight, an innkeeper from the Harz Mountains, a superb skier who had lied about his age to join up and had served with Radl in Russia.

Radl sat down behind his desk and gazed morosely at a picture of his wife and three daughters, safe in Bavaria in the mountains. Hofer, who knew the signs, gave him a cigarette and poured him a small brandy from a bottle of Courvoisier kept in the bottom drawer of the desk.

'As bad as that, Herr Oberst?'

'As bad as that, Karl,' Radl answered, then he swallowed his brandy and told him the worst.

*

And there it might have rested had it not been for an extraordinary coincidence. On the morning of the 22nd, exactly one week after his interview with Canaris, Radl was seated at his desk, fighting his way through a mass of paperwork which had accumulated during a three-day visit to Paris.

He was not in a happy mood and when the door opened and Hofer entered, he glanced up with a frown and said impatiently, 'For God's sake, Karl, I asked to be left in peace. What is it now?'

'I'm sorry, Herr Oberst. It's just that a report has come to my notice which I thought might interest you.'

'Where did it come from?'

'Abwehr One.'

Which was the department which handled espionage abroad and Radl was aware of a faint, if reluctant, stirring of interest. Hofer stood there waiting, hugging the manilla folder to his chest and Radl put down his pen with a sigh. 'All right, tell me about it.'

Hofer placed the file in front of him and opened it. 'This is the latest report from an agent in England. Code name Starling.'

Radl glanced at the front sheet as he reached for a cigarette from the box on the table. 'Mrs Joanna Grey.'

'She's situated in the northern part of Norfolk close to the coast, Herr Oberst. A village called Studley Constable.'

'But of course,' Radl said, suddenly rather more enthusiastic. 'Isn't she the woman who got the details of the Oboe installation?' He turned over the first two or three pages briefly and frowned. 'There's a hell of a lot of it. How does she manage that?'

'She has an excellent contact at the Spanish Embassy who puts her stuff through in the diplomatic bag. It's as good as the post. We usually take delivery within three days.'

'Remarkable,' Radl said. 'How often does she report?'

'Once a month. She also has a radio link, but this is seldom used, although she follows normal procedure and keeps her channel open three times a week for one hour in case she's needed. Her link man at this end is Captain Meyer.'

'All right, Karl,' Radl said. 'Get me some coffee and I'll read it.'

'I've marked the interesting paragraph in red, Herr Oberst. You'll find it on page three. I also put in a large-scale, British ordnance survey map of the area,' Hofer told him and went out.

The report was very well put together, lucid and full of information of worth. A general description of conditions in the area, the location of two new American B17 squadrons south of the Wash, a B24 squadron near Sheringham. It was all good, useful stuff without being terribly exciting. And then he came to page three and that brief paragraph, underlined in red, and his stomach contracted in a spasm of nervous excitement.

It was simple enough. The British Prime Minister, Winston Churchill, was to inspect a station of RAF Bomber Command near the Wash on the morning of Saturday 6 November. Later on the same day, he was scheduled to visit a factory near King's Lynn and make a brief speech to the workers.

Then came the interesting part. Instead of returning to London he intended to spend the week-end at the home of Sir Henry Willoughby, Studley Grange, which was just five miles outside the village of Studley Constable. It was a purely private visit, the details supposedly secret. Certainly no one in the village was aware of the plan, but Sir Henry, retired naval commander, had apparently been unable to resist confiding in Joanna Grey, who was, it seemed, a personal friend.

Radl sat staring at the report for a few moments, thinking about it, then he took out the ordnance survey map Hofer had provided and unfolded it. The door opened and Hofer appeared with the coffee. He placed the tray on the table, filled a cup and stood waiting, face impassive.

Radl looked up. 'All right, damn you. Show me where the place is. I expect you know.'

'Certainly, Herr Oberst.' Hofer placed a finger on the Wash and ran it south along the coast. 'Studley Constable, and here are Blakeney and Cley on the coast, the whole forming a triangle. I have looked at Mrs Grey's report on the area from before the war. An isolated place – very rural. A lonely coastline of vast beaches and salt marshes.'

Radl sat there staring at the map for a while and then came to a decision. 'Get me Hans Meyer, I'd like to have a word with him, only don't even hint what it's about.'

'Certainly, Herr Oberst.'

Hofer moved to the door. 'And Karl,' Radl added, 'every report she's ever sent. Everything we have on the entire area.'

The door closed and suddenly it seemed very quiet in the room. He reached for one of his cigarettes. As usual they were Russian, half-tobacco, half-cardboard tube. An affectation with some people who had served in the East. Radl smoked them because he liked them. They were far too strong and made him cough. That was a matter of indifference to him: the doctors had already warned of a considerably shortened lifespan due to his massive injuries.

He went and stood at the window feeling curiously deflated. It was all such a farce really. The Führer, Himmler, Canaris – like shadows behind the white sheet in a Chinese play. Nothing substantial. Nothing real and this silly business – this Churchill thing. While good men were dying on the Eastern Front in their thousands he was playing damned stupid games like this which couldn't possibly come to anything.

He was full of self-disgust, angry with himself for no known reason and then a knock at the door pulled him up short. The man who entered was of medium height and wore a Donegal tweed suit. His grey hair was untidy and the horn-rimmed spectacles made him seem curiously vague.

'Ah, there you are, Meyer. Good of you to come.'

Hans Meyer was at that time fifty years of age. During the First World War he had been a U-boat commander, one of the youngest in the German Navy. From 1922 onwards he had been wholly employed in intelligence work and was considerably sharper than he looked.

'Herr Oberst,' he said formally.

'Sit down, man, sit down,' Radl indicated a chair. 'I've been reading the lastest report from one of your agents – Starling. Quite fascinating.'

'Ah, yes.' Meyer took off his spectacles and polished them with a grubby handkerchief. 'Joanna Grey. A remarkable woman.'

'Tell me about her.'

Meyer paused, a slight frown on his face. 'What would you like to know, Herr Oberst?'

'Everything!' Radl said.

Meyer hesitated for a moment, obviously on the point of asking why and then thought better of it. He replaced his spectacles and started to talk.

*

Joanna Grey had been born Joanna Van Oosten in March, 1875, at a small town called Vierskop in the Orange Free State. Her father was a farmer and pastor of the Dutch Reform Church and, at the age of ten, had taken part in the Great Trek, the migration of some ten thousand Boer farmers between 1836 and 1838 from Cape Colony to new lands north of the Orange River to escape British domination.

She had married, at twenty, a farmer named Dirk Jansen. She had one child, a daughter born in 1898, a year before the outbreak of hostilities with the British of the following year that became known as the Boer War.

Her father raised a mounted commando and was killed near Bloemfontein in May, 1900. From that month the war was virtually over, but the two years which followed proved to be the most tragic of the whole conflict for, like others of his countrymen, Dirk Jansen fought on, a bitter guerrilla war in small groups, relying upon outlying farms for shelter and support.

The British cavalry patrol who called at the Jansen homestead on 11 June 1901, were in search of Dirk Jansen, ironically, and unknown to his wife, already dead of wounds in a mountain camp two months earlier. There was only Joanna, her mother and the child at home. She had refused to answer the corporal's questions and had been taken into the barn for an interrogation that had involved being raped twice.

Her complaint to the local area commander was turned down and, in any case, the British were at that time attempting to combat the guerrillas by burning farms, clearing whole areas and placing the population in what soon became known as concentration camps.

The camps were badly run – more a question of poor administration than of any deliberate ill-will. Disease broke out and in fourteen months over twenty thousand people died, amongst them Joanna Jansen's mother and daughter. Greatest irony of all, she would have died herself had it not been for the careful nursing she had received from an English doctor named Charles Grey who had been brought into her camp in an attempt to improve things after a public outcry in England over the disclosure of conditions.

Her hatred of the British was now pathological in its intensity, burned into her forever. Yet she married Grey when he proposed to her. On the other hand, she was twenty-eight years of age and broken by life. She had lost husband and child, every relative she had in the world, had not a penny to her name.

That Grey loved her there can be no doubt. He was fifteen years older and made few demands, was courteous and kind. Over the years she developed a certain affection for him, mixed with the kind of constant irritation and impatience one feels for an unruly child.

He accepted work with a London Bible Society as a medical missionary and for some years held a succession of appointments in Rhodesia and Kenya and finally amongst the Zulu. She could never understand his preoccupation with what to her were kaffirs, but accepted it, just as she accepted the drudgery of the teaching she was expected to do to help his work.

In March, 1925, he died of a stroke and on the conclusion of his affairs, she was left with little more than one hundred and fifty pounds to face life at the age of fifty. Fate had struck her another bitter blow, but she fought on, accepting a post as governess to an English civil servant's family in Cape Town.

During this time she started to interest herself in Boer nationalism, attending meetings held regularly by one of the more extreme organizations engaged in the campaign to take South Africa out of the British Empire. At one of these meetings she met a German civil engineer named Hans Meyer. He was ten years her junior and yet a romance flowered briefly, the first genuine physical attraction she had felt for anyone since her first marriage.

Meyer was in reality an agent of German Naval Intelligence, in Cape Town to obtain as much information as he could about naval installations in South Africa. By chance, Joanna Grey's employer worked for the Admiralty and she was able, at no particular risk, to take from the safe at his house certain interesting documents which Meyer had copied before she returned them.

She was happy to do it because she felt a genuine passion for him, but there was more to it than that. For the first time in her life she was striking a blow against England. Some sort of return for everything she felt had been done to her.

Meyer had gone back to Germany and continued to write to her and then, in 1929, when for most people the world was cracking into a thousand pieces as Europe nose-dived into a depression, Joanna Grey had the first piece of genuine good fortune of her entire life.

She received a letter from a firm of solicitors in Norwich, informing her that her late husband's aunt had died leaving her a cottage outside the village of Studley Constable in North Norfolk and an income of a little over four thousand pounds a year. There was only one snag. The old lady had had a sentimental regard for the house and it was a strict provision of the will that Joanna Grey would have to take up residence.

To live in England. The very idea made her flesh crawl, but what was the alternative? To continue her present life of genteel slavery, her only prospect a poverty-stricken old age? She obtained a book on Norfolk from the library and read it thoroughly, particularly the section covering the northern coastal area.

The names bewildered her. Stiffkey, Morston, Blakeney, Cley-next-the-Sea, salt marshes, shingle beaches. None of this made any kind of sense for her so she wrote to Hans Meyer with her problem and Meyer wrote back at once, urging her to go and promising to visit her as soon as he could.

It was the best thing she had ever done in her life. The cottage turned out to be a charming five-bedroomed Georgian house set in half an acre of walled garden. Norfolk at that time was still the most rural county in England, had changed comparatively little since the nineteenth century so that in a small village like Studley Constable she was regarded as a wealthy woman, a person of some importance. And another, stranger thing happened. She found the salt marshes and the shingle beaches fascinating, fell in love with the place, was happier than at any other time in her life.

Meyer came to England in the autumn of that year and visited her several times. They went for long walks together. She showed him everything. The endless beaches stretching into infinity, the salty marshes, the dunes of Blakeney Point. He never once referred to the period in Cape Town when she had helped him obtain the information he needed, she never once asked him about his present activities.

They continued to correspond and she visited him in Berlin in 1935. He showed her what National Socialism was doing for Germany. She was intoxicated by everything she saw, the enormous rallies, uniforms everywhere, handsome boys, laughing, happy women and children. She accepted completely that this was the new order. This was how it should be.

And then, one evening as they strolled back along Unter den Linden after an evening at the opera in which she had seen the Führer himself in his box, Meyer had calmly told her he was now with the Abwehr, and asked her if she would consider working for them as an agent in England.

She had said yes instantly, without needing to think about it, her whole body pulsing with an excitement that she had never known in her life before. So, at sixty, she had become a spy, this upper-class English lady, for so she was considered, with the pleasant face, walking the countryside in sweater and tweed skirt with her black retriever at her heels. A pleasant, white-haired lady who had a wireless transmitter and receiver in a small cubbyhole behind the panelling in her study and a contact in the Spanish Embassy in London who passed anything of a bulky nature out to Madrid in the diplomatic bag from where it was handed on to German Intelligence.

Her results had been consistently good. Her duties as a member of the Women's Voluntary Service took her into many military installations and she had been able to pass out details of most RAF heavy bomber stations in Norfolk and a great deal of additional relevant information. Her greatest coup had been at the beginning of 1943 when the RAF had introduced two new blind bombing devices which were hoped to greatly increase the success of the night bombing offensive against Germany.

The most important of these, Oboe, operated by linking up with two ground stations in England. One was in Dover and known as Mouse, the other was situated in Cromer on the North Norfolk coast and rejoiced in the name of Cat.

It was amazing how much information RAF personnel were willing to give to a kindly WVS lady handing out library books and cups of tea, and during half-a-dozen visits to the Oboe installation at Cromer, she was able to put one of her miniature cameras to good use. A single phone call to Señor Lorca, the clerk at the Spanish Embassy who was her contact, a trip by train to London for the day, a meeting in Green Park, was all it took.

Within twenty-four hours the information on Oboe was leaving England in the Spanish diplomatic bag. Within thirty-six, a delighted Hans Meyer was laying it on the desk of Canaris himself in his office at the Tirpitz Ufer.

*

When Hans Meyer had finished, Radl laid down the pen with which he had been making brief notes. 'A fascinating lady,' he said 'Quite remarkable. Tell me one thing – how much training has she done?'

'An adequate amount, Herr Oberst,' Meyer told him. 'She holidayed in the Reich in 1936 and 1937. On each occasion she received instruction in certain obvious matters. Codes, use of radio, general camera work, basic sabotage techniques. Nothing too advanced admittedly, except for her morse code which is excellent. On the other hand, her function was never intended to be a particularly physical one.'

'No, I can see that. What about use of weapons?'

'Not much need for that. She was raised on the veld. Could shoot the eye out of a deer at a hundred yards by the time she was ten years old.'

Radl nodded, frowning into space and Meyer said tentatively, 'Is there something special involved here, Herr Oberst? Perhaps I could be of assistance?'

'Not now,' Radl told him, 'but I could well need you in the near future, I'll let you know. For the moment, it will be sufficient to pass all files on Joanna Grey to this office and no radio communication until further orders.'

Meyer was aghast and quite unable to contain himself. 'Please, Herr Oberst, if Joanna is in any kind of danger . . .'

'Not in the slightest,' Radl said. 'I understand your concern, believe me, but there is really nothing more I can say at this time. A matter of the highest security, Meyer.'

Meyer recovered himself enough to apologize. 'Of course, Herr Oberst. Forgive me, but as an old friend of the lady . . .'

He withdrew. A moment or so after he had gone, Hofer came in from the anteroom carrying several files and a couple of rolled-up maps under his arm. 'The information you wanted, Herr Oberst, and I've also brought two British Admiralty charts which cover the coastal area – numbers one hundred and eight and one hundred and six.'

'I've told Meyer to let you have everything he has on Joanna Grey and I've told him no more radio communication,' Radl said. 'You take over from now on.'

He reached for one of those eternal Russian cigarettes and Hofer produced a lighter made from a Russian 7.62 mm cartridge case. 'Do we proceed, then, Herr Oberst?'

Radl blew a cloud of smoke and looked up at the ceiling. 'Are you familiar with the works of Jung, Karl?'

'The Herr Oberst knows I sold good beer and wine before the war.'

'Jung speaks of what he calls synchronicity. Events sometimes having a coincidence in time and, because of this, the feeling that some much deeper motivation is involved.'

'Herr Oberst?' Hofer said politely.

'Take this affair. The Führer, whom heaven protect naturally, has a brainstorm and comes up with the comical and absurd suggestion that we should emulate Skorzeny's exploit at Gran Sasso by getting Churchill, although whether alive or dead has not been specified. And the synchronicity rears its ugly head in a routine Abwehr report. A brief mention that Churchill will be spending a week-end no more than seven or eight miles from the coast at a remote country house in as quiet a part of the country as one could wish. You take my meaning? At any other time that report of Mrs Grey's would have meant nothing.'

'So we do proceed then, Herr Oberst?'

'It would appear that fate has taken a hand, Karl,' Radl said. 'How long did you say Mrs Grey's reports take to come in through the Spanish diplomatic bag?'

'Three days, Herr Oberst, if someone is waiting in Madrid to collect. No more than a week, even if circumstances are difficult.'

'And when is her next radio contact time?'

'This evening, Herr Oberst.'

'Good – send her this message.' Radl looked up at the ceiling again, thinking hard, trying to compress his thoughts. 'Very interested in your visitor of sixth November. Like to drop some friends in to meet him in the hope that they might persuade him to come back with them. Your early comments looked for by usual route with all relevant information.'

'Is that all, Herr Oberst?'

'I think so.'

*

That was Wednesday and it was raining in Berlin, but the following morning when Father Philip Vereker limped out through the lychgate of St Mary's and All the Saints, Studley Constable, and walked down through the village, the sun was shining and it was that most beautiful of all things, a perfect autumn day.

At that time, Philip Vereker was a tall, gaunt young man of thirty, the gauntness emphasized even more by the black cassock. His face was strained and twisted with pain as he limped along,

leaning heavily on his stick. He had only been discharged from
a military hospital four months earlier.

The younger son of a Harley Street surgeon, he had been a
brilliant scholar who at Cambridge had shown every sign of an
outstanding future. Then, to his family's dismay, he had
decided to train for the priesthood, had gone to the English
College in Rome and joined the Society of Jesus.

He had entered the army as a padre in 1940 and had finally
been assigned to the Parachute Regiment and had seen action
only once in November, 1942, in Tunisia when he had jumped
with units of the First Parachute Brigade with orders to seize
the airfield at Oudna, ten miles from Tunis. In the end, they
had been compelled to make a fighting retreat over fifty miles
of open country, strafed from the air every yard of the way and
under constant attack from ground forces.

One hundred and eighty made it to safety. Two hundred and
sixty didn't. Vereker was one of the lucky ones, in spite of a
bullet which had passed straight through his left ankle, chipping bone. By the time he reached a field hospital, sepsis had
set in. His left foot was amputated and he was invalided out.

Vereker found it difficult to look pleasant these days. The
pain was constant and would not go away, and yet he did
manage a smile as he approached Park Cottage and saw
Joanna Grey emerge pushing her bicycle, her retriever at her
heels.

'How are you, Philip?' she said. 'I haven't seen you for
several days.'

She wore a tweed skirt, polo-necked sweater underneath a
yellow oilskin coat and a silk scarf was tied around her white
hair. She really did look very charming with that South
African tan of hers that she never really lost.

'Oh, I'm all right,' Vereker said. 'Dying by inches of
boredom more than anything else. One piece of news since I
last saw you. My sister, Pamela. Remember me speaking of
her? She's ten years younger than me. A corporal in the
WAAF.'

'Of course I remember,' Mrs Grey said. 'What's happened?'

'She's been posted to a bomber station only fifteen miles from here at Pangbourne, so I'll be able to see something of her. She's coming over this week-end. I'll introduce you.'

'I'll look forward to that.' Joanna Grey climbed on to her bike.

'Chess tonight?' he asked hopefully.

'Why not? Come around eight and have supper as well. Must go now.'

She pedalled away along the side of the stream, the retriever, Patch, loping along behind. Her face was serious now. The radio message of the previous evening had come as an enormous shock to her. In fact, she had decoded it three times to make sure she hadn't made an error.

She had hardly slept, certainly not much before five and had lain there listening to the Lancasters setting out across the sea to Europe and then, a few hours later, returning. The strange thing was that after finally dozing off, she had awakened at seven-thirty full of life and vigour.

It was as if for the first time she had a really important task to handle. This – this was so incredible. To kidnap Churchill - snatch him from under the very noses of those who were supposed to be guarding him.

She laughed out loud. Oh, the damned English wouldn't like that. They wouldn't like that one little bit, with the whole world amazed.

As she coasted down the hill to the main road, a horn sounded behind her and a small saloon car passed and drew into the side of the road. The man behind the wheel had a large white moustache and the florid complexion of one who consumes whisky in large quantities daily. He was wearing the uniform of a lieutenant-colonel in the Home Guard.

'Morning, Joanna,' he called jovially.

The meeting could not have been more fortunate. In fact it saved her a visit to Studley Grange later in the day. 'Good morning, Henry,' she said and dismounted from her bike.

He got out of the car. 'We're having a few people on Saturday night. Bridge and so on. Supper afterwards. Nothing very special. Jean thought you might like to join us.'

'That's very kind of her. I'd love to,' Joanna Grey said. 'She must have an awful lot on, getting ready for the big event at the moment.'

Sir Henry looked slightly hunted and dropped his voice a little. 'I say, you haven't mentioned that to anyone else, have you?'

Joanna Grey managed to look suitably shocked. 'Of course not. You did tell me in confidence, remember.'

'Shouldn't have mentioned it at all actually, but then I knew I could trust you, Joanna.' He slipped an arm about her waist. 'Mum's the word on Saturday night, old girl, just for me, eh. Any of that lot get a hint of what's afoot and it will be all over the county.'

'I'd do anything for you, you know that,' she said calmly.

'Would you, Joanna?' His voice thickened and she was aware of his thigh pushed against her, trembling slightly. He pulled away suddenly. 'Well, I'll have to be off. Got an area command meeting in Holt.'

'You must be very excited,' she said, 'at the prospect of having the Prime Minister.'

'Indeed I am. Very great honour.' Sir Henry beamed. 'He's hoping to do a little painting and you know how pretty the views are from the Grange.' He opened the door and got back into the car. 'Where are you off to, by the way?'

She'd been waiting for exactly that question. 'Oh, a little bird watching as usual. I may go down to Cley or the marsh. I haven't made up my mind yet. There are some interesting passage migrants about at the moment.'

'You damn well watch it.' His face was serious. 'And remember what I told you.'

As local Home Guard commander he had plans covering every aspect of coastal defence in the area, including details of all mined beaches and – more importantly – beaches which were only supposedly mined. On one occasion, full of solicitude for her welfare, he had spent two careful hours going over the maps with her, showing her exactly where not to go on her bird-watching expeditions.

'I know the situation changes all the time,' she said. 'Perhaps you could come round to the cottage again with those maps of yours and give me another lesson.'

His eyes were slightly glazed. 'Would you like that?'

'Of course. I'm at home this afternoon, actually.'

'After lunch,' he said. 'I'll be there about two,' and he released the handbrake and drove rapidly away.

Joanna Grey got back on her bicycle and started to pedal down the hill towards the main road, Patch running behind. Poor Henry. She was really quite fond of him. Just like a child and so easy to handle.

Half-an-hour later, she turned off the coast road and cycled along the top of a dyke through desolate marshes known locally as Hobs End. It was a strange, alien world of sea creeks and mudflats and great pale barriers of reeds higher than a man's head, inhabited only by the birds, curlew and redshank and brent geese coming south from Siberia to winter on the mud flats.

Half-way along the dyke, a cottage crouched behind a mouldering flint wall, sheltered by a few sparse pine trees, It looked substantial enough with outbuildings and a large barn, but the windows were shuttered and there was a general air of desolation about it. This was the marsh warden's house and there had been no warden since 1940.

She moved on to a high ridge lined with pines. She dismounted from her bicycle and leaned it against a tree. There were sand dunes beyond and then a wide, flat beach stretching with the tide out a quarter of a mile towards the sea. In the distance she could see the Point on the other side of the estuary, curving in like a great bent forefinger, enclosing an area of channels and sand-banks and shoals that, on a rising tide, was probably as lethal as anywhere on the Norfolk coast.

She produced her camera and took a great many pictures from various angles. As she finished, the dog brought her a stick to throw, which he laid carefully down between her feet. She crouched and fondled his ears. 'Yes, Patch,' she said softly. 'I really think this will do very well indeed.'

She tossed the stick straight over the line of barbed wire which prevented access to the beach and Patch darted past the post with the notice board that said *Beware of mines*. Thanks to Henry Willoughby, to her certain knowledge there wasn't a mine on the beach.

To her left was a concrete blockhouse and a machine-gun post, a very definite air of decay to both of them, and in the gap between the pine trees, the tank trap had filled with drifting sand. Three years earlier, after the Dunkirk debacle, there would have been soldiers here. Even a year ago, Home Guard, but not now.

In June, 1940, an area up to twenty miles inland from the Wash to the Rye was declared a Defence Area. There were no restrictions on people living there, but outsiders had to have a good reason for visiting. All that had altered considerably and now, three years later, virtually no one bothered to enforce the regulations for the plain truth was that there was no longer any need.

Joanna Grey bent down to fondle the dog's ears again. 'You know what it is, Patch? The English just don't expect to be invaded any more.'

3

It was the following Tuesday before Joanna Grey's report arrived at the Tirpitz Ufer. Hofer had put a red flag out for it. He took it straight in to Radl who opened it and examined the contents.

There were photos of the marsh at Hobs End and the beach approaches, their position indicated only by a coded map reference. Radl passed the report itself to Hofer.

'Top priority. Get that deciphered and wait while they do it.'

The Abwehr had just started using the new Sonlar coding unit that took care in a matter of minutes of a task that had previously taken hours. The machine had a normal typewriter keyboard. The operator simply copied the coded message, which was automatically deciphered and delivered in a sealed reel. Even the operator did not see the actual message involved.

Hofer was back in the office within twenty minutes and waited in silence while the colonel read the report. Radl looked up with a smile and pushed it across the desk. 'Read that, Karl, just you read that. Excellent – really excellent. What a woman.'

He lit one of his cigarettes and waited impatiently for Hofer to finish. Finally the sergeant glanced up. 'It looks quite promising.'

'Promising? Is that the best you can do? Good God, man, it's a definite possibility. A very real possibility.'

He was more excited now than he had been for months, which was bad for him, for his heart, so appallingly strained by his massive injuries. The empty eye socket under the black patch throbbed, the aluminium hand inside the glove seemed to come alive, every tendon taut as a bow string. He fought for breath and slumped into his chair.

Hofer had the Courvoisier bottle out of the bottom drawer in an instant, half-filled a glass and held it to the colonel's lips. Radl swallowed most of it down, coughed heavily, then seemed to get control of himself again.

He smiled wryly. 'I can't afford to do that too often, eh, Karl? Only two more bottles left. It's like liquid gold these days.'

'The Herr Oberst shouldn't excite himself so,' Hofer said and added bluntly. 'You can't afford to.'

Radl swallowed some more of the brandy. 'I know, Karl, I know, but don't you see? It was a joke before – something the Führer threw out in an angry mood on a Wednesday, to be forgotten by Friday. A feasibility study, that was Himmler's suggestion and only because he wanted to make things awkward for the Admiral. The Admiral told me to get something down on paper. Anything, just so long as it showed we were doing our job.'

He got up and walked to the window. 'But now it's different, Karl. It isn't a joke any longer. It could be done.'

Hofer stood stolidly on the other side of the desk, showing no emotion. 'Yes, Herr Oberst, I think it could.'

'And doesn't that prospect move you in any way at all?' Radl shivered. 'God, but it frightens me. Bring me those Admiralty charts and the ordnance survey map.'

Hofer spread them on the desk and Radl found Hobs End and examined it in conjunction with the photos. 'What more could one ask for? A perfect dropping zone for parachutists and that week-end the tide comes in again by dawn and washes away any signs of activity.'

'But even quite a small force would have to be conveyed in a transport type of aircraft or a bomber,' Hofer pointed out. 'Can you imagine a Dornier or a Junkers lasting for long over the Norfolk coast these days, with so many bomber stations protected by regular night fighter patrols?'

'A problem,' Radl said, 'I agree, but hardly insurmountable. According to the Luftwaffe target chart for the area there is no low-level radar on that particular section of coast, which means an approach under six hundred feet would be undetected. But that kind of detail is immaterial at the moment. It can be handled later. A feasibility study, Karl, that's all we need at this stage. You agree that in theory it would be possible to drop a raiding party on that beach?'

Hofer said, 'I accept that as a proposition, but how do we get them out again? By U-boat?'

Radl looked down at the chart for a moment, then shook his head. 'No, not really practical. The raiding party would be too large. I know that they could all be crammed on board somehow, but the rendezvous would need to be some distance off-shore and there would be problems getting so many out there. It needs to be something simpler, more direct. An E-boat, perhaps. There's plenty of E-boat activity in that area in the coastal shipping lanes. I don't see any reason why one couldn't slip in between the beach and the Point. It would be on a rising tide and according to the report, there are no mines in that channel, which would simplify things considerably.'

'One would need Navy advice on that,' Hofer said cautiously. 'Mrs Grey does say in her report that those are dangerous waters.'

'Which is exactly what good sailors are for. Is there anything else you're not happy with?'

'Forgive me. Herr Oberst, but it would seem to me that there is a time factor involved which could be quite crucial to the success of the entire operation and frankly, I don't see how it could be reconciled.' Hofer pointed to Studley Grange on the ordnance survey map. 'Here is the target, approximately eight miles from the dropping zone. Considering the unfamiliar territory and the darkness, I would say it would take the raiding party two hours to reach it and however brief the visit, it would still take as long for the return journey. My estimate would be an action span of six hours. If one accepts that the drop would have to be made around midnight for security reasons, this means that the rendezvous with the E-boat would take place at dawn if not after, which would be completely unacceptable. The E-boat must have at least two hours of darkness to cover her departure.'

Radl had been lying back in the chair, face turned up to the ceiling, eyes closed. 'Very lucidly put, Karl. You're learning.' He sat up. 'You're absolutely right, which is why the drop would have to be made the night before.'

'Herr Oberst?' Hofer said, astonishment on his face. 'I don't understand.'

'It's quite simple. Churchill will arrive at Studley Grange during the afternoon or evening of the sixth and spend the night there. Our party drops in on the previous night, November fifth.'

Hofer frowned, considering the point. 'I can see the advantage, of course, Herr Oberst. The additional time would give them room to manoeuvre in case of any unlooked-for eventuality.'

'It would also mean that there would no longer be any problem with the E-boat,' Radl said. 'They could be picked up as early as ten or eleven o'clock on the Saturday.' He smiled and took another cigarette from the box. 'So, you agree that this, too, is feasible?'

'There would be a grave problem of concealment on the Saturday itself,' Hofer pointed out. 'Especially for a sizeable group.'

'You're absolutely right,' Radl stood up and started to pace up and down the room again. 'But it seems to me there's a rather obvious answer. Let me ask you a question as an old forester, Karl? If you wanted to hide a pine tree, what would be the safest place on earth?'

'In a forest of pines, I suppose.'

'Exactly. In a remote and isolated area like this a stranger – any stranger – stands out like a sore thumb, especially in wartime. No holidaymakers, remember. The British, like good Germans, spend their holidays at home to help the war effort. And yet, Karl, according to Mrs Grey's report, there are strangers constantly passing through the lanes and the villages every week who are accepted without question.' Hofer looked mystified and Radl continued. 'Soldiers, Karl, on manoeuvres, playing war-games, hunting each other through the hedgerows.' He reached for Joanna Grey's report from the desk and turned the pages. 'Here, on page three, for example, she speaks of this place Meltham House eight miles from Studley Constable. During the past year used as a training establishment for commando-type units on four occasions. Twice by British commandos, once by a similar unit composed of Poles and Czechs with English officers and once by American Rangers.'

He passed the report across and Hofer looked at it.

'All they need are British uniforms to be able to pass through the countryside with no difficulty. A Polish commando unit would do famously.'

'It would certainly take care of the language problem,' Hofer said. 'But that Polish unit Mrs Grey mentioned had English officers, not just English-speaking. If the Herr Oberst will forgive me for saying so, there's a difference.'

'Yes, you're right,' Radl told him. 'All the difference in the world. If the officer in charge is English or apparently English, then that would make the whole thing so much tighter.'

Hofer looked at his watch. 'If I might remind the Herr Oberst, the Heads of Section weekly meeting is due to start in the Admiral's office in precisely ten minutes.'

'Thank you, Karl.' Radl tightened his belt and stood up. 'So, it would appear that our feasibility study is virtually complete. We seem to have covered everything.'

'Except for what is perhaps the most important item of all, Herr Oberst.'

Radl was half-way to the door and now he paused. 'All right, Karl, surprise me.'

'The leader of such a venture, Herr Oberst. He would have to be a man of extraordinary abilities.'

'Another Otto Skorzeny,' Radl suggested.

'Exactly,' Hofer said. 'With, in this case, one thing more. The ability to pass as an Englishman.'

Radl smiled beautifully. 'Find him for me, Karl. I'll give you forty-eight hours.' He opened the door quickly and went out.

*

As it happened, Radl had to go to Munich unexpectedly the following day and it was not until after lunch on Thursday that he re-appeared in his office at the Tirpitz Ufer. He was extremely tired, having slept very little in Munich the night before. The Lancaster bombers of the RAF had pressed their attentions on that city with more than usual severity.

Hofer produced coffee instantly and poured him a brandy. 'Good trip, Herr Oberst?'

'Fair,' Radl said. 'Actually, the most interesting happening was when we were landing yesterday. Our Junkers was buzzed by an American Mustang fighter. Caused more than a little panic, I can tell you. Then we saw that it had a Swastika on the tailplace. Apparently it was one which had crash-landed and the Luftwaffe had put it into working order and were flight testing.'

'Extraordinary, Herr Oberst.'

Radl nodded. 'It gave me an idea, Karl. That little problem you had about Dorniers or Junkers surviving over the Norfolk coast.' And then he noticed a fresh green manilla folder on the desk. 'What's this?'

'The assignment you gave me, Herr Oberst. The officer who could pass as an Englishman. Took some digging out, I can tell you, and there's a report of some court martial proceedings which I've indented for. They should be here this afternoon.'

'Court martial?' Radl said. 'I don't like the sound of that.' He opened the file. 'Who on earth is this man?'

'His name is Steiner. Lieutenant-Colonel Kurt Steiner,' Hofer said, 'and I'll leave you in peace to read about him. It's an interesting story.'

*

It was more than interesting. It was fascinating.

Steiner was the only son of Major-General Karl Steiner, at present area commander in Brittany. He had been born in 1916 when his father was a major of artillery. His mother was American, daughter of a wealthy wool merchant from Boston who had moved to London for business reasons. In the month that her son was born, her only brother had died on the Somme as a captain in a Yorkshire infantry regiment.

The boy had been educated in London, spending five years at St Paul's during the period his father was military attaché at the German Embassy, and spoke English fluently. After his mother's tragic death in a car crash in 1931, he had returned to Germany with his father, but had continued to visit relatives in Yorkshire until 1938.

For a while, he had studied art in Paris, maintained by his father, the bargain being that if it didn't work out he would enter the Army. That was exactly what had happened. He had a brief period as a second lieutenant in the Artillery and in 1936 had answered the call for volunteers to do parachute training at Stendhal, more to relieve the boredom of military life than anything else.

It had become obvious immediately that he had a talent for that kind of freebooter soldiery. He'd seen ground action in Poland and parachuted into Narvik in the Norwegian campaign. As a full lieutenant he'd crash-landed by glider with the group that took the Albert Canal in 1940 during the big push for Belgium and had been wounded in the arm.

Greece came next – the Corinth Canal, and then a new kind of hell. May, 1941, a captain by then, in the big drop over Crete, severely wounded in savage fighting for Maleme airfield.

Afterwards, the Winter War. Radl was aware of a sudden chill in his bones at the very name. *God, will we ever forget Russia? he asked himself, those of us who were there then?*

As an acting major Steiner had led a special assault group of three hundred volunteers, dropped by night to contact and lead out two divisions cut off during the battle for Leningrad. He had emerged from that affair with a bullet in the right leg which had left him with a slight limp, a Knight's Cross and a reputation for that kind of cutting-out operation.

He had been in charge of two further affairs of a similar nature and had been promoted lieutenant-colonel in time to go to Stalingrad where he had lost half his men, but had been ordered out several weeks before the end when there were still planes running. In January, he and the one hundred and sixty-seven survivors of his original assault group were dropped near Kiev, once again to contact and lead out two infantry divisions which had been cut off. The end product was a fighting retreat for three hundred blood-stained miles and during the last week in April, Kurt Steiner had crossed into German lines with only thirty survivors of his original assault force.

There was an immediate award of the Oak Leaves to his Knight's Cross and Steiner and his men had been packed off to Germany by train as soon as possible, passing through Warsaw on the morning of the 1st of May. He had left it with his men that same evening under close arrest by order of Jurgen Stroop, SS Brigade-Führer and Major-General of Police.

There had been a court martial the following week. The details were missing, only the verdict was on file. Steiner and his men had been sentenced to serve as a penal unit to work on Operation Swordfish on Alderney in the German-occupied Channel Islands. Radl sat looking at the file for a moment, then closed it and pressed the buzzer for Hofer who came in at once.

'Herr Oberst?'

'What happened in Warsaw?'

'I'm not sure, Herr Oberst. I'm hoping to have the court martial papers available later this afternoon.'

'All right,' Radl said. 'What are they doing in the Channel Islands?'

'As far as I can find out, Operation Swordfish is a kind of suicide unit, Herr Oberst. Their purpose is the destruction of allied shipping in the Channel.'

'And how do they achieve that?'

'Apparently they sit on a torpedo with the charge taken out, Herr Oberst, and a glass cupola fitted to give the operator some protection. A live torpedo is slung underneath which during an attack, the operator is supposed to release, turning away at the last moment himself.'

'Good God Almighty,' Radl said in horror. 'No wonder they had to make it a penal unit.'

He sat there in silence for a while looking down at the file. Hofer coughed and said tentatively. 'You think he could be a possibility?'

'I don't see why not,' Radl said. 'I should imagine that anything would seem like an improvement on what he's doing now. Do you know if the Admiral is in?'

'I'll find out, Herr Oberst.'

'If he is, try and get me an appointment this afternoon. Time I showed him how far we've got. Prepare me an outline – nice and brief. One page only and type it yourself. I don't want anyone else getting wind of this thing. Not even in the Department.'

*

At that precise moment Lieutenant-Colonel Kurt Steiner was up to his waist in the freezing waters of the English Channel, colder than he had ever been in his life before, colder even than in Russia, cold eating into his brain as he crouched behind the glass cupola on his torpedo.

His exact situation was almost two miles to the north-east of Braye Harbour on the island of Alderney, and north of the smaller off-shore island of Burhou, although he was cocooned in a sea-fog of such density that for all he could see, he might as well have been at the end of the world. At least he was not alone.

Lifelines of hemp rope disappeared into the fog on either side of him like umbilical cords connecting him with Sergeant Otto Lemke on his left and Lieutenant Ritter Neumann on his right.

Steiner had been amazed to get called out that afternoon. Even more astonishing was the evidence of a radar contact, indicating a ship so close inshore, for the main route up-channel was much further north. As it transpired later, the vessel in question, an eight-thousand-ton Liberty ship *Joseph Johnson* out of Boston for Plymouth with a cargo of high explosives, had sustained damage to her steering in a bad storm near Land's End three days earlier. Her difficulties in this direction and the heavy fog had conspired to put her off course.

North of Burhou, Steiner slowed, jerking on the lifelines to alert his companions. A few moments later, they coasted out of the fog on either side to join him. Ritter Neumann's face was blue with cold in the black cowl of his rubber suit. 'We're close, Herr Oberst,' he said. 'I'm sure I can hear them.'

Sergeant Lemke drifted in to join them. The curly black beard, of which he was very proud, was a special dispensation from Steiner in view of the fact that Lemke's chin was badly deformed by a Russian high-velocity bullet. He was very excited, eyes sparkling, and obviously looked upon the whole thing as a great adventure.

'I, too, Herr Oberst.'

Steiner raised a hand to silence him and listened. The muted throbbing was quite close now for the *Joseph Johnson* was taking it very steady indeed.

'An easy one, Herr Oberst.' Lemke grinned in spite of the fact that his teeth were chattering in the cold. 'The best touch we've had yet. She won't even know what's hit her.'

'You speak for yourself, Lemke,' Ritter Neumann said. 'If there's one thing I've learned in my short and unhappy life it's never to expect anything and to be particularly suspicious of that which is apparently served up on a plate.'

As if to prove his words, a sudden flurry of wind tore a hole in the curtain of the fog. Behind them was the grey-green sweep of Alderney, the old Admiralty breakwater poking out like a granite finger for a thousand yards from Braye, the Victorian naval fortification of Fort Albert clearly visible.

No more than a hundred and fifty yards away, the *Joseph Johnson* moved on a north-westerly course for the open Channel at a steady eight or ten knots. It could only be a matter of moments before they were seen. Steiner acted instantly. 'All right, straight in, release torpedoes at fifty yards and out again and no stupid heroics, Lemke. There aren't any medals to be had in the penal regiments, remember. Only coffins.'

He increased power and surged forward, crouching behind the cupola as waves started breaking over his head. He was aware of Ritter Neumann on his right, roughly abreast of him, but Lemke had surged on and was already fifteen or twenty yards in front.

'The silly young bastard,' Steiner thought. 'What does he think this is, the Charge of the Light Brigade?'

Two of the men at the rail of the *Joseph Johnson* had rifles in their hands and an officer came out of the wheelhouse and stood on the bridge firing a Thompson sub-machine-gun with a drum magazine. The ship was picking up speed now, driving through a light curtain of mist, as the blanket of fog began to settle again. Within another few moments she would have disappeared altogether. The riflemen at the rail were having difficulty in taking aim on a heaving deck at a target so low in the water and their shots were very wide of the mark. The Thompson, not too accurate at the best of times, was doing no better and making a great deal of noise about it.

Lemke reached the fifty-yard line several lengths in front of the others and kept right on going. There wasn't a thing Steiner could do about it. The riflemen started to get the range and a bullet ricocheted from the body of his torpedo in front of the cupola.

He turned and waved to Neumann. 'Now!' he cried and fired his torpedo.

The one upon which he was seated, released from the weight it had been carrying, sprang forward with new energy and he turned to starboard quickly, following Neumann round in a great sweeping curve intended to take them away from the ship as fast as possible.

Lemke was turning away now also, no more than twenty-five yards from the *Joseph Johnson*, the men at the rail firing at him for all they were worth. Presumably one of them scored a hit, although Steiner could never be sure. The only certain thing was that one moment Lemke was crouched astride his torpedo, surging away from danger. The next, he wasn't there any more.

A second later one of the three torpedoes scored a direct hit close to the stern and the stern hold contained hundreds of tons of high explosive bombs destined for use by Flying Fortresses of bombardment groups of the 1st Air Division of the American 8th Air Force in Britain. As the *Joseph Johnson* was swallowed by the fog, she exploded, the sound re-echoing from the island again and again. Steiner crouched low as the blast swept over, swerving when an enormous piece of twisted metal hurtled into the sea in front of him.

Debris cascaded down. The air was full of it and something struck Neumann a glancing blow on the head. He threw up his hands with a cry and catapulted backwards into the sea, his torpedo running away from him, plunging over the next wave and disappearing.

Although unconscious, blood on his forehead from a nasty gash, he was kept afloat by his inflatable jacket. Steiner coasted in beside him, looped one end of a line under the lieutenant's jacket and kept on going, pushing towards the breakwater and Braye, already fading as the fog rolled in towards the island again.

The tide was ebbing fast. Steiner didn't have one chance in hell of reaching Braye Harbour and he knew it, as he wrestled vainly against a tide that must eventually sweep them far out into the Channel beyond any hope of return.

He suddenly realized that Ritter Neumann was conscious again and staring up at him. 'Let me go!' he said faintly. 'Cut me loose. You'll make it on your own.'

Steiner didn't bother to reply at first, but concentrated on turning the torpedo over towards the right. Burhou was somewhere out there in that impenetrable blanket of fog. There was a chance the ebbing tide might push them in, a slim one perhaps, but better than nothing.

He said calmly, 'How long have we been together now, Ritter?'

'You know damn well,' Ritter said. 'The first time I clapped eyes on you was over Narvik when I was afraid to jump out of the plane.'

'I remember now,' Steiner said. 'I persuaded you otherwise.'

'That's one way of putting it,' Ritter said. 'You threw me out.'

His teeth were chattering and he was very cold and Steiner reached down to check the line. 'Yes, a snotty eighteen-year-old Berliner, fresh from the University. Always with a volume of poetry in your hip pocket. The professor's son who crawled fifty yards under fire to bring me a medical kit when I was wounded at the Albert Canal.'

'I should have let you go,' Ritter said. 'Look what you got me into. Crete, then a commission I didn't want, Russia and now this. What a bargain.' He closed his eyes and added softly, 'Sorry, Kurt, but it's no good.'

Quite suddenly, they were caught in a great eddy of water that swept them in towards the rocks of L'Equet on the tip of Burhou. There was a ship there, or half one; all that was left of a French coaster that had run on the reef in a storm earlier in the year. What was left of her stern deck sloped into deep water. A wave swept them in, the torpedo high on the swell and Steiner rolled away from it, grabbing for the ship's rail with one hand and hanging on to Neumann's lifeline with the other.

The wave receded, taking the torpedo with it. Steiner got to his feet and went up the sloping deck to what was left of the wheelhouse. He wedged himself in the broken doorway and hauled his companion after him. They crouched in the roofless shell of the wheelhouse and it started to rain softly.

'What happens now?' Neumann asked weakly.

'We sit tight,' Steiner said. 'Brandt will be out with the recovery boat as soon as this fog clears a little.'

'I could do with a cigarette,' Neumann said, and then he stiffened suddenly and pointed out through the broken doorway. 'Look at that.'

Steiner went to the rail. The water was moving fast now as the tide ebbed, twisting and turning amongst the reefs and rocks, carrying with it the refuse of war, a floating carpet of wreckage that was all that was left of the *Joseph Johnson*.

'So, we got her,' Neumann said. Then he tried to get up. 'There's a man down there, Kurt, in a yellow lifejacket. Look, under the stern.'

Steiner slid down the deck into the water and turned under the stern, pushing his way through a mass of planks to the man who floated there, head back, eyes closed. He was very young with blond hair plastered to the skull. Steiner grabbed him by the life-jacket and started to tow him towards the safety of the shattered stern, and he opened his eyes and stared at him. Then he shook his head, trying to speak.

Steiner floated beside him for a moment. 'What is it?' he said in English.

'Please,' the boy whispered. 'Let me go.'

His eyes closed again and Steiner swam with him to the stern. Neumann, watching from the wheelhouse, saw Steiner start to drag him up the sloping deck. He paused for a long moment, then slid the boy gently back into the water. A current took him away and out of sight beyond the reef, and Steiner clambered wearily back up the deck again.

'What was it?' Neumann demanded weakly.

'Both legs were gone from the knees down.' Steiner sat very carefully and braced his feet against the rail. 'What was that poem of Eliot's that you were always quoting at Stalingrad? The one I didn't like?'

'I think we are in rat's alley,' Neumann said, 'Where the dead men lost their bones.'

'Now I understand it,' Steiner told him. 'Now I see exactly what he meant.'

They sat there in silence. It was colder now, the rain increasing in force, clearing the fog rapidly. About twenty minutes later they heard an engine not too far away. Steiner took the small signalling pistol from the pouch on his right leg, charged it with a waterproof cartridge and fired a maroon.

A few moments later, the recovery launch appeared from the fog and slowed, drifting in towards them. Sergeant-Major Brandt was in the prow with a line ready to throw. He was an enormous figure of a man, well over six feet tall and broad in proportion, rather incongruously wearing a yellow oilskin coat with *Royal National Lifeboat Institution* on the back. The rest of the crew were all Steiner's men. Sergeant Sturm at the wheel, Lance-Corporal Briegel and Private Berg acting as deckhands. Brandt jumped for the sloping deck of the wreck and hitched the line about the rail as Steiner and Neumann slid down to join him.

'You made a hit, Herr Oberst. What happened to Lemke?'

'Playing heroes as usual,' Steiner told him. 'This time he went too far. Careful with Lieutenant Neumann. He's had a bad crack on the head.'

'Sergeant Altmann's out in the other boat with Riedel and Meyer. They might see some sign of him. He has the Devil's own luck, that one.' Brandt lifted Neumann up over the rail with astonishing strength. 'Get him in the cabin.'

But Neumann wouldn't have it and slumped down on the deck with his back against the stern rail. Steiner sat beside him and Brandt gave them cigarettes as the motor boat pulled away. Steiner felt tired. More tired than he he had been in a very long time. *Five years of war.* Sometimes it seemed as if it was not only all there was, but all there ever had been.

They rounded the end of the Admiralty breakwater and followed the thousand yards or so of its length into Braye. There was a surprising number of ships in the harbour, French coasters mostly, carrying building supplies from the continent for the new fortifications that were being raised all over the island.

The small landing stage had been extended. An E-boat was tied up there and as the motor boat drifted in astern, the sailors on deck raised a cheer and a young, bearded lieutenant in a heavy sweater and salt-stained cap stood smartly to attention and saluted.

'Fine work, Herr Oberst!'

Steiner acknowledged the salute as he went over the rail. 'Many thanks, Koenig.'

He went up the steps to the upper landing stage, Brandt following, supporting Neumann with a strong arm. As they came out on top a large black saloon car, an old Wolseley, turned on to the landing stage and braked to a halt. The driver jumped out and opened the rear door.

The first person to emerge was the man who at that time was acting-commandant of the island, Hans Neuhoff, a full colonel of artillery. Like Steiner, a Winter War veteran, wounded in the chest at Leningrad, he had never recovered his health, his lungs damaged beyond repair, and his face had the permanently resigned look of a man who is dying by inches and knows it. His wife got out of the car after him.

Ilse Neuhoff was at that time twenty-seven years of age, a slim, aristocratic-looking blonde with a wide, generous mouth and good cheekbones. Most people turned to look at her twice and not only because she was beautiful, but because she usually seemed familiar. She had enjoyed a successful career as a film starlet working for UFA in Berlin. She was one of those odd people that everyone likes and she had been much in demand in Berlin society. She was a friend of Goebbels. The Führer himself had admired her.

She had married Hans Neuhoff out of a genuine liking that went far beyond sexual love, something of which he was no longer capable anyway. She had nursed him back on his feet after Russia, supported him every step of the way, used all her influence to secure him his present post, had even obtained a pass to visit him by influence of Goebbels himself. They had an understanding – a warm and mutual understanding and it was because of this that she was able to go forward to Steiner and kiss him openly on the cheek.

'You had us worried, Kurt.'

Neuhoff shook hands, genuinely delighted. 'Wonderful work, Kurt. I'll get a signal off to Berlin at once.'

'Don't do that for God's sake,' Steiner said in mock alarm. 'They might decide to send me back to Russia.'

Ilse took his arm. 'It wasn't in the cards when I last read Tarot for you, but I'll look again tonight if you like.'

There was a hail from the lower landing stage and they moved forward to the edge in time to see the second recovery boat coming in. There was a body on the stern deck covered with a blanket and Sergeant Altmann, another of Steiner's men, came out of the wheelhouse. 'Herr Oberst?' he called, awaiting orders.

Steiner nodded and Altmann raised the blanket briefly. Neumann had moved to join Steiner and now he said bitterly. 'Lemke. Crete, Leningrad, Stalingrad – all those years and this is how it ends.'

'When your name's on the bullet, that's it,' Brandt said.

Steiner turned to look into Ilse Neuhoff's troubled face. 'My poor Ilse, better to leave those cards of yours in the box. A few more afternoons like this and it won't be so much a question of *will* the worst come to pass as *when*.'

He took her arm, smiling cheerfully and led her towards the car.

*

Canaris had a meeting with Ribbentrop and Goebbels during the afternoon and it was six o'clock before he could see Radl. There was no sign of Steiner's court martial papers.

At five minutes to six Hofer knocked on the door and entered Radl's office. 'Have they come?' Radl demanded eagerly.

'I'm afraid not, Herr Oberst.'

'Why not, for God's sake?' Radl said angrily.

'It seems that as the original incident was concerned with a complaint from the SS, the records are at Prinz Albrechtstrasse.'

'Have you got the outline that I asked you for?'

'Herr Oberst.' Hofer handed him a neatly typed sheet of paper.

Radl examined it quickly. 'Excellent, Karl. Really excellent.' He smiled and straightened his already immaculate uniform. 'You're off duty now, aren't you?'

'I'd prefer to wait until the Herr Oberst returns,' Hofer said.

Radl smiled and clapped him on the shoulder. 'All right, let's get it over with.'

*

The Admiral was being served with coffee by an orderly when Radl went in. 'Ah, there you are, Max,' he said cheerfully. 'Will you join me?'

'Thank you, Herr Admiral.'

The orderly filled another cup, adjusted the blackout curtains and went out. Canaris sighed and eased himself back in the chair, reaching down to fondle the ears of one of his dachshunds. He seemed weary and there was evidence of strain in the eyes and around the mouth.

'You look tired,' Radl told him.

'So would you if you'd been closeted with Ribbentrop and Goebbels all afternoon. Those two really get more impossible every time I see them. According to Goebbels we're still winning the war, Max. Was there ever anything more absurd?' Radl didn't really know what to say but was saved by the Admiral carrying straight on. 'Anyway, what did you want to see me about?'

Radl placed Hofer's typed outline on the desk and Canaris started to read it. After a while he looked up in obvious bewilderment. 'What is it, for God's sake?'

'The feasibility study you asked for, Herr Admiral. The Churchill business. You asked me to get something down on paper.'

'Ah, yes.' There was understanding on the Admiral's face now and he looked again at the paper. After a while he smiled. 'Yes, very good, Max. Quite absurd, of course, but on paper it does have a kind of mad logic to it. Keep it handy in case Himmler reminds the Führer to ask me if we've done anything about it.'

'You mean that's all, Herr Admiral?' Radl said. 'You don't want me to take it any further?'

Canaris had opened a file and now he looked up in obvious surprise. 'My dear Max, I don't think you quite get the point. The more absurd the idea put forward by your superiors in this game, the more rapturously should you receive it, however crazy. Put all your enthusiasm – assumed, of course – into the project. Over a period of time allow the difficulties to show, so that very gradually your masters will make the discovery for themselves that it just isn't on. As nobody likes to be involved in failure if he can avoid it, the whole project will be discreetly dropped.' He laughed lightly and tapped the outline with one finger. 'Mind you, even the Führer would need to be having a very off-day indeed to see any possibilities in such a mad escapade as this.'

Radl found himself saying. 'It would work, Herr Admiral. I've even got the right man for the job.'

'I'm sure you have, Max, if you've been anything like as thorough as you usually are.' He smiled and pushed the outline across the desk. 'I can see that you've taken the whole thing too seriously. Perhaps my remarks about Himmler worried you. But there's no need, believe me. I can handle him. You've got enough on paper to satisfy them if the occasion arises. Plenty of other things you can get on with now – really important matters.'

He nodded in dismissal and picked up his pen. Radl said stubbornly, 'But surely, Herr Admiral, if the Führer wishes it . . .'

Canaris exploded angrily, throwing down his pen. 'God in heaven, man, kill Churchill when we have already lost the war? In what way is that supposed to help?'

He had jumped up and leaned across the desk, both hands braced. Radl stood rigidly to attention, staring woodenly into space a foot above the Admiral's head. Canaris flushed, aware that he had gone too far, that there had been treason implicit in his angry words and too late to retract them.

'At ease,' he said.

Radl did as he was ordered. 'Herr Admiral.'

'We've known each other a long time, Max.'

'Yes, sir.'

'So trust me now. I know what I'm doing.'

'Very well, Herr Admiral,' Radl said crisply.

He stepped back, clicked his heels, turned and went out. Canaris stayed where he was, hands braced against the desk, suddenly looking haggard and old. 'My God,' he whispered. 'How much longer?'

When he sat down and picked up his coffee, his hand was trembling so much that the cup rattled in the saucer.

*

When Radl went into the office, Hofer was straightening the papers on his desk. The sergeant turned eagerly and then saw the expression on Radl's face.

'The Admiral didn't like it, Herr Oberst?'

'He said it had a certain mad logic, Karl. Actually, he seemed to find it quite amusing.'

'What happens now, Herr Oberst?'

'Nothing, Karl,' Radl said wearily and sat down behind his desk. 'It's on paper, the feasibility study they wanted and may never ask for again and that's all we were required to do. We get on with something else.'

He reached for one of his Russian cigarettes and Hofer gave him a light. 'Can I get you anything, Herr Oberst?' he said, his voice sympathetic, but careful.

'No, thank you, Karl. Go home now. I'll see you in the morning.'

'Herr Oberst.' Hofer clicked his heels and hesitated.

Radl said, 'Go on, Karl, there's a good fellow and thank you.'

Hofer went out and Radl ran a hand over his face. His empty socket was burning, the invisible hand ached. Sometimes he felt as if they'd wired him up wrongly when they'd put him back together again. Amazing how disappointed he felt. A sense of real, personal loss.

'Perhaps it's as well,' he said softly, 'I was beginning to take the whole damn thing too seriously.'

He sat down, opened Joanna Grey's file and started to read it. After a while he reached for the ordnance survey map and began to unfold it. He stopped suddenly. He'd had enough of this tiny office for one day, enough of the Abwehr. He pulled his briefcase from under the desk, stuffed the files and map inside and took his leather greatcoat down from behind the door.

It was too early for the RAF and the city seemed unnaturally quiet when he went out of the front entrance. He decided to take advantage of the brief calm and walk home to his small apartment instead of calling for a staff car. In any case his head was splitting and the light rain which was falling was really quite refreshing. He went down the steps, acknowledging the sentry's salute and passed under the shaded street light at the bottom. A car started up somewhere further along the Tirpitz Ufer and pulled in beside him.

It was a black Mercedes saloon, as black as the uniforms of the two Gestapo men who got out of the front seats and stood waiting. As Radl saw the cuff-title of the one nearest to him, his heart seemed to stop beating. RFSS. Reichsführer der SS. The cuff-title of Himmler's personal staff.

The young man who got out of the rear seat wore a slouch hat and a black leather coat. His smile had the kind of ruthless charm that only the genuinely insincere possess. 'Colonel Radl?' he said. 'So glad we were able to catch you before you left. The Reichs-führer presents his compliments. If you could find it convenient to spare him a little time, he'd appreciate it.' He deftly removed the briefcase from Radl's hand. 'Let me carry that for you.'

Radl moistened dry lips and managed a smile. 'But of course,' he said and got into the rear of the Mercedes.

The young man joined him, the other got into the front and they moved away. Radl noticed that the one who wasn't driving had an Erma police sub-machine-gun across his knees. He breathed deeply in an effort to control the fear that rose inside him.

'Cigarette, Herr Oberst?'

'Thank you,' Radl said. 'Where are we going, by the way?'

'Prinz Albrechtstrasse.' The young man gave him a light and smiled. 'Gestapo Headquarters.'

4

When Radl was ushered into the office on the first floor at Prinz Albrechtstrasse, he found Himmler seated behind a large desk, a stack of files in front of him. He was wearing full uniform as Reichsführer SS, a devil in black in the shaded light, and when he looked up the face behind the silver pince-nez was cold and impersonal.

The young man in the black leather coat who had brought Radl in gave the Nazi salute and placed the briefcase on the table. 'At your orders, Herr Reichsführer.'

'Thank you, Rossman,' Himmler replied. 'Wait outside. I may need you later.'

Rossman went out and Radl waited as Himmler moved the files very precisely to one side of the desk, as if clearing the decks for action. He pulled the briefcase forward and looked at it thoughtfully. Strangely enough, Radl had got back some of his nerve, and a certain black humour that had been a saving grace to him on many occasions surfaced now.

'Even the condemned man is entitled to a last cigarette, Herr Reichsführer.'

Himmler actually smiled, which was quite something considering that tobacco was one of his pet aversions. 'Why not?' He waved a hand. 'They told me you were a brave man, Herr Oberst. You earned your Knight's Cross during the Winter War?'

'That's right, Herr Reichsführer.' Radl got his cigarette case out, one-handed, and opened it deftly.

'And have worked for Admiral Canaris ever since?'

Radl waited, smoking his cigarette, trying to make it last while Himmler stared down at the briefcase again. The room was really quite pleasant in the shaded light. An open fire burned brightly and above it there was an autographed picture of the Führer in a gilt frame.

Himmler said, 'There is not much that happens at the Tirpitz Ufer these days that I don't know about. Does that surprise you? For example, I am aware that on the twenty-second of this month you were shown a routine report from an Abwehr agent in England, a Mrs Joanna Grey, in which the magic name of Winston Churchill figured.'

'Herr Reichsführer, I don't know what to say,' Radl told him.

'Even more fascinating, you had all her files transferred from Abwehr One into your custody, and relieved Captain Meyer, who had been this lady's link man for many years, of duty. I understand he's most upset.' Himmler placed a hand on the briefcase. 'Come, Herr Oberst, we're too old to play games. You know what I'm talking about. Now, what have you got to tell me?'

Max Radl was a realist. He had no choice at all in the matter. He said, 'In the briefcase, the Reichsführer will find all that there is to know except for one item.'

'The court martial papers of Lieutenant-Colonel Kurt Steiner of the Parachute Regiment?' Himmler picked up the top file from the pile at the side of his desk and handed it over. 'A fair exchange. I suggest you read it outside.' He opened the briefcase and started to extract the contents. 'I'll send for you when I need you.'

Radl almost raised his arm, but one last stubborn grain of self-respect turned it into a smart, if conventional salute. He turned on his heel, opened the door and went out into the anteroom.

Rossman sprawled in an easy chair reading a copy of *Signal*, the Wehrmacht magazine. He glanced up in surprise. 'Leaving us already?'

'No such luck,' Radl dropped the file on to a low coffee table and started to unbuckle his belt. 'It seems I've got some reading to do.'

Rossman smiled amiably. 'I'll see if I can find us some coffee. It looks to me as if you could be with us for quite some time.'

He went out and Radl lit another cigarette, sat down and opened the file.

*

The date chosen for the final erasing of the Warsaw Ghetto from the face of the earth was the 19th April. Hitler's birthday was on the 20th and Himmler hoped to present him with the good news as a suitable present. Unfortunately when the commander of the operation, SS Oberführer von Sammern-Frankenegg and his men marched in, they were chased out again by the Jewish Combat Organization, under the command of Mordechai Anielewicz.

Himmler immediately replaced him with SS Brigadeführer and Major-General of Police, Jurgen Stroop, who, aided by a mixed force of SS and renegade Poles and Ukrainians, applied himself seriously to the task in hand: to leave not one brick standing, not one Jew alive. To be able to report to Himmler personally that *The Warsaw Ghetto is no more*. It took him twenty-eight days to accomplish.

Steiner and his men arrived in Warsaw on the morning of the Thirteenth Day on a hospital train from the Eastern Front bound for Berlin. There was a stopover time of between one to two hours, depending on how long it took to rectify a fault in the engine's cooling system, and orders were broadcast over the loudspeaker that no one was to leave the station. There were military police on the entrances to see that the order was obeyed.

Most of his men stayed inside the coach, but Steiner got out to stretch his legs and Ritter Neumann joined him. Steiner's jump boots were worn through, his leather coat had definitely seen better days and he was wearing a soiled white scarf and sidecap of a type more common amongst NCOs than officers.

The military policeman guarding the main entrance held his rifle across his chest in both hands and said roughly, 'You heard the order, didn't you? Get back in there!'

'It would seem they want to keep us under wraps for some reason, Herr Oberst,' Neumann said.

The military policeman's jaw dropped and he came to attention hurriedly. 'I ask the Herr Oberst's pardon. I didn't realize.'

There was a quick step behind them and a harsh voice demanded, 'Schultz – what's all this about?'

Steiner and Neumann ignored it and stepped outside. A pall of black smoke hung over the city, there was a crump of artillery in the distance, the rattle of small arms fire. A hand on Steiner's shoulder spun him round and he found himself facing an immaculately uniformed major. Around his neck was suspended on a chain the gleaming brass gorget plate of the military police. Steiner sighed and pulled away the white scarf at his neck exposing not only the collar patches of his rank, but also the Knight's Cross with Oak Leaves for a second award.

'Steiner,' he said. 'Parachute Regiment.'

The major saluted politely, but only because he had to. 'I'm sorry, Herr Oberst, but orders are orders.'

'What's your name?' Steiner demanded.

There was an edge to the colonel's voice now in spite of the lazy smile, that hinted at the possibility of a little unpleasantness. 'Otto Frank, Herr Oberst.'

'Good, now that we've established that, would you be kind enough to explain exactly what's going on here? I thought the Polish Army surrendered in thirty-nine?'

'They are razing the Warsaw Ghetto to the ground,' Frank said.

'Who is?'

'A special task force. SS and various other groups commanded by Brigadeführer Jurgen Stroop. Jewish bandits, Herr Oberst. They've been fighting from house to house, in the cellars, in the sewers, for thirteen days now. So we're burning them out. Best way to exterminate lice.'

During convalescent leave after being wounded at Leningrad, Steiner had visited his father in France and had found him considerably changed. The General had had his doubts about the new order for some considerable time. Six months earlier he had visited a concentration camp at Auschwitz in Poland.

'The commander was a swine named Rudolf Hoess, Kurt. Would you believe it, a murderer serving a life sentence and released from gaol in the amnesty of nineteen-twenty-eight. He was killing Jews by the thousand in specially constructed gas chambers, disposing of their bodies in huge ovens. After extracting such minor items as gold teeth and so forth.'

The old general had been drunk by then and yet not drunk. 'Is this what we're fighting for, Kurt? To protect swine like Hoess? And what will the rest of the world say when the time comes? That we are all guilty? That Germany is guilty because we stood by? Decent and honourable men stood by and did nothing? Well not me, by God. I couldn't live with myself.'

Standing there in the entrace to Warsaw Station, the memory of all this welling up inside, Kurt Steiner produced an expression on his face that sent the major back a couple of steps. 'That's better,' Steiner said, 'and if you could make it downwind as well I'd be obliged.'

Major Frank's look of astonishment quickly turned to anger as Steiner walked past him, Neumann at his side. 'Easy, Herr Oberst. Easy,' Neumann said.

On the platform at the other side of the track, a group of SS were herding a line of ragged and filthy human beings against a wall. It was virtually impossible to differentiate between the sexes and as Steiner watched, they all started to take their clothes off.

A military policeman stood on the edge of the platform watching and Steiner said, 'What's going on over there?'

'Jews, Herr Oberst,' the man replied. 'This morning's crop from the Ghetto. They'll be shipped out to Treblinka to finish them off later today. They make them strip like that before a search mainly because of the women. Some of them have been carrying loaded pistols inside their pants.'

There was brutal laughter from across the track and someone cried out in pain. Steiner turned to Neumann in disgust and found the lieutenant staring along the platform to the rear of the troop train. A young girl of perhaps fourteen or fifteen, with ragged hair and smoke-blackened face, wearing a cut-down man's overcoat tied with string, crouched under a coach. She had presumably slipped away from the group opposite and her intention was obviously to make a bid for freedom by riding the rods under the hospital train when it pulled out.

In the same moment the military policeman on the edge of the platform saw her and raised the alarm, jumping down on to the track and grabbing for her. She screamed, twisting from his grasp, scrambled up to the platform and ran for the entrance, straight into the arms of Major of Police Frank as he came out of his office.

He had her by the hair and shook her like a rat. 'Dirty little Jew bitch. I'll teach you some manners.'

Steiner started forward, 'No, Herr Oberst!' Neumann said, but he was too late.

Steiner got a firm grip on Frank's collar, pulling him off balance so that he almost fell down, grabbed the girl by the hand and stood her behind him.

Major Frank scrambled to his feet, his face contorted with rage. His hand went to the Walther in the holster at his belt, but Steiner produced a Luger from the pocket of his leather coat and touched him between the eyes. 'You do,' he said, 'and I'll blow your head off. Come to think of it, I'd be doing humanity a favour.'

At least a dozen military policemen ran forward, some carrying machine pistols, others rifles and paused in a semi-circle three or four yards away. A tall sergeant aimed his rifle and Steiner got a hand in Frank's tunic and held him close, screwing the barrel of the Luger in hard.

'I wouldn't advise it.'

An engine coasted through the station at five or six miles an hour hauling a line of open wagons loaded with coal. Steiner said to the girl without looking at her, 'What's your name, child?'

'Brana,' she told him. 'Brana Lezemnikof.'

'Well, Brana,' he said, 'if you're half the girl I think you are, you'll grab hold of one of those coal trucks and hang on till you're out of here. The best I can do for you.' She was gone in a flash and he raised his voice. 'Anyone takes a shot at her puts one in the major here as well.'

The girl jumped for one of the trucks, secured a grip and pulled herself up between two of them. The train coasted out of the station. There was complete silence.

Frank said, 'They'll have her off at the first station, I'll see to it personally.'

Steiner pushed him away and pocketed his Luger. Immediately the military policemen closed in and Ritter Neumann called out, 'Not today, gentlemen.'

Steiner turned and found the lieutenant holding an MP-40 machine pistol. The rest of his men were ranged behind him, all armed to the teeth.

At that point, anything might have happened, had it not been for a sudden disturbance in the main entrance. A group of SS stormed in, rifles at the ready. They took up position in a V formation and a moment later, SS Brigadeführer and Major-General of Police Jurgen Stroop entered, flanked by three or four SS officers of varying ranks, all carrying drawn pistols. He wore a field cap and service uniform and looked surprisingly nondescript.

'What's going on here, Frank?'

'Ask him, Herr Brigadeführer,' Frank said, his face twisted with rage. 'This man, an officer of the German Army, has just allowed a Jewish terrorist to escape.'

Stroop looked Steiner over, noting the rank badges and the Knight's Cross plus the Oak Leaves, 'Who are you?' he demanded.

'Kurt Steiner – Parachute Regiment,' Steiner told him, 'And who might you be?'

Jurgen Stroop was never known to lose his temper. He said calmly, 'You can't talk to me like that, Herr Oberst. I'm a Major-General as you very well know.'

'So is my father,' Steiner told him, 'so I'm not particularly impressed. However, as you've raised the matter, are you Brigadeführer Stroop, the man in charge of the slaughter out there?'

'I am in command here, yes.'

Steiner wrinkled his nose. 'I rather thought you might be. You know what you remind me of?'

'No, Herr Oberst,' Stroop said. 'Do tell me.'

'The kind of thing I occasionally pick up on my shoe in the gutter,' Steiner said. 'Very unpleasant on a hot day.'

Jurgen Stroop, still icy calm, held out his hand. Steiner sighed, took the Luger from his pocket and handed it across. He looked over his shoulder to his men. 'That's it, boys, stand down.' He turned back to Stroop. 'They feel a certain loyalty for some reason unknown to me. Is there any chance you could content yourself with me and overlook their part in this thing?'

'Not the slightest,' Brigadeführer Jurgen Stroop told him.

'That's what I thought,' Steiner said. 'I pride myself I can always tell a thoroughgoing bastard when I see one.'

*

Radl sat with the file on his knee for a long time after he'd finished reading the account of the court martial. Steiner had been lucky to escape execution but his father's influence would have helped and after all, he and his men were war heroes. Bad for morale to have to shoot a holder of the Knight's Cross with Oak Leaves. And Operation Swordfish, in the Channel Islands, was just as certain in the long run for all of them. A stroke of genius on somebody's part.

Rossman sprawled in the chair opposite, apparently asleep, the black slouch hat tipped over his eyes, but when the light at the door flashed, he was on his feet. He went straight in without knocking and was back in a moment.

'He wants you.'

The Reichsführer was still seated behind the desk. He now had the ordnance survey map spread out in front of him. He looked up. 'And what did you make of friend Steiner's little escapade in Warsaw?'

'A remarkable story,' Radl said carefully. 'An – an unusual man.'

'I would say one of the bravest you are ever likely to encounter,' Himmler said calmly. 'Gifted with high intelligence, courageous, ruthless, a brilliant soldier – and a romantic fool. I can only imagine that to be the American half of him.' The Reichsführer shook his head. 'The Knight's Cross with Oak Leaves. After that Russian affair the Führer had asked to meet him personally. And what does he do? Throws it all away, career, future, everything, for the sake of a little Jewish bitch he'd never clapped eyes on in his life before.'

He looked up at Radl as if waiting for a reply and Radl said lamely, 'Extraordinary, Herr Reichsführer.'

Himmler nodded and then, as if dismissing the subject completely, rubbed his hands together and leaned over the map. 'The Grey woman's reports are really quite brilliant. An outstanding agent.' He leaned down, eyes very close to the map. 'Will it work?'

'I think so,' Radl replied without hesitation.

'And the Admiral? What does the Admiral think?'

Radl's mind raced as he tried to frame a suitable reply. 'That's a difficult question to answer.'

Himmler sat back, hands folded. For a wild moment Radl felt as if he were back in short trousers and in front of his old village schoolmaster.

'You don't need to tell me, I think I can guess. I admire loyalty, but in this case you would do well to remember that loyalty to Germany, to your Führer, comes first.'

'Naturally, Herr Reichsführer,' Radl said hastily.

'Unfortunately there are those who would not agree,' Himmler went on. 'Subversive elements at every level in our society. Even amongst the generals of the High Command itself. Does that surprise you?'

Radl, genuinely astonished, said, 'But Herr Reichsführer, I can hardly believe. . .'

'That men who have taken an oath of personal loyalty to the Führer can behave in such a dastardly fashion?' He shook his head almost sadly. 'I have every reason to believe that in March of this year, high ranking officers of the Wehrmacht placed a bomb on the Führer's plane, set to explode during its flight from Smolensk to Rastenburg.'

'God in heaven,' Radl said.

'The bomb failed to explode and was removed by the individuals concerned later. Of course, it makes one realize more strongly than ever that we cannot fail, that ultimate victory must be ours. That the Führer was saved by some divine intervention seems obvious. That doesn't surprise me of course. I have always believed that some higher being is behind nature, don't you agree?'

'Of course, Herr Reichsführer,' Radl said.

'Yes, if we refused to recognize that we would be no better than Marxists. I insist that all members of the SS believe in God.' He removed his pince-nez for a moment and stroked the bridge of his nose gently with one finger. 'So, traitors everywhere. In the Army and in the Navy, too, at the highest level.'

He replaced his pince-nez and looked up at Radl. 'So you see, Radl,' Himmler went on, 'I have the very best of reasons for being sure that Admiral Canaris must have vetoed this scheme of yours.'

Radl stared at him dumbly. His blood ran cold. Himmler said gently, 'It would not be in accordance with his general aim and that aim is not the victory of the German Reich in this war, I assure you.'

That the Head of the Abwehr was working against the State? The idea was monstrous. But then Radl remembered the Admiral's acid tongue. The derogatory remarks about high state officials, about the Führer himself on occasions. His reaction earlier that evening. *We have lost the war.* And that from the Head of the Abwehr.

Himmler pressed the buzzer and Rossman came in. 'I have an important phone call to make. Show the Herr Oberst around for ten minutes then bring him back.' He turned to Radl, 'You haven't seen the cellars here, have you?'

'No, Herr Reichsführer.'

He might have added that the Gestapo cellars at Prinz Albrechtstrasse were the last places on earth he wanted to see. But he knew that he was going to whether he liked it or not, knew from the slight smile on Rossman's mouth that it was all arranged.

*

On the ground floor they went along a corridor that led to the rear of the building. There was an iron door guarded by two Gestapo men wearing steel helmets and armed with machine pistols. 'Are you expecting a war or something?' Radl enquired.

Rossman grinned. 'Let's say it impresses the customers.'

The door was unlocked and he led the way down. The passage at the bottom was brilliantly lit, brickwork painted white, doors opening to right and left. It was extraordinarily quiet.

'Might as well start in here,' Rossman said and opened the nearest door and switched on the light.

It was a conventional enough looking cellar painted white except for the opposite wall which had been faced with concrete in a surprisingly crude way, for the surface was uneven and badly marked. There was a beam across the ceiling near that wall, chains hanging down and coil spring stirrups on the end.

'Something they're supposed to have a lot of success with lately,' Rossman took out a packet of cigarettes and offered Radl one. 'I think it's a dead loss myself. I can't see much point in driving a man insane when you want him to talk.'

'What happens?'

'The suspect is suspended in those stirrups, then they simply turn the electricity on. They throw buckets of water on that concrete wall to improve the electrical flow or something. Extraordinary what it does to people. If you look close you'll see what I mean.'

When Radl approached the wall he saw that what he had taken to be a crudely finished surface was in fact a patina of hand prints in raw concrete where victims had clawed in agony.

'The Inquisition would have been proud of you.'

'Don't be bitter, Herr Oberst, it doesn't pay, not down here. I've seen generals on their knees down here and begging.' Rossman smiled genially. 'Still, that's neither here nor there.' He walked to the door. 'Now what can I show you next?'

'Nothing, thank you,' Radl said. 'You've made your point, wasn't that the object of the exercise? You can take me back now.'

'As you say, Herr Oberst.' Rossman shrugged and turned out the light.

*

When Radl went back into the office, he found Himmler busily writing in a file. He looked up and said calmly, 'Terrible the things that have to be done. It personally sickens me to my stomach. I can't abide violence of any sort. It is the curse of greatness, Herr Oberst, that it must step over dead bodies to create new life.'

'Herr Reichsführer,' Radl said. 'What do you want of me?'

Himmler actually smiled, however slightly, contriving to look even more sinister. 'Why, it's really very simple. This Churchill business. I want it seeing through.'

'But the Admiral doesn't.'

'You have considerable autonomy, is it not so? Run your own office? Travel extensively? Munich, Paris, Antwerp within the past fortnight?' Himmler shrugged. 'I see no reason why you shouldn't be able to manage without the Admiral realizing what's going on. Most of what needs to be done could be handled in conjunction with other business.'

'But why, Herr Reichsführer, why is it so important that it be done this way?'

'Because, in the first place, I think the Admiral totally wrong in this affair. This scheme of yours could work if everything falls right for it, just like Skorzeny at Gran Sasso. If it succeeds, if Churchill is either killed or kidnapped – and personally, I'd sooner see him dead – then we have a world sensation. An incredible feat of arms.'

'Which if the Admiral had had his way would never have taken place,' Radl said. 'I see now. Another nail in his coffin?'

'Would you deny that he would have earned it in such circumstances?'

'What can I say?'

'Should such men be allowed to get away with it? Is that what you want, Radl, as a loyal German officer?'

'But the Herr Reichsführer must see what an impossible position this puts me in,' Radl said. 'My relations with the Admiral have always been excellent.' It occurred to him, too late, that that was hardly the point to make under the circumstances and he added hurriedly, 'Naturally my personal loyalty is beyond question, but what kind of authority would I have to carry such a project through?'

Himmler took a heavy manilla envelope from his desk drawer. He opened it and produced a letter which he handed to Radl without a word. It was headed by the German Eagle with the Iron Cross in gold.

FROM THE LEADER AND THE CHANCELLOR
OF THE STATE MOST SECRET

Colonel Radl is acting under my direct and personal orders in a matter of the utmost importance to the Reich. He is answerable only to me. All personnel, military and civil, without distinction of rank, will assist him in any way he sees fit.   Adolf Hitler.

Radl was stunned. It was the most incredible document he had ever held in his hand. With such a key, a man could open any door in the land, be denied nothing. His flesh crawled and a strange thrill ran through him.

'As you can see, anyone who wishes to query that document would have to be prepared to take it up with the Führer himself.' Himmler rubbed his hands together briskly. 'So, it is settled. You are prepared to accept this duty your Führer places on you?'

There was really nothing to be said except the obvious thing. 'Of course, Herr Reichsführer.'

'Good.' Himmler was obviously pleased. 'To business then. You are right to think of Steiner. The very man for the job. I suggest that you go and see him without delay.'

'It occurs to me,' Radl said cheerfully, 'that in view of his recent history he may not be interested in such an assignment.'

'He will have no choice in the matter,' Himmler said. 'Four days ago his father was arrested on suspicion of treason against the state.'

'General Steiner?' Radl said in astonishment.

'Yes, the old fool seems to have got himself involved with entirely the wrong sort of people. He's being brought to Berlin at the moment.'

'To – to Prinz Albrechtstrasse?'

'But of course. You might point out to Steiner that not only would it be in his own best interests to serve the Reich in any way he can at the moment. Such evidence of loyalty might well affect the outcome of his father's case.' Radl was genuinely horrified, but Himmler carried straight on. 'Now, a few facts. I would like you to elaborate on this question of disguise that you mention in your outline. That interests me.'

Radl was aware of a feeling of total unreality. No one was safe – no one. He had known of people, whole families, who had disappeared after the Gestapo called. He thought of Trudi, his wife, his three cherished daughters and the same fierce courage that had brought him through the Winter War flowed through him again. For them, he thought, I've got to survive for them. Anything it takes – anything.

He started to speak, amazed at the calmness in his own voice. 'The British have many commando regiments as the Reichsführer is aware, but perhaps one of the most successful has been the unit formed by a British officer named Stirling to operate behind our lines in Africa. The Special Air Service.'

'Ah, yes, the man they called the Phantom Major. The one Rommel thought so highly of.'

'He was captured in January of this year, Herr Reichsführer. I believe he is in Colditz now, but the work he started has not only continued, but expanded. According to our present information there are due to return to Britain soon, probably to prepare for an invasion of Europe, the First and Second SAS Regiments and the Third and Fourth French Parachute Battalions. They even have a Polish Independent Parachute Squadron.'

'And the point you are trying to make?'

'Little is known of such units by the more conventional branches of the army. It is accepted that their purposes are secret, therefore less likely that they would be challenged by anyone.'

'You would pass off our men as Polish members of this unit?'

'Exactly, Herr Reichsführer.'

'And uniforms?'

'Most of these people are now wearing camouflage smock and trousers in action, rather similar to SS pattern. They also wear the English parachutists' red beret with a special badge. A winged dagger with the inscription *Who dares – wins*.'

'How dramatic,' Himmler said drily.

'The Abwehr has ample supplies of such clothing from those taken prisoner during SAS operations in the Greek Islands, Yugoslavia and Albania.'

'And equipment?'

'No problem. The British Special Operations Executive still do not appreciate the extent to which we have penetrated the Dutch resistance movement.'

'Terrorist movement,' Himmler corrected him. 'But carry on.'

'Almost nightly they drop further supplies of arms, sabotage equipment, radios for field use, even money. They still don't realize that all the radio messages they receive are from the Abwehr.'

'My God,' Himmler said, 'and still we continue to lose the war.' He got up, walked to the fire and warmed his hands. 'This whole question of wearing enemy uniform is a matter of great delicacy and it is forbidden under the Geneva Convention. There is only one penalty. The firing squad.'

'True, Herr Reichsführer.'

'In this case it seems to me a compromise would be in order. The raiding party will wear normal uniform underneath these British camouflage outfits. That way they will be fighting as German soldiers, not gangsters. Just before the actual attack, they could remove these disguises. You agree?'

Radl personally thought it probably the worst idea he'd ever heard of, but realized the futility of argument. 'As you say, Herr Reichsführer.'

'Good. Everything else seems to me simply a question of organization. The Luftwaffe and the Navy for transportation. No trouble there. The Führer's Directive will open all doors for you. Is there anything you wish to raise with me?'

'As regards Churchill himself,' Radl said. 'Is he to be taken alive?'

'If possible,' Himmler said. 'Dead if there is no other way.'

'I understand.'

'Good, then I may safely leave the matter in your hands. Rossman will give you a special phone number on the way out. I wish to be kept in daily touch with your progress.' He replaced the reports and the map in the briefcase and pushed it across.

'As you say, Herr Reichsführer.'

Radl folded the precious letter, put it back in the manilla envelope which he slipped inside his tunic. He picked up the briefcase and his leather greatcoat and moved to the door.

Himmler, who had started writing again, said, 'Colonel Radl.'

Radl turned. 'Herr Reichsführer?'

'Your oath as a German soldier, to your Führer and the State. You remember it?'

'Of course, Herr Reichsführer.'

Himmler looked up, the face cold, enigmatic. 'Repeat it now.'

'I swear by God this holy Oath. I will render unconditional obedience to the Führer of the German Reich and People. Adolf Hitler, the Supreme Commander of the Armed Forces and will be ready, as a brave soldier, to stake my life at any time to this oath.'

His eye socket was on fire again, his dead hand ached. 'Excellent, Colonel Radl. And remember one thing. Failure is a sign of weakness.'

Himmler lowered his head and continued to write. Radl got the door open as fast as he could and stumbled outside.

*

He changed his mind about going home to his apartment. Instead he got Rossman to drop him at the Tirpitz Ufer, went up to his office and bedded down on the small camp bed that he kept for such emergencies. Not that he slept much. Every time he closed his eyes he saw the silver pince-nez, the cold eyes, the calm, dry voice making its monstrous statements.

One thing was certain, or so he told himself at five o'clock when he finally surrendered and reached for the bottle of Courvoisier. He had to see this thing through, not for himself, but for Trudi and the children. Gestapo surveillance was bad enough for most people. 'But me,' he said as he put the light out again. 'I have to have Himmler himself on my tail.'

After that he slept and was awakened by Hofer at eight o'clock with coffee and hot rolls. Radl got up and walked across to the window eating one of the rolls. It was a grey morning and raining heavily.

'Was it a bad raid, Karl?'

'Not too bad. I hear eight Lancasters were shot down.'

'If you look in the inside breast pocket of my tunic you'll find an envelope,' Radl said. 'I want you to read the letter inside.'

He waited, peering out into the rain and turned after a moment or so. Hofer was staring down at the letter, obviously shaken. 'But what does this mean, Herr Oberst?'

'The Churchill affair, Karl. It proceeds. The Führer wishes it so. I had that from Himmler himself last night.'

'And the Admiral, Herr Oberst?'

'Is to know nothing.'

Hofer stared at him in honest bewilderment, the letter in one hand. Radl took it from him and held it up. 'We are little men, you and I, caught in a very large web and we must tread warily. This directive is all we need. Orders from the Führer himself. Do you follow me?'

'I think so.'

'And trust me?'

Hofer sprang to attention. 'I have never doubted you, Herr Oberst. Never.'

Radl was aware of a surge of affection. 'Good, then we proceed as I have indicated and under conditions of the strictest secrecy.'

'As you say, Herr Oberst.'

'Good, Karl, then bring me everything. Everything we have, and we'll go over it again.'

He moved to the window, opened it and took a deep breath. There was the acrid tang of smoke on the air from last night's fires. Parts of the city that he could see were a desolate ruin. Strange how excited he felt.

*

'She needs a man, Karl.'

'Herr Oberst?' Hofer said.

They were leaning over the desk, the reports and charts spread before them. 'Mrs Grey,' Radl explained. 'She needs a man.'

'Ah, I see now, Herr Oberst,' Hofer said. 'Someone with broad shoulders. A blunt instrument?'

'No.' Radl frowned and took one of his Russian cigarettes from the box on the table. 'Brains as well – that is essential.'

Hofer lit the cigarette for him. 'A difficult combination.'

'It always is. Who does Section One have working for them in England at the moment, who might be able to help? Someone thoroughly reliable?'

'There are perhaps seven or eight agents who may be so considered. People like Snow White, for example. He's been working in the offices at the Naval Department in Portsmouth for two years. We receive regular and valuable information on North Atlantic convoys from him.'

Radl shook his head impatiently. 'No, no one like that. Such work is too important to be jeopardized in any way. Surely to God there are others?'

'At least fifty.' Hofer shrugged. 'Unfortunately the BIA section of M15 has had a remarkably successful run during the past eighteen months.'

Radl got up and went to the window. He stood there tapping one foot impatiently. He was not angry – worried more than anything else. Joanna Grey was sixty-eight years of age and no matter how dedicated, no matter how reliable, she needed a man. As Hofer had put it, a blunt instrument. Without him the whole enterprise could founder.

His left hand was hurting, the hand which was no longer there, a sure sign of stress, and his head was splitting. Failure is a sign of weakness, *Colonel.* Himmler had said that, the dark eyes cold. Radl shivered uncontrollably, fear almost moving his bowels as he remembered the cellars at Prinz Albrechtstrasse.

Hofer said diffidently, 'Of course, there is always the Irish Section.'

'What did you say?'

'The Irish Section, sir. The Irish Republican Army.'

'Completely useless,' Radl said. 'The whole IRA connection was aborted long ago, you know that, after that fiasco with Goertz and the other agents. A total failure, the entire enterprise.'

'Not quite, Herr Oberst.'

Hofer opened one of the filing cabinets, leafed through it quickly and produced a manilla folder which he laid on the desk. Radl sat down with a frown and opened it.

'But, of course . . . and he's still here? At the university?'

'So I understand. He also does a little translation work when needed.'

'And what does he call himself now?'

'Devlin. Liam Devlin.'

'Get him!'

'Now, Herr Oberst?'

'You heard me. I want him here within the hour. I don't care if you have to turn Berlin upside down. I don't care if you have to call in the Gestapo.'

Hofer clicked his heels and went out quickly. Radl lit another cigarette with trembling fingers and started to go through the file.

*

He had not been far wrong in his earlier remarks, for every German attempt to make terms with the IRA since the beginning of the war had come to nothing and the whole business was probably the biggest tale of woe in Abwehr files.

None of the German agents sent to Ireland had achieved anything worth having. Only one had remained at large for any length of time, Captain Goertz, who had been parachuted from a Heinkel over Meath in May, 1940, and who had succeeded in remaining at large for nineteen wasted months.

Goertz found the IRA exasperatingly amateur and unwilling to take any kind of advice. As he was to comment years later, they knew how to die for Ireland, but not how to fight for her and German hopes of regular attacks on British military installations in Ulster faded away.

Radl was familiar with all this. What really interested him was the man who called himself Liam Devlin. Devlin had actually parachuted into Ireland for the Abwehr, had not only survived, but had eventually made his way back to Germany, a unique achievement.

Liam Devlin had been born in Lismore in County Down in the North of Ireland in July, 1908, the son of a small tenant farmer who had been executed in 1921 during the Anglo-Irish War for serving with an IRA flying column. The boy's mother had gone to keep house for her brother, a Catholic priest in the Falls Road area of Belfast and he had arranged for him to attend a Jesuit boarding school in the South. From there Devlin had moved to Trinity College, Dublin, where he had taken an excellent degree in English Literature.

He'd had a little poetry published, was interested in a career in journalism, would probably have made a successful writer if it had not been for one single incident which had altered the course of his entire life. In 1931 while visiting his home in Belfast during a period of serious sectarian rioting, he had witnessed an Orange mob sack his uncle's church. The old priest had been so badly beaten that he had lost an eye. From that moment Devlin had given himself completely to the Republican cause.

In a bank raid in Derry in 1932 to gather funds for the movement, he was wounded in a gun battle with the police and sentenced to ten years imprisonment. He had escaped from the Crumlin Road gaol in 1934 and while on the run, led the defence of Catholic areas in Belfast during the rioting of 1935.

Later that year he had been sent to New York to execute an informer who had been put on a boat to America by the police for his own good after selling information which had led to the arrest and hanging of a young IRA volunteer named Michael Reilly. Devlin had accomplished this mission with an efficiency that could only enhance a reputation that was already becoming legendary. Later that year he repeated the performance. Once in London and again in America, although this time the venue was Boston.

In 1936 he had taken himself to Spain, serving in the Lincoln Washington Brigade. He had been wounded and captured by Italian troops who, instead of shooting him, had kept him intact, hoping to effect an exchange for one of their own officers. Although this had never come to anything, it meant that he survived the war, being eventually sentenced to life imprisonment by the Franco government.

He had been freed at the instigation of the Abwehr in the autumn of 1940 and brought to Berlin, where it was hoped he might prove of some use to German Intelligence. It was at this stage that things had gone sadly wrong, for according to the record, Devlin, while having little sympathy with the Communist cause, was very definitely anti-fascist, a fact which he had made abundantly clear during his interrogation. A bad risk, then considered fit only for minor translation duties and English tutoring at the University of Berlin.

But the position had changed drastically. The Abwehr had made several attempts to get Goertz out of Ireland. All had failed. In desperation, the Irish Section had called in Devlin and asked him to parachute into Ireland with forged travel documents, contact Goertz and get him out via a Portuguese ship or some similar neutral vessel. He was dropped over County Meath on the 18 October 1941 but some weeks later, before he could contact Goertz, the German was arrested by the Irish Special Branch.

Devlin had spent several harrowing months on the run, betrayed at every turn, for so many IRA supporters had been interned in the Curragh by the Irish Government that there were few reliable contacts left. Surrounded by police in a farmhouse in Kerry in June, 1942, he wounded two of them and was himself rendered unconscious when a bullet creased his forehead. He had escaped from a hospital bed, made his way to Dun Laoghaire and had managed to get passage on a Brazilian boat bound for Lisbon. From there he had passed through Spain via the usual channels until he once more stood in the offices at the Tirpitz Ufer.

From then on, Ireland was a dead end as far as the Abwehr was concerned and Liam Devlin was sent back to kick his heels in translation duties and occasionally, so farcical can life be, to take tutorials again in English literature at the University of Berlin.

*

It was just before noon when Hofer came back into the office, 'I've got him, Herr Oberst.'

Radl looked up and put down his pen. 'Devlin?' He stood up and walked to the window, straightening his tunic, trying to work out what he was going to say. This had to go right, had to work. Yet Devlin would require careful handling. He was, after all, a neutral. The door clicked open and he turned.

Liam Devlin was smaller than he had imagined. No more than five feet five or six. He had dark, wavy hair, pale face, eyes of the most vivid blue that Radl had ever seen and a slight, ironic smile that seemed to permanently lift the corner of his mouth. The look of a man who had found life a bad joke and had decided that the only thing to do was laugh about it. He was wearing a black, belted trenchcoat and the ugly puckered scar of the bullet

wound that he had picked up on his last trip to Ireland showed
clearly on the left side of his forehead.

'Mr Devlin,' Radl went round the desk and held out his hand.
'My name is Radl – Max Radl. It's good of you to come.'

'That's nice,' Devlin said in excellent German. 'The impression
I got was that I didn't have much choice in the matter.' He moved
forward, unbuttoning his coat. 'So this is Section Three where it
all happens?'

'Please, Mr Devlin.' Radl brought a chair forward and offered
him a cigarette.

Devlin leaned forward for a light. He coughed, choking as the
harsh cigarette smoke pulled at the back of his throat. 'Mother
Mary, Colonel, I knew things were bad, but not that bad. What's
in them or shouldn't I ask?'

'Russian,' Radl said. 'I picked up the taste for them during the
Winter War.'

'Don't tell me,' Devlin said. 'They were the only thing that kept
you from falling asleep in the snow.'

Radl smiled, warming to the man. 'Very likely.' He produced
the bottle of Courvoisier and two glasses. 'Cognac?'

'Now you're being too nice.' Devlin accepted the glass, swallowed, closing his eyes for a moment. 'It isn't Irish, but it'll do to
be going on with. When do we get to the nasty bit? The last time I
was at Tirpitz Ufer they asked me to jump out of a Dornier at five
thousand feet over Meath in the dark and I've a terrible fear of
heights.'

'All right, Mr Devlin,' Radl said. 'We do have work for you if
you're interested.'

'I've got work.'

'At the university? Come now, for a man like you that must be
rather like being a thoroughbred racing horse that finds itself
pulling a milk cart.'

Devlin threw back his head and laughed out loud. 'Ah,
Colonel, you've found my weak spot instantly. Vanity, vanity.
Stroke me any more and I'll purr like my Uncle Sean's old tomcat.
Are you trying to lead up, in the nicest way possible, to the fact
that you want me to go back to Ireland? Because if you are you can

forget it. I wouldn't stand a chance, not for any length of time the way things are now, and I've no intention of sitting on my arse in the Curragh for five years. I've had enough of prisons to last me quite some time.'

'Ireland is still a neutral country, Mr de Valera had made it quite clear that she will not take sides.'

'Yes, I know,' Devlin said, 'which is why a hundred thousand Irishmen are serving in the British forces. And another thing – every time an RAF plane crash-lands in Ireland, the crew are passed over the border in a matter of days. How many German pilots have they sent you back lately?' Devlin grinned. 'Mind you, with all that lovely butter and cream and the colleens, they probably think they're better off where they are.'

'No, Mr Devlin, we don't want you to go back to Ireland,' Radl said. 'Not the way you mean.'

'Then what in the hell do you want?'

'Let me ask you something first. You are still a supporter of the IRA.'

'Soldier of,' Devlin corrected him. 'We have a saying back home, Colonel. Once in, never out.'

'So, your total aim is victory against England?'

'If you mean a united Ireland, free and standing on her own two feet, then I'll cheer for that: I'll believe it when it happens, mind you, but not before.'

Radl was mystified. 'Then why fight?'

'God save us, but don't you ask the questions?' Devlin shrugged. 'It's better than fist-fighting outside Murphy's Select Bar on Saturday nights. Or maybe it's just that I like playing the game.'

'And which game would that be?'

'You mean to tell me you're in this line of work and you don't know?'

For some reason Radl felt strangely uncomfortable so he said hurriedly, 'Then the activities of your compatriots in London, for instance, don't commend themselves to you?'

'Hanging round Bayswater making Paxo in their landlady's saucepans?' Devlin said. 'Not my idea of fun.'

'Paxo?' Radl was bewildered.

'A joke. Paxo is a well-known package gravy, so that's what the boys call the explosive they mix. Potassium chlorate, sulphuric acid and a few other assorted goodies.'

'A volatile brew.'

'Especially when it goes up in your face.'

'This bombing campaign your people started with the ultimatum they sent to the British Prime Minister in January, 1939 . . .'

Devlin laughed. 'And Hitler and Mussolini and anyone else they thought might be interested including Uncle Tom Cobley.'

'Uncle Tom Cobley?'

'Another joke,' Devlin said. 'A weakness of mine, never having been able to take anything too seriously.'

'Why, Mr Devlin? That interests me.'

'Come now, Colonel,' Devlin said. 'The world was a bad joke dreamed up by the Almighty on an off-day. I've always felt myself that he probably had a hangover that morning. But what was your point about the bombing campaign?'

'Did you approve of it?'

'No. I don't like soft target hits. Women, kids, passers-by. If you're going to fight, if you believe in your cause and it is a just one, then stand up on your two hind legs and fight like a man.'

His face was white and very intense, the bullet scar in his head glowing like a brand. He relaxed just as suddenly and laughed. 'There you go, bringing out the best in me. Too early in the morning to be serious.'

'So, a moralist,' Radl said. 'The English would not agree with you. They bomb the heart out of the Reich every night.'

'You'll have me in tears if you keep that up. I was in Spain fighting for the Republicans remember. What in the hell do you think those German Stukas were doing flying for Franco? Ever heard of Barcelona or Guernica?'

'Strange, Mr Devlin, you obviously resent us and I had presumed it was the English you hated.'

'The English?' Devlin laughed. 'Sure and they're just like your mother-in-law. Something you put up with. No I don't *hate* the English – it's the bloody British Empire I hate.'

'So, you wish to see Ireland free?'

'Yes.' Devlin helped himself to another of the Russian cigarettes.

'Then would you accept that from your point of view the best way of achieving that aim would be for Germany to win this war?'

'And pigs might fly one of these days,' Devlin told him, 'but I doubt it.'

'Then why stay here in Berlin?'

'I didn't realize that I had any choice?'

'But you do, Mr Devlin,' Colonel Radl said quietly. 'You can go to England for me.'

Devlin stared at him in amazement, for once in his life stopped dead in his tracks. 'God save us, the man's mad.'

'No, Mr Devlin, quite sane I assure you.' Radl pushed the Courvoisier bottle across the desk and placed the manilla file next to it. 'Have another drink and read that file then we'll talk again.'

He got up and walked out.

                              *

When at the end of a good half-hour there was no sign of Devlin, Radl steeled himself to open the door and go back in. Devlin was sitting with his feet on the desk, Joanna Grey's reports in one hand, a glass of Courvoisier in the other. The bottle looked considerably depleted.

He glanced up. 'So there you are? I was beginning to wonder what had happened to you.'

'Well, what do you think?' Radl demanded.

'It reminds me of a story I heard when I was a boy,' Devlin said. 'Something that happened during the war with the English back in nineteen-twenty-one. May, I think. It concerned a man called Emmet Dalton. He that was a General in the Free State Army later. Did you ever hear tell of him?'

'No, I'm afraid not,' said Radl with ill-concealed impatience.

'What we Irish would call a lovely man. Served as a major in the British Army right through the war, awarded the Military Cross for bravery, then he joined the IRA.'

'Forgive me, Mr Devlin, but is any of this relevant?'

Devlin didn't seem to have heard him. 'There was a man in Mountjoy prison in Dublin called McEoin, another lovely man, but in spite of that he only had the gallows before him.' He helped himself to more Courvoisier. 'Emmet Dalton had other ideas. He stole a British armoured car, put on his old major's uniform, dressed a few of the boys as *Tommis*, bluffed his way into the prison and right into the governor's office. Would you believe that?'

By now Radl was interested in spite of himself. 'And did they save this McEoin?'

'By bad luck, it was the one morning his application to see the governor was refused.'

'And these men – what happened to them?'

'Oh, there was a little shooting, but they got clean away. Bloody cheek, though.' He grinned and held up Joanna Grey's report. 'Just like this.'

'You think it would work?' Radl demanded eagerly. 'You think it possible?'

'It's impudent enough.' Devlin threw the report down. 'And I thought the Irish were supposed to be the crazy ones. To tumble the great Winston Churchill out of his bed in the middle of the night and away with him.' He laughed out loud. 'Now that would be something to see. Something that would stand the whole world on its ear in amazement.'

'And you'd like that?'

'A great ploy, surely.' Devlin smiled hugely and was still smiling when he added, 'Of course, there is the point that it wouldn't have the slightest effect on the course of the war. The English will simply promote Attlee to fill the vacancy, the Lancasters will still come over by night and the Flying Fortresses by day.'

'In other words it is your considered opinion that we'll still lose the war?' Radl said.

'Fifty marks on that any time you like.' Devlin grinned. 'On the other hand I'd hate to miss this little jaunt, if you're really serious, that is?'

'You mean you're willing to go?' Radl was by now thoroughly bewildered. 'But I don't understand. Why?'

'I know, I'm a fool,' Devlin said. 'Look what I'm giving up. A nice safe job at the University of Berlin with the RAF bombing by night, the Yanks by day, food getting shorter, the Eastern Front crumbling.'

Radl raised both hands, laughing. 'All right, no more questions, the Irish are quite obviously mad. I was told it, now I accept it.'

'The best thing for you and, of course, we mustn't forget the twenty thousand pounds you're going to deposit to a numbered account in a Geneva bank of my choosing.'

Radl was aware of a feeling of acute disappointment. 'So, Mr Devlin, you also have your price like the rest of us?'

'The movement I serve has always been notoriously low on funds.' Devlin grinned. 'I've seen revolutions started on less than twenty thousand pounds, Colonel.'

'Very well,' Radl said. 'I will arrange it. You will receive confirmation of the deposit before you leave.'

'Fine,' Devlin said. 'So what's the score then?'

'Today is the first October. That gives us exactly five weeks.'

'And what would my part be?'

'Mrs Grey is a first-rate agent, but she is sixty-eight years of age. She needs a man.'

'Someone to do the running around? Handle the rough stuff?'

'Exactly.'

'And how do you get me there and don't tell me you haven't been thinking about it?'

Radl smiled. 'I must admit I've given the matter considerable thought. See how this strikes you. You're an Irish citizen who has served with the British Army. Badly wounded and given a medical discharge. That scar on your forehead will help there.'

'And how does this fit in with Mrs Grey?'

'An old family friend who has found you some sort of employment in Norfolk. We'll have to put it to her and see what she comes up with. We'll fill the story out, supply you with every possible document from an Irish passport to your army discharge papers. What do you think?'

'It sounds passable enough.' Devlin said. 'But how do I get there?'

'We'll parachute you into Southern Ireland. As close to the Ulster border as possible. I understand it to be extremely easy to walk across the border without passing through a customs post.'

'No trouble there,' Devlin said. 'Then what?'

'The night boat from Belfast to Heysham, train to Norfolk, everything straight and above board.'

Devlin pulled the ordnance survey map forward and looked down at it. 'All right, I'll buy that. When do I go?'

'A week, ten days at the most. For the moment, you will obviously observe total security. You must also resign your post at the University and vacate your present apartment. Drop completely out of sight. Hofer will arrange other accommodation for you?'

'Then what?'

I'm going to see the man who will probably command the assault group. Tomorrow or the next day depending on how soon I can arrange flights to the Channel Islands. You might as well come too. You're going to have a lot in common. You agree?'

'And why shouldn't I, Colonel? Won't the same bad old roads all lead to hell in the end?' He poured what was left of the Courvoisier into his glass.

5

Alderney is the most northerly of the Channel Islands and the closest to the French coast. As the German Army rolled inexorably westward in the summer of 1940 the islanders had voted to evacuate. When the first Luftwaffe plane landed on the tiny grass strip on top of the cliffs on 2 July 1940, the place was deserted, the narrow cobbled streets of St Anne eerily quiet.

By the autumn of 1942 there was a garrison of perhaps three thousand, mixed Army, Navy and Luftwaffe personnel and several Todt camps employing slave labour from the continent to work on the massive concrete gun emplacements of the new fortifications. There was also a concentration camp staffed by members of the SS and Gestapo, the only such establishment ever to exist on British soil.

Just after noon on Sunday Radl and Devlin flew in from Jersey in a Stork spotter plane. It was only a half-hour run and as the Stork was unarmed the pilot did the entire trip at sea level only climbing up to seven hundred feet at the last moment.

As the Stork swept in over the enormous breakwater Alderney was spread out for them like a map. Braye Bay, the harbour, St Anne, the island itself, perhaps three miles long and a mile and a half wide, vividly green, great cliffs on one side, the land sliding down into a series of sandy bays and coves on the other.

The Stork turned into the wind and dropped down on to one of the grass runways of the airfield on top of the cliffs. It was one of the smallest Radl had ever seen, hardly deserving of the name. A tiny control tower, a scattering of prefabricated buildings and no hangars.

There was a black Wolseley car parked beside the control tower and as Radl and Devlin went towards it, the driver, a sergeant of Artillery, got out and opened the rear door. He saluted, 'Colonel Radl? The commandant asks you to accept his compliments. I'm to take you straight to the Feldkommandantur.'

'Very well,' Radl said.

They got in and were driven away, soon turning into a country lane. It was a fine day, warm and sunny, more like late spring than early autumn.

'It seems a pleasant enough place,' Radl commented.

'For some.' Devlin nodded over towards the left where hundreds of Todt workers could be seen in the distance labouring on what looked like some enormous concrete fortification.

The houses in St Anne were a mixture of French Provincial and English Georgian, streets cobbled, gardens high-walled against the constant winds. There were plenty of signs of war – concrete pillboxes, barbed wire, machine-gun posts, bomb damage in the harbour far below – but it was the Englishness of it all that fascinated Radl. The incongruity of seeing two SS men in a field car parked in Connaught Square and of a Luftwaffe private giving another a light for his cigarette under a sign that said 'Royal Mail.'

Feldkommandantur 515, the German civilian administration for the Channel Islands, had its local headquarters in the old Lloyds Bank premises in Victoria Street and as the car drew up outside, Neuhoff himself appeared in the entrance.

He came forward, hand outstretched. 'Colonel Radl? Hans Neuhoff, temporarily in command here, Good to see you.'

Radl said, 'This gentleman is a colleague of mine.'

He made no other attempt to introduce Devlin and a certain alarm showed in Neuhoff's eyes instantly, for Devlin, in civilian clothes and a black leather military greatcoat Radl had procured for him, was an obvious curiosity. The logical explanation would seem to be that he was Gestapo. During the trip from Berlin to Brittany and then on to Guernsey, the Irishman had seen the same wary look on other faces and had derived a certain malicious satisfaction from it.

'Herr Oberst,' he said, making no attempt to shake hands.

Neuhoff, more put out than ever, said hurriedly, 'This way, gentlemen, please.'

Inside, three clerks worked at the mahogany counter. Behind them on the wall was a new Ministry of Propaganda poster showing an eagle, with a swatika in its talons, rearing proudly above the legend *Am ende der Sieg!* At the end stands victory.

'My God,' Devlin said softly, 'some people will believe anything.'

A military policeman guarded the door of what had presumably been the manager's office. Neuhoff led the way in. It was sparsely furnished, a workroom more than anything else. He brought two chairs forward. Radl took one, but Devlin lit a cigarette and went and stood at the window.

Neuhoff glanced at him uncertainly and tried to smile. 'Can I offer you gentlemen a drink? Schnapps or a Cognac perhaps?'

'Frankly I'd like to get straight down to business,' Radl told him.

'But, of course, Herr Oberst.'

Radl unbuttoned his tunic, took the manilla envelope from his inside pocket and produced the letter. 'Please read that.'

Neuhoff picked it up, frowning slightly and ran his eyes over it. 'The Führer himself commands.' He looked up at Radl in amazement. 'But I don't understand. What is it that you wish of me?'

'Your complete co-operation, Colonel Neuhoff,' Radl said. 'And no questions. You have a penal unit here, I believe? Operation Swordfish.'

There was a new kind of wariness in Neuhoff's eyes, Devlin noticed it instantly, and the colonel seemed to stiffen. 'Yes, Herr Oberst, that is so. Under the command of Colonel Steiner of the Parachute Regiment.'

'So I understand,' Radl said. 'Colonel Steiner, a Lieutenant Neumann and twenty-nine paratroopers.'

Neuhoff corrected him. 'Colonel Steiner, Ritter Neumann and fourteen paratroopers.'

Radl stared at him in surprise. 'What are you saying? Where are the others?'

'Dead, Herr Oberst,' Neuhoff said simply. 'You know about Operation Swordfish? You know what they do, these men? They sit astride torpedoes and . . .'

'I'm aware of that.' Radl stood up, reached for the Führer Directive and replaced it in its envelope, 'Are there any operations planned for today?'

'That depends on whether there is a radar contact.'

'No more,' Radl said. 'It stops now, from this moment.' He held up the envelope. 'My first order under this directive.'

Neuhoff actually smiled. 'I am delighted to comply with such an order.'

'I see,' Radl said. 'Colonel Steiner is a friend?'

'My privilege,' Neuhoff said simply. 'If you knew the man, you'd know what I mean. There is also the point of view that someone of his extraordinary gifts is of more use to the Reich alive than dead.'

'Which is exactly why I am here,' Radl said. 'Now, where can I find him?'

'Just before you get to the harbour there's an inn. Steiner and his men use it as their headquarters. I'll take you down there.'

'No need,' Radl said. 'I'd like to see him alone. Is it far?'

'A quarter of a mile.'

'Good, then we'll walk.'

Neuhoff stood up. 'Have you any idea how long you will be staying?'

'I have arranged for the Stork to pick us up first thing in the morning,' Radl said. 'It is essential that we're at the airfield in Jersey no later than eleven. Our plane for Brittany leaves then.'

'I'll arrange accommodation for you and your – your friend.' Neuhoff glanced at Devlin. 'Also, if you would care to dine with me tonight? My wife would be delighted and perhaps Colonel Steiner could join us.'

'An excellent idea,' Radl said. 'I'll look forward to it.'

As they walked down Victoria Street past the shuttered shops and empty houses Devlin said, 'What's got into you? You were laying it on a bit strong, weren't you? Are we feeling our oats today?'

Radl laughed, looked slightly shamefaced. 'Whenever I take that damned letter out I feel strange. A feeling of – of power comes over me. Like the centurion in the Bible, who says do this and they do it, go there and they go.'

As they turned into Braye Road a fieldcar drove past them, the artillery sergeant who brought them in from the airfield at the wheel.

'Colonel Neuhoff sending a warning of our coming,' Radl commented. 'I wondered whether he would.'

'I think he thought I was Gestapo,' Devlin said. 'He was afraid.'

'Perhaps,' Radl said. 'And you, Herr Devlin? Are you ever afraid?'

'Not that I can remember.' Devlin laughed, without mirth. 'I'll tell you something I've never told another living soul. Even at the moment of maximum danger and, God knows, I've known enough of those in my time, even when I'm staring Death right between the eyes, I get the strangest feeling. It's as if I want to reach out and take his hand. Now isn't that the funniest thing you ever heard of?'

*

Ritter Neumann, wearing a black rubber wet suit, was sitting astride a torpedo moored to the number one recovery boat tinkering with its engine, when the fieldcar roared along the jetty and braked to a halt. As Neumann looked up, shading his eyes against the sun, Sergeant-Major Brandt appeared.

'What's your hurry?' Neumann called. 'Is the war over?'

'Trouble, Herr Leutnant,' Brandt said. 'There's some staff officer flown in from Jersey. A Colonel Radl. He's come for the Colonel. We've just had a tip-off from Victoria Street.'

'Staff officer?' Neumann said and he pulled himself over the rail of the recovery boat and took the towel that Private Riedel handed him. 'Where's he from?'

'Berlin!' Brandt said grimly, 'And he has someone with him who looks like a civilian, but isn't.'

'Gestapo?'

'So it would appear. They're on their way down now – walking.'

Neumann pulled on his jump boots and scrambled up the ladder to the jetty. 'Do the lads know?'

Brandt nodded, a savage look on his face, 'And don't like it. If they find he's come to put the screws in the Colonel they're quite likely to push him and his pal off the end of the jetty with sixty pounds of chain apiece around their ankles.'

'Right,' said Neumann. 'Back to the pub as fast as you can and hold them. I'll take the fieldcar and get the Colonel. He went for a walk along the breakwater with Frau Neuhoff.'

Steiner and Ilse Neuhoff were at the very end of the break-water. She was sitting above the rampart, those long legs dangling into space, the wind off the sea ruffling the blonde hair, tugging at her skirt. She was laughing down at Steiner. He turned as the fieldcar braked to a halt.

Neumann scrambled out and Steiner took one look at his face and smiled sardonically. 'Bad news, Ritter, and on such a lovely day.'

'There's some staff officer in from Berlin looking for you, a Colonel Radl,' Neumann said grimly. 'They say he has a Gestapo man with him.'

Steiner wasn't put out in the slightest. 'That certainly adds a little interest to the day.'

He put up his hands to catch Ilse as she jumped down, and held her close for a moment. Her face was full of alarm. 'For God's sake, Kurt, can't you ever take anything seriously?'

'He's probably only here for a head count. We should all be dead by now. They must be very put out at Prinz Albrechtstrasse.'

*

The old inn stood at the side of the road on the approach to the harbour backing on to the sands of Braye Bay. It was strangely quiet as Radl and the Irishman approached.

'As nice a looking pub as I've seen,' Devlin said. 'Would you think it possible they might still have a drink on the premises?'

Radl tried the front door. It opened and they found themselves in a dark passageway. A door clicked open behind them. 'In here, Herr Oberst,' a soft, cultured voice said.

Sergeant Hans Altmann leaned against the outside door as if to bar their exit. Radl saw the Winter War ribbon, the Iron Cross, First and Second Class, silver wound badge which meant at least three wounds, the Air Force Ground Combat badge and, most coveted honour of all amongst paratroopers, the *Kreta* cuff-title, proud mark of those who had spearheaded the invasion of Crete in May, 1941.

'Your name?' Radl said crisply.

Altmann didn't reply, but simply pushed with his foot so that the door marked 'Saloon Bar' swung open and Radl, sensing something, but uncertain what, stuck out his chin and advanced into the room.

The room was only fair-sized. There was a bar counter to the left, empty shelves behind it, a number of framed photographs of old wrecks on the walls, a piano in one corner. There were a dozen or so paratroopers scattered around the room, all remarkably unfriendly. Radl, looking them over coolly, was impressed. He'd never before seen a group of men with so many decorations between them. There wasn't a man there who didn't have the Iron Cross, First Class and such minor items as wound badges and tank destruction badges were ten a penny.

He stood in the centre of the room, his briefcase under his arm, his hands in his pockets, coat collar still turned up. 'I'd like to point out,' he said mildly, 'that men have been shot before now for this kind of behaviour.'

There was a shout of laughter. Sergeant Sturm, who was behind the bar cleaning a Luger said, 'That really is very good, Herr Oberst. Do you want to hear something funny? When we went operational here ten weeks ago, there were thirty-one of us, including the Colonel. Fifteen now, in spite of a lot of lucky breaks. What can you and this Gestapo shit offer that's worse than that?'

'Don't go including me in this thing,' Devlin said. 'I'm neutral.'

Sturm, who had worked the Hamburg barges since the age of twelve and was inclined to be a trifle direct in his speech, went on, 'Listen to this because I'm only going to say it once. The Colonel isn't going anywhere. Not with you. Not with anyone.' He shook his head. 'You know that's a pretty hat, Herr Oberst, but you've been polishing a chair with your backside for so long there in Berlin that you've forgotten how real soldiers feel. You've come to the wrong place if you're hoping for a chorus from the *Horst Wessel.*'

'Excellent,' Radl said. 'However, your completely incorrect reading of the present situation argues a lack of wit which I, for one, find deplorable in someone of your rank.'

He dumped his briefcase on the counter, opened the buttons of his coat with his good hand and shrugged it off. Sturm's jaw dropped as he saw the Knight's Cross, the Winter War ribbon. Radl moved straight into the attack.

'Attention!' he barked. 'On your feet, all of you.' There was an instant burst of activity and in the same moment the door swung open and Brandt rushed in. 'And you, Sergeant-Major,' Radl snarled.

There was pin-drop silence as every man stood rigidly to attention and Devlin, thoroughly enjoying this new turn events had taken, pulled himself up on to the bar and lit a cigarette.

Radl said. 'You think you are German soldiers, a natural error in view of the uniforms you wear, but you are mistaken.' He moved from one man to another, pausing as if committing each face to memory. 'Shall I tell you what you are?'

Which he did in simple and direct terms that made Sturm look like a beginner. When he paused for breath after two or three minutes, there was a polite cough from the open doorway and he turned to find Steiner there, Ilse Neuhoff behind him.

'I couldn't have put it better myself, Colonel Radl. I can only hope that you are willing to put down anything which has happened here to misguided enthusiasm and let it go at that. Their feet won't touch the ground when I get through with them, I promise you.' He held out his hand and smiled with considerable charm. 'Kurt Steiner.'

Radl was always to remember that first meeting. Steiner possessed that strange quality to be found in the airborne troops of every country. A kind of arrogant self-sufficiency bred of the hazards of the calling. He was wearing a blue-grey flying blouse with the yellow collar patches bearing the wreath and two stylized wings of his rank, jump trousers and the kind of sidecap known as a *Schiff,* an affectation of many of the old-timers. The rest, for a man who had every conceivable decoration in the book, was extraordinarily simple. The *Kreta* cuff title, the ribbon for the Winter War and the silver and gold eagle of the paratroopers' qualification badge. The Knight's Cross with Oak Leaves was concealed by a silk scarf tied loosely about his neck.

'To be honest, Colonel Steiner, I've rather enjoyed putting these rogues of yours in their place.'

Ilse Neuhoff chuckled. 'An excellent performance, Herr Oberst, if I may say so.'

Steiner made the necessary introductions and Radl kissed her hand. 'A great pleasure, Frau Neuhoff.' He frowned. 'Have we by any chance met before?'

'Undoubtedly,' Steiner said and pulled forward Ritter Neumann who had been lurking in the background in his rubber wet suit. 'And this, Herr Oberst, is not as you may imagine, a captive Atlantic seal, but Oberleutnant Ritter Neumann.'

'Lieutenant.' Radl glanced at Ritter Neumann briefly, remembering the citation for the Knight's Cross that had been quashed because of the court martial, wondering whether he knew.

'And this gentleman?' Steiner turned to Devlin who jumped down from the counter and came forward.

'Actually everyone round here seems to think I'm your friendly neighbourhood Gestapo man,' Devlin said. 'I'm not sure I find that too flattering.' He held out his hand. 'Devlin, Colonel. Liam Devlin.'

'Herr Devlin is a colleague of mine,' Radl explained quickly.

'And you?' Steiner said politely.

'From Abwehr Headquarters. And now, if it is convenient, I would like to talk to you privately on a matter of grave urgency.'

Steiner frowned and again, there was that pin-drop silence in the room. He turned to Ilse. 'Ritter will see you home.'

'No, I'd rather wait until your business with Colonel Radl is over.'

She was desperately worried, it showed in her eyes. Steiner said gently, 'I shouldn't imagine I'll be very long. Look after her, Ritter.' He turned to Radl. 'This way, Herr Oberst.'

Radl nodded to Devlin and they went after him.

'All right, stand down,' Ritter Neumann said. 'You damned fools.'

There was a general easing of tension. Altmann sat at the piano and launched into a popular song which assured everyone that everything would get better by and by. 'Frau Neuhoff,' he called. 'What about a song?'

Ilse sat on one of the bar stools. 'I'm not in the mood,' she said. 'You want to know something, boys? I'm sick of this damned war. All I want is a decent cigarette and a drink, but that would be too much like a miracle, I suppose.'

'Oh, I don't know, Frau Neuhoff.' Brandt vaulted clean over the bar and turned to face her. 'For you, anything is possible. Cigarettes, for example, London gin.'

His hands went beneath the counter and came up clutching a carton of Gold Flake and a bottle of Beefeater.

'Now will you sing for us, Frau Neuhoff?' Hans Altmann called.

*

Devlin and Radl keaned on the parapet looking down into the water, clear and deep in the pale sunshine. Steiner sat on a bollard at the end of the jetty working his way through the contents of Radl's briefcase. Across the bay, Fort Albert loomed on the headland and below, the cliffs were splashed with birdlime, seabirds wheeling in great clouds, gulls, shags, razorbills and oyster-catchers.

Steiner called, 'Colonel Radl.'

Radl moved towards him and Devlin followed, stopping two or three yards away to lean on the wall. Radl said. 'You have finished?'

'Oh, yes.' Steiner put the various papers back into the brief-case. 'You're serious, I presume?'

'Of course.'

Steiner reached forward and tapped a forefinger on Radl's Winter War ribbon. 'Then all I can say is that some of that Russian cold must have got into your brain, my friend.'

Radl took the manilla envelope from his inside pocket and produced the Führer Directive. 'I think you had better have a look at that.'

Steiner read it, with no evidence of emotion, and shrugged as he handed it back. 'So what?'

'But Colonel Steiner,' Radl said. 'You are a German soldier. We swore the same oath. This is a direct order from the Führer himself.'

'You seem to have forgotten one highly important thing,' Steiner told him, 'I'm in a penal unit, under suspended sentence of death, officially disgraced. In fact, I only retain my rank because of the peculiar circumstances of the job in hand.' He produced a crumpled packet of French cigarettes from his hip pocket and put one in his mouth. 'Anyway, I don't like Adolf. He has a loud voice and bad breath.'

Radl ignored this remark. 'We must fight. We have no other choice.'

'To the last man?'

'What else can we do?'

'We can't win.'

Radl's good hand was clenched into a fist, he was filled with nervous excitement. 'But we can force them to change their views. See that some sort of settlement is better than this continual slaughter.'

'And knocking off Churchill would help?' Steiner said with obvious scepticism.

'It would show them we still have teeth. Look at the furore when Skorzeny lifted Mussolini off the Gran Sasso. A sensation all over the world.'

Steiner said, 'As I heard it, General Student and a few paratroopers had a hand in that as well.'

'For God's sake,' Radl said impatiently. 'Imagine how it would look. German troops dropping into England for one thing, but with such a target. Of course, perhaps you don't think it could be done.'

'I don't see why not,' Steiner said calmly. 'If those papers I've just looked at are accurate and if you've done your homework correctly, the whole thing could go like a Swiss watch. We could really catch the *Tommis* with their pants down. In and out again before they know what's hit them, but that isn't the point.'

'What is?' demanded Radl, completely exasperated. 'Is thumbing your nose at the Führer more important because of your court martial? Because you're here? Steiner, you and your men are dead men if you stay here. Thirty-one of you eight weeks ago. How many left – fifteen? You owe it to your men, to yourself, to take this last chance to live.'

'Or die in England instead.'

Radl shrugged. 'Straight in, straight out, that's the way it could go. Just like a Swiss watch, you said that yourself.'

'And the terrible thing about those is that if anything goes wrong with even the tiniest part, the whole damn thing stops working,' Devlin put in.

Steiner said, 'Well put, Mr Devlin. Tell me something. Why are you going?'

'Simple,' Devlin said. 'Because it's there. I'm the last of the great adventurers.'

'Excellent,' Steiner laughed delightedly. 'Now that, I can accept. To play the game. The greatest game of all. But it doesn't help, you see,' he went on. 'Colonel Radl here tells me that I owe it to my men to do the thing because it is a way out from certain death here. Now, to be perfectly frank with you, I don't think I owe anything to anybody.'

'Not even your father?' Radl said.

There was a silence, only the sea washing over the rocks below. Steiner's face turned pale, the skin stretched tight on the cheekbones, eyes dark. 'All right, tell me.'

'The Gestapo have him at Prinz Albrechstrasse. Suspicion of treason.'

And Steiner, remembering the week he had spent at his father's headquarters in France in 'forty-two, remembering what the old man had said, knew instantly that it was true.

'Ah, I see now,' he said softly. 'If I'm a good boy and do as I'm told, it would help his case.' Suddenly his face changed and he looked about as dangerous as any man could and when he reached for Radl, it was in a kind of slow motion. 'You bastard. All of you, bastards.'

He had Radl by the throat. Devlin moved in fast and found that it took all his considerable strength to pull him off. 'Not him, you fool. He's under the boot as much as you. You want to shoot somebody, shoot Himmler. He's the man you want.'

Radl fought to get his breath and leaned against the parapet, looking very ill. 'I'm sorry,' Steiner put a hand on his shoulder in genuine concern. 'I should have known.'

Radl raised his dead hand. 'See this, Steiner, and the eye? And other damage that you can't see. Two years if I'm lucky, that's what they tell me. Not for me. For my wife and daughters because I wake up at night sweating at the thought of what might happen to them. That's why I'm here.'

Steiner nodded slowly. 'Yes, of course, I understand. We're all up the same dark alley looking for a way out.' He took a deep breath. 'All right, we'll go back. I'll put it to the lads.'

'Not the target,' Radl said. 'Not at this stage.'

'The destination then. They're entitled to know that. As for the rest – I'll only discuss it with Neumann for the moment.'

He started to walk away and Radl said, 'Steiner, I must be honest with you.' Steiner turned to face him. 'In spite of everything I've said, I also think it's worth a try, this thing. All right, as Devlin says, getting Churchill, alive or dead, isn't going to win us the war, but perhaps it will give them a shake. Make them think again about a negotiated peace.'

Steiner said, 'My dear Radl, if you believe that you'll believe anything. I'll tell you what this affair, even if it's successful, will buy you from the British. Damn all!'

He turned and walked away along the jetty.

*

The saloon bar was full of smoke. Hans Altmann was playing the piano and the rest of the men were crowded round Ilse, who was sitting at the bar, a glass of gin in one hand, recounting a slightly unsavoury story current in high society and relevant only to Reichsmarschall Hermann Goering's love life, such as it was. There was a burst of laughter as Steiner entered the room followed by Radl and Devlin. Steiner surveyed the scene in astonishment, particularly the array of bottles on the bar counter.

'What the hell's going on here?'

The men eased away from the bar, Ritter Neumann, who was standing behind it with Brandt said, 'Altmann found a trap door under that old rush mat behind the bar this morning, sir, and a cellar below that we didn't know about. Two parcels of cigarettes not even unwrapped. Five thousand in each.' He waved a hand along the counter. 'Gordon's gin, Beefeater, White Horse Scotch Whisky, Haig and Haig.' He picked up a bottle and spelled out the English with difficulty. 'Bushmills Irish Whiskey, Pot distilled.'

Liam Devlin gave a howl of delight and grabbed it from him. 'I'll shoot the first man that touches a drop,' he declared. 'I swear it. It's all for me.'

There was a general laugh and Steiner calmed them with a raised hand. 'Steady down, there's something to discuss. Business.' He turned to Ilse Neuhoff. 'Sorry, my love, but this is top security.'

She was enough of a soldier's wife not to argue. 'I'll wait outside. But I refuse to let that gin out of my sight.' She exited, the bottle of Beefeater in one hand, her glass in the other.

There was silence, now, in the saloon bar, everyone suddenly sober, waiting to hear what he had to say. 'It's simple,' Steiner told them. 'There's a chance to get out of here. A special mission.'

'Doing what, Herr Oberst?' Sergeant Altmann asked.

'Your old trade. What you were trained to do.'

There was an instant reaction, a buzz of excitement. Someone whispered, 'Does that mean we'll be jumping again?'

'That's exactly what I mean,' Steiner said. 'But it's volunteers only. A personal decision for every man here.'

'Russia, Herr Oberst?' Brandt asked.

Steiner shook his head. 'Somewhere no German solider has ever fought.' The faces were full of curiosity, tight, expectant as he looked from one to the other. 'How many of you speak English?' he asked softly.

There was a stunned silence and Ritter Neumann so far forgot himself as to say in a hoarse voice. 'For God's sake, Kurt, you've got to be joking.'

Steiner shook his head. 'I've never been more serious. What I tell you now is top secret, naturally. To be brief, in approximately five weeks we'd be expected to do a night drop over a very isolated part of the English coast across the North Sea from Holland. If everything went according to plan we'd be taken off again the following night.'

'And if not?' Neumann said.

'You'd be dead, naturally, so it wouldn't matter.' He looked around the room. 'Anything else?'

'Can we be told the purpose of the mission, Herr Oberst?' Altmann asked.

'The same sort of thing Skorzeny and those lads of the Paratroop School Battalion pulled at Gran Sasso. That's all I can say.'

'Well, it's enough for me.' Brandt glared around the room. 'If we go, we might die, if we stay here we die for certain. If you go – we go.'

'I agree,' Ritter Neumann echoed and snapped to attention.

Every man in the room followed suit. Steiner stood there for a long moment, staring into some dark secret place in his own mind and then he nodded. 'So be it. Did I hear someone mention White Horse Whisky?'

The group broke for the bar and Altmann sat down and started to play *We march against England* on the piano. Someone threw his cap at him and Sturm called, 'You can stick that load of old crap. Let's have something worth listening to.'

The door opened and Ilse Neuhoff appeared. 'Can I come in now?'

There was a roar from the whole group. In a moment she was lifted up on to the bar. 'A song!' they chorused.

'All right,' she said, laughing. 'What do you want?'

Steiner got in before everyone, his voice sharp and quick. *'Alles ist verrückt.'*

There was a sudden silence. She looked down at him, face pale. 'You're sure?'

'Highly appropriate,' he said. 'Believe me.'

Hans Altmann moved into the opening chords, giving it every-thing he had and Ilse paraded slowly up and down the bar, her hands on her hips, as she sang that strange melancholy song known to every man who had served in the Winter War.

What are we doing here? What is it all about? Alles ist verrückt. Everything's crazy. Everything's gone to hell.

There were tears in her eyes now. She spread her arms wide as if she would embrace them all and suddenly everyone was singing, slow and deep, looking up at her, Steiner, Ritter, all of them – even Radl.

Devlin looked from one face to the other in bewilderment then turned, pulled open the door and lurched outside. 'Am I crazy or are they?' he whispered.

*

It was dark on the terrace because of the blackout, but Radl and Steiner went out there to smoke a cigar after dinner, more for privacy than anything else. Through the thick curtains that covered the French windows they could hear Liam Devlin's voice, Ilse Neuhoff and her husband laughing gaily.

'A man of considerable charm,' Steiner said.

Radl nodded. 'He has other qualities also. Many more like him and the British would have thankfully got out of Ireland years ago. You had a mutually profitable meeting after I left you this after-noon, I trust?'

'I think that you could say that we understand each other,' Steiner said, 'and we examined the map together very closely. It will be of great assistance to have him as an advance party, believe me.'

'Anything else I should know?'

'Yes, young Werner Briegel's actually been to that area.'

'Briegel?' Radl said. 'Who's he?'

'Lance-corporal. Twenty-one. Three years service. Comes from a place called Barth on the Baltic. He says some of that coastline is rather similar to Norfolk. Enormous lonely beaches, sand dunes and lots of birds.'

'Birds?' Radl said.

Steiner smiled through the darkness. 'I should explain that birds are the passion of young Werner's life. Once, near Leningrad, we were saved from a partisan ambush because they disturbed a huge flock of starlings. Werner and I were temporarily caught in the open, under fire and flat on our faces in the mud. He filled in the time by giving me chapter and verse on how the starlings were probably migrating to England for the winter.'

'Fascinating,' Radl said ironically.

'Oh, you may laugh. but it passed a nasty thirty minutes rather quickly for us. That's what took him and his father to North Norfolk in nineteen-thirty-seven, by the way. The birds. Apparently the whole coast is famous for them.'

'Ah, well,' Radl said. 'Each one to his own taste. What about this question of who speaks English? Did you get that sorted out?'

'Lieutenant Neumann, Sergeant Altmann and young Briegel all speak good English, but with accents, naturally. No hope of passing for natives. Of the rest, Brandt and Klugel both speak the broken variety. Enough to get by. Brandt, by the way, was a deck hand on cargo boats as a youngster, Hamburg to Hull.'

Radl nodded. 'It could be worse. Tell me, has Neuhoff questioned you at all?'

'No, but he's obviously very curious. And poor Ilse is beside herself with worry. I'll have to make sure she doesn't try to take the whole thing up with Ribbentrop in a misguided attempt to save me from what she knows not what.'

'Good,' Radl said. 'You sit tight then and wait. You'll have movement orders within a week to ten days, depending on how quickly I can find a suitable base in Holland. Devlin, as you know, will probably go over in about a week. I think we'd better go in now.'

Steiner put a hand on his arm. 'And my father?'

Radl said, 'I would be dishonest if I led you to believe I have any influence in the matter. Himmler is personally responsible. All that I can do – and I will certainly do this – is make it plain to him how co-operative you are being.'

'And do you honestly think that will be enough?'

'Do you ?' Radl said.

Steiner's laugh had no mirth in it at all. 'He has no conception of honour.'

It seemed a curiously old-fashioned remark, and Radl was intrigued. 'And you?' he said. 'You have?'

'Perhaps not. Perhaps it's too fancy a word for what I mean. Simple things like giving your word and keeping it, standing by friends whatever comes. Does the sum of these things total honour?'

'I don't know, my friend,' Radl said. 'All I can confirm with any certainty is the undoubted fact that you are too good for the Reichsführer's world, believe me.' He put an arm around Steiner's shoulders. 'And now, we'd really better go in.'

Ilse, Colonel Neuhoff and Devlin were seated at a small round table by the fire and she was busy laying out a Celtic Circle from the Tarot pack in her left hand.

'Go on, amaze me.' Devlin was saying.

'You mean you are not a believer, Mr Devlin?' she asked him.

'A decent Catholic lad like me? Proud product of the best the Jesuits could afford, Frau Neuhoff?' He grinned, 'Now what do you think?'

'That you are an intensely superstitious man, Mr Devlin.' His smile slipped a little. 'You see,' she went on, 'I am what is known as a sensitive. The cards are not important. They are a tool only.'

'Go on then.'

'Very well, your future on one card, Mr Devlin. The seventh I come to.'

She counted them out quickly and turned the seventh card over. It was a skeleton carrying a scythe and the card was upside down.

'Isn't he the cheerful one?' Devlin remarked, trying to sound unconcerned and failing.

'Yes, Death,' she said, 'but reversed it doesn't mean what you imagine.' She stared down at the card for a full half-minute and then said very quickly. 'You will live long, Mr Devlin. Soon for you begins a lengthy period of inertia, of stagnation even and then, in the closing years of your life, revolution, perhaps assassination.' She looked up calmly. 'Does that satisfy you?'

'The long life bit does,' Devlin said cheerfully. 'I'll take my chance on the rest.'

'May I join in, Frau Neuhoff,' Radl said.

'If you like.'

She counted out the cards. This time the seventh was the Star reversed. She looked at it for another long moment. 'Your health is not good, Herr Oberst.'

'That's true,' Radl said.

She looked up and said simply, 'I think you know what is here?'

'Thank you, I believe I do,' he said, smiling calmly.

There was a slightly uncomfortable atmosphere then, as if a sudden chill had fallen and Steiner said, 'All right, Ilse, what about me?'

She reached for the cards as if to gather them up. 'No, not now, Kurt. I think we've had enough for one night.'

'Nonsense,' he said. 'I insist.' He picked up the cards. 'There, I hand you the pack with my left hand, isn't that right?'

Very hesitantly she took it, looked at him in mute appeal, then started to count. She turned the seventh card over quickly, long enough to glance at it herself and put it back on the top of the pack. 'Lucky in cards as well, it seems, Kurt. You drew Strength. Considerable good fortune, a triumph in adversity, sudden success.' She smiled brightly. 'And now, if you gentlemen will excuse me, I'll see to the coffee,' and she walked out of the room.

Steiner reached down and turned the card over. It was The Hanged Man. He sighed heavily. 'Women,' he said, 'can be very silly at times. Is it not so, gentlemen?'

*

There was fog in the morning. Neuhoff had Radl wakened just after dawn and broke the bad news to him over coffee.

'A regular problem here, I'm afraid,' he said. 'But there it is and the general forecast is lousy. Not a hope of anything getting off the ground here before evening. Can you wait that long?'

Radl shook his head. 'I have to be in Paris by this evening and to do that it's essential that I catch the transport leaving Jersey at eleven to make the necessary connection in Brittany. What else can you offer?'

'I could arrange passage by E-boat if you insist,' Neuhoff told him. 'Something of an experience, I warn you, and rather hazardous. We've more trouble with the Royal Navy than we do with the RAF in this area. But it would be essential to leave without delay if you are to make St Helier in time.'

'Excellent,' Radl said. 'Please make all necessary arrangements at once and I'll rouse Devlin.'

*

Neuhoff drove them down to the harbour himself in his staff car shortly after seven, Devlin huddled in the rear seat showing every symptom of a king-size hangover. The E-boat waited at the lower jetty. When they went down the steps they found Steiner in sea boots and reefer jacket, leaning on the rail talking to a young bearded naval lieutenant in heavy sweater and salt-stained cap.

He turned to greet them. 'A nice morning for it. I've just been making sure Koenig realizes he's carrying precious cargo.'

The lieutenant saluted. 'Herr Oberst.'

Devlin, the picture of misery, stood with his hands pushed deep into his pockets. 'Not too well this morning, Mr Devlin?' Steiner enquired.

Devlin moaned. 'Wine is a mocker; strong drink is raging.'

Steiner said. 'You won't be wanting this then?' He held up a bottle. 'Brandt found another Bushmills.'

Devlin relieved him of it instantly. 'I wouldn't dream of allowing it to do to anyone else what it's done to me.' He shook hands. 'Let's hope that when you're coming down I'll be looking up,' and he clambered over the rail and sat in the stern.

Radl shook hands with Neuhoff, then turned to Steiner, 'You'll hear from me soon. As for the other matter, I'll do everything I can.'

Steiner said nothing. Did not even attempt to shake hands and Radl hesitated, then scrambled over the rail. Koenig issued orders crisply, leaning out of the open window in the wheelhouse. The lines were cast off and the E-boat slipped away into the mist of the harbour.

*

They rounded the end of the breakwater and picked up speed. Radl looked about him with interest. The crew were a rough-looking lot, half of them bearded, and all attired in either Guernseys or thick fishermen's sweaters, denim pants and sea boots. In fact, there was little of the Navy about them at all and the craft itself, festooned with strange aerials, was like no E-boat he had ever seen before now that he examined it thoroughly.

When he went on to the bridge he found Koenig leaning over the chart table, a large black-bearded seaman at the wheel who wore a faded reefer jacket that carried a chief petty officer's rank badges. A cigar jutted from between his teeth, something else which, it occurred to Radl, did not seem very naval.

Koenig saluted decently enough. 'Ah, there you are. Herr Oberst. Everything all right?'

'I hope so,' Radl leaned over the chart table. 'How far is it?'

'About fifty miles.'

'Will you get us there on time?'

Koenig glanced at his watch. 'I estimate we'll arrive at St Helier just before ten, Herr Oberst, as long as the Royal Navy doesn't get in the way.'

Radl looked out of the window. 'Your crew, Lieutenant, do they always dress like fishermen? I understood the E-boats to be the pride of the Navy.'

Koenig smiled. 'But this isn't an E-boat, Herr Oberst. Only classed as one.'

'Then what in the hell is it?' Radl demanded in bewilderment.

'Actually we're not too sure, are we, Muller?' The petty officer grinned and Koenig said, 'A motor gun boat, as you can see, Herr Oberst, constructed in Britain for the Turks and commandeered by the Royal Navy.'

'What's the story?'

'Ran aground on a sandbank on an ebb tide near Morlaix in Brittany. Her captain couldn't scuttle her, so he fired a demolition charge before abandoning her.'

'And?'

'It didn't go off and before he could get back on board to rectify the error an E-boat turned up and grabbed him and his crew.'

'Poor devil,' Radl said. 'I almost feel sorry for him.'

'But the best is yet to come, Herr Oberst,' Koenig told him. 'As the captain's last message was that he was abandoning his ship and blowing her up, the British Admiralty naturally assumed that he had succeeded.'

'Which leaves you free to make the run between the islands in what is to all intents and purposes a Royal Navy boat? I see now.'

'Exactly. You were looking at the jack staff earlier and were no doubt puzzled to find that it is the White Ensign of the Royal Navy we keep ready to unfurl.'

'And it's saved you on occasion?'

'Many times. We hoist the White Ensign, make a courtesy signal and move on. No trouble at all.'

Radl was aware of that cold finger of excitement moving inside him again. 'Tell me about the boat,' he said. 'How fast is she?'

'Top speed was originally twenty-five knots, but the Navy yard at Brest did enough work on her to bring that to thirty. Still not up to E-boat, of course, but not bad. A hundred and seventeen feet long and as for armaments, a six-pounder, a two-pounder, two twin point five machine-guns, twin twenty millimetre anti-aircraft cannon.'

'Fine,' Radl cut him off. 'A gun boat indeed. What about range?'

'A thousand miles at twenty-one knots. Of course, with the silencers on, she burns up much more fuel.'

'And what about that lot?' Radl pointed to the aerials which festooned her.

'Navigational some of them. The rest are S-phone aerials. It's a micro-wave wireless set for two-way voice communication between a moving ship and an agent on land. Far better than anything we've got. Obviously used by agents to talk them in before a landing. I'm sick of singing its praises at Naval Headquarters in Jersey. Nobody takes the slighest interest. No wonder we're . . .'

He stopped himself just in time. Radl glanced at him and said calmly, 'At what range does this remarkable gadget function?'

'Up to fifteen miles on a good day; for reliability I'd only claim half that distance, but at that range it's as good as a telephone call.'

Radl stood there for a long moment, thinking about it all and then he nodded abruptly, 'Thank you, Koenig,' he said and went out.

He found Devlin in Koenig's cabin, flat on his back, eyes closed, hands folded over a bottle of Bushmills. Radl frowned, annoyance and even a certain alarm stirring inside him and then saw that the seal on the bottle was unbroken.

'It's all right, Colonel dear,' Devlin said without apparently opening his eyes. 'The Devil hasn't got me by the big toe yet.'

'Did you bring my briefcase with you?'

Devlin squirmed to pull it from beneath him. 'Guarding it with my life.'

'Good,' Radl moved back to the door. 'They've got a wireless in the wheelhouse that I'd like you to look at before we land.'

'Wireless?' Devlin grunted.

'Oh, never mind,' Radl said. 'I'll explain later.'

When he went back to the bridge Koenig was seated at the chart table in a swivel chair drinking coffee from a tin mug. Muller still had the wheel.

Koenig got up, obviously surprised, and Radl said, 'The officer commanding naval forces in Jersey – what's his name?'

'Kapitän zur See Hans Olbricht.'

'I can see – can you get us to St Helier half an hour earlier than your estimated time of arrival?'

Koenig glanced dubiously at Muller. 'I'm not sure, Herr Oberst. We could try. Is it essential?'

'Absolutely. I must have time to see Olbricht to arrange your transfer.'

Koenig looked at him in astonishment. 'Transfer, Herr Oberst? To which command?'

'My command.' Radl took the manilla envelope from his pocket and produced the Führer Directive. 'Read that.'

He turned away impatiently and lit a cigarette. When he turned again, Koenig's eyes were wide. 'My God!' he whispered.

'I hardly think He enters into the matter.' Radl took the letter from him and replaced it in the envelope. He nodded at Muller. 'This big ox is to be trusted?'

'To the death, Herr Oberst.'

'Good,' Radl said. 'For a day or two you'll stay in Jersey until orders are finalized, then I want you to make your way along the coast to Boulogne where you will await my instructions. Any problems in getting there?'

Koenig shook his head. 'None that I can see. An easy enough trip for a boat like this staying inshore.' He hesitated. 'And afterwards, Herr Oberst?'

'Oh, somewhere on the North Dutch coast near Den Helder. I haven't found a suitable place yet. Do you know it?'

It was Muller who cleared his throat and said, 'Begging the Herr Oberst's pardon, but I know that coast like the back of my hand. I used to be the first mate on a Dutch salvage tug out of Rotterdam.'

'Excellent. Excellent.'

He left them, then went and stood in the prow beside the six-pounder smoking a cigarette. 'It marches,' he said softly. 'It marches,' and his stomach was hollow with excitement.

6

Just before noon on Wednesday 6 October Joanna Grey took possession of a large envelope deposited inside a copy of *The Times* left on a certain bench in Green Park by her usual contact at the Spanish Embassy.

Once in possession of the package she went straight back to Kings Cross station and caught the first express north, changing at Peterborough to a local train for King's Lynn where she had left her car, taking advantage of the surplus she had managed to accumulate from the petrol allocation given to her for WVS duties.

When she turned into the yard at the back of Park Cottage it was almost six o'clock and she was dog tired. She let herself in through the kitchen where she was greeted enthusiastically by Patch. He trailed at her heels when she went into the sitting-room and poured herself a large Scotch – of which, thanks to Sir Henry Willoughby, she had a plentiful supply. Then she climbed the stairs to the small study next to her bedroom.

The panelling was Jacobean and the invisible door in the corner was none of her doing, but part of the original, a common device of the period and designed to resemble a section of panelling. She took a key from a chain around her neck and unlocked the door. A short wooden stairway gave access to a cubby-hole loft under the roof. Here she had a radio receiver and transmitter. She sat down at an old deal table, opened a drawer in it, pushing a loaded Luger to one side and rummaged for a pencil, then took out her code books and got to work.

When she sat back an hour later her face was pinched with excitement. 'My God!' she said to herself in Afrikaans. 'They meant it – they actually meant it.'

Then she took a deep breath, pulled herself together and went back downstairs. Patch was waiting patiently at the door and followed at her heels all the way to the sitting-room where she picked up the telephone and dialled the number of Studley Grange. Sir Henry Willoughby himself answered.

She said, 'Henry – it's Joanna Grey.'

His voice warmed immediately. 'Hello there, my dear. I hope you're not ringing to say you won't be coming over for bridge or something. You hadn't forgotten? Eight-thirty?'

She had, but that didn't matter. She said, 'Of course not, Henry. It's just that I've got a little favour to ask and I wanted to speak to you privately about it.'

His voice deepened. 'Fire away, old girl. Anything I can do.'

'Well, I've heard from some Irish friends of my late husband and they've asked me to try and do something for their nephew. In fact, they're sending him over. He'll be arriving in the next few days.'

'Do what exactly?'

'His name is Devlin – Liam Devlin, and the thing is, Henry, the poor man was very badly wounded serving with the British Army in France. He received a medical discharge and he's been convalescing for almost a year. He's quite fit now though and ready for work, but it needs to be the outdoor variety.'

'And you thought I might be able to fix him up?' said Sir Henry jovially. 'No difficulty there, old girl. You know what it's like getting any kind of workers for the estate these days.'

'He wouldn't be able to do much at first,' she said. 'Actually I was wondering about the marsh warden's job at Hobs End. That's been vacant since young Tom King went off to the Army two years ago, hasn't it, and there's the house standing empty? It would be good to have somebody in. It's getting very run down.'

'I'll tell you what, Joanna, I think you might have something there. We'll go into the whole thing in depth. No sense in discussing it over bridge with other people there. Are you free tomorrow afternoon?'

'Of course,' she said. 'You know, it's so good of you to help in this way, Henry. I always seem to be bothering you with my problems these days.'

'Nonsense,' he told her sternly. 'That's what I'm here for. Woman needs a man to smooth over the rough spots for her.' His voice was shaking slightly.

'I'd better go now,' she said. 'I'll see you soon.'

'Goodbye, my dear.'

She put down the receiver and patted Patch on the head and he trailed along at her heels when she went back upstairs. She sat at the transmitter and made the briefest of signals on the frequency of the Dutch beacon for onward transmission to Berlin. An acknowledgement that her instructions had been safely received and a given code word that meant that the business of Devlin's employment had been taken care of.

*

In Berlin it was raining, black, cold rain drifting across the city pushed by a wind so bitter that it must have come all the way from the Urals. In the ante-room outside Himmler's office at Prinz Albrechtstrasse, Max Radl and Devlin sat facing each other, as they had been sitting for more than an hour now.

'What in the hell goes on?' Devlin said. 'Does he want to see us or doesn't he?'

'Why don't you knock and ask?' Radl suggested.

Just then the outer door opened and Rossman came in, beating rain from his slouch hat, his coat dripping water. He smiled brightly, 'Still here, you two?'

Devlin said to Radl, 'He's got the great wit to him, that one, isn't it a fact?'

Rossman knocked at the door and went in. He didn't bother closing it. 'I've got him, Herr Reichsführer.'

'Good,' they heard Himmler say. 'Now I'll see Radl and this Irish fellow.'

'What in the hell is this?' Devlin muttered. 'A command performance?'

'Watch your tongue,' Radl said, 'and let me do the talking.'

He led the way into the room, Devlin at his heels, and Rossman closed the door behind them. Everything was exactly the same as on that first night. The room in half-darkness, the open fire flickering, Himmler seated behind the desk.

The Reichsführer said, 'You've done well, Radl. I'm more than pleased with the way things are progressing. And this is Herr Devlin?'

'As ever was,' Devlin said cheerfully. 'Just a poor, old Irish peasant, straight out of the bog, that's me, your honour.'

Himmler frowned in puzzlement. 'What on earth is the man talking about?' he demanded of Radl.

'The Irish, Herr Reichsführer, are not as other people,' Radl said weakly.

'It's the rain,' Devlin told him.

Himmler stared at him in astonishment, then turned to Radl. 'You are certain he is the man for this?'

'Perfectly.'

'And when does he go?'

'On Sunday.'

'And your other arrangements? They are proceeding satisfactorily?'

'So far. My trip to Alderney I combined with Abwehr business in Paris and I have perfectly legal reasons for visiting Amsterdam next week. The Admiral knows nothing. He has been preoccupied with other matters.'

'Good.' Himmler sat staring into space, obviously thinking about something.

'Was there anything else, Herr Reichsführer?' Radl asked as Devlin stirred impatiently.

'Yes, I brought you here for two reasons tonight. In the first place I wanted to see Herr Devlin for myself. But secondly, there is the question of the composition of Steiner's assault group.'

'Maybe I should leave,' Devlin suggested.

'Nonsense,' Himmler said brusquely. 'I would be obliged if you would simply sit in the corner and listen. Or are the Irish incapable of such a feat?'

'Oh, it's been known,' Devlin said. 'But not often.'

He went and sat by the fire, took out a cigarette and lit it. Himmler glared at him, seemed about to speak and obviously thought better of it. He turned back to Radl.

'You were saying, Herr Reichsführer?'

'Yes, there seems to me one weakness in the composition of Steiner's group. Four or five of the men speak English to some degree, but only Steiner can pass as a native. This isn't good enough. In my opinion he needs the backing of someone of similar ability.'

'But people with that sort of ability are rather thin on the ground.'

'I think I have a solution for you,' Himmler said. 'There is a man called Amery – John Amery. Son of a famous English politician. He ran guns for Franco. Hates the Bolsheviks. He's been working for us for some time now.'

'Is he of any use?'

'I doubt it, but he came up with the idea of founding what he called the British Legion of St George. The idea was to recruit Englishmen from the prisoner of war camps, mainly to fight on the Eastern Front.'

'Did he get any takers?'

'A few – not many and mostly rogues. Amery has nothing to do with it now. For a while the Wehrmacht was responsible for the unit, but now the SS has taken over.'

'These volunteers – are there many?'

'Fifty or sixty as I last heard. They now rejoice in the name British Free Corps.' Himmler opened a file in front of him and took out a record card. 'Such people do have their uses on occasion. This man, for instance, Harvey Preston. When captured in Belgium he was wearing the uniform of a captain in the Cold-stream Guards, and having what I am informed are the voice and mannerisms of the English aristocrat, no one doubted him for some time.'

'And he was not what he seemed?'

'Judge for yourself.'

Radl examined the card. Harvey Preston had been born in Harrogate, Yorkshire in 1916, the son of a railway porter. He had left home at fourteen to work as a prop boy with a touring variety company. At eighteen he was acting in repertory in Southport. In 1937 he was sentenced to two years imprisonment at Winchester Assizes on four charges of fraud.

Discharged in January, 1939, he was arrested a month later and sentenced to a further nine months on a charge of impersonating an RAF officer and obtaining money by false pretences. The judge had suspended the sentence on condition that Preston joined the forces. He had gone to France as an orderly room clerk with an RASC transport company and, when captured, held the rank of acting corporal.

His prison camp record was bad or good according to which side you were on, for he had informed on no fewer than five separate escape attempts. On the last occasion this had become known to his comrades and if he had not volunteered to serve in the Free Corps, he would in any case have had to be moved for reasons of his own safety.

Radl walked across to Devlin and handed him the card, then turned to Himmler. 'And you want Steiner to take this . . . this . . .'

'Rogue,' Himmler said, 'who is quite expendable, but who simulates the English aristocrat quite well? He really does have presence, Radl. The sort of man to whom policemen touch their helmets the moment he opens his mouth. I've always understood that the English working classes know an officer and a gentleman when they see one, and Preston should do very well.'

'But Steiner and his men, Herr Reichsführer, are soldiers – real soldiers. You know their record. Can you see such a man fitting in? Taking orders?'

'He will do as he is told,' Himmler said. 'That goes without question. We'll have him in, shall we?'

He pressed the buzzer and a moment later, Rossman appeared in the doorway. 'I'll see Preston now.' Rossman went out, leaving the door open, and a moment later Preston entered the room, closed the door behind him and gave the Nazi Party salute.

He was at that time twenty-seven years of age, a tall, handsome man in a beautifully-tailored uniform of field grey. It was the uniform particularly which fascinated Radl. He had the death's head badge of the SS in his peaked cap and collar patches depicting the three leopards. Under the eagle on his left sleeve was a Union Jack shield and a black and silver cuff-title carried the legend in Gothic lettering, *Britishes Freikorps*.

'Very pretty,' Devlin said, but so softly that only Radl heard.

Himmler made the introductions. 'Untersturmführer Preston – Colonel Radl of the Abwehr and Herr Devlin. You will be familiar with the role each of these gentlemen plays in the affair at hand from the documents I gave you to study earlier today.'

Preston half-turned to Radl, inclined his head and clicked his heels. Very formal, very military, just like someone playing a Prussian officer in a play.

'So,' Himmler said. 'You have had ample opportunity to consider this matter. You understand what is required of you?'

Preston said carefully, 'Do I take it that Colonel Radl is looking for volunteers for this mission?' His German was good, although the accent could have been improved on.

Himmler removed his pince-nez, stroked the bridge of his nose gently with a forefinger and replaced them with great care. It was a gesture somehow infinitely sinister. His voice, when he spoke, was dry leaves brushed by the wind. 'What exactly are you trying to say, Untersturmführer?'

'It's just that I find myself in rather a difficulty here. As the Reichsführer knows, members of the British Free Corps were given a guarantee that at no time would they have to wage war or take part in any armed act against Britain or the Crown or indeed to support any act detrimental to the interest of the British people.'

Radl said, 'Perhaps this gentleman would be happier serving on the Eastern Front, Herr Reichsführer? Army Group South, under Field Marshal von Manstein. Plenty of hot spots there for those who crave real action.'

Preston, realizing that he had made a very bad mistake, hastily tried to make amends. 'I can assure you, Herr Reichsführer, that . . .'

Himmler didn't give him a chance. 'You talk of volunteering, where I see only an act of sacred duty. An opportunity to serve the Führer and the Reich.'

Preston snapped to attention. It was an excellent performance and Devlin, for one, was thoroughly enjoying himself. 'Of course, Herr Reichsführer. It is my total aim.'

'I am right, am I not, in assuming that you have taken an oath to this effect? A holy oath?'

'Yes, Herr Reichsführer.'

'Then nothing more need be said. You will from this moment consider yourself to be under the orders of Colonel Radl here.'

'As you say, Herr Reichsführer.'

'Colonel Radl, I'd like to have a word with you in private.' Himmler glanced at Devlin. 'Herr Devlin, if you would be kind enough to wait in the ante-room with Untersturmführer Preston.'

Preston gave him a crisp Heil Hitler, turned on heel with a precision that would not have disgraced the Grenadier Guards, and went out. Devlin followed, closing the door behind them.

There was no sign of Rossman and Preston kicked the side of one of the armchairs viciously and threw his cap down on the table. He was white with anger and when he produced a silver case and extracted a cigarette, his hand trembled slightly.

Devlin strolled across and helped himself to a cigarette before Preston could close the case. He grinned. 'By God, the old bugger's got you by the balls.'

He had spoken in English and Preston, glaring at him, replied in the same language. 'What in the hell do you mean?'

'Come on, son,' Devlin said. 'I've heard of your little lot. Legion of St George; British Free Corps. How was it they bought you? Unlimited booze and as many women as you can handle, if you're not too choosy, that is. Now it's all got to be paid for.'

At an inch above six feet, Preston was able to look down with some contempt at the Irishman. His left nostril curled. 'My God, the people one has to deal with – straight out of the bogs, too, from the smell. Now go away and try playing nasty little Irishmen elsewhere, there's a good chap, or I might have to chastise you.'

Devlin, in the act of putting a match to his cigarette, kicked Preston with some precision under the right kneecap.

*

In the office Radl had just come to the end of a progress report. 'Excellent,' Himmler said, 'and the Irishman leaves on Sunday?'

'By Dornier from a Luftwaffe base outside Brest – Laville. A north-westerly course from there will take them to Ireland without the necessity of passing over English soil. At twenty-five thousand feet for most of the way they should have no trouble.'

'And the Irish Air Force?'

'What air force, Herr Reichsführer?'

'I see,' Himmler closed the file. 'So, things seem to be really moving at last. I'm very pleased with you, Radl. Continue to keep me informed.'

He picked up his pen in a dismissive gesture and Radl said, 'There is one other matter.'

Himmler looked up. 'And what is that?'

'Major-General Steiner.'

Himmler laid down his pen. 'What about him?'

Radl didn't know how to put it, but he had to make the point somehow. He owed it to Steiner. In fact, considering the circumstances, the intensity with which he wanted to keep that promise surprised him. 'It was the Reichsführer himself who suggested I make it clear to Colonel Steiner that his conduct in this affair could have a significant effect on his father's case.'

'That is so,' Himmler said calmly. 'But what is the problem?'

'I promised Colonel Steiner, Herr Reichsführer,' Radl said lamely. 'Gave him an assurance that . . . that . . .'

'Which you had no authority to offer,' Himmler said. 'However, under the circumstances, you may give Steiner that assurance in my name.' He picked up his pen again. 'You may go now and tell Preston to remain. I want another word with him. I'll have him report to you tomorrow.'

When Radl went out into the ante-room, Devlin was standing at the window peering through a chink in the curtains and Preston was sitting in one of the armchairs. 'Raining cats and dogs out there,' he said cheerfully. 'Still, it might keep the RAF at home for a change. Are we going?'

Radl nodded and said to Preston, 'You stay. He wants you. And don't come to Abwehr Headquarters tomorrow. I'll get in touch with you.'

Preston was on his feet, very military again, arm raised. 'Very well, Herr Oberst. Heil Hitler!'

Radl and Devlin moved to the door and as they went out, the Irishman raised a thumb and grinned amiably. 'Up the Republic, me old son!'

Preston dropped his arm and swore viciously. Devlin closed the door and followed Radl down the stairs. 'Where in the hell did they find him? Himmler must have lost his wits entirely.'

'God knows,' Radl said as they paused beside the SS guards in the main entrance to turn up their collars against the heavy rain. 'There is some merit in the idea of another officer who is obviously English, but this Preston.' He shook his head. 'A badly flawed man. Second-rate actor, petty criminal. A man who has spent most of his life living some sort of private fantasy.'

'And we're stuck with him,' Devlin said. 'I wonder what Steiner will make of it?'

They ran through the rain as Radl's staff car approached and settled themselves in the back. 'Steiner will cope,' Radl said. 'Men like Steiner always do. But now to business. We fly to Paris tomorrow afternoon.'

'Then what?'

'I've important business in Holland. As I told you, the entire operation will be based on Landsvoort, which is the right kind of end-of-the-world spot. During the operational period I shall be there myself, so, my friend, if you make a transmission, you'll know who is on the other end. As I was saying, I'll leave you in Paris when I fly to Amsterdam. You, in your turn, will be ferried down to the airfield at Laville near Brest. You take off at ten o'clock on Sunday night.'

'Will you be there?' Devlin asked.

'I'll try, but it may not be possible.'

They arrived at Tirpitz Ufer a moment later and hurried through the rain to the entrance just as Hofer, in cap and heavy greatcoat, was emerging. He saluted and Radl said, 'Going off duty, Karl? Anything for me?'

'Yes, Herr Oberst, a signal from Mrs Grey.'

Radl was filled with excitement. 'What is it, man, what does she say?'

'Message received and understood, Herr Oberst and the question of Herr Devlin's employment has been taken care of.'

Radl turned triumphantly to Devlin, rain dripping from the peak of his mountain cap. 'And what do you have to say to that, my friend?'

'Up the Republic,' Devlin said morosely. 'Right up! Is that patriotic enough for you? If so, could I go in now and have a drink?'

*

When the office door clicked open Preston was sitting in the corner reading an English-language edition of *Signal*. He glanced up and finding Himmler there watching him, jumped to his feet. 'Your pardon, Herr Reichsführer.'

'For what?' Himmler said, 'Come with me, I want to show you something.'

Puzzled and also faintly alarmed, Preston followed him downstairs and along the ground floor corridor to the iron door guarded by two Gestapo men. One of them got the door open, they sprang to attention, Himmler nodded and started down the steps.

The white-painted corridor seemed quiet enough and then Preston became aware of a dull, rhythmic slapping, strangely remote, as if it came from a great distance. Himmler paused outside a cell door and opened a metal gate. There was a small window of armoured glass.

A grey-haired man of sixty or so in a tattered shirt and military breeches was sprawled across a bench while a couple of heavily muscled SS man beat him systematically across the back and buttocks with rubber truncheons. Rossman stood watching, smoking a cigarette, his shirt sleeves rolled up.

'I detest this sort of mindless violence,' Himmler said. 'Don't you, Herr Untersturmführer?'

Preston's mouth had gone dry and his stomach heaved. 'Yes, Herr Reichsführer. Terrible.'

'If only these fools would listen. A nasty business, but how else can one deal with treason against the State? The Reich and the Führer demand an absolute and unquestioning loyalty and those who give less than this must accept the consequences. You understand me?'

Which Preston did – perfectly. And when the Reichsführer turned and went back up the stairs he stumbled after him, a handkerchief to his mouth in an attempt to stop himself from being sick.

In the darkness of his cell below, Major-General of Artillery Karl Steiner crawled into a corner and crouched there, arms folded as if to stop himself from falling apart. 'Not one word,' he said softly through swollen lips. 'Not one word – I swear it.'

*

At precisely 02.20 hours on the morning of Saturday 9 October Captain Peter Gericke of Night Fighter Group 7, operating out of Grandjeim on the Dutch coast made his thirty-eighth confirmed kill. He was flying a Junkers 88 in heavy cloud, one of those apparently clumsy, black, twin-engined planes festooned with strange radar aerials, that had proved so devastating in their attacks on RAF bombing groups engaged on night raids over Europe.

Not that Gericke had had any luck earlier that night. A blocked fuel pipe in the port engine had kept him grounded for thirty minutes while the rest of the Staffel had taken off to pounce upon a large force of British bombers returning home across the Dutch coast after a raid on Hanover.

By the time Gericke reached the area most of his comrades had turned for home. And yet there were always stragglers, so he remained on patrol for a while longer.

Gericke was twenty-three years of age. A handsome, rather saturnine young man whose dark eyes seemed full of impatience, as if life itself were too slow for him. Just now he was whistling softly between his teeth the first movement of the Pastoral Symphony.

Behind him, Haupt, the radar operator, huddled over the Lichtenstein set gave an excited gasp. 'I've got one.'

In the same moment base took over smoothly and the familiar voice of Major Hans Berger, ground controller of NJG7, crackled over Gericke's headphones. 'Wanderer Four, this is Black Knight. I have a Kurier for you. Are you receiving?'

'Loud and clear,' Gericke told him.

'Steer nought-eight-seven degrees. Target range ten kilo-metres.'

The Junkers burst out of cloud cover only seconds later and Bohmler, the observer, touched Gericke's arm. Gericke saw his prey instantly, a Lancaster bomber limping home in bright moon-light, a feathered plume of smoke drifting from the port outer motor.

'Black Knight, this is Wanderer Four,' Gericke said. 'I have visual sighting and require no further assistance.'

He slipped back into the clouds, descended five hundred feet then banked steeply to port, emerging a couple of miles to the rear and below the crippled Lancaster. It was a sitting target, drifting above them like a grey ghost, that plume of smoke trailing gently.

During the second half of 1943, many German night fighters began operating with a secret weapon that was known as *Schraege Musik*, a pair of twenty millimetre cannon mounted in the fusel-age and arranged to fire upwards at an angle of between ten and twenty degrees. This weapon enabled night fighters to attack from below, from which position the bomber presented an enormous target and was virtually blind. As tracer rounds were not used, scores of bombers were brought down without their crews even knowing what hit them.

So it was now. For a split second, Gericke was on target, then as he turned away to port, the Lancaster banked steeply and plunged towards the sea three thousand feet below. There was one para-chute, then another. A moment later, the plane itself exploded in a brilliant ball of orange fire. Fuselage dropped down towards the sea, one of the parachutes ignited and flared briefly.

'Dear God in heaven!' Bohmler said in horror.

'What God?' Gericke demanded savagely. 'Now send base a fix on that poor sod down there so someone can pick him up and let's go home.'

*

When Gericke and his two crewmen reported to the Intelligence Room in the Operations building it was empty except for Major Adler, the senior Intelligence officer, a jovial fifty-year old with the slightly frozen face of someone who had been badly burned.

He had actually flown during the First War in von Richthofen's Staffel and wore the Blue Max at his throat.

'Ah, there you are, Peter,' he said. 'Better late than never. Your kill's been confirmed by radio from an E-boat in the area.'

'What about the man who got clear?' Gericke demanded. 'Have they found him?'

'Not yet, but they're searching. There's an air-sea rescue launch in the area, too.'

He pushed a sandalwood box across his desk. It contained very long, pencil-slim Dutch cheroots. Gericke took one.

Adler said, 'You seem concerned, Peter. I had never imagined you a humanitarian.'

'I'm not,' Gericke told him bluntly as he put a match to his cheroot, 'but tomorrow night that could be me. I like to think those air-sea rescue bastards are on their toes.'

As he turned away, Adler said, 'Prager wants to see you.'

Lieutenant-Colonel Otto Prager was Gruppenkommandant of Grandjeim, responsible for three Staffeln including Gericke's. He was a strict disciplinarian and an ardent National Socialist, neither of which qualities Gericke found particularly pleasing. He atoned for these minor irritations by being a first-rate pilot in his own right, totally dedicated to the welfare of the aircrew in his Gruppe.

'What does he want?'

Adler shrugged. 'I couldn't say, but when he telephoned, he made it plain it was to be at the earliest possible moment.'

'I know,' Bohmler said, 'Goering's been on the phone. Invited you to Karinhall for the weekend and about time.'

It was a well-known fact that when a Luftwaffe pilot was awarded the Knight's Cross, the Reichsmarschall, as an old flyer himself, liked to hand it over in person.

'That'll be the day,' Gericke said grudgingly. The fact was that men with fewer kills to their credit than he had received the coveted award. It was a distinctly sore point.

'Never mind, Peter,' Adler called as they went out. 'Your day will come.'

'If I live that long,' Gericke said to Bohmler as they paused on the steps of the main entrance to the Operations building. 'What about a drink?'

'No, thanks,' Bohmler said. 'A hot bath and eight hours sleep are my total requirements. I don't approve of it at this time in the morning. You know that even if we are living backwards way round.'

Haupt was already yawning and Gericke said morosely, 'Bloody Lutheran. All right, sod both of you.'

As he started to walk away, Bohmler called. 'Don't forget Prager wants to see you.'

'Later,' Gericke said. 'I'll see him later.'

'He's really asking for it,' Haupt remarked as they watched him go. 'What's got into him lately?'

'Like the rest of us, he lands and takes off too often,' Bohmler said.

Gericke walked towards the officers' mess wearily, his flying boots drubbing on the tarmac. He felt unaccountably depressed, stale, somehow at the final end of things. It was strange how he couldn't get that *Tommi*, the sole survivor of the Lancaster, out of his mind. What he needed was a drink. A cup of coffee, very hot, and a large schnapps or perhaps a Steinhager?

He walked into the ante-room and the first person he saw was Colonel Prager sitting in an easy chair in the far corner with another officer, their heads together as they talked in subdued tones. Gericke hesitated, debating whether to turn tail, for the Gruppenkommandant was particularly strict on the question of flying clothes being worn in the mess. Prager looked up and saw him.

'There you are, Peter. Come and join us.'

He snapped his finger for the mess waiter who hovered nearby and ordered coffee as Gericke approached. He didn't approve of alcohol where pilots were concerned. 'Good morning, Herr Oberst,' Gericke said brightly, intrigued by the other officer, a lieutenant-colonel of Mountain Troops with a black patch over one eye and a Knight's Cross to go with it.

'Congratulations,' Prager said. 'I hear you've got another confirmed kill.'

'That's right, a Lancaster. One man got clear, I saw his chute open. They're looking for him now.'

'Colonel Radl,' Prager said.

Radl held out his good hand and Gericke shook it briefly. 'Herr Oberst.'

Prager was more subdued than he had ever known him. In fact, he was very obviously labouring under some kind of strain, easing himself in the chair as if in acute physical discomfort as the mess waiter brought a tray with a fresh pot of coffee and three cups.

'Leave it, man, leave it!' Prager ordered curtly.

There was a slight strained silence after the waiter had departed. Then the Gruppenkommandeur said abruptly, 'The Herr Oberst here is from the Abwehr. With fresh orders for you.'

'Fresh orders, Herr Oberst?'

Prager got to his feet. 'Colonel Radl can tell you more than I can, but obviously you're being given an extraordinary opportunity to serve the Reich.' Gericke stood up and Prager hesitated then stuck out his hand. 'You've done well here, Peter. I'm proud of you. As for the other business – I've recommended you three times now so it's right out of my hands.'

'I know, Herr Oberst,' Gericke said warmly, 'and I'm grateful.'

Prager walked away and Gericke sat down. Radl said. 'This Lancaster makes thirty-eight confirmed kills, is it not so?'

'You seem remarkably well informed, Herr Oberst,' Gericke said. 'Will you join me in a drink?'

'Why not? A cognac, I think.'

Gericke called to the waiter and gave the order.

'Thirty-eight confirmed kills and no Knight's Cross,' Radl commented. 'Isn't that unusual?'

Gericke stirred uncomfortably. 'The way it goes sometimes.'

'I know,' Radl said. 'There is also the fact to be taken into consideration that during the summer of nineteen-forty, when you were flying ME one-o-nines out of a base near Calais, you told Reichsmarschall Goering who was inspecting your Staffel, that in your opinion, the Spitfire was a better aircraft.' He smiled gently.

'People of his eminence don't forget junior officers who make remarks like that.'

Gericke said, 'With all due respect, might I point out to the Herr Oberst that in my line of work I can only rely on today because tomorrow I might very possibly be dead, so some idea of what all this is about would be appreciated.'

'It's simple enough,' Radl said. 'I need a pilot for a rather special operation.'

'*You* need?'

'All right, the Reich,' Radl told him. 'Does that please you any better?'

'Not particularly.' Gericke held up his empty schnapps glass to the waiter and signalled for another. 'As it happens, I'm perfectly happy where I am.'

'A man who consumes schnapps in such an amount at four o'clock in the morning? I doubt that. In any case, you've no choice in the matter.'

'Is that so?' Gericke said angrily.

'You are perfectly at liberty to confirm this with the Gruppenkommandant,' Radl said.

The waiter brought him the second glass of schnapps, Gericke poured it down in one quick swallow and made a face. 'God, how I hate that stuff.'

'Then why drink it?' Radl asked.

'I don't know. Maybe I've been out there in the dark too much or flying too long.' He smiled sardonically. 'Or perhaps I just need a change, Herr Oberst.'

'I think I may say without any exaggeration that I can certainly offer you that.'

'Fine.' Gericke swallowed the rest of his coffee. 'What's the next move?'

'I have an appointment in Amsterdam at nine o'clock. Our destination after that is about twenty miles north of the city, on the way to Den Helder.' He glanced at his watch. 'We'll need to leave here no later than seven-thirty.'

'That gives me time for breakfast and a bath,' Gericke said, 'I can catch a little sleep in the car if that's all right with you.'

As he got up, the door opened and an orderly came in. He saluted and passed the young captain a signal flimsy. Gericke read it and smiled. 'Something important?' Radl asked.

'The *Tommi* who parachuted out of that Lancaster I shot down earlier. They've picked him up. A Pilot Officer navigator.'

'His luck is good,' Radl commented.

'A good omen,' Gericke said. 'Let's hope mine is.'

*

Landsvoort was a desolate little place about twenty miles north of Amsterdam between Schagen and the sea. Gericke slept soundly for the entire journey, only coming awake when Radl shook his arm.

There was an old farmhouse and barn, two hangars roofed with rusting corrugated iron and a single runway of crumbling concrete, grass growing between the cracks. The wire perimeter fence was nothing very special and the steel and wire swing gate, which looked new, was guarded by a sergeant with the distinctive gorget plate of the military police hanging around his neck. He was armed with a Schmeisser machine pistol and held a rather savage-looking Alsatian on the end of a steel chain.

He checked their papers impassively while the dog growled deep in its throat, full of menace. Radl drove on through the gate and pulled up in front of the hangars. 'Well, this is it.'

The landscape was incredibly flat, stretching out towards the distant sand dunes and the North Sea beyond. As Gericke opened the door and got out, rain drifted in off the sea in a fine spray and there was the tang of salt to it. He walked across to the edge of the crumbling runway and kicked with his foot until a piece of concrete broke away.

'It was built by a shipping magnate in Rotterdam for his own use ten or twelve years ago,' Radl said as he got out of the car to join him. 'What do you think?'

'All we need now are the Wright brothers.' Gericke looked out towards the sea, shivered and thrust his hands deep into the pockets of his leather coat. 'What a dump – the last place on God's list, I should imagine.'

'Therefore exactly right for our purposes,' Radl pointed out. 'Now, let's get down to business.'

He led the way across to the first hangar which was guarded by another military policeman complete with Alsatian. Radl nodded and the man pulled back one of the sliding doors.

It was damp and rather cold inside, rain drifting in through a hole in the roof. The twin-engine aircraft which stood there looked lonely and rather forlorn, and very definitely far from home. Gericke prided himself that he had long since got past being surprised at anything in this life, but not that morning.

The aircraft was a Douglas DC3, the famous Dakota, probably one of the most successful general transport planes ever built, as much a workhorse for the Allied Forces during the war as was the Junkers 52 to the German Army. The interesting thing about this one was that it carried Luftwaffe insignia on the wings and a Swastika on the tail.

Peter Gericke loved aeroplanes as some men love horses, with a deep and unswerving passion. He reached up and touched a wing gently and his voice was soft when he said, 'You old beauty.'

'You know this aircraft?' Radl said.

'Better than any woman.'

'Six months with the Landros Air Freight Company in Brazil from June to November, nineteen-thirty-eight. Nine hundred and thirty flying hours. Quite something for a nineteen-year-old. That must have been hard flying.'

'So that's why I was chosen?'

'All on your records.'

'Where did you get her?'

'RAF Transport Command, dropping supplies to the Dutch Resistance four months ago. One of your night fighter friends got her. Superficial engine damage only. Something to do with the fuel pump, I understand. The observer was too badly wounded to jump so the pilot managed to bring her down in a ploughed field. Unfortunately for him he was nextdoor to an SS barracks. By the time he got his friend out, it was too late to blow her up.'

The door was open and Gericke pulled himself inside. In the cockpit, he sat behind the controls and for a moment he was back in Brazil, green jungle below, the Amazon twisting through it like a great, silver snake from Manaus down to the sea.

Radl took the other seat. He produced a silver case and offered Gericke one of his Russian cigarettes. 'You could fly this thing, then?'

'Where to?'

'Not very far. Across the North Sea to Norfolk. Straight in, straight out.'

'To do what?'

'Drop sixteen paratroopers.'

In his astonishment, Gericke inhaled too deeply and almost choked, the harsh Russian tobacco catching at the back of his throat.

He laughed wildly. 'Operation Sealion at last. Don't you think it's a trifle late in the war for the invasion of England?'

'This particular section of the coast has no low level radar cover,' Radl said calmly. 'No difficulty at all if you go in below six hundred feet. Naturally I'll have the plane cleaned up and the RAF roundels replaced on the wings. If anyone does see you, they see an RAF aircraft presumably going about its lawful business.'

'But why?' said Gericke. 'What in the hell are they going to do when they get there?'

'None of your affair,' Radl said firmly. 'You are just a bus driver, my friend.'

He got up and went out and Gericke followed him. 'Now look here, I think you could do better than that.'

Radl walked to the Mercedes without replying. He stood looking out across the airfield to the sea. 'Too tough for you?'

'Don't be stupid,' Gericke told him angrily. 'I just like to know what I'm getting into, that's all.'

Radl opened his coat and unbuttoned his tunic. From the inside pocket he took out the stiff manilla envelope that housed the precious letter and handed it to Gericke. 'Read that,' he said crisply.

When Gericke looked up, his face was suddenly bleak. 'That important? No wonder Prager was so disturbed.'

'Exactly.'

'All right, how long have I got?'

'Approximately four weeks.'

'I'll need Bohmler, my observer, to fly with me. He's the best bloody navigator I've ever come across.'

'Anything you need. Just ask. Top secret, the whole thing, of course. I can get you a week's leave if you like. After that, you stay here, at the farm under strict security.'

'Can I test flight?'

'If you must, but only at night and preferably only once. I'll have a team of the finest aircraft mechanics the Luftwaffe can supply. Anything you need. You'll be in charge of that side. I don't want engines failing for some absurd mechanical reason when you're four hundred feet above a Norfolk marsh. We'll go back to Amsterdam now.'

He opened the car door and Gericke said, 'One thing – security doesn't seem up to much here.'

Radl frowned. 'I don't agree. In this sort of country, it is impossible to hide. Too flat. You'd be seen coming for miles.' He nodded towards the military policeman, whose Alsatian was straining towards them, a noise like distant thunder deep down in its throat. 'There are twenty more like him patrolling the wire and those dogs can kill a man in three seconds, remember.'

'So they tell me.' Gericke walked towards the policeman and the Alsatian. The policeman cried out in alarm, the dog reared up on the chain with a snarl. Gericke snapped his fingers, whistling softly a strange, lonely sound that for some reason set Radl's teeth on edge. The Alsatian stood very still, staring up at him, then subsided. Gericke crouched down and fondled its ears, whispering softly to it.

The policeman seemed considerably put out and Radl said, 'I wouldn't have believed it if I hadn't seen it with my own eyes.'

'I was raised in the Harz Mountains,' Gericke said. 'On my grandfather's estate. Lots of dogs. I first found I could do that when I was six years old. Very strange.'

He got into the Mercedes and Radl climbed behind the wheel. 'Something of an understatement,' he said as he pressed the starter. 'In the Middle Ages they'd have burned you.'

'It certainly proves one thing,' Gericke said as they slowed for the main gate to open.

'What's that?'

Gericke nodded out at the sentry and his formidable-looking Alsatian. 'That you can't depend on anything in this life.'

He leaned back in the seat, tipped the peak of his cap over his eyes and went to sleep and Radl drove on through the flat, dreary landscape, his face sober.

*

It was just before nine-thirty on the following night when Radl flew into Laville airfield outside Brest in a Ju.52 transport on a normal passenger run. He was tired – very tired and exasperated by a series of unlooked for delays that had hampered his progress all the way from Amsterdam. An hour late leaving Le Bourget and even now, ground control made them fly circuits while a Dornier 215 bomber took off, one of the famous Flying Pencils, so nicknamed because of its slim fuselage.

Devlin was due off at ten which wasn't going to give them much time and Radl waited, fuming, as the Junkers landed and rolled to a halt. When the door was opened he was first down the steps and was immediately greeted by a Luftwaffe major in a sidecap and black leather coat. 'Colonel Radl? Major Hans Rudel, Gruppenkommandant here at Laville.'

'What about my Irishman?' Radl demanded. 'How is he?'

'Gone, Herr Oberst, not five minutes ago.'

'In the Dornier which just took off?' Radl cried. 'But that isn't possible. Flight time was ten o'clock.'

'We had a very bad met report earlier,' Rudel explained. 'A cold front on its way in from the Atlantic. Rain and some fog later. I thought they'd better get off while they could.'

Radl nodded. 'Yes, I see that. Would it be possible for me to get a message to him?'

'Of course, Herr Oberst, if you would be so kind as to follow me.' Rudel led the way quickly toward the control tower.

Five minutes later, Liam Devlin – who was lying on his back on the floor of the Dornier in flying suit and helmet, eyes closed, hands folded around the bottle of Bushmills Steiner had given him – felt a touch on his shoulder. He opened his eyes and found the wireless operator bending over him, a piece of paper in one hand.

'A message for you,' he cried over the noise of the engines.

'All right,' Devlin shouted back. 'Read it to me.'

'It just says: Sorry I was late. Missed you by a whisker.' The wireless operator hesitated. 'I don't understand the last bit.'

'Read it anyway.'

'Good luck and up the Republic. Does that make any sense?'

'All the sense in the whole wide world, son,' Liam Devlin told him and closed his eyes again, smiling.

*

At precisely two forty-five on the following morning, Seumas O'Broin, a sheep farmer of Conroy in County Monaghan was endeavouring to find his way home across a stretch of open moorland. And making a bad job of it.

Which was understandable enough for when one is seventy-six, friends have a tendency to disappear with monotonous regularity and Seumas O'Broin was on his way home from a funeral wake for one who had just departed – a wake which had lasted for seventeen hours.

He had not only, as the Irish so delightfully put it, drink taken. He had consumed quantities so vast that he was not certain whether he was in this world or the next; so that when what he took to be a large, white bird sailed out of the darkness over his head without a sound and plunged into the field beyond the next wall, he felt no fear at all, only a mild curiosity.

Devlin made an excellent landing, the supply bag dangling twenty feet below from a line clipped to his belt, hitting the ground first, warning him to be ready. He followed a split second later, rolling in springy Irish turf, scrambling to his feet instantly and unfastening his harness.

The clouds parted at that moment, exposing a quarter-moon which gave him exactly the right amount of light to do what had to be done. He opened the supply bag, took out a small trenching shovel, his dark raincoat, a tweed cap, a pair of shoes and a large, leather Gladstone bag.

There was a thorn hedge nearby, a ditch beside it and he quickly scraped a hole in the bottom with the shovel. Then he unzipped his flying overalls. Underneath he was wearing a tweed suit and he transferred the Walther which he had carried in his belt to his right-hand pocket. He pulled on his shoes and then put the overalls, the parachute and the flying boots into the bag and dropped it into the hole, raking the soil back into place quickly. He scraped a mass of dry leaves and twigs over everything, just to finish things off and tossed the spade into a nearby copse.

He pulled on his raincoat, picked up the Gladstone bag and turned to find Seumas O'Broin leaning on the wall watching him. Devlin moved fast, his hand on the butt of the Walther. But then the aroma of good Irish whiskey, the slurred speech told him all he needed to know.

'What are ye, man or divil?' the old farmer demanded, each word slow and distinct. 'Of this world or the next?'

'God save us, old man, but from the smell of you, if one of us lit a match right now we'd be in hell together soon enough. As for your question, I'm a little of both. A simple Irish boy, trying a new way of coming home after years in foreign parts.'

'Is that a fact?' O'Broin said.

'Aren't I telling you?'

The old man laughed delightedly. '*Cead mile failte sa bhaile romhat*,' he said in Irish. 'A hundred thousand welcomes home to you.'

Devlin grinned. '*Go raibh maith agat*,' he said. 'Thanks.' He picked up the Gladstone bag, vaulted over the wall and set off across the meadow briskly, whistling softly between his teeth. It was good to be home, however brief the visit.

The Ulster border, then, as now, was wide open to anyone who knew the area. Two and a half hours of brisk walking by country lanes and field paths and he was in the county of Armagh and standing on British soil. A lift in a milk truck had him in Armagh itself by six o'clock. Half-an-hour later, he was climbing into a third-class compartment on the early morning train to Belfast.

7

On Wednesday it rained all day and in the afternoon mist drifted in off the North Sea across the marshes at Cley and Hobs End and Blakeney.

In spite of the weather, Joanna Grey went into the garden after lunch. She was working in the vegetable patch beside the orchard, lifting potatoes, when the garden gate creaked. Patch gave a sudden whine and was off like a flash. When she turned, a smallish, pale-faced man with good shoulders, wearing a black, belted trenchcoat and tweed cap was standing at the end of the path. He carried a Gladstone bag in his left hand and had the most startling blue eyes she had ever seen.

'Mrs Grey?' he enquired in a soft, Irish voice. 'Mrs Joanna Grey?'

'That's right.' Her stomach knotted with excitement. For a brief moment she could hardly breathe.

He smiled. 'I shall light a candle of understanding in the heart which shall not be put out.'

'*Magna est veritas et praevalet.*'

'Great is Truth and mighty above all things,' Liam Devlin smiled. 'I could do with a cup of tea, Mrs Grey. It's been one hell of a trip.'

*

Devlin had been unable to secure a ticket for the night crossing from Belfast to Heysham on Monday and the situation was no better on the Glasgow route. But the advice of a friendly booking clerk had sent him up to Larne where he'd had better luck, obtaining a passage on the Tuesday morning boat on the short run to Stranraer in Scotland.

The exigencies of wartime travel by train had left him with a seemingly interminable journey from Stranraer to Carlisle, changing for Leeds. And in that city, a lengthy wait into the small hours of Wednesday morning before making a suitable connection for Peterborough where he had made the final change to a local train for Kings Lynn.

Much of this passed through his mind again when Joanna Grey turned from the stove where she was making tea and said, 'Well, how was it?'

'Not too bad,' he said. 'Surprising in some ways.'

'How do you mean?'

'Oh, the people, the general state of things. It wasn't quite as I expected.'

He thought particularly of the station restaurant at Leeds, crowded all night with travellers of every description, all hopefully waiting for a train to somewhere, the poster on the wall which had said with particular irony in his case: *It is more than ever vital to ask yourself: Is my journey really necessary?* He remembered the rough good humour, the general high spirits and contrasted it less than favourably with his last visit to the central railway station in Berlin.

'They seem to be pretty sure they're going to win the war,' he said as she brought the tea tray to the table.

'A fool's paradise,' she told him calmly. 'They never learn. They've never had the organization, you see, the discipline that the Führer has given to Germany.'

Remembering the bomb-scarred Chancellery as he had last seen it, the considerable portions of Berlin that were simply heaps of rubble after the Allied bombing offensive, Devlin felt almost constrained to point out that things had changed rather a lot since the good old days. On the other hand, he got the distinct impression that such a remark would not be well received.

So, he drank his tea and watched her as she walked to a corner cupboard, opened it and took down a bottle of Scotch, marvelling that this pleasant-faced, white-haired woman in the neat, tweed skirt and Wellington boots could be what she was.

She poured a generous measure into two glasses and raised one in a kind of salute. 'To the English Enterprise,' she said, her eyes shining.

Devlin could have told her that the Spanish Armada had been so described, but remembering what had happened to that ill-fated venture decided, once again, to keep his mouth shut.

'To the English Enterprise,' he said solemnly.

'Good.' She put down her glass. 'Now let me see all your papers. I must make sure you have everything.'

He produced his passport, army discharge papers, a testimonial purporting to be from his old commanding officer, a similar letter from his parish priest and various documents relating to his medical condition.

'Excellent,' she said. 'These are really very good. What happens now is this. I've fixed you up with a job working for the local squire, Sir Henry Willoughby. He wants to see you as soon as you arrive so we'll get that over with today. Tomorrow morning I'll run you into Fakenham, that's a market town about ten miles from here.'

'And what do I do there?'

'Report to the local police station. They'll give you an alien's registration form which all Irish citizens have to fill in and you'll also have to provide a passport photo, but we can get that with no trouble. Then you'll need insurance cards, an identity card, ration book, clothing coupons.'

She numbered them off on the fingers of one hand and Devlin grinned. 'Heh, hold on now. It sounds like one hell of a lot of trouble to me. Three weeks on Saturday, that's all, and I'll be away from here so fast they'll think I've never been.'

'All these things are essential,' she said. 'Everyone has them, so you must. It only needs one petty clerk in Fakenham or Kings Lynn to notice that you haven't applied for something and put an enquiry in hand and then where would you be?'

Devlin said cheerfully. 'All right, you're the boss. Now what about this job?'

'Warden of the marshes at Hobs End. It couldn't be more isolated. There's a cottage to go with it. Not much, but it will do.'

'And what will be expected of me?'

'Gamekeeping duties in the main and there's a system of dyke gates that needs regular checking. They haven't had a warden for two years since the last one went off to the war. And you'll be expected to keep the vermin in check. The foxes play havoc with the wild-fowl.'

'What do I do? Throw stones at them?'

'No, Sir Henry will supply you with a shotgun.'

'That's nice of him. What about transport?'

'I've done the best I can. I've managed to persuade Sir Henry to allocate you one of the estate motor-bikes. As an agricultural worker it's legitimate enough. Buses have almost ceased to exist, so most people are allowed a small monthly ration to help them get into town occasionally for essential purposes.'

A horn sounded outside. She went into the sitting-room and was back in an instant. 'It's Sir Henry. Leave the talking to me. Just act properly servile and speak only when you're spoken to. He'll like that. I'll bring him in here.'

She went out and Devlin waited. He heard the front door open and her feigned surprise. Sir Henry said, 'Just on my way to another command meeting in Holt, Joanna. Wondered if there was anything I could get you?'

She replied much more quietly so that Devlin couldn't hear what she said. Sir Henry dropped his voice in return, there was a further murmur of conversation and then they came into the kitchen.

Sir Henry was in uniform as a lieutenant-colonel in the Home Guard, medal ribbons for the First World War and India making a splash of colour above his left breast pocket. He glanced piercingly at Devlin, one hand behind his back, the other brushing the wide sweep of his moustache.

'So you're Devlin?'

Devlin lurched to his feet and stood there twisting and untwisting his tweed cap in his two hands. 'I'd like to thank you, sir,' he said, thickening the Irish accent noticeably. 'Mrs Grey's told me how much you've done for me. It's more than kind.'

'Nonsense, man,' Sir Henry said brusquely although it was observable that he stretched to his full height and placed his feet a little further apart. 'You did your best for the old country, didn't you? Caught a packet in France, I understand?'

Devlin nodded eagerly and Sir Henry leaned forward and examined the furrow on the left side of the forehead made by an Irish Special Branch detective's bullet. 'By heavens,' he said softly. 'You're damn lucky to be here if you ask me.'

'I thought I'd settle him in for you,' Joanna Grey said. 'If that's all right, Henry? Only you're so busy, I know.'

'I say, would you, old girl?' He glanced at his watch. 'I'm due in Holt in half an hour.'

'No more to be said. I'll take him along to the cottage, show him around the marsh generally and so on.'

'Come to think of it you probably know more about what goes on at Hobs End than I do.' He forgot himself for a moment and slipped an arm about her waist, then withdrew it hastily and said to Devlin, 'Don't forget to present yourself to the police in Fakenham without delay. You know all about that?'

'Yes, sir.'

'Anything you want to ask me?'

'The gun, sir,' Devlin said. 'I understand you want me to do a little shooting.'

'Ah, yes. No trouble there. Call at the Grange tomorrow afternoon and I'll see you fixed up. You can pick the bike up tomorrow afternoon, too. Mrs Grey's told you about that, has she? Only three gallons of petrol a month, mind you, but you'll have to make out the best way you can. We've all got to make sacrifices,' He brushed his moustache again. 'A single Lancaster, Devlin, uses two thousand gallons of petrol to reach the Ruhr. Did you know that?'

'No, sir.'

'There you are, then. We've all got to be prepared to do our best.'

Joanna Grey took his arm. 'Henry, you're going to be late.'

'Yes, of course, my dear.' He nodded to the Irishman. 'All right, Devlin, I'll see you tomorrow afternoon.'

Devlin actually touched his forelock and waited until they'd gone out of the front door before moving into the sitting-room. He watched Sir Henry drive away and was lighting a cigarette when Joanna Grey returned.

'Tell me something,' he said. 'Are he and Churchill supposed to be friends?'

'As I understand it, they've never met. Studley Grange is famous for its Elizabethan gardens. The Prime Minister fancied the idea of a quiet weekend and a little painting before returning to London.'

'With Sir Henry falling over himself to oblige? Oh, yes, I can see that.'

She shook her head. 'I thought you were going to say begorrah any minute. You're a wicked man, Mr Devlin.'

'Liam,' he said. 'Call me Liam. It'll sound better, especially if I still call you Mrs Grey. He fancies you, then, and at his age?'

'Autumn romance is not completely unheard of.'

'More like winter, I should have thought. On the other hand it must be damn useful.'

'More than that – essential,' she said. 'Anyway, bring your bag and I'll get the car and take you along to Hobs End.'

*

The rain pushed in on the wind from the sea was cold and the marsh was shrouded in mist. When Joanna Grey braked to a halt in the yard of the old marsh warden's cottage, Devlin got out and looked about him thoughtfully. It was a strange, mysterious sort of place, the kind that made the hair lift on the back of his head. Sea creeks and mudflats, the great, pale reeds merging with the mist and somewhere out there, the occasional cry of a bird, the invisible beat of wings.

'I see what you mean about being isolated.'

She took a key from under a flat stone by the front door and opened it, leading the way into a flagged passageway. There was rising damp and the whitewash was flaking from the wall. On the left a door opened into a large kitchen-cum-living room. Again, the floor was stone flags, but there was a huge open-hearth fireplace and rush mats. At the other end of the room was an iron cooking stove and a chipped, white pot sink with a single tap. A large pine table flanked by two benches and an old wing-backed chair by the fire were the only furniture.

'I've news for you,' Devlin said. 'I was raised in a cottage exactly like this in County Down in the North of Ireland. All it needs is a bloody good fire to dry the place out.'

'And it has one great advantage – seclusion,' she said. 'You probably won't see a soul the whole time you're here.'

Devlin opened the Gladstone bag and took out some personal belongings, clothing and three or four books. Then he ran a finger through the lining to find a hidden catch, and removed a false bottom. In the cavity he revealed was a Walther P38, a Sten gun, the silenced version, in three parts, and a land agent's S-phone receiver and transmitter which was no more than pocket size. There was a thousand pounds in pound notes and another thousand in fivers. There was also something in a white cloth which he didn't bother to unwrap.

'Operating money,' he said.

'To obtain the vehicles?'

'That's right. I've been given the address of the right sort of people.'

'Where from?'

'The kind of thing they have on file at Abwehr Headquarters.'

'Where is it?'

'Birmingham. I thought I'd take a run over there this weekend. What do I need to know?'

She sat on the edge of the table and watched as he screwed the barrel unit of the Sten into the main body and slotted the shoulder stock in place. 'It's a fair way,' she said. 'Say three hundred miles the round trip.'

'Obviously my three gallons of petrol isn't going to get me very far. What can I do about that?'

'There's plenty of black market petrol available, at three times the normal price, if you know the right garages. The commercial variety is dyed red to make it easy for the police to detect wrongful use, but you can get rid of the dye by straining the petrol through an ordinary civilian gas mask filter.'

Devlin rammed a magazine into the Sten, checked it, then took the whole thing to pieces again and replaced it in the bottom of the bag.

'A wonderful thing, technology,' he observed. 'That thing can be fired at close quarters and the only sound you can hear is the bolt clicking. It's English, by the way. Another of the items SOE fondly imagine it's been dropping in to the Dutch underground.' He took out a cigarette and put it in his mouth. 'What else should I know when I make this trip? What are the risks?'

'Very few,' she said. 'The lights on the machine will have the regulation blackout fittings so there's no problem there. The roads, particularly in country areas, are virtually traffic free. And white lines have been painted down the centre of most of them. That helps.'

'What about the police or the security forces?'

She gazed at him blankly. 'Oh, there's nothing to worry about there. The military would only stop you if you tried to enter a restricted area. Technically this still *is* a Defence Area, but nobody bothers with the regulations these days. As for the police, they're entitled to stop you and ask for your identity card or they might stop a vehicle on the main road as part of a spot check in the campaign against misuse of petrol.'

She almost sounded indignant and, remembering what he had left, Devlin had to fight an irresistible compulsion to open her eyes a little. Instead he said, 'Is that all?'

'I think so. There's a twenty-mile-an-hour speed limit in built-up areas and of course you won't find signposts anywhere, but they started putting place names up again in many places earlier this summer.'

'So, the odds are that I shouldn't have any trouble?

'No one's stopped me. Nobody bothers now.' She shrugged. 'There's no problem. At the local WVS aid centre we have all sorts of official forms from the old Defence Area days. There was one that allowed you to visit relatives in hospital. I'll make one out referring to some brother in hospital in Birmingham. That and those medical discharge papers from the Army should be enough to satisfy anyone. Everybody has a soft spot for a hero these days.'

Devlin grinned. 'You know something, Mrs Grey? I think we're going to get on famously.' He went and rummaged in the cupboard under the sink and returned with a rusty hammer and a nail. 'The very thing.'

'For what?' she demanded.

He stepped inside the hearth and drove the nail partially home at the back of the smoke-blackened beam which supported the chimney breast. Then he hung the Walther up there by its trigger guard. 'What I call my ace-in-the-hole. I like to have one around, just in case. Now, show me round the rest of the place.'

There was an assortment of outbuildings, mostly in decay, and a barn in quite reasonable condition. There was another standing behind it on the very edge of the marsh, a decrepit building of considerable age, the stonework green with mildew. Devlin got one half of the large door open with difficulty. Inside it was cold and damp and obviously hadn't been used for anything for years.

'This will do just fine,' he said. 'Even if old Sir Willoughby comes poking his nose in I shouldn't think he'd go this far.'

'He's a busy man,' she said. 'County affairs, magistrate, running the local Home Guard. He still takes that very seriously. Doesn't really have much time for anything else.'

'But you,' he said. 'The randy old bastard still has enough time left for you.'

She smiled. 'Yes, I'm afraid that's only too true.' She took his arm. 'Now, I'll show you the dropping zone.'

They walked up through the marsh along the dyke road. It was raining quite hard now and the wind carried with it the damp, wet smell of rotting vegetation. Some Brent geese flew in out of the mist in formation like a bombing squadron going in for the kill and vanished into the grey curtain.

They reached the pine trees, the pill boxes, the sand-filled tank trap, the warning *Beware of Mines* so familiar to Devlin from the photographs he had seen. Joanna Grey tossed a stone out over the sands and Patch bounded through the wire to retreive it.

'You're sure?' Devlin said.

'Absolutely.'

He grinned crookedly. 'I'm a Catholic, remember that if it goes wrong.'

'They all are here. I'll see you're put down properly.'

He stepped over the coils of wire, paused on the edge of the sand, and walked forward. He paused again, then started to run, leaving wet footprints for the tide had no long ebbed. He turned, ran back and once again negotiated the wire.

He was immensely cheerful and put an arm around her shoulders. 'You were right – from the beginning. It's going to work, this thing. You'll see.' He looked out to sea across the creeks and the sandbanks, through the mist towards the Point. 'Beautiful. The thought of leaving all this must break your heart.'

'Leave?' She looked up at him blankly. 'What do you mean?'

'But you can't stay,' he said. 'Not afterwards. Surely you must see that?'

She looked out to the Point as if for the last time. Strange, but it had never occurred to her that she would have to leave. She shivered as the wind drove rain in hard off the sea.

*

It was raining at Landsvoort, too, as Steiner and Ritter Neumann made their first tour of inspection of the general area surrounding the airstrip. They had arrived an hour previously by truck after a flight in a Ju.52 transport from Cherbourg to Amsterdam, and Steiner had left the immediate problem of settling the men in the capable hands of Sergeant-Major Brandt.

He and Ritter followed a track which led from the farmhouse to the shore perhaps a quarter of a mile away. It was an incredibly desolate landscape, flat and barren. There was little shelter anywhere.

Neumann said, 'What a dump. It's going to be a long three weeks.'

'It needn't be if you and Brandt organize it properly,' Steiner said. 'A good hard schedule and lots of ground-jump training practice. Most of them could do with that. We haven't jumped for some time, remember. Then there are the British weapons to come to terms with. Target briefing and so on. I think the three weeks should be filled rather well.'

'When are you going to tell them; about the target, I mean? Will you leave it till the last possible moment?'

'I don't think so. About a week before we go would be a good time. That would sharpen them up for the last few days. You know how men get when they're kept under strict security for an operation like this.'

'You don't need to rub it in,' Neumann said. 'Remember what things were like at Hildesheim airbase at the beginning of the war when we were preparing for the Eben Emael assault and the Albert Canal bridges? How long did they keep us in quarantine for that one? Six months?'

'But it paid off, remember. It worked to perfection, right down to the last detail.' Steiner sighed. 'A long time ago, Ritter. Like something out of an old story. A different war.'

The track snaked between dunes of pure white sand, tufts of grass sticking through here and there, a barrier between the land and the sea. There was an inlet on the other side, deep water and a broken concrete pier.

'What was it used for?' Neumann asked.

'Barges came up the coast from the Hague and Rotterdam to fill up with sand,' Steiner told him. 'It should suit young Koenig admirably.'

'When does he arrive?'

'Radl wasn't sure when he spoke to me on the telephone. Certainly within the next week. The thing is, Koenig may find it better to come up with one of the coastal convoys than on his own.'

Their footsteps boomed hollowly on the boardwalk along the centre of the pier. There was the heavy salt smell of the sea, the murmur of the waves as they swirled between the concrete piles below. Steiner stood at the very end and looked out into the curtain of grey mist and rain. 'There it is, Ritter, waiting for us. A hundred and sixty miles due west, that's all.'

'And will this work to perfection, too, Herr Oberst?' Ritter Neumann said. 'Like Eben Emael, right down to the last detail?'

'It worked for Skorzeny at Gran Sasso.'

'That isn't what I asked.'

'All right, let's see if I can do any better.' Steiner took his time over lighting a cigarette and flicked the match out into space. 'Men generally die in war when they cannot help it and are defeated by a disadvantageous situation.'

'And what in the hell is that supposed to mean?'

'That you need luck, Ritter, always that, because no matter how well you plan there remains the unexpected. The one thing you hadn't looked for. The stupid, silly, unimportant items that can destroy you.' He smiled. 'Having made that point, it is a fact that with any kind of luck this whole thing could go beautifully. We could be in and out so fast that they won't know we've been till we've gone.'

'And if it doesn't go like that?'

'Then all your problems will be over and you won't have a thing to worry about.' Steiner smiled slightly. 'And now, I think we'd better get back.' He turned and walked away along the pier.

*

At twenty to eight that evening Max Radl, in his office at the Tirpitz Ufer, decided he'd had enough for the day. He'd not felt well since his return from Brittany and the doctor he'd gone to see had been horrified at his condition.

'If you carry on like this, Herr Oberst, you will kill yourself,' he had declared firmly. 'I think I can promise you that.'

Radl had paid his fee and taken the pills – three different kinds – which with any kind of luck might keep him going. As long as he could stay out of the hands of the Army medics he had a chance, but one more physical check-up with that lot and he was finished. They'd have him into a civilian suit before he knew where he was.

He opened a drawer, took out one of the pill bottles and popped two into his mouth. They were supposed to be pain killers, but just to make sure, he half-filled a tumbler with Courvoisier to wash them down. There was a knock on the door and Hofer entered. His normally composed face was full of emotion and his eyes were bright.

'What is it, Karl, what's happened ?' Radl demanded.

Hofer pushed a signal flimsy across the desk. 'It's just in, Herr Oberst. From Starling – Mrs Grey. He's arrived safely. He's with her now.'

Radl looked down at the flimsy in a kind of awe. 'My God, Devlin,' he whispered. 'You brought it off. It worked.'

A sense of physical release surged through him. He reached inside his bottom drawer and found another glass. 'Karl, this very definitely calls for a drink.'

He stood up, full of fierce joy, aware that he had not felt like this in years, not since that incredible euphoria when racing for the French coast at the head of his men in the summer of 1940.

He raised his glass and said to Hofer, 'I give you a toast, Karl. To Liam Devlin and "Up the Republic".'

*

As a staff officer in the Lincoln Washington Brigade in Spain, Devlin had found a motor-cycle the most useful way of keeping contact between the scattered units of his command in difficult mountain country. Very different from Norfolk, but there was that same sense of freedom, of being off the leash, as he rode from Studley Grange through quiet country lanes towards the village.

He'd obtained a driving licence in Holt that morning along with his other documents, without the slightest difficulty. Wherever he'd gone, from the police station to the local labour exchange, his cover story of being an ex-infantryman, discharged because of wounds, had worked like a charm. The various officials had really put themselves out to push things through for him. It was true what they said. In wartime, everyone loved a soldier, and a wounded hero even more so.

The motor-cycle was pre-war, of course, and had seen better days. A 350 cc BSA, but when he took a chance and opened the throttle wide on the first straight, the needle swung up to sixty with no trouble at all. He throttled back quickly once he'd established that the power was there if needed. No sense in asking for trouble. There was no village policeman in Studley Constable, but Joanna Grey had warned him that one occasionally appeared from Holt on a motor-cycle.

He came down the steep hill into the village itself past the
old mill with the waterwheel which didn't seem to be turning
and slowed for a young girl in a pony and trap carrying three
milk churns. She wore a blue beret and a very old, First
World War trenchcoat at least two sizes too big for her. She
had high cheekbones, large eyes, a mouth that was too wide
and three of her fingers poked through holes in the woollen
gloves she wore.

'Good day to you, *a colleen,*' he said cheerfully as he
waited for her to cross his path to the bridge. 'God save the
good work.'

Her eyes widened in a kind of astonishment, her mouth
opened slightly. She seemed bereft of speech and clicked her
tongue, urging the pony over the bridge and into a trot as
they started up the hill past the church.

'A lovely, ugly little peasant,' he quoted softly, 'who
turned my head not once, but twice.' He grinned. 'Oh, no,
Liam, me old love. Not that. Not now.'

He swung the motor-cycle in towards the Studley Arms and
became aware of a man standing in the window glaring at
him. An enormous individual of thirty or so with a tangled
black beard. He was wearing a tweed cap and an old reefer
coat.

And what in the hell have I done to you, son? Devlin asked
himself. The man's gaze travelled to the girl and the trap just
breasting the hill beside the church and moved back again. It
was enough. Devlin pushed the BSA up on to its stand,
unstrapped the shotgun in its canvas bag which was hanging
about his neck, tucked it under his arm and went inside.

There was no bar, just a large comfortable room with a
low-beamed ceiling, several high-backed benches, a couple of
wooden tables. A wood fire burned brightly on an open
hearth.

There were only three people in the room. The man sitting
beside the fire playing a mouth organ, the one with the black
beard at the window and a short, stocky man in shirt sleeves
who looked to be in his late twenties.

'God bless all here,' Devlin announced, playing the bog Irishman to the hilt.

He put the gun in its canvas bag on the table and the man in the shirt sleeves smiled and stuck out his hand. 'I'm George Wilde the publican here and you'll be Sir Henry's new warden down on the marshes. We've heard all about you.'

'What, already?' Devlin said.

'You know how it is in the country.'

'Or does he?' the big man at the window said harshly.

'Oh, I'm a farm boy from way back myself,' Devlin said.

Wilde looked troubled, but attempted the obvious introduction. 'Arthur Seymour and the old goat by the fire is Laker Armsby.'

As Devlin discovered later, Laker was in his late forties, but looked older. He was incredibly shabby, his tweed cap torn, his coat tied with string and his trousers and shoes were caked with mud.

'Would you gentlemen join me in a drink?' Devlin suggested.

'I wouldn't say no to that,' Laker Armsby told him. 'A pint of brown ale would suit me fine.'

Seymour drained his flagon and banged it down on the table. 'I buys my own.' He picked up the shotgun and hefted it in one hand. 'The Squire's really looking after you, isn't he? This and the bike. Now I wonder why you should rate that, an incomer like you, when there's those amongst us who've worked the estate for years and still must be content with less.'

'Sure and I can only put it down to my good looks,' Devlin told him.

Madness sparked in Seymour's eyes, the Devil looked out, hot and wild. He had Devlin by the front of the coat and pulled him close. 'Don't make fun of me, little man. Don't ever do that or I'll step on you as I'd step on a slug.'

Wilde grabbed his arm, 'Now come on, Arthur,' but Seymour pushed him away.

'You walk soft round here, you keep your place and we might get on. Understand me?'

Devlin smiled anxiously. 'Sure and if I've given offence, I'm sorry.'

'That's better,' Seymour released his grip and patted his face. 'That's much better. Only in future, remember one thing. When I come in, you leave.'

He went out, the door banged behind him and Laker Armsby cackled wildly, 'He's a bad bastard is Arthur.'

George Wilde vanished into the back room and returned with a bottle of Scotch and some glasses. 'This stuff's hard to come by at the moment, but I reckon you've earned one on me, Mr Devlin.'

'Liam,' Devlin said. 'Call me Liam.' He accepted the glass of whisky. 'Is he always like that?'

'Ever since I've known him.'

'There was a girl outside in a pony and trap as I came in. Does he have some special interest there?'

'Fancies his chances.' Laker Armsby chuckled. 'Only she won't have any of it.'

'That's Molly Prior,' Wilde said. 'She and her mother have a farm a couple of miles this side of Hobs End. Been running it between them since last year when her father died. Laker gives them a few hours when he isn't busy at the church.'

'Seymour does a bit for them as well. Some of the heavy stuff.'

'And thinks he owns the place, I suppose? Why isn't he in the Army?'

'That's another sore point. They turned him down because of a perforated eardrum.'

'Which he took as an insult to his great manhood, I suppose?' Devlin said.

Wilde said awkwardly, as if he felt some explanation was necessary, 'I picked up a packet myself with the Royal Artillery at Narvik in April, nineteen-forty. Lost my right knee-cap, so it was a short war for me. You got yours in France I understand?'

'That's right,' Devlin said calmly. 'Near Arras. Came out through Dunkirk on a stretcher and never knew a thing about it.'

'And over a year in hospitals Mrs Grey tells me?'

Devlin nodded. 'A grand woman. I'm very grateful to her. Her husband knew my people back home years ago. If it wasn't for her I wouldn't have this job.'

'A lady,' Wilde said. 'A real lady. There's nobody better liked round here.'

Laker Armsby said, 'Now me, I copped my first packet on the Somme in nineteen-sixteen. With the Welsh Guards, I was.'

'Oh, no.' Devlin took a shilling from his pocket, slapped it down on the table and winked at Wilde, 'Give him a pint, but I'm off. Got work to do.'

He slung the shotgun over his back again, kicked the motor-cycle into life and drove down to Park Cottage. Joanna Grey was in WVS uniform, standing in the garden drinking a cup of tea. She crossed to the gate with a bright smile. 'Everything all right?'

'Yes, I've seen the old boy and picked up the bike and the gun, so that's covered. Only snag so far was just now down at the pub. A big ox called Seymour who doesn't like strangers.'

'Keep out of his way,' she said. 'He's quite unbalanced. When are you going to Birmingham?'

'Overnight Saturday. I'll be back Sunday afternoon or evening.'

'Good,' she said calmly. 'Then if you drive round to the back I'll give you that form I promised and you'll find a couple of two-gallon cans of petrol in the garage. That should cover you for the Birmingham trip and to spare.'

'What in the hell would I do without you?' he asked her.

'Exactly, Mr Devlin.'

She turned and walked back into the house and Devlin pushed the BSA round to the rear.

*

As a member of the IRA, Liam Devlin had been officially denied the Sacraments for a considerable number of years and his espousal of the Republican cause in Spain had hardly helped his situation. It was always possible to find the odd priest here and there who, sympathetic to the cause itself, was willing to overlook such evidence of human frailty, but Devlin had never bothered.

The urge was simply not there. Had not been for some considerable time.

Having said that, churches in their own right had always given
him a certain aesthetic pleasure. He liked the cold spirituality of
them, what he called the smell of the ages. The sense of history
through people's lives to be found there and when he pushed open
the door and went into St Mary and All the Saints, he was not
disappointed.

'Would you look at that now?' he said softly, gazing about him
with a conscious pleasure, dipping his hand in the Holy Water and
crossing himself mechanically.

It really was very beautiful. Time holding its breath, waiting for
the next thing to happen. The flickering candles, the ruby light of
the sanctuary lamp and he sat down into the nearest pew, arms
folded, filled with a pleasant nostalgia.

There was the click of a door behind him, approaching
footsteps. He turned and found Father Vereker approaching.
Devlin got to his feet. 'Good afternoon to you, Father.'

'Can I help you?'

'Not really. I was just watching a little lad going down the aisle
there in a scarlet cassock and white cotta, a bucket of holy water in
his hand and wondering if it was ever me.'

'I know that kind of feeling only too well.' Vereker smiled and
held out his hand. 'You will be Mr Devlin. Mrs Grey told me
you'd be coming.'

Devlin shook hands. 'That was nice of her.'

Vereker was nothing if not direct. He said, 'I presume you're a
Catholic?'

'Because I'm Irish, Father?' Devlin smiled. 'I mind me one or
two who weren't. There was a fella named Wolfe Tone I heard of a
time or two.'

'I take the point.' Vereker managed a smile with some difficulty, for on some days the aluminium foot they'd given him
played the very devil – and this was one of them. 'We have a small
congregation here. Never more than fifteen or twenty for Mass.
People find it difficult to get in from the outlying farms in the
evening with the lack of transport so you will be very welcome.

Times of Confession are on the board outside.'

'Sorry, Father, but that's a service I haven't used for some considerable time.'

Vereker frowned, immediately serious. 'May I ask why?'

'Sure and if I told you, you would never believe me. Let's just say Liam Devlin and Holy Mother Church haven't seen eye to eye on a few things for quite a while now and leave it at that.'

'But that is something I cannot and will not do, Mr Devlin.'

'Well, here's one soul you'll have the devil's own luck in saving from the fire, Father, believe me.' Devlin grinned. 'I'll be away now. Nice meeting you.'

He had got as far as the door when Father Vereker called, 'Mr Devlin.'

Devlin turned, the door half-open. 'Yes, Father.'

'Another time. Something I have plenty of.'

Devlin sighed. 'I know, Father. That's the trouble with you fellas. You always do.'

*

When he reached the coast road, Devlin took the first dyke path that he came to at the northerly end of Hobs End marsh and drove out towards the fringe of pine trees. It was a crisp, autumnal sort of day, cold but bracing, white clouds chasing each other across a blue sky. He opened the throttle and roared along the narrow dyke path. A hell of a risk, for one wrong move and he'd be into the marsh. Stupid really, but that was the kind of mood he was in, and the sense of freedom was exhilarating.

He throttled back, braking to turn into another path, working his way along the network of dykes towards the coast, when a horse and rider suddenly appeared from the reeds thirty or forty yards to his right and scrambled up on top of the dyke. It was the girl he'd last seen in the village in the pony and trap, Molly Prior. As he slowed, she leaned low over the horse's neck and urged it into a gallop, racing him on a parallel course.

Devlin responded instantly, opening the throttle and surging forward in a burst of speed, kicking dirt out in a great spray into the marsh behind him. The girl had an advantage, in that the dyke she was on ran straight to the pine trees, whereas Devlin had to work his way through a maze, turning from one path into another and he lost ground.

She was close to the trees now and as he skidded out of one path broadside on and finally found a clear run, she plunged her mount into the water and mud of the marsh, urging it through the reeds in a final short cut. The horse responded well and a few moments later, bounded free and disappeared into the pines.

Devlin left the dyke path at speed, shot up the inside of the first sand dune, travelled some little distance through the air and alighted in soft white sand, going down on one knee in a long slide.

Molly Prior was sitting at the foot of a pine tree gazing out to sea, her chin on her knees. She was dressed exactly as she had been when Devlin had last seen her except that she had taken off the beret, exposing short-cropped, tawny hair. The horse grazed on a tuft of grass that pushed up through the sand.

Devlin got the bike up on its stand and threw himself down beside her. 'A fine day, thanks be to God.'

She turned and said calmly, 'What kept you?'

Devlin had taken off his cap to wipe sweat from his forehead and he looked up at her in astonishment, 'What kept me, is it? Why, you little . . .'

And then she smiled. More than that, threw back her head and laughed and Devlin laughed too. 'By God, and I'll know you till the crack of Doomsday, that's for sure.'

'And what's that supposed to mean?' She spoke with the strong and distinctive Norfolk accent that was still so new to him.

'Oh, a saying they have where I come from.' He found a packet of cigarettes and put one in his mouth. 'Do you use these things?'

'No.'

'Good for you, they'd stunt your growth and you with your green years still ahead of you.'

'I'm seventeen, I'll have you know,' she told him. 'Eighteen in February.'

Devlin put a match to his cigarette and lay back pillowing his head on his hands, the peak of his cap over his eyes. 'February what?'

'The twenty-second.'

'Ah, a little fish, is it? Pisces. We should do well together, me being a Scorpio. You should never marry a Virgo, by the way. No chance of them and Pisces hitting it off at all. Take Arthur, now. I've a terrible hunch he's a Virgo. I'd watch it there if I were you.'

'Arthur?' she said. 'You mean Arthur Seymour? Are you crazy?'

'No, but I think he is,' Devlin replied and carried on. 'Pure, clean, virtuous and not very hot, which is a terrible pity from where I'm lying.'

She had turned round to look down at him and the old coat gaped open. Her breasts were full and firm, barely contained by the cotton blouse she was wearing.

'Oh, girl dear, you'll have a terrible problem with your weight in a year or two if you don't watch your food.'

Her eyes flashed, she glanced down and instinctively pulled her coat together. 'You bastard,' she said, somehow drawing the word out. And then she saw his lips quiver and leaned down to peer under the peak of the cap. 'Why, you're laughing at me!' She pulled off his cap and threw it away.

'And what else would I do with you, Molly Prior?' He put out a hand defensively. 'No, don't answer that.'

She sat back against the tree, her hands in her pockets. 'How did you know my name?'

'George Wilde told me at the pub.'

'Oh, I see now. And Arthur – was he there?'

'You could say that. I get the impression he looks upon you as his personal property.'

'Then he can go to hell,' she said, suddenly fierce. 'I belong to no man.'

He looked up at her from where he lay, the cigarette hanging from the corner of his mouth, and smiled. 'Your nose turns up, has anyone ever told you that? And when you're angry, your mouth goes down at the corners.'

He had gone too far, touched some source of secret inner hurt. She flushed and said bitterly, 'Oh, I'm ugly enough, Mr Devlin. I've sat all night long at dances in Holt without being asked, too often not to know my place. You wouldn't throw me out on a wet

Saturday night, I know. But that's men for you. Anything's better than nothing.'

She started to get up, Devlin had her by the ankle and dragged her down, pinning her with one strong arm as she struggled. 'You know my name? How's that?'

'Don't let it go to your head. Everybody knows about you. Everything there is to know.'

'I've news for you,' he said pushing himself up on one elbow and leaning over her. 'You don't know the first thing about me because if you did, you'd know I prefer fine autumn afternoons under the pine trees to wet Saturday nights. On the other hand, the sand has a terrible way of getting where it shouldn't.' She went very still. He kissed her briefly on the mouth and rolled away. 'Now get the hell out of it before I let my mad passion run away with me.'

She grabbed her beret, jumped to her feet and reached for the horse's bridle. When she turned to glance at him her face was serious, but after she'd scrambled into the saddle and pulled her mount round to look at him again, she was smiling. 'They told me all Irishmen were mad. Now I believe them. I'll be at Mass Sunday evening. Will you?'

'Do I look as though I will?'

The horse was stamping, turning in half-circles, but she held it well. 'Yes,' she said seriously, 'I think you do,' and she gave the horse its head and galloped away.

'Oh, you idiot, Liam,' Devlin said softly as he pushed his motor-cycle off its stand and shoved it alongside the sand dune, through the trees and on to the path. 'Won't you ever learn?'

He drove back along the main dyke top, sedately this time, and ran the motor-cycle into the barn. He found the key where he'd left it under the stone by the door and let himself in. He put the shotgun in the hallstand, went into the kitchen, unbuttoning his raincoat, and paused. There was a pitcher of milk on the table, a dozen brown eggs in a white bowl.

'Mother Mary,' he said softly. 'Would you look at that now?'

He touched the bowl gently with one finger, but when he finally turned to take off his coat, his face was bleak.

8

The Sunday morning weather forecast from Wilhelmshaven for the North Sea area generally had been far from promising. Winds five-to-six with rain squalls and off the Dutch coast the weather was about as dirty as it could be, heavy dark clouds swollen with rain, merging with the sea on the horizon.

Dawn was at six-fifteen, but visibility, even by nine-thirty, was bad enough to keep even the RAF at home; so that no one could have been blamed for failing to spot the lone Mosquito coming in low off the sea astern of the convoy. The pilot ripped up the decks of the fourth and fifth coasters in line with cannon shell and banked to turn for a second run.

Koenig, in his bunk below trying to snatch an hour's sleep, was awake in an instant and making for the companionway. As he reached the deck, the gun crew were already running for the twin 20mm anti-aircraft cannon. Koenig beat them to it, was into the bucket seat in a second, hands clamping around the trigger handles.

As the Mosquito came in off the water for a second time, he started to fire along with everyone else in the convoy, swinging to follow its flight as its cannon ripped into the superstructure of another ship up front. Not that he hit anything, which was hardly surprising as the Mosquito was making its pass at something like four hundred miles an hour. It curved away to port through puffballs of black smoke and fled into the grey morning like a departing spirit.

All firing stopped and one of the escorting destroyers surged ahead to where a column of black smoke curled up into the morning from the fourth coaster in line. Koenig could clearly see the crew unscrambling the hoses.

He stood up and turned to Leading Seaman Kranz who was in charge of the anti-aircraft cannon. 'You were five seconds too slow getting to your post, you and your lads, Kranz, and one day that could be the end of all of us. Do I need to say more?'

The men of the gun crew shuffled uneasily and Kranz rammed his heels together. 'No, Herr Leutnant. It won't happen again.'

'If it does,' Koenig assured him, 'you'll be back where you started three years ago. That's a promise.'

He went on the bridge where Muller had the wheel and slumped into the chart-table chair. When he lit a cigarette, his hands were trembling.

'A lone wolf,' Muller said.

Koenig nodded. 'They're not going to turn planes out in any kind of force on a morning like this. They'd lose too many to the weather.'

'I'm sorry about that gun crew,' Muller said. 'No excuse. I'll have a word with Kranz.'

'Let it go. They've had a rough trip. They need a rest, that's all.'

Which was something of an understatement. The trip from Jersey to Cherbourg and on to Boulogne had been bad enough because of extremely poor weather conditions with force eight winds on occasion, but the run with the convoy from Boulogne had been hell for most of the way.

The coastal minefields were an effective enough barrier as far as keeping the Royal Navy at bay was concerned, but they didn't mean a thing to the RAF. The convoy had been strafed twice by fighter bombers on the way through the Straits of Dover and again near Dunkirk and had lost two ships.

A young sailor came in with a couple of mugs of coffee which he put on the table. Koenig's eyes were gritty from lack of sleep, his back ached, but by some minor miracle known only to the navy, the coffee was real. He suddenly began to feel human again.

He turned and found that Muller was looking sideways at him, a trifle anxiously. 'Better, Herr Leutnant?'

Koenig grinned. 'Much better – as always.'

'You should get something to eat.'

'No, you first. I'll take the wheel for a while.'

Muller looked as if he might argue and Koenig stood up. 'I want to be by myself for a while, Erich. I want to think. You understand?'

'Yes, Herr Leutnant.' Muller handed over the wheel without further argument and went out.

Koenig lit another cigarette and opened one of the side windows breathing in the good salt air. They had got the fire on the fourth coaster under control now and the eighteen vessels of the convoy forged on without any slackening of speed, perfectly on station, the two destroyers and four armed trawlers who were the escort, circling to take up position again after the brief taste of battle.

It came to him, with a kind of wonder, that he was actually enjoying himself, in spite of the hunger, the constant fatigue, the aching back, the stress that must already have taken years off his life. Before the war he'd been a trainee accountant in a Hamburg bank, but now the sea was his life. Meat and drink to him, more important than any woman. It was the circumstance of war which had given him this, but the war wouldn't last forever.

He said softly, 'What in the hell am I going to do when it's all over?'

The lead destroyer swept past at that moment, signal lamp flashing on its bridge. Koenig leaned out of the side window and spoke to Teusen, the leading telegraphist on duty at the rail. 'What's he saying?'

' "Altering course for Rotterdam now. Goodbye and good luck." '

Koenig waved. 'Make; "Many thanks and heartiest congratulations on a good job well done." '

Teusen's signal lamp clattered, and there was an acknowledgement as the destroyer turned away, leading the convoy round towards the Dutch coast. As Koenig altered course a couple of points and increased speed, the E-boat plunging over the waves into the grey curtain of rain, it occurred to him, with a certain gloomy satisfaction, that his problem might very well be solved for him. After all, when he considered the task that waited for him at Landsvoort, it seemed highly unlikely that he would survive the war anyway.

*

In Birmingham the weather was no better, a cold wind drifting across the city hurling rain again the great plate glass window of Ben Garvald's flat above the garage in Saltley. In the silk dressing gown and with a scarf at the throat, the dark, curly hair carefully combed, he made an imposing figure; the broken nose added a sort of rugged grandeur. A closer inspection was not so flattering, the fruits of dissipation showing clearly on the fleshy arrogant face.

But there was more there this morning – a considerable annoyance with the world at large – and not just because it was Sunday, although he loathed Sunday at the best of times. At eleven-thirty on the previous night, one of his business ventures, a small illegal gaming club in a house in an apparently respectable street in Aston had been turned over by the City of Birmingham Police. Not that Garvald was in any personal danger of being arrested himself. That was what the front man was paid for and he would be taken care of. Much more serious was the three and a half thousand pounds on the gaming tables which had been confiscated by the police.

The kitchen door swung open and a young girl of seventeen or eighteen came in. She wore a pink lace dressing gown, her peroxide-blonde hair was tousled and her face was blotched, the eyes swollen from weeping. 'Can I get you anything else, Mr Garvald?' she said in a low voice.

'Get me anything?' he said. 'That's good. That's bloody rich, that is, seeing as how you haven't bleeding well *given* me anything yet.'

He spoke without turning round. His interest had been caught by a man on a motor-cycle who had just ridden into the yard below and parked beside one of the trucks.

The girl, who had found herself quite unable to cope with some of Garvald's more bizarre demands of the previous night said tearfully, 'I'm sorry, Mr Garvald.'

The man below had walked across the yard and disappeared now. Garvald turned and said to the girl, 'Go on, get your clothes on and piss off.' She was frightened to death, shaking with fear and staring at him, mesmerized. A delicious feeling of power, almost sexual in its intensity, flooded through him. He grabbed her hair and twisted it cruelly. 'And learn to do as you're told. Understand?'

As the girl fled, the outer door opened and Reuben Garvald, Ben's younger brother, entered. He was small and sickly-looking, one shoulder slightly higher than the other, but the black eyes in the pale face were constantly on the move, missing nothing.

His eyes followed the girl disapprovingly as she disappeared into the bedroom. 'I wish you wouldn't, Ben. A dirty little cow like that. You might catch something.'

'That's what they invented penicillin for,' Garvald said. 'Anyway, what do you want?'

'There's a bloke to see you. Just came in on a motor-cycle.'

'So I noticed. What's he want?'

'Wouldn't say. Cheeky little Mick with too much off.' Reuben held out half a five pound note. 'Told me to give you that. Said you could have the other half if you'd see him.'

Garvald laughed, quite spontaneously, and plucked the torn banknote from his brother's hand. 'I like it. Yes, I very definitely go for that.' He took it to the window and examined it. 'It looks Kosher, too.' He turned, grinning. 'I wonder if he's got any more, Reuben? Let's see.'

Reuben went out and Garvald crossed to a sideboard in high good humour and poured himself a glass of Scotch. Maybe the morning was not going to turn out to be such a dead loss after all. It might even prove to be quite entertaining. He settled himself in an easy chair by the window.

The door opened and Reuben ushered Devlin into the room. He was wet through, his raincoat saturated, and he took off his tweed cap and squeezed it over a Chinese porcelain bowl filled with bulbs. 'Would you look at that now?'

'All right,' Garvald said. 'I know all you bleedin' Micks are cracked. You needn't rub it in. What's the name?'

'Murphy, Mr Garvald,' Devlin told him. 'As in spuds.'

'And I believe that, too,' Garvald said. 'Take that coat off, for Christ's sake. You'll ruin the bloody carpet. Genuine Axminster. Costs a fortune to get hold of that these days.'

Devlin removed his dripping trenchcoat and handed it to Reuben, who looked mad but took it anyway and draped it over a chair by the window.

'All right, sweetheart,' Garvald said. 'My time's limited so let's get to it.'

Devlin rubbed his hands dry on his jacket and took out a packet of cigarettes. 'They tell me you're in the transport business,' he said. 'Amongst other things.'

'Who tells you?'

'I heard it around.'

'So?'

'I need a truck. Bedford three-tonner. Army type.'

'Is that all?' Garvald was still smiling, but his eyes were watchful.

'No, I also want a jeep, a compressor plus spray equipment and a couple of gallons of khaki-green paint. And I want both trucks to have service registration.'

Garvald laughed out loud. 'What are you going to do, start the Second Front on your own or something?'

Devlin took a large envelope from his inside breast pocket and held it out. 'There's five hundred quid on account in there, just so you know I'm not wasting your time.'

Garvald nodded to his brother who took the envelope, opened it and checked the contents. 'He's right, Ben. In brand new fivers, too.'

He pushed the money across. Garvald weighed it in his hand then dropped it on the coffee table in front of him. He leaned back. 'All right, let's talk. Who are you working for?'

'Me,' Devlin said.

Garvald didn't believe him for a moment and showed it, but he didn't argue the point. 'You must have something good lined up to be going to all this trouble. Maybe you could do with a little help.'

'I've told you what I need, Mr Garvald,' Devlin said. 'One Bedford three-ton truck, a jeep, a compressor, and a couple of gallons of khaki-green paint. Now if you don't think you can help, I can always try elsewhere.'

Reuben said angrily, 'Who the hell do you think you are? Walking in here's one thing. Walking out again isn't always so easy.'

Devlin's face was very pale and when he turned to look at Reuben, the blue eyes seemed to be fixed on some distant point, cold and remote. 'Is that a fact, now?'

He reached for the bundle of fivers, his left hand in his pocket on the butt of the Walther. Garvald slammed a hand down across them hard. 'It's cost you,' he said softly. 'A nice, round figure. Let's say two thousand quid.'

He held Devlin's gaze in a kind of challenge, there was a lengthy pause and then Devlin smiled. 'I bet you had a mean left hand in your prime.'

'I still do, boy.' Garvald clenched his fist. 'The best in the business.'

'All right,' Devlin said. 'Throw in fifty gallons of petrol in Army jerrycans and you're on.'

Garvald held out his hand. 'Done. We'll have a drink on it. What's your pleasure?'

'Irish if you've got it. Bushmills for preference.'

'I got everything, boy. Anything and everything.' He snapped his fingers. Reuben hesitated, his face set and angry, and Garvald said in a low, dangerous voice. 'The Bushmills, Reuben.'

His brother went over to the sideboard and opened the cupboard, disclosing dozens of bottles underneath. 'You do all right for yourself,' Devlin observed.

'The only way,' Garvald took a cigar from a box on the coffee table. 'You want to take delivery in Birmingham or someplace else?'

'Somewhere near Peterborough on the A1 would do,' Devlin said.

Reuben handed him a glass. 'You're bloody choosy, aren't you?'

Garvald cut in. 'No, that's all right. You know Norman Cross? That's on the A1 about five miles out of Peterborough. There's a garage called Fogarty's a couple of miles down the road. It's closed at the moment.'

'I'll find it,' Devlin said.

'When do you want to take delivery?'

'Thursday the twenty-eighth and Friday the twenty-ninth. I'll take the truck and the compressor and the jerrycans the first night, the jeep on the second.'

Garvald frowned slightly. 'You mean you're handling the whole thing yourself?'

'That's right.'

'Okay – what kind of time were you thinking of?'

'After dark. Say about nine to nine-thirty.'

'And the cash?'

'You keep that five hundred on account. Seven-fifty when I take delivery of the truck, the same for the jeep and I want delivery licences for each of them.'

'That's easy enough,' Garvald said. 'But they'll need filling in with purpose and destination.'

'I'll see to that myself when I get them.'

Garvald nodded slowly, thinking about it. 'That looks all right to me. Okay, you're on. What about another snort?'

'No, thanks,' Devlin said. 'I've places to go.'

He pulled on the wet trenchcoat and buttoned it quickly. Garvald got up and went to the sideboard and came back with the freshly opened bottle of Bushmills. 'Have that on me, just to show there's no ill will.'

'The last thought in my mind,' Devlin told him. 'But thanks anyway. A little something in return.' He produced the other half of the five pound note from his breast pocket. 'Yours, I believe.'

Garvald took it and grinned. 'You've got the cheek of the Devil, you know that, Murphy?'

'It's been said before.'

'All right, we'll see you at Norman Cross on the twenty-eighth. Show him out, Reuben. Mind your manners.'

Reuben moved to the door sullenly and opened it and went out. Devlin followed him, but turned as Garvald sat down again. 'One more thing, Mr Garvald.'

'What's that?'

'I keep my word.'

'That's nice to know.'

'See that you do.'

He wasn't smiling now, the face bleak for the moment longer that he held Garvald's gaze before turning and going out.

Garvald stood up, walked to the sideboard and pured himself another Scotch, then he went to the window and looked down into the yard. Devlin pulled his motor-cycle off the stand and kicked the engine into life. The door opened and Reuben entered the room.

He was thoroughly aroused now. 'What's got into you, Ben? I don't understand. You let a little Mick, so fresh out of the bogs he's still got mud on his boots, walk all over you. You took more from him than I've seen you take from anyone.'

Garvald watched Devlin turn into the main road and ride away through the heavy rain. 'He's on to something, Reuben, boy,' he said softly. 'Something nice and juicy.'

'But why the Army vehicles?'

'Lots of possibilities there. Could be almost anything. Look at that case in Shropshire the other week. Some bloke dressed as a soldier drives an Army lorry into a big NAAFI depot and out again with thirty thousand quid's worth of Scotch on board. Imagine what that lot would be worth on the black market.'

'And you think he could be on to something like that?'

'He's got to be,' Garvald said, 'and whatever it is, I'm in, whether he likes it or not.' He shook his head in a kind of bewilderment. 'Do you know, he threatened me, Reuben – me! We can't have that, now can we?'

*

Although it was only mid-afternoon, the light was beginning to go as Koenig took the E-boat in towards the low-lying coastline. Beyond, thunderclouds towered into the sky, black and swollen and edged with pink.

Muller who was bending over the chart table said, 'A bad storm soon, Herr Leutnant.'

Koenig peered out of the window. 'Another fifteen minutes before it breaks. We'll be well up by then.'

Thunder rumbled ominously, the sky darkened and the crew,

waiting on deck for the first glimpse of their destination, were strangely quiet.

Koenig said, 'I don't blame them. What a bloody place after St Helier.'

Beyond the line of sand dunes the land was flat and bare, swept clean by the constant wind. In the distance he could see the farmhouse and the hangars at the airstrip, black against a pale horizon. The wind brushed across the water and Koenig reduced speed as they approached the inlet. 'You take her in, Erich.'

Muller took the wheel. Koenig pulled on an old pilot coat and went out on deck and stood at the rail smoking a cigarette. He felt strangely depressed. The voyage had been bad enough, but in a sense his problems were only beginning. The people he was to work with, for example. That was of crucial importance. In the past he'd had certain unfortunate experiences in similar situations.

The sky seemed to split wide open and rain began to fall in torrents. As they coasted in towards the concrete pier, a field car appeared on the track between the dunes. Muller cut the engines and leaned out of the window shouting orders. As the crew bustled to get a line ashore, the field car drove on to the pier and braked to a halt. Steiner and Ritter Neumann got out and walked to the edge.

'Hello, Koenig, so you made it?' Steiner called cheerfully 'Welcome to Landsvoort.'

Koenig, halfway up the ladder, was so astonished that he missed his footing and almost fell into the water. 'You, Herr Oberst, but . . .' And then as the implication struck home, he started to laugh. 'And here was I worrying like hell about who I was going to have to work with.'

He scrambled up the ladder and grabbed Steiner's hand.

*

It was half past four when Devlin rode down through the village past the Studley Arms. As he went over the bridge he could hear the organ playing and lights showed very dimly at the windows of the church for it was not yet dark. Joanna Grey had told him that evening Mass was held in the afternoon to avoid the blackout. As he went up the hill he remembered Molly Prior's remark. Smiling, he pulled up outside the church. She was there, he knew, because the pony stood patiently in the shafts of the trap, its nose in a feed bag. There were two cars, a flat-backed truck and several bicycles parked there also.

When Devlin opened the door, Father Vereker was on his way down the aisle with three young boys in scarlet cassocks and white cottas, one of them carrying a bucket of holy water, Vereker sprinkling the heads of the congregation as he passed, washing them clean. '*Asperges me*,' he intoned and Devlin slipped down the right-hand aisle and found a pew.

There were no more than seventeen or eighteen people in the congregation. Sir Henry and a woman who was presumably his wife and a young, dark-haired girl in her early twenties in the uniform of the Women's Auxiliary Air Force who sat with them and who was obviously Pamela Vereker. George Wilde was there with his wife. Laker Armsby sat with them, scrubbed clean in stiff white collar and an ancient, black suit.

Molly Prior was across the aisle with her mother, a pleasant, middle-aged woman with a kind face. Molly wore a straw hat decorated with some kind of fake flowers, the brim tilted over her eyes, and a flowered cotton dress with a tightly buttoned bodice and a rather short skirt. Her coat was folded neatly over the pew.

I bet she's been wearing that dress for at least three years now, he told himself. She turned suddenly and saw him. She didn't smile, simply looked at him for a second or so, then glanced away.

Vereker in his faded rose cope was up at the altar, hands together as he commenced Mass. 'I confess to Almighty God, and to you, my brothers and sisters, that I have sinned through my own fault.'

He struck his breast and Devlin, aware that Molly Prior's eyes had swivelled sideways under the brim of the straw hat to watch him, joined in out of devilment, asking Blessed Mary ever Virgin, all the Angels and Saints and the rest of the congregation to pray for him to the Lord our God.

When she went down on her knees on the hassock, she seemed to descend in slow motion, lifting her skirt perhaps six inches too high. He had to choke back his laughter at the demureness of it. But he sobered soon enough when he became aware of Arthur Seymour's mad eyes glaring from the shadows beside a pillar on the far aisle.

When the service was over, Devlin made sure he was first out. He was astride the motor-cycle and ready for off when he heard her call, 'Mr Devlin, just a minute.' He turned as she hurried towards him, an umbrella over her head, her mother a few yards behind her. 'Don't be in such a rush to be off,' Molly said. 'Are you ashamed or something?'

'Damn glad I came,' Devlin told her.

Whether she blushed or not, it was impossible to say for the light was bad. In any case, her mother arrived at that moment. 'This is my mum,' Molly said. 'And this is Mr Devlin.'

'I know all about you,' Mrs Prior said. 'Anything we can do, you just ask now. Difficult for a man on his own.'

'We thought you might like to come back and have tea with us,' Molly told him.

Beyond them, he saw Arthur Seymour standing by the lychgate, glowering. Devlin said, 'It's very nice of you, but to be honest, I'm in no fit state.'

Mrs Prior reached out to touch him. 'Lord bless us, boy, but you're soaking. Get you home and into a hot bath on the instant. You'll catch your death.'

'She's right.' Molly told him fiercely. 'You get off and mind you do as she says.'

Devlin kicked the starter. 'God protect me from this monstrous regiment of women,' he said and rode away.

*

The bath was an impossibility. It would have taken too long to heat the copper of water in the back scullery. He compromised by lighting an enormous, log fire on the huge stone hearth; then he stripped, towelled himself briskly and dressed again in a navy-blue flannel shirt and trousers of dark worsted.

He was hungry, but too tired to do anything much about it, so

he took a glass and the bottle of Bushmills Garvald had given him
and one of his books and sat in the old wing-back chair and roasted
his feet and read by the light of the fire. It was perhaps an hour
later that a cold wind touched the back of his neck briefly. He had
not heard the latch, but she was there, he knew that.

'What kept you?' he said without turning round.

'Very clever, I'd have thought you could have done better than
that after I've walked a mile and a quarter over wet fields in the
dark to bring you your supper.'

She moved round to the fire. She was wearing her old raincoat,
Wellington boots and a headscarf and carried a basket in one
hand. 'A meat and potato pie, but then I suppose you've eaten?'

He groaned aloud. 'Don't go on. Just get it in the oven as quick
as you can.'

She put the basket down and pulled off her boots and unfastened the raincoat. Underneath she was wearing the flowered
dress. She pulled off the scarf, shaking her hair. 'That's better.
What are you reading?'

He handed her the book. 'Poetry,' he said, 'by a blind Irishman
called Raftery who lived a long time ago.'

She peered at the page in the firelight. 'But I can't understand
it,' she said. 'It's in a foreign language.'

'Irish,' he said. 'The language of kings.' He took the book from
her and read,

Anois, teacht an Earraigh, beidh an la dul chun sineadh,
is tar eis feile Bride, ardochaidh me mo sheol . . .
. . . Now, in the springtime, the day's getting longer,
On the feastday of Bridget, up my sail will go,
Since my journey's decided, my step will get stronger,
Till once more I stand in the plains of Mayo . . .

'That's beautiful,' she said. 'Really beautiful.' She dropped
down on the rush mat beside him, leaning against the chair, her
left hand touching his arm. 'Is that where you come from, this
place Mayo?'

'No,' he said, keeping his voice steady with some difficulty.
'From rather farther north, but Raftery had the right idea.'

'Liam,' she said. 'Is that Irish, too?'

'Yes, m'am.'

'What does it mean?'

'William.'

She frowned. 'No, I think I prefer Liam. I mean, William's so ordinary.'

Devlin hung on to the book in his left hand and caught hold of her hair at the back with his right. 'Jesus, Joseph and Mary aid me.'

'And what's that supposed to mean?' she asked, all innocence.

'It means, girl dear, that if you don't get that pie out of the oven and on to the plate this instant, I won't be responsible.'

She laughed suddenly, deep in the throat, leaning over for a moment, her head on his knee. 'Oh, I do like you,' she said. 'Do you know that? From the first moment I saw you, Mr Devlin, sir, sitting astride that bike outside the pub, I liked you.'

He groaned, closing his eyes and she got to her feet, eased the skirt over her hips and got his pie from the oven.

*

When he walked her home over the fields it had stopped raining and the clouds had blown away, leaving a sky glowing with stars. The wind was cold and beat amongst the trees over their heads as they followed the field path, showering them with twigs. Devlin had the shotgun over his shoulder and she hung on to his left arm.

They hadn't talked much after the meal. She'd made him read more poetry to her, leaning against him, one knee raised. It had been infinitely worse than he could have imagined. Not in his scheme of things at all. He had three weeks, that was all, and a great deal to do in that time and no room for distraction.

They reached the farmyard wall and paused beside the gate.

'I was wondering. Wednesday afternoon if you've nothing on, I could do with some help in the barn. Some of the machinery needs moving for winter storage. It's a bit heavy for Mum and me. You could have your dinner with us.'

It would have been churlish to refuse. 'Why not?' he said.

She reached a hand up behind his neck, pulling his face down and kissed him with a fierce, passionate, inexperienced urgency that was incredibly moving. She was wearing some sort of lavender perfume, infinitely sweet, probably all she could afford. He was to remember it for the rest of his life.

She leaned against him and he said into her ear gently, 'You're seventeen and I'm a very old thirty-five. Have you thought about that?'

She looked up at him, eyes blind, 'Oh you're lovely,' she said. 'So lovely.'

A silly, banal phrase, laughable in other circumstances, but not now. Never now. He kissed her again, very lightly on the mouth. 'Go in!'

She went without any attempt at protest, wakening only the chickens as she crossed the farmyard. Somewhere on the other side of the house, a dog barked hollowly, a door banged, Devlin turned and started back.

It began to rain again as he skirted the last meadow above the main road. He crossed to the dyke path opposite with the old wooden sign, *Hobs End Farm*, which no one had ever thought worth taking down. Devlin trudged along, head bowed against the rain. Suddenly there was a rustling in the reeds to his right and a figure bounded into his path.

In spite of the rain, the cloud cover was only sparse and in the light of the quarter moon he saw that Arthur Seymour crouched in front of him. 'I told you,' he said. 'I warned you, but you wouldn't take no notice. Now you'll have to learn the hard way.'

Devlin had the shotgun off his shoulder in a second. It wasn't loaded, but no matter. He thumbed the hammers back with a very definite double click and rammed the barrel under Seymour's chin.

'Now you be careful,' he said. 'Because I've a licence to shoot vermin here from the squire himself and you're on the squire's property.'

Seynour jumped back. 'I'll get you, see if I don't. And that dirty little bitch. I'll pay you both out.'

He turned and ran into the night. Devlin shouldered his gun and moved on towards the cottage, head down as the rain increased in force. Seymour was mad – no, not quite – just not responsible. He wasn't worried about his threats in the slightest, but then he thought of Molly and his stomach went hollow.

'My God,' he said softly. 'If he harms her, I'll kill the bastard. I'll kill him.'

9

The Sten machine carbine was probably the greatest mass produced weapon of the Second World War and the standby of most British infantrymen. Shoddy and crude it may have looked, but it could stand up to more ill-treatment than any other weapon of its type. It came to pieces in seconds and would fit into a handbag or the pocket of an overcoat – a fact which made it invaluable to the various European resistance groups to whom it was parachuted by the British. Drop it in the mud, stamp on it and it would still kill as effectively as the most expensive Thompson gun.

The MK IIS version was specially developed for use by commando units, fitted with a silencer which absorbed the noise of the bullet explosions to an amazing degree. The only sound when it fired was the clicking of the bolt and that could seldom be heard beyond a range of twenty yards.

The one which Staff Sergeant Willi Scheid held in his hands on the improvised firing range amongst the sand dunes at Landsvoort on the morning of Wednesday 20 October, was a mint specimen. There was a row of targets at the far end, lifesize replicas of charging *Tommis*. He emptied the magazine into the first five, working from left to right. It was an eerie experience to see the bullets shredding the target and to hear only the clicking of the bolt. Steiner and the rest of his small assault force, standing in a semi-circle behind him, were suitably impressed.

'Excellent!' Steiner held out his hand and Scheid passed the Sten to him. 'Really excellent!' Steiner examined it and handed it to Neumann.

Neumann cursed suddenly. 'Dammit, the barrel's hot.'

'That is so, Herr Oberleutnant,' Scheid said. 'You must be careful to hold only the canvas insulating cover. The silencer tubes heat rapidly when the weapon is fired on full automatic.'

Scheid was from the Ordnance Depot at Hamburg, a small, rather insignificant man in steel spectacles and the shabbiest uniform Steiner had ever seen. He moved across to a groundsheet on which various weapons were displayed. 'The Sten gun, in both the silenced and normal versions, will be the machine pistol you will use. As regards a light machine-gun, the Bren. Not as good a general purpose weapon as our own MG-forty-two, but an excellent section weapon. It fires in either single shots or bursts of four or five rounds so it's very economical and highly accurate.'

'What about rifles?' Steiner asked.

Before Scheid could reply, Neumann tapped Steiner on the shoulder and the Colonel turned in time to see the Stork come in low from the direction of the Ijsselmeer and turn for its first circuit over the airstrip.

Steiner said, 'I'll take over for a moment, Sergeant.' He turned to the men. 'From now on what Staff Sergeant Scheid says goes. You've got a couple of weeks, and by the time he's finished with you I'll expect you to be able to take these things apart and put them together again with your eyes closed.' He glanced at Brandt. 'Any assistance he wants, you see that he gets it, understand?'

Brandt sprang to attention. 'Herr Oberst.'

'Good,' Steiner's glance seemed to take in each man as an individual. 'Most of the time Oberleutnant Neumann and myself will be in there with you. And don't worry. You'll know what it's all about soon enough, I promise you.'

Brandt brought the entire group to attention. Steiner saluted, then turned and hurried across to the field car which was parked nearby, followed by Neumann. He got into the passenger seat, Neumann climbed behind the wheel and drove away. As they approached the main entrance to the airstrip the military policeman on duty opened the gate and saluted awkwardly, hanging on to his snarling guard dog with the other hand.

'One of these days that brute is going to get loose,' Neumann said, 'and frankly, I don't think it knows which side it's on.'

The Stork dropped in for an excellent landing and four or five Luftwaffe personnel raced out to meet it in a small truck. Neumann followed in the field car and pulled up a few yards away from the Stork. Steiner lit a cigarette as they waited for Radl to disembark.

Neumann said, 'He's got someone with him.'

Steiner looked up with a frown as Max Radl came towards him, a cheerful smile on his face. 'Kurt, how goes it?' he called, hand outstretched.

But Steiner was more interested in his companion, the tall, elegant young man with the deathshead of the SS in his cap. 'Who's your friend, Max?' he asked softly.

Radl's smile was awkward as he made the necessary introduction. 'Colonel Kurt Steiner – Untersturmführer Harvey Preston of the British Free Corps.'

*

Steiner had had the old living-room of the farmhouse converted into the nerve centre for the entire operation. There were a couple of army cots at one end of the room for himself and Neumann and two large tables placed down the centre were covered with maps and photos of the Hobs End and Studley Constable general area. There was also a beautifully made three-dimensional mock-up as yet only half completed. Radl leaned over it with interest, a glass of brandy in one hand. Ritter Neumann stood on the other side of the table and Steiner paced up and down by the window, smoking furiously.

Radl said, 'This model is really superb. Who's working on it?'

'Private Klugl,' Neumann told him. 'He was an artist, I think, before the war.'

Steiner turned impatiently. 'Let's stick to the matter in hand, Max. Do you seriously expect me to take that – that object out there?'

'It's the Reichsführer's idea, not mine,' Radl said mildly. 'In matters like this, my dear Kurt, I take orders, I don't give them.'

'But he must be mad.'

Radl nodded and went to the sideboard to help himself to more cognac. 'I believe that has been suggested before.'

'All right,' Steiner said. 'Let's look at it from the purely practical angle. If this thing is to succeed it's going to need a highly disciplined body of men who can move as one, think as one, act as one and that's exactly what we've got. Those lads of mine have been to hell and back. Crete, Leningrad, Stalingrad and a few placcs in between and I was with them every step of the way. Max, there are times when I don't even have to give a spoken order.'

'I accept that completely.'

'Then how on earth do you expect them to function with an outsider at this stage, especially one like Preston?' He picked up the file Radl had given him and shook it. 'A petty criminal, a poseur who's acted since the day he was born, even to himself.' He threw the file down in disgust. 'He doesn't even know what real soldiering is.'

'What's more to the point at the moment, or so it seems to me,' Ritter Neumann put it, 'he's never jumped out of an aeroplane in his life.'

Radl took out one of his Russian cigarettes and Neumann lit it for him. 'I wonder, Kurt, whether you're letting your emotions run away with you in this matter.'

'All right,' Steiner said. 'So my American half hates his lousy guts because he's a traitor and a turncoat and my German half isn't too keen on him either.' He shook his head in exasperation. 'Look, Max, have you any idea what jump training is like?' He turned to Neumann. 'Tell him, Ritter.'

'Six jumps go into the paratroopers qualification badge and after that, never less than six a year if he wants to keep it.' Neumann said. 'And that applies to everyone from private to general officer. Jump pay is sixty-five to one hundred and twenty Reichsmarks per month, according to rank.'

'So?' Radl said.

'To earn it you train on the ground for two months, make your first jump alone from six hundred feet. After that, five jumps in groups and in varying light conditions, including darkness, bringing the altitude down all the time and then the grand finale. Nine plane-loads dropping together in battle conditions at under four hundred feet.'

'Very impressive,' Radl said. 'On the other hand, Preston has to jump only once, admittedly at night, but to a large and very lonely beach. A perfect dropping zone as you have admitted yourselves. I would have thought it not beyond the bounds of possibility to train him sufficiently for that single occasion.'

Neumann turned in despair to Steiner, 'What more can I say?'

'Nothing,' Radl said, 'because he goes. He goes because the Reichsführer thinks it a good idea.'

'For God's sake,' Steiner said. 'It's impossible, Max, can't you see that?'

'I'm returning to Berlin in the morning.' Radl replied. 'Come with me and tell him yourself if that's how you feel. Or would you rather not?'

Steiner's face was pale. 'Damn you to hell, Max, you know I can't and you know why.' For a moment he seemed to have difficulty in speaking. 'My father – he's all right? You've seen him?'

'No,' Radl said, 'But the Reichsführer instructed me to tell you that you have his personal assurance in this matter.'

'And what in the hell is that supposed to mean?' Steiner took a deep breath and smiled ironically. 'I know one thing. If we can take Churchill, who I might as well tell you now is a man I've always personally admired, and not just because we both had an American mother, then we can drop in on Gestapo Headquarters in Prinz Albrechtstrasse and grab that little shit any time we want. Come to think of it, that's quite an idea.' He grinned at Neumann.

'What do you think, Ritter?'

'Then you'll take him?' Radl said eagerly. 'Preston, I mean?'

'Oh, I'll take him all right,' Steiner said, 'only by the time I've finished, he'll wish he'd never been born.' He turned to Neumann. 'All right, Ritter. Bring him in and I'll give him some idea of what hell is going to be like.'

*

When Harvey Preston was in repertory he'd once played a gallant young British officer in the trenches of the First World War in that great play *Journey's End*. A brave, war-weary young veteran, old beyond his years, able to meet death with a wry smile on his face and a glass raised, at least symbolically, in his right hand. When the roof of the dug-out finally collapsed and the curtain fell, you simply picked yourself up and went back to the dressing room to wash the blood off.

But not now. This was actually happening, terrifying in its implication and quite suddenly he was sick with fear. It was not that he had lost any faith in Germany's ability to win the war. He believed in that totally. It was simply that he preferred to be alive to see the glorious day for himself.

It was cold in the garden and he paced nervously up and down, smoking a cigarette and waiting impatiently for some sign of life from the farmhouse. His nerves were jagged. Steiner appeared at the kitchen door. 'Preston!' he called in English. 'Get in here.'

He turned without another word. When Preston went into the living-room, he found Steiner, Radl and Ritter Neumann grouped around the map table.

'Herr Oberst,' he began.

'Shut up!' Steiner told him coldly. He nodded to Radl. 'Give him his orders.'

Radl said formally, 'Untersturmführer Harvey Preston of the British Free Corps, from this moment you are to consider yourself under the total and absolute command of Lieutenant-Colonel Steiner of the Parachute Regiment. This by direct order of Reichsführer Heinrich Himmler himself. You understand?'

As far as Preston was concerned Radl might as well have worn a black cap, for his words were like a death sentence. There was sweat on his forehead as he turned to Steiner and stammered, 'But Herr Oberst, I've never made a parachute jump.'

'The least of your deficiencies,' Steiner told him grimly. 'But we'll take care of all of them, believe me.'

'Herr Oberst, I must protest,' Preston began and Steiner cut in on him like an axe falling.

'Shut your mouth and get your feet together. In future you speak when you're spoken to and not before.' He walked round behind Preston who was by now standing rigidly to attention. 'All you are at the moment is excess baggage. You're not even a soldier, just a pretty uniform. We'll have to see if we can change that, won't we?' There was silence and he repeated the question quite softly into Preston's left ear. 'Won't we?'

He managed to convey an infinite menace, and Preston said hurriedly, 'Yes, Herr Oberst.'

'Good. So now we understand each other.' Steiner walked round to the front of him again. 'Point number one – at the moment the only people at Landsvoort who know the purpose for which this whole affair had been put together are the four of us present in this room. If anyone else finds out before I'm ready to tell them because of a careless word from you, I'll shoot you myself. Understand?'

'Yes, Herr Oberst.'

'As regards rank, you cease to hold any for the time being. Lieutenant Neumann will see that you're provided with parachutists' overalls and a jump smock. You'll therefore be indistinguishable from the rest of your comrades with whom you will be training. Naturally there will be certain additional work necessary in your case, but we'll come to that later. Any questions?'

Preston's eyes burned, he could hardly breathe so great was his rage. Radl said gently, 'Of course. Herr Untersturmführer, you could always return to Berlin with me if dissatisfied and take up the matter personally with the Reichsführer.'

In a choked whisper, Preston said, 'No questions.'

'Good,' Steiner turned to Ritter Neumann. 'Get him kitted out, then hand him over to Brandt. I'll speak to you about his training schedule later.' He nodded to Preston. 'All right, you're dismissed.'

Preston didn't give the Nazi party salute because it suddenly occurred to him that it would very possibly not be appreciated. Instead he saluted, turned and stumbled out. Ritter Neumann grinned and went after him.

As the door closed, Steiner said, 'After that I really do need a drink,' and he moved across to the sideboard and poured a cognac.

'Will it work out, Kurt?' Radl asked.

'Who knows?' Steiner smiled wolfishly. 'With luck he might break a leg in training.' He swallowed some of his brandy. 'Anyway, to more important matters. How's Devlin doing at the moment? Any more news?'

*

In her small bedroom in the old farmhouse above the marsh at Hobs End, Molly Prior was trying to make herself presentable for Devlin, due to arrive for his dinner as promised at any moment. She undressed quickly and stood in front of the mirror in the old mahogany wardrobe for a moment in pants and bra and examined herself critically. The underwear was neat and clean, but showed signs of numerous repairs. Well, that was all right and the same for everybody. There were never enough clothing coupons to go round. It was what was underneath that mattered and that wasn't too bad. Nice, firm breasts, round hips, good thighs.

She placed a hand on her belly and thought of Devlin touching her like that and her stomach churned. She opened the top drawer of the dresser, took out her only pair of pre-war silk stockings, each one darned many times and rolled them on carefully. Then she got the cotton dress that she had worn on Saturday from the wardrobe.

As she pulled it over her head, there was the sound of a car horn. She peered out of the window in time to see an old Morris drive into the farmyard. Father Vereker was at the wheel. Molly cursed softly, eased the dress over her head, splitting a seam under one arm and pulled on her Sunday shoes with the two-inch heels.

As she went downstairs she ran a comb through her hair, wincing as it snagged on the tangles. Vereker was in the kitchen with her mother and he turned and greeted her with what for him was a surprisingly warm smile.

'Hello, Molly, how are you?'

'Hard pressed and hard worked, Father.' She tied an apron about her waist and said to her mother, 'That meat and tatie pie. Ready is it? He'll be here any minute.'

'Ah, you're expecting company.' Vereker stood up, leaning on his stick. 'I'm in the way. A bad time.'

'Not at all, Father,' Mrs Prior said. 'Only Mr Devlin, the new warden at Hobs End. He's having his dinner here, then giving us an afternoon's work. Was there anything special?'

Vereker turned to look at Molly, speculatively, noting the dress, the shoes and there was a frown on his face as if he disapproved of what he saw. Molly flared angrily. She put her left hand on her hip and faced him belligerently.

'Was it me you wanted, Father?' she asked, her voice dangerously calm.

'No, it was Arthur I wanted a word with. Arthur Seymour. He helps you up here Tuesdays and Wednesdays, doesn't he?'

He was lying, she knew that instantly. 'Arthur Seymour doesn't work here any more, Father. I'd have thought you'd have known that. Or didn't he tell you I sacked him?'

Vereker was very pale. He would not admit it, yet he was not prepared to lie to her face. Instead he said. 'Why was that, Molly?'

'Because I didn't want him round here any more.'

He turned to Mrs Prior enquiringly. She looked uncomfortable, but shrugged. 'He's not fit company for man nor beast.'

He made a bad mistake then and said to Molly, 'The feeling in the village is that he's been hard done to. That you should have a better reason than preference for an outsider. Hard on a man who's bided his time and helped where he could, Molly.'

'Man,' she said. 'Is that what he is, Father? I never realized. You could tell 'em he was always sticking his hand up my skirt and trying to feel me.' Vereker's face was very white now, but she carried on remorselessly. 'Of course, people in the village might think that all right, him having acted no different round females since he was twelve years old and no one ever did a thing about it. And you don't seem to be shaping no better.'

'Molly!' her mother cried, aghast.

'I see,' Molly said. 'One mustn't offend a priest by telling him the truth, is that what you're trying to say?' There was contempt on her face when she looked at Vereker. 'Don't tell me you don't know what he's like, Father. He never misses Mass Sundays so you must confess him often enough.'

She turned from the furious anger in his eyes as there was a knock at the door, smoothing her dress over her hips as she hurried to answer. But when she opened the door it wasn't Devlin, but Laker Armsby who stood there rolling a cigarette beside the tractor with which he'd just towed in a trailer loaded with turnips.

He grinned. 'Where you want this lot then, Molly?'

'Damn you, Laker, you choose your times, don't you? In the barn. Here, I'd better show you myself or you're bound to get it wrong.'

She started across the yard, picking her way through the mud in her good shoes and Laker trailed after her. 'Dressed up like a dog's dinner today. Now I wonder why that should be, Molly?'

'You mind your business, Laker Armsby,' she told him, 'and get this door open.'

Laker tipped the holding bar and started to open one of the great barn doors. Arthur Seymour was standing on the other side, his cap pulled low over the mad eyes, the massive shoulders straining the seams of the old reefer coat.

'Now then, Arthur,' Laker said warily.

Seymour shoved him to one side and grabbbed Molly by the right wrist, pulling her towards him. 'You get in here, you bitch. I want words with you.'

Laker pawed at his arm ineffectually, 'Now look here, Arthur,' he said. 'No way to behave.'

Seymour slapped him back-handed, bringing blood from his nose in a sudden gush. 'Get out of it!' he said and shoved Laker backwards into the mud.

Molly kicked out furiously. 'You let me go!'

'Oh, no,' he said. He pushed the door closed behind him and shot the bolt. 'Never again, Molly.' He grabbed for her hair with his left hand. 'Now you be a good girl and I won't hurt you. Not so long as you give me what you've been giving that Irish bastard.'

His fingers were groping for the hem of her skirt.

'You stink,' she said. 'You know that? Like an old sow that's had a good wallow.'

She leaned down and bit his wrist savagely. He cried out in pain, releasing his grip, but clutched at her with his other hand as she turned, dress tearing, and ran for the ladder to the loft.

*

Devlin, on his way across the fields from Hobs End, reached the crest of the meadow above the farm in time to see Molly and Laker Armsby crossing the farmyard to the barn. A moment later Laker was propelled from the barn to fall flat on his back in the mud and the great door slammed. Devlin tossed his cigarette to one side and went down the hill on the run.

By the time he was vaulting the fence into the farmyard, Father Vereker and Mrs Prior were at the barn. The priest hammered on the door with his stick. 'Arthur?' he shouted, 'Open the door – stop this foolishness.'

The only reply was a scream from Molly. 'What's going on?' Devlin demanded.

'It's Seymour,' Laker told him, holding a bloody handkerchief to his nose. 'Got Molly in there, he has, and he's bolted the door.'

Devlin tried a shoulder and realized at once that he was wasting his time. He glanced about him desperately as Molly cried out again and his eyes lit on the tractor where Laker had left it, engine ticking over. Devlin was across the yard in a moment, scrambled up into the high seat behind the wheel and rammed the stick into gear, accelerating so savagely that the tractor shot forward, trailer swaying, turnips scattering across the yard like cannon balls. Vereker, Mrs Prior and Laker got out of the way just in time as the tractor collided with the doors, bursting them inwards and rolling irresistibly forward.

Devlin braked to a halt. Molly was up in the loft, Seymour down below trying to reposition the ladder which she had obviously thrown down. Devlin switched off the engine and Seymour turned and looked at him, a strange, dazed look in his eyes.

'Now then, you bastard,' Devlin said.

Vereker limped in. 'No, Devlin, leave this to me!' he called and turned to Seymour. 'Arthur, this won't do, will it?'

Seymour paid not the slightest heed to either of them. It was as if they didn't exist and he turned and started to climb the ladder. Devlin jumped down from the tractor and kicked the ladder from under him. Seymour fell heavily to the ground. He lay there for a moment or so, shaking his head. Then his eyes cleared.

As Seymour got to his feet, Father Vereker lurched forward, 'Now, Arthur, I've told you . . .'

It was as far as he got for Seymour hurled him so violently to one side that he fell down. 'I'll kill you, Devlin!'

He gave a cry of rage and rushed in, great hands outstretched to destroy. Devlin dodged to one side and the weight of Seymour's progress carried him into the tractor. Devlin gave him a left and right to the kidneys and danced away as Seymour cried out in agony.

He came in with a roar and Devlin feinted with his right and smashed his left fist into the ugly mouth, splitting the lips so that blood spurted. He followed up with a right under the ribs that sounded like an axe going into wood.

He ducked in under Seymour's next wild punch and hit him under the ribs again. 'Footwork, timing and hitting, that is the secret. The Holy Trinity, we used to call them, Father. Learn those and ye shall inherit the earth as surely as the meek. Always helped out by a little dirty work now and then, of course.'

He kicked Seymour under the right kneecap and as the big man doubled over in agony, put a knee into the descending face, lifting him back through the door into the mud of the yard. Seymour got to his feet slowly and stood there like a dazed bull in the centre of the plaza, blood on his face.

Devlin danced in. 'You don't know when to lie down, do you, Arthur, but that's hardly surprising with a brain the size of a pea?'

He advanced his right foot, slipped in the mud and went down on one knee. Seymour delivered a stunning blow to his forehead that put him flat on his back. Molly screamed and rushed in, hands clawing at Seymour's face. He threw her away from him and raised a foot to crush Devlin. But the Irishman got a hand to it and twisted, sending him staggering into the barn entrance again.

When he turned, Devlin was reaching for him, no longer smiling, the white killing face on him now. 'All right, Arthur. Let's get it over with. I'm hungry.'

Seymour tried to rush him again and Devlin circled, driving him across the yard, giving him neither quarter nor peace, evading his great swinging punches with ease, driving his knuckles into the face again and again until it was a mask of blood.

There was an old zinc water trough near the back door and Devlin pushed him towards it relentlessly. 'And now you will listen to me, you bastard!' he said. 'Touch that girl again, harm her in any way and I'll take the shears to you myself. Do you understand me?' He punched under the ribs again and Seymour groaned, his hands coming down. 'And in future, if you are in a room and I enter, you get up and walk out. Do you understand that too?'

His right connected twice with the unprotected jaw and Seymour fell across the trough and rolled on to his back.

Devlin dropped to his knees and pushed his face into the rainwater in the trough. He surfaced for air to find Molly crouched beside him, and Father Vereker bending over Seymour. 'My God, Devlin, you might have killed him,' the priest said.

'Not than one,' Devlin said. 'Unfortunately.'

As if anxious to prove him right, Seymour groaned and tried to sit up. At the same moment Mrs Prior came out of the house with a double-barrelled shotgun in her hands. 'You get him out of here,' she told Vereker. 'And tell him from me, when his brains are unscrambled, that if he comes back here bothering my girl again, I'll shoot him like a dog and answer for it.'

Laker Armsby dipped an old enamel bucket into the trough and emptied it over Seymour. 'There you go, Arthur,' he said cheerfully. 'First bath you've had since Michaelmas, I dare say.'

Seymour groaned and grabbed for the trough to pull himself up. Father Vereker said, 'Help me, Laker,' and they took him between them across to the Morris.

Quite suddenly, the earth moved for Devlin, like the sea turning over. He closed his eyes. He was aware of Molly's cry of alarm, her strong, young shoulder under his arm and then her mother was on the other side of him and they were walking him towards the house between them.

He surfaced to find himself in the kitchen chair by the fire, his face against Molly's breasts, while she held a damp cloth to his forehead. 'You can let me go now, I'm fine,' he told her.

She looked down at him, face anxious. 'God, but I thought he'd split your skull with that one punch.'

'A weakness of mine,' Devlin told her, aware of her concern and momentarily serious. 'After periods of intense stress I sometimes keel over, go out like a light. Some psychological thing.'

'What's that?' she demanded, puzzled.

'Never mind,' he said. 'Just let me put my head back where I can see your right nipple.'

She put a hand to her torn bodice and flushed, 'You devil.'

'You see,' he said. 'Not much difference between Arthur and me when it comes right down to it.'

She tapped a finger very gently between his eyes. 'I never heard such rubbish from a grown man in all my life.'

Her mother bustled into the kitchen fastening a clean apron about her waist. 'By God, boy, but you must have a powerful hunger on you after that little bout. Are you ready for your meat and potato pie now, then?'

Devlin looked up at Molly and smiled. 'Thank you kindly, ma'am. As a matter of fact, I think I could say with some truth that I'm ready for anything.'

The girl choked back laughter, shook a clenched fist under his nose and went to help her mother.

*

It was late evening when Devlin returned to Hobs End. It was very still and quiet on the marsh as if rain threatened and the sky was dark and thunder rumbled uneasily on the far horizon. He took the long way round to check the dyke gates that controlled the flow into the network of waterways and when he finally turned into the yard, Joanna Grey's car was parked by the door. She was wearing WVS uniform and leaning on the wall looking out to sea, the retriever sitting beside her patiently. She turned to look at him as he joined her. There was a sizeable bruise on his forehead where Seymour's fist had landed.

'Nasty,' she said. 'Do you try to commit suicide often?'

He grinned. 'You should see the other fella.'

'I have.' She shook her head. 'It's got to stop, Liam.'

He lit a cigarette, match flaring in cupped hands. 'What has?'

'Molly Prior. You're not here for that. You've got a job to do.'

'Come off it,' he said. 'I haven't a thing to lay hand to before my meeting with Garvald on the twenty-eighth.'

'Don't be silly. People in places like this are the same the world over, you know that. Distrust the stranger and look after your own. They don't like what you did to Arthur Seymour.'

'And I didn't like what he tried to do to Molly.' Devlin half-laughed in a kind of astonishment. 'God save us, woman, if only half the things Laker Armsby told me about Seymour this afternoon are true, they should have locked him up years ago and thrown away the key. Sexual assaults of one kind or another too numerous to mention and he's crippled at least two men in his time.'

'They never use the police in places like this. They handle it themselves.' She shook her head impatiently. 'But this isn't getting us anywhere. We can't afford to alienate people so do the sensible thing. Leave Molly alone.'

'Is that an order, ma'm?'

'Don't be an idiot. I'm appealing to your good sense, that's all.'

She walked to the car, put the dog in the back and got behind the wheel. 'Any news from the Sir Henry front?' Devlin asked as she switched on the engine.

She smiled, 'I'm keeping him warm, don't worry. I'll be on the radio to Radl again on Friday night. I'll let you know what comes up.'

She drove away and Devlin unlocked the door and let himself in. Inside he hesitated for a long moment and then shot the bolt and went into the living-room. He pulled the curtain, lit a small fire and sat in front of it, a glass of Garvald's Bushmills in his hand.

It was a shame – one hell of a shame, but perhaps Joanna Grey was right. It would be silly to go looking for trouble. He thought of Molly for one brief moment, then resolutely selected a copy of *The Midnight Court* in Irish from his small stock of books and forced himself to concentrate.

It started to rain, brushing the window pane. It was about seven-thirty when the handle of the front door rattled vainly. After a while, there was a tap at the window on the other side of the curtain and she called his name softly. He kept on reading, straining to follow the words in the failing light of the small fire and after a while, she went away.

He swore softly, black rage in his heart and threw the book at the wall, resisting with every fibre of his being the impulse to run to the door, unlock it and go after her. He poured himself another large whiskey and stood at the window, feeling suddenly lonelier than he had ever felt in his life before, as rain hurtled in across the marsh in a sudden fury.

*

And at Landsvoort there was a gale blowing in off the sea, with the kind of bitter drenching rain that cut to the bone like a surgeon's knife. Harvey Preston, on guard duty at the garden gate of the old farmhouse, huddled against the wall, cursing Steiner, cursing Radl, cursing Himmler and whatever else had combined to reduce him to this, the lowest and most miserable level of his entire life.

10

During the Second World War, the German paratrooper differed from his British counterpart in one highly important aspect – the type of parachute used.

The German version, unlike that issued to Luftwaffe pilots and aircrew, did not have straps, known as lift webs, fastening the shroud lines to the harness. Instead, the shroud lines connected directly to the pack itself. It made the whole process of jumping entirely different and because of that, on Sunday morning at Landsvoort, Steiner arranged for a demonstration of the standard British parachute in the old barn at the back of the farmhouse.

The men stood in front of him in a semi-circle, Harvey Preston in the centre, dressed, like the others, in jump boots and overalls. Steiner faced them, Ritter Neumann and Brandt on either side of him.

Steiner said, 'The whole point of this operation, as I've already explained, is that we pass ourselves off as a Polish unit of the Special Air Service. Because of this, not only will all your equipment be British – you'll jump using the standard parachute used by British airborne forces.' He turned to Ritter Neumann. 'All yours.'

Brandt picked up a parachute pack and held it aloft. Neumann said, 'X Type parachute as used by British Airborne forces. Weighs around twenty-eight pounds and as the Herr Oberst says, very different from ours.'

Brandt pulled the ripcord, the pack opened, disgorging the khaki chute. Neumann said, 'Note the way the shroud lines are fastened to the harness by shoulder straps, just like the Luftwaffe.'

'The point being,' Steiner put in, 'that you can manipulate the chute, change direction, have the kind of control over your own destiny that you just don't get with the one you're used to.'

'Another thing,' Ritter said, 'With our parachute the centre of gravity is high which means you get snagged up in the shroud lines unless you exit in a partially face-down position, as you all know. With the X type, you can go out in the standing posture and that's what we're going to practise now.'

He nodded to Brandt, who said, 'All right, let's have you all down here.'

There was a loft perhaps fifteen feet high at the far end of the barn. A rope had been looped over a beam above it, an X type parachute harness fastened to one end. 'A trifle primitive,' Brandt announced jovially, 'but good enough. You jump off the loft and there'll be half a dozen of us on the other end to make sure you don't hit the dirt too hard. Who's first?'

Steiner said, 'I'd better claim that honour, mainly because I've things to do elsewhere.'

Ritter helped him into the harness, then Brandt and four others got on the other end of the rope and hauled him up to the loft. He paused on the edge for a moment or so, Ritter signalled and Steiner swung out into space. The other end of the rope went up, taking three of the men with it, but Brandt and Sergeant Sturm hung on, cursing. Steiner hit the dirt, rolled over in a perfect fall and sprang to his feet.

'All right,' he told Ritter. 'Usual stick formation. I've time to see everyone do it once. Then I must go.'

He moved to the rear of the group and lit a cigarette as Neumann buckled himself into the harness. From the back of the barn it looked reasonably hair-raising as the Oberleutnant was hoisted up to the loft, but there was a roar of laughter when Ritter made a mess of his landing and ended up flat on his back.

'See?' Private Klugl said to Werner Briegel. 'That's what riding those damn torpedoes does for you. The Herr Leutnant's forgotten everything he ever knew.'

Brandt went next and Steiner observed Preston closely. The Englishman was very pale, sweat on his face – obviously terrified. The group worked through with varying success, the men on the end of the rope in one unfortunate lapse mistaking the signal and leaving go at the wrong moment so that Private Hagl descended the full fifteen feet under his own power with all the grace of a sack of potatoes. But he picked himself up, none the worse for his experience.

Finally, it was Preston's turn. The good humour faded abruptly. Steiner nodded to Brandt. 'Up with him.'

The five men on the end of the rope hauled with a will and Preston shot up, banging against the loft on the way, finishing just below the roof. They lowered him till he stood on the edge, gazing down at them wildly.

'All right, English,' Brandt called. 'Remember what I told you. Jump when I signal.'

He turned to instruct the men on the rope, and there was a cry of alarm from Briegel as Preston simply fell forward into space. Ritter Neumann jumped for the rope. Preston came to rest three feet above the ground, swinging like a pendulum, arms hanging at his side head down.

Brandt put a hand under the chin and looked into the Englishman's face. 'He's fainted.'

'So it would appear,' Steiner said.

'What do we do with him, Herr Oberst?' Ritter Neumann demanded.

'Bring him round,' Steiner said calmly. 'Then put him up again. As many times as it takes until he can do it satisfactorily – or breaks a leg.' He saluted. 'Carry on, please,' turned and went out.

*

The rooks in the beech trees were the only sign of life as Devlin went through the lychgate of St Mary and All the Saints. They lifted into the sky noisily as if conscious that he was a stranger and annoyed about it. When he opened the door and went into the church it was very quiet and his footsteps on the stone flags echoed hollowly between the pillars.

Our Lady seemed to float above the flickering candles in the half-light of the side chapel, the beautiful medieval face eternally peaceful. Vereker knelt before her in prayer. He crossed himself as Devlin approached then stood up with difficulty and turned, leaning on the stick. His face was drawn – in fact he looked quite haggard and was obviously in some pain.

'You wanted to see me,' Devlin said.

'It was good of you to come.'

Devlin made no reply, and Vereker swayed slightly, as if almost losing his balance, reached for the end of a pew to steady himself and sat down. 'I'm sorry. I don't feel too well. You'll have to excuse me.'

It was the first reference Devlin had known him to make to his physical state and completely unexpected, for in his short acquaintance with Vereker, he had formed the impression that the priest resented his infirmity so much, he preferred to act as if it did not exist.

'That's all right, what did you want?'

'No sense in beating about the bush,' Vereker said. 'It's to do with Molly – Molly Prior.'

'Well?' Devlin said. 'What about her?'

'I don't want you to see her again.'

'*You* don't want me to see her again.' Devlin laughed out loud.

Vereker's face was pale, the eyes flared. 'Mind your manners.'

'Oh, I'm sorry, sir.' Devlin rolled out the bog Irish accent in deliberate mockery. 'If I had me cap on, I'd touch it to your honour.'

'Stay away from her.' Vereker was thoroughly angry now.

'Would you mind giving me a reason?'

'A hatful if you like. For one thing, you're old enough to be her father.'

Devlin's laughter echoed up into the nave and he slapped his cap against his thigh. 'By God, Father, for that to be true I'd have had to start damned early.'

'Watch your language,' Vereker said. 'Remember you are in God's house.' His knuckles gleamed white as they tightened over the handle of the stick. 'You're not fit, Devlin, either for her, or for this place.'

'Because I don't pour my guts out to you once a week and come to Mass like a good Catholic boy?' Devlin said. 'Like Arthur Seymour? He turns up regular as clockwork, Wednesdays and Sundays, isn't that a fact? That makes what he does all right, is that what you're saying?'

Vereker was able to speak only with great difficulty. 'Arthur Seymour is a poor, unfortunate wretch not responsible for his actions. I try to help him. We all do. That is something you, as an outsider, cannot understand. Here, we all help each other.'

'Here you all rot together on your own stinking little dung heap, you mean.' Devlin's anger was like a fuse, slow-burning. 'You know what that animal was trying to do to Molly the other day? What he's tried elsewhere before and succeeded by all accounts. But does anyone do anything about it?'

'It's the village's business and no one else's,' Vereker said. 'They know how to handle Arthur. We all do. You don't, so stay out.'

'You can't even handle yourself,' Devlin said contemptuously. 'Look at you, self-pity eating the insides out of you. My father went to war for something he believed in and they hanged him like a dog. All you lost out there in Tunisia was a foot, or was it something else?' He frowned suddenly. 'Your self-respect, maybe? Were you afraid, Father, was that it?' He nodded. 'Yes, I can imagine someone like you taking a thing like that hard, you always having had such a grand opinion of yourself.'

There were beads of sweat on Vereker's face; his eyes seemed to start from their sockets. 'I think you'd better go,' he said hoarsely.

'Oh, I will, never fret,' Devlin told him. 'It's suddenly a trifle close for me in here.'

'Get out!' Vereker cried, in a kind of agony.

'House of God, did you say, Father?' Devlin walked away, his steps echoing. When he opened the door and went out into the porch, Pamela Vereker was coming up the path. She was wearing sweater and slacks and carried a riding crop.

She smiled. 'Mr Devlin, isn't it?'

'I sometimes wonder,' he said, 'especially on days like this. If you want your brother, you'll find him inside. He looked in need of a little tea and sympathy to me.'

She frowned in puzzlement, he touched a finger to the peak of his cap with exaggerated courtesy, went down the path to his motor-cycle and rode away.

*

There were at least a dozen men in the tap room of the Studley Arms when Devlin went in. Laker Armsby in his usual place by the fire with his mouth organ, the rest seated around the two large tables playing dominoes. Arthur Seymour was staring out of the window, a pint in his hand.

'God save all here!' Devlin announced cheerfully. There was complete silence, every face in the room turned towards him except for Seymour's. 'God save you kindly, was the answer to that one,' Devlin said. 'Ah, well.'

There was a step behind him and he turned to find George Wilde emerging from the back room, wiping his hands on a butcher's apron. His face was grave and steady, no emotion there at all. 'I was just closing, Mr Devlin,' he said politely.

'Time for a jar, surely,'

'I'm afraid not. You'll have to leave, sir.'

The room was very quiet. Devlin put his hands in his pockets and hunched his shoulders, head down. And when he looked up, Wilde took an involuntary step back, for the Irishman's face had turned very pale, the skin stretched tight over the cheek bones, blue eyes glittering.

'There is one man here who will leave,' Devlin said quietly, 'and it is not me.'

Seymour turned from the window. One eye was still completely closed, his lips scabbed and swollen. His entire face seemed lopsided and was covered with purple and green bruises. He stared at Devlin dully, then put down his half-finished pint of ale and shuffled out.

Devlin turned back to Wilde. 'I'll have that drink, now, Mr Wilde. A drop of Scotch, Irish being something you'll never have heard of here at the edge of your own little world, and don't try to tell me you don't have a bottle or two under the counter for favoured customers.'

Wilde opened his mouth as if to speak and obviously thought

better of it. He went into the back and returned with a bottle of White Horse and a small glass. He poured out a single measure and placed the glass on the shelf next to Devlin's head.

Devlin produced a handful of change. 'One shilling and sixpence,' he said cheerfully, counting it out on the nearest table. 'The going price for a nip. I'm taking it for granted, of course, that such a fine, upstanding pillar of the church as yourself wouldn't be dealing in black market booze.'

Wilde made no reply. The whole room waited. Devlin picked up the glass, held it to the light, then emptied it in a golden stream to the floor. He put the glass down carefully on the table. 'Lovely,' he said. 'I enjoyed that.'

Laker Armsby broke into a wild cackle of laughter, Devlin grinned. 'Thank you, Laker, my old son. I love you too,' he said and walked out.

*

It was raining hard at Landsvoort as Steiner drove across the airstrip in his field car. He braked to a halt outside the first hangar and ran for its shelter. The starboard engine of the Dakota was laid bare and Peter Gericke, in a pair of old overalls, grease up to his elbows, worked with a Luftwaffe sergeant and three mechanics.

'Peter?' Steiner called. 'Have you got a moment? I'd like a progress report.'

'Oh, things are going well enough.'

'No problems with the engines?'

'None at all. They're nine-hundred horsepower Wright Cyclones. Really first class and as far as I can judge, they've done very little time. We're only stripping as a precaution.'

'Do you usually work on your own engines?'

'Whenever I'm allowed.' Gericke smiled. 'When I flew these things in South America you had to service your own engines, because there was nobody else who could.'

'No problems?'

'Not as far as I can see. She's scheduled to have her new paint job some time next week. No rush on that and Bohmler's fitting a Lichtenstein set so we'll have good radar coverage. A milk run.

An hour across the North Sea, an hour back. Nothing to it.'

'In an aircraft whose maximum speed is half that of most RAF or Luftwaffe fighters.'

Gericke shrugged. 'It's all in how you fly them, not in how fast they go.'

'You want a test flight, don't you?'

'That's right.'

'I've been thinking,' Steiner said. 'It might be a good idea to combine it with a practice drop. Preferably one night when the tide is well out. We could use the beach north of the sand pier. It will give the lads a chance to try out these British parachutes.'

'What altitude are you thinking of?'

'Probably four hundred feet. I want them down fast and from that height fifteen seconds is all it takes.'

'Rather them than me. I've only had to hit the silk three times in my career and it was a lot higher than that.' The wind howled across the airstrip, driving rain before it, and he shivered. 'What a bloody awful place.'

'It serves its purpose.'

'And what's that?'

Steiner grinned. 'You ask me that at least five times a day. Don't you ever give up?'

'I'd like to know what it's all about, that's all.'

'Maybe you will, one day, that's up to Radl, but for the moment we're here because we're here.'

'And Preston?' Gericke said. 'I wonder what his reason is? What makes a man do what he's done.'

'All sorts of things,' Steiner said. 'In his case, he's got a pretty uniform, officer status. He's somebody for the first time in his life, that means a lot when you've been nothing. As regards the rest – well, he's here as the result of a direct order from Himmler himself.'

'What about you?' Gericke asked. 'The greater good of the Third Reich? A life for the Führer?'

Steiner smiled. 'God knows. War is only a matter of perspective. After all, if it had been my father who was American and my mother German, I'd have been on the other side. As for the

Parachute Regiment – I joined that because it seemed like a good idea at the time. After a while, of course, it grows on you.'

'I do it because I'd rather fly anything than nothing,' Gericke said, 'and I suppose it's much the same for most of those RAF lads on the other side of the North Sea. But you . . .' He shook his head. 'I don't really see it. Is it a game to you, then, just that and nothing more?'

Steiner said wearily. 'I used to know, now I'm not so sure. My father was a soldier of the old school. Prussian blue. Plenty of blood and iron, but honour, too.'

'And this task they've given you to do,' Gericke said, 'this – this English business, whatever it is. You have no doubts?'

'None at all. A perfectly proper military venture, believe me. Churchill himself couldn't fault it, in principle, at least,' Gericke tried to smile and failed and Steiner put a hand on his shoulder. 'I know, there are days when I could weep myself – for all of us,' and he turned and walked away through the rain.

*

In the Reichsführer's private office, Radl stood in front of the great man's desk while Himmler read through his report. 'Excellent, Herr Oberst,' he said finally. 'Really quite excellent.' He laid the report down. 'Everything would appear to be progressing more than satisfactorily. You have heard from the Irishman?'

'No, only from Mrs Grey, that is the arrangement. Devlin has an excellent radio-telephone set. Something which we picked up from the British SOE, which will keep him in touch with the E-boat on its way in. That is part of the operation he will handle as regards communication.'

'The Admiral has not become suspicious in any way? Has picked up no hint of what is happening? You're sure of that?'

'Perfectly, Herr Reichsführer. My visits to France and Holland, I've been able to handle in conjunction with Abwehr business in Paris and Antwerp or Rotterdam. As the Reichsführer is aware, I have always had considerable latitude from the Admiral as regards running my own section.'

'And when do you go to Landsvoort again?'

'Next weekend. By a fortunate turn of events, the Admiral goes to Italy on the first or second of November. This means I can afford to stay at Landsvoort myself during the final crucial days and indeed, for the period of the operation itself.'

'No coincidence, the Admiral's visit to Italy, I can assure you.' Himmler smiled thinly. 'I suggested it to the Führer at exactly the right moment. Within five minutes he'd quite decided he'd thought of it himself.' He picked up his pen. 'So, it progresses, Radl. Two weeks from today and it will all be over. Keep me informed.'

He bent over his work and Radl licked dry lips and yet it had to be said. 'Herr Reichsführer.'

Himmler sighed heavily. 'I'm really very busy, Radl. What is it now?'

'General Steiner, Herr Reichsführer. He is – he is well?'

'Of course,' Himmler said calmly. 'Why do you ask?'

'Colonel Steiner,' Radl explained, his stomach churning. 'He is naturally extremely anxious . . .'

'There is no need to be.' Himmler said gravely. 'I gave you my personal assurance, is that not so?'

'Of course.' Radl backed to the door. 'Thank you again,' and he turned and got out as fast as he could.

Himmler shook his head, sighed in a kind of exasperation and returned to his writing.

*

When Devlin went into the church, Mass was almost over. He slipped down the right-hand aisle and eased into a pew. Molly was on her knees beside her mother dressed exactly as she had been on the previous Sunday. Her dress showed no evidence of the rough treatment it had received from Arthur Seymour. He was present also, in the same position he usually occupied and he saw Devlin instantly. He showed no emotion at all, but simply got to his feet and slipped down the aisle in the shadows and went out.

Devlin waited, watching Molly at prayer, all innocence kneeling there in the candlelight. After a while, she opened her eyes and turned very slowly as if physically aware of his presence. Her eyes widened, she looked at him for a long moment, then turned away again.

Devlin left just before the end of the service and went out quickly. By the time the first of the congregation exited, he was already at his motor-cycle. It was raining slightly and he turned up the collar of his trenchcoat and sat astride the bike and waited. When Molly finally came down the path with her mother she ignored him completely. They got into the trap, her mother took the reins and they drove away.

'Ah, well, now,' Devlin told himself softly. 'And who would blame her?'

He kicked the engine into life, heard his name called and found Joanna Grey bearing down on him. She said in a low voice, 'I had Philip Vereker at me for two hours this afternoon. He wanted to complain to Sir Henry about you.'

'I don't blame him.'

She said, 'Can't you ever be serious for more than five minutes at any one time?'

'Too much of a strain,' he said and she was prevented from continuing the conversation by the arrival of the Willoughbys.

Sir Henry was in uniform. 'Now then, Devlin, how's it working out?'

'Fine, sir,' Devlin rolled out the Irish. 'I can't thank you enough for this wonderful opportunity to make good.'

He was aware of Joanna Grey standing back, tight-lipped, but Sir Henry liked it well enough. 'Good show, Devlin. Getting excellent reports on you. Excellent. Keep up the good work.'

He turned to speak to Joanna Grey and Devlin, seizing his opportunity, rode away.

*

It was raining very heavily by the time he reached the cottage, so he put the motor-cycle in the first barn, changed into waders and an oilskin coat, got his shotgun and started out into the marsh. The dyke gates needed checking in such heavy rain and trudging round in such conditions was a nice negative sort of occupation to take his mind off things.

It didn't work. He couldn't get Molly Prior out of his thoughts. The image recurred constantly of her dropping to her knees in prayer the previous Sunday in a kind of slow motion, the skirt sliding up her thighs. Would not go away.

'Holy Mary and all the Saints,' he said softly. 'If this is what love is really like, Liam my boy, you've taken one hell of a long time finding out about it.'

As he came back along the main dyke towards the cottage he smelt woodsmoke heavy on the damp air. There was a light at the window in the evening gloom, the tiniest chink where the blackout curtains had failed to come together. When he opened the door he could smell cooking. He put the shotgun in the corner, hung the oilskin coat up to dry and went into the living room.

She was on one knee at the fire, putting on another log. She turned to look over her shoulder gravely. 'You'll be wet through.'

'Half an hour in front of that fire and a couple of whiskies inside me and I'll be fine.'

She went to the cupboard, got the bottle of Bushmills and a glass. 'Don't pour it on the floor,' she said. 'Try drinking it this time.'

'So you know about that?'

'Not much you don't hear in a place like this. Irish stew on the go. That all right?'

'Fine.'

'Half an hour, I'd say.' She crossed to the sink and reached for a glass dish. 'What went wrong, Liam? Why did you keep out of the way?'

He sat down in the old wing-back chair, legs wide to the fire, steaming rising from his trousers. 'I thought it best at first.'

'Why?'

'I had my reasons.'

'And what went wrong today?'

'Sunday, bloody Sunday. You know how it is.'

'Damn your eyes.' She crossed the room, drying her hands on her apron and looked down at the steam rising from Devlin's trousers. 'You'll catch your death if you don't change those. Rheumatism at least.'

'Not worth it,' he said. 'I'll go to bed soon. I'm tired.'

She reached out hesitantly and touched his hair. He seized her hand and kissed it. 'I love you, you know that?'

It was as if a lamp had been switched on inside her. She glowed, seemed to expand and take on an entirely new dimension. 'Well, thank God for that. At least it means I can go to bed now with a clear conscience.'

'I'm bad for you, girl dear, there's nothing in it. No future, I warn you. There should be a notice above that bedroom door. Abandon hope all ye who enter here.'

'We'll see about that,' she said. 'I'll get your stew,' and she moved across to the stove.

*

Later, lying in the old brass bed, an arm about her, watching the shadow patterns on the ceiling from the fire, he felt more content, more at peace with himself than he had done for years.

There was a radio on a small table at her side of the bed. She switched it on, then turned her stomach against his thigh and sighed, eyes closed. 'Oh, that was lovely. Can we do it again some time?'

'Would you give a fella time to catch his breath?'

She smiled and ran a hand across his belly. 'The poor old man. Just listen to him.'

A record was playing on the radio.

When that man is dead and gone . . .
Some fine day the news will flash,
Satan with a small moustache
Is asleep beneath the tomb.

'I'll be glad when that happens,' she said drowsily.

'What?' he asked.

'Satan with a small moustache asleep beneath the tomb. Hitler. I mean, it'll all be over then, won't it?' She snuggled closer. 'What's going to happen to us, Liam? When the war's over?'

'God knows.'

He lay there staring at the fire. After a while her breathing steadied and she was asleep. *After the war was over.* Which war? He'd been on the barricades one way or another for twelve years now. How could he tell her that? It was a nice little farm, too, and they needed a man. God, the pity of it. He held her close and the wind moaned about the old house, rattling the windows.

*

And in Berlin, at Prinz Albrechtstrasse, Himmler still sat at his desk, methodically working his way through dozens of reports and sheets of statistics, mainly those relating to the extermination squads who, in the occupied lands of Eastern Europe and Russia, liquidated Jews, gypsies, the mentally and physically handicapped and any others who did not fit into the Reichsführer's plan for a Greater Europe.

There was a polite knock at the door and Karl Rossman entered. Himmler looked up. 'How did you get on?'

'I'm sorry, Herr Reichsführer, he won't budge and we really have tried just about everything. I'm beginning to think he might be innocent after all.'

'Not possible.' Himmler produced a sheet of paper. 'I received this document earlier this evening. A signed confession from an artillery sergeant who was his batman for two years and who during that time engaged in work prejudicial to State Security on Major-General Karl Steiner's direct order.'

'So what now, Herr Reichsführer?'

'I'd still prefer a signed confession from General Steiner himself. It makes everything that much tighter.' Himmler frowned slightly. 'Let's try a little more psychology. Clean him up, get an SS doctor to him, plenty of food. You know the drill. The whole thing has been a shocking mistake on somebody's part. Sorry you have still to detain him, but one or two points still remain to be cleared up.'

'And then?'

'When he's had say ten days of that, go to work on him again. Right out of the blue. No warning. The shock might do it.'

'I'll do as you suggest, Herr Reichsführer,' Rossman said.

11

At four o'clock on the afternoon of Thursday, the twenty-eighth October, Joanna Grey drove into the yard of the cottage at Hobs End and found Devlin in the barn working on the motor-cycle.

'I've been trying to get hold of you all week,' she said. 'Where have you been?'

'Around,' he told her cheerfully, wiping grease from his hands on an old rag. 'Out and about. I told you there was nothing for me to do till my meeting with Garvald so I've been having a look at the countryside.'

'So I've heard,' she said grimly. 'Riding around on that motorcycle with Molly Prior on the pillion. You were seen in Holt at a dance on Tuesday night.'

'A very worthy cause,' he said, 'Wings for Victory. Actually your friend Vereker turned up and made an impassioned speech about how God would help us crush the bloody Hun. I found that ironic in view of the fact that everywhere I went in Germany I used to see signs saying *God with us.*'

'I told you to leave her alone.'

'I tried that, it didn't work. Anyway, what did you want? I'm busy. I'm having a certain amount of magneto trouble and I want this thing to be in perfect working order for my run to Peterborough tonight.'

'Troops have moved into Meltham House,' she said. 'They arrived on Tuesday night.'

He frowned. 'Meltham House – isn't that the place where Special Force outfits train?'

'That's right. It's about eight miles up the coast road from Studley Constable.'

'Who are they?'

'American Rangers.'

'I see. Should it make any difference, their being here?'

'Not really. They usually stay up at that end, the units who use the facilities. There's a heavily wooded area, a salt marsh and a good beach. It's a factor to be considered, that's all.'

Devlin nodded. 'Fair enough. Let Radl know about it in your next broadcast and there's your duty done. And now, I must get on.'

She turned to go to the car and hesitated. 'I don't like the sound of this man Garvald.'

'Neither do I, but don't worry, my love. If he's going to turn nasty, it won't be tonight. It will be tomorrow.'

She got into the car and drove away and he returned to his work on the motor-cycle. Twenty minutes later Molly rode up out of the marsh, a basket hanging from her saddle. She slipped to the ground and tied the horse to a hitching ring in the wall above the trough. 'I've brought you a shepherds pie.'

'Yours or your mother's?' She threw a stick at him and he ducked. 'It'll have to wait. I've got to go out tonight. Put it in the oven for me and I'll heat it up when I get in.'

'Can I go with you?'

'Not a chance. Too far. And besides, it's business.' He slapped her behind. 'A cup of tea is what I crave, woman of the house, or maybe two, so off with you and put the kettle on.'

He reached for her again, she dodged him, grabbed her basket and ran for the cottage. Devlin let her go. She went into the living-room and put the basket on the table. The Gladstone bag was at the other end and as she turned to go to the stove, she caught it with her left arm, knocking it to the floor. It fell open disgorging packets of banknotes and the Sten gun parts.

She knelt there, stunned for the moment, suddenly icy cold, as if aware by some kind of precognition that nothing ever would be the same again.

There was a step in the doorway and Devlin said quietly, 'Would you put them back, now, like a good girl?'

She looked up, white-faced, but her voice was fierce. 'What is it? What does it mean?'

'Nothing,' he said, 'for little girls.'

'But all this money.'

She held up a packet of fivers. Devlin took the bag from her, stuffed the money and the weapons back inside and replaced the bottom. Then he opened the cupboard under the window, took out a large envelope and tossed it to her.

'Size ten. Was I right?'

She opened the envelope, peered inside and there was an immediate look of awe on her face. 'Silk stockings. Real silk and two pairs. Where on earth did you get these?'

'Oh, a man I met in a pub in Fakenham. You can get anything you want if you know where to look.'

'The black market,' she said. 'That's what you're mixed up in, isn't it?'

There was a certain amount of relief in her eyes and he grinned. 'The right colour for me. Now would you kindly get the tea on and hurry? I want to be away by six and I've still got work to do on the bike.'

She hesitated, clutching the stockings and moved close. 'Liam, it's all right, isn't it?'

'And why wouldn't it be?' He kissed her briefly, turned and went out, cursing his own stupidity.

And yet as he walked towards the barn, he knew in his heart that there was more to it than that. For the first time he had been brought face to face with what he was doing to this girl. Within little more than a week, her entire world was going to be turned upside down. That was absolutely inevitable and nothing he could do about it except leave her, as he must, to bear the hurt of it alone.

Suddenly, he felt physically sick and kicked out at a packing case savagely. 'Oh, you bastard,' he said. 'You dirty bastard, Liam.'

*

Reuben Garvald opened the judas in the main gate of the workshop of Fogarty's garage and peered outside. Rain swept across the cracked concrete of the forecourt where the two rusting petrol pumps stood forlornly. He closed the judas hurriedly and stepped back inside.

The workshop had once been a barn and was surprisingly

spacious. A flight of wooden steps led up to a loft, but in spite of a wrecked saloon car in one corner, there was still plenty of room for the three-ton Bedford truck and the van in which Garvald and his brother had travelled from Birmingham. Ben Garvald himself walked up and down impatiently, occasionally beating his arms together. In spite of the heavy overcoat and scarf he wore, he was bitterly cold.

'Christ what a dump,' he said. 'Isn't there any sign of that little Irish sod?'

'It's only a quarter to nine, Ben,' Reuben told him.

'I don't care what bleeding time it is.' Garvald turned on a large, hefty young man in a sheepskin flying jacket who leaned against the truck reading a newspaper. 'You get me some heat in here tomorrow night, Sammy boy, or I'll have your balls. Understand?'

Sammy, who had long dark sideburns and a cold, rather dangerous-looking face seemed completely unperturbed. 'Okay, Mr Garvald. I'll see to it.'

'You'd better, sweetheart, or I'll send you back to the Army.' Garvald patted his face. 'And you wouldn't like that, would you?'

He took out a packet of Gold Flake, selected one and Sammy gave him a light with a fixed smile. 'You're a card, Mr Garvald. A real card.'

Reuben called urgently from the door. 'He's just turned on to the forecourt.'

Garvald tugged at Sammy's arm. 'Get the door open and let's have the bastard in.'

Devlin entered in a flurry of rain and wind. He wore oilskin leggings with his trenchcoat, an old leather flying helmet and goggles which he'd bought in a secondhand shop in Fakenham. His face was filthy and when he switched off and pushed up his goggles, there were great white circles round his eyes.

'A dirty night for it, Mr Garvald,' he said as he shoved the BSA on its stand.

'It always is, son,' Garvald replied cheerfully. 'Nice to see you.' He shook hands warmly. 'Reuben you know and this is Sammy Jackson, one of my lads. He drove the Bedford over for you.'

There was an implication that Jackson had somehow done him a great personal favour and Devlin responded in kind, putting on the Irish as usual. 'Sure and I appreciate that. It was damn good of you,' he said, wringing Sammy's hand.

Jackson looked him over contemptuously but managed a smile and Garvald said, 'All right then, I've got business elsewhere and I don't expect you want to hang around. Here's your truck. What do you think?'

The Bedford had definitely seen better days, the paintwork badly fading and chipped, but the tyres weren't too bad and the canvas tilt was almost new. Devlin heaved himself over the tailboard and noted the Army jerrycans, the compressor and the drum of paint he'd asked for.

'It's all there, just like you said.' Garvald offered him a cigarette. 'Check the petrol if you want.'

'No need, I'll take your word for it.'

Garvald wouldn't have tried any nonsense with the petrol, he was sure of that. After all, he wanted him to return on the following evening. He went round to the front and lifted the bonnet. The engine seemed sound enough.

'Try it,' Garvald invited.

He switched on and tapped the accelerator, and the engine broke into a healthy enough roar as he had expected. Garvald would be much too interested in finding out exactly what he was up to to spoil things by trying to push second-class goods at this stage.

Devlin jumped down and looked at the truck again, noting the military registration. 'All right?' Garvald asked.

'I suppose so.' Devlin nodded slowly. 'From the state of it, it looks as if it's been having a hard time in Tobruk or somewhere.'

'Very probably, old son,' Garvald kicked a wheel. 'But these things are built to take it.'

'Have you got the delivery licence I asked for?'

'Sure thing,' Garvald snapped a finger. 'Let's have that form, Reuben.'

Reuben produced it from his wallet and said sullenly, 'When do we see the colour of his money?'

'Don't be like that, Reuben. Mr Murphy here is as sound as a bell.'

'No, he's right enough, a fair exchange.' Devlin took a fat manilla envelope from his breast pocket and passed it to Reuben. 'You'll find seven hundred and fifty in there in fivers, as agreed.'

He pocketed the form Reuben had given him after glancing at it briefly and Ben Garvald said, 'Aren't you going to fill that thing in?'

Devlin tapped his nose and tried to assume an expression of low cunning. 'And let you see where I'm going? Not bloody likely, Mr Garvald.'

Garvald laughed delightedly. He put an arm about Devlin's shoulder. The Irishman said, 'If someone could give me a hand to put my bike in the back, I'll be off.'

Garvald nodded to Jackson who dropped the tailboard of the Bedford and found an old plank. He and Devlin ran the BSA up and laid it on its side. Devlin clipped the tailboard in place and turned to Garvald. 'That's it then, Mr Garvald, same time tomorrow.'

'Pleasure to do business with you, old son,' Garvald told him, wringing his hand again. 'Get the door open, Sammy.'

Devlin climbed behind the wheel and started the engine. He leaned out of the window. 'One thing, Mr Garvald. I'm not likely to find the military police on my tail, now am I?'

'Would I do that to you, son?' Garvald beamed. 'I ask you.' He banged the side of the truck with the flat of his hand. 'See you tomorrow night. Repeat performance. Same time, same place and I'll bring you another bottle of Bushmills.'

Devlin drove out into the night and Sammy Jackson and Reuben got the doors closed. Garvald's smile disappeared. 'It's up to Freddy now.'

'What if he loses him?' Reuben asked.

'Then there's tomorrow night, isn't there.' Garvald patted him on the face. 'Where's that half of brandy you brought?'

'Lose him?' Jackson said. 'That little squirt?' He laughed harshly. 'Christ, he couldn't even find the way to the men's room unless you showed him.'

*

Devlin, a quarter of a mile down the road, was aware of the dim lights behind him indicating the vehicle which had pulled out of a lay-by a minute or so earlier as he passed, exactly as he expected.

An old ruined windmill looked out of the night on his left and a flat stretch of cleared ground in front of it. He switched off all his lights suddenly, swung the wheel and drove into the cleared area blind, and braked. The other vehicle carried straight on, increasing its speed and Devlin jumped to the ground, went to the back of the Bedford and removed the bulb from the rear light. Then he got back behind the wheel, turned the truck in a circle on to the road and only switched on his lights when he was driving back towards Norman Cross.

A quarter of a mile this side of Fogarty's he turned right into a side road, the B660, driving through Holme, stopping fifteen minutes later outside Doddington to replace the bulb. When he returned to the cab, he got out the delivery licence form and filled it in in the light of a torch. There was the official stamp of a Service Corps unit near Birmingham at the bottom and the signature of the commanding officer, a Major Thrush. Garvald had thought of everything. Well, not quite everything. Devlin grinned and filled in his destination as the RAF radar station at Sheringham ten miles further along the coast road from Hobs End.

He got back behind the wheel and drove away again. Swaffham first, then Fakenham. He'd worked it all out very carefully on the map and he sat back and took it steadily because the black-out visors on his headlamps didn't give him a great deal of light to work by. Not that it mattered. He'd all the time in the world. He lit a cigarette and wondered how Garvald was getting on.

*

It was just after midnight when he turned into the yard outside the cottage at Hobs End. The journey had proved to be completely uneventful and in spite of the fact that he had boldly used the main roads for most of the way, he had passed no more than a handful of vehicles during the entire trip. He coasted round to the old barn on the very edge of the marsh, jimped out into the heavy rain and unlocked the padlock. He got the doors open and drove inside.

There were only a couple of round loft windows and it had been easy enough to black those out. He primed two Tilley lamps, pumped them until he had plenty of light, went outside to check that nothing showed, then he went back in and got his coat off.

Within half an hour, he had the truck unloaded, running the BSA out on an old plank and sliding the compressor to the ground the same way. The jerrycans, he stacked in a corner, covering them with an old tarpaulin. Then he washed down the truck. When he was satisfied that it was as clean as he was going to get it he brought newspapers and tape which he had laid by earlier and proceeded to mask the windows. He did this very methodically, concentrating all the time and when he was finished went across to the cottage and had some of Molly's shepherds pie and a glass of milk.

It was still raining very hard when he ran back to the barn, hissing angrily into the waters of the marsh, filling the night with sound. Conditions were really quite perfect. He filled the compressor, primed the pump and turned its motor over, then he put the spraying equipment together and mixed some paint. He started on the tailboard first, taking his time, but it really worked very well indeed and within five minutes he had covered it with a glistening new coat of khaki green.

'God save us,' he said to himself softly. 'It's a good thing I haven't a criminal turn of mind for I could be making a living at this sort of thing and that's a fact.'

He moved round to the left and started on the side panels.

*

After lunch on Friday, he was touching up the numbers on the truck with white paint when he heard a car drive up. He wiped his hands and let himself out of the barn quickly, but when he went round the corner of the cottage it was only Joanna Grey. She was trying the front door, a trim and surprisingly youthful figure in the green WVS uniform.

'You always look your best in that outfit,' he said. 'I bet it has old Sir Henry crawling up the wall.'

She smiled. 'You're on form, anyway. Things must have gone well.'

'See for yourself?'

He opened the barn door and led her in. The Bedford, in its fresh coat of khaki green paint really looked very well indeed. 'As my information has it, Special Forces vehicles don't usually carry divisional flashes or insignia. Is that so?'

'That's true,' she said. 'The stuff I've seen operating out of Meltham House in the past have never advertised who they are.' She was obviously very impressed. 'This is really good, Liam. Did you have any trouble?'

'He had someone try to follow me, but I soon shook him off. The big confrontation should be tonight.'

'Can you handle it?'

'This can.' He picked up a cloth bundle lying on the packing case beside his brushes and tins of paint, unwrapped it and took out a Mauser with a rather strange bulbous barrel. 'Ever seen one of these before?'

'I can't say I have.' She weighed it in her left hand with professional interest and took aim.

'Some of the SS security people use them,' he said, 'but there just aren't enough to go round. Only really efficient silenced handgun I've ever come across.'

She said dubiously, 'You'll be on your own.'

'I've been on my own before.' He wrapped the Mauser in the cloth again and went to the door with her. 'If everything goes according to plan I should be back with the jeep around midnight. I'll check with you first thing in the morning.'

'I don't think I can wait that long.'

Her face was tense and anxious. She put out her hand impulsively and he held it tight for a moment. 'Don't worry. It'll work. I have the sight, or so my old grannie used to say. I know about these things.'

'You rogue,' she said and leaned forward and kissed him on the cheek in genuine affection. 'I sometimes wonder how you've survived so long.'

'That's easy,' he said. 'Because I've never particularly cared whether I do or not.'

'You say that as if you mean it.'

'Tomorrow.' He smiled gently. 'I'll be round first thing. You'll see.'

He watched her drive away, then kicked the door of the barn shut behind him and stuck a cigarette in his mouth. 'You can come out now,' he called.

There was a moment's delay and then Molly emerged from the rushes on the far side of the yard. Too far to have heard anything which was why he had let it go. He padlocked the door, then walked towards her. He stopped a yard away, hands pushed into his pockets. 'Molly, my own sweet girl,' he said gently. 'I love you dearly, but any more games like this and I'll give you the thrashing of your young life.'

She flung her arms around his neck. 'Is that a promise?'

'You're entirely shameless.'

She looked up at him, hanging on. 'Can I come over tonight?'

'You can't,' he said 'because I won't be here,' and he added a half-truth. 'I'm going to Peterborough on private business and I won't be back until the small hours.' He tapped the end of her nose with a finger. 'And that's between us. No advertising.'

'More silk stockings?' she said, 'or is it Scotch whisky this time.'

'Five quid a bottle the Yanks will pay, so they tell me.'

'I wish you wouldn't.' Her face was troubled. 'Why can't you be nice and normal like everyone else?'

'Would you have me in my grave so early?' He turned her round. 'Go and put the kettle on the stove and if you're a good girl, I'll let you make dinner – or something.'

She smiled briefly over her shoulder, looking suddenly quite enchanting, then ran across to the cottage. Devlin put the cigarette back into his mouth, but didn't bother to light it. Thunder rumbled far out on the horizon, heralding more rain. *Another wet ride.* He sighed and went after her across the yard.

*

In the workshop at Fogarty's garage it was even colder than it had been on the previous night, in spite of Sammy Jackson's attempts to warm things up by punching holes in an old oil drum and lighting a coke fire. The fumes it gave off were quite something.

Ben Garvald, standing beside it, a half-bottle of brandy in one hand, a plastic cup in the other, retreated hastily. 'What in the hell are you trying to do, poison me?'

Jackson, who was sitting on a packing case on the opposite side of the fire nursing a sawn-off, double-barrelled shotgun across his knees, put it down and stood up. 'Sorry, Mr Garvald. It's the coke – that's the trouble. Too bloody wet.'

Reuben, at the judas, called suddenly, 'Here, I think he's coming.'

'Get that thing out of the way,' Garvald said quickly, 'and remember you don't make your move till I tell you.' He poured some more brandy into the plastic cup and grinned. 'I want to enjoy this, Sammy boy. See that I do.'

Sammy put the shotgun under a piece of sacking beside him on the packing case and hurriedly lit a cigarette. They waited as the sound of the approaching engine grew louder, then moved past and died away into the night.

'For Christ's sake,' Garvald said in disgust. 'It wasn't him. What time is it?'

Reuben checked his watch. 'Just on nine. He should be here any moment.'

If they had but known it Devlin was, in fact, already there, standing in the rain at the broken rear window which had been roughly boarded up with planks. His vision, through a crack, was limited, but at least covered Garvald and Jackson beside the fire. And he'd certainly heard every word spoken during the past five minutes.

Garvald said, 'Here, you might as well do something useful while we're waiting, Sammy. Top up the jeep's tank with a couple of those jerrycans so you're ready for the run back to Brum.'

Devlin withdrew, worked his way through the yard, negotiating with caution the wrecks of several cars, regained the main road and ran back along the verge to the lay-by, a quarter of a mile away where he had left the BSA.

He unbuttoned the front flap of his trenchcoat, took out the Mauser and checked it in the light of the headlamp. Satisfied, he pushed it back inside, but left the flap unbuttoned, then he got back in the saddle. He wasn't afraid, not in the slightest. A little excited, true, but only enough to put an edge to him. He kicked the starter and turned into the road.

*

Inside the workshop, Jackson had just finished filling the jeep's tank when Reuben turned from the judas again excitedly. 'It's him. Definitely this time. He's just turned on to the forecourt.'

'Okay, get the doors open and let's have him in,' Garvald said.

The wind was so strong it caused a massive draught when Devlin entered that had the coke crackling like dried wood. Devlin switched off and shoved the bike up on its stand. His face was in an even worse state than it had been in the night before, plastered with mud. But when he pushed up his goggles he was smiling cheerfully.

'Hello there, Mr Garvald.'

'Here we are again.' Garvald passed him the half of brandy. 'You look as if you could do with a nip.'

'Did you remember my Bushmills?'

'Course I did. Get those two bottles of Irish out of the van for Mr Murphy, Reuben.'

Devlin took a quick pull at the brandy bottle while Reuben went to the van and returned with the two bottles of Bushmills. His brother took them from him. 'There you are, boy, just like I promised.' He went across to the jeep and put the bottles down on the passenger seat. 'Everything went off all right last night, then?'

'No problems at all,' Devlin said.

He approached the jeep. Like the Bedford, its coachwork was badly in need of a fresh coat of paint, but otherwise it was fine. It had a strip canvas roof with open sides and a mounting point for a machine gun. The registration, in contrast to the rest of the vehicle, had been freshly painted and when Devlin looked closely he could see traces of another underneath.

'There's a thing now, Mr Garvald,' he said. 'Would some Yank airbase be missing one of these?'

'Now, look here, you,' Reuben put in angrily.

Devlin cut him off. 'Come to think of it, Mr Garvald, there was a moment last night when I thought someone was trying to follow me. Nerves, I suppose. Nothing came of it.'

He turned back to the jeep and had another quick pull at the bottle. Garvald's anger, contained with considerable difficulty, overflowed now. 'You know what you need?'

'And what would that be?' Devlin enquired softly. He turned, still holding the half of brandy, clutching one lapel of his trench-coat with his right hand.

'A lesson in manners, sweetheart,' Garvald said. 'You need putting in place and I'm just the man to do it.' He shook his head. 'You should have stayed back home in the bogs.'

He started to unbutton his overcoat and Devlin said, 'Is that a fact now? Well, before you start. I'd just like to ask Sammy boy, here, if that shotgun he's got under the sacking is cocked or not, because if it isn't, he's in big trouble.'

In that single, frozen moment in time, Ben Garvald suddenly knew beyond any shadow of a doubt that he'd just made the worst mistake of his life. 'Take him, Sammy!' he cried.

Jackson was way ahead of him, had already grabbed for the shotgun under the sacking – already too late. As he frantically thumbed back the hammers, Devlin's hand was inside his trench-coat and out again. The silenced Mauser coughed once, the bullet smashed into Jackson's left arm, turning him in a circle. The second shot shattered his spine, driving him headfirst into the wrecked car in the corner. In death his finger tightened convulsively on the triggers of the shotgun, discharging both barrels into the ground.

The Garvald brothers backed away slowly, inching towards the door. Reuben was shaking with fear, Garvald watchful, waiting for any kind of chance to seize on.

Devlin said, 'That's far enough.'

In spite of his size, the old flying helmet and goggles, the soaking-wet coat, he seemed a figure of infinite menace as he faced them from the other side of the fire, the Mauser with the bulbous silencer in his hand.

Garvald said, 'All right, I made a mistake.'

'Worse than that, you broke your word,' Devlin said. 'And where I come from, we have an excellent specific for people who let us down.'

'For God's sake, Murphy . . .'

He didn't get any further because there was a dull thud as Devlin fired again. The bullet splintered Garvald's right kneecap. He went back against the door with a stifled cry and fell to the ground. He rolled over, clutching at his knee with both hands, blood pumping between his fingers.

Reuben crouched, hands raised in futile protection, head down. He spent two or three of the worst moments of his life in that position and when he finally had the courage to look up, discovered Devlin positioning an old plank at the side of the jeep. As Reuben watched, the Irishman ran the BSA up and into the rear.

He came forward and opened one half of the garage doors. Then he snapped his fingers at Reuben. 'The delivery licence.'

Reuben produced it from his wallet with shaking fingers and handed it over. Devlin checked it briefly, then took out an envelope which he dropped at Garvald's feet. 'Seven hundred and fifty quid, just to keep the books straight. I told you, I'm a man of my word. You should try it some time.' He got into the jeep, pressed the starter and drove out into the night.

'The door,' Garvald said to his brother through clenched teeth. 'Get the bloody door closed or you'll have every copper for miles turning up to see what the light is.'

Reuben did as he was told, then turned to survey the scene. The air was full of hazy blue smoke and the stench of cordite.

Reuben shuddered. 'Who was that bastard, Ben?'

'I don't know and I don't really care.' Garvald pulled free the white silk scarf he wore around his neck. 'Use this to bandage this bloody knee.'

Reuben looked at the wound in fascinated horror. The 7·63mm cartridge had gone in one side and out of the other, and the kneecap had fragmented, spinters of white bone protruding through flesh and blood.

'Christ, it's bad, Ben. You need a hospital.'

'Like hell I do. You carry me into any casualty department in this country with a gunshot wound and they'll shout for the coppers so fast you'll think you're standing still.' There was sweat on his face. 'Go on, bandage it for Christ's sake.'

Reuben started to wind the scarf round the shattered knee, He was almost in tears. 'What about Sammy, Ben?'

'Leave him where he is. Just cover him with one of the tarpaulins for the moment. You can get some of the boys over here tomorrow to get rid of him.' He cursed as Reuben tightened the scarf. 'Hurry up, and let's get out of here.'

'Where to, Ben?'

'We'll go straight to Birmingham. You can take me to that nursing home in Aston. The one that Indian doctor runs. What's his name?'

'You mean Das?' Reuben shook his head. 'He's in the abortion racket, Ben. No good to you.'

'He's a doctor, isn't he?' Ben said. 'Now give me a hand up and let's get out of here.'

*

Devlin drove into the yard at Hobs End half an hour after midnight. It was a dreadful night with gale-force winds, torrential rain and when he had unlocked the doors of the barn and driven inside, he had all on to get them closed again.

He lit the Tilley lamps and manoeuvred the BSA out of the back of the jeep. He was tired and bitterly cold, but not tired enough to sleep. He lit a cigarette and walked up and down, strangely restless.

It was quiet in the barn, only the rain drumming against the roof, the quiet hissing of the Tilley lamps. The door opened in a flurry of wind and Molly entered, closing it behind her. She wore her old trenchcoat, wellington boots and a headscarf and was soaked to the skin so that she shook with cold, but it didn't seem to matter. She walked to the jeep, a puzzled frown on her face.

She gazed at Devlin dumbly. 'Liam?' she said.

'You promised,' he told her. 'No more prying. It's useful to know how you keep your word.'

'I'm sorry, but I was so frightened, and then all this.' She gestured at the vehicles. 'What does it mean?'

'None of your business,' he told her brutally. 'As far as I'm concerned you can clear off right now. If you want to report me to the police – well, you must do as you see fit.'

She stood staring at him, eyes very wide, mouth working. 'Go on!' he said, 'If that's what you want. Get out of it!'

She ran into his arms, bursting into tears. 'Oh, no Liam, don't send me away. No more questions, I promise and from now on I'll mind my own business, only don't send me away.'

It was the lowest point in his life and the self-contempt he felt as he held her in his arms was almost physical in its intensity. But it had worked. She would cause him no more trouble, of that he was certain.

He kissed her on the forehead. 'You're freezing. Get on over to the house with you and build up the fire, I'll be with you in a few minutes.'

She gazed up at him searchingly, then turned and went out. Devlin sighed and went over to the jeep and picked up one of the bottles of Bushmills. He eased the cork and took a long swallow.

'Here's to you, Liam, old son,' he said with infinite sadness.

*

In the tiny operating theatre in the nursing home in Aston, Ben Garvald lay back on the padded table, eyes closed. Reuben stood beside him while Das, a tall cadaverous Indian in an immaculate white coat, cut away the trouser leg with surgical scissors.

'Is it bad?' Reuben asked him, his voice shaking.

'Yes, very bad,' Das replied calmly. 'He needs a first-rate surgeon, if he is not to be crippled. There is also the question of sepsis.'

'Listen, you bleeding wog bastard,' Ben Garvald said, eyes opening. 'It says physician and surgeon on that fancy brass plate of yours by the door, doesn't it?'

'True, Mr Garvald,' Das told him calmly. 'I have degrees of the Universities of Bombay and London, but that is not the point. You need specialist assistance in this instance.'

Garvald pushed himself up on one elbow. He was in considerable pain and sweat was pouring down his face. 'You listen to me and listen good. A girl died in here three months ago. What the law would call an illegal operation. I know about that and a lot more. Enough to put you away for seven years at least, so if you don't want the coppers in here, get moving on this leg.'

Das seemed quite unperturbed. 'Very well, Mr Garvald, on your own head be it. I'll have to give you an anaesthetic. You understand this?'

'Give me anything you bleeding well like, only get on with it.'

Garvald closed his eyes. Das opened a cupboard, took out a gauze face mask and a bottle of chloroform. He said to Reuben, 'You'll have to help. Add chloroform to the pad as I tell you, drop by drop. Can you manage it?'

Reuben nodded, too full to speak.

12

It was still raining on the following morning when Devlin rode over to Joanna Grey. He parked his bike by the garage and went to the back door. She opened it instantly and drew him inside. She was still in her dressing gown and her face was strained and anxious.

'Thank God, Liam.' She took his face between her two hands and shook him. 'I hardly slept a wink. I've been up since five o'clock drinking whisky and tea alternately. A hell of a mixture at this time in the morning.' She kissed him warmly. 'You rogue, it's good to see you.'

The retriever swung its hindquarters frantically from side-to-side, anxious to be included. Joanna Grey busied herself at the stove and Devlin stood in front of the fire.

'How was it?' she asked.

'All right.'

He was deliberately noncommital, for it seemed likely she might not be too happy about the way he had handled things.

She turned, surprise on her face. 'They didn't try anything?'

'Oh, yes,' he said. 'But I persuaded them otherwise.'

'Any shooting?'

'No need,' he said calmly. 'One look at that Mauser of mine was enough. They're not used to guns, the English criminal fraternity. Razors are more their style.'

She carried the tea things on a tray across to the table. 'God, the English. Sometimes I despair of them.'

'I'll drink to that in spite of the hour. Where's the whisky?'

She went and got the bottle and a couple of glasses. 'This is disgraceful at this time of day, but I'll join you. What do we do now?'

'Wait,' he said. 'I've got the jeep to fix up, but that's all. You'll need to squeeze old Sir Henry dry right up to the last moment, but other than that, all we can do is bite our nails for the next six days.'

'Oh, I don't know,' she said. 'We can always wish ourselves luck.' She raised her glass. 'God bless you, Liam, and long life.'

'And you, my love.'

She raised her glass and drank. Suddenly something moved inside Devlin like a knife in his bowels. In that moment he knew, beyond any shadow of a doubt, that the whole bloody thing was going to go about as wrong as it could do.

*

Pamela Vereker had a thirty-six-hour pass that weekend, coming off duty at seven a.m., and her brother had driven over to Pangbourne to pick her up. Once at the presbytery, she couldn't wait to get out of uniform and into a pair of jodhpurs and a sweater.

In spite of this symbolic turning away, however temporarily, from the dreadul facts of daily life on a heavy bomber station, she still felt edgy and extremely tired. After lunch she cycled six miles along the coast road to Meltham Vale Farm where the tenant, a parishioner of Vereker's, had a three-year-old stallion badly in need of exercise.

Once over the dunes behind the farm, she gave the stallion his head and galloped along the winding track through the tangled gorse, climbing towards the wooded ridge above. It was completely exhilarating, with the rain beating in her face, and for a while she was back in another, safer place, the world of her childhood that had ended at four forty-five on the morning of 1 September 1939 when General Gerd von Rundsted's Army Group South had invaded Poland.

She entered the trees, following the old forestry commisssion track and the stallion slowed as it approached the crest of the hill. There was a pine tree across the track a yard or two further on, a windfall. It was no more than three feet high and the stallion took it in its stride. As it landed on the other side, a figure stood up in the undergrowth on the right. The stallion swerved. Pamela Vereker lost her stirrups and was tossed to one side. A rhododendron bush broke her fall, but for a moment she was winded and lay there fighting for breath, aware of voices all around.

'You stupid bastard, Krukowski,' someone said. 'What were you trying to do, kill her?'

The voices were American. She opened her eyes and found a ring of soldiers in combat jackets and steel helmets surrounding her, faces daubed with camouflage cream, all heavily armed. Kneeling beside her was a large rugged Negro with a master sergeant's stripes on his arm. 'You all right, miss?' he asked anxiously.

She frowned and shook her head, and suddenly felt rather better. 'Who are you?'

He touched his helmet in a kind of half-salute. 'Name's Garvey. Master Sergeant. Twenty-first Specialist Raiding Force. We're based at Meltham House for a couple of weeks for field training.'

A jeep arrived at that moment, skidding to a halt in the mud. The driver was an officer, she could tell that, although not sure of his rank, having had little to do with American forces during her service career. He wore a forage cap and normal uniform and was certainly not dressed for manoeuvres.

'What in the hell is going on here?' he demanded.

'Lady got thrown from her horse, Major,' Garvey replied. 'Krukowski jumped out of the bushes at the wrong moment.'

Major, she thought, surprised at his youth. She scrambled to her feet. 'I'm all right, really I am.'

She swayed and the major took her arm. 'I don't think so. Do you live far, ma'am?'

'Studley Constable. My brother is parish priest there.'

He guided her firmly towards the jeep. 'I think you'd better come with me. We've got a medical officer down at Meltham House. I'd like him to make sure you're still in one piece.'

The flash on his shoulder said *Rangers* and she remembered having read somewhere that they were the equivalent of the British Commandos. 'Meltham House?'

'I'm sorry, I should introduce myself, Major Harry Kane, attached to the Twenty-first Specialist Raiding Force under the command of Colonel Robert E. Shafto. We're here for field training.'

'Oh, yes,' she said, 'My brother was telling me that Meltham was being used for some such purpose these days.' She closed her eyes. 'Sorry, I feel a little faint.'

'You just relax. I'll have you there in no time.'

It was a nice voice. Most definitely. For some absurd reason it made her feel quite breathless. She lay back and did exactly as she was told.

*

The five acres of garden at Meltham House were surrounded by a typical Norfolk flint wall, some eight feet in height. It had been spiked with barbed wire at the top for extra security. Meltham itself was of modest size, a small manor house dating from the early part of the seventeenth century. Like the wall, a great deal of split flint had been used, the construction of the building, particularly the design of the gable ends, showed the Dutch influence typical of the period.

Harry Kane and Pamela strolled through the shrubbery towards the house. He had spent a good hour showing her over the estate and she had enjoyed every minute of it. 'How many of you are there?'

'At the present time, about ninety. Most of the men are under canvas, of course, in the camp area I pointed out on the other side of the spinney.'

'Why wouldn't you take me down there? Secret training or something?'

'Good God, no.' He chuckled. 'You're entirely too good-looking, it's as simple as that.'

A young soldier hurried down the steps of the terrace and came towards them. He saluted smartly. 'Colonel's back, sir. Master Sergeant Garvey is with him now.'

'Very well, Appleby.'

The boy returned Kane's salute, turned and doubled away.

'I thought Americans were supposed to take things terribly easy,' Pamela said.

Kane grinned. 'You don't know Shafto. I think they must have coined the term martinet especially for him.'

As they went up the steps to the terrace, an officer came out through the French windows. He stood facing them, slapping a riding crop against his knee, full of a restless animal vitality. Pamela did not need to be told who he was. Kane saluted. 'Colonel Shafto, allow me to present Miss Vereker.'

Robert Shafto was at that time forty-four years of age, a handsome, arrogant-looking man; a flamboyant figure in polished top boots and riding breeches. He wore a forage cap slanted to his left eye and the two rows of medal ribbons above his left pocket made a bright splash of colour. Perhaps the most extraordinary thing about him was the pearl handled Colt .45 he carried in an open holster on his left hip.

He touched his riding crop to his brow and said gravely, 'I was distressed to hear of your accident, Miss Vereker. If there is anything I can do to make up for the clumsiness of my men . . .'

'That's most kind of you,' she said. 'However, Major Kane here has very kindly offered to run me back to Studley Constable, if you can spare him, that is. My brother is priest there.'

'The least we can do.'

She wanted to see Kane again and there seemed to be only one sure way she could accomplish that. She said, 'We're having a little party at the presbytery tomorrow night. Nothing very special. Just a few friends for drinks and sandwiches. I was wondering whether you and Major Kane would care to join us.' Shafto hesitated. It seemed obvious that he was going to make some excuse and she carried on hurriedly. 'Sir Henry Willoughby will be there, the local squire. Have you met yet?'

Shafto's eyes lit up. 'No, I haven't had that pleasure.'

'Miss Vereker's brother was a padre with the First Parachute Brigade,' Kane said. 'Dropped with them at Oudna in Tunisia last year. You remember that one, Colonel?'

'I certainly do,' Shafto said. 'That was one hell of an affair. Your brother must be quite a man to have survived that, young lady.'

'He was awarded the Military Cross,' she said. 'I'm very proud of him.'

'And so you should be. I'll be happy to attend your little soirée tomorrow night and have the pleasure of meeting him. You make the necessary arrangements, Harry.' He saluted again with the riding crop. 'And now you must excuse me. I have work to do.'

*

'Were you impressed?' Kane asked her as they drove back along the coast road in his jeep.

I'm not sure,' she said. 'He's rather a flamboyant figure, you must admit.'

'The understatement of this or any other year,' he said. 'Shafto is what is known in the trade as a fighting soldier. The kind of guy who used to lead his men over the top of some trench in Flanders in the old days armed with a swagger stick. Like that French General said at Balaclava, magnificent, but it isn't war.'

'In other words he doesn't use his head?'

'Well, he does have one hell of a fault from the Army's point of view. He can't take orders – from anybody. Fighting Bobby Shafto, the pride of the infantry. Got himself out of Bataan back

in April last year when the Japs overran the place. Only trouble
was, he left an infantry regiment behind. That didn't sit too well at
the Pentagon. Nobody wanted him so they shipped him over to
London to work on the staff at Combined Operations.'
     'Which he didn't like?'
     'Naturally. Used it as a stepping stone to further glory. He
discovered the British had their Small Scale Raiding Force slipping over the Channel by night playing Boy Scouts and decided
the American Army should have the same. Unfortunately some
imbecile at Combined Operations thought it was a good idea.'
     'Don't you?' she said.
     He seemed to evade the question. 'During the past nine
months, men from the Twenty-first have raided across the Channel on no fewer than fourteen separate occasions.'
     'But that's incredible.'
     'Which includes,' he carried on, 'the destruction of an empty
lighthouse in Normandy and several landings on uninhabited
French islands.'
     'You don't think much of him, it seems?'
     'The great American public certainly does. Three months ago
some war reporter, in London and short of a story, heard how
Shafto had captured the crew of a lightship off the Belgian coast.
There were six of them and as they happened to be German
soldiers, it looked pretty good, especially the photos of the landing craft coming into Dover in the grey dawn, Shafto and his boys,
one helmet strap dangling, the prisoners looking suitably cowed.
Straight off Stage Ten at MGM.' He shook his head. 'How the
folks back home bought that one. Shafto's Raiders. *Life, Colliers,
Saturday Evening Post.* You name it, he was in there someplace.
The people's hero. Two DSCs, Silver Star with Oak Leaf clusters.
Everything but the Congressional Medal of Honour and he'll have
that before he's through, even if he has to kill the lot of us doing
it.'
     She said stiffly, 'Why did you join this unit, Major Kane?'
     'Stuck behind a desk,' he said. 'That about sums it up. Guess I'd
have done just about anything to get out – and did.'
     'So you weren't on any of the raids you mention?'

'No, ma'am.'

'Then I suggest you think twice in future before dismissing so lightly the actions of a brave man, especially from the vantage point of a desk.'

He pulled into the side of the road and braked to a halt. He turned to her, smiling cheerfully. 'Heh, I like that. Mind if I write it down to use in that great novel we journalists are always going to write?'

'Damn you, Harry Kane.'

She raised a hand as if to strike him, and he pulled out a pack of Camels and shook one out. 'Have a cigarette instead. Soothes the nerves.'

She took it and the light which followed and inhaled deeply, staring out over the salt marsh towards the sea. 'Sorry, I suppose I am reacting too strongly, but this war has become very personal for me.'

'Your brother?'

'Not only that, My job. When I was on duty yesterday afternoon, I got a fighter pilot on the RT. Badly shot up in a dogfight over the North Sea. His Hurricane was on fire and he was trapped in the cockpit. He screamed all the way down.'

'It started out by being a nice day,' Kane said. 'Suddenly it isn't.'

He reached for the steering wheel and she put her hand on his impulsively. 'I'm sorry – really I am.'

'That's okay.'

Her expression changed to one of puzzlement and she raised his hand. 'What's wrong with your fingers? Several of them are crooked. Your nails . . . Good God, Harry, what happened to your nails?'

'Oh, that?' he said. 'Somebody pulled them out for me.'

She stared at him in horror. 'Was it – was it the Germans, Harry?' she whispered.

'No.' He switched on the engine. 'As a matter of fact they were French, but working for the other side, of course. It's one of life's more distressing discoveries, or so I've found, that it very definitely takes all sorts to make a world.'

He smiled crookedly and drove away.

*

On the evening of the same day in his private room in the nursing home at Aston, Ben Garvald took a decided turn for the worse. He lost consciousness at six o'clock. His condition was not discovered for another hour. It was eight before Doctor Das arrived in answer to the nurse's urgent phone call, ten past when Reuben walked in and discovered the situation.

He had been back to Fogarty's on Ben's instructions, with a hearse and a coffin obtained from the funeral firm which was another of the Garvald brothers' many business ventures. The unfortunate Jackson had just been disposed of at a local private crematorium in which they also had an interest, not the first time, by any means, that they had got rid of an inconvenient corpse in this way.

Ben's face was bathed in sweat and he groaned, moving from side to side. There was a faint unpleasant odour like rotten meat, Reuben caught a glimpse of the knee as Das lifted the dressing. He turned away, fear rising into his mouth like bile.

'Ben?' he said.

Garvald opened his eyes. For a moment he didn't seem to recognize his brother and then he smiled. 'You got it done, Reuben boy? Did you get rid of him?'

'Ashes to ashes, Ben.'

Garvald closed his eyes and Reuben turned to Das. 'How bad is it?'

'Very bad. There is a chance of gangrene here. I warned him.'

'Oh, my God,' Reuben said. 'I knew he should have gone to hospital.'

Ben Garvald's eyes opened and he glared feverishly. He reached for his brother's wrist. 'No hospital, you hear me? What do you want to do? Give those bleeding coppers the opening they've been looking for for years?'

He fell back, eyes closed again. Das said, 'There is one chance. There is a drug called penicillin. You have heard of it?'

'Sure I have. They say it'll cure anything. Fetches a fortune on the black market.'

'Yes, it has quite miraculous results in cases like this. Can you get hold of some? Now – tonight?'

'If it's in Birmingham, you'll have it within an hour.' Reuben walked to the door and turned. 'But if he dies, then you go with him, son. That's a promise.'

He went out and the door swung behind him.

*

At the same moment in Landsvoort the Dakota lifted off the runway and turned out to sea. Gericke didn't waste any time. Simply took her straight up to a thousand feet, banked to starboard and dropped down towards the coast. Inside, Steiner and his men made ready. They were all dressed in full British paratroop gear, all weapons and equipment stowed in suspension bags in the British manner. 'All right,' Steiner called.

They all stood and clipped their static lines to the anchor line cable, each man checking the comrade in front of him, Steiner seeing to Harvey Preston who was last in line. The Englishman was trembling. Steiner could feel it as he tightened his straps for him.

'Fifteen seconds,' he said, 'So you haven't got long – understand? And get this straight, all of you. If you're going to break a leg, do it here. Not in Norfolk.'

There was a general laugh and he walked to the front of the line where Ritter Neumann checked his straps. Steiner slid back the door as the red light blinked above his head and there was the sudden roaring of the wind.

In the cockpit, Gericke throttled back and went in low. The tide was out, the wide, wet lonely beaches pale in the moonlight, stretching into infinity. Bohmler, beside him, was concentrating on the altimeter. 'Now!' Gericke cried and Bohmler was ready for him.

The green light flared above Steiner's head, he slapped Ritter on the shoulder. The young Oberleutnant went out followed by the entire stick, very fast, ending with Brandt. As for Preston, he stood there, mouth gaping, staring out into the night.

'Go on!' Steiner cried and grabbed for his shoulder.

Preston pulled away, holding on to a steel strut to support himself. He shook his head, mouth working. 'Can't!' he finally managed to say. 'Can't do it!'

Steiner struck him across the face back-handed, grabbed him by the right arm and slung him towards the open door. Preston hung there, bracing himself with both hands. Steiner put a foot in his rear and shoved him out into space. Then he clipped on to the anchor line and went after him.

*

When you jump at four hundred feet there isn't really time to be frightened. Preston was aware of himself somersaulting, the sudden jerk, the slap of the 'chute catching air and then he was swinging beneath the dark khaki umbrella.

It was fantastic. The moon pale on the horizon, the flat wet sands, the creamy line of the surf. He could see the E-boat by the sand pier quite clearly, men watching and further along the beach a line of collapsed parachutes as the others gathered them in. He glanced up and caught a glimpse of Steiner above him and to the left and then seemed to be going in very fast.

The supply bag, swinging twenty feet below at the end of a line clipped to his waist, hit the sand with a solid thump warning him to get ready. He went in hard, too hard, or so it seemed, rolled and miraculously found himself on his feet, the parachute billowing up like some pale flower in the moonlight.

He moved in quickly to deflate it as he had been taught and suddenly paused there on his hands and knees, a sense of overwhelming joy, of personal power sweeping through him of a kind he had never known in his life before.

'I did it!' he cried aloud. 'I showed the bastards. I did it! I did it! I did it!'

*

In the bed at the nursing home in Aston, Ben Garvald lay very still. Reuben stood at the end and waited as Doctor Das probed for a heartbeat with his stethoscope.

'How is he?' Reuben demanded.

'Still alive, but only just.'

Reuben made his decision and acted on it. He grabbed Das by the shoulder and shoved him at the door. 'You get an ambulance round here quick as you like. I'm having him in hospital.'

'But that will mean the police, Mr Garvald,' Das pointed out.

'Do you think I care?' Reuben said hoarsely. 'I want him alive, understand? He's my brother. Now get moving!'

He opened the door and pushed Das out. When he turned back to the bed there were tears in his eyes. 'I promise you one thing, Ben,' he said brokenly. 'I'll have that little Irish bastard for this if it's the last thing I do.'

13

At forty-five, Jack Rogan had been a policeman for nearly a quarter of a century – a long time to work a three-shift system and be disliked by the neighbours. But that was the policeman's lot, and only to be expected, as he frequently pointed out to his wife.

It was nine-thirty on Tuesday 2 November when he entered his office at Scotland Yard. By rights, he shouldn't have been there at all. Having spent a lengthy night at Muswell Hill interrogating members of an Irish club, he was entitled to a few hours in bed, but there was a little paperwork to clear up first.

He'd just settled down at his desk when there was a knock at the door and his assistant, Detective Inspector Fergus Grant, entered. Grant was the younger son of a retired Indian Army colonel. Winchester and Hendon Police College. One of the new breed who were supposed to revolutionize the Force. In spite of this, he and Rogan got on well together.

Rogan put up a hand defensively. 'Fergus, all I want to do is sign a few letters, have a cup of tea and go home to bed. Last night was hell.'

'I know, sir,' Grant said. 'It's just that we've had a rather unusual report in from the City of Birmingham Police. I thought it might interest you.'

'You mean me in particular or the Irish Section?'

'Both.'

'All right.' Rogan pushed back his chair and started to fill his pipe from a worn, leather pouch. I'm not in the mood for reading so tell me about it.'

'Ever hear of a man called Garvald, sir?'

Rogan paused. 'You mean Ben Garvald? He's been bad news for years. Biggest villain in the Midlands.'

'He died early this morning. Gangrene as the result of a gunshot wound. The hospital got their hands on him too late.'

Rogan struck a match. 'There are people I know who might say that was the best bit of news they'd heard in years, but how does it affect us?'

'He was shot in the right kneecap, by an Irishman.'

Rogan stared at him. 'That *is* interesting. The statutory IRA punishment when someone tries to cross you.' He cursed as the match in his left hand burned down to his fingers and dropped it. 'What was his name, this Irishman?'

'Murphy, sir.'

'It would be. Is there more?'

'You could say that,' Grant told him. 'Garvald had a brother who's so cut up about his death that he's singing like a bird. He wants friend Murphy nailing to the door.'

Rogan nodded. 'We'll have to see if we can oblige him. What was it all about?'

Grant told him in some detail and by the time he had finished, Rogan was frowning. 'An Army truck, a jeep, khaki-green paint? What would he want with that little lot?'

'Maybe they're going to try a raid on some army camp, sir, to get arms.'

Rogan got up and walked to the window. 'No, I can't buy that, not without firm evidence. They're just not active enough at the moment. Not capable of that kind of ploy, you know that.' He came back to the desk. 'We've broken the back of the IRA here in England and in Ireland, de Valera's put most of them in internment at the Curragh.' He shook his head. 'It wouldn't make sense that kind of operation at this stage. What did Garvald's brother make of it?'

'He seemed to think Murphy was organizing a raid on a NAAFI depot or something like that. You know the sort of thing? Drive in dressed as soldiers in an army truck.'

'And drive out again with fifty thousand quid's worth of scotch and cigarettes. It's been done before,' Rogan said.

'So Murphy's just another thief on the take, sir? Is that your hunch?'

'I'd accept that if it wasn't for the bullet in the kneecap. That's pure IRA. No, my left ear's twitching about this one, Fergus. I think we could be on to something.'

'All right, sir, what's the next move?'

Rogan walked over to the window thinking about it. Outside it was typical autumn weather, fog drifting across the rooftops from the Thames, rain dripping from the sycamore trees.

He turned. 'I know one thing. I'm not having Birmingham cock this up for us. You handle it personally. Book a car from the pool and get up there today. Take the files with you, photos, the lot. Every known IRA man not under wrappers. Maybe Garvald can pick him out for us.'

'And if not, sir?'

'Then we start asking questions at this end. All the usual channels. Special Branch in Dublin will help all they can. They hate the IRA worse than ever since they shot Detective Sergeant O'Brien last year. You always feel worse when it's one of your own.'

'Right, sir,' Grant said. 'I'll get moving.'

*

It was eight that evening when General Karl Steiner finished the meal which had been served to him in his room on the second floor at Prinz Albrechtstrasse. A chicken leg, potatoes fried in oil, just as he liked them, a tossed salad and a half-bottle of Riesling, served ice-cold. Quite incredible. And real coffee to follow.

Things had certainly changed since the final terrible night when he had collapsed after the electrical treatment. The following morning he had awakened to find himself lying between clean sheets in a comfortable bed. No sign of that bastard Rossman and his Gestapo bully boys. Just an Obersturmbannführer named Zeidler, a thoroughly decent type, even if he was SS. A gentleman.

He had been full of apologies. A dreadful mistake had been made. False information had been laid with malicious intent. The Reichsführer himself had ordered the fullest possible enquiry. Those responsible would undoubtedly be apprehended and punished. In the meantime, he regretted the fact that the Herr General had still to be kept under lock and key, but this would only be for a matter of a few days. He was sure he understood the situation.

Which Steiner did perfectly. All they had ever had against him was innuendo, nothing concrete. And he hadn't said a word in spite of everything Rossman had done, so the whole thing was going to look like one God-Almighty foul-up on someone's part. They were hanging on to him now to make sure he looked good for when they released him. Already, the bruises had almost faded. Except for the rings around his eyes he looked fine. They'd even given him a new uniform.

The coffee was really quite excellent. He started to pour another cup and the key rattled in the lock and the door opened behind him. There was an uncanny silence. The hair seemed to lift on the back of his head.

He turned slowly and found Karl Rossman standing in the doorway. He was wearing his slouch hat, the leather coat over his shoulders and a cigarette dangled from the corner of his mouth. Two Gestapo men in full uniform stood on either side of him.

'Hello, there, Herr General,' Rossman said. 'Did you think we'd forgotten you?'

Something seemed to break inside Steiner. The whole thing became dreadfully clear. 'You bastard!' he said and threw the cup of coffee at Rossman's head.

'Very naughty,' Rossman said. 'You shouldn't have done that.'

One of the Gestapo men moved in quickly. He rammed the end of his baton into Steiner's groin, who dropped to his knees with a scream of agony. A further blow to the side of the head put him down completely.

'The cellars,' Rossman said simply, and went out.

The two Gestapo men got an ankle apiece and followed, dragging the General behind them face-down, keeping in step with a military precision that didn't even falter when they reached the stairs.

*

Max Radl knocked at the door of the Reichsführer's office and went in. Himmler was standing in front of the fire, drinking coffee. He put down his cup and crossed to the desk. 'I had hoped that you would have been on your way by now.'

'I leave on the overnight flight for Paris,' Radl told him. 'As the Herr Reichsführer is aware, Admiral Canaris only flew to Italy this morning.'

'Unfortunate,' Himmler said. 'However, it should still leave you plenty of time.' He removed his pince-nez and polished them as meticulously as usual. 'I've read the report you gave Rossman this morning. What about these American Rangers who have appeared in the area? Show me.'

He unfolded the ordnance survey map in front of him and Radl put a finger on Meltham House. 'As you can see, Herr Reichsführer, Meltham House is eight miles to the north along the coast from Studley Constable. Twelve or thirteen from Hobs End. Mrs Grey anticipates no trouble whatsoever in that direction in her latest radio message.'

Himmler nodded. 'Your Irishman seems to have earned his wages. The rest is up to Steiner.'

'I don't think he'll let us down.'

'Yes, I was forgetting,' Himmler said dryly. 'He has, after all, a personal stake in this.'

Radl said, 'May I be permitted to enquire after Major-General Steiner's health?'

'I last saw him yesterday evening,' Himmler replied with perfect truth, 'although I must confess he did not see me. At that time he was working his way through a meal consisting of roast potatoes, mixed vegetables and a rather large rump steak.' He sighed. 'If only these meat eaters realized the effect on the system of such a diet. Do you eat meat, Herr Oberst?'

'I'm afraid so.'

'And smoke sixty or seventy of those vile Russian cigarettes a day and drink. What is your brandy consumption now?' He shook his head as he shuffled his papers into a neat pile in front of him, 'Ah, well, in your case I don't suppose it really matters.'

Is there anything the swine doesn't know? Radl thought. 'No. Herr Reichsführer.'

'What time do they leave on Friday?'

'Just before midnight. A one-hour flight, weather permitting.'

Himmler looked up instantly, eyes cold. 'Colonel Radl, let me make one thing perfectly plain. Steiner and his men go in as arranged, weather or no weather. This is not something that can be postponed until another night. This is a once in a lifetime opportunity. There will be a line kept open to these headquarters at all times. From Friday morning you will communicate with me each hour on the hour and continue so doing until the operation is successfully concluded.'

'I will, Herr Reichsführer.'

Radl turned for the door and Himmler said, 'One more thing. I have not kept the Führer informed of our progress in this affair for many reasons. These are hard times, Radl, the destiny of Germany rests on his shoulders. I would like this to be, how can I put it, a surprise for him?'

For a moment, Radl though he must be going out of his mind. Then realized that Himmler was serious. 'It is essential that we don't disappoint him,' Himmler went on. 'We are all in Steiner's hands now. Please impress that on him.'

'I will, Herr Reichsführer.' Radl choked back an insane desire to laugh.

Himmler flipped up his right arm in a rather negligent party salute. 'Heil Hitler!'

Radl, in what he afterwards swore to his wife was the bravest action of his entire life, gave him a punctilious military salute, turned to the door and got out as fast as he could.

*

When he went into his office at the Tirpitz Ufer, Hofer was packing an overnight bag for him. Radl got out the Courvoisier and poured himself a large one. 'Is the Herr Oberst all right?' Hofer enquired anxiously.

'You know what our esteemed Reichsführer has just let slip, Karl? He hasn't told the Führer about how far along the road we are with this thing. He wants to surprise him. Now isn't that sweet?'

'Herr Oberst, for God's sake.'

Radl raised his glass. 'To our comrades, Karl, the three hundred and ten of the regiment who died in the Winter War, I'm not sure what for. If you find out, let me know.' Hofer stared at him and Radl smiled. 'All right, Karl, I'll be good. Did you check the time of my Paris flight?'

'Ten-thirty from Tempelhof. I've ordered a car for nine-fifteen. You have plenty of time.'

'And the onward flight to Amsterdam?'

'Some time tomorrow morning. Probably about eleven, but they couldn't be sure.'

'That's cutting it fine. All I need is a little dirty weather and I won't get to Landsvoort till Thursday. What's the met report?'

'Not good. A cold front coming in from Russia.'

'There always is,' Radl told him bleakly. He opened the desk drawer and took out a sealed envelope. 'That's for my wife. See that she gets it. Sorry you can't come with me, but you must hold the fort here, you understand that?'

Hofer looked down at the letter and there was fear in his eyes. 'Surely the Herr Oberst doesn't think . . .'

'My dear, good Karl,' Radl told him. 'I think nothing. I simply prepare for any unpleasant eventuality. If this thing goes wrong then it seems to me that those connected with it might not be

considered – how shall I put it? – persona grata at court. In any
such eventuality your own line should be to deny all knowledge
of the affair. Anything I've done, I've done alone.'

'Herr Oberst, please,' Hofer said hoarsely. There were tears
in his eyes.

Radl took out another glass, filled it and handed it to him.
'Come now, a toast. What shall we drink to?'

'God knows, Herr Oberst.'

'Then I shall tell you. To life, Karl, and love and friendship
and hope.' He smiled wryly. 'You know, it's just occurred to
me that the Reichsführer very probably doesn't know the first
thing about any one of those items. Ah, well . . .'

He threw back his head and emptied his glass at a single
swallow.

*

Like most senior officers at Scotland Yard, Jack Rogan had a
small camp bed in his office for use on those occasions when air
raids made travelling home a problem. When he came back
from the Assistant Commissioner, Special Branch's, weekly
coordinating meeting with section heads on Wednesday morning just before noon, he found Grant asleep on it, eyes closed.

Rogan stuck his head out of the door and told the duty
constable to make some tea. Then he gave Grant a friendly
kick and went and stood at the window filling his pipe. The fog
was worse than ever. A real London particular, as Dickens had
once aptly phrased it.

Grant got up, adjusting his tie. His suit was crumpled and he
needed a shave. 'Hell of a journey back. The fog was really
quite something.'

'Did you get anywhere?'

Grant opened his briefcase, took out a file and produced a
card which he laid on Rogan's desk. A photo of Liam Devlin
was clipped to it. Strangely enough he looked older. There
were several different names typed underneath. 'That's Murphy, sir.'

Rogan whistled softly. 'Him? Are you sure?'

'Reuben Garvald is.'

'But this doesn't make sense,' Rogan said. 'Last I heard, he was in trouble in Spain, fighting for the wrong side. Serving a life sentence on some penal farm.'

'Evidently not, sir.'

Rogan jumped up and walked to the window. He stood there, hands in pockets, for a moment. 'You know, he's one of the few top-liners in the movement I've never met. Always the mystery man. All those bloody aliases for one thing.'

'Went to Trinity College according to his file, which is unusual for a Catholic,' Grant said. 'Good degree in English Literature. There's irony, considering he's in the IRA.'

'That's the bloody Irish for you.' Rogan turned, prodding a finger into his skull. 'Puddled from birth. Round the twist. I mean his uncle's a priest, he has a university degree and what is he? The most cold-blooded executioner the movement's had since Collins and his Murder Squad.'

'All right, sir.' Grant said. 'How do we handle it?'

'First of all get in touch with the Special Branch in Dublin. See what they've got.'

'And next?'

'If he's here legally he must have registered with his local police, wherever that is. Alien's registration form plus photograph.'

'Which are then passed on to the headquarters of the force concerned.'

'Exactly.' Rogan kicked the desk. 'I've been arguing for two years now that we should have them on a central file, but with nearly three-quarters of a million micks working over here nobody wants to know.'

'That means circulating copies of this photo to all city and county forces and asking for someone to go through every registration on file.' Grant picked up the card. 'It'll take time.'

'What else can we do, stick it in the paper and say: *Has anybody seen this man*? I want to know what he's up to, Fergus, I want to catch him at it, not frighten him off.'

'Of course, sir.'

'Just get on with it. Top Priority. Give it a National Security Red File rating. That will make the buggers jump to it.'

Grant went out and Rogan picked up Devlin's file, leaned back in the chair and started to read it.

*

In Paris, all aircraft were grounded and the fog was so thick that when Radl walked out of the entrance of the departure lounge at Orly he couldn't see his hand in front of his face. He went back inside and spoke to the Duty Officer. 'What do you think?'

'I'm sorry, Herr Oberst, but on the basis of the latest met report, nothing before morning. To be honest with you, there could be further delays even then. They seem to think this fog could last for some days.' He smiled amiably. 'It keeps the *Tommis* at home, anyway.'

Radl made his decision and reached for his bag. 'Absolutely essential that I'm in Rotterdam no later than tomorrow afternoon. Where's the motor pool?'

Ten minutes later he was holding the Führer Directive under the nose of a middle-aged transport captain and twenty minutes after that was being driven out of the main gate of Orly Airport in a large, black Citroën saloon.

*

At the same moment in the sitting-room of Joanna Grey's cottage at Studley Constable, Sir Henry Willoughby was playing bezique with Father Vereker and Joanna Grey. He had had more to drink than was perhaps good for him and was in high good humour.

'Let me see now, I had a Royal Marriage – forty points and now a sequence in trumps.'

'How many is that?' Vereker demanded.

'Two hundred and fifty,' Joanna Grey said. 'Two-ninety with his Royal Marriage.'

'Just a minute,' Vereker said. 'He's got a ten above the Queen.'

'But I explained that earlier,' Joanna told him. 'In bezique, the ten *does* come before the Queen.'

Philip Vereker shook his head in disgust. 'It's no good. I'll never understand this damned game.'

Sir Henry laughed delightedly. 'A gentleman's game, my boy. The aristocrat of card games.' He jumped up, knocking his chair over and righted it. 'Mind if I help myself, Joanna?'

'Of course not, my dear,' she said brightly.

'You seem pleased with yourself tonight.' Vereker remarked.

Sir Henry, warming his backside in front of the fire, grinned. 'I am, Philip, I am and good cause to be.' It all came flowing out of him in a sudden burst. 'Don't see why I shouldn't tell you. You'll know soon enough now.'

God, the old fool. Joanna Grey's alarm was genuine as she said hastily. 'Henry, do you think you should?'

'Why not? he said. 'If I can't trust you and Philip, who can I trust.' He turned to Vereker. 'Fact is, the Prime Minister is coming to stay the weekend on Saturday.'

'Good heavens. I'd heard he was speaking at King's Lynn, of course.' Vereker was astounded. 'To be honest, sir, I didn't realize you knew Mr Churchill.'

'I don't,' Sir Henry said. 'Thing is he fancied a quiet weekend and a little painting before going back to town. Naturally he'd heard about the gardens at Studley, I mean who hasn't? Laid down in the Armada year. When Downing Street got in touch to ask if he could stay, I was only too delighted.'

'Naturally,' Vereker said.

'Now you must keep it to yourselves, I'm afraid,' Sir Henry said. 'Villagers can't know till he's gone. They're most insistent about that. Security, you know. Can't be too careful.'

He was very drunk now, slurring his words. Vereker said, 'I suppose he'll be quite heavily guarded.'

'Not at all,' Sir Henry said. 'Wants as little fuss as possible. He'll only have three or four people with him. I've arranged for a platoon of my Home Guard chaps to guard the perimeter of the Grange while he's there. Even they don't know what it's all about. Think it's an exercise.

'Is that so?' Joanna said.

'Yes, I'm to go up to King's Lynn on Saturday to meet him. We'll come back by car.' He belched and put down his glass. 'I say, would you excuse me? Don't feel too good.'

'Of course,' Joanna Grey said.

He walked to the door, turned and put a finger to his nose. 'Mum's the word now.'

After he'd gone, Vereker said, 'That is a turn-up for the book.'

'He's really very naughty,' Joanna said. 'He isn't supposed to say a word and yet he told me in exactly similar circumstances when he'd had too much to drink. Naturally I felt bound to keep quiet about it.'

'Of course,' he said. 'You were absolutely right.' He stood up, groping for his stick. I'd better run him home. He's not fit to drive.'

'Nonsense.' She took his arm and steered him to the door. 'That would mean you having to walk up to the presbytery to get your own car out. There's no need. I'll take him.'

She helped him into his coat. 'If you're sure, then?'

'Of course.' She kissed his cheek. I'm looking forward to seeing Pamela on Saturday.'

He limped away into the night. She stood at the door listening as the sound of his progress faded. It was so still and quiet, almost as quiet as the veldt when she was a young girl. Strange, but she hadn't though of that for years.

She went back inside and closed the door. Sir Henry appeared from the downstairs cloakroom and weaved an unsteady path to his chair by the fire. 'Must go, old girl.'

'Nonsense,' she said. 'Always time for another one.' She poured two fingers of Scotch into his glass and sat on one arm of the chair, gently stroking his neck. 'You know, Henry, I'd love to meet the Prime Minister. I think I'd like that more than anything else in the world.'

'Would you, old girl?' He gazed up at her foolishly.

She smiled and gently brushed her lips along his forehead. 'Well, almost anything.'

*

It was very quiet in the cellars at Prinz Albrechtstrasse as Himmler went down the stairs. Rossman was waiting at the bottom. His sleeves were rolled up to the elbows and he was very pale.

'Well?' Himmler demanded.

'He's dead, I'm afraid, Herr Reichsführer.'

Himmler was not pleased and showed it. 'That seems singularly careless of you, Rossman. I told you to take care.'

'With all due respect, Herr Reichsführer, it was his heart which gave out. Dr Prager will confirm this, I sent for him at once. He's still in there.'

He opened the nearest door. Rossman's two Gestapo assistants stood at one side, still wearing rubber gloves and aprons. A small, brisk-looking man in a tweed suit was leaning over the body on the iron cot in the corner, probing the naked chest with a stethoscope.

He turned as Himmler entered and gave the party salute. 'Herr Reichsführer.'

Himmler stood looking down at Steiner for a while. The General was stripped to the waist and his feet were bare. His eyes were partly open, fixed, staring into eternity.

'Well?' Himmler demanded.

'His heart, Herr Reichsführer. No doubt about it.'

Himmler removed his pince-nez and gently rubbed between his eyes. He'd had a headache all afternoon and it simply would not go away. 'Very well, Rossman,' he said. 'He was guilty of treason against the State, of plotting against the life of the Führer himself. As you know, the Führer has decreed a statutory punishment for this offence and Major-General Steiner cannot evade this, even in death.'

'Of course, Herr Reichsführer.'

'See that the sentence is carried out. I won't stay myself, I am summoned to Rastenburg but take photographs and dispose of the body in the usual way.'

They all clicked their heels in the party salute and left.

*

'He was arrested where?' Rogan said in astonishment. It was just before five and already dark enough for the blackout curtains to be drawn.

'At a farmhouse near Caragh Lake in Kerry in June last year, after a gunfight in which he shot two policemen and was wounded himself. He escaped from the local hospital the following day and dropped out of sight.'

'Dear God and they call themselves policemen,' Rogan said in despair.

'The thing is, Special Branch, Dublin, weren't involved in any of this, sir. They only identified him later by the prints on the revolver. The arrest was made by a patrol from the local *Garda* barracks checking for an illicit still. One other point, sir, Dublin say they checked with the Spanish Foreign Office, our friend supposedly being in gaol over there. They were reluctant to come across, you know how difficult they can be about this kind of thing. They finally admitted that he'd escaped from a penal farm in Granada in the autumn of 1940. Their information was that he'd made it to Lisbon and taken passage to the States.'

'And now he's back,' Rogan said. 'But what for, that's the thing. Have you heard from any of the provincial forces yet?'

'Seven, sir – all negative, I'm afraid.'

'All right. There's nothing more we can do at the moment except hope. The moment you have anything, contact me instantly. Day or night, no matter where I am.'

'Very well, sir.'

14

It was precisely eleven-fifteen on Friday morning at Meltham Grange when Harry Kane, who was supervising a squad's progress over the assault course, received an urgent summons to report to Shafto at once. When he reached his commanding officer's outer office he found things in something of a turmoil. The clerks looked frightened and Master-Sergeant Garvey paced up and down, smoking a cigarette nervously.

'What's happened?' Kane demanded.

'God knows, Major. All I know is he blew his stack about fifteen minutes ago after receiving an urgent despatch from Headquarters. Kicked young Jones clean out of the office. And I mean kicked.'

Kane knocked at the door and went in. Shafto was standing at the window, his riding crop in one hand, a glass in the other. He turned angrily and then his expression changed. 'Oh, it's you, Harry.'

'What is it, sir?'

'It's simple. Those bastards up at Combined Operations who've been trying to get me out of the way have finally managed it. When we finish here next weekend, I hand over command to Sam Williams.'

'And you, sir?'

'I'm to go back Stateside. Chief Instructor in Fieldcraft at Fort Benning.'

He kicked a wastepaper bin clean across the room and Kane said, 'Isn't there anything you can do about it, sir?'

Shafto turned on him like a madman. 'Do about it?' He picked up the order and pushed it into Kane's face. 'See the signature on that? Eisenhower himself.' He crumpled it into a ball and threw it away. 'And you know something, Kane? He's never been in action. Not once in his entire career.'

*

At Hobs End Devlin was lying in bed writing in his personal notebook. It was raining hard and outside, mist draped itself over the marsh in a damp, clinging shroud. The door was pushed open and Molly came in. She was wearing Devlin's trenchcoat and carried a tray which she put down on the table beside the bed.

'There you are, O lord and master. Tea and toast, two boiled eggs, four and a half minutes as you suggested, and cheese sandwiches.'

Devlin stopped writing and looked at the tray appreciatively. 'Keep up this standard and I might be tempted to take you on permanently.'

She took off the trenchcoat. Underneath she was only wearing pants and bra and she picked up her sweater from the end of the bed and pulled it over her head. 'I'll have to get moving. I told Mum I'd be in for my dinner.'

He poured himself a cup of tea and she picked up the notebook. 'What's this?' She opened it. 'Poetry?'

He grinned. 'A matter of opinion in some quarters.'

'Yours?' she said and there was genuine wonder on her face. She opened it at the place where he had been writing that morning. 'There is no certain knowledge of my passing, where I have walked in woodland after dark.' She looked up. 'Why, that's beautiful, Liam.'

'I know,' he said. 'Like you keep telling me, I'm a lovely boy.'

'I know one thing, I could eat you up.' She flung herself on top of him and kissed him fiercely. 'You know what today is? The fifth of November only we can't have no bonfire because of rotten old Adolf.'

'What a shame,' he jeered.

'Never you mind.' She wriggled into a comfortable position, her legs stradding him. 'I'll come round tonight and cook you supper and we'll have a nice little bonfire all our own.'

'No you won't' he said. 'Because I shan't be here.'

Her face clouded, 'Business?'

He kissed her lightly. 'Now you know what you promised.'

'All right,' she said. 'I'll be good. I'll see you in the morning.'

'No, I probably won't get back till tomorrow afternoon. Far better to leave it that I'll call for you – all right?'

She nodded reluctantly. 'If you say so.'

'I do.'

He kissed her and there was the sound of a horn outside. Molly darted to the window and came back in a hurry grabbing for her denim trousers. 'My God, it's Mrs Grey.'

'That's what's called being caught with your pants down,' Devlin told her, laughing.

He pulled on a sweater. Molly reached for her coat. 'I'm off. I'll see you tomorrow, beautiful. Can I take this? I'd like to read the others.'

She held up his notebook of poetry. 'God, but you must like punishment,' he said.

She kissed him hard and he followed her out, opening the back door for her, standing watching her run through the reeds to the dyke, knowing that this could well be the end. 'Ah, well,' he said softly. 'The best thing for her.'

He turned and went to open the door in answer to Joanna Grey's repeated knocking. She surveyed him grimly as he tucked his shirt into his trousers. 'I caught a glimpse of Molly on the dyke path a second ago.' She walked past him. 'You really should be ashamed of yourself.'

'I know,' he said as he followed her into the sitting-room. 'I'm a terrible bad lot. Well, the big day. I'd say that warrants a little nip. Will you join me?'

'Quarter of an inch in the bottom of the glass and no more,' she said sternly.

He brought the Bushmills and two glasses and poured a couple of drinks. 'Up the Republic!' he told her, 'both the Irish and South African varieties. Now, what's the news?'

'I switched to the new wavelength last night as ordered, transmitting directly to Landsvoort. Radl himself is there now.'

'And it's still on?' Devlin said. 'In spite of the weather?'

Her eyes were shining. 'Come hell or high water, Steiner and his men will be here at approximately one o'clock.'

*

Steiner was addressing the assault group in his quarters. The only person present other than those actually making the drop was Max Radl. Even Gericke had been excluded. They all stood around the map table. There was an atmosphere of nervous excitement as Steiner turned from the window where he had been talking to Radl in a low voice and faced them. He indicated Gerhard Klugl's model, the photos, the maps.

'All right. You all know where you're going. Every stick, every stone of it, which has been the object of the exercise for the past few weeks. What you don't know is what we're supposed to do when we get there.'

He paused, glancing at each face in turn, tense, expectant. Even Preston, who, after all, had known for some time, seemed caught by the drama of the occasion.

So Steiner told them.

*

Peter Gericke could hear the roar from as far away as the hangar.
'Now what's happening, for God's sake?' Bohmler said.
'Don't ask me,' Gericke replied sourly. 'Nobody tells me anything around here.' The bitterness suddenly overflowed. 'If we're
good enough to risk our necks flying the sods in, you'd think we
might at least be told what it's all about.'

'If it's as important as that,' Bohmler said, 'I'm not sure I want
to know. I'm going to check the Lichtenstein set.'

He climbed into the plane and Gericke lit a cigarette and moved
a little further away, looking the Dakota over again. Sergeant
Witt had done a lovely job on the RAF roundels. He turned and
saw the field car moving across the airstrip towards him, Ritter
Neumann at the wheel, Steiner beside him, Radl in the rear. It
braked to a halt a yard or two away. No one got out.

Steiner said, 'You don't look too pleased with life, Peter.'
'Why should I?' Gericke said. 'A whole month I've spent in this
dump, worked all the hours God sends on that plane in there and
for what?' His gesture took in the mist, the rain, the entire sky. 'In
this kind of shit I'll never even get off the ground.'

'Oh, we have every confidence that a man of your very special
calibre will be able to accomplish that.'

They started to get out of the field wagon and Ritter particularly
was having the greatest difficulty in holding back his laughter.
'Look, what's going on here?' Gericke said truculently. 'What's it
all about?'

'Why, it's really quite simple, you poor, miserable, hard-done-
to-son of a bitch,' Radl said. 'I have the honour to inform you that
you have just been awarded the Knight's Cross.'

Gericke stared at him, open-mouthed and Steiner said gently,
'So you see, my dear Peter, you get your weekend at Karinhall
after all.'

*

Koenig leaned over the chart table with Steiner and Radl and
Chief Petty Officer Muller stood at a respectful distance, but
missing nothing.

The young lieutenant said, 'Four months ago a British armed trawler was torpedoed off the Hebrides by a U-boat under the command of Horst Wengel, an old friend of mine. There were only fifteen in the crew so he took them all prisoner. Unfortunately for them, they hadn't managed to get rid of their documents, which included some interesting charts of the British coastal minefields.'

'That was a break for somebody,' Steiner said.

'For all of us, Herr Oberst, as these latest charts from Wilhelmshaven prove. See, here, east of the Wash where the minefield runs parallel to the coast to protect the inshore shipping lane? There is a route through quite clearly marked. The British Navy made it for their own purposes, but units of the Eighth E-boat Flotilla out of Rotterdam have used it with perfect safety for some time now. In fact, as long as navigation is accurate enough, one may proceed at speed.'

'There would seem to be an argument for saying that the minefield itself in such circumstances will afford you considerable protection,' Radl said.

'Exactly, Herr Oberst.'

'And what about the estuary approach behind the Point to Hobs End?'

'Difficult certainly, but Muller and I have studied the Admiralty Charts until we know them by heart. Every sounding, every sandbank. We will be going in on a rising tide, remember, if we are to make the pick-up at ten.'

'You estimate eight hours for the passage which would mean your leaving here at what – one o'clock?'

'If we are to have a margin at the other end in which to operate. Of course, this is a unique craft as you know. She could do the trip in seven hours if it comes to that. I'm just playing safe.'

'Very sensible.' Radl said, 'because Colonel Steiner and I have decided to modify your orders. I want you off the Point and ready to go in for the pick-up at *any* time between nine and ten. You'll get your final run-in orders from Devlin on the S-phone. Be guided by him.'

'Very well, Herr Oberst.'

'You shouldn't be in any particular danger under cover of darkness,' Steiner said and smiled. 'After all, this is a British ship.'

Koenig grinned, opened a cupboard under the chart table and took out a British Navy White Ensign. 'And we'll be flying this, remember.'

Radl nodded. 'Radio silence from the moment you leave. Under no circumstances must you break it until you hear from Devlin. You know the code sign, of course.'

'Naturally, Herr Oberst.'

Koenig was being polite and Radl clapped him on the shoulder. 'Yes, I know, to you I am a nervous, old man. I'll see you tomorrow before you leave. You'd better say goodbye to Colonel Steiner now.'

Steiner shook hands with both of them. 'I don't quite know what to say except be on time for God's sake.'

Koenig gave him a perfect naval salute. 'I'll see you on that beach, Herr Oberst. I promise you.'

Steiner smiled wryly. 'I damn well hope so.' He turned and followed Radl outside.

As they walked along the sand pier towards the field car Radl said, 'Well, is it going to work, Kurt?'

At that moment Werner Briegel and Gerhard Klugl came over the sand dunes. They were wearing ponchos and Briegel's Zeiss fieldglasses were slung around his neck.

'Let's seek their opinion,' Steiner suggested and called out in English, 'Private Kunicki! Private Moczar! Over here, please!' Briegel and Klugl doubled across without hesitation. Steiner looked them over calmly and continued in English, 'Who am I?'

'Lieutenant-Colonel Howard Carter, in command of the Polish Independent Parachute Squadron, Special Air Service Regiment,' Briegel replied promptly in good English.

Radl turned to Steiner with a smile, 'I'm impressed.'

Steiner said, 'What are you doing here?'

'Sergeant-Major Brandt,' Briegel began and hastily corrected himself. 'Sergeant-Major Kruczek told us to relax.' He hesitated then added in German. 'We're looking for shorelarks, Herr Oberst.'

'Shorelarks?' Steiner said.

'Yes, they're quite easy to distinguish. A most striking black and yellow pattern on face and throat.'

Steiner exploded into laughter. 'You see, my dear Max? Shorelarks. How can we possibly fail?'

*

But the elements seemed determined to make sure that they did. As darkness fell, fog still blanketed most of Western Europe. At Landsvoort, Gericke inspected the airstrip constantly from six o'clock onwards, but in spite of the heavy rain the fog was as thick as ever.

'There's no wind, you see,' he informed Steiner and Radl at eight o'clock. 'That's what we need now to clear this damn stuff away. Lots of wind.'

*

Across the North Sea in Norfolk things were no better. In the secret cubbyhole in the loft of her cottage, Joanna Grey sat by the radio receiver in her headphones and filled in the time reading a book Vereker had lent her in which Winston Churchill described how he had escaped from a prison camp during the Boer War. It was really quite enthralling and she was conscious of a rather reluctant admiration.

Devlin, at Hobs End, had been out to check on the weather as frequently as Gericke, but nothing changed and the fog seemed as impenetrable as ever. At ten o'clock he went along the dyke to the beach for the fourth time that night, but conditions didn't seem to have altered.

He flashed his torch into the gloom then shook his head and said softly to himself, 'A good night for dirty work, that's about all you can say for it.'

*

It seemed obvious that the whole thing was a washout and it was hard to escape that conclusion at Landsvoort, too. 'Are you trying to say you can't take off?' Radl demanded when the young Hauptmann came back inside the hangar from another inspection.

'No problem there,' Gericke told him. 'I can take off blind. Not particularly hazardous in country as flat as this. The difficulty's going to be at the other end. I can't just drop those men and hope for the best. We could be a mile out to sea. I need to see the target, however briefly.'

Bohmler opened the judas in one of the big hangar doors and peered in. 'Herr Hauptmann.'

Gericke moved to join him. 'What is it?'

'See for yourself.'

Gericke stepped through, Bohmler had switched on the outside light and in spite of its dimness, Gericke could see the fog swirling in strange patterns. Something touched his cheek coldly. 'Wind!' he said. 'My God, we've got wind.'

There was a sudden gap torn in the curtain and he could see the farmhouse for a moment. Dimly, but it was there. 'Do we go?' Bohmler demanded.

'Yes,' Gericke said. 'But it's got to be now,' and he turned and plunged back through the judas to tell Steiner and Radl.

*

Twenty minutes later, at exactly eleven o'clock, Joanna Grey straightened abruptly as her earphones started to buzz. She dropped her book, reached for a pencil and wrote on the pad in front of her. It was a very brief message, decoded in seconds. She sat staring at it, momentarily spellbound, then she made an acknowledgement.

She went downstairs quickly and took her sheepskin coat from behind the door. The retriever sniffed at her heels. 'No, Patch, not this time,' she said.

She had to drive carefully because of the fog and it was twenty minutes later before she turned into the yard at Hobs End. Devlin was getting his gear together on the kitchen table when he heard the car. He reached for the Mauser quickly and went out into the passageway.

'It's me, Liam,' she called.

He opened the door and she slipped in. 'What's all this?'

'I've just received a message from Landsvoort, timed eleven o'clock exactly,' she said. 'The Eagle has flown.'

He stared at her, astonished. 'They must be crazy. It's like pea soup up there on the beach.'

'It seemed a little clearer to me as I turned along the dyke.'

He went out quickly and opened the front door. He was back in a moment, face pale with excitement. 'There's a wind coming in off the sea, not much, but it could get stronger.'

'Don't you think it will last?' she said.

'God knows.' The silenced Sten gun was assembled on the table and he handed it to her. 'You know how to work these?'

'Of course.'

He picked up a bulging rucksack and slung it over his shoulders. 'Right then, let's you and me get to it. We've got work to do. If your timing's right, they'll be over that beach in forty minutes.' As they moved into the passage, he laughed harshly. 'By God, but they mean business, I'll say that for them.'

He opened the door and they plunged out into the fog.

*

'I'd close my eyes if I were you,' Gericke told Bohmler cheerfully, above the rumbling of the engines warming up as he made his final check before take-off. 'This one's going to be pretty hair-raising.'

The flares to mark the take-off run had been lit, but only the first few could be seen. Visibility was still no more than forty or fifty yards. The door behind them opened and Steiner poked his head into the cockpit.

'Everything strapped down back there?' Gericke asked him.

'Everything and everybody. We're ready when you are.'

'Good, I don't want to be an alarmist, but I should point out that anything could happen and very probably will.'

He increased his engine revs and Steiner grinned, shouting to make himself heard above the roaring. 'We have every faith in you.'

He closed the door and retired. Gericke boosted power instantly and let the Dakota go. To plunge headlong into that grey wall was probably the most terrifying thing he had ever done in his life. He needed a run of several hundred yards, a speed of around eighty miles an hour for lift-off.

'My God,' he thought. 'Is this it? Is this finally it?'

The vibrations as he gave her more power seemed unbearable. Up came the tail as he pushed the column forward. Just a touch. She yawed to starboard in a slight crosswind and he applied a little rudder correction.

The roar of the engines seemed to fill the night. At eighty, he eased back slightly, but held on. And then, as that feeling flowed through him, that strange sixth sense, the product of several thousand hours of flying that told you when things were just right, he hauled back on the column.

'Now!' he cried.

Bohmler, who had been waiting tensely, his hand on the undercarriage lever, responded frantically, retracting the wheels. Suddenly they were flying. Gericke kept her going, straight into that grey wall, refusing to sacrifice power for height, hanging on till the last possible moment, before pulling the column right back. At five hundred feet they burst out of the fog, he stamped on the right rudder and turned out to sea.

Outside the hangar, Max Radl sat in the passenger seat of the field car staring up into the fog, a kind of awe on his face. 'Great God in heaven!' he whispered. 'He did it!'

He sat there for a moment longer, listening as the sound of the engines faded into the night, then nodded to Witt behind the wheel. 'Back to the farmhouse as quickly as you like, Sergeant. I've got things to do.'

*

In the Dakota there was no easing of tension. There had been none in the first place. They talked amongst themselves in low tones with all the calm of veterans who had done this sort of thing so many times that it was second nature. As nobody had been allowed to have German cigarettes on his person, Ritter Neumann and Steiner moved amongst them handing them out singly.

Altmann said, 'He's a flyer, that Hauptmann, I'll say that for him. A real ace to take off in that fog.'

Steiner turned to Preston sitting at the end of the stick. 'A cigarette, Lieutenant?' he said in English.

'Thanks very much, sir, I think I will.' Preston replied in a beautifully clipped voice that suggested he was playing the Coldstream Guards Captain again.

'How do you feel?' Steiner asked in a low voice.

'In excellent spirits, sir.' Preston told him calmly. 'Can't wait to get stuck in.'

Steiner gave up and retreated to the cockpit where he found Bohmler passing Gericke coffee from a Thermos flask. They were flying at two thousand feet. Through occasional gaps in the clouds, stars could be seen and a pale sickle moon. Below, fog covered the sea like smoke in a valley, a spectacular sight.

'How are we doing?' Steiner asked.

'Fine. Another thirty minutes. Not much of a wind though. I'd say about five knots.'

Steiner nodded down into the cauldron below. 'What do you think? Will it be clear enough when you go down?'

'Who knows?' Gericke grinned. 'Maybe I'll end up on that beach with you.'

At that moment Bohmler, huddled over the Lichtenstein set, gave an excited gasp. 'I've got something, Peter.'

They entered a short stretch of cloud. Steiner said. 'What's it likely to be?'

'Probably a night fighter, as he's on his own,' Gericke said, 'Better pray it isn't one of ours. He'll blow us out of the sky.'

They emerged from the clouds into clear air and Bohmler tapped Gericke's arm. 'Coming in like a bat out of hell on the starboard quarter.'

Steiner turned his head and after a few moments, could plainly see a twin-engine aircraft levelling out to starboard.

'Mosquito,' Gericke said and added calmly, 'Let's hope he knows a friend when he sees one.'

The Mosquito held course with them for only a few more moments, then waggled its wingtips and swung away to starboard at great speed, disappearing into heavy cloud.

'See,' Gericke smiled up at Steiner. 'All you have to do is live right. Better get back to your lads and make sure they're ready to go. If everything works, we should pick up Devlin on the S-phone twenty miles out. I'll call you when we do. Now get the hell out of here. Bohmler's got some fancy navigating to do.'

Steiner returned to the main cabin and sat down beside Ritter Neumann. 'Not long now.' He passed him a cigarette.

'Thanks very much,' Steiner said. 'Just what I needed.'

*

It was cold on the beach and the tide was about two-thirds of the way in. Devlin walked up and down restlessly to keep warm, holding the receiver in his right hand, the channel open. It was almost ten to twelve and Joanna Grey, who had been sheltering from the light rain in the trees, came towards him.

'They must be close now.'

As if in direct answer, the S-phone crackled and Peter Gericke said with astonishing clarity, 'This is Eagle, are you receiving me, Wanderer?'

Joanna Grey grabbed Devlin's arm. He shook her off and spoke into the S-phone. 'Loud and clear.'

'Please report conditions over nest.'

'Visibility poor,' Devlin said. 'One hundred to one hundred and fifty yards, wind freshening.'

'Thank you, Wanderer. Estimated time of arrival, six minutes.'

Devlin shoved the S-phone into Joanna Grey's hand. 'Hang on to that while I lay out the markers.'

Inside his rucksack he had a dozen cycle lamps. He hurried along the beach, putting them down at intervals of fifteen yards in a line following the direction of the wind, switching each one on. Then he turned and went back in a parallel line at a distance of twenty yards.

When he rejoined Joanna Grey he was slightly breathless. He took out a large and powerful spotlight and ran a hand over his forehead to wipe sweat from his eyes.

'Oh, this damn fog,' she said. 'They'll never see us. I know they won't.'

It was the first time he'd seen her crack in any way and he put a hand on her arm. 'Be still, girl.'

Faintly, in the distance, there was the rumble of engines.

*

The Dakota was down to a thousand feet and descending through intermittent fog. Gericke said over his shoulder. 'One pass, that's all I'll get, so make it good.'

'We will,' Steiner told him.

'Luck, Herr Oberst. I've got a bottle of Dom Perignon back there at Landsvoort on ice, remember. We'll drink it together, Sunday morning.'

Steiner clapped him on the shoulder and went out. He nodded to Ritter who gave the order. Everyone stood and clipped his static line to the anchor cable. Brandt slid back the exit door and as fog and cold air billowed in, Steiner moved down the line checking each man personally.

Gericke went in very low, so low that Bohmler could see the white of waves breaking in the gloom. Ahead was only fog and more darkness. 'Come on!' Bohmler whispered, hammering his clenched fist on his knee, 'Come on, damn you!'

As if some unseen power had decided to take a hand, a sudden gust of wind tore a hole in the grey curtain and revealed Devlin's parallel line of cycle lamps, clear in the night, a little to starboard.

Gericke nodded. Bohmler pressed the switch and the red light in the cabin flashed above Steiner's head. 'Ready!' he cried.

Gericke banked to starboard, throttled back until his airspeed indicator stood at a hundred and made his pass along the beach at three hundred and fifty feet. The green light flashed, Ritter Neumann jumped into darkness, Brandt followed, the rest of the men tumbled after them. Steiner could feel the wind on his face, smell the salt tang of the sea and waited for Preston to falter. The Englishman stepped into space without a second's hesitation. It was a good omen. Steiner clipped on to the anchor line and went after him.

Bohmler, peering out through the open door of the cockpit tapped Gericke on the arm. 'All gone, Peter. I'll go and close the door.'

Gericke nodded and swung out towards the sea again. It was no more than five minutes later that the S-phone receiver crackled and Devlin said clearly. 'All fledglings safe and secure in the nest.'

Gericke reached for the mike. 'Thank you, Wanderer. Good luck.'

He said to Bohmler, 'Pass that on to Landsvoort at once. Radl must have been walking on hot bricks for the past hour.'

*

In his office at Prinz Albrechtstrasse, Himmler worked alone in the light of the desk lamp. The fire was low, the room rather cold, but he seemed oblivious of both those facts and wrote on steadily. There was a discreet knock at the door and Rossman entered.

Himmler looked up. 'What is it?'

'We've just heard from Radl at Landsvoort, Herr Reichsführer. The Eagle has landed.'

Himmler's face showed no emotion whatsoever. 'Thank you, Rossman,' he said. 'Keep me informed.'

'Yes, Herr Reichsführer.'

Rossman withdrew and Himmler returned to his work, the only sound in the room the steady scratching of his pen.

*

Devlin, Steiner and Joanna Grey stood together at the table examining a large-scale map of the area. 'See here, behind St Mary's,' Devlin was saying, 'Old Woman's Meadow. It belongs to the church and the barn with it which is empty at the moment.'

'You move in there tomorrow,' Joanna Grey said. 'See Father Vereker and tell him you're on exercises and wish to spend the night in the barn.'

'And you're certain he'll agree?' Steiner said.

Joanna Grey nodded. 'No question of it. That sort of thing happens all the time. Soldiers appear either on exercises or forced marches, disappear again. No one ever really knows who they are. Nine months ago we had a Czechoslovakian unit through here and even their officers could only speak a few words of English.'

'Another thing, Vereker was a paratrooper padre in Tunisia,' Devlin added, 'so he'll be leaning over backwards to assist when he sees those red berets.'

'There's an even stronger point in our favour where Vereker's concerned,' Joanna Grey said. 'He knows the Prime Minister is spending the weekend at Studley Grange which is going to work on our behalf very nicely. Sir Henry let it slip the other night at my house when he'd been drinking a little bit too much. Of course Vereker was sworn to secrecy. Can't even tell his own sister until after the great man's gone.'

'And how will this help us?' Steiner asked.

'It's simple,' Devlin said. 'You tell Vereker you're here for the weekend on some exercise or other and ordinarily he would accept that at face value. But this time, remember, he knows that Churchill is visiting the area incognito, so what interpretation does he put on the presence of a crack outfit like the SAS?'

'Of course,' Steiner said. 'Special security.'

'Exactly.' Joanna Grey nodded. 'Another point in our favour. Sir Henry is giving a small dinner party for the Prime Minister tomorrow night.' She smiled and corrected herself. 'Sorry, I mean tonight. Seven-thirty for eight and I'm invited. I'll go only to make my excuses. Say that I've had a call to turn out on night duty for the WVS emergency service. It's happened before, so Sir Henry and Lady Willoughby will accept it completely. It means, of course, that if we make contact in the vicinity of the Grange, I'll be able to give you a very exact description of the immediate situation there.'

'Excellent,' Steiner said. 'The whole thing seems more plausible by the minute.'

Joanna Grey said, 'I must go.'

Devlin brought her coat and Steiner took it from him and held it open for her courteously. 'Is there no danger for you in driving round the countryside alone at this hour of the morning?'

'Good heavens no.' She smiled. 'I'm a member of the WVS motor pool. That's why I'm allowed the privilege of running a car at all, but it means that I'm required to provide an emergency service in the village and surrounding area. I often have to turn out in the early hours to take people to hospital. My neighbours are perfectly used to it.'

The door opened and Ritter Neumann entered. He was wearing a camouflaged jump jacket and trousers and there was an SAS winged dagger badge in his red beret.

'Everything all right out there?' Steiner asked.

Ritter nodded. 'Everyone bedded down snugly for the night. Only one grumble. No cigarettes.'

'Of course. I knew there was something I'd forgotten. I left them in the car.' Joanna Grey hurried out.

She was back in a few moments and put two cartons of Players on the table, five hundred in each in packets of twenty.

'Holy Mother,' Devlin said in awe. 'Did you ever see the like? They're like gold those things. Where did they come from?'

'WVS stores. You see, now I've added theft to my accomplishments.' She smiled. 'And now, gentlemen, I must leave you. We'll meet again, by accident, of course, tomorrow when you are in the village.'

Steiner and Ritter Neumann saluted and Devlin took her out to her car. When he returned, the two Germans had opened one of the cartons and were smoking by the fire.

'I'll have a couple of packets of these myself,' Devlin said.

Steiner gave him a light. 'Mrs Grey is a remarkable woman. Who did you leave in charge out there, Ritter? Preston or Brandt?'

'I know who thinks he is.'

There was a light tap on the door and Preston entered. The camouflaged jump jacket, the holstered revolver at his waist, the red beret slanted at just the right angle towards the left eye, made him seem more handsome than ever.

'Oh, yes,' Devlin said. 'I like it. Very dashing. And how are you, me old son? Happy to be treading your native soil again, I dare say?'

The expression on Preston's face suggested that Devlin reminded him of something that needed scraping off his shoe. 'I didn't find you particularly entertaining in Berlin, Devlin. Even less so now. I'd be pleased if you would transfer your attentions elsewhere.'

'God save us,' Devlin said, amazed. 'Who in the hell does the lad think he's playing now?'

Preston said to Steiner, 'Any further orders, sir?'

Steiner picked up the two cartons of cigarettes and handed them to him. 'I'd be obliged if you'd give these out to the men,' he said gravely.

'They'll love you for that,' Devlin put in.

Preston ignored him, put the cartons under his left arm and saluted smartly. 'Very well, sir.'

*

In the Dakota, the atmosphere was positively euphoric. The return trip had passed completely without incident. They were thirty miles out from the Dutch coast and Bohmler opened the Thermos and passed Gericke another cup of coffee. 'Home and dry,' he said.

Gericke nodded cheerfully. Then the smile vanished abruptly. Over his headphones he heard a familiar voice. Hans Berger, the controller at his old unit, NJG7.

Bohmler touched his shoulder. 'That's Berger, isn't it?'

'Who else?' Gericke said. 'You've listened to him often enough.'

'Steer o-eight-three degrees.' Berger's voice crackled through the static.

'Sounds as if he's leading a night fighter in for the kill,' Bohmler said. 'On our heading.'

'Target five kilometres.'

Suddenly Berger's voice seemed like the hammer on the last nail in a coffin, crisp, clear, final. Gericke's stomach knotted in a cramp that was almost sexual in its intensity. And he was not afraid. It was as if after years of looking for Death, he was now gazing upon his face with a kind of yearning.

Bohmler grabbed his arm convulsively. 'It's us, Peter!' he screamed. 'We're the target!'

The Dakota rocked violently from side to side as cannon shell punched through the floor of the cockpit, tearing the instrument panel apart, shattering the windscreen. Shrapnel ripped into Gericke's right thigh and a heavy blow shattered his left arm. Another part of his brain told him exactly what was happening. *Schraege Musik*, delivered from below by one of his own comrades – only this time he was on the receiving end.

He wrestled with the control column, heaving it back with all his strength as the Dakota started to go down. Bohmler was struggling to rise to his feet, blood on his face.

'Get out!' Gericke shouted above the roaring of the wind through the shattered windscreen. 'I can't hold her for long.'

Bohmler was on his feet now and trying to speak. Gericke lashed out wildly with his left arm, catching him across the face. The pain was excruciating and he screamed again, 'Get out! That's an order.'

Bohmler turned and moved back along the Dakota to the exit. The plane was in a hell of a state, great holes ripped in the body, pieces of fuselage rattling in the turbulence. He could smell smoke and burning oil. Panic gave him new strength, as he wrestled with the release handles on the hatch.

'Dear God, don't let me burn,' he thought. 'Anything but that.' Then the hatch eased back and he poised for a moment and tumbled into the night.

The Dakota corkscrewed and the port wing lifted. Bohmler somersaulted, his head caught the tailplane a violent blow even as his right hand fastened convulsively on the metal ring. He pulled his ripcord in the very moment of dying. The parachute opened like a strange, pale flower and carried him gently down into darkness.

The Dakota flew on, descending now, the port engine on fire, flames spreading along the wing, reaching for the main body of the plane. Gericke sat at the controls, still fighting to hold her, unaware that his left arm was broken in two places.

There was blood in his eyes. He laughed weakly as he strained to peer through the smoke. *What a way to go*. No visit to Karinhall now, no Knight's Cross. His father would be disappointed about that. Though they'd simply award the damn thing posthumously.

Suddenly, the smoke cleared and he could see the sea through intermittent fog. The Dutch coast couldn't be far away. There were ships down there, at least two. A line of tracer arched up towards him. Some bloody E-boat showing it had teeth. It was really very funny.

He tried to move in his seat and found that his left foot was trapped by a piece of twisted fuselage. Not that it mattered, for by now he was too far down to jump. He was only three hundred feet above the sea, aware of the E-boat to starboard racing him like a greyhound, firing with everything it had got, cannon shells ripping into the Dakota.

'Bastards!' Gericke shouted. 'Stupid bastards!' He laughed weakly again and said softly, as if Bohmler was still there on his left. 'Who in the hell am I supposed to be fighting, anyway?'

Quite suddenly, the smoke was torn away in a violent cross wind and he saw the sea no more than a hundred feet below and coming up to meet him fast.

At that moment he became a great pilot for the only time in his life when it really mattered. Every instinct for survival surged up to give him new strength. He pulled on the column and in spite of the agony of his left arm throttled back and dropped what was left of his flaps.

The Dakota almost stalled, the tail started to fall. He gave a final burst of power to straighten her up as she dropped in to the waves and pulled hard on the column again. She bounced three times, skimming the water like a gigantic surfboard and came to a halt, the burning engine hissing angrily as a wave slopped across it.

Gericke sat there for a moment. Everything wrong, nothing by the book and yet he had done it and against every conceivable odds. There was water around his ankles. He tried to get up, but his left foot was securely held. He pulled the fire axe on his right from its holding clip and smashed at the crumpled fuselage, and his foot, breaking the ankle in the process. By then he was beyond reason.

It came as no surprise to find himself standing, the foot free. He got the hatch open – no trouble at all, and fell out into the water, bumping against the wing clumsily, pulling at the quick release ring of his life-jacket. It inflated satisfactorily and he kicked out at the wing, pushing himself away as the Dakota started to go under.

When the E-boat arrived behind him he didn't even bother to turn, but floated there watching the Dakota slide under the surface.

'You did all right, old girl. All right,' he said.

A rope splashed into the water beside him and someone called in English with a heavy German accent. 'Catch hold, *Tommi,* and we'll haul you in. You're safe now.'

Gericke turned and looked up at the young German naval lieutenant and half a dozen sailors who leaned over the rail above him.

'Safe, is it?' he demanded in German. 'You stupid bastards – I'm on your side.'

15

It was just after ten on Saturday morning when Molly rode down through the fields towards Hobs End. The heavy rain of the previous night had slackened into a light drizzle, but the marsh itself was still blanketed in fog.

She'd risen early and worked hard all morning, had fed the livestock and seen to the milking herself, for Laker Armsby had a grave to dig. Her decision to ride down to the marsh had been a sudden impulse for, in spite of the fact that she had promised Devlin to wait until he called for her, she was terrified that something might happen to him. Conviction of those involved in black market activities usually meant a heavy prison sentence.

She took the horse down into the marsh and came to the cottage from the rear through the reed barrier, letting the animal choose its own way. The muddy water came up to its belly and some slopped inside her wellington boots. She paid no heed and leaned over the horse's neck, peering through the fog. She was sure she could smell woodsmoke. Then the barn and the cottage gradually materialized from the fog, and there *was* smoke ascending from the chimney.

She hesitated, momentarily undecided. Liam was at home, obviously back earlier than he had intended, but if she went in now he would think she had been snooping again. She dug her heels into her horse's flanks and started to turn it away.

*

In the barn the men were getting their equipment ready for the move out. Brandt and Sergeant Altmann were supervising the mounting of a Browning M2 heavy machine-gun on the jeep. Preston stood watching, hands clasped behind his back, giving the impression of being somehow in charge of the whole thing.

Werner Briegel and Klugl had partially opened one of the rear shutters and Werner surveyed what he could of the marsh through his Zeiss fieldglasses. There were birds in the *suaeda* bushes, the reedy dykes. Enough to content even him. Grebes and moorhens, curlews, widgeon, brent geese.

'There's a good one,' he said to Klugl. 'A green sandpiper. Passage migrant, usually in the autumn, but they've been known to winter here.' He continued his trajectory and Molly jumped into view. 'Christ, we're being watched.'

In a moment Brandt and Preston were at his side. Preston said 'I'll get her,' and he turned and ran for the door.

Brandt grabbed at him, too late, and Preston was across the yard and into the reeds in a matter of moments. Molly turned, reining in. Her first thought was that it was Devlin. Preston grabbed for the reins and she looked down at him in astonishment.

'All right, let's have you.'

He reached for her and she tried to back her mount away. 'Here, you leave me be. I haven't done anything.'

He grabbed her right wrist and pulled her out of the saddle, catching her as she fell. 'We'll see about that, shall we?'

She started to struggle and he tightened his grip. He slung her over his shoulder and carried her kicking and shouting through the reeds to the barn.

Devlin had been up to the beach at first light to make certain that the tide had covered all traces of the previous night's activities. He had gone up again with Steiner after breakfast to show him as much of the general pick-up area of the estuary and the Point as could be seen in the fog. They were on their way back, only thirty yards from the cottage when Preston emerged from the marsh with the girl on his shoulder.

'What is it?' Steiner demanded.

'It's Molly Prior, the girl I told you about.'

He started to run, entering the yard as Preston reached the entrance. 'Put her down, damn you!' Devlin shouted.

Preston turned. 'I don't take orders from you.'

But Steiner, hard on Devlin's heel into the yard, took a hand. 'Lieutenant Preston,' he called in a voice like iron. 'You will release the lady now.'

Preston hesitated, then set Molly down reluctantly. She promptly slapped his face. 'And you keep your hands to yourself, you bugger,' she stormed at him.

There was immediate laughter from inside the barn and she turned to see through the open door, a line of grinning faces, the truck beyond, the jeep with the Browning machine-gun mounted.

Devlin arrived and shoved Preston out of the way. 'Are you all right, Molly?'

'Liam,' she said in bewilderment. 'What is it? What's going on?'

But it was Steiner who handled it, smooth as silk. 'Lieutenant Preston,' he said coldly. 'You will apologize to this young lady at once.' Preston hesitated and Steiner really laid it on, 'At once, Lieutenant!'

Preston got his feet together. 'Humble apologies, ma'am. My mistake,' he said with some irony, turned and went inside the barn.

Steiner saluted gravely. 'I can't tell you how sorry I am about this whole unfortunate incident.'

'This is Colonel Carter, Molly,' Devlin explained.

'Of the Polish Independent Parachute Squadron,' Steiner said. 'We're here in this area for tactical field training and I'm afraid Lieutenant Preston gets rather carried away when it comes to a question of security.'

She was more bewildered than ever now, 'But, Liam,' she began.

Devlin took her by the arm. 'Come on now, let's catch that horse and get you back into the saddle.' He pushed her towards the edge of the marsh where her mount nibbled peacefully at the tussocks of grass. 'Now look what you've done,' he scolded her. 'Didn't I tell you to wait for me to call this afternoon? When will you learn to stop sticking your nose into things that don't concern you?'

'But I don't understand.' she said. 'Paratroopers – here, and that truck and the jeep you painted?'

He gripped her arm fiercely. 'Security, Molly, for God's sake. Didn't you get the drift of what the Colonel was saying? Sure and why do you think that lieutenant reacted like he did? They've a very special reason for being here. You'll find out when they've gone, but for the moment it's top secret and you mustn't mention seeing them here to a living soul. As you love me, promise me that.'

She stared up at him and there was a kind of understanding in her eyes. 'I see the way of it now,' she said. 'All these things you've been doing, the trips at night and so on. I thought it was something to do with the black market and you let me think it. But I was wrong. You're still in the army, that's it, isn't it?'

'Yes,' he said with some truth. 'I'm afraid I am.'

Her eyes were shining. 'Oh, Liam, can you ever forgive me thinking you some cheap spiv peddling silk stockings and whisky round the pubs?'

Devlin took a very deep breath, but managed a smile. 'I'll think about it. Now go home like a good girl and wait until I call, no matter how long.'

'I will, Liam. I will.'

She kissed him, one hand behind his neck and swung up into the saddle. Devlin said, 'Mind now, not a word.'

'You can rely on me.' She kicked her heels into the horse's belly and moved away through the reeds.

Devlin went back across the yard walking very fast. Ritter had joined Steiner from the cottage and the Colonel said, 'Is it all right?'

Devlin brushed past him and plunged into the barn. The men were talking together in small groups and Preston was in the act of lighting a cigarette, the match flaring in his cupped hands. He looked up with a slight, mocking smile. 'And we all know what you've been getting up to during the past few weeks. Was it nice, Devlin?'

Devlin got in one beautiful right hand that landed high on Preston's cheekbone and sent the Englishman sprawling over someone's outstretched foot. Then Steiner had him by the arm.

'I'll kill the bastard!' Devlin said.

Steiner got in front of him, both hands on the Irishman's shoulders and Devlin was astonished at the strength. 'Go up to the cottage,' he said calmly. 'I'll handle it.'

Devlin glared at him, that bone-white killing face on him again and then the eyes dulled a little. He turned and went out, breaking into a run across the yard. Preston got to his feet, a hand to his face. There was total silence.

Steiner said, 'There is a man who will kill you if he can, Preston. Be warned. Step out of line once more and if he doesn't, I'll shoot you myself.' He nodded to Ritter, 'Take command!'

When he went into the cottage, Devlin was at the Bushmills. The Irishman turned with a shaky grin. 'God, but I would have killed him. I must be going to pieces.'

'What about the girl?'

'No worries there. She's convinced I'm still in the army and up to my neck in official secrets.' The self-disgust was plain on his face. 'Her lovely boy, that's what she called me. I'm that all right.' He started to pour another whiskey, hesitated then corked the bottle firmly. 'All right,' he said to Steiner. 'What now?'

'We'll move up to the village around noon and go through the motions. My own feeling is that you should keep completely out of the way for the time being. We can meet up again this evening, after dark, when we're closer to making the assault.'

'All right,' Devlin said. 'Joanna Grey is certain to contact you at the village somehow during the afternoon. Tell her I'll be at her place by six-thirty. The E-boat should be available any time between nine and ten. I'll bring the S-phone with me so that you can contact Koenig direct from the scene of operations and fix a pick-up time to fit the circumstances.'

'Fine,' Steiner said and appeared to hesitate. 'There's one thing.'

'What's that?'

'My orders regarding Churchill. They're quite explicit. They'd like to have him alive, but if that isn't possible . . .'

'You've got to put a bullet in him. So what's the problem?'

'I wasn't sure whether there might be one for you?'

'Not in the slightest,' Devlin said. 'This time everyone's a soldier, and takes a soldier's chances. That includes old Churchill.'

*

In London, Rogan was clearing his desk, thoughts of lunch in his mind, when the door opened with no preliminary knock and Grant entered. His face was tense with excitement. 'Just in over the teleprinter, sir.' He slapped the message down in front of Rogan. 'We've got him.'

'Norfolk Constabulary, Norwich,' Rogan said.

'That's where his registration particulars ended up, but he's some distance from there, right up on the North Norfolk coast near Studley Constable and Blakeney. Very isolated sort of place.'

'Do you know the area?' Rogan asked as he read the message.

'Two holidays in Sheringham when I was a nipper, sir.'

'So, he's calling himself Devlin and he's working as a marsh warden for Sir Henry Willoughby, the local squire. He's certainly due for a shock. How far is this place?'

'I'd say about a couple of hundred miles.' Grant shook his head. 'What in the hell could he be up to?'

'We'll find that out soon enough,' Rogan looked up from the report.

'What's the next move, sir? Shall I get the Norfolk Constabulary to pick him up?'

'Are you mad?' Rogan said in amazement. 'You know what these country police are like? Turnip heads. No, we'll handle this one ourselves, Fergus. You and me. It's a while since I've had a weekend in the country. It'll make a nice change.'

'You've got an appointment at the Attorney General's office after lunch,' Grant reminded him. 'Evidence for the Halloran case.'

'I'll be out of there by three o'clock. Three-thirty at the latest. You get a car from the pool and be ready and waiting and we can get straight off.'

'Should I clear it with the Assistant Commissioner, sir?'

Rogan flared in irritation. 'For Christ's sake, Fergus, what's wrong with you? He's in Portsmouth, isn't he? Now get moving.'

Unable to explain his strange reluctance to himself, Grant made an effort. 'Very well, sir.'

He had a hand on the door when Rogan added, 'And Fergus.'

'Yes, sir?'

'Call in at the armoury and draw a couple of Browning Hi-Powers. This character shoots first and asks what you wanted afterwards.'

Grant swallowed hard. 'I'll see to that, sir,' he said, his voice shaking slightly and went out.

Rogan pushed back his chair and went to the window. He flexed the fingers of both hands, full of tension. 'Right you bastard,' he said softly. 'Let's see if you're as good as they say you are.'

*

It was just before noon when Philip Vereker opened the door at the end of the presbytery hall under the back stairs and went down to the cellar. His foot was giving him hell and he had hardly slept at all during the night. That was his own fault. The doctor had offered a plentiful supply of morphine tablets, but Vereker had a morbid fear of becoming addicted.

So he suffered. At least Pamela was coming for the weekend. She'd telephoned early that morning, not only to confirm it, but to tell him that Harry Kane had offered to pick her up from Pang-bourne. At least it saved Vereker a gallon of petrol, and that was something. And he liked Kane. Had done instinctively, which was rare for him. It was nice to see Pamela taking an interest in someone at last.

A large torch hung from a nail at the bottom of the cellar steps. Vereker took it down, then opened an ancient, black, oak cupboard opposite, stepped inside and closed the door. He switched on the torch, felt for a hidden catch and the back of the cupboard swung open to reveal a long, dark tunnel with Norfolk flint walls that glistened with moisture.

It was one of the finest remaining examples of such a structure in the country, a priest's tunnel linking the presbytery with the church, a relic of the days of Roman Catholic persecution under Elizabeth Tudor. The secret of it was handed on from one incumbent to the next. From Vereker's point of view it was simply a very great convenience.

At the end of the tunnel, he mounted a flight of stone steps and paused in surprise, listening carefully. Yes, there could be no mistake. Someone was playing the organ, and very well indeed. He went up the rest of the stairs, opened the door at the top (which was in fact a section of the oak-panelled wall in the sacristy), closed it behind him, opened the other door and moved into the church.

When Vereker went up the aisle he saw to his astonishment that a paratrooper sergeant in camouflaged jump jacket was sitting at the organ, his red beret on the seat beside him. He was playing a Bach choral prelude, one highly appropriate to the season, for it was usually sung to the old Advent hymn *Gottes Sohn ist kommen*.

Hans Altmann was thoroughly enjoying himself. A superb instrument, a lovely church. Then he glanced up and in the organist's mirror saw Vereker at the bottom of the chancel steps. He stopped playing abruptly and turned.

'I'm sorry, Father, but I just couldn't help myself.' He spread his hands. 'One doesn't often get the chance in my – my present occupation.' His English was excellent but with a definite accent.

Vereker said, 'Who are you?'

'Sergeant Emil Janowski, Father.'

'Polish?'

'That's right.' Altmann nodded. 'Came in here looking for you with my C.O. You were not here, of course, so he told me to wait on while he tried the presbytery.'

Vereker said, 'You play very well indeed. Bach needs to be played well, a fact I constantly remember with bitterness each time I take that seat.'

'Ah, you play yourself?' Altmann said.

'Yes,' Vereker said. 'I'm very fond of the piece you were playing.'

Altmann said. 'A favourite of mine.' He started to play, singing at the same time, *'Gott, durch deine Güte, wolst uns arme Leute . . .'*

'But that's a Trinity Sunday hymn,' Vereker said.

'Not in Thuringia, Father.' At that moment the great oak door creaked open and Steiner entered.

He moved down the aisle, a leather swagger stick in one hand, his beret in the other. His boots rang on the flagstones and as he came towards them, the shafts of light, slanted down through the gloom from the clerestory windows above, touched with fire his pale, fair hair.

'Father Vereker?'

'That's right.'

'Howard Carter, in command Independent Polish Parachute Squadron of the Special Air Service Regiment.' He turned to Altmann. 'You been behaving yourself, Janowski?'

'As the Colonel knows, the organ is my principal weakness.'

Steiner grinned. 'Go on, cut along and wait outside with the others.' Altmann departed and Steiner looked up into the nave. 'This is really quite beautiful.'

Vereker looked him over curiously, noting the crown and pip of a lieutenant-colonel on the epaulettes of the jump jacket. 'Yes, we're rather proud of it. SAS. Aren't you and your chaps rather a long way from your usual haunts? I thought the Greek Islands and Yugoslavia were your stamping ground?'

'Yes, well so did I until a month or so ago and then the powers-that-be in their wisdom decided to bring us home for special training, although perhaps home isn't exactly the right word to use, my lads all being Polish.'

'Like Janowski?'

'Not at all. He speaks really very good English. Most of the others manage *Hello* or *Will you come out with me tonight* and that's it. They don't seem to think they need any more.' Steiner smiled. 'Paratroopers can be a pretty arrogant lot, Father. Always the trouble with elite units.'

'I know,' Vereker said. 'I was one myself. Padre to the First Parachute Brigade.'

'Were you, by God?' Steiner said. 'You served in Tunisia then?'

'Yes, at Oudna, which was where I got this.' Vereker tapped his stick against his aluminium foot. 'And now I'm here.'

Steiner reached for his hand and shook it. 'It's a pleasure to meet you. Never expected anything like this.'

Vereker managed one of his rare smiles. 'What can I do for you?'

'Put us up for the night, if you will. You've a barn in the field next door that's had similar use before, I believe.'

'You're on exercise?'

Steiner smiled lightly. 'Yes, you could call it that. I've only got a handful of men with me here. The rest are scattered all over North Norfolk. At a given time tomorrow everyone's supposed to race like hell for a certain map reference, just to see how fast we can come together.'

'So you'll only be here this afternoon and tonight?'

'That's it. We'll try not to be a nuisance, of course. I'll probably give the lads a few tactical exercises round the village and so on, just to keep them occupied. You don't think anyone will mind?'

It worked, exactly as Devlin had predicted. Philip Vereker

smiled. 'Studley Constable has been used for military manoeuvres of one kind or another many times before, Colonel. We'll all be only too happy to help in any way we can.'

*

When Altmann came out of the church he went down the road to where the Bedford stood beside the five-barred gate at the entrance to the track which gave access to the barn in Old Woman's Meadow. The jeep waited beside the lychgate, Klugl at the wheel, Werner Briegel behind the Browning M2.

Werner had his Zeiss fieldglasses trained on the rookery in the beech trees. 'Very interesting,' he said to Klugl. 'I think I'll take a closer look. Are you coming?'

He'd spoken in German as there was no one around and Klugl answered in the same language. 'Do you think we should?'

'What harm?' Werner said.

He got out, went in through the lychgate and Klugl followed him reluctantly. Laker Armsby was digging a grave up at the west end of the church. They threaded their way between the tombstones and Laker, seeing them coming, stopped work and took a half-smoked cigarette from behind his ear.

'Hello, there,' Werner said.

Laker squinted up at them. 'Foreigner, eh? Thought you was British boys in them uniforms.'

'Poles,' Werner told him, 'so you'll have to excuse my friend. He doesn't speak English.' Laker fiddled ostentatiously with the dog-end and the young German took the hint and produced a packet of Players. 'Have one of these.'

'Don't mind if I do.' Laker's eyes sparkled.

'Take another.'

Laker needed no second bidding. He put one cigarette behind his ear and lit the other. 'What's your name, then?'

'Werner.' There was a nasty pause as he realized his mistake and added, 'Kunicki.'

'Oh, aye,' Laker said. 'Always thought Werner was a German name. I took a prisoner once in France in nineteen-fifteen. He was called Werner. Werner Schmidt.'

'My mother was German,' Werner explained.

'Not your fault that,' Laker replied. 'We can't choose who brings us into this world.'

'The rookery,' Werner said. 'Can I ask you how long it has been here?'

Laker looked at him in puzzlement, then stared up at the trees. 'Since I were a lad, that is a fact. Are you interested in birds or something?'

'Certainly,' Werner told him. 'The most fascinating of living creatures. Unlike man, they seldom fight with each other, they know no boundaries, the whole world is their home.'

Laker looked at him as if he was mad and laughed. 'Go on. Who'd want to get worked up over a few tatty old rooks?'

'But are they, my friend?' Werner said. 'Rooks are an abundant and widespread resident of Norfolk, true, but many arrive during the late autumn and winter from as far afield as Russia.'

'Get away,' Laker told him.

'No, it's true. Many rooks in this area before the war were found to have been ringed around Leningrad, for example.'

'You mean some of those old ragbags sitting above my head could have come from there?' Laker demanded.

'Most certainly.'

'Well. I never did.'

'So, my friend, in future you must treat them with the respect they deserve as much-travelled ladies and gentlemen, these rooks from Leningrad,' Werner told him.

There was a shout, 'Kunicki – Moczar,' and they turned and found Steiner and the priest standing outside the church porch. 'We're leaving,' Steiner called and Werner and Klugl doubled back through the cemetery to the jeep.

Steiner and Father Vereker started to walk down the path together. A horn sounded and another jeep came up the hill from the direction of the village and pulled in at the opposite side of the road. Pamela Vereker got out in WAAF uniform. Werner and Klugl eyed her appreciatively and then they stiffened as Harry Kane came round from the other side. He was wearing a side cap, combat jacket and jump boots.

As Steiner and Vereker reached the gate, Pamela joined them and reached up to kiss her brother on the cheek. 'Sorry I'm late, but Harry wanted to see a little more of Norfolk than he's been able to manage so far.'

'And you took him the long way round?' Vereker said affectionately.

'At least I got her here, Father,' Kane said.

'I'd like you both to meet Colonel Carter of the Polish Independent Parachute Squadron,' Vereker said. 'He and his men are on exercise in this district. They'll be using the barn in Old Woman's Meadow. My sister Pamela, Colonel, and Major Harry Kane.'

'Twenty-first Specialist Raiding Force.' Kane shook hands. 'We're up the road at Meltham House. I noticed your boys on the way up, Colonel. Your guys have sure got it made with those crazy red berets. I bet the girls go wild.'

'It's been known to happen,' Steiner said.

'Polish, eh? We've one or two Polish guys in our outfit. Krukowski for instance. He's from Chicago. Born and raised there and yet his Polish is as good as his English. Funny people. Maybe we can have some sort of get together.'

'I'm afraid not,' Steiner said. 'I'm under special orders. Exercises this afternoon and this evening, move on to join up with other units under my command tomorrow. You know how it is.'

'I certainly do,' Kane said, 'being in exactly the same position myself.' He glanced at his watch. 'In fact, if I'm not back at Meltham House within twenty minutes the Colonel will have me shot.'

Steiner said pleasantly, 'Nice to have met you anyway. Miss Vereker. Father.' He got into the jeep and nodded to Klugl who released the brake and moved away.

'Try to remember it's the left-hand side of the road you drive on here, Klugl,' Steiner said calmly.

*

The walls of the barn were three feet thick in places. Tradition had it that during the Middle Ages it had been part of a manor house. It was certainly adequate enough for their purposes. There was the usual smell of old hay and mice. A broken wagon stood in one corner and a large loft with round, glassless windows let in light.

They left the Bedford outside with a man on guard, but took the jeep inside. Steiner stood in it and addressed them all.

'So far, so good. From now on we've got to make the whole thing look as natural as possible. First, get the field stoves out and cook a meal.' He looked at his watch. 'That should take us somewhere up towards three o'clock. Afterwards, some field training. That's what we're here for and that's what people will expect to see. Basic infantry tactics across the fields, by the stream, amongst the houses. Another thing – be careful at all times about speaking German. Keep your voices low. Use hand signals wherever possible during the field exercises. The only spoken orders to be in English naturally. The field telephones are for emergency only and I mean emergency. Oberleutnant Neumann will give section leaders the necessary call signs.'

Brandt said, 'What's the drill if people try to speak to us?'

'Pretend you don't understand, even if you've got good English, I'd rather you did that than get involved.'

Steiner turned to Ritter. I'll leave the field training organization to you. Make sure each group has at least one person who speaks good English. You should be able to manage that.' He turned back to the men. 'Remember it will be dark by six to six-thirty. We have only to look busy until then.'

He jumped down and went outside. He walked down the track and leaned on the gate. Joanna Grey was toiling up the hill on her bicycle, a large bunch of flowers in the basket which hung from her handlebars, Patch running along behind.

'Good afternoon, ma'am.' Steiner saluted.

She dismounted and came forward, pushing the machine. 'How's everything progressing?'

'Fine.'

She held out her hand as if introducing herself formally. At a distance it must have looked very natural. 'And Philip Vereker?'

'Couldn't be more helpful. Devlin was right. I think he's decided we're here to keep an eye on the great man.'

'What happens now?'

'You'll see us playing soldiers round the village. Devlin said he'll be up to see you at six-thirty.'

'Good.' She held out her hand again. 'I'll see you later.'

Steiner saluted, turned and went back to the barn and Joanna remounted and continued up the hill to the church. Vereker was standing in the porch waiting for her and she leaned her cycle against the wall and went towards him with the flowers.

'They're nice,' he said. 'Where on earth did you get them?'

'Oh, a friend in Holt. Iris. Raised under glass, of course. Dreadfully unpatriotic. I suppose she should have put the time in on potatoes or cabbages.'

'Nonsense, man does not live by bread alone.' Strange how pompous he could sound. 'Did you see Sir Henry before he left?'

'Yes, he called in on his way. Full uniform, too. He really looked very splendid.'

'And he'll be back with the great man himself before night-fall,' Vereker said. 'A brief line in some biography of him one of these days. *Spent the night at Studley Grange.* The villagers don't know a thing about it and yet a little piece of history is being made here.'

'Yes, I suppose you're right if you look at it that way.' She smiled beautifully. 'Now, shall we arrange these flowers on the altar.'

He opened the door for her and they went inside.

16

At Landsvoort the fog had cleared, but a light sea mist kept
visibility down to about a hundred yards. On the E-boat, the crew
were making ready to cast off under Muller's supervision. Koenig
walked up and down the sand pier in the light rain, smoking. In his
sea boots, old reefer coat and salt-stained cap he looked anything
but a naval officer.

'We're ready when you are, Herr Leutnant,' Muller called.

'We'll have to wait,' Koenig replied. 'I must know about
Hauptmann Gericke before we go.'

At that moment the field car came down the track between the
sand dunes and braked to a halt at the shore end of the pier.
Sergeant Witt was at the wheel, Radl in the passenger seat. The
colonel got out and Koenig went to meet him.

'How is he?'

'I've had him moved to a private ward in the best hospital in
Amsterdam. The finest surgeon in the Luftwaffe, a real expert on
aircrew crash injuries, is flying in from Paris. He'll be with us by
this evening.'

'Yes, but how is he?' Koening demanded.

'All right,' Radl said wearily. 'If you want the facts. His right
thigh is fractured, an ankle reduced to matchwood and his left arm
appears to be in pieces.'

'Will he survive?'

'They seem to think so, but he'll never fly again.'

'My God,' Koenig said. 'And flying is his whole life.'

Radl tried to put a good face on it. 'Yes, a great shame.
Naturally, I'll see that the full facts of his remarkable flight are
brought to the attention of Reichsmarschall Goering. With any
luck Gericke should be awarded the Oak Leaves to his Knight's
Cross.'

'That's good,' Koenig said. 'Marvellous. That should really set
him up for life.'

'I'm sorry, Paul,' Radl said quietly. 'Truly I am, but in this war there are no victors. Only victims. We are all victims.' He held out his hand. 'Good luck.'

'Herr Oberst.' Koenig saluted navy-style, turned and vaulted over the rail of the E-boat. He went straight into the wheelhouse and Muller supervised casting-off.

Radl stood for a long time watching it go and only when it had disappeared from sight into the mist did he return to the field car. 'I'll walk back,' he told Witt.

The field car moved off and he stood looking out to sea filled with an indescribable feeling of bitterness. Someone always suffered — always. His hand ached, the eye socket burned. 'God, how I wish it was all over,' he said to himself softly and he turned and walked away.

*

In London, as Big Ben struck three, Rogan came out of the Royal Courts of Justice and hurried along the pavement to where Fergus Grant waited at the wheel of a Humber saloon. In spite of the heavy rain the Chief Inspector was in high good humour as he opened the door.

'Everything go off all right, sir?' Fergus asked him.

Rogan grinned smugly. 'If friend Halloran draws less than ten years I'm a monkey's uncle. Did you get them?'

'Glove compartment, sir.'

Rogan opened it and found a Browning Hi-Power automatic. He checked the clip, rammed it back into the butt. Strange how good it felt in his hand. How right. He hefted it for a moment, then slipped it into his inside breast pocket.

'All right, Fergus, now for friend Devlin.'

*

At the same moment Molly was approaching St Mary and All the Saints on horseback by way of the field paths. Because of the light drizzle she wore her old trenchcoat and a scarf around her hair and carried a rucksack on her back covered with a piece of sacking.

She tethered her horse under the trees at the back of the presbytery and went through the back gate into the graveyard. As she went round to the porch, a shouted command drifted up the hill and she paused and looked down towards the village. The paratroops were advancing in skirmishing order towards the old mill by the stream, their red berets very clear against the green of the meadow. She could see Father Vereker, George Wilde's boy, Graham, and little Susan Turner standing on the footbridge above the weir watching. There was another shouted command and the paratroopers flung themselves down.

When she went inside the church she found Pamela Vereker on her knees at the altar polishing the brass ralls, 'Hello, Molly,' she said. 'Come to help?'

'Well, it is my mum's weekend for the altar,' Molly said, slipping her arms out of the rucksack, 'only she has a bad cold and thought she'd spend the day in bed.'

Another shouted order echoed faintly from the village. 'Are they still at it out there?' Pamela asked. 'Wouldn't you think there was enough war to get on with and still they have to play their stupid games. Is my brother down there?'

'He was when I came in.'

A shadow crossed Pamela Vereker's face, 'I wonder about that sometimes. Wonder if he somehow resents being out of it all now.' She shook her head. 'Men are strange creatures.'

*

There were no obvious signs of life in the village except for smoke here and there from a chimney. For most people it was a working day. Ritter Neumann had split the assault group into three sections of five, all linked to each other by field telephone. He and Harvey Preston were deployed amongst the cottages with one section each. Preston was rather enjoying himself. He crouched by the wall at the side of the Studley Arms, revolver in hand and gave his section a hand signal to move forward. George Wilde leaned on the wall watching and his wife, Betty, appeared in the doorway, wiping her hands on her apron.

'Wish you was back in action then?'

Wilde shrugged. 'Maybe.'

'Men,' she said in disgust. 'I'll never understand you.'

The group in the meadow consisted of Brandt, Sergeant Sturm, Corporal Becker and Privates Jansen and Hagl. They were deployed opposite the old mill. It had not been in use for thirty years or more and there were holes in the roof where slates were missing.

Usually the massive waterwheel stood still, but during the night the rushing water of the stream, flooded by many days of heavy rain, had exerted such pressure that the locking bar, already eaten away by rust, had snapped. Now the wheel was moving round again with an unearthly creaking and groaning, churning the water into foam.

Steiner, who had been sitting in the jeep examining the wheel with interest, turned to watch Brandt correcting young Jansen's technique in the prone firing position. Higher up the stream above the weir, Father Vereker and the two children also watched. George Wilde's son, Graham, was eleven and considerably excited by the activities of the paratroops.

'What are they doing now, Father?' he asked Vereker.

'Well, Graham, it's a question of having the elbows in the right position,' Vereker said. 'Otherwise he won't be able to get a steady aim. See, now he's demonstrating the leopard crawl.'

Susan Turner was bored with the entire proceedings and, hardly surprising in a five-year-old girl, was more interested in the wooden doll her grandfather had made for her the evening before. She was a pretty, fair-haired child, an evacuee from Birmingham. Her grandparents, Ted and Agnes Turner, ran the village Post Office and general store and small telephone exchange. She'd been with them for a year now.

She crossed to the other side of the footbridge, ducked under the rail and squatted at the edge. The floodwaters rushed past not more than two feet below, brown and foam-flecked. She dangled the doll by one of its movable arms just above the surface, chuckling as water splashed across its feet. She leaned still lower, clutching the rail above her head, dipping the doll's legs right into the water now. The rail snapped and with a scream she went head first into the water.

Vereker and the boy turned in time to see her disappear. Before the priest could move she was swept under the bridge. Graham, more by instinct than courage, jumped in after her. At that point the water was usually no more than a couple of feet deep. During the summer he had fished there for tadpoles. But now all was changed. He grabbed the tail of Susan's coat and hung on tight. His feet were scrabbling for the bottom, but there was no bottom and he cried out in fear as the current swept them towards the weir above the bridge.

Vereker, frozen with horror, had not uttered a sound, but Graham's cry alerted Steiner and his men instantly. As they all turned to see what the trouble was the two children went over the edge of the weir and slid down the concrete apron into the mill pool.

Sergeant Sturm was on his feet and running for the edge of the pool, tearing off his equipment. He had no time to unzip his jump jacket. The children, with Graham still hanging on to Susan, were being carried relentlessly by the current into the path of the water wheel.

Sturm plunged in without hesitation and struck out towards them. He grabbed Graham by the arm. Brandt plunged waist deep into the water behind him. As Sturm pulled Graham in, the boy's head dipped momentarily under the water. He panicked, kicking and struggling, releasing his grip on the girl. Sturm swung him round in an arc so that Brandt could catch hold of him, then plunged on after Susan.

She had been saved by the enormous force of the current, which had kept her on the surface. She was screaming as Sturm's hand fastened on her coat. He pulled her into his arms and tried to stand. But he went right under and when he surfaced again, he felt himself being drawn inexorably into the path of the water wheel.

He was aware of a cry above the roaring, turned and saw that his comrades on the bank had the boy, that Brandt was back in the water again and pushing towards him. Walter Sturm summoned up everything he had, every ounce of strength and hurled the child bodily through the air to the safety of Brandt's arms. A moment later and the current took him in a giant hand and swept him in. The wheel thundered down and he went under.

*

George Wilde had gone into the pub to get a bucket of water to swill the front step. He came out again in time to see the children go over the weir. He dropped the bucket, called out to his wife and ran across the road to the bridge. Harvey Preston and his section, who had also witnessed the mishap, followed.

Except for being soaked to the skin, Graham Wilde seemed none the worse for his experience. The same held true for Susan, though she was crying hysterically. Brandt thrust the child into George Wilde's arms and ran along the bank to join Steiner and the others, searching beyond the water wheel for Sturm. Suddenly he floated to the surface in calm water. Brandt plunged in and reached for him.

Except for a slight bruise on the forehead there wasn't a mark on him, but his eyes were closed, his lips slightly parted. Brandt waded out of the water holding him in his arms, and everyone seemed to arrive at once. Vereker, then Harvey Preston and his men and, finally, Mrs Wilde, who took Susan from her husband.

'Is he all right?' Vereker demanded.

Brandt ripped the front of the jump jacket open and got a hand inside the blouse, feeling for the heart. He touched the small bruise on the forehead and the skin was immediately suffused with blood, the flesh and bone soft as jelly. In spite of this Brandt remained sufficiently in control to remember where he was.

He looked up at Steiner and said in fair English, 'I'm sorry, sir, but his skull is crushed.'

For a moment, the only sound was the mill wheel's eerie creaking. It was Graham Wilde who broke the silence, saying loudly, 'Look at his uniform, Dad. Is that what the Poles wear?'

Brandt, in his haste, had committed an irretrievable blunder. Beneath the open jump jacket was revealed Paul Sturm's *Fliegerbluse*, with the Luftwaffe eagle badge on the right breast. The blouse had been pierced to take the red, white and black ribbon of the Iron Cross 2nd Class. On the left breast was the Iron Cross Ist Class, the ribbon for the Winter War, the paratrooper's qualification badge, the silver wound badge. Under the jump jacket, full uniform, as Himmler himself had insisted.

'Oh, my God,' Vereker whispered.

The Germans closed round in a circle. Steiner said in German to Brandt, 'Put Sturm in the jeep.' He snapped his fingers at Jansen who was carrying one of the field telephones. 'Let me have that. Eagle One to Eagle Two,' he called. 'Come in please.'

Ritter Neumann and his section were at work out of sight on the far side of the cottage. He replied almost instantly. 'Eagle Two, I hear you.'

'The Eagle is blown,' Steiner said. 'Meet me at the bridge now.'

He passed the phone back to Jansen. Betty Wilde said in bewilderment, 'What is it, George? I don't understand?'

'They're Germans,' Wilde said. 'I've seen uniforms like that before, when I was in Norway.'

'Yes,' Steiner said. 'Some of us were there.'

'But what do you want?' Wilde said. 'It doesn't make sense. There's nothing for you here.'

'You poor stupid bastard,' Preston jeered. 'Don't you know who's staying at Studley Grange tonight? Mr Lord-God-Almighty-Winston-bloody-Churchill himself.'

Wilde stared at him in astonishment and then he actually laughed. 'You must be bloody cracked. I never heard such nonsense in all my life. Isn't that so, Father?'

'I'm afraid he's right.' Vereker got the words out slowly and with enormous difficulty. 'Very well, Colonel. Do you mind telling me what happens now? To start with, these children must be chilled to the bone.'

Steiner turned to Betty Wilde. 'Mrs Wilde, you may take your son and little girl home now. When the boy has changed, take Susan in to her grandparents. They run the Post Office and general store, is this not so?'

She glanced wildly at her husband, still bemused by the whole thing. 'Yes, that's right.'

Steiner said to Preston, 'There are only six telephones in the general village area. All calls come through a switchboard at the Post Office and are connected by either Mr Turner or his wife.'

'Shall we rip it out?' Preston suggested.

'No, that might attract unnecessary attention. Someone might send a repair man. When the child is suitably changed, send her and her grandmother up to the church. Keep Turner himself on the switchboard. If there are any incoming calls, he's to say that whoever they want isn't in or something like that. It should do for the moment. Now get to it and try not to be melodramatic about it.'

Preston turned to Betty Wilde. Susan had stopped crying and he held out his hands and said with a dazzling smile. 'Come on, beautiful, I'll give you a piggyback.' The child responded instinctively with a delighted smile. 'This way, Mrs Wilde, if you'd be so kind.'

Betty Wilde, after a desperate glance at her husband, went after him, holding her son by the hand. The rest of Preston's section, Dinter, Meyer, Riedel and Berg followed a yard or two behind.

Wilde said hoarsely, 'If anything happens to my wife . . .'

Steiner ignored him. He said to Brandt, 'Take Father Vereker and Mr Wilde up to the church and hold them there. Becker and Jansen can go with you. Hagl, you come with me.'

Ritter Neumann and his section had arrived at the bridge. Preston had just reached them and was obviously telling the Oberleutnant what had happened.

Philip Vereker said, 'Colonel, I've a good mind to call your bluff. If I walk off now you can't afford to shoot me out of hand. You'll arouse the whole village.'

Steiner turned to face him. 'There are sixteen houses or cottages in Studley Constable, Father. Forty-seven people in all and most of the men aren't even here. They are working on any one of a dozen farms within a radius of five miles from here. Apart from that . . .' He turned to Brandt, 'Give him a demonstration.'

Brandt took Corporal Becker's Mk IIS Sten from him, turned and fired from the hip, spraying the surface of the mill pool. Fountains of water spurted high in the air, but the only sound was the metallic chattering as the bolt reciprocated.

'Remarkable, you must admit,' Steiner said. 'And a British invention. But there's an even surer way, Father. Brandt puts a knife under your ribs in just the right way to kill you instantly and without a sound. He knows how, believe me. He's done it many times. Then we walk you to the jeep between us, set you up in the passenger seat and drive off with you. Is that ruthless enough for you?'

'It will do to be going on with, I fancy,' Vereker said.

'Excellent.' Steiner nodded to Brandt. 'Get going, I'll be up in a few minutes.'

He turned and hurried towards the bridge, walking very fast so that Hagl had to trot to keep up with him. Ritter came to meet them. 'Not so good. What happens now?'

'We take over the village. You know what Preston's orders are?'

'Yes, he told me. What do you want us to do?'

'Send a man up for the truck, then start at one end of the village and work your way through house by house. I don't care how you do it, but I want everybody out and up in that church within fifteen to twenty minutes.'

'And afterwards?'

'A road block at each end of the village. We'll make it look nice and official, but anyone who comes in stays.'

'Shall I tell Mrs Grey?'

'No, leave her for the time being. She needs to stay free to use the radio. I don't want anyone to know she's on our side until it's absolutely necessary. I'll see her myself later.' He grinned. 'A tight one, Ritter.'

'We've known them before, Herr Oberst.'

'Good.' Steiner saluted formally. 'Get to it then.' He turned and started up the hill to the church.

*

In the living room of the Post Office and General Stores Agnes Turner wept as she changed her granddaughter's clothes. Betty Wilde sat beside her, hanging on tightly to Graham. Privates Dinter and Berg stood on either side of the door waiting for them.

'I'm that feared, Betty,' Mrs Turner said. 'I've read such terrible things about them. Murdering and killing. What are they going to do to us?'

In the tiny room behind the Post Office counter that held the switchboard, Ted Turner said in some agitation, 'What's wrong with my missus?'

'Nothing,' Harvey Preston said. 'And there isn't likely to be as long as you do exactly as you're told. If you try shouting a message into the phone when someone rings through. Any tricks at all.' He took the revolver from his webbing holster. 'I won't shoot you – I'll shoot your wife and that's a promise.'

'You swine,' the old man said. 'Call yourself an Englishman?'

'A better one than you, old man.' Harvey struck him across the face with the back of his hand. 'Remember that.'

He sat back in the corner, lit a cigarette and picked up a magazine.

*

Molly and Pamela Vereker had finished at the altar and used up what remained of the reeds and marsh grasses Molly had brought to create a display by the font. Pamela said, 'I know what it needs. Ivy leaves. I'll get some.'

She opened the door, went out through the porch and plucked two or three handfuls of leaves from the vine which climbed the tower at that spot. As she was about to go into the church again, there was a squeal of brakes and she turned to see the jeep draw up. She watched them get out, her brother and Wilde, and at first concluded that the paratroopers had merely given them a lift. Then it occurred to her that the huge sergeant-major was covering her brother and Wilde with the rifle he held braced against his hip. She would have laughed at the absurdity of it had it not been for Becker and Jansen who followed the others through the lychgate carrying Sturm's body.

Pamela retreated through the partly opened door, bumping into Molly. 'What is it?' Molly demanded.

Pamela hushed her. 'I don't know, but something's wrong – very wrong.'

Half-way along the path, George Wilde attempted to make a break for it, but Brandt, who had been expecting such a move, deftly tripped him. He leaned over Wilde, prodding him under the chin with the muzzle of the M1. 'All right, *Tommi,* you're a brave man. I salute you. But try anything like that again and I blow your head off.'

Wilde, helped by Vereker, scrambled to his feet and the party moved on towards the porch. Inside Molly looked at Pamela in consternation. 'What's it mean?'

Pamela hushed her again. 'Quick, in here,' she said and opened the sacristy door. They slipped inside, she closed it and slid home the bolt. A moment later they heard voices clearly.

Vereker said, 'All right, now what?'

'You wait for the Colonel,' Brandt told him. 'On the other hand, I don't see why you shouldn't fill in the time by doing what's right for poor old Sturm. As it happens, he was a Lutheran, but I don't suppose it matters. Catholic or Protestant, German or English. It's all the same to the worms.'

'Bring him to the Lady Chapel,' Vereker said.

The footsteps died away and Molly and Pamela crouched against the door, looked at each other. 'Did he say German?' Molly said. 'That's crazy.'

Footsteps echoed hollowly on the flags of the porch and the outer door creaked open. Pamela put a finger to her lips and they waited.

Steiner paused by the font and looked around him, tapping his swagger stick against his thigh. He hadn't bothered to remove his beret this time. 'Father Vereker,' he called. 'Down here, please.' He moved to the sacristy door and tried the handle. On the other side the two girls eased back in alarm. As Vereker limped down the aisle, Steiner said, 'This seems to be locked. Why? What's in there?'

The door had never been locked to Vereker's knowledge because the key had been lost for years. That could only mean that someone had bolted it from the inside. Then he remembered that he had left Pamela working on the alter when he had gone to watch the paratroopers. The conclusion was obvious.

He said clearly. 'It is the sacristy, Herr Oberst. Church registers, my vestments, things like that. I'm afraid the key is over at the presbytery. Sorry for such inefficiency. I suppose you order things better in Germany?'

'You mean we Germans have a passion for order, Father?' Steiner said. 'True. I, on the other hand, had an American mother although I went to school in London. In fact, lived there for many years. Now, what does that mixture signify?'

'That it is highly unlikely that your name is Carter.'

'Steiner, actually. Kurt Steiner.'

'What of, the SS?'

'It seems to have a rather morbid fascination for you people. Do you imagine all German soldiers serve in Himmler's private army?'

'No, perhaps it is just that they behave as if they do.'

'Like Sergeant Sturm, I suppose.' Vereker could find nothing to say to that. Steiner added, 'For the record, we are not SS. We are Fallschirmjäger. The best in the business, with all due respect to your Red Devils.'

Vereker said, 'So, you intend to assassinate Mr Churchill at Studley Grange tonight?'

'Only if we have to,' Steiner said. 'I'd much prefer to keep him in one piece.'

'And now the planning's gone slightly awry? The best laid schemes and so on . . .'

'Because one of my men sacrificed himself to save the lives of two children of this village, or perhaps you don't wish to know about that? Why should that be, I wonder? Because it destroys this pitiful delusion that all German soldiers are savages whose sole occupation is murder and rape? Or is it something deeper? Do you hate all of us because it was a German bullet that crippled you?'

'Go to hell!' Vereker said.

'The Pope, Father, would not be at all pleased with such a sentiment. To answer your original question. Yes, the plan has gone a little awry, but improvisation is the essence of our kind of soldiering. As a paratrooper yourself, you must know that.'

'For heavens sakes, man, you've had it,' Vereker said. 'No element of surprise.'

'There still will be,' Steiner told him calmly. 'If we hold the entire village incommunicado, so to speak, for the required period.'

Vereker was, for the moment, rendered speechless by the audacity of this suggestion. 'But that is impossible.'

'Not at all. My men are at this very moment rounding up everyone at present in Studley Constable. They'll be up here within the next fifteen or twenty minutes. We control the telephone system, the roads, so that anyone entering will be immediately apprehended.'

'But you'll never get away with it.

'Sir Henry Willoughby left the Grange at eleven this morning to travel to King's Lynn where he was to have lunch with the Prime Minister. They were due to leave in two cars with an escort of four Royal Military Police motor-cyclists at three-thirty.' Steiner looked at his watch. 'Which, give or take a minute or two, is right now. The Prime Minister has expressed a particular desire to pass through Walsingham, by the way, but forgive me, I must be boring you with all this.'

'You seem to be very well informed?'

Oh, I am. So, you see, all we have to do is to hang on until this evening as arranged, and the prize will still be ours. Your people, by the way, have nothing to fear as long as they do as they are told.'

'You won't get away with it,' Vereker said stubbornly.

'Oh, I don't know. It's been done before. Otto Skorzeny got Mussolini out of an apparently impossible situation. Quite a feat of arms as Mr Churchill himself conceded in a speech at Westminster.'

'Or what's left of it after your damned bombs,' Vereker said.

'Berlin isn't looking too good either these days,' Steiner pointed out, 'and if your friend Wilde is interested, tell him that the five-year-old daughter and wife of the man who died to save his son, were killed by RAF bombs four months ago.' Steiner held out his hand. 'I'll have the keys of your car. It might come in useful.'

'I haven't got them with me,' Vereker began.

'Don't waste my time, Father. I'll have my lads strip you if I have to.'

Vereker reluctantly produced his keys and Steiner slipped them into his pocket. 'Right, I have things to do.' He raised his voice. 'Brandt, hold the fort here. I'll send Preston to relieve you, then report to me in the village.'

He went out, and Private Jansen came and stood against the door with his M1. Vereker walked up the aisle slowly, past Brandt and Wilde who was sitting in one of the pews, shoulders hunched. Sturm was lying in front of the altar in the Lady Chapel. The priest stood looking down at him for a moment, then knelt, folded his hands and in a firm, confident voice, began to recite the prayers for the dying.

*

'So now we know,' Pamela Vereker said as the door banged behind Steiner.

'What are we going to do?' Molly said dully.

'Get out of here, that's the first thing.'

'But how?'

Pamela moved to the other side of the room, found the concealed catch and a section of the panelling swung back to reveal the entrance to the priest's tunnel. She picked up the torch her brother had left on the table. Molly was gaping in amazement. 'Come on,' Pamela said impatiently. 'We must get moving.'

Once inside, she closed the door and led the way quickly along the tunnel. They exited through the oak cupboard in the presbytery cellar and went up the stairs to the hall. Pamela put the torch on the table beside the telephone and when she turned, saw that Molly was crying bitterly.

'Molly, what is it?' she said, taking the girl's hands in hers.

'Liam Devlin,' Molly said. 'He's one of them. Must be. They were at his place, you see. I saw them.'

'When was this?'

'Earlier today. He let me think he was still in the army. Some kind of secret job.' Molly pulled her hands free and clenched them into fists. 'He used me. All the time he was using me. God help me, but I hope they hang him.'

'Molly, I'm sorry,' Pamela said. 'Truly I am. If what you say is true then he'll be taken care of. But we've got to get out of here.' She looked down at the telephone. 'No use trying to get through to the police or somebody on that, not if they control the village exchange. And I haven't got the keys of my brother's car.'

'Mrs Grey has a car,' Molly said.

'Of course.' Pamela's eyes glinted with excitement. 'Now if I could only get down to her house.'

'Then what would you do? There isn't a phone for miles.'

'I'd go straight to Meltham House,' Pamela said. 'There are American Rangers there. A crack outfit. They'd show Steiner and his bunch a thing or two. How did you get here?'

'Horseback. He's tied up in the woods behind the presbytery.'

'All right, leave him. We'll take the field path back of Hawks Wood and see if we can get to Mrs Grey's without being seen.'

Molly didn't argue. Pamela tugged her sleeve, they darted across the road into the shelter of Hawks Wood.

The path was centuries old and cut deep into the earth, giving complete concealment. Pamela led the way, running very fast, not stopping until they came out into the trees on the opposite side of the stream from Joanna Grey's cottage. There was a narrow footbridge and the road seemed deserted.

Pamela said, 'All right, let's go. Straight across.'

Molly grabbed her arm. 'Not me, I've changed my mind.'

'But why?'

'You try this way. I'll go back for my horse and try another. Two bites of the apple.'

Pamela nodded. 'That makes sense. All right then, Molly.' She kissed her on the cheek impulsively. 'Only watch it! They mean business, this lot.'

Molly gave her a little push and Pamela darted across the road and disappeared round the corner of the garden wall. Molly turned and started to run back up the track through Hawks Wood. *Oh, Devlin, you bastard, she thought, I hope they crucify you.*

By the time she reached the top, the tears, slow, sad and incredibly painful were oozing from her eyes. She didn't even bother to see if the road was clear, but simply dashed across and followed the line of the garden wall round to the wood at the back. Her horse was waiting patiently where she'd tethered him, cropping the grass. She untied him quickly, scrambled into the saddle and galloped away.

*

When Pamela went into the yard at the rear of the cottage the Morris saloon was standing outside the garage. When she opened the car door the keys were in the ignition. She started to get behind the wheel and an indignant voice called, 'Pamela, what on earth are you doing?'

Joanna Grey was standing at the back door. Pamela ran towards her. 'I'm sorry, Mrs Grey, but something absolutely terrible has happened. This Colonel Carter and his men who are exercising in the village. They're not SAS at all. His name is Steiner and they're German paratroopers here to kidnap the Prime Minister.'

Joanna Grey drew her into the kitchen and closed the door. Patch fawned about her knees. 'Now calm down,' Joanna said. 'This really is a most incredible story. The Prime Minister isn't even here.'

She turned to her coat hanging behind the door and fumbled in the pocket. 'Yes, but he will be this evening,' Pamela said. 'Sir Henry is bringing him back from King's Lynn.'

Joanna turned, a Walther automatic in her hand. 'You have been busy, haven't you?' She reached behind and got the cellar door open. 'Down you go.'

Pamela was thunderstruck. 'Mrs Grey, I don't understand.

'And I don't have time to explain. Let's just say we're on different sides in this affair and leave it at that. Now get down those stairs. I won't hesitate to shoot if I have to.'

Pamela went down, Patch scampering in front of her, and Joanna Grey followed. She switched on a light at the bottom and opened a door opposite. Inside was a dark windowless storeroom filled with junk. 'In you go.'

Patch, circling his mistress, managed to get between her feet. She stumbled against the wall. Pamela gave her a violent push through the doorway. As she fell back, Joanna Grey fired at point-blank range. Pamela was aware of the explosion that half-blinded her, the sudden touch of a white-hot poker against the side of her head, but she managed to slam the door in Joanna Grey's face and ram home the bolt.

The shock of a gunshot wound is so great that it numbs the entire central nervous system for a while. There was a desperate air of unreality to everything as Pamela stumbled upstairs to the kitchen. She leaned on a chest of drawers to stop herself from falling, and looked in the mirror above it. A narrow strip of flesh had been gouged out of the left side of her forehead and bone showed through. There was surprisingly little blood and, when she touched it gently with a fingertip, no pain. *That would come later.*

'I must get to Harry,' she said aloud. 'I must get to Harry.'

Then, like something in a dream, she found herself behind the wheel of the Morris driving out of the yard, as if in slow motion.

*

As he walked down the road Steiner saw her go and made the natural assumption that Joanna Grey was at the wheel. He swore softly, turned and went back to the bridge where he had left the jeep with Werner Briegel manning the machine-gun and Klugl at the wheel. As he arrived, the Bedford came back down the hill from the church. Ritter Neumann standing on the running-board and hanging on to the door. He jumped down.

'Twenty-seven people up at the church now, Herr Oberst,' including the two children. Five men, nineteen women.'

'Ten children at harvest camp,' Steiner said. 'Devlin estimated a present population of forty-seven. If we allow for Turner in the exchange, and Mrs Grey, that leaves eight people who are certain to turn up at some time. Mostly men, I would imagine. Did you find Vereker's sister?'

'No sign of her at the presbytery and when I asked him where she was, he told me to go to hell. Some of the women were more forthcoming. It seems she goes riding on Saturday afternoons when she's at home.'

'You'll have to keep an eye out for her as well, then,' Steiner said.

'Have you seen Mrs Grey?'

'I'm afraid not.' Steiner explained what had happened. 'I made a bad mistake there. I should have allowed you to go and see her when you suggested it. I can only hope she returns soon.'

'Perhaps she's gone to see Devlin?'

'That's a point. Worth checking on. We'll have to let him know what's happening anyway.' He slapped the swagger stick against his palm.

There was a crash of breaking glass and a chair came through the window of Turner's shop. Steiner and Ritter Neumann drew their Brownings and ran across the road.

*

For most of the day Arthur Seymour had been felling the trees of a small plantation on a farm to the east of Studley Constable. He sold the logs to his own benefit in and around the village. Mrs Turner had given him an order only that morning. When he was finished at the plantation, he filled a couple of sacks, put them on his handcart and went down to the village across the field tracks, coming into the yard at the back of the Turners' shop from the rear.

He kicked open the kitchen door without knocking and walked in, a sack of logs on his shoulder – and came face-to-face with Dinter and Berg who were sitting on the edge of the table drinking coffee. If anything, they were more surprised than Seymour.

'Here, what's going on?' he demanded.

Dinter, who had his Sten slung across his chest, moved it on target and Berg picked up his M1. At the same moment Harvey Preston appeared in the door. He stood there, hands on hips, looking Seymour over. 'My God,' he said. 'The original walking ape.'

Something stirred in Seymour's dark mad eyes. 'You watch your mouth, soldier boy.'

'It can talk as well,' Preston said. 'Wonders will never cease. All right, put him with the others.'

He turned to go back into the exchange and Seymour tossed the sack of logs at Dinter and Berg and jumped on him, one arm clamping around Preston's throat, a knee in his back. He snarled like an animal. Berg got to his feet and slammed the butt of his M1 into Seymour's kidneys. The big man cried out in pain, released his hold on Preston and launched himself at Berg with such force that they went through the open door behind into the shop, a display cabinet collapsing beneath them.

Berg lost his rifle but managed to get to his feet and back away. Seymour advanced on him, sweeping the counter clear of the pyramids of tinned goods and packages, growling deep in his throat. Berg picked up the chair Mrs Turner habitually sat on behind the counter. Seymour knocked it aside in mid-flight and it went out through the shop window. Berg drew his bayonet and Seymour crouched.

Preston took a hand then, moving in from behind, Berg's M1 in his hands. He raised it high and drove the butt into the back of Seymour's skull. Seymour cried out and swung round. 'You bloody great ape,' Preston cried. 'We'll have to teach you your manners, won't we?'

He smashed the butt into Seymour's stomach and as the big man started to fold, hit him again in the side of the neck. Seymour fell back, grabbed for support and only succeeded in bringing a shelf and its contents down on top of him as he slid to the floor.

Steiner and Ritter Neumann burst in through the shop doorway at that moment, guns ready. The place was a shambles, cans of various descriptions, sugar, flour, scattered everywhere. Harvey Preston handed Berg his rifle. Dinter appeared in the doorway, swaying slightly, a streak of blood on his forehead.

'Find some rope,' Preston said, 'and tie him up or next time you might not be so lucky.'

Old Mr Turner was hovering in the door of the exchange. There were tears in his eyes as he surveyed the shambles. 'And who's going to pay for that lot.'

'Try sending the bill to Winston Churchill, you never know your luck,' Preston said brutally. 'I'll have a word with him for you if you like. Press your case.'

The old man slumped down in a chair in the small exchange, the picture of misery and Steiner said, 'All right, Preston, I won't need you down here any more. Get on up to the church and take that specimen behind the counter with you. Relieve Brandt. Tell him to report to Oberleutnant Neumann.'

'What about the switchboard?'

'I'll send Altmann in. He speaks good English. Dinter and Berg can keep an eye on things until then.'

Seymour was stirring, pushing himself up on his knees and making the discovery that his hands were lashed behind his back. 'Comfortable, are we?' Preston kicked him in the backside and hauled him to his feet. 'Come on, ape, start putting one foot in front of the other.'

*

At the church, the villagers sat in pews as instructed and awaited their fate, talking to each other in low voices. Most of the women were plainly terrified. Vereker moved amongst them, bringing what comfort he could. Corporal Becker stood guard near the chancel steps, a Sten gun in his hands, Private Jansen at the door. Neither spoke English.

After Brandt had departed, Harvey Preston found a length of rope in the bell room at the bottom of the tower, lashed Seymour's ankles together, then turned him over and dragged him on his face to the Lady Chapel where he dumped him beside Sturm. There was blood on Seymour's cheek where the skin had rubbed away and there were gasps of horror, particularly from the women.

Preston ignored them and kicked Seymour in the ribs. 'I'll cool you down before I'm through, I promise you.'

Vereker limped forward and grabbed him by the shoulder, turning him round. 'Leave that man alone.'

'Man?' Preston laughed in his face. 'That isn't a man, it's a thing.' Vereker reached down to touch Seymour and Preston knocked him away and drew his revolver. 'You just won't do as you're told, will you?'

One of the women chocked back a scream. There was a terrible silence as Preston thumbed back the hammer. A moment in time. Vereker crossed himself and Preston laughed again and lowered the revolver. 'A lot of good that will do you.'

'What kind of man are you?' Vereker demanded. 'What moves you to act like this?'

'What kind of man?' Preston said. 'That's simple. A special breed. The finest fighting men that ever walked the face of the earth. The Waffen SS in which I have the honour to hold the rank of Untersturmführer.'

He walked up the aisle, turned at the chancel steps, unzipped his jump jacket and took it off, revealing the tunic underneath, the collar patches with the three leopards, the eagle on his left arm, the Union Jack shield beneath and the black and silver cuff-title.

It was Laker Armsby sitting beside George Wilde who said, 'Here, he's got a Union Jack on his sleeve.'

Vereker moved forward, a frown on his face and Preston held out his arm. 'Yes, he's right. Now read the cuff-title.'

'Britisches Freikorps,' Vereker said aloud and glanced up sharply. 'British Free Corps?'

'Yes, you damned fool. Don't you realize? Don't any of you realize? I'm English, like you, only I'm on the right side. The only side.'

Susan Turner started to cry. George Wilde came out of his pew, walked up the aisle slowly and deliberately and stood looking up at Preston. 'The Jerries must be damned hard up, because the only place they could have found you was under a stone.'

Preston shot him at point-blank range. As Wilde fell back across the steps below the roodscreen, blood on his face, there was pandemonium. Women were screaming hysterically. Preston fired another shot into the air. 'Stay where you are!'

There was the kind of frozen silence produced by complete panic. Vereker got down on one knee awkwardly and examined Wilde as he groaned and moved his head from side to side. Betty Wilde ran up the aisle, followed by her son, and dropped to her knees beside her husband.

'He'll be all right, Betty, his luck is good,' Vereker told her. 'See, the bullet has just gouged his cheek.'

At that moment the door at the other end of the church crashed open and Ritter Neumann rushed in, his Browning in his hand. He ran up the centre aisle and paused. 'What's going on here?'

'Ask your colleague from the SS,' Vereker suggested.

Ritter glanced at Preston, then dropped to one knee and examined Wilde. 'Don't you touch him, you – you bloody German swine,' Betty said.

Ritter took a field dressing from one of his breast pockets and gave it to her. 'Bandage him with that. He'll be fine.' He stood up and said to Vereker, 'We are Fallschirmjäger, Father, and proud of our name. This gentleman, on the other hand . . .' He turned in an almost casual gesture and struck Preston a heavy blow across the face with the Browning. The Englishman cried out and crumpled to the floor.

The door opened again and Joanna Grey ran in. 'Herr Oberleutnant,' she called in German. 'Where's Colonel Steiner? I must speak with him.'

Her face was streaked with dirt and her hands were filthy. Neumann went down the aisle to meet her. 'He isn't here. He's gone to see Devlin. Why?'

Vereker said, 'Joanna?' There was a question in his voice, but more than that, a kind of dread as if he was afraid to know for certain what he feared.

She ignored him and said to Ritter, 'I don't know what's been going on here, but about forty-five minutes ago, Pamela Vereker turned up at the cottage and she knew everything. Wanted my car to go to Meltham House to get the Rangers.'

'What happened?'

'I tried to stop her and ended up locked in the cellar. I only managed to break out five minutes ago. What are we going to do?'

Vereker put a hand on her arm and pulled her round to face him. 'Are you saying you're one of them?'

'Yes,' she said impatiently. 'Now will you leave me alone? I've work to do.' She turned back to Ritter.

'But why?' Vereker said. 'I don't understand. You're British . . .'

She rounded on him then. 'British?' she shouted. 'Boer, damn you! Boer! How could I be British? You insult me with that name.'

There was a genuine horror on virtually every face there. The agony in Philip Vereker's eyes was plain for all to see. 'Oh, my God,' he whispered.

Ritter took her by the arm. 'Back to your house fast. Contact Landsvoort on the radio. Let Radl know the position. Keep the channel open.'

She nodded and hurried out. Ritter stood there, for the first time in his military career totally at a loss. *What in the hell are we going to do?* he thought. But there was no answer. Couldn't be without Steiner.

He said to Corporal Becker. 'You and Jansen stay here,' and he hurried outside.

There was silence in the church. Vereker walked up the aisle, feeling inexpressibly weary. He mounted the chancel steps and turned to face them. 'At times like these there is little left, but prayer,' he said. 'And it frequently helps. If you would all please kneel.'

He crossed himself, folded his hands and began to pray aloud in a firm and remarkably steady voice.

17

Harry Kane was supervising a course in field tactics in the wood behind Meltham Farm when he received Shafto's urgent summons to report to the house and bring the training squad with him. Kane left the sergeant, a Texan named Hustler from Fort Worth, to follow with the men and went on ahead.

As he arrived, Sections which had been training on various parts of the estate were all coming in together. He could hear the revving of engines from the motor pool in the stabling block at the rear. Several jeeps turned into the gravel drive in front of the house and drew up line abreast.

The crews started to check their machine-guns and equipment. An officer jumped out of the lead vehicle, a captain named Mallory.

'What gives, for Christ's sake?' Kane demanded.

'I haven't the slightest idea,' Mallory said. 'I get the orders, I follow them through. He wants you in a hurry, I know that.' He grinned. 'Maybe it's the Second Front.'

Kane went up the steps on the run. The outer office was a scene of frenzied activity. Master Sergeant Garvey paced up and down outside Shafto's door, nervously smoking a cigarette. His face brightened as Kane entered.

'What in the hell is going on?' Kane demanded. 'Have we orders to move out or something?'

'Don't ask me, Major. All I know is that lady friend of yours arrived in one hell of a state about fifteen minutes ago and nothing's been the same since.'

Kane opened the door and went in. Shafto, in breeches and riding boots, was standing at the desk with his back to him. When he swung round Kane saw that he was loading the pearl-handled Colt. The change in him was extraordinary. He seemed to crackle with electricity, his eyes sparkled as if he was in a high fever, his face was pale with excitement.

'Fast action, Major, that's what I like.'

He reached for belt and holster and Kane said. 'What is it, sir? Where's Miss Vereker?'

'In my bedroom. Under sedation and badly shocked.'

'But what happened?'

'She took a bullet in the side of the head.' Shafto buckled his belt quickly, easing the holster low down on his right hip. 'And the finger on the trigger was that friend of her brother's, Mrs Grey. Ask her yourself. I can only spare you three minutes.'

Kane opened the bedroom door. Shafto followed him in. The curtains had been partially drawn and Pamela was in bed, the blankets up to her chin. She looked pale and very ill and there was a bandage around her head, a little blood soaking through.

As Kane approached, her eyes opened and she stared up at him fixedly. 'Harry?'

'It's all right.' He sat on the edge of the bed.

'No, listen to me.' She pushed herself up and tugged at his sleeve and when she spoke, her voice was remote, far-away. 'Mr Churchill leaves King's Lynn at three-thirty for Studley Grange with Sir Henry Willoughby. They'll be coming by way of Walsingham. You must stop him.'

'Why must I?' Kane said gently.

'Because Colonel Steiner and his men will get him if you don't. They're waiting at the village now. They're holding everyone prisoner at the church.'

'Steiner?'

'The man you know as Colonel Carter. And his men, Harry. They aren't Poles. They're German paratroops.'

'But Pamela,' Kane said. 'I met Carter. He's as English as you are.'

'No, his mother was American and he went to school in London. Don't you see? That explains it.' There was a kind of exasperation in her voice now. 'I overheard them talking in the church, Steiner and my brother. I was hiding with Molly Prior. After we got away, we split up and I went to Joanna's, only she's one of them. She shot me and I – I locked her in the cellar.' She frowned, trying hard. 'Then I took her car and came here.'

There was a sudden release that was almost physical in its intensity. It was as if she had been holding herself together by willpower alone and now it didn't matter. She lay back against the pillows and closed her eyes. Kane said, 'But how did you get away from the church, Pamela?'

She opened her eyes and stared at him, dazed, uncomprehending. 'The church? Oh, the – the usual way.' Her voice was the merest whisper. 'And then I went to Joanna's and she shot me.' She closed her eyes again. 'I'm so tired, Harry.'

Kane stood up and Shafto led the way back into the other room. He adjusted his sidecap in the mirror. 'Well, what do you think? That Grey woman for a start. She must be the great original bitch of all time.'

'Who have we notified? The War Office and GOC East Anglia for a start and . . .'

Shafto cut right in. 'Have you any idea how long I'd be on the phone while those chair-bound bastards at Staff try to decide whether I've got it right or not?' He slammed a fist down on the table. 'No, by Godfrey. I'm going to nail these Krauts myself, here and now and I've got the men to do it. Action this day!' He laughed harshly. 'Churchill's personal motto. I'd say that's rather appropriate.'

Kane saw it all then. To Shafto it must have seemed like a dispensation from the gods themselves. Not only the salvaging of his career, but the making of it. The man who had saved Churchill. A feat of arms that would take its place in the history books. Let the Pentagon try to keep that general's star from him after this and there would be rioting in the streets.

'Look, sir,' Kane said stubbornly. 'If what Pamela said is true, this must be just about the hottest potato of all time. If I might respectfully suggest, the British War Office won't take too kindly . . .'

Shafto's fist slammed down on the desk again. 'What's got into you? Maybe those Gestapo boys did a better job than they knew?' He turned to the window restlessly, then swung back as quickly, smiling like a contrite schoolboy. 'Sorry, Harry, that was uncalled for. You're right, of course.'

'Okay, sir, what do we do?'

Shafto looked at his watch. 'Four-fifteen. That means the Prime Minister must be getting close. We know the road he's coming on. I think it might be a good idea if you took a jeep and headed him off. From what the girl said you should be able to catch him this side of Walsingham.'

'I agree, sir. At least we can offer him one hundred and ten per cent security here.'

'Exactly.' Shafto sat down behind the desk and picked up the telephone. 'Now get moving and take Garvey with you.'

'Colonel.'

As Kane opened the door he heard Shafto say, 'Get me the General Officer commanding East Anglia District and I want him personally – no one else.'

When the door closed Shafto removed his left index finger from the telephone rest. The operator's voice crackled in his ear. 'Did you want something, Colonel?'

'Yes, get Captain Mallory in here on the double.'

Mallory was with him in about forty-five seconds. 'You wanted me, Colonel?'

'That's right, plus a detail of forty men ready to move out five minutes from now. Eight jeeps should do it. Cram 'em in.'

'Very well, sir.' Mallory hesitated, breaking one of the strictest rules. 'Is it permitted to ask what the Colonel intends?'

'Well, let's put it this way,' Shafto said. 'You'll be a major by nightfall – or dead.'

Mallory went out, his heart pumping and Shafto went to the cupboard in the corner and took out a bottle of Bourbon and half-filled a glass. Rain beat against the window and he stood there, drinking his Bourbon, taking his time. Within twenty-four hours he would probably have the best-known name in America. His day had come, he knew that with absolute conviction.

*

When he went outside three minutes later the jeeps were drawn up in line, the crews on board. Mallory was standing in front talking to the unit's youngest officer, a second lieutenant named

Chalmers. They sprang to attention and Shafto paused at the top of the steps.

'You're wondering what all this is about. I'll tell you. There's a village named Studley Constable about eight miles from here. You'll find it marked plainly enough on your maps. Most of you will have heard that Winston Churchill was visiting an RAF station near King's Lynn today. What you don't know is that he's spending tonight at Studley Grange. This is where it gets interesting. There are sixteen men from the Polish Independent Parachute Squadron of the SAS training in Studley Constable. You can't miss them in those pretty red berets and camouflage uniforms.' Somebody laughed and Shafto paused until there was complete silence again. 'I've got news for you. Those guys are Krauts. German paratroops here to get Churchill and we're going to nail them on the wall.' The silence was total and he nodded slowly. 'One thing I can promise you boys. Handle this right and by tomorrow, your names will ring from California to Maine. Now get ready to move out.'

There was an instant burst of activity as engines roared into life. Shafto went down the steps and said to Mallory, 'Make sure they go over those maps on the way. No time for any fancy briefing when we get there.' Mallory hurried away and Shafto turned to Chalmers. 'Hold the fort, boy, until Major Kane gets back.' He slapped him on the shoulder. 'Don't look too disappointed. He'll have Mr Churchill with him. You see he gets the hospitality of the house.' He jumped into the lead jeep and nodded to the driver. 'Okay, son, let's move out.'

They roared down the drive, the sentries on the massive front gate got it open fast and the convoy turned into the road. A couple of hundred yards farther on, Shafto waved them to a halt and told his driver to pull in close to the nearest telephone pole. He turned to Sergeant Hustler in the rear seat. 'Give me that Thompson gun.'

Hustler handed it over. Shafto cocked it, took aim and sprayed the top of the pole, reducing the crossbars to matchwood. The telephone lines parted, springing wildly through the air.

Shafto handed the Thompson back to Hustler. 'I guess that takes care of any unauthorized phone calls for a while.' He slapped the side of the vehicle. 'Okay, let's go, let's go, let's go!'

*

Garvey handled the jeep like a man possessed, roaring along the narrow country lanes at the kind of speed which assumed that nothing was coming the other way. Even then, they almost missed their target, for as they drove along the final stretch to join the Walsingham road, the small convoy flashed past at the end of the lane. Two military policemen on motor-cycles leading the way, two Humber saloon cars, two more policemen bringing up the rear.

'It's him!' Kane cried.

The jeep skidded into the main road, Garvey rammed his foot down hard. It was only a matter of moments before they caught up the convoy. As they roared up behind, the two military policemen at the rear glanced over their shoulders. One waved them back.

Kane said, 'Sergeant, pull out and overtake and if you can't stop them any other way you have my permission to ram that front car.'

Dexter Garvey grinned. 'Major, I'm going to tell you something. If this goes wrong we'll end up in that Leavenworth stockade so fast you won't know which day it is.'

He swerved out to the right past the motor-cyclists and pulled alongside the rear Humber. Kane couldn't see much of the man in the back seat because the side curtains were pulled forward just sufficiently to ensure privacy. The driver, who was in dark blue chauffeur's uniform, glanced sideways in alarm and the man in the grey suit in the front passenger seat drew a revolver.

'Try the next one,' Kane ordered and Garvey pulled alongside the front saloon, blaring his horn.

There were four men in there, two in army uniform, both colonels, one with the red tabs of a staff officer. The other turned in alarm and Kane found himself looking at Sir Henry Willoughby. There was instant recognition and Kane shouted to Garvey, 'Okay, pull out in front. I think they'll stop now.'

Garvey accelerated, overtaking the military policemen at the head of the small covoy. A horn blared three times behind them, obviously some pre-arranged signal. When Kane looked over his shoulder they were pulling in at the side of the road. Garvey braked and Kane jumped out and ran back.

The military policemen had a Sten gun apiece trained on him before he was anywhere close and the man in the grey suit, presumably the Prime Minister's personal detective, was already out of the rear car, revolver in hand.

The staff colonel with the red tabs got out of the first car, Sir Henry in Home Guard uniform at his heels. 'Major Kane,' Sir Henry said in bewilderment. 'What on earth are you doing here?'

The staff colonel said curtly, 'My name is Corcoran, Chief Intelligence Officer to the GOC, East Anglia District. Will you kindly explain yourself, sir?'

'The Prime Minister mustn't go to Studley Grange,' Kane told him. 'The village has been taken over by German paratroops and . . .'

'Good God,' Sir Henry interrupted. 'I've never heard such nonsense . . .'

Corcoran waved him to silence. 'Can you substaniate this statement, Major?'

'Dear God Almighty,' Kane shouted. 'They're here to get Churchill like Skorzeny dropped in for Mussolini, don't you understand? What in the hell does it take to convince you guys? Won't anybody listen?'

A voice from behind, a voice that was entirely familiar to him said, 'I will, young man. Tell your story to me.'

Harry Kane turned slowly, leaned down at the rear window and was finally face-to-face with the great man himself.

*

When Steiner tried the door of the cottage at Hobs End it was locked. He went round to the barn, but there was no sign of the Irishman there either. Briegel shouted, 'Herr Oberst, he's coming.'

Devlin was riding the BSA across the network of narrow dyke paths. He turned into the yard, shoved the bike up on its stand and pushed up his goggles. 'A bit public, Colonel.'

Steiner took him by the arm and led him across to the wall where, in a few brief sentences, he filled him in on the situation. 'Well,' he said when he was finished 'What do you think?'

'Are you sure your mother wasn't Irish?'

'*Her* mother was.'

Devlin nodded. 'I might have known. Still, who knows? We might get away with it.' He smiled. 'I know one thing. My fingernails will be down to the quick by nine tonight.'

Steiner jumped into the jeep and nodded to Klugl. 'I'll keep in touch.'

From the wood on the hill on the other side of the road Molly stood beside her horse and watched Devlin take out his key and unlock the front door. She had intended to confront him, filled with the desperate hope that even now she might be mistaken, but the sight of Steiner and his two men in the jeep was the ultimate truth of things.

*

A half mile outside Studley Constable Shafto waved the column to a halt and gave his orders. 'No time for any nonsense now. We've got to hit them and hit them hard before they know what's happening. Captain Mallory, you take three jeeps and fifteen men, cross the fields to the east of the village using those farm tracks marked on the map. Circle round till you come out on the Studley Grange road north of the watermill. Sergeant Hustler, the moment we reach the edge of the village, you dismount and take a dozen men on foot and make your way up this sunken track through Hawks Wood to the church. The remaining men stay with me. We'll plug the road by the Grey woman's house.'

'So we've got them completely bottled up, Colonel,' Mallory said.

'Bottled up hell. When everyone's in position and I give the signal on field telephone, we go in and finish this thing fast.'

There was silence. It was Sergeant Hustler who finally broke it. 'Begging the Colonel's pardon, but wouldn't some sort of reconnaissance be in order?' He tried to smile. 'I mean, from what we hear, these Kraut paratroopers ain't exactly Chesterfields.'

'Hustler,' Shafto said coldly. 'You ever query an order of mine again and I'll have you down to private so fast you won't know your own first name.' A muscle twitched in his right cheek as his glance took in the assembled NCOs one by one. 'Hasn't anybody got any guts here?'

'Of course, sir,' Mallory answered. 'We're right behind you, Colonel.'

'Well you'd better be,' Shafto said, 'Because I'm going in there now on my own with a white flag.'

'You mean you're going to invite them to surrender, sir?'

'Surrender, my backside, Captain. While I do some talking, the rest of you will be getting into position and you've got exactly ten minutes from the moment I enter that dump so let's get to it.'

*

Devlin was hungry. He heated a little soup, fried an egg and made a sandwich of it with two thick slices of bread, Molly's own baking. He was eating it in the chair by the fire when a cold draught on his left cheek told him that the door had opened. When he looked up, she was standing there.

'So there you are?' he said cheerfully. 'I was having a bit before coming looking for you.' He held up the sandwich. 'Did you know these things were invented by a belted earl, no less?'

'You bastard!' she said. 'You dirty swine! You used me.'

She flung herself on him, hands clawing at his face. He grabbed her wrists and fought to control her. 'What is it?' he demanded. Yet in his heart, he knew.

'I know all about it. Carter isn't his name – it's Steiner and he and his men are bloody Germans come for Mr Churchill. And what's your name? Not Devlin, I'll be bound.'

He pushed her away from him, went and got the Bushmills and a glass. 'No, Molly, it isn't.' He shook his head. 'You weren't meant to be any part of this, my love. You just happened.'

'You bloody traitor!'

He said in a kind of exasperation. 'Molly, I'm Irish, that means I'm as different from you as a German is from a Frenchman. I'm a foreigner. We're not the same just because we both speak English with different accents. When will you learn, you people?'

There was uncertainty in her eyes now, but still she persisted. 'Traitor!'

His face was bleak then, the eyes very blue, the chin tilted. 'No traitor, Molly. I am a soldier of the Irish Republican Army. I serve a cause as dear to me as yours.'

She needed to hurt him, to wound and had the weapon to do it. 'Well, much good may it do you and your friend Steiner. He's finished or soon will be. You next.'

'What are you talking about?'

'Pamela Vereker was with me up at the church when he and his men took her brother and George Wilde up there. We overheard enough to send her flying off to Meltham to get those Yankee Rangers.'

He grabbed her by the arms. 'How long ago?'

'You go to hell!'

'Tell me, damn you!' he shook her roughly.

'I'd say they must be there by now. If the wind was in the right direction you could probably hear the shooting, so there isn't a bloody thing you can do about it except run while you have the chance.'

He released her and said wryly. 'Sure and it would be the sensible thing to do, but I was never one for that.'

He pulled on his cap and goggles, his trenchcoat, and belted it around his waist. He crossed to the fireplace and felt under a pile of old newspapers behind the log basket. There were two hand grenades there which Ritter Neumann had given him. He primed them and placed them carefully inside the front flap of his trenchcoat. He put the Mauser into his right pocket and lengthened the sling on his Sten, suspending it around his neck almost to waist level so that he could fire it one-handed if necessary.

Molly said, 'What are you going to do?'

'Into the valley of death, Molly, my love, rode the six hundred and all that sort of good old British rubbish.' He poured himself a glass of Bushmills and saw the look of amazement on her face. 'Did you think I'd run for the hills and leave Steiner in the lurch?' He shook his head. 'God, girl, and I thought you knew something about me.'

'You can't go up there.' There was panic in her voice now. 'Liam, you won't stand a chance.' She caught hold of him by the arm.

'Oh, but I must, my pet.' He kissed her on the mouth and pushed her firmly to one side. He turned at the door. 'For what it's worth, I wrote you a letter. Not much, I'm afraid, but if you're interested, it's on the mantelpiece.'

The door banged, she stood there rigid, frozen. Somewhere in another world the engine roared into life and moved away.

She found the letter and opened it feverishly. It said: *Molly, my own true love. As a great man once said, I have suffered a sea-change and nothing can ever be the same again. I came to Norfolk to do a job, not to fall in love for the first and last time in my life with an ugly little peasant girl that should have known better. By now you'll know the worst of me, but try not to think it. To leave you is punishment enough. Let it end there. As they say in Ireland, we knew the two days. Liam.*

The words blurred, there were tears in her eyes. She stuffed the letter into her pocket and stumbled outside. Her horse was at the hitching ring. She untied him quickly, scrambled up on his back and urged him into a gallop, beating her clenched fist against his neck. At the end of the dyke she took him straight across the road, jumped the hedge and galloped for the village, taking the shortest route across the fields.

*

Otto Brandt sat on the parapet of the bridge and lit a cigarette as if he didn't have a care in the world. 'So what do we do, run for it?'

'Where to?' Ritter looked at his watch. 'Twenty to five. It should be dark by six-thirty at the latest. If we can hang on until then, we could fade away in twos and threes and make for Hobs End across country. Maybe some of us could catch that boat.'

'The Colonel could have other ideas,' Sergeant Altmann said.

Brandt nodded. 'Exactly, only he isn't here, so for the moment it seems to me we'd better get ready to do a little fighting.'

'Which raises an important point,' Ritter said. 'We fight only as German soldiers. That was made clear from the beginning. It seems to me that the time has come to drop the pretence.'

He took off his red beret and jump jacket, revealing his *Fliegerbluse*. From his hip pocket he produced a Luftwaffe sidecap or *Schiff* and adjusted it to the correct angle.

'All right,' he said to Brandt and Altmann. 'The same for everybody, so you'd better get moving.'

Joanna Grey had witnessed the entire scene from her bedroom window and the sight of Ritter's uniform brought a chill to her heart. She watched Altmann go in to the Post Office. A moment later Mr Turner emerged. He crossed the bridge and started up the hill to the church.

Ritter was in an extraordinary dilemma. Ordinarily in such circumstances he would have ordered an immediate withdrawal, but as he had said to Brandt, where to? Including himself, he had twelve men to guard the prisoners and hold the village. An impossible situation. *But so was the Albert Canal and Eban Emael,* that's what Steiner would have said. It occurred to him and not for the first time, how much he had come to depend on Steiner over the years.

He tried to raise him again on the field telephone. 'Come in Eagle One,' he said in English. 'This is Eagle Two.'

There was no reply. He handed the phone back to Private Hagl who lay in the shelter of the bridge wall, the barrel of his Bren protruding through a drainage hole giving him a fair field of fire. A supply of magazines was neatly stacked beside him. He, too, had divested himself of the red beret and jump jacket and wore *Schiff* and *Fliergerbluse* while still retaining his camouflaged trousers.

'No luck, Herr Oberleutnant?' he said and then stiffened. 'I think that's a jeep I hear now.'

'Yes, but from the wrong direction entirely,' Ritter told him grimly.

He vaulted over the wall beside Hagl, turned and saw a jeep come round the corner by Joanna Grey's cottage. A white hand-kerchief fluttered at the end of the radio aerial. There was one occupant only, the man at the wheel. Ritter stepped from behind the wall and waited, hands on hips.

Shafto hadn't bothered swopping to a tin hat and still wore his sidecap. He took a cigar from one of his shirt pockets, and put it between his teeth purely for effect. He took his time over lighting it, then got out of the jeep and came forward. He stopped a yard or two away from Ritter and stood, legs apart, looking him over.

Ritter noted the collar tabs and saluted formally. 'Colonel.'

Shafto returned the salute. His glance took in the two Iron Crosses, the Winter War ribbon, the wound badge in silver, the combat badge for distinguished service in ground battles, the paratroopers qualification badge, and knew that in this fresh-faced young man he was looking on a hardened veteran.

'So, no more pretence, Herr Oberleutnant? Where's Steiner? Tell him Colonel Robert E. Shafto, in command Twenty-first Specialist Raiding Force, would like to speak with him.'

'I am in charge here, Herr Oberst. You must deal with me.'

Shafto's eyes took in the barrel of the Bren poking through the drainage hole in the bridge parapet, swivelled to the Post Office, the first floor of the Studley Arms where two bedroom windows stood open. Ritter said politely, 'Is there anything else, Colonel, or have you seen enough?'

'What happened to Steiner? Has he run out on you or some-thing?' Ritter made no reply and Shafto went on, 'Okay, son, I know how many men you have under your command and if I have to bring my boys in here you won't last ten minutes. Why not be practical and throw in the towel?'

'So sorry,' Ritter said, 'But the fact is I left in such a hurry that I forgot to put one in my overnight bag.'

Shafto tapped ash from his cigar. 'Ten minutes, that's all I'll give you, then we come in.'

'And I'll give you two, Colonel,' Ritter said. 'To get the hell out of here before my men open fire.'

There was the metallic click of weapons being cocked. Shafto looked up at the windows and said grimly, 'Okay, sonny, you asked for it.'

He dropped the cigar, stamped it very deliberately into the ground, walked back to the jeep and got behind the wheel. As he drove away he reached for the mike on the field radio. 'This is Sugar One. Twenty seconds and counting. Nineteen, eighteen, seventeen . . .'

He was passing Joanna Grey's cottage at twelve, disappeared round the bend in the road on ten.

She watched him go from the bedroom window, turned and went into the study. She opened the secret door to the cubbyhole loft, closed it behind her and locked it. She went upstairs, sat down at the radio, took the Luger from the drawer and laid it down on the table where she could reach it quickly. Strange, but now that it had come to this she wasn't in the least afraid. She reached for a bottle of Scotch and as she poured a large one, firing started outside.

*

The lead jeep in Shafto's section roared round the corner into the straight. There were four men inside and the two in the rear were standing up working a Browning machine-gun. As they passed the garden of the cottage next to Joanna Grey's, Dinter and Berg stood up together, Dinter supporting the barrel of a Bren gun across his shoulder while Berg did the firing. He loosed one long continuous burst that knocked the two men at the Browning off their feet. The jeep bounced over the verge and rolled over, coming to rest upside down in the stream.

The next jeep in line swerved away wildly, the driver taking it round in a circle over the grass bank that almost had it into the stream with the other. Berg swung the barrel of the Bren, continuing to fire in short bursts, driving one of the jeep's machine gun crew over the side of the vehicle and smashing its windscreen before it scrambled round the corner to safety.

In the rubble of Stalingrad, Dinter and Berg had learned that the essence of success in such situations was to make your hit, then get out fast. They exited immediately through a wrought-iron gate in the wall and worked their way back to the Post Office, using the cover of the back garden hedges at the rear of the cottages.

Shafto, who had witnessed the entire debacle from a rise in the woods further down the road, ground his teeth with rage. It had suddenly become all too obvious that Ritter had let him see exactly what he had wanted him to see. 'Why, that little bastard was setting me up,' he said softly.

The jeep which had just been shot-up pulled in at the side of the road in front of number three. Its driver had a bad cut on the face. A sergeant named Thomas was putting a field dressing on it. Shafto shouted down, 'For Christ's sake, Sergeant, what are you playing at? There's a machine-gun behind the wall of the garden of the second cottage along. Go forward with three men on foot now and take care of it.'

Krukowski, who waited behind him with the field telephone, winced. *Five minutes ago we were thirteen. Now it's nine. What in the hell does he think he's playing at?*

There was heavy firing from the other side of the village. Shafto raised his fieldglasses, but could see little except for a piece of the road curving beyond the bridge and the roof of the mill standing up beyond the end houses. He snapped a finger and Krukowski passed him the phone. 'Mallory, do you read me?'

Mallory answered instantly. 'Affirmative, Colonel.'

'What in the hell goes on up there? I expected you with bells on by now.'

'They've got a strong point set up in the mill on the first floor. Commands one hell of a field of fire. They knocked out the lead jeep. It's blocking the road now. I've already lost four men.'

'Then lose some more,' Shafto yelled into the phone. 'Get in there, Mallory. Burn them out. Whatever it takes.'

The firing was very heavy now as Shafto tried the other section. 'You there, Hustler?'

'Colonel, this is Hustler.' His voice sounded rather faint.

'I expected to see you up on the hill at that church by now.'

'It's been tough going, Colonel. We started across the fields like you said and got tangled up in a bog. Just approaching the south end of Hawks Wood now.'

'Well, get the lead out, for Christ's sake!'

He handed the phone back to Krukowski. 'Christ Jesus!' he said bitterly. 'You can't rely on anybody: when it comes right down to it, anything I need doing right, I've got to see to myself.'

He slid down the bank into the ditch as Sergeant Thomas and the three men he'd taken with him returned. 'Nothing to report, Colonel.'

'What do you mean, nothing to report?'

'No one there, sir, just these.' Thomas held out a handful of .303 cartridge cases.

Shafto struck his hand violently, spilling them to the ground. 'Okay, I want both jeeps out in front, two men to each Browning. I want that bridge plastering. I want you to lay down such a field of fire that even a blade of grass won't be able to stand up.'

'But Colonel,' Thomas began.

'And you take four men and work your way on foot back of the cottages. Hit that Post Office by the bridge from the rear. Krukowski stays with me.' He slammed his hand down hard on the bonnet of the jeep. 'Now move it!'

*

Otto Brandt had Corporal Walther, Meyer and Riedel with him in the mill. From a defence point of view it was perfect: the ancient stone walls were about three feet thick and downstairs the oak doors were bolted and barred. The windows of the first floor commanded an excellent field of fire and Brandt had a Bren gun set up there.

Down below a jeep burned steadily, blocking the road. One man was still inside, two more sprawled in the ditch. Brandt had disposed of the jeep personally, making no sign at first, letting Mallory and his men come roaring in, only lobbing down a couple of grenades from the loft door at the last moment. The effect had been catastrophic. From behind the hedges further up the road the Americans poured in a considerable amount of fire to little effect because of those massive stone walls.

'I don't know who's in charge down there, but he doesn't know his business,' Walther oberved as he reloaded his M1.

'Well, what would you have done?' Brandt asked him, squinting along the barrel of the Bren as he loosed off a quick burst.

'There's the stream, isn't there? No windows on that side. They should be moving in from the rear . . .'

Brandt held up his hand. 'Everyone stop firing.'

'Why?' Walther demanded.

'Because they have, or hadn't you noticed?'

There was a deathly silence and Brandt said softly, 'I'm not sure I really believe this, but get ready.'

A moment later, with a rousing battlecry, Mallory and eight or nine men emerged from shelter and ran for the next ditch, firing from the hip. In spite of the fact that they were getting covering fire from the Brownings of the two remaining jeeps on the other side of the hedge, it was an incredible act of folly.

'My God!' Brandt said. 'Where do they think they are? The Somme?'

He put a long, almost leisurely burst into Mallory and killed him instantly. Three more went down as the Germans all fired at once. One of them picked himself up and staggered back to the safety of the first hedge as the survivors retreated.

In the quiet which followed, Brandt reached for a cigarette. 'I make that seven. Eight if you count the one who dragged himself back.'

'Crazy.' Walther said. 'Suicide. I mean, why are they in such a hurry? All they have to do is wait.'

*

Kane and Colonel Corcoran sat in a jeep two hundred yards down the road from the main gate at Meltham House and looked up at the shattered telephone pole. 'Good God!' Corcoran said. 'It's really quite incredible. What on earth was he thinking of?'

Kane could have told him, but refrained. He said, 'I don't know, Colonel. Maybe some notion he had about security. He sure was anxious to get to grips with those paratroopers.'

A jeep turned out of the main gate and moved towards them. Garvey was at the wheel and when he braked, his face was serious. 'We just got a message in the radio room.'

'From Shafto?'

Garvey shook his head. 'Krukowski, of all people. He asked for you, Major, personally. It's a mess down there. He says they walked right into it. Dead men all over the place.'

'And Shafto?'

'Krukowski was pretty hysterical. Kept saying the colonel was acting like a crazy man. Some of it didn't make much sense.'

Dear God, Kane thought, he's gone riding straight in, guidons fluttering in the breeze. He said to Corcoran, 'I think I should get down there, Colonel.'

'So do I,' Corcoran said. 'Naturally, you'll leave adequate protection for the Prime Minister.'

Kane turned to Garvey. 'What have we got left in the motor pool?'

'A White Scout car and three jeeps.'

'All right, we'll take them plus a detail of twenty men. Ready to move out in five minutes if you please, Sergeant.'

Garvey swung the jeep in a tight circle and drove away fast. 'That leaves twenty-five for you, sir,' Kane told Corcoran. 'Will that be all right?'

'Twenty-six with me,' Corcoran said. 'Perfectly adequate, especially as I shall naturally assume command. Time someone licked you colonials into shape.'

'I know, sir,' Harvey Kane said as he switched on the engine. 'Nothing but a mass of complexes since Bunker Hill.' He let in the clutch and drove away.

18

The village was still a good mile and a half away when Steiner first became aware of the persistent electronic buzz from the Grauman field phone. Someone was on channel, but too far away to be heard. 'Put your foot down,' he told Klugl. 'Something's wrong.'

When they were a mile away, the rattle of small arms fire in the distance confirmed his worst fears. He cocked his Sten gun and looked up at Werner. 'Be ready to use that thing. You might have to.'

Klugl had the jeep pushed right up to its limit, his foot flat on the boards. 'Come on, damn you! Come on!' Steiner cried.

The Grauman had ceased the buzz and as they drew closer to the village, he tried to make voice contact. 'This is Eagle One. Come in Eagle Two.'

There was no reply. He tried again, but with no better success. Klugl said, 'Maybe they're too busy. Herr Oberst.'

A moment later they topped the rise at Garrowby Heath three hundred yards west of the church at the top of the hill and the whole panorama was spread below. Steiner raised his field glasses, took in the mill and Mallory's detail in the field beyond. He moved on, noting the Rangers behind the hedges at the rear of the Post Office and the Studley Arms and Ritter, young Hagl beside him, pinned down behind the bridge by the heavy concentration of machine-gun fire from the Brownings of Shafto's two remaining jeeps. One of them had been sited alongside Joanna Grey's garden wall from where the gun crew were able to fire over the top and yet remain in good cover. The other employed the same technique against the wall of the next cottage.

Steiner tried the Grauman again. 'This is Eagle One. Do you read me?'

On the first floor of the mill, his voice crackled in the ear of Riedel, who had just switched on during a lull in the fighting. 'It's the Colonel,' he cried to Brandt and said into the phone. 'This is Eagle Three, in the water mill. Where are you?'

'On the hill above the church,' Steiner said. 'What is your situation?'

Several bullets passed through the glassless windows and ricochetted from the wall. 'Give it to me!' Brandt called from his position flat on the floor behind the Bren.

'He's on the hill,' Riedel said. 'Trust Steiner to turn up to pull us out of the shit.' He crawled along to the loft door above the waterwheel and kicked it open.

'Come back here,' Brandt called.

Riedel crouched to peer outside. He laughed excitedly and raised the Grauman to his mouth. 'I can see you, Herr Oberst, we're . . .'

There was a heavy burst of automatic fire from outside, blood and brains sprayed across the wall as the back of Riedel's skull disintegrated and he went head-first out of the loft, still clutching the field phone.

Brandt flung himself across the room and peered over the edge. Riedel had fallen on top of the waterwheel. It kept on turning, carrying him with it, down into the churning waters. When it came round again, he was gone.

*

On the hill, Werner tapped Steiner on the shoulder. 'Below, Herr Oberst, in the wood on the right. Soldiers.'

Steiner swung his field glasses. With the height advantage the hill gave him it was just possible to see down into one section of the sunken track through Hawks Wood about half-way along. Sergeant Hustler and his men were passing through.

Steiner made his decision and acted on it. 'It seems we're Fallschirmjäger again, boys.'

He tossed his red beret away, unbuckled his webbing belt and the Browning in its holster and took off his jump jacket. Underneath he was wearing his *Fliegerbluse*, the Knight's Cross with Oak Leaves at his throat. He took a *Schiff* from his pocket and jammed it down on his head. Klugl and Werner followed his example.

Steiner said, 'Right, boys, the grand tour. Straight down that track through the wood, across the footbridge for a few words with those jeeps. I think you can make it, Klugl, if you go fast enough, then on to Oberleutnant Neumann.' He looked up at Werner. 'And don't stop firing. Not for anything.'

*

The jeep was doing fifty as they went down the final stretch towards the church. Corporal Becker was outside the porch. He crouched in alarm, Steiner waved, then Klugl swung the wheel and turned the jeep into the Hawks Wood track.

They bounced over a slight rise, hurtled round a bend between the steep walls and there was Hustler with his men, no more than twenty yards away, strung out on either side of the track. Werner started to fire at point blank range, had no more than a few seconds in which to take aim because by then, the jeep was into them. Men were jumping for their lives, trying to scramble up the steep banks. The offside front wheel bounced over a body and then they were through, leaving Sergeant Horace Hustler and seven of his men dead or dying behind them.

The jeep emerged from the end of the track like a thunderbolt. Klugl kept right on going as ordered, straight across the four-foot wide footbridge over the stream, snapping the rustic pole handrails like matchsticks, and shot up the bank to the road, all four wheels clear of the ground as they bounced over the rise.

The two men comprising the machine-gun crew of the jeep sheltering behind Joanna Grey's garden wall swung their Browning frantically, already too late as Werner raked the wall with a sustained burst that knocked them both off their feet.

But the fact of their dying gave the crew of the second jeep, positioned at the side of the next garden wall, the two or three precious seconds to react – the seconds that meant the difference between life and death. They had their Browning round and were already firing as Klugl swung the wheel and drove back towards the bridge.

It was the Rangers' turn now. Werner got in a quick burst as they flashed past that caught one of the machine-gun crew, but the other kept on firing his Browning, bullets hammering into the Germans' jeep, shattering the windscreen. Klugl gave a sudden sharp cry and fell forward across the steering wheel, the jeep swerved wildly and smashed into the parapet at the end of the bridge. It seemed to hang there for a moment, then tipped over on to its side very slowly.

Klugl lay huddled in the shelter of the jeep and Werner crouched over him, blood on his face where flying glass had cut him. He looked up at Steiner. 'He's dead, Herr Oberst,' he said and his eyes were wild.

He reached for a Sten gun and started to stand. Steiner dragged him down. 'Pull yourself together, boy. He's dead, you're alive.'

Werner nodded dully. 'Yes, Herr Oberst.'

'Now get this Browning set up and keep them busy down there.'

As Steiner turned, Ritter Neumann crawled out from behind the parapet carrying a Bren gun. 'You certainly created hell back there.'

'They had a section moving up through the wood to the church,' Steiner said. 'We didn't do them any good either. What about Hagl?'

'Done for, I'm afraid.' Neumann nodded to where Hagl's boots protruded from behind the parapet.

Werner had the Browning set up at the side of the jeep now and started to fire in short bursts. Steiner said, 'All right, Herr Oberleutnant, and what exactly did you have in mind?'

'It should be dark in an hour,' Ritter said. 'I thought if we could hold on till then and slip away in twos and threes. We could lie low in the marsh at Hobs End under cover of darkness. Still make that boat if Koenig arrives as arranged. After all, we'll never get near the old man now.' He hesitated and added rather awkwardly. 'It gives us some sort of chance.'

'The only one,' Steiner said. 'But not here. I think it's time we re-grouped again. Where is everybody?'

Ritter gave him a quick run-down on the general situation and when he was finished, Steiner nodded. 'I managed to raise them in the mill on the way in. Got Riedel on the Grauman plus a lot of machine-gun fire. You get Altmann and his boys and I'll see if I can get through to Brandt.'

Werner gave Ritter covering fire as the Oberleutnant darted across the road and Steiner tried to raise Brandt on the Grauman. He had no success at all and as Neumann emerged from the door of the Post Office with Altmann, Dinter and Berg, there was an outbreak of heavy firing up at the mill.

They all crouched behind the parapet and Steiner said, 'I can't raise Brandt. God knows what's happening. I want the rest of you to make a run for it to the church. You've good cover for most of the way if you keep to the hedge. You're in charge, Ritter.'

'What about you?'

'I'll keep them occupied with the Browning for a while then I'll follow on.'

'But Herr Oberst,' Ritter began.

Steiner cut him off short. 'No buts about it. Today's my day for playing hero. Now get the hell out of it, all of you and that's an order.'

Ritter hesitated, but only fractionally. He nodded to Altmann then slipped past the jeep and ran across the bridge, crouching behind the parapet. Steiner got down to the Browning and started to fire.

At the other end of the bridge there was a stretch of open ground, no more than twenty-five feet before the safety of the hedge. Ritter, crouching on one knee, said, 'Taking it one by one is no good because after he's seen the first, that joker on the machine-gun will be ready and waiting for whoever comes next. When I give the word, we all go together.'

A moment later he was out of cover and dashing across the road, vaulting the stile and dropping into the safety of the hedge, Altmann right on his heels and followed by the others. The Ranger on the Browning at the other end of the village was a corporal named Bleeker, a Cape Cod fisherman in happier times. Just now, he was nearly out of his mind with pain, a piece of glass having buried itself just beneath his right eye. More than anything else in the world he hated Shafto for bringing him to this, but right now any target would do. He saw the Germans crossing the road and swung the Browning, too late. In his rage and frustration he raked the hedge anyway.

On the other side, Berg tripped and fell and Dinter turned to help him. 'Give me your hand, you daft bastard,' he said. 'Two left feet as usual.'

Berg stood up to die with him as bullets shredded the hedge, hammering into them, driving them both back across the meadow in a last frenzied dance. Werner turned with a cry and Altmann grabbed him by the shoulder and pushed him after Ritter.

*

From the loft entrance above the waterwheel, Brandt and Meyer saw what had happened in the meadow. 'So now we know,' Meyer said. 'From the looks of things I'd say we've taken up permanent residence here.'

Brandt watched Ritter, Altmann and Briegel toil up the long run of the hedge and scramble over the wall into the churchyard. 'They made it,' he said. 'Wonders will never cease.'

He moved across to Meyer, who was propped against a box in the middle of the floor. He'd been shot in the stomach. His blouse was open and there was an obscene hole with swollen purple lips just below his navel. 'Look at that,' he said, sweat on his face. 'At least I'm not losing any blood. My mother always did say I had the luck of the Devil.'

'So I've observed,' Brandt put a cigarette in Meyer's mouth, but before he could light it, heavy firing started again from outside.

*

Shafto crouched in the shelter of the wall in Joanna Grey's front garden, stunned by the enormity of the news one of the survivors of Hustler's section had just brought him. The catastrophe seemed complete. In little over half-an-hour he had lost at least twenty-two dead or wounded. More than half his command. The consequences were too appalling to contemplate.

Krukowski, crouching behind him with the field telephone, said, 'What are you going to do, Colonel?'

'What do you mean, what am *I* going to do?' Shafto demanded. 'It's always me when it comes right down to it. Leave things to other people, people with no conception of discipline or duty, and see what happens.'

He slumped against the wall and looked up. At that exact moment Joanna Grey peered from behind the bedroom curtain. She drew back instantly, too late. Shafto growled deep in his throat. 'My God, Krukowski, that goddamned, double-dealing bitch is still in the house.'

He pointed up at the window as he scrambled to his feet. Krukowski said, 'I can't see anyone, sir.'

'You soon will, boy!' Shafto cried, drawing his pearl-handled Colt. 'Come on!' and he ran up the path to the front door.

*

Joanna Grey locked the secret door and went up the stairs quickly to the cubbyhole loft. She sat down at the radio and started to transmit on the Landsvoort channel. She could hear noise downstairs. Doors were flung open and furniture knocked over as Shafto ransacked the house. He was very close now, stamping about in the study. She heard his cry of rage quite clearly as he went out on the stairs.

'She's got to be in here someplace.'

A voice echoed up the stairs. 'Heh, Colonel, there was this dog locked in the cellar. He's on the way up to you now like a bat out of hell.'

Joanna Grey reached for the Luger and cocked it, continuing to transmit without faltering. On the landing, Shafto stood to one side as Patch scurried past him. He followed the retriever into the study and found him scratching at the panelling in the corner.

Shafto examined it quickly and found the tiny keyhole almost at once. 'She's here, Krukowski!' There was a savage, almost insane joy in his voice. 'I've got her!'

He fired three shots point blank in the general area of the keyhole. The wood splintered as the lock disintegrated and the door swung open of its own accord, just as Krukowski entered the room, his M1 ready.

'Take it easy, sir.'

'Like hell I will.' Shafto started up the stairs, the Colt held out in from of him as Patch flashed past. 'Come down out of there, you bitch!'

As his head rose above floor level, Joanna Grey shot him between the eyes. He tumbled back down into the study. Krukowski poked the barrel of his M1 round the corner and loosed off a fifteen-round clip so fast that it sounded like one continuous burst. The dog howled, there was the sound of a body falling, and then silence.

*

Devlin arrived outside the church as Ritter, Altmann and Werner Briegel ran through the tombstones towards the porch. They veered towards him as Devlin braked to a halt at the lychgate. 'It's a mess,' Ritter said. 'And the Colonel's still down there by the bridge.'

Devlin looked down to the village where Steiner continued to fire the Browning from behind the damaged jeep and Ritter grabbed his arm and pointed. 'My God, look what's coming!'

Devlin turned and saw, on the other side of the bend in the road beyond Joanna Grey's cottage, a White Scout Car and three jeeps. He revved his motor and grinned. 'Sure and if I don't go now I might think better of it and that would never do.'

He went straight down the hill and skidded broadside on into the entrance to Old Woman's meadow, leaving the track within a few yards and taking the direct route straight across the field to the footbridge above the weir. He seemed to take off again and again as the machine bounced over the tussocky grass and Ritter watched from the lychgate, marvelling that he remained in the saddle.

The Oberleutnant ducked suddenly as a bullet chipped the woodwork beside his head. He dropped into the shelter of the wall with Werner and Altmann and started to return the fire as the survivors of Hustler's section, finally re-grouped, reached the fringe of the wood opposite the church.

*

Devlin shot across the footbridge and followed the track through the wood on the other side. There were men up there by the road, he was sure of it. He pulled one of the grenades from inside his coat and yanked the pin with his teeth. And then he was through the trees and there was a jeep on the grass verge, men turning in alarm.

He simply dropped the grenade behind him. He took out the other. There were more Rangers behind the hedge on his left and he tossed the second grenade over towards them as the first exploded. He kept right on going, down the road past the mill and round the corner, skidding to a halt behind the bridge where Steiner still crouched with the machine-gun.

Steiner didn't say a word. He simply stood up, holding the Browning in both hands and emptied it in a long burst of such savagery that it sent Corporal Bleeker diving for cover behind the garden wall. In the same moment, Steiner tossed the Browning to one side and swung a leg over the pillion. Devlin gunned the motor, swerved across the bridge and went straight up the hill as the White Scout Car nosed round the corner of Joanna Grey's Cottage. Harry Kane stood up to watch them go.

'And what in the hell was *that*?' Garvey demanded.

Corporal Bleeker fell out of his jeep and stumbled towards them, blood on his face. 'Is there a medic there, sir? I think maybe I lost my right eye. I can't see a thing.'

Someone jumped down to hold him and Kane surveyed the shambles of the village. 'The crazy, stupid bastard,' he whispered.

Krukowski came out of the front gate and saluted. 'Where's the Colonel?' Kane asked.

'Dead, sir, upstairs in the house. The lady in there – she shot him.'

Kane got down in a hurry. 'Where is she?'

'I – I killed her, Major,' Krukowski said, and there were tears in his eyes.

Kane couldn't think of a single damn thing to say. He patted Krukowski on the shoulder and went up the path to the cottage.

*

As the top of the hill, Ritter and his two comrades were still firing from behind the wall at the Rangers in the wood when Devlin and Steiner arrived on the scene. The Irishman changed gear, got his foot down and let the bike drift, turning at just the right moment for a clear run through the lychgate and up the path to the porch. Ritter, Altmann and Werner retreated steadily using the tombstones for cover and finally made the safety of the porch without further casualties.

Corporal Becker had the door open, they all passed inside and he slammed it shut and bolted it. The firing resumed outside with renewed intensity. The villagers huddled together, tense and anxious. Philip Vereker limped down the aisle to confront Devlin, his face white with anger. 'Another damned traitor!'

Devlin grinned. 'Ah, well,' he said. 'It's nice to be back amongst friends.'

*

In the mill everything was quiet. 'I don't like it,' Walther commented.

'You never do,' Brandt said and frowned. 'What's that?'

There was the sound of a vehicle approaching. Brandt tried to peer out of the loft entrance over the road and immediately came under fire. He drew back. 'How's Meyer?'

'I think he's dead.'

Brandt reached for a cigarette as the noise of the approaching vehicle drew close. 'Just think,' he said. 'The Albert Canal, Crete, Stalingrad and where does the end of the road turn out to be? Studley Constable.' He put a light to his cigarette.

The White Scout Car was doing at least forty when Garvey swung the wheel and smashed it straight through the mill doors. Kane stood in the back behind a Browning anti-aircraft machine-gun and was already firing up through the wooden floor above, the enormous .50 calibre rounds smashing their way through with ease, ripping the planking to pieces. He was aware of the cries of agony, but kept on firing, working the gun from side to side, only stopping when there were great gaping holes in the floor.

A bloodstained hand showed at one of them. It was very quiet. Garvey took a Thompson gun from one of the men, jumped down and went up the flight of wooden steps in the corner. He came down again almost instantly.

'That's it, Major.'

Harry Kane's face was pale, but he was completely in command of himself. 'All right,' he said. 'Now for the church.'

*

Molly arrived on Garrowby Heath in time to see a jeep drive up the hill, a white handkerchief fluttering from its radio aerial. It pulled up at the lychgate and Kane and Dexter Garvey got out. As they went up the path through the churchyard Kane said softly, 'Use your eyes, Sergeant. Make sure you'd know this place again if you saw it.'

'Affirmative, Major.'

The church door opened and Steiner moved out of the porch and Devlin leaned against the wall behind him smoking a cigarette. Harry Kane saluted formally. 'We've met before, Colonel.'

Before Steiner could reply, Philip Vereker pushed past Becker at the door and limped forward. 'Kane, where's Pamela? Is she all right?'

'She's fine, Father,' Kane told him. 'I left her back at Meltham House.'

Vereker turned to Steiner, face pinched and very white. There was a glitter of triumph in his eyes. 'She fixed you beautifully, didn't she, Steiner? Without her you might actually have got away with it.'

Steiner said calmly, 'Strange how the perspective changes with the point of view. I thought we failed because a man called Karl Sturm sacrificed himself to save two children's lives.' He didn't wait for an answer, but turned to Kane. 'What can I do for you?'

'Surely that's obvious. Surrender. There's no point in further useless bloodshed. The men you left down in the mill are all dead. So is Mrs Grey.'

Vereker caught him by the arm. 'Mrs Grey is dead? How?'

'She killed Colonel Shafto when he tried to arrest her, died herself in the exchange of gunfire which followed.' Vereker turned away, a look of utter desolation on his face and Kane said to Steiner. 'You are quite alone now. The Prime Minister is safe at Meltham House under as heavy a guard as he's likely to see in his lifetime. It's all over.'

Steiner thought of Brandt and Walther and Meyer, Gerhard Klugl, Dinter and Berg and nodded, his face very pale. 'Honourable terms?'

'No terms!' Vereker shouted it aloud like a cry to heaven. 'These men came here in British uniform, must I remind you of that, Major?'

'But did not fight in them,' Steiner cut in. 'We fought only as German soldiers, in German uniforms. As Fallschirmjäger. The other was a legitimate *ruse de guerre*.'

'And a direct contravention of the Geneva Convention,' Vereker answered. 'Which not only expressly forbids the wearing of an enemy's uniform in time of war, but also prescribes the death penalty for offenders.'

Steiner saw the look on Kane's face and smiled gently. 'Don't worry, Major, not your fault. The rules of the game and all that.' He turned to Vereker. 'Well now, Father, your God is a God of Wrath indeed. You would dance on my grave, it seems.'

'Damn you, Steiner!' Vereker lurched forward, raising his stick to strike, stumbled over the long skirts of his cassock and fell, striking his head on the edge of a tombstone.

Garvey dropped to one knee beside him and made a quick examination. 'Out for the count.' He looked up. 'Somebody should check him out, though. We've got a good medic down in the village.'

'Take him by all means,' Steiner said. 'Take all of them.'

Garvey glanced at Kane, then picked Vereker up and carried him to the jeep. Kane said, 'You'll let the villagers go?'

'The obvious thing to do since a further outbreak of hostilities seems imminent.' Steiner looked faintly amused. 'Why, did you think we'd hold the entire village hostage or come out fighting, driving the women in front of us? The brutal Hun? Sorry I can't oblige.' He turned. 'Send them out, Becker, all of them.'

The door swung open with a crash and the villagers started to pour through, led by Laker Armsby. Most of the women were crying hysterically as they rushed past. Betty Wilde came last with Graham and Ritter Neumann supported her husband, who looked dazed and ill. Garvey hurried back up the path and got an arm round him and Betty Wilde reached for Graham's hand and turned to Ritter.

'He'll be all right, Mrs Wilde,' the young Oberleutnant said. 'I'm sorry about what happened in there, believe me.'

'That's all right,' she said. 'It wasn't your fault. Would you do something for me? Would you tell me your name?'

'Neumann,' he said. 'Ritter Neumann.'

'Thank you,' she said simply. I'm sorry I said the things I did.' She turned to Steiner. 'And I want to thank you and your men for Graham.'

'He's a brave boy,' Steiner said. 'He didn't even hesitate. He jumped straight in. That takes courage and courage is something that never goes out of fashion.'

The boy stared up at him. 'Why are you a German?' he demanded. 'Why aren't you on our side?'

Steiner laughed out loud. 'Go on, get him out of here,' he said to Betty Wilde. 'Before he completely corrupts me.'

She took the boy by the hand and hurried away. Beyond the wall the women streamed down the hill. At that moment the White Scout Car emerged from the Hawks Wood track and stopped, its anti-aircraft gun and heavy machine-gun traversing on to the porch.

Steiner nodded wryly. 'So, Major, the final act. Let battle commence then.' He saluted and went back into the porch where Devlin had been standing throughout the entire conversation without saying a word.

'I don't think I've ever heard you silent for so long before,' Steiner said.

Devlin grinned. 'To tell you the truth I couldn't think of a single damned thing to say except *Help*. Can I go in now and pray?'

*

From her vantage point on the heath Molly watched Devlin disappear inside the porch with Steiner and her heart sank like a stone. *Oh, God, she thought, I must do something.* She got to her feet and at the same moment, a dozen Rangers headed by the big black sergeant, cut across the road from the wood well up from the church where they couldn't be seen. They ran back along the wall and entered the presbytery garden through the wicket gate.

But they didn't go into the house. They slipped over the wall into the cemetery, approaching the church from the tower end and worked their way round to the porch. The big sergeant had a coil of rope over his shoulder and as she watched, he jumped for the porch guttering and pulled himself over, then scrambled fifteen feet up the ivy vine to the lower leads. Once there, he uncoiled the rope and tossed the end down and the other Rangers began to follow.

Seized by a sudden new determination, Molly swung into the saddle and urged her horse across the heath, turning down to the woods at the rear of the presbytery.

*

It was very cold inside the church, a place of shadows, only the flickering candles, the ruby light of the sanctuary lamp. There were eight of them left now including Devlin. Steiner and Ritter, Werner Briegel, Altmann, Jansen, Corporal Becker and Preston. There was also, unknown to any of them, Arthur Seymour who, overlooked in the stampede to get out, still lay beside Sturm in the darkness of the Lady Chapel, his hands and feet bound. He had managed to push himself into a sitting position against the wall and was working on his wrists, his strange mad eyes fixed on Preston.

Steiner tried the tower door and the sacristy, both of which appeared to be locked and looked behind the curtain at the foot of the tower where ropes soared through holes in the wooden floor thirty feet up to bells which hadn't rung since 1939.

He turned and walked up the aisle to face them. 'Well, all I can offer you is another fight.'

Preston said. 'It's a ludicrous situation. How can we fight? They've got the men, the equipment. We couldn't hold this place for ten minutes once they really start.'

'It's quite simple,' Steiner said. 'We don't have any other choice. As you heard, under the terms of the Geneva Convention we have put ourselves gravely at risk by wearing British uniforms.'

'We fought as German soldiers,' Preston insisted. 'In German uniforms. You said that yourself.'

'A neat point,' Steiner said. 'I'd hate to stake my life on it, even with a good lawyer. If it's to be a bullet, rather now than from a firing squad later.'

'I don't know what you're getting so worked up about anyway, Preston,' Ritter said. 'it's the Tower of London for you without a doubt. The English, I'm afraid, have never held traitors in particularly high regard. They'll hang you so high the crows won't be able to get at you.'

Preston sank down in a pew, head in hands.

The organ rumbled into life and Hans Altmann, sitting high above the choir stalls, called, 'A choral prelude of Johan Sebastian Bach, particularly appropriate to our situation as it is entitled *For the Dying*.'

His voice echoed up into the nave as the music swelled. *Ach wie nichtig, ach wie fluchtig. O how cheating, O how fleeting are our days departing . . .*

One of the clerestory windows high up in the nave smashed. A burst of automatic fire knocked Altmann off the seat into the choir stalls. Werner turned, crouching, firing his Sten. A Ranger pitched headlong through the window and landed between two pews. In the same moment, several more clerestory windows crashed in and heavy fire was poured down into the church. Werner was hit in the head as he ran along the south aisle and fell on his face without a cry. Someone was using a Thompson gun up there now, spraying it back and forth.

Steiner crawled to Werner, turned him over, then moved on, dodging up the chancel steps to check on Altmann. He returned by way of the south aisle, keeping down behind the pews as intermittent firing continued.

Devlin crawled to meet him. 'What's the situation up there?'
'Altmann and Briegel both gone.'
'It's a bloodbath,' the Irishman said. 'We don't stand a chance. Ritter's been hit in the legs and Jansen's dead.'

Steiner crawled back with him to the rear of the church and found Ritter on his back behind the pews binding a field dressing round one thigh. Preston and Corporal Becker crouched beside him.

'Are you all right, Ritter?' Steiner asked.

'They'll run out of wound badges, Herr Oberst.' Ritter grinned, but was obviously in great pain.

They were still firing from above and Steiner nodded towards the sacristy door, barely visible now in the shadows and said to Becker. 'See if you can shoot your way in through that door. We can't last long out here, that's for certain.'

Becker nodded and slipped through the shadows behind the font, keeping low. There was that strange metallic clicking of the bolt reciprocating as he fired the silenced Sten; he stamped against the sacristy door; it swung open.

All firing stopped and Garvey called from high above. 'You had enough yet, Colonel? This is like shooting fish in a barrel and I'd rather not, but we'll carry you out on a plank if we have to.'

Preston cracked then, jumped to his feet and ran out into the open by the font. 'Yes, I'll come! I've had enough!'

'Bastard!' Becker cried and he ran out of the shadows by the sacristy door and rammed the butt of his rifle against the side of Preston's skull. The Thompson gun rattled, a short burst only but it caught Becker full in the back, driving him headlong through the curtains at the base of the tower. He grabbed at the ropes in dying as if trying to hang on to life itself and somewhere overhead, a bell tolled sonorously for the first time in years.

There was silence again and Garvey called, 'Five minutes, Colonel.'

'We'd better got moving,' Steiner said to Devlin in a low voice. 'We'll do better inside that sacristy than out here.'

'How long for?' Devlin asked.

There was a slight eerie creaking and straining his eyes, Devlin saw that someone was standing in the entrance to the sacristy where the broken door swung crazily. A familiar voice whispered, 'Liam?'

'My God,' he said to Steiner. 'It's Molly. Where in the hell did she spring from?' He crawled across the floor to join her and was back in a moment. 'Come on!' he said, getting a hand under Ritter's left arm. 'The little darling's got a way out for us. Now let's have this one on his feet and get moving while those lads up on the leads are still waiting.'

They slipped through the shadows, Ritter between them, and moved into the sacristy. Molly waited by the secret panel. Once they were inside, she closed it and led the way down the stairs and along the tunnel.

It was very quiet when they came out into the hall at the presbytery. 'Now what?' Devlin said. 'We'll not get far with Ritter like this.'

'Father Vereker's car is in the yard at the back,' Molly said.

And Steiner, remembering, put a hand in his pocket. 'And I've got his keys.'

'Don't be silly,' Ritter told him. 'The moment you start the motor you'll have Rangers swarming all over you.'

'There's a gate at the back,' Molly said. 'A track over the fields beside the hedge. We can push that little Morris Eight of his between us for a couple of hundred yards. Nothing to it.'

They were at the bottom of the first meadow and a hundred and fifty yards away, when shooting began again at the church. Only then did Steiner start the engine and drive away, following Molly's directions, sticking to farm tracks across the fields, all the way down to the coast road.

*

After the tiny click of the panel door in the sacristy closing, there was a stirring in the Lady Chapel and Arthur Seymour stood up, hands free. He padded down the north aisle without a sound, holding in his left hand the coil of rope with which Preston had bound his feet.

It was totally dark now, the only light the candles at the altar and the sanctuary lamp. He leaned down to satisfy himself that Preston was still breathing, picked him up and slung him over one massive shoulder. Then he turned and walked straight up the centre aisle towards the altar.

On the leads, Garvey was beginning to worry. It was so dark down there that you couldn't see a damn thing. He snapped his fingers for the field telephone and spoke to Kane who was at the gate with the White Scout Car. 'Silent as the grave in here, Major. I don't like it.'

'Try a burst. See what happens,' Kane told him.

Garvey pushed the barrel of his Thompson through the clerestory window and fired. There was no response and then the man on his right grabbed his arm. 'Down there, Sergeant, near the pulpit. Isn't someone moving?'

Garvey took a chance and flashed his torch. The young private on his right gave a cry of horror. Garvey ran the torch quickly along the south aisle, then said into the field phone, 'I don't know what's happening, Major, but you'd better get in there.'

A moment later, a burst from a Thompson gun shattered the lock on the main door, it crashed back and Harry Kane and a dozen Rangers moved in fast, ready for action. But there was no Steiner and no Devlin. Only Arthur Seymour kneeling in the front pew in the guttering candlelight, staring up into the hideously swollen face of Harvey Preston hanging by his neck from the centre pole of the rood screen.

19

The Prime Minister had taken the library overlooking the rear terrace at Meltham House for his personal use. When Harry Kane came out at seven-thirty Corcoran was waiting. 'How was he?'

'Very interested,' Kane said. 'Wanted chapter and verse on the whole battle. He seems fascinated by Steiner.'

'Aren't we all. What I'd like to know is where the damn man is now and that Irish scoundrel.'

'Nowhere near the cottage he's been living in, that's for sure. I had a report over the radio from Garvey just before I went in. It seems that when they went to check out this cottage of Devlin's, they found two inspectors from Special Branch waiting for him.'

'Good God,' Corcoran said. 'How on earth did they get on to him?'

'Some police investigation or other. Anyway, he's highly unlikely to turn up there now. Garvey is staying in the area and setting up a couple of road blocks on the coast road, but we can't do much more till we get more men.'

'They're coming in, my boy, believe me.' Corcoran said. 'Since your chaps got the telephones working again, I've had several lengthy discussions with London. Another couple of hours should see the whole of North Norfolk sealed up tight. By morning most of this area will be, to all intents and purposes, under martial law. And it will certainly stay that way until Steiner is caught.'

Kane nodded. 'There's no question that he could get anywhere near the Prime Minister. I've got men on his door, on the terrace outside and at least two dozen prowling out there in the garden, with blackened faces and Thompson guns. I've given it to them straight. They shoot first. Accidents we can argue about afterwards.

The door opened and a young coporal entered, a couple of typewritten sheets in his hand. 'I've got the final lists if you'd like to see them, Major.'

He went out and Kane looked at the first sheet. 'They've had Father Vereker and some of the villagers look at the German bodies.'

'How is he?' Corcoran asked.

'Concussed, but otherwise he seems okay. From what they say everyone is accounted for except for Steiner, his second in command, Neumann, and the Irishman, of course. The other fourteen are all dead.'

'But how in the hell did they get away, that's what I'd like to know?'

'Well, they blasted their way into the sacristy to get out of the line of fire from Garvey and his men up on the leads. My theory is that when Pamela and the Prior girl got out through this priest's tunnel, they were in such a hurry they didn't close the secret door properly.'

Corcoran said, 'I understand the young Prior girl was rather sweet on this scoundrel Devlin. You don't think she could be involved in any way?'

'I wouldn't have thought so. According to Pamela the kid was really bitter and about the whole thing.'

'I suppose so,' Corcoran said. 'Anyway, what about casualties on your side?'

Kane glanced at the second list. 'Including Shafto and Captain Mallory, twenty-one dead, eight wounded.' He shook his head. 'Out of forty. There's going to be one God Almighty rumpus when this gets out.'

'*If* it gets out.'

'What do you mean?'

'London is already making it clear they want a very low profile on this one. They don't want to alarm the people for one thing. I ask you, German Fallschirmjäger dropping into Norfolk to seize the Prime Minister. And coming too damn close for comfort. And what about this British Free Corps? Englishmen in the SS. Can you imagine how *that* would look in the papers?' He shuddered. 'I'd have hung the damn man myself.'

'I see what you mean.'

'And look at it from the Pentagon's point of view. A crack American unit, the elite of the elite, takes on a handful of German paratroopers and sustains a seventy per cent casualty rate.'

'I don't know,' Kane shook his head. 'It's expecting a hell of a lot of people to keep quiet.'

'There's a war on, Kane,' Corcoran said. 'And in wartime, people can be made to do as they are told, it's as simple as that.'

The door opened, the young corporal looked in. 'London on the phone again, Colonel.'

Corcoran went out in a hurry, and Kane followed. He lit a cigarette which he held in the palm of his hand when he went out of the front door and down the steps past the sentries. It was raining hard and very dark, but he could smell fog on the air as he walked across the front terrace. Maybe Corcoran was right? It could happen that way. A world at war was crazy enough for anything to be believable.

He went down the steps and in a moment had an arm about his throat, a knee in his back. A knife gleamed dully. Someone said, 'Identify yourself.'

'Major Kane.'

A torch flicked on and off. 'Sorry, sir. Corporal Bleeker.'

'You should be in bed, Bleeker. How's that eye?'

'Five stitches in it, Major, but it's going to be fine. I'll move on now, sir, with your permission.'

He faded away and Kane stared into the darkness. 'I will never,' he said softly, 'to the end of my days even begin to understand my fellow human beings.'

*

In the North Sea area generally, as the weather report had it, the winds were three to four with rain squalls and some sea fog persisting till morning. The E-Boat had made good time and by eight o'clock they were through the minefields and into the main coastal shipping lane.

Muller was at the wheel and Koenig looked up from the chart table where he had been laying off their final course with great care. 'Ten miles due east of Blakeney Point, Erich.'

Muller nodded, straining his eyes into the murk ahead. 'This fog isn't helping.'

'Oh, I don't know,' Koenig said. 'You might be glad of it before we're through.'

The door banged open and Teusen, the leading telegraphist, entered. He held out a signal flimsy. 'Message from Landsvoort, Herr Leutnant.'

He held out the flimsy, Koenig took it from him and read it in the light of the chart table. He looked down at it for a long moment, then crumpled it into a ball in his right hand.

'What is it?' Muller asked.

'The Eagle is blown. The rest is just words.'

There was a short pause. Rain pattered against the window. Muller said, 'And our orders?'

'To proceed as I see fit.' Koenig shook his head. 'Just think of it. Colonel Steiner, Ritter Neumann – all those fine men.'

For the first time since childhood he felt like crying. He opened the door and stared out into the darkness, rain beating against his face. Muller said carefully, 'Of course, it's always possible some of them might make it. Just one or two. You know how these things go?'

Koenig slammed the door. 'You mean you'd still be willing to go in there?' Muller didn't bother to reply and Koenig turned to Teusen. 'You, too?'

Teusen said, 'We've been together a long time, Herr Leutnant. I've never asked where we were going before.'

Koenig was filled with a wild elation. He slapped him on the back. 'All right, then send this signal.'

*

Radl's condition had deteriorated steadily during the late afternoon and evening, but he had refused to remain in bed in spite of Witt's pleadings. Since Joanna Grey's final message he had insisted on staying in the radio room, lying back in an old armchair Witt had brought in while the operator tried to raise Koenig. The pain in his chest was not only worse, but had spread to his left arm. He was no fool. He knew what that meant. Not that it mattered. Not that anything mattered now.

At five minutes to eight, the operator turned, a smile of triumph on his face. 'I've got them, Herr Oberst. Message received and understood.'

'Thank God,' Radl said and fumbled to open his cigarette case, but suddenly his fingers seemed too stiff and Witt had to do it for him.

'Only one left, Herr Oberst,' he said as he took out the distinctive Russian cigarette and put it in Radl's mouth.

The operator was writing feverishly on his pad. He tore off the sheet and turned, 'Reply, Herr Oberst.'

Radl felt strangely dizzy and his vision wasn't good. He said, 'Read it, Witt.'

'Will still visit nest. Some fledglings may need assistance. Good luck.' Witt looked bewildered. 'Why does he add that, Herr Oberst?'

'Because he is a very perceptive young man who suspects I'm going to need it as much as he does.' He shook his head slowly. 'Where do we get them from, these boys? To dare so much, sacrifice everything and for what?'

Witt looked troubled. 'Herr Oberst, please.'

Radl smiled. 'Like this last of my Russian cigarettes, my friend, all good things come to an end sooner or later.' He turned to the radio operator and braced himself to do what should have been done at least two hours earlier. 'Now you can get me Berlin.'

*

There was a decaying farm cottage on the eastern boundary of Prior Farm, at the back of the wood on the opposite side of the main road above Hobs End. It provided some sort of shelter for the Morris.

It was seven-fifteen when Devlin and Steiner left Molly to look after Ritter and went down through the trees to make a cautious reconnaisance. They were just in time to see Garvey and his men go up the dyke road to the cottage. They retreated through the trees and crouched in the lee of a wall to consider the situation.

'Not so good,' Devlin said.

'You don't need to go to the cottage. You can cut through the marsh on foot and still reach that beach in time,' Steiner pointed out.

'For what?' Devlin sighed. 'I've a terrible confession to make, Colonel. I went off in such a devil of a hurry that I left the S-phone at the bottom of a carrier-bag filled with spuds that's hanging behind the kitchen door.'

Steiner laughed softly. 'My friend, you are truly yourself alone. God must have broken the mould after turning you out.'

'I know,' Devlin said. 'A hell of a thing to live with, but staying with the present situation, I can't call Koenig without it.'

'You don't think he'll come in without a signal?'

'That was the arrangement. Any time between nine and ten as ordered. Another thing. Whatever happened to Joanna Grey, it's likely she got some sort of a message off to Landsvoort. If Radl has passed it on to Koenig, he and his boys could be already on their way back.'

'No,' Steiner said. 'I don't think so. Koenig will come. Even if he fails to get your signal, he will come to that beach.'

'Why should he?'

'Because he told me he would,' Steiner said simply. 'So you see, you could manage without the S-phone. Even if the Rangers search the area, they won't bother with the beach because the signs say it is mined. If you get there in good time you can walk along the estuary for at least a quarter of a mile with the tide as it is.'

'With Ritter in his state of health?'

'All he needs is a stick and a shoulder to lean on. Once in Russia he walked eighty miles in three days through snow with a bullet in his right foot. When a man knows he'll die if he stays where he is, it concentrates his mind wonderfully on moving somewhere else. You'll save a considerable amount of time. Meet Koenig on his way in.'

'You're not going with us.' It was a statement of fact, not a question.

'I think you know where I must go, my friend.'

Devlin sighed. 'I was always the great believer in letting a man go to hell his own way, but I'm willing to make an exception in your case. You won't even get close. They'll have more guards round him than there are flies on a jam jar on a hot summer day.'

'In spite of that I must try.'

'Why, because you think it might help your father's case back home? That's an illusion. Face up to it. Nothing you do can help him if that old sod at Prinz Albrechtstrasse decides otherwise.'

'Yes, you're very probably right. I think I've always known that.'

'Then why?'

'Because I find it impossible to do anything else.'

'I don't understand.'

'I think you do. This game you play. Trumpets on the wind, the tricolour fluttering bravely in the grey morning. Up the Republic. Remember Easter nineteen-sixteen. But tell me this, my friend. In the end, do you control the game, or does the game possess you? Can you stop, if you want, or must it always be the same? Trenchcoats and Thompson guns, my life for Ireland until the day you lie in the gutter with a bullet in your back?'

Devlin said hoarsely, 'God knows, I don't.'

'But I do, my friend. And now, I think, we should rejoin the others. You will naturally say nothing about my personal plans. Ritter could prove difficult.'

'All right,' Devlin said reluctantly.

They moved back through the night to the ruined cottage where they found Molly rebandaging one of Ritter's thighs. 'How are you doing?' Steiner asked him.

'Fine,' Ritter answered, but when Steiner put a hand on his forehead it was damp with sweat.

Molly joined Devlin in the angle of the two walls where he sheltered from the rain, smoking a cigarette. 'He's not good,' she said. 'Needs a doctor if you ask me.'

'You might as well send for an undertaker,' Devlin said. 'But never mind him. It's you I'm worried about now. You could be in serious trouble from this night's work.'

She was curiously indifferent. 'Nobody saw me get you out of

the church, nobody can prove I did. As far as they're concerned
I've been sitting on the heath in the rain crying my heart out at
finding the truth about my lover.'

'For God's sake, Molly.'

'Poor, silly little bitch, they'll say Got her fingers burned and
serves her right for trusting a stranger.'

He said awkwardly, 'I haven't thanked you.'

'It doesn't matter. I didn't do it for you. I did it for me.' She was
a simple girl in many ways and content to be so and yet now, more
than at any other time in her life, she wanted to be able to express
herself with complete certainty. 'I love you. That doesn't mean I
like what you are or what you've done or even understand it.
That's something different. The love is a separate issue. It's in a
compartment of its own. That's why I got you out of that church
tonight. Not because it was right or wrong, but because I couldn't
have lived with myself if I'd stood by and let you die.' She pulled
herself free. 'I'd better check on how the lieutenant is getting on.'

She walked over to the car and Devlin swallowed hard. Wasn't
it the strange thing? The bravest speech he'd ever heard in his life,
a girl to cheer from the rooftops and here he felt more like crying
at the tragic waste of it all.

*

At twenty past eight, Devlin and Steiner went down through the
trees again. The cottage out there in the marsh was in darkness but
on the main road, there were subdued voices, the dim shape of a
vehicle. 'Let's move a little closer,' Steiner whispered.

They got to the boundary wall between the wood and the road
and peered over. It was raining hard now. There were two jeeps,
one on either side of the road and several Rangers were sheltering
under the trees. A match flared in Garvey's cupped hands, lighting his face for a brief moment.

Steiner and Devlin retreated. 'The big negro,' Steiner said 'The
Master Sergeant who was with Kane, waiting to see if you show
up.'

'Why not at the cottage?'

'He probably has men out there, too. This way he covers the
road as well.'

'It doesn't matter,' Devlin said. 'We can cross the road further down. Make it to the beach on foot as you said.'

'Easier if you had a diversion.'

'Such as?'

'Me in a stolen car passing through that road block. I could do with your trenchcoat, by the way, if you'd consider a permanent loan.'

Devlin couldn't see his face in the darkness and suddenly didn't want to. 'Damn you, Steiner, go to hell your own way,' he said wearily. He unslung his Sten gun, took off the trenchcoat and handed it over. 'You'll find a silenced Mauser in the right-hand pocket and two extra magazines.'

'Thank you,' Steiner took off his *Schiff* and pushed it inside his *Fliegerbluse*. He pulled on the trenchcoat and belted it. 'So, the final end of things. We'll say goodbye here, I think.'

'Tell me one thing,' Devlin said. 'Has it been worth it? Any of it?'

'Oh, no.' Steiner laughed lightly. 'No more philosophy, please.' He held out his hand. 'May you find what you are searching for, my friend.'

'I already have and lost it in the finding,' Devlin told him.

'Then from now on, nothing really matters,' Steiner said. 'A dangerous situation. You will have to take care,' and he turned and went back to the ruined cottage.

They got Ritter out of the car and pushed it to where the track started to slope to a five-barred gate, the road on the other side. Steiner ran down and opened it, pulling a six-foot length of rail off the fence which he gave to Ritter when he got back.

'How's that?' he asked.

'Fine,' Ritter said bravely. 'Do we go now?'

'You, not me. There are Rangers down there on the road. I thought I might arrange a small diversion while you get across. I'll catch up with you later.'

Ritter grabbed his arm and there was panic in his voice. 'No, Kurt, I can't let you do this.'

Steiner said, 'Oberleutnant Neumann, you are undoubtedly the finest soldier I've ever known. From Narvik to Stalingrad, you've never shirked your duty or disobeyed an order of mine and I haven't the slightest intention of letting you start now.'

Ritter tried to straighten up, bracing himself against the rail. 'As the Herr Oberst wishes,' he said formally.

'Good,' Steiner said. 'Go now, please, Mr Devlin, and good luck.'

He opened the car door and Ritter called softly, 'Herr Oberst.'

'Yes?'

'A privilege to serve with you, sir.'

'Thank you, Herr Oberleutnant.'

Steiner got into the Morris, released the brake and the car started to roll down the track.

*

Devlin and Molly went through the trees, Ritter between them, and paused at the side of the low wall. Devlin whispered, 'Time for you to go, girl.'

'I'll see you to the beach, Liam,' she said firmly.

He had no chance to argue because the car engine started forty yards up the road and the Morris's slotted headlights were turned on. One of the Rangers took a red lamp from under his cape and waved it. Devlin had expected the German to drive straight on, but to his astonishment, he slowed. Steiner was taking a coldly calculated risk, something designed to draw every last man there. There was only one way he could do that. He waited for Garvey's approach, his left hand on the wheel, his right holding the Mauser.

Garvey said as he approached. 'Sorry, but you'll have to identify yourself.'

He switched on the torch in his left hand, picking Steiner's face out of the darkness. The Mauser coughed once as Steiner fired, apparently at point blank range, but a good two inches to one side, the wheels skidded as he stamped on the accelerator and was away.

'That was Steiner himself, Goddammit!' Garvey cried. 'Get after him!' There was a mad scramble as everyone jumped to get on board, Garvey's jeep was away first, the other hard behind. The sound dwindled into the night.

Devlin said, 'Right, let's get out of it then,' and he and Molly helped Ritter over the wall and started across the road.

*

Built in 1933, the Morris was still on the road only because of the wartime shortage of new cars. Her engine was virtually worn out and although she suited Vereker's requirements adequately enough, they were not those of Steiner that night. With his foot flat on the boards, the needle hovered on forty and obstinately refused to move beyond that point.

He had minutes only, not even that, for as he debated the merits of stopping suddenly and taking to the woods on foot, Garvey, in the lead jeep, started to fire its Browning. Steiner ducked over the wheel, bullets hammered through the body, the windscreen dissolved in a snowstorm of flying glass.

The Morris swerved to the right, smashed through some wooden railings and lumbered down a slope of young firs. The braking effect of these was such that the speed was not very great. Steiner got the car door open and tumbled out. He was on his feet in a moment, moving away through the trees into the darkness as the Morris went into the flooded waters of the marsh below and started to sink.

The jeeps skidded to a halt on the road above. Garvey was first out, going down the bank fast, the torch ready in his hand. As he reached the bank, the muddy waters of the marsh closed over the roof of the Morris.

He took off his helmet and started to unbuckle his belt and Krukowski, sliding down after him, grabbed him by the arm. 'Don't even think it. That isn't just water down there. The mud in some of these places is deep enough to swallow a man whole.'

Garvey nodded slowly. 'Yes, I suppose you're right.' He played his torch on the surface of the muddy pool where bubbles broke through, then turned and went back up the slope to radio in.

*

Kane and Corcoran were having supper in the ornate front drawing room, when the corporal from the radio room rushed in with the signal. Kane looked at it briefly then slid it across the polished surface of the table.

'My God, and he was pointing in this direction, you realize that?' Corcoran frowned in distaste. 'What a way for such a man to go.'

Kane nodded. He should have been pleased and felt curiously depressed. He said to the corporal, 'Tell Garvey to stay where he is, then get the motor pool to send some sort of recovery vehicle out to him. I want Colonel Steiner's body out of there.'

The corporal went out and Corcoran said, 'What about the other one and the Irishman?'

'I don't think we need worry. They'll turn up, but not here.' Kane sighed. 'No, in the end it was Steiner on his own, I think. The sort of man who never knows when to give up.'

Corcoran went to the sideboard and poured two large whiskies. He handed one to Kane. 'I won't say cheers because I think I know how you feel. A strange sense of personal loss.'

'Exactly.'

'I've been at this game for too long, I think.' Corcoran shivered and downed his whisky. 'Will you tell the Prime Minister or shall I?'

'Your privilege, I fancy, sir.' Kane managed a smile. 'I'd better let the men know.'

When he went out of the front door it was pouring with rain and he stood at the top of the steps in the porch and shouted, 'Corporal Bleeker?'

'Bleeker ran out of the darkness within a few moments and came up the steps. His combat jacket was soaked, his helmet shiny with rain and the dark camouflage cream on his face had streaked.

Kane said, 'Garvey and his boys got Steiner back along the coast road. Spread the word.'

Bleeker said, 'That's it then. Do we stand down, sir?'

'No, but you can phase the guard system now. Work it so you get some time off in turns for a hot meal and so on.'

Bleeker started down the steps and vanished into the darkness. The Major stayed there for quite some time, staring out into the rain and then finally turned and went back inside.

*

The cottage at Hobs End was in total darkness as Devlin, Molly and Ritter Neumann approached. They paused by the wall and Devlin whispered. 'It looks quiet enough to me.'

'Not worth the risk,' Ritter whispered.

But Devlin, thinking of the S-phone, said stubbornly, 'And bloody daft we'd be and no one in the place. You two keep moving along the dyke. I'll catch you up.'

He slipped away before either of them could protest, and went across the yard cautiously and listened at the window. All was quiet, only the rain falling, not a chink of light anywhere. The front door opened to his touch with a slight creak and he moved into the hall, the Sten gun ready.

The living room door stood ajar, a few embers from the dying fire glowing redly on the hearth. He stepped inside and knew instantly that he had made a very bad mistake. The door slammed behind him, the muzzle of a Browning was rammed into the side of his neck and the Sten plucked from his hand.

'Hold it right there,' Jack Rogan said. 'All right, Fergus, let's have a little light on the situation.'

A match flared as Fergus Grant touched the wick of the oil lamp and replaced the glass chimney. Rogan put his knee into Devlin's back and sent him staggering across the room. 'Let's have a look at you.'

Devlin half-turned, a foot on the hearth. He put a hand on the mantelpiece. 'I haven't had the honour.'

'Chief Inspector Rogan, Inspector Grant, Special Branch.'

'The Irish Section, is it?'

'That's right, son, and don't ask for my warrant card or I'll belt you.' Rogan sat on the edge of the table, holding his Browning against his thigh. 'You know, you've been a very naughty boy from what I hear.'

'Do you tell me?' Devlin said, leaning a little further into the hearth, knowing that even if he got to the Walther his chances were of the slimmest. Whatever Rogan might be doing, Grant was taking no chances and had him covered.

'Yes, you really give me a pain, you people,' Rogan said. 'Why can't you stay back there in the bogs where you belong?'

'It's a thought,' Devlin said.

Rogan took a pair of handcuffs out of his coat pocket. 'Get over here.'

A stone crashed through the window on the other side of the blackout curtain and both policemen turned in alarm. Devlin's hand reached for the Walther hanging on the nail at the back of the beam that supported the chimney breast. He shot Rogan in the head, knocking him back off the table, but Grant was already turning. He got off one wild shot that caught the Irishman in the right shoulder and Devlin fell back in the easy chair, still firing, shattering the young inspector's left arm, putting another bullet into the shoulder on the same side.

Grant fell back against the wall and slid down to the floor. He seemed in deep shock and gazed across the room uncomprehendingly at Rogan lying on the other side of the table. Devlin picked up the Browning and stuffed it in his waistband, then went to the door, took down the carrier bag and emptied the potatoes on the floor. The small canvas bag at the bottom contained the S-phone and a few other odds and ends and he slung it over his shoulder.

'Why don't you kill me as well?' Fergus Grant said weakly.

'You're nicer than he was,' Devlin said. 'I'd find a better class of work, son, if I was you.'

He went out quickly. When he opened the front door, Molly was standing against the wall. 'Thank God!' she said, but he put a hand to her mouth and hurried her away. They reached the wall where Ritter waited. Molly said, 'What happened?'

'I killed a man, wounded another, that's what happened,' Devlin told her. 'Two Special Branch detectives.'

'I helped you do that?'

'Yes,' he said. 'Will you go now, Molly, while you still can?'

She turned from him suddenly and started to run back along the dyke. Devlin hesitated and then, unable to contain himself, went after her. He caught her within a few yards and pulled her into his arms. Her hands went to his neck, she kissed him with a passion that was all-consuming. He pushed her away. 'Go now, girl, and God go with you.'

She turned without a word and ran into the night and Devlin went back to Ritter Neumann. 'A very remarkable young woman,' the Oberleutnant said.

'Yes, you could say that,' Devlin told him, 'And you'd be making the understatement of the age.' He got the S-phone out of the bag and switched on to channel. 'Eagle to Wanderer. Eagle to Wanderer. Come in please.'

On the bridge of the E-boat where the S-phone receiver had been situated, his voice sounded as clearly as if he was just outside the door. Koenig reached for the mike quickly, his heart beating. 'Eagle, this is Wanderer. What is your situation?'

'Two fledglings still in the nest,' Devlin said. 'Can you come immediately?'

'We're on our way,' Koenig told him. 'Over and out.' He put the mike back on its hook and turned to Muller. 'Right, Erich, switch to silences and break out the White Ensign. We're going in.'

*

As Devlin and Neumann reached the trees, the Irishman glanced back and saw car headlights turn out of the main road and move along the dyke path. Ritter said, 'Who do you think it is?'

'God knows,' Devlin told him.

Garvey, waiting a couple of miles along the road for the recovery vehicle, had decided to send the other jeep back to check on the two Special Branch men.

Devlin got a hand under Ritter's arm. 'Come on, son, we'd better get out of this.' He cursed suddenly at the searing pain in his shoulder now that the shock was beginning to wear off.

'Are you all right?' Ritter asked.

'Bleeding like Mrs O'Grady's pig. I stopped one in the shoulder back there, but never mind that now. Nothing like a sea voyage to cure what ails you.'

They went past the warning notice, picked their way gingerly through the barbed wire and started across the beach. Ritter was gasping with pain at every step. He leaned heavily on the rail Steiner had given him, yet he never faltered. The sands stretched wide and flat before them, fog rolling in on the wind, and then they were walking on water, only an inch or two at first, rather more in the depressions.

They paused to take stock and Devlin looked back and saw lights moving in the trees, 'Christ almighty,' he said. 'Don't they ever give up?'

They stumbled on towards the estuary across the sands and as the tide flowed in, the water grew deeper. At first knee-deep and then it was up to their thighs. They were well out into the estuary now and Ritter groaned suddenly and fell to one knee, dropping his rail. 'It's no good, Devlin. I've had it. I've never known such pain.'

Devlin crouched beside him and raised the S-phone to his mouth again. 'Wanderer, this is Eagle. We are waiting for you in the estuary a quarter of a mile off-shore. Signalling now.'

From the canvas bag he took out a luminous signal ball, another gift from the Abwehr by courtesy of SOE, and held it up in the palm of his right hand. He glanced round towards the shore, but the fog had rolled in now, blanketing everything back there.

*

Twenty minutes later, the water was up to his chest. He had never been so cold in his life before. He stood on the sandbank, legs apart, his left arm supporting Ritter, his right hand holding the luminous signalling ball high, the tide flowing around them.

'It's no good,' Ritter whispered. 'I can't feel a thing. I'm finished. I can't take any more.'

'As Mrs O'Flynn said to the Bishop,' Devlin said. 'Come on, boy, don't give in now. What would Steiner say?'

'Steiner?' Ritter coughed, choking a little as salt water slopped over his chin and into his mouth. 'He'd have swum across.'

Devlin forced a laugh. 'That's the way, son, keep smiling.' He started to sing at the top of his voice, 'And down the glen rode Sarsfield's men all in their jackets green.'

A wave passed right over his head and they went under. Oh, Christ, he thought, this is it, but when it had rolled on, still managed to find his feet, his right hand holding the signalling ball high, although by now, the water was up to his chin.

It was Teusen who caught sight of the light to port and ran to the bridge instantly. Three minutes later, the E-boat slid out of the darkness and someone shone a torch down on the two men. A net was thrown over, four seamen clambered down and willing hands reached for Ritter Neumann.

'Watch him,' Devlin urged. 'He's in a bad way.'

When he went over the rail himself a couple of moments later and collapsed, it was Koenig who knelt beside him with a blanket, 'Mr Devlin, drink some of this.' He passed him a bottle.

'Cead mile Failte,' Devlin said.

Koenig leaned close. 'I'm sorry, I don't understand.'

'And how would you? It's Irish, the language of kings. I simply said, a hundred thousand welcomes.'

Koenig smiled through the darkness. 'I am glad to see you, Mr Devlin. A miracle.'

'The only one you're likely to get this night.'

'You are certain?'

'As the coffin lid closing.'

Koenig stood up. 'Then we will go now. Please excuse me.'

A moment later, the E-boat swung round and surged forward. Devlin got the cork out of the bottle and sniffed at the contents. *Rum*. Not one of his favourites, but he swallowed deep and huddled against the stern rail looking back towards the land.

In her bedroom at the farm, Molly sat up suddenly, then moved across the room and drew the curtains. She threw the windows open and leaned out into the rain, a tremendous feeling of elation, of release filling her and at that very moment, the E-boat moved from behind the Point and turned out towards the open sea.

*

In his office at Prinz Albrechtstrasse, Himmler worked at his eternal files in the light of the desk lamp. There was a knock at the door and Rossman entered.

'Well?' Himmler said.

'I'm sorry to disturb you, Herr Reichsführer, but we've had a signal from Landsvoort. The Eagle is blown.'

Himmler showed no emotion whatsoever. He laid down his pen carefully and held out his hand. 'Let me see.' Rossman gave him the signal and Himmler read it through. After a while, he looked up. 'I have an errand for you.'

'Herr Reichsführer.'

'Take two of your most trusted men. Fly to Landsvoort at once and arrest Colonel Radl. I will see that you have all the necessary authorization before you leave.'

'Of course, Herr Reichsführer. And the charge?'

'Treason against the state. That should do for a start. Report to me as soon as you get back.' Himmler picked up his pen and started to write again and Rossman withdrew.

*

Just before nine o'clock Corporal George Watson of the Military Police ran his motor-cycle into the side of the road a couple of miles south from Meltham House and pushed it up on its stand. Having ridden from Norwich with almost torrential rain the whole way, he was soaked to the skin, in spite of his long dispatch rider's coat – bitterly cold and very hungry. He was also lost.

He opened his map case in the light of his headlamp and leaned down to check it. A slight movement to his right made him look up. A man in a trenchcoat was standing there. 'Hello,' he said. 'Lost, are you?'

'I'm trying to find Meltham House,' Watson told him. 'All the way from Norwich in this bloody rain. These country districts all look the same with the damned signposts missing.'

'Here, let me show you,' Steiner said.

Watson leaned down to examine the map again in the light from the headlamp, the Mauser rose and fell across the back of his neck. He lay in a puddle of water and Steiner pulled his dispatch case over his head and examined the contents quickly. There was only one letter heavily sealed and marked *Urgent*. It was addressed to Colonel William Corcoran, Meltham House.

Steiner got hold of Watson under the armpits and dragged him into the shadows. When he re-appeared a few moments later, he was wearing the dispatch rider's long raincoat, helmet and goggles and leather gauntlets. He pulled the sling of the dispatch case over his head, pushed the motor-cycle off its stand, kicked the engine into life and rode away.

*

At the side of the road they had a spotlight set up and as the Scammel recovery truck's winch started to revolve, the Morris came up out of the march on the bank. Garvey stayed up on the road, waiting.

The corporal in charge had the door open. He peered inside and looked up. 'There's nothing here.'

'What in the hell are you talking about?' Garvey demanded and he moved down through the trees quickly.

He looked inside the Morris, but the corporal was right. Lots of stinking mud, a certain amount of water, but no Steiner. 'Oh, my God,' Garvey said as the full implication hit him and he turned, scrambled up the bank, and grabbed for the mike on his jeep's radio.

*

Steiner turned in at the gate of Meltham House, which was closed, and halted. The Ranger on the other side shone a torch on him and called, 'Sergeant of the Guard.'

Sergeant Thomas came out of the lodge and approached the gate. Steiner sat there, anonymous in helmet and goggles. 'What is it?' Thomas demanded.

Steiner opened his dispatch case, took out the letter and held it close to the bars. 'Dispatch from Norwich for Colonel Corcoran.'

Thomas nodded, the Ranger next to him unbolted the gate. 'Straight up to the front of the house. One of the sentries will take you in.'

Steiner rode up the drive and turned away from the front door, following a branch that finally brought him to the motor pool at the rear of the building. He stopped beside a parked truck, switched off and pushed the motor-cycle up on its stand, then turned and followed the path round towards the garden. When he'd gone a few yards, he stepped into the shelter of the rhododendrons.

He removed the crash helmet, the raincoat and gauntlets, took his *Schiff* from inside his *Fliegerbluse* and put it on. He adjusted the Knight's Cross at his throat and moved off, the Mauser ready.

He paused on the edge of a sunken garden below the terrace to get his bearings. The blackout wasn't too good, chinks of light showing at several windows. He took a step forward and someone said. 'That you, Bleeker?'

Steiner grunted. A dim shape moved forward. The Mauser coughed in his right hand, there was a startled gasp as the Ranger slumped to the ground. In the same moment, a curtain was pulled back and light fell across the terrace above.

When Steiner looked up, he saw the Prime Minister standing at the balustrade smoking a cigar.

*

When Corcoran came out of the Prime Minister's room he found Kane waiting. 'How is he?' Kane asked.

'Fine. Just gone out on the terrace for a last cigar and then he's going to bed.'

They moved into the hall. 'He probably wouldn't sleep too well if he heard my news, so I'll keep it till morning,' Kane told him. 'They hauled that Morris out of the marsh and no Steiner.'

Corcoran said. 'Are you suggesting he got away? How do you know he isn't still down there? He might have been thrown out or something.'

The front door opened and Sergeant Thomas came in. He unbuttoned his coat to shake the rain from it. 'You wanted me, Major?'

'Yes,' Kane said. 'When they got the car out, Steiner was missing. We're taking no chances and doubling the guard. Nothing to report from the gate?'

'Not a damn thing since the recovery Scammel went out. Only that military policeman from Norwich with the dispatch for Colonel Corcoran.'

Corcoran stared at him, frowning. 'That's the first I've heard of it. When was this?'

'Maybe ten minutes ago, sir.'

'Oh, my God!' Kane said. 'He's here! The bastard's here!' And he turned, tugging at the Colt automatic in the holster at his waist and ran for the library door. *

Steiner went up the steps to the terrace slowly. The scent of the good Havana cigar perfumed the night. As he put foot on the top step it crunched in gravel. The Prime Minister turned sharply and looked at him.

He removed the cigar from his mouth, that implacable face showing no kind of reaction, and said, 'Oberstleutnant Kurt Steiner of the Fallschirmjäger, I presume?'

'Mr Churchill.' Steiner hesitated. 'I regret this, but I must do my duty, sir.'

'Then what are you waiting for?' the Prime Minister said calmly.

Steiner raised the Mauser, the curtains at the French windows billowed and Harry Kane stumbled through, firing wildly. His first bullet hit Steiner in the right shoulder spinning him round, the second caught him in the heart, killing him instantly, pushing him back over the balustrade.

Corcoran arrived on the terrace a moment later, revolver in hand, and below in the sunken garden, Rangers appeared from the darkness on the run, to pause and stand in a semi-circle. Steiner lay in the pool of light from the open window, the Knight's Cross at his throat, the Mauser still gripped firmly in his right hand.

'Strange,' the Prime Minister said. 'With his finger on the trigger, he hesitated. I wonder why?'

'Perhaps that was his American half speaking, sir?' Harry Kane said.

The Prime Minister had the final word. 'Whatever else may be said, he was a fine soldier and a brave man. See to him, Major.' He turned and went back inside.

20

As regards the historical characters involved in this story, the whole world knows of the events in the Führer-bunker in Berlin during those last few mad days in April, 1945. Admiral Wilhelm Canaris finally fell from grace when the Abwehr was dissolved in February 1944 and was arrested with hundreds of others during the wave of hysteria following the attempt on Hitler's life of July, 1944. Less than a month before the end of the war, after a summary SS trial at Flossenburg concentration camp, he was dragged from his cell naked on 9 April and hanged.

Heinrich Himmler tried to lose himself in the chaos that was Germany in the days immediately after the end of hostilities, wearing a black eyepatch and private's uniform. Apprehended by the British, he committed suicide by swallowing a vial of potassium cyanide concealed in his gums.

Rossman fared rather better. He survived the war and was an officer of the Hamburg Police Department for several years until 1955, when on the arrest and trial of former colleagues, particularly those involved in the execution of Canaris and others at Flossenburg, he dropped out of sight and was transported to South America by the 'Odessa' organization of ex-members of the SS. The documents relating to the execution of Major General of Artillery Karl Steiner were found, with similar records, at Prinz Albrechstrasse. They are now on file at Ludwigsburg with the Central Federal Agency that attempts, with a rather conspicuous lack of success, to do something about crimes committed during the Nazi era.

Jurgen Stroop, that monstrous creature whom Steiner faced on the platform at the railway station in Warsaw that memorable day, was convicted at Nuremburg, the only evidence necessary being the beautifully bound book he'd prepared for the Führer entitled *The Jewish Ghetto in Warsaw No Longer Exists* in which he described in meticulous detail, in diary form, exactly what he had done. A record he was obviously proud of, therefore it is hardly surprising that he fails to mention a German colonel named Steiner and his men who had so disgraced themselves.

I have been to Warsaw, examined the spot where they finally hanged Stroop, looked upon the memorial to the dead of the Ghetto. As for Steiner, when I mentioned the events of that day to my host, an ex-member of the Polish Home Army, he remembered the story well. Brana Lezemnikof, the little Jewish girl Steiner saved, had jumped from the train seven miles out of the city and had been found in a ditch with a broken ankle by members of a partisan unit. She survived the war and was last heard of in 1947 on leaving Warsaw for Marseilles with a group of other Jews, their intention being to take passage on one of the boats attempting to run the British blockade into Palestine. I hope she made it.

*

There are few official records covering anything I've mentioned earlier. An item here, another there. Tiny pieces of a vast jigsaw. Vereker stated the British point of view very adequately, while the débâcle of Shafto's attack on the village and the shattering losses suffered by his men were enough to make Washington put down a blanket security cover just as tight.

Germany in November 1943 needed victories, not defeats. Studley Constable was not Gran Sasso and so Himmler used all his extraordinary powers of life and death to make sure that it had never happened at all.

That Max Radl survived until December 1945 can only be put down to the extraordinary fact that when Rossman and his Gestapo aides arrived in Holland to arrest him he was already in an Amsterdam hospital under intensive care after suffering a massive heart attack. As he was not expected to live, he was left to die in peace.

He survived, as an invalid, for almost two years with his beloved Trudi and their three daughters in the beautiful village of Holzbach in the Bavarian Alps. Here, he spent much of his time completing and editing his diary account of those crucial weeks, the diary that his widow, after much persuasion, finally allowed me to read during one memorable weekend in June 1973.

Armed with such detailed information, the rest was comparatively easy, for people who were not prepared to talk about the affair at first usually changed their minds when I told them how much I already knew.

So many were dead, of course. Ritter Neumann was killed fighting as a sergeant in a French Foreign Legion parachute regiment at Dien Bien Phu in 1954 and Paul Koenig, the brave young sailor who took the gamble of his life that dark night, died three days after D-day making a torpedo run on British transports using Mulberry Harbour when his E-boat was blown out of the water by the guns of an American destroyer.

Erich Muller survived, however, and I traced him to Rotterdam where he is now managing director of one of the largest deep-sea salvage operations in Europe and also a naturalized Dutchman. He talked easily enough over dinner on one of the canal boats that run through the city and told me pretty well everything.

It was towards the end that he made the remark that seemed so extraordinary to me. 'Tell me,' he said, 'because after all these years I'd love to know. What was it all about?'

'You honestly don't know?' I said.

'All we were told was where to pick them up. Nothing about the purpose of the whole thing. Reich security and so on. Not to be talked about under any circumstances or else, as those Gestapo bastards who turned up when we got back made very clear.'

I told him and when I was finished, he said, 'So that was it?'

'The biggest prize of all.'

He shook his head. 'In the salvage game we have a saying. No save, no pay. It doesn't mean a damn thing if you don't bring the boat back with you.' He shook his head, echoing Koenig's words. 'All those fine men and all for nothing.' He reached for his glass. 'At least we can drink to them and to Paul Koenig, the best sailor I ever knew. And here's luck to you too, my friend, because you're going to need it.' He grinned. 'Nobody will ever believe you.'

*

John Amery, founding father of the British Legion of St George, was sentenced to death for high treason by Mr Justice Humphreys in No. 1 Court at the Old Bailey in November 1945, and Harvey Preston's comrades of the British Free Corps fared no better. In spite of intensive recruiting, the SS never succeeded in raising it beyond a strength of two platoons. Those who survived the war received sentences varying from life down to a year or two. An interesting photo still exists showing twenty men and a sergeant serving with the SS Panzer grenadier division Nordland. When this unit was sent to Berlin to take part in the last terrible battle for the city, the British contingent was ordered to Templin on 15 April 1945, and their names disappear from the Division's records. Preston was, perhaps, in some ways luckier than he knew.

After one brilliant commando exploit following another, Otto Skorzeny stood in the dock at Dachau in 1947 for no greater crime than that he had been responsible for operations in which his men had worn American uniforms. The prosecution was discomfited to find that the chief witness for the defence was a British officer and holder of the George Cross, Wing Commander Yeo-Thomas, the brilliant secret service agent known as the White Rabbit. Betrayed to the Gestapo, tortured, he had escaped from Buchenwald and disclosed to the court that he had known of operations in which British agents and members of the French resistance wore German uniforms. The case against Skorzeny collapsed and he was acquitted of all charges against him. He was luckier than those of his men captured wearing GI uniforms in the Ardennes in 1944, who were executed out of hand by the Americans for this breach of the Geneva Convention. Vereker had known what he was talking about.

Karl Hofer disappeared as if wiped off the face of the earth, a victim of Rossman and his Gestapo aides, no doubt, for if ever a man knew too much, it was Hofer.

But Harry Kane's luck held, for he finished the war a full colonel, as they told me when I checked with the Pentagon Records Department in Washington. He was living in California, it seemed, so I flew to San Francisco, hired a car and took a chance by driving down to the house at Big Sur on the first Sunday and throwing the whole thing right at him.

It worked beautifully, for he was vastly intrigued. He'd been a writer for years. Filmscripts to start with, then television, and he was now more involved in the production side. He'd married Pamela Vereker in 1945. He spoke quite openly about it as we walked on the beach that afternoon. My impression was that it had not worked out too well, but in any event, she had died of leukaemia in 1948.

He was fascinated to hear my story, the German side of the affair that he'd never known anything about, and willingly filled in gaps for me, not only as regards the final stages of the battle at Studley Constable, but subsequent events at Meltham House later that night.

'It's ironic when you think of it,' he said. 'I saved the life of one of the greatest men of my generation with half a second to spare and because of the security clampdown, I didn't even get a mention in dispatches.'

'Was it as bad as that?'

'Brother, you've got no idea. Every single individual interviewed personally where it was made plain that the whole thing had the highest possible security classification. Ten years in the stockade for any guy who opened his mouth. Not that it mattered. After the Studley Constable affair, the outfit was officially disbanded, then regrouped as a kind of élite airborne pathfinding unit which, in case you don't know, is just a highly specialized way of committing suicide. There were only about ninety in the outfit before Studley Constable, remember. The way I see it, some bright boy at the Pentagon thought it was a good way of getting rid of the rest of us.'

'Did he succeed?'

'You could say that. On the night before D-day we went in as pathfinders for the 82nd and 101st Airborne Divisions near St Mère Église. There was too much wind and on top of that somebody got his navigation slightly wrong. Anyway, we were dropped five miles off target right in the lap of a crack German outfit. Panzergrenadiers.' He shook his head. 'The worst hand-to-hand fighting I've ever seen. Most of our guys were dead before morning.'

'Was Dexter Garvey there?'

'Still is. I visited his grave when I was in France last year. Sergeant Thomas. Corporal Bleeker. A bad business.'

It began to rain so we started back towards the house. 'But surely,' I said, 'after all these years, haven't you ever felt tempted to write the whole thing up?'

'Still classified information. Not that that would worry me after thirty years, but I'll show you something when we get back.'

Which he did. A typewritten memoir of the affair, the edges of the paper yellow with age. 'So you did write it up?' I said.

'About twelve years ago; and then this happened around the same time.' He tossed across a magazine, one of the how-I-won-the-war variety with a girl on the front in her underwear spraying a bunch of Gestapo men with a Tommy-gun held in one hand, while she cut the bonds of her rugged GI lover with a knife held in the other.

'Page twenty,' Kane said.

The article was entitled: 'How I saved Winston Churchill'. It was a hair-raising and inaccurate account of events in which even the place names were wrong. The writer had placed the action, for example, in Melton Constable, a small Norfolk market town, obviously confusing this with Studley Constable. Steiner had become Oberst von Stagen of the SS and so on.

'Who on earth wrote this rubbish?'

He showed me the name which I'd missed because it was right under the title and to one side in the small print. *Jerzy Krukowski. Shafto's radio man. The boy who had shot Joanna Grey.* I passed it back. 'Did you get in touch with him?'

'Oh, yes. Found him living on his disability pension in Phoenix. He sustained a bad head wound on that D-day drop. The poor devil actually thought this was going to make his fortune.'

'What happened?'

'Nothing.' Kane waved the magazine at me. 'Who ever believes what's in these things?' He shook his head. 'Let me tell you something, Higgins. In spite of everything the army tried, that story leaked almost as soon as it happened. You used to hear it around in distorted versions, but nobody believed it. The air was full of stories like that in those days. Otto Skorzeny was going to get Eisenhower, someone had tried for Patton. In the end, there was so much fiction around, the truth kind of drowned in it, I guess.' He tossed his script to me. 'Anyway, you can have that and good luck to you, but I haven't said a word. Now, let's have another drink.'

*

Sir Henry Willoughby had died in 1953, but Brigadier William Corcoran I found living in retirement at Rock in Cornwall across the Camel estuary from Padstowe. He was eighty-two years of age and received me courteously enough. Even allowed me to tell my story. At the end, he just as courteously and firmly told me that I must be stark, staring, raving mad and showed me the door.

I fared no better with ex-Inspector Fergus Grant of the Irish Section of the Special Branch, now managing director of one of the largest private security companies in the country. When I wrote asking for an appointment, I received by return a letter informing me that under no circumstances did he wish any kind of communication with me, so somebody had got to him. On the other hand, he'd obviously taken Devlin's advice to heart and got himself into a better class of work entirely.

*

And Devlin? Strangely enough I got on to him through Peter Gericke, who was, I discovered, living in Hamburg; improbably, for an ex-flyer, a Planning Director with a shipping firm specializing in cruises. He was in the Far East when I first tried to see him and it was two months before we had our first meeting. He had a house at Blankenese on the Elbe, a pleasant enough place, and took me for a meal in one of the restaurants that is built out over the river on pilings.

And the difference between Gericke and most of the others was that he knew everything. Almost as much as I did, for it seemed that into the private ward where he lay in the hospital in Amsterdam they had carried Ritter Neumann and Liam Devlin. From all accounts, a high old time of it the three of them had during the time they were cooped up in there. It was over the coffee that he dropped his bombshell.

'I'm surprised Liam has lasted as long as he has. I saw him in Sweden at a party last year, quite by chance, taking a rest from Belfast.'

'Belfast?' I said.

'But surely you knew? Here, just a moment.'

He opened his wallet, went through the contents quickly and produced a folded newspaper clipping. I opened it out and my heart turned to stone. The face was that of a man I'd heard of since childhood, one of the great mythological figures of the underworld of Irish politics, a prime architect of the Provisional IRA movement, chased by the British Army from one end of Ulster to the other for four years now.

'And *he* is Liam Devlin?' I said, stunned by the enormity of it.

'Yes, since 1943 I've seen him a dozen or fifteen times. We've kept in fairly close touch.'

'What happened to him? Afterwards, I mean?'

'We all expected the worst the Reichsführer could offer. What saved me personally, I think, was that my right leg gave such trouble they had to take it off.' He tapped his knee and smiled. 'You hadn't noticed. It kept me in hospital for over a year. The same thing applied to Ritter to a certain extent. He had six months in bed, but Liam was on his feet in a matter of a few weeks and feared the worst, so he simply walked out one night. He told me years later that after considerable difficulties, he made his way to Lisbon where he took ship for America. He stayed there for some years, teaching, I believe, in a small Indiana college. He returned to Ireland for a brief period during the IRA campaign of the late fifties. When that failed, he went back to America.'

'And returned when things really started to warm up again?'

'And as they say, has never looked back.'

It was still difficult to believe. 'It's a miracle he's still alive.'

'You intend to see him?'

'Yes, I think so.'

'Give him my best and tell him . . . tell him—' He appeared to hesitate.

'What?' I said, curious.

He suddenly looked very sad indeed. 'No, what would be the point? I tried to say it all years ago. This senseless violence, the dark path he walks.' He shook his head. 'There can only be one end, you know.'

                                    *

But before Belfast I returned to Studley Constable, for there was still one other person left to see. Someone very special indeed. Prior Farm must have changed a lot since Devlin's time. There was a silage tower, numerous outbuildings and the yard had been concreted. When I knocked at the front door it was opened by a young woman in an overall with a child on her hip.

'Yes?' she said politely enough.

'I don't know if you can help me?' I told her. 'Actually, I'm trying to get in touch with Molly Prior.'

She burst into laughter. 'My goodness, you are out of date.' She called, 'Mum, someone to see you.'

The woman who came into the hall had iron-grey hair and wore an apron. Her sleeves were rolled up and there was flour to her elbows. 'Molly Prior?' I asked.

She really did look astonished. 'Not since 1944, that was when I changed my name to Howard.' She smiled. 'What's all this about?'

I opened my wallet and extracted a newspaper cutting similar to the one Gericke had shown me. 'I thought you might find this interesting.'

Her eyes widened, she wiped her hands on her apron and caught my arm. 'Come in. Please do come in.'

We sat in the front parlour and talked while she held the clipping in her hand. 'It's strange,' she said. 'I do believe I've heard that name, but I never connected it with Liam.'

'And you've never seen a newspaper picture like this of him before?'

'We only get the local paper and I never read that. Always too busy.'

'Then how can you be certain it's him? How could you even be certain he was alive?'

'He wrote to me,' she said simply. 'In 1945 from America. Just the once. He said he was sorry for keeping me in suspense for so long and asked me to go out there and marry him.'

I was completely thrown by the calm and matter-of-fact way she said it. 'Did you reply?'

'No,' she said.

'Why not?'

'No point. I was already married to a good, kind man twenty years my elder who didn't mind damaged goods.' And then I saw everything. 'Yes,' she said. 'That was the way of it.'

She got up, opened a cupboard and produced an old jewellery box which she opened with a key hidden behind the clock on the mantlepiece. She took out various things, passing them to me to examine. The exercise book of poetry, the letter he had left that fateful day, the one from America and there were photos there also.

She passed one across. 'I took that with a Box Brownie.' It was Devlin in cap, goggles and raincoat, standing beside the BSA.

She handed me another. Devlin again, driving a tractor and then I saw a subtle difference. 'My son William,' she said simply.

'Does he know?' I asked.

'As much as he needs to. I told him after my husband passed on seven years ago. Will you be seeing Liam?'

'I hope so.'

'Give him that photo.' She sighed. 'He was a lovely man. There hasn't been a day of my life I haven't wondered where he was and what was happening to him.'

She took me to the door and shook hands. I'd got to the car when she called and as I turned, the sun came out and for a moment, the years faded and standing there, half in shadow, half in light, she seemed Devlin's beautiful ugly little peasant girl again.

'And tell him, Mr Higgins,' she called. 'Tell him I hope he finally finds those Plains of Mayo he was always looking for.'

She closed the door and I got into the car and drove away.

*

Once booked into the Europa in Belfast, I made the right phone calls to the right people, told them what I wanted, then sat back and waited nervously for two days during which the city saw eighteen separate bombing incidents and three soldiers shot dead – and that wasn't counting the civilians.

On the evening of the second day the call came and I took a cab to the Royal Hospital where I was picked up by a bread van which dropped me outside a small terraced house in a mean side street off the Falls Road five minutes later. Inside, I was searched with considerable expertise by two hard and danger-ous-looking young men, before being allowed to step into the tiny living room.

The man who had called himself Liam Devlin was sitting at the window in shirtsleeves, writing in an exercise book. He wore reading glasses and there was a Smith & Wesson .38 revolver on the table close to his hand. He put down his pen, took off his glasses and turned. I looked into that face, ravaged by the years, to see some sign of that other man, and it was there in the bright blue eyes, the ironic quirk.

'You'll know me next time.'

'I will so,' I told him.

'I read that book of yours. Not bad for an Orange boy off the Albertbridge Road. I can't see why you don't take the oath and join the movement. It was good enough for Wolfe Tone and he was a damned Prod too.' He stuck a cigarette in his mouth and put a match to it. 'Now, what's all this about? You said it was urgent, so if it's an interview you're after, I'll have your balls for wasting my time.'

I produced the photo Molly had given me and put it on the desk. 'Your son,' I said, 'Molly thought you'd like to have it.'

He reeled as from a physical blow, his face turned very pale. He sat staring at the photo for a very long time. Finally he said, 'You'd better tell me what it's all about.'

Which I did, and during the telling he constantly interrupted me, correcting the odd fact here, inserting one there. When I came to the final act and Steiner on the terrace at Meltham House he jumped from his seat and got a bottle of Bushmills and two glasses from a cupboard. 'He came that close, did he? By

God, he was a man, that one.' He splashed whiskey into the glasses. 'We'll drink to him.'

Which we did. I said. 'I hear you tried teaching in the States for a few years after the war?'

'There was little enough to do here, God knows.'

'And the Churchill affair?' I said. 'Didn't it ever occur to you to let the facts be known?'

'From me?' he said. 'One of the most wanted men in the IRA? Now who in the hell would ever have believed in a story like that coming from me?'

Which was fair enough. 'Tell me,' I said. 'How does a man who told Max Radl in October 1947 that he disapproved of soft target bombing come to be one of the prime architects of the Provisional IRA's present campaign, where the bomb, after all, has been your main weapon?'

There was pain in his eyes and his smile was more savage than anything else. 'As the times change, all men change with them. Some idiot said that, I forget who.'

'Has it been worth it?' I said. 'All these years? The violence, the killings?'

'The cause I represent is a just one,' he said. 'I fight for an ideal of freedom . . .' Quite suddenly, he broke down and sagged into a chair, his shoulders shaking.

At first I thought that he was crying, but then he looked up and I saw that he was laughing his head off. 'God save us, but all of a sudden I was standing six feet away and listening to myself. I tell you, son, you should try it some time. It's a salutory experience.' He poured himself another whiskey. 'Steiner was right. It's just a bloody senseless game after all and when it gets you by the ballocks it won't let go.'

'Have you any message for Molly?'

'After all these years? From a walking corpse like me? Be your age, son, and now get out of this. I've work to do.'

There was the rattle of small arms fire in the distance, the crump of an explosion. I paused at the door. 'Sorry, I almost forgot, Molly sent you a message.'

He looked up, face expressionless. 'Did she?'

'Yes, she said she hoped you finally find those Plains of Mayo.'

He smiled a smile of infinite and terrible sadness and I swear there were tears in his eyes. 'If you see her,' he said simply, 'give her my love. She had it then, she has it now.' He reached for his glasses. 'Now get to hell out of here.'

*

It was almost a year to the day since I had made that astonishing discovery in the churchyard at St Mary and All the Saints when I returned to Studley Constable, this time by direct invitation of Father Philip Vereker. I was admitted by a young priest with an Irish accent.

Vereker was sitting in a wing-back chair in front of a huge fire in the study, a rug about his knees, a dying man if ever I've seen one. The skin seemed to have shrunk on his face, exposing every bone and the eyes were full of pain. 'It was good of you to come.'

'I'm sorry to see you so ill,' I said.

'I have a cancer of the stomach. Nothing to be done. The Bishop has been very good in allowing me to end it here, arranging for Father Damian to assist with parish duties, but that isn't why I sent for you. I hear you've had a busy year.'

'I don't understand,' I said. 'When I was here before you wouldn't say a word. Drove me out, in fact.'

'It's really very simple. For years I've only known half the story myself. I suddenly discover that I have an insatiable curiosity to know the rest before it is too late.'

So I told him because there didn't really seem any reason why I shouldn't. By the time I had finished, the shadows were falling across the grass outside and the room was half in darkness.

'Remarkable,' he said. 'How on earth did you find it all out?'

'Not from any official source, believe me. Just from talking to people, those who are still alive and who were willing to talk. The biggest stroke of luck was in being privileged to read a very comprehensive diary kept by the man responsible for the organization of the whole thing, Colonel Max Radl. His widow is still alive in Bavaria. What I'd like to know now is what happened here afterwards.'

'There was a complete security clampdown. Every single villager involved was interviewed by the intelligence and security people. The Official Secrets Act invoked. Not that it was really necessary. These are a peculiar people. Drawing together in adversity, hostile to strangers, as you have seen. They looked upon it as their business and no one else's.'

'And there was Seymour.'

'Exactly. Did you know that he was killed last February?'

'No.'

'Driving back from Holt one night drunk. He ran his van off the coast road into the marsh and was drowned.'

'What happened to him after the other business?'

'He was quietly certified. Spent eighteen years in an institution before he managed to obtain his release when the mental health laws were relaxed.'

'But how could people stand having him around?'

'He was related by blood to at least half the families in the district. George Wilde's wife, Betty, was his sister.'

'Good God,' I said. 'I didn't realize.'

'In a sense, the silence of the years was also a kind of protection for Seymour.'

'There is another possibility,' I said. 'That the terrible thing he did that night was seen as a reflection on all of them. Something to hide rather than reveal.'

'That, too.'

'And the tombstone?'

'The military engineers who were sent here to clean up the village, repair damage and so on, placed all the bodied in a mass grave in the churchyard. Unmarked, of course and we were told it was to remain so.'

'But you thought differently?'

'Not just me. All of us. Wartime propaganda was a pernicious thing then, however necessary. Every war picture we saw at the cinema, every book we read, every newspaper, portrayed the average German soldier as a ruthless and savage barbarian, but these men were not like that. Graham Wilde is alive today, Susan Turner married with three children because one of Steiner's men gave his life to save them. And at the church, remember, he let the people go.'

'So, a secret monument was decided on?'

'That's right. It was easy enough to arrange. Old Ted Turner was a retired monumental mason. It was laid, dedicated by me at a private service, then concealed from the casual observer as you know. The man Preston is down there, too, but was not included on the monument.'

'And you all agreed with this?'

IIe managed one of his rare, wintry smiles. 'As some kind of personal penance if you like. Dancing on his grave was the term Steiner used and he was right. I hated him that day. Could have killed him myself.'

'Why?' I said. 'Because it was a German bullet that crippled you?'

'So I pretended until the day I got down on my knees and asked God to help me face the truth.'

'Joanna Grey?' I said gently.

His face was completely in shadow. I found it impossible to see his expression. 'I am more used to hearing confessions than making them, but yes, you are right. I worshipped Joanna Grey. Oh, not in any silly superficial sexual way. To me she was the most wonderful woman I'd ever known. I can't even begin to describe the shock I experienced on discovering her true role.'

'So in a sense, you blamed Steiner?'

'I think that was the psychology of it.' He sighed. 'So long ago. How old were you in nineteen-forty-three? Twelve, thirteen? Can you remember what it was like?'

'Not really – not in the way you mean.'

'People were tired because the war seemed to have gone on for ever. Can you possibly imagine the terrible blow to national morale if the story of Steiner and his men and what took place here, had got out? That German paratroopers could land in England and come within an ace of snatching the Prime Minister himself?'

'Could come as close as the pull of a finger on the trigger to blowing his head off.'

He nodded. 'Do you still intend to publish?'

'I don't see why not.'

'It didn't happen, you know. No stone any more and who is to say it ever existed? And have you found one single official document to substantiate any of it?'

'Not really,' I said cheerfully. 'But I've spoken to a lot of people and together they've told me what adds up to a pretty convincing story.'

'It could have been.' He smiled faintly. 'If you hadn't missed out on one very important point.'

'And what would that be?'

'Look up any one of two dozen history books on the last war and check what Winston Churchill was doing during the weekend in question. But perhaps that was too simple, too obvious.'

'All right,' I said. 'You tell me.'

'Getting ready to leave in HMS *Renown* for the Teheran conference. Called at Algiers on the way, where he invested Generals Eisenhower and Alexander with special versions of the North Africa ribbon and arrived at Malta, as I remember, on the seventeenth November.'

It was suddenly very quiet. I said, 'Who was he?'

'His name was George Howard Foster, known in the profession as the Great Foster.'

'The profession?'

'The stage, Mr Higgins. Foster was a music hall act, an impressionist. The war was his salvation.'

'How was that?'

'He not only did a more than passable imitation of the Prime Minister. He even looked like him. After Dunkirk, he started doing a special act, a kind of grand finale to the show. *I have nothing to offer but blood, sweat and tears. We will fight them on the beaches.* The audiences loved it.'

'And Intelligence pulled him in?'

'On special occasions. If you intend to send the Prime Minister to sea at the height of the U-boat peril, it's useful to have him publicly appearing elsewhere.' He smiled. 'He gave the performance of his life that night. They all believed it was him, of course. Only Corcoran knew the truth.'

'All right,' I said. 'Where's Foster now?'

'Killed, along with a hundred and eight other people when a flying bomb hit a little theatre in Islington in nineteen-forty-four. So you see, it's all been for nothing. It never happened. Much better for all concerned.'

He went into a bout of coughing that racked his entire body. The door opened and the nun entered. She leaned over him and whispered. He said, 'I'm sorry, it's been a long afternoon. I think I should rest. Thank you for coming and filling in the gaps.'

He started to cough again so I left as quickly as I could and was ushered politely to the door by young Father Damian. On the step I gave him my card. 'If he gets worse.' I hesitated. 'You know what I mean? I'd appreciate hearing from you.'

*

I lit a cigarette and leaned on the flint wall of the churchyard beside the lychgate. I would checks the facts, of course, but Vereker was telling the truth, I knew that beyond any shadow of a doubt and did it really change anything? I looked towards the porch where Steiner had stood that evening so long ago in confrontation with Harry Kane, thought of him on the terrace at Meltham House, the final, and for him, fatal hesitation. *And even if he had pulled that trigger it would still all have been for nothing.*

There's irony for you, as Devlin would have said. I could almost hear his laughter. Ah, well, in the final analysis there was nothing I could find to say that would be any improvement on the words of a man who had played his own part so well on that fatal night.

Whatever else may be said, he was a fine soldier and a brave man. Let it end there. I turned and walked away through the rain.

Jack
Higgins

Luciano's
Luck

For Sacha and George

SICILY – 1943

In July 1943, American forces landed on the southern coast of Sicily and in an advance of incredible rapidity, reached Palermo in only seven days. That their success was due in no small measure to the co-operation of the Sicilian Mafia acting under the direct orders of Charles Lucky Luciano, then serving a sentence of thirty to fifty years in Great Meadow Penitentiary in New York State, is a matter of historical fact. What is particularly fascinating about this strange episode is that in Sicily to this day, there are those who insist that they saw Luciano in person with the American units during the early part of the invasion ...

1

It was just before evening, when the jeep carrying Harry Carter turned in through the gates of the great Moorish villa called dar el Ouad outside Algiers, and braked to a halt at the ornate, arched entrance.

'Wait for me,' Carter told the driver and went up the steps past the sentries.

In the cool, dark hall inside, a young captain in summer uniform sat at a desk working on some papers. The plaque in front of him said, *Captain George Cusak*. He glanced up at Carter, noted the uniform, the crowns on his shoulder, the purple and white ribbon of the Military Cross with a silver rosette for a second award, and stood up.

'What can I do for you, Major?'

Carter produced his pass. 'I think you'll find General Eisenhower is expecting me.'

The captain examined the pass briefly and nodded. 'Ten minutes to go, Major. If you'll take a seat, I'll tell him you're here.'

Harry Carter walked out on to the terrace through the open french windows and sat down in one of the wicker-work chairs. After a moment's hesitation he took out an old silver case from his breast pocket and selected a cigarette.

He was forty-two, of medium height, a handsome man with a calm, pleasant face which always seemed about to break into a smile, but never quite made it. And he suited the uniform to perfection which was surprising for he was the second son of a prosperous Yorkshire mill-owner, a scholar by nature, educated at Leeds Grammar School until thirteen and then Winchester. From there he had absconded in 1917, joining the Army under a false age, serving the last eighteen months of the First World War as an infantry private on the Western Front.

Afterwards came Cambridge and a brilliant academic career which had included spells at Harvard as visiting Professor of Greek Archaeology, the University of Florence and then a return to Cambridge as a Fellow of Trinity and Claverhouse Professor of Ancient History at thirty-five.

Just after Munich, he had been approached by British Intelligence and had worked with Masterman at MI5, helping to destroy the German spy network in England. He then moved to Special Operations Executive, eventually transferring to Cairo to take responsibility for the Italian section Sicily had come later, had never really been on the cards at all.

And it was beginning to show; in the weariness in the grey eyes, the flecks of silver in the dark hair. He flicked what remained of his cigarette out into the garden.

'Careful, Harry,' he said softly. 'Next thing, you'll be starting to feel sorry for yourself.'

There was a movement behind him and he glanced up as Captain Cusak appeared.

'Major Carter, General Eisenhower will see you now, sir.'

*   *   *

The room was as ornate and Moorish in its furnishings as was the rest of the villa. The only signs that it was the nerve centre of the headquarters of the Supreme Allied Commander for the North African Theatre were to be found in the maps of the Mediterranean pinned to one wall and the three trestle tables covered with more maps, which had been placed by the terrace windows to serve as a desk.

Eisenhower was standing outside on the terrace as they went in, smoking a cigarette, wearing boots and riding breeches for he rode most afternoons. He turned and walked in briskly, his face illuminated by that famous and inimitable smile.

'Coffee, George,' he said to Cusak. 'Or maybe Major Carter would prefer tea?'

'No, coffee would be fine, sir.'

Cusak went out and Eisenhower indicated a chair and opened a file on his desk.

'And just how does a man with your background get by as a Sicilian peasant?'

'Oh, you can thank the University Dramatic Society for that, General. There was a wild moment there when I was tempted to turn professional.'

'You were that good.'

'I wouldn't be here if I wasn't, sir,' Carter said calmly.

'When SOE sent you out to Cairo to take charge of the Italian section I don't think they envisaged your personal invasion of Sicily on ...' here he glanced again at the file, '... three separate occasions?'

'I know, sir,' Carter said. 'But we didn't really have any choice. When it came to Sicily, there wasn't anyone else who knew the language or the people as well. I did a lot of work on archaeological digs there during the thirties.'

'And now you're going in again. Don't you think you're getting a little old for this sort of thing?'

Eisenhower pushed a document across the desk and Carter picked it up. It was a typical SOE operation order in sparse, no-nonsense Civil Service English.

OPERATION INSTRUCTION NO. 592

For Major Harry Carter.
Operation: Swordarm
Field Name: FORTUNATO
Name on Papers: Giovanni Ciccio

I. INFORMATION

We have discussed with you the possibility of your returning to Sicily to finalize the mission you were originally given when you left for that island in February of this year; namely, to co-ordinate the organization of resistance groups in the general area of the Cammarata so that the maximum co-operation is available to Allied troops in the event of invasion. You have made it quite clear that in your view, nothing prevents you from returning to the same area to carry out this task.

2. METHOD

From Maison Blanche you will proceed to Sicily in a Halifax of 138 (Special Duties) Squadron and will land by parachute at a point 10 kilometres west of Bellona where you will be received by elements of the local resistance movement. You have been given a cover story and papers in the name of Giovanni Ciccio which will enable you to live a normal life in the field.

INTERCOMMUNICATIONS

Your channel of communication with the resistance movement in the Palermo area will be through the Contessa di Bellona who is at the present time in residence at her villa outside that town.

Your channel of communication with HQ will be by W/T radio transmission handled by Vito Barbera, co-ordinator, Bellona area.

WEAPONS

At your discretion, but only those you consider essential for hand-to-hand combat.

CONCLUSION

You are aware of the importance of this mission and nothing must take precedence over it. We anticipate completion in two weeks. Your return will be by submarine pick-up and details of this will be transmitted by radio in field-code at the appropriate time.

NOW DESTROY ... NOW DESTROY ... NOW DESTROY

Carter took a cigarette lighter from his pocket, flicked it with his thumb and touched the flame to the corner of the document. When it was well alight, he crossed to the empty fireplace and dropped it into the grate.

'Even you shouldn't have that, General.'

The door opened and Cusak returned with coffee on a brass Arabic tray. 'Thanks, George, I'll take care of it,' Eisenhower said.

He poured the coffee himself and lit another cigarette. 'I'd say it's a reasonable assumption that you know more about what's happening over there at the moment than anyone else in North Africa. So let's talk.'

'What would you like to know, General?'

'I'd like you to explain the Mafia to me.'

'You have a file on the Mafia connection, presumably?'

'Yes.'

Carter lit a cigarette himself without thinking. 'Mafia began as a kind of secret society during a period of real oppression. In those days it was the only weapon the peasant had, his only means of justice.'

'Go on.'

'You have to understand the landscape, sir. It's another world. Sterile, barren, where the struggle is not so much for a living as for survival. A world where the key word is *omerta* which means manliness, honour, and never, never seek official help. If you have a problem, you go to the *capo*.'

'The *capo*?' Eisenhower frowned.

'*Capo* means boss, chief, put it how you like. Wherever you go in Sicily there will be a *capo mafia* who rules the roost.'

'And still does?'

'Mussolini tried to crush the movement but it simply went under the surface. You can talk of Separatists, Communists and other political factions as much as you like, but in Sicily, it's still the Mafia which has the real influence.'

Eisenhower sat staring into space, brooding.

Finally, as if coming to a decision, he tapped the brown manila folder in front of him.

'This is the file you referred to as the Mafia connection. Are you familiar with an individual mentioned in it known as Lucky Luciano?'

Carter nodded. 'A New York Sicilian gangster and probably the most important *capo* in American Mafia. He's serving a thirty-to-fifty year sentence in Dannemora Penitentiary at the moment. I believe the charge was organized prostitution.'

'Not now, he isn't,' Eisenhower said. 'According to the file, he's been moved to Great Meadow at Comstock. It seems that after the liner Normandie was burned out on the Hudson last year, Naval Intelligence became worried about increasing sabotage on the New York waterfront.'

'I know, General, and when they approached the docker's unions, they discovered that the man to see was Luciano, inside prison or out.'

Eisenhower said, 'Quite incredible. In the middle of the greatest war in history they have to go to a crook for help. As if that wasn't enough, I now find that our people have been putting agents into Sicily for some time now, usually Americans with an ethnic Sicilian background. Were you aware of this?'

'It's a specifically American project, General, but yes, I did know about it. The aim is, I believe, to ensure Mafia co-operation in the event of an invasion.'

Eisenhower exploded angrily. 'Aren't we supposed to be fighting the same war, for God's sake?' He took another cigarette and struck the match so forcibly that it snapped. 'They approached Luciano in the penitentiary again about giving his assistance. They seem to think he has some influence in Sicily also.'

'Considerable, General. If he appeared in some of those mountain villages it would be like the second coming.'

'Our Intelligence people certainly seem to think so. Apparently a yellow scarf with the initial L in black, which is Luciano's calling card, will be dropped extensively in appropriate areas at the right time.'

'And they think this will help?' Carter asked.

Eisenhower turned back to the map. 'The theory is sound enough. The terrain Patton and his army have to pass through to reach Palermo is a soldier's nightmare. The area around the Cammarata particularly is a warren of ravines and mountains. It could take months to hack a way through it. On the other hand, if the Mafia used its power to promote an uprising of the people and to persuade Italian units to surrender, the Germans would have no other recourse but to get the hell out of it.'

'Yes, General,' Carter said.

'You don't sound too certain. Don't you think the Mafia can deliver?'

'Frankly, sir, not as the people in Washington who dreamed this thing up seem to expect. One major weakness. If you take the Mafia boss, the *capo*, in one particular district, you may find he doesn't have much influence elsewhere. Another thing, your Intelligence people have been recruiting American service personnel with Sicilian or Italian ethnic backgrounds.'

'And what's wrong with that?' Eisenhower demanded.

'It's better than nothing, of course, but being Italian doesn't cut much ice in Sicily and as regards the language, there are at least five Sicilian dialects in Palermo alone.'

'But surely the idea of using Luciano was to get over such difficulties by having someone whose name meant something to everyone.'

'I don't happen to think it's enough.'

'But Washington does?'

'So it would appear.'

There was a brief silence, Eisenhower frowning down thoughtfully at the file and then he looked up.

'All right, Major, you've had one briefing. Now I'm going to give you another. I want the facts on this Mafia thing and straight from the horse's mouth. When you return in two weeks or whatever, I want you back here Priority One with a first hand assessment of the situation in the field. You understand me?'

'Perfectly, General.'

'Good. You'd better get moving, then.'

Carter saluted. Eisenhower nodded and picked up his pen. As Carter reached the door and opened it, the General called softly, 'One thing more, Major.'

Carter turned to face him. 'Yes, sir?'

'Leave the rough stuff to other people. I'd be considerably inconvenienced if you failed to keep our next appointment.'

2

It started to rain as Carter went over the ridge, a heavy, drenching downpour, sheet lightning flickering beyond the mountain peaks. He leaned the cumbersome bicycle against a tree and took the field-glasses from his pocket. When he focused them the houses of Bellona three miles away jumped into view. He followed the valley road to where it disappeared into pine trees, but there was no sign of life. Not even a shepherd.

He replaced the field-glasses in his pack, moved back through the trees to the other side of the ridge and looked down at the villa in the hollow below, quiet in the evening light, waiting for him.

He was tired and yet filled with a sudden fierce exhilaration, faced at last with the final end of things. He started down the slope through pine trees, pushing the bicycle before him.

He entered the grounds by a gate in the rear wall and followed a path round to the front of the house. The garden was Moorish, lush, semi-tropical vegetation pressing in everywhere. Palms swayed gently above his head and in the heavy downpour water gurgled in the old conduits, splashing from numerous fountains.

He emerged into the courtyard at the front of the house, leaned the bicycle against the baroque fountain, and went up the steps to the front door. There was already a light in the hall and he pulled on the bell chain and waited. There was the sound of footsteps approaching and the door opened.

The man who stood there was perhaps forty, his heavy moustache and hair already grey. He wore a black bow tie and alpaca jacket and looked Carter over with total disapproval.

'What do you want?'

Carter removed his cloth cap and when he spoke, his voice was rough and hoarse, pure Sicilian. 'I have a message for the Contessa.'

The manservant held out his hand. 'Give it to me.'

Carter shook his head, assuming an expression of peasant cunning. 'My orders were to deliver it personally. She's expecting me. Tell her Ciccio is here.'

The manservant shrugged. 'All right, come in. I'll see what she has to say.'

Carter stepped inside and stood there, dripping rain on to the black and white ceramic tiles. The manservant frowned his displeasure, walked across the hall and went through a green baize door into a large kitchen. He paused just inside the door, took a Walther automatic from his pocket, checked it quickly then opened a cupboard beside the old-fashioned iron stove and took out a military field telephone. He wound the handle and waited, whistling softly to himself, tapping the Walther against his thigh.

There was the murmur of a voice at the other end and he said in German, 'Schaefer – at the villa. Carter's turned up at last. No problem. I'll hold him till you get here.'

He replaced the telephone in the cupboard, turned and still whistling softly, moved back to the door.

*   *   *

Carter shivered, suddenly cold, aware for the first time that the rain had soaked through to his skin. *Almost over now. God, but he was tired.* In the gilt mirror on the other side of the hall he could see his reflection. A middle-aged Sicilian peasant, badly in need of a shave, hair too long, with sullen, brutalized features, patched tweed suit and leather leggings, a shotgun, the traditional *lupara* with sawn-off barrels, hanging from his left shoulder.

But not for much longer. Soon there would be Cairo, Shepherd's Hotel, hot baths, clean sheets, seven-course meals and ice-cold champagne. Dom Perignon 35. He still had, after all, an infallible source of supply.

The green baize door opened in the mirror behind him and

the manservant came through. Carter turned. 'The Contessa will see me?'

'She would if she could, only she isn't here. We took her away three days ago.' His right hand came up holding the Walther and now he was speaking in English. 'The shotgun, Major Carter. On the floor, very gently, then turn, hands against the wall.'

Strange, but now that it had happened, this moment that he had always known would come one day, Carter was aware of a curious sensation of relief. He didn't even attempt ot play Ciccio anymore, but put down the *lupara* as instructed and turned to face the wall.

'German?' he asked.

'I'm afraid so.' A hand searched him expertly. 'Schäfer. *Geheimefeldpolizei*. I was beginning to think you weren't coming.' He stepped back and Carter turned to face him.

'The Contessa?'

'The Gestapo have her. They've been waiting for you in Bellona for three days now. I've just telephoned through from the kitchen. They'll be here in twenty minutes.'

'I see,' Carter said. 'So what do we do now?'

'We wait.' Schäfer motioned him through into the dining room.

Carter paused, looking down at the open fire, steam rising from his damp clothes and behind him, Schäfer sat at the end of the long dining table, took out a pack of cigarettes, lit one, then pushed the pack along the table. Carter took one gratefully and when he struck the match, his fingers trembled slightly.

Schäfer said, 'There's brandy on the sideboard. You look as if you could do with it.'

Carter went round the table and helped himself. The brandy was the local variety, raw and pungent, it burned as it went down and he coughed, struggling for breath. He poured himself another and turned to Schäfer.

'What about you?'

'Why not?'

Carter found another glass and moved to the table. 'Say when,' he said and started to pour.

Schäfer still covered him with the Walther. Raising the glass to his lips he said, 'I'm sorry about this, Major. I don't like those Gestapo bastards any more than you do, but I've got a job to do.'

'Haven't we all,' Carter said.

He swung the decanter in an arc against the German's skull, at the same time grabbing for the wrist of the hand that held the Walther, desperately trying to deflect it.

He swung the decanter again so that it splintered into dozens of pieces, brandy spurting across Schäfer's head and face, mingling with the blood. Incredibly, Schäfer's left fist managed a punch of considerable force high on Carter's right cheek, splitting the flesh to the bone, before clutching him by the throat.

They fell across the table and rolled over the edge to the floor and Carter was aware of one blow after another to the body and the pistol exploding between them. Somehow, he found himself up on one knee, twisting the other's wrist up and around until the bone cracked and the Walther jumped into the air, landing in the hearth.

The German screamed, his head going back, and Carter punched him in the open throat with knuckles extended. Schäfer rolled over on to his face and lay still and Carter turned and ran into the hall. He grabbed for the shotgun, slinging it over his shoulder as he made for the front door.

There was a dreamlike quality to everything. It was as if he was moving in slow motion, no strength to him, so that even opening the front door was an effort. He leaned against the balustrade of the porch, aware now that the front of his jacket was soaked with blood, not Schäfer's but his own. When he slipped a hand inside his shirt he could feel the lips of the wound like raw meat where a bullet had ripped through his left side.

No time for that, not now for he was aware of the sound of vehicles approaching on the road, very fast. He went lurching down the steps, picked up the bicycle and hurriedly retraced his steps through the garden to the rear gate.

He reached the shelter of the pine trees below the villa, turned in time to see a truck and two *kubelwagens* appear on the main road above him. Carter didn't wait to see what would happen, simply pushed on through the trees until he came to the woodcutter's track that ran all the way down through the forest to Bellona. Just enough light to see by if he was lucky. He flung a leg over the broken leather saddle of the old bicycle and rode away.

*   *   *

There wasn't a great deal to remember of that ride. The trees crowding in on either side, deepening the evening gloom, the rush of the heavy rain. It was rather like being on the kind of monumental drunk where, afterwards, only occasional images surface.

He opened his eyes to find himself lying on his back, the rain falling on his upturned face, in a ditch on the edge of the village, the bicycle beside him.

The pain of the gunshot wound was intense now, worse than he would have believed possible. There was no sign of the shotgun and he forced himself to his feet and stumbled along the track through the swiftly falling darkness.

The smell of wood smoke hung on the damp air and a dog barked hollowly in the distance, but otherwise there was no sign of life except for the occasional light in a window. And yet there were people up there, watching from behind the shutters, waiting.

He made it across the main square, pausing at the fountain in the centre to put his head under the jet of cold water that gushed from the mouth and nostrils of a bronze dryad, continued past the church and turned into a narrow side street. There was an entrance to a courtyard a few houses along, barred by an oaken gate, a blue lamp above it. The sign painted on the wall in ornate black letters read *Vito Barbera – Mortician*.

A small judas gate stood next to the main door. Carter leaned against it and pulled the bell chain. There was silence for a while and he held on to the grille with one hand, staring up at the rain falling in a silver spray through the lamplight. A footstep sounded inside and the grille opened.

Barbera said, 'What is it?'

'Me, Vito.'

'Harry, is that you?' Barbera said, this time in the kind of

English that came straight from the Bronx. 'Thank God. I thought they must have lifted you.'

He opened the judas gate and Carter stepped inside. 'A damn near-run thing, Vito, just like Waterloo,' he said and fainted.

*   *   *

Carter surfaced slowly and found himself looking up at a cracked plaster ceiling. It was very cold and there was a heavy, medicinal smell to everything that he soon recognized as formaldehyde. He was lying on one of the tables in the mortuary preparation room, his neck pillowed on a wooden block, his stomach and chest expertly bandaged.

He turned his head and found Barbera, wearing a long rubbei apron, working on the corpse of an old man at the next table Carter pushed himself up.

Barbera said cheerfully, 'I wouldn't if I were you. He shot you twice. The one in the side went straight through, but the second is somewhere in the left lung. You'll need a top surgeon.'

'Thanks a million,' Carter said. 'That really does make me feel a whole lot better.'

On a trolley beside Barbera were the tools of the embalmer's trade laid out neatly on a white cloth: forceps, scalpels, surgical needles, artery tubes and a glass jar containing a couple of gallons of embalming fluid.

There was a look of faint surprise on the corpse's face that many people show in death, jaw dropped, mouth gaping as if in astonishment that this could be happening. Barbera took a long curved needle and passed it from behind the lower lip, up through the nasal septum and down again so that when he tightened the thread and tied it off, the jaw was lifted.

'So you raise people from the dead, too?' Carter eased himself off the table. 'I always knew you were a man of parts.'

Barbera smiled, a small, intense-looking man of fifty whose tangled iron-grey beard appeared strangely at odds with the Bronx accent.

'You fucking English, Harry! I mean, when are you going to learn? The days of Empire are over. What were you trying to do up there, win the war on your own?'

'Something like that.'

The door opened and a young girl entered. Sixteen or seventeen, no more. Small, dark-haired with a ripe, full body that strained at the seams of the old cotton dress. She had a wide mouth, dark brown eyes in a face of considerable character and yet there was the impression of one who had seen too much of life at its worst too early.

She carried a tray containing an old brass coffee pot, brown sugar and glasses. There was also a bottle of cognac – Courvoisier.

Barbera carried on working. 'Rosa, this is Major Carter. My niece, arrived from Palermo since you were last here.'

'Rosa,' Carter said.

She poured coffee and handed it to him without a word.

Barbera said, 'Good girl. Now go back to the gate and watch the square. Anything – anything at all, you let me know.'

She went out and Carter poured himself a brandy, sipping it slowly for the pain in his lung was so intense that he could hardly breathe. 'I never knew you had a niece. How old is she?'

'Oh, a hundred and fifty, or sixteen. Take your pick. Her father was my youngest brother. Killed in an auto accident in thirty-seven in Naples. I lost sight of his wife. She died of consumption in Palermo three years ago.'

'And Rosa?'

'I only heard about her two months ago through Mafia friends in Palermo. She's been a street whore since she was thirteen. I figured it was time she came home.'

'You still think of this place as home after Tenth Avenue?'

'Oh, sure, no regrets. Something Rosa can't understand. New York is still the promised land to her, whereas to me, it was somewhere to leave.'

He was working cream into the old man's face now, touching the cheeks with rouge.

Carter said, 'What about the Contessa?'

'The Gestapo took her to Palermo.'

'Bad for you if they break her.'

'Not possible.' Barbera shook his head. 'A friend passed her a cyanide capsule in the women's prison yesterday afternoon.'

Carter took a long, shuddering breath to steady his nerves. 'I was hoping she'd have news for me of Luca.'

Barbera paused and glanced at him in some surprise. 'You waste your time. No one has news of Luca because that is the way he wants it.'

'Mafia again?'

'Yes, my friend, Mafia again and you would do well to remember that. What are your plans?'

'I was supposed to go to Agrigento tonight. I'm due to put to sea with a tuna boat out of Porto Stefano at midnight.'

'Submarine pick-up?'

'That's it.'

Barbera frowned thoughtfully. 'I don't see how, Harry, not tonight. The roads will be crawling with Krauts. Maybe tomorrow.' He gestured to the corpse. 'I've got to take the old boy here down to Agrigento anyway.'

Before Carter could reply, the door burst open and Rosa looked in. 'They are here in the square. Many Germans.'

Barbera moved to the window and parted the curtain slightly. Carter struggled up with difficulty and limped to join him. Several vehicles had pulled up in the square, *kubelwagens* and troop carriers and two armoured cars. Soldiers had gathered in a semi-circle and were being addressed from the back of a field car by an officer.

Carter said, 'SS paratroopers. Where in the hell did they come from?'

'The mainland last month. Specially selected by Kesselring to clear the mountains of partisans. The one doing the talking is their commanding officer, Major Koenig. He's good. They call him the Hunter in the Cammarata.'

As they watched, the SS broke away to commence searching the village. Koenig sat down and his *kubelwagen* started across the square, followed by another.

Barbera closed the curtain. 'Looks as if he's coming this way.' He turned to Carter. 'Did you leave anybody dead up there at the villa, by any chance?'

'Probably.' Carter caught him by the sleeve. 'He'll take it out on the village if I don't turn up.'

Barbera smiled sadly. 'Not his style. Very definitely a man of honour. Makes it difficult to stick a knife in his back. Now you stay here with Rosa and keep quiet.'

He took the lamp and went out, leaving them in darkness.

        ★   ★   ★

They were already knocking at the outer gate as he crossed the courtyard. He eased back the massive bolt and the gate swung open to reveal the first *kubelwagen*, Koenig seated beside the driver. He got out and moved forward.

'Ah, there you are, Signor Barbera. I've brought some custom for you, I'm afraid,' he said in fair Italian.

The two *kubelwagens* drove into the courtyard. Barbera saw that there was a body strapped to a stretcher on one of them and covered with a blanket.

Two SS ran round to lift it down and Barbera said, 'If you'd follow me, Major.'

He crossed the courtyard and led the way in through a short passage. When he opened the door at the end, there was the taint of death on the air.

The room which he entered was quiet, a single oil lamp on a table in the centre the only light. It was a waiting mortuary of a type common in Sicily. There were at least a dozen coffins, each one open and containing a corpse, fingers entwined in a pulley arrangement that stretched overhead to an old brass bell by the door.

Koenig entered behind him. His NCO's field cap was an affectation of some of the old timers, silver death's head badge glinting in the lamplight. The scarlet and black ribbon of the Knight's Cross made a brave show at his throat. He wore a leather greatcoat which had seen long service and paratroopers' jumpboots. He lit a cigarette, pausing just inside the door, and flicked a finger against the bell which echoed eerily.

'Has it ever rung?'

'Frequently,' Barbera said. 'Limbs behave strangely as they stiffen in death. If what the Major means is has anyone returned to life, that, too. A girl of twelve and on another occasion, a man of forty. Both revived after death had been pronounced. That, after all, is the purpose of these places.'

'You Sicilians seem to me to have an excessive pre-occupation with death,' Koenig said.

'Not to the extent that we are excited by the idea of being buried alive.'

From the preparation room, peering through the crack in the door, Carter leaned against Rosa, fighting the pain, and watched them place the stretcher on a table and uncover Schäfer, the *feldpolizei* sergeant. The face was streaked with blood, the eyes staring. Barbera closed them with a practised movement.

'Sergeant Schäfer was a good man,' Koenig said. 'I need hardly point out that it would be most unfortunate for anyone found harbouring the man who did this.'

Barbera said, 'What would you like me to do with him, Major?'

'Clean him up and deliver him to *Geheimefeldpolizei* headquarters in Agrigento.'

Barbera covered Schäfer with the blanket again. 'I have a previous engagement tomorrow. The family of the Contessa di Bellona wish me to fetch her body from the women's prison in Palermo. A matter of some delicacy.'

'Understandably,' Koenig said.

'In the circumstances, I had intended taking another corpse down to Agrigento tonight. See, in here.'

He moved to the door of the preparation room, opened it and led the way in, holding the lamp high so that Koenig could see the corpse of the old man. In the darkness of the rear cupboard, Carter slumped against Rosa and her arms tightened about him.

'I could take Sergeant Schäfer at the same time,' Barbera said. 'Of course, I would need a pass, Major. I presume your men will be active on all roads tonight.'

He followed Koenig out and Carter waited there in the dark, the pain in his lung like a living thing. *God, he thought, perhaps I'm dying.* He clutched desperately at the girl as if she was life itself, conscious of the softness of her flesh, her breasts tight against him.

He groaned, struggling to control the pain, and she fastened her mouth over his as if to hold the sound in, her tongue working furiously. In spite of the agony, his flesh reacted to her practised hands.

After a while she opened the door cautiously and led him out. Carter propped himself against one of the tables, aware of the sound of vehicles driving away down there in the courtyard.

'What were you trying to do, kill me or cure me?' he croaked.

She wiped sweat from his face with one of Barbera's towels. 'We have a saying, Colonel. There is the big death and then there is the small death which may be repeated many times. Which would you prefer?'

He stared down into that old-young face, but before he could reply Barbera came back, holding a piece of paper.

'Signed by Major Koenig himself. Good for any road block between here and Agrigento. With luck, you should make that submarine after all.'

'How?' Carter said.

'I wouldn't dream of having a hearse without a hidden compartment. Comes in handy. Of course, you'll be lying flat on your back with two corpses in coffins just inches above your nose, but I can guarantee you won't smell a thing.' He grinned. 'Stick with me, old buddy and you'll live for ever.'

3

The JU52 which flew in from Rome with Field Marshal Albert Kesselring landed at the Luftwaffe base at Punta Raisi outside Palermo just after nine in the morning. An hour later, he was at German Army headquarters in the old Benedictine Monastery near Monte Pellegrino, drinking coffee in the office of Major General Karl Walther who was temporarily in command.

'Beautiful,' Kesselring said, indicating the view. 'Quite remarkable, and so is the coffee.'

'Yemeni mocha.' Walther poured him another cup. 'We still manage some of the finer things in life here.'

'We had some difficulty driving through the town. There seemed to be religious processions everywhere.'

'Some sort of holy week. They hold them all the time. Everything grinds to a halt. They're a very religious people.'

'So it would appear,' Kesselring said. 'When one of the processions passed us I noticed a rather unusual feature. The Image of the Virgin they were carrying had a knife through its heart.'

'Typically Sicilian,' Walther replied. 'The cult of death everywhere.'

Kesselring put down his cup. 'All right, what have I got?'

'There are eight this morning. All Iron Crosses. First Class, except for the two in whom the Field Marshal has a special interest.'

'Let's take a look.'

Walther opened the door and ushered him out on to a stone-flagged terrace, an ironwork grille between the pillars. Below in the courtyard eight men were drawn up.

'Koenig on the far end, Herr Field Marshal Walther said.

'The man next to him is Sturmscharführer Brandt.'
'Who receives the Knight's Cross?'
'The third occasion that Koenig has put him forward.'
'So,' Kesselring nodded. 'Then let's get on with it.'

                    *   *   *

Major Max Koenig was twenty six and looked ten years older.
He had seen action in Poland, France and Holland and had
transferred to the newly formed 21st SS Paratroop Battalion in
time for the drop over Maleme airfield in Crete in 1941 where he
was seriously wounded. Then came the Winter War in Russia.
Two years of it and it showed: in the gold wound badge that said
he'd been a casualty on five separate occasions; in the general air
of weariness, the empty look in the dark eyes.

Except for the silver death's head badge in his service cap and
the SS runes and rank badges on his collar, he was all *fallschirmjäger*: flying blouse, jump trousers tucked into paratroop
boots. On his left sleeve was the *Kreta* cuff title, proud badge of
those who had spearheaded the invasion of Crete. The gold and
silver eagle of the paratroopers' qualification badge was pinned
to his left breast beside the Iron Cross. The Knight's Cross with
Oak Leaves hung at his throat.

Standing at ease at the end of the line waiting to receive the
Swords, he felt strangely indifferent and yet strove to find the
right thing to say to Sergeant-major Brandt for whom this was a
moment of supreme importance.

'So, Rudi,' he whispered. 'The great occasion at last.'

'Thanks to you, Major,' Brandt replied. He was an
innkeeper's son from the Austrian Tyrol, a small, wiry man who
could climb all day with no need of rest. He and Koenig had
been together for more than two years now.

There was a clatter of boots on the stone stairs as Kesselring
and General Walther appeared and someone called the parade to
attention.

It was a pleasant enough affair, for Kesselring was in good
humour, full of his usual charm. He had a word for each man as
he pinned on the ribbon. They responded well, as was only to be
expected, for he was, after all, Commander-in-Chief South and

arguably one of the best half-dozen generals on either side during the Second World War.

They had reached Brandt now and Kesselring did a marvellous thing, throwing all distinctions of rank to one side, clapping Brandt on the shoulders and shaking him warmly by the hand before hanging the coveted cross around his neck.

'My dear Brandt, a real pleasure, I assure you as one soldier to another, and long overdue.'

Brandt was overcome and Koenig was unable to keep a fleeting smile from his lips. A master stroke, but Kesselring knew how to handle men. Then the Field Marshal was standing in front of him, a slightly wry smile on his face as if he had noticed Koenig's reaction and was asking him to bear with him.

'What on earth can I say, Major? You are only the thirtieth recipient of the swords since the award was created. Normally, our Führer himself would wish to decorate you personally, but these are extraordinary times. I can only say how delighted I am that the honour falls to me.'

He held Koenig by the shoulders for a moment and then, as if in a sudden excess of emotion, embraced him.

*　　*　　*

Later, back in Walther's office having a cognac before lunch, Kesselring said, 'A very impressive young man.'

'He's certainly that,' Walther agreed.

'Decent, honourable, chivalrous. A superb soldier. What every member of the Waffen SS would like to imagine himself to be. Let's have him in and get it over with.'

Walther pressed a buzzer on his desk and a moment later an aide looked in.

'Major Koenig,' Walther said.

The aide withdrew and Koenig entered. He paused at the desk, clicked his heels, and his hand went to the peak of his fieldcap in a military salute.

The Field Marshal said, 'Pull up a chair, Major, and sit down.'

Koenig did as he was told. Kesselring turned to the large-

scale military map of Sicily on the wall. 'I see you've applied for
a transfer already.'

'Yes, Herr Field Marshal.'

'Well, it's denied.'

'May I be permitted to ask why?'

'I could say because that silver plate they had to put in your
skull after your last exploit in Russia makes you unsuitable for
jumping out of aeroplanes any more. But I don't need to. Your
task here in Sicily is of vital importance.'

General Walther said, 'There is still too much partisan
activity here in the central mountains, particularly in the region
of the Cammarata. It would be fatal to our interests in the event
of an invasion.'

'I thought the Allies intend to try Sardinia first, General?'
queried Koenig.

Walther and Kesselring glanced at each other and Kesselring
laughed. 'Go on, tell him. I don't see why not.'

Walther said, 'Actually, you're not far wrong, Major. The
high command in Berlin, the Führer himself, feel that Sardinia
will be the invasion point.'

'A few weeks ago, the body of a British courier was washed up
on a Spanish beach,' Kesselring went on. 'A Royal Marine
Major. He was carrying letters to General Alexander in Tunisia.
There was another from Lord Louis Mountbatten to Sir
Andrew Cunningham, Commander-in-Chief of the British
Mediterranean Fleet. The gist of these letters indicates firmly
that the target for the Allied invasion will be Sardinia and
Greece. Any attack on Sicily will be diversionary.'

There was a heavy silence. General Walther said, 'We'd be
interested in your opinion. Feel free to speak.'

'What can I say, Herr General.' Koenig shrugged. 'Miracles
do occur on occasions, even in this day and age. Presumably this
British Major's body being so conveniently washed up on a
Spanish beach where our agents could have a sight of the letters
he was carrying, was one of them.'

'But on the whole,' Kesselring said, 'you don't believe in
miracles.'

'Not since I stopped reading the fairy tales of the Brothers
Grimm, Herr Field Marshal.'

'Good.' Kesselring was all business now. 'Give me your personal assessment of the situation here.'

Koenig stood up and moved round to the map. 'As regards partisan activity, two important groups. The Separatists, who want an independent Sicily, and the Communists. We all know what *they* want.

'They cut each other's throats as cheerfully as they do ours.'

'General Walther was explaining to me about this Mafia movement,' Kesselring said. 'Are they a force to be reckoned with?'

'Yes, I think they have very real power under the surface of things and again, they are peculiarly Sicilian. Mainland Italy and Mussolini mean nothing to them.'

'And if an invasion comes, they will fight?'

'Oh, yes, I think so.' Koenig nodded. 'All of them. Our main worry would be the Italian Army itself.'

'You think so?' Kesselring asked.

Koenig took a deep breath and jumped in with both feet. 'Frankly, Herr Field Marshal, I think the fact must be faced that the Italian people as a whole, have lost any interest they ever had in the war and all enthusiasm for Mussolini.'

There was a slight pause and then Kesselring smiled. 'An accurate enough assessment. I wouldn't disagree with that. So, you think invasion will come to Sicily?'

Koenig ran a finger along the road south from Palermo to Agrigento. 'Here is the most vital road in the whole of Sicily, passing through the Cammarata, one of the wildest and most primitive places in the island. There has been considerable partisan activity in that area recently. According to our informants, a number of American agents have been dropped by parachute during the past few weeks. So far, we haven't succeeded in catching any of them.'

Kesselring picked up a folder from the desk. 'And yet you almost had this man.' He opened the file. 'Major Harry Carter, in charge of the Italian desk at Special Operations Executive in Cairo. You had him, Koenig, and let him slip through your fingers.'

'With respect, Herr Field Marshal,' Koenig corrected him firmly, 'my task was to provide back-up forces on the ground.

The affair was in the hands of the *Geheimefeldpolizei* and Gestapo. And I would remind you, sir, that thanks to Russia, I have only thirty-five men remaining in what was once a battalion. Not a single officer is left on the strength except myself.'

'The capture of Carter would have been an intelligence coup of the first order and Berlin, in the person of Reichsführer Himmler, is not pleased. To that end he has ordered the transfer of one of his most trusted intelligence officers from the Rome Office to work with you here.'

'I see, Herr Field Marshal,' Koenig said. 'Gestapo?'

'Oh, no,' Kesselring told him gravely. 'Rather more important than that.' He turned to Walther. Show Major Meyer in.'

The man who entered was broad and squat with a flat Slav face and cold blue eyes. Koenig recognized the type at once for the security service was full of them; ex-police officers, more used to the criminal underworld than anything else. He wore SS field uniform and his only decoration was the Order of Blood, a much coveted Nazi medal specially struck for those who had served prison sentences for political crimes in the old Weimar Republic. The most interesting fact about him was his cuff-title which carried the legend RFSS picked out in silver thread. Reichsführer der SS, the symbol of Himmler's personal staff.

'Major Franz Meyer, Major Koenig.' Walther made the introductions while Kesselring stood looking out of the window, smoking a cigarette.

Meyer took in everything about Koenig with the policeman's practised eye: the highly irregular SS uniform, the Knight's Cross with Oak Leaves and Swords.

'A pleasure, Major,' he said.

Koenig turned to Kesselring. 'There is a difficulty here, I think, Herr Field Marshal. Who is to be in charge? Meyer and I would appear to carry the same rank.'

'No difficulty there, I hope?' Kesselring said, smoothly. 'I see you as performing separate functions; you being responsible for the purely military side of the operation and Major Meyer for the, how shall I put it? The more political aspects.'

'There will be no problem from my point of view, I can assure the Herr Field Marshal of that,' Meyer said.

'Excellent.' Kesselring managed a wintry smile. 'And now, if you would leave us, Meyer. There are still matters I wish to discuss with Major Koenig.'

Meyer clicked his heels, delivered an impressive Heil Hitler and departed. When he'd gone, Kesselring said, 'I know what you're going to say, Koenig, and you're quite right. It places you in a most difficult situation.'

'Almost impossible, Herr Field Marshal. I will have no authority of rank, which means the wretched man can interfere as much as he likes.'

He was angry and it showed. Kesselring said, 'Rank has little to do with the matter. As a member of the Reichsführer's personal staff, he will always have considerable influence in certain situations, even were I myself concerned. However, I have done the best I can for you in the circumstances.'

He nodded to Walther who handed Koenig a buff envelope. Koenig started to open it and Kesselring said, 'No, keep it for later.' He held out his hand in another of those unexpected gestures. 'I wish you luck. You're going to need it.'

'Herr Field Marshal – General.' Koenig saluted, turned and went out.

*   *   *

Franz Meyer stood in the hall, pretending to read the notice-board as he waited for Koenig.

His dislike for the Major had been immediate and it went beyond any personal jealousy of Koenig's military distinction. The truth was far deeper. Koenig was a gentleman, son of a Major General of the Luftwaffe. Meyer, on the other hand, was the third son of a Hamburg shoemaker who had served the last two years of the First World War in the trenches, who had starved like thousands of others in Germany during the twenties, thanks to the British and the French and the Jews until the Führer had come along, a man of the people, giving hope to the people. And Meyer had served him since those first days, one of the earliest party members in Hamburg. The Führer himself had pinned the Blood Order on him. The Koenigs of the world, who thought themselves so far above him, had a lesson to learn.

He turned as Koeing approached. 'Ah, there you are, Major. I would very much appreciate an opportunity to discuss my duties at the earliest possible moment. This Carter affair, for example.'

'Gestapo business, not mine,' Koenig said, pulling on his gloves. 'I merely provided ground support.'

Meyer said, 'A valuable field officer murdered, Carter allowed to get clean away, yet you took no hostages in Bellona. Exacted no reprisals.'

'I'm a soldier, not a butcher,' Koenig said. 'If the distinction doesn't appeal to you, take it up with the Field Marshal.'

'There are perhaps others I could take it up with,' Meyer replied calmly. 'Reichsführer Himmler might well be interested in an officer of SS who expresses such sentiments.'

'Then you must discuss it with him,' Koenig said, 'as I'm sure you will,' and he went out of the entrance, down the steps and crossed to where Brandt waited for him behind the wheel of a *kubelwagen.*

*   *   *

Koenig smoked a cigarette as they drove down towards Palermo. Finally, he said, 'Pull over, Rudi. I must walk for a while.'

Brandt turned in at the entrance of the Pellegrino cemetery and Koenig got out and walked through the gates between even lines of Cyprus trees.

He stood looking up at a white marble tomb with a life-size statue of Santa Rosalia of Pellegrino on top. Brandt moved in behind him.

Koenig said, 'The most vulgar thing I've ever seen in my life.'

Brandt asked, 'What happened back there?'

'Oh, nothing much. They've hung a Major called Meyer from Himmler's personal staff on my back, that's all. The Field Marshal was very sorry, but there wasn't much he could do about it.'

He reached into his pocket for matches and the envelope Kesselring had given him fell out. Brandt picked it up as Koenig lit a cigarette.

'Major,' he said, holding the envelope out.

'Kesselring's parting gift,' Koenig told him. 'Open it and let's see what it was he didn't have the courage to tell me personally.'

He turned, looking out towards the sea, aware of Brandt ripping open the envelope and then the sergeant major's incredulous explosion of delight. Koenig swung round and Brandt held out the letter, smiling.

'It's your promotion, Lieutenant-Colonel.'

Koenig stared at him for a long moment, then snatched the letter from him. The formality of the language meant nothing to him. The important thing was that Brandt was right. Kesselring had promoted him. When he looked at the envelope, he saw now that it was addressed to Obersturmbannführer Max Koenig. What was it Kesselring had said? *I have done the best I can for you in the circumstances.*

He clapped Brandt on the shoulder. 'A celebration, Rudi, is very definitely in order.' As they started to walk back towards the *kubelwagen* he laughed. 'My God, but I'd like to see Meyer's face when he hears about this.'

4

It was four weeks later when the jeep carrying Harry Carter deposited him at the ornate entrance of the villa at dar el Ouad. He went up the steps slowly, taking his time and passed into the cool darkness.

Cusak looked up from his desk and got to his feet instantly. 'Major Carter. Good to see you, sir.'

'I believe I'm expected.'

'That's right, sir. I'll tell General Eisenhower you're here.'

He moved away and Carter went out on the terrace. *Was it only six weeks since he'd stood here?* He had that pain in his chest again and in spite of the fact, or because of it, he took the old silver case from his breast pocket, selected a cigarette and lit it, inhaling with great deliberation.

There was a quick step behind him and as he turned, Cusak said, 'The General will see you now, Major.'

* * *

Standing in front of the desk, Carter was filled with a strange sense of déja vu. Eisenhower, looking up at him, frowned. 'You don't look too good, Major.'

'I'll be all right, sir. I was just wondering whether it was then or now.'

Eisenhower smiled. 'Oh, yes, you've been here before, I can assure you. I get days like that myself. Sit down.' He pulled a file forward and opened it. 'I read your report with considerable interest.'

Carter pulled forward a chair. 'Thank you, sir.' He hesitated. 'Is the Sicilian invasion on, General?'

Eisenhower looked up and said calmly, 'During the next few weeks the British under General Montgomery will invade at the Eastern end of the island, while General Patton and the Seventh Army will land in the South and strike for Palermo. Are you surprised?'

'Not really, sir, although there's been a strong opinion in Sicily for months now, which I might say the Germans seem to hold also, that Sardinia would be the target.'

'Which is exactly what we want them to think. But let's get back to the original question I put to you when you were last here. According to your report, you seem certain that Washington is hoping for too much with the Mafia connection.'

'I'm afraid so, General.'

There was a brief silence, while Eisenhower stared down at the file. 'All right, what's your solution?'

'Well, there is a man, General, named Luca. Don Antonio Luca. He's what's known in Sicily as *Capo di Tutti Capi*. Boss of all the bosses. The fascists imprisoned him in 1940. Sent him to prison on the mainland – Naples. He escaped later that year and returned to Sicily where he's been in hiding ever since. He's the one man they'll all listen to. I don't wish to blaspheme, but in Sicily he could pull a larger audience than the Pope.'

'Then find him,' Eisenhower said.

'He doesn't want to be found, sir.'

'Could you find him?'

'I've tried. Total silence so far. I've got a better chance than most people though. He doesn't care for Americans. It seems he had a young brother called Cesare, who was a rum-runner on the Great Lakes during Prohibition. One night in 1929 Cesare was ambushed by a rival gang outside Chicago and personally shot three men dead. He died himself in the electric chair the following year.'

Eisenhower stood up. He paced up and down a couple of times, then turned to the map and stood looking up at it. 'Still, one thing's for sure. If George Patton and his boys have to fight their way through those mountains to Palermo, they'll die by the thousands.'

He repeated the phrase in a whisper as if to himself. Carter knew that in his mind's eye, Eisenhower was seeing again the

American dead on the battlefield of Kasserine, that terrible debacle in which untried boys had found themselves faced with the cream of the Afrika Corps.

Carter cleared his throat. 'With respect, General, I do have a suggestion.'

Eisenhower turned, suddenly alert. 'And what might that be?'

'After all is said and done, Luciano still seems to me the key figure in the whole affair. His influence with the Sicilian Mafia is unquestioned. He might provide the right link with Luca. Enough to make Luca come out of hiding and declare himself for us. If he does that, General, then we have Mafia on our side one hundred and ten percent.'

Eisenhower stood there for a long moment, staring at him, then nodded slowly. 'Damn me, Major, but I have a sneaking suspicion you might be right.'

'Then you'll put Intelligence in Washington on to it right away, sir?' Carter said. 'They could approach Luciano again during the next couple of days.'

'I'll think about it.' Eisenhower glanced at his watch. 'And now you must excuse me. This is the time of day when the telephone lines start hotting up to Washington. I talk to the President most days. He likes to be kept informed.'

'I'll go then, sir.'

Carter got up, put on his cap and saluted. Eisenhower acknowledged the salute perfunctorily, already busy with papers again, and Carter walked to the door.

As he got it open, Eisenhower called, 'I'd like you back here at eleven.'

Carter turned in surprise. 'You mean eleven tonight, General?'

'That's it, Major,' Eisenhower replied without looking up.

Carter closed the door, paused, then crossed the hall to the entrance and went down the steps to his jeep. He climbed in beside the driver and glanced at his watch. It was just after six. Almost five hours to kill.

'Where to now, sir?' asked the driver, a private first class who looked at most sixteen years of age.

'Do you know the RAF base at Maison Blanche?'

'Sure do, Major. About an hour and a half from here.'
'Fine,' Carter said. 'Take me there.'

*   *   *

The Douglas DC3, the famous Dakota, was probably the most successful general transport plane ever built, but the one which Wing commander Harvey Grant was bringing back from Malta to his base at Maison Blanche just before dark had definitely seen better days.

Not that it was in any sense his regular plane. The old Dakota did a milk run to Malta and back three times a week with medical supplies. The duty pilot had been taken ill that morning, and as there was no replacement readily available, Grant had seized the opportunity to vacate the Squadron Commander's desk and do the flight himself. Which was very much contrary to regulations, for Grant had been forbidden any further operational flying by the Air Officer Commanding Middle East Theatre himself only six weeks previously.

He sat at the controls now, alone and happy, whistling tunelessly between his teeth, the two supply sergeants forming his crew asleep in the rear.

Harvey Grant was twenty-six, a small man whose dark eyes seemed perpetually full of life. Son of a wheat farmer in Parker, Iowa, the greatest influence on his life had been his father's younger brother, Templeton Grant, who had flown with the Royal Flying Corps in France.

At an early age, Grant learnt that you always watched the sun and never crossed the line alone under 10,000 feet. He soloed at sixteen, thanks to his uncle's tuition, then moved on to Harvard to study law, more to please his father than anything else. He was at the Sorbonne in Paris when war broke out, and promptly joined the RAF.

He was shot down twice piloting Hurricanes and had eleven German fighters to his credit before the Battle of Britain was over. He'd then transferred to Bomber Command, completing a tour in Wellingtons, a second in Lancasters, by which time he was a Squadron Leader with a DSO and two DFC's to his name.

After that had come his posting to 138 (Special Duties) Squadron at Tempsford, the famous Moon Squadron that specialized in dropping agents into occupied Europe or picking them up again, as the occasion required.

Grant had flown over thirty such missions from Tempsford before being promoted and posted to Maison Blanche to handle the same kind of work, flying black-painted Halifaxes from the Algerian mainland to Sardinia, Sicily and Italy.

But all that was behind him. Now he was officially grounded. Too valuable to risk losing, that's what the AOC had said, although in Grant's opinion, it was simply another manoeuvre on the part of the American Army Air Corps to force him to transfer, a fate he was determined to avoid.

He was south-west of Pantellaria just before dusk, a quarter-moon touching the clouds with a pale luminosity, when a roaring filled the night. The Dakota bucked wildly so that it took everything Grant had to hold her as a dark shadow banked away to port.

He recognized it at once, a Junkers 88, one of those apparently clumsy, black, twin-engined planes festooned with strange radar aerials that had proved so devastating in their attacks on RAF bombers engaged on night raids over Europe. And he didn't have a thing to fight with except skill, for the Dakota carried no kind of armament.

The cabin door swung open behind him and the two supply sergeants peered in.

'Hang on!' Grant said. 'I'm going to see if I can make him do something stupid.'

He went down fast and was aware of the Junkers, turning and coming in fast, firing his cannon too soon, his speed so excessive that he had to bank to port to avoid collision.

Which was exactly what Grant was counting on. He kept on going down, was at six hundred feet when the Junkers came in on his tail. This time the Dakota staggered under the impact of cannon shell. The Junkers curved away to starboard again and appeared to take up station.

'Come on, you bastard! Come on!' Grant said softly.

Behind him one of the sergeants appeared, blood on his face where a splinter had caught him. 'Johnson's bought it.'

'Okay,' Grant said. 'He's coming in again so get down on your face and hang on.'

He was no more than five hundred feet above the waves as the Junkers came in for the kill, judging his speed perfectly now, sliding in on the Dakota's tail, opening up with more cannon shell. As the aircraft started to shudder under their impact, Grant dropped his flaps.

The Dakota seemed to stop in mid-air. The pilot of the Junkers banked steeply to starboard to avoid a collision and, with no space left to work in at such a speed, kept right on going, ploughing straight into the sea.

*   *   *

Grant, depressed, walked towards the officers' mess at Maison Blanche, his flying boots drubbing on the tarmac. He kept thinking of the way that Junkers had gone in, imagining the men inside. That was no good at all. He started up the steps to the mess and found Harry Carter standing at the top.

'Harry!' Grant said in delight. 'I heard you were in hospital in Cairo.'

'Not any more,' Carter told him. 'I had business with the man himself at dar el Ouad and as I have an hour or two to spare, I thought I'd see how you were getting on.'

On the two occasions that Carter had dropped by parachute into Sicily, Grant had flown the plane, which was something of a bond.

'Feel like a drink?' he asked.

'Not really. Let's take a walk.'

They moved towards the hangars. Carter said, 'I hear you got another one this evening.'

'In a manner of speaking.'

'And you're supposed to be grounded.'

'Damn nonsense. I had to see Air Marshal Sloane a few weeks ago on squadron business and he said I had a muscle twitching in my right cheek. Insisted I had a medical and the bastards stood me down.'

He was angry and it showed. Carter said, 'We can win the war without you, Harvey, but only just.' He put a hand on the

American's shoulder for a moment. 'What's wrong? What's really wrong?'

'I keep thinking about the men in that Junkers this evening,' Grant said. 'I don't know how to explain this, Harry, but for the first time it was as if it was me. Does that make any kind of sense?'

'Perfectly,' Carter told him. 'It means that the doctor who stood you down knew what he was talking about.'

Grant said, 'And what about you? Are you going back over there again?'

'I shouldn't think it's likely.'

'And a good thing, too.' They were passing a hangar in which ground crew worked under floodlights repairing a badly damaged Halifax. Half the tail plane was missing and the rear gunner's compartment shattered. 'Rear gunner and navigator both killed on a supply drop to Sicily two nights ago. The Luftwaffe really do have things their own way over there, Harry. We've lost four planes in ten days, all shot down, and in each case the agents they were to drop were still inside. If you asked me to fly you in again, I'd give us no better than an even chance of reaching the target and dropping you.'

'Oh, well,' Carter said. 'Someone else can worry about that one.'

They had reached the end of the main hangar and he saw, to his surprise, a Junkers 88 night fighter standing there in the gloom, RAF rondels painted on the fuselage and wings.

'What's this, for God's sake?'

'Forced down up the coast a few weeks ago after dropping a couple of Arab agents by parachute. See where they cut a special door in the fuselage. This is a Ju88S, one of their best night fighters, capable of around four hundred miles an hour. We've been doing evaluation flights.'

'You have, you mean.'

'Well, an hour here and there.' Grant shrugged. 'Who's to notice?' He clapped Carter on the shoulder. 'So, what are you up to now? Something so secret the whole future of the war depends on it?'

Carter smiled. 'There's no such animal, Harvey. Wars aren't

won by men any more. They're run by large corporations, just like big business.'

'Maybe you're right,' Grant tossed his cigarette away. 'You want to know something, Harry? I feel tired – I mean really tired. So I don't care any more.'

'It's the war, Harvey. It's gone on too long.'

'Good,' Grant said. 'I mean, that really does make me feel a whole lot better. Now let's get back to the mess and I'll buy you a drink.'

*   *   *

When the jeep dropped Carter in the courtyard outside the villa, there was a big Packard staff car outside. Carter went up the steps past the sentries and found Cusak still sitting at the desk.

'Doesn't anyone work around here except you?' Carter enquired.

Cusak smiled. 'I must admit it feels that way some days. He won't be long, sir. He has General Patton with him.'

Carter moved out on the terrace, wondering what it was Eisenhower wanted to see him about. A further discussion of the Sicilian situation perhaps and, yet, what more was there to say? It was all decided. Within the next few weeks, the big battalions would roll, the invasion would take place and, an unknown quantity of dead men later, Sicily would be in Allied hands. The Germans had lost the war, so much was obvious, so why didn't everyone simply get off at the next stop?

The door to Eisenhower's office opened and General George Patton walked across the hall. He wore field cap and heavy military greatcoat, his hands pushed deep into its pockets as if cold.

As Carter moved out of the shadows, Patton paused. 'Are you Carter?'

'That's right, sir.'

Patton stood there looking him over, a slight frown on his face. For a moment, it was as if he was about to speak; then he thought better of it, turned and walked out without another word.

The telephone buzzed, Cusak picked it up. 'Yes, General?' He smiled briefly at Carter. 'He'll see you now, Major.'

*   *   *

The room was dark, the only light the table lamp on the desk where Eisenhower sat working on a file in a haze of cigarette smoke. He glanced up as Carter entered and put down his pen.

'You know, one thing they omitted to tell us when I was a cadet at West Point was the amount of paperwork that went into being Commander-in-Chief.'

'If they did, maybe nobody would want the job, General.'

'Exactly,' Eisenhower grinned briefly and was then all business. 'There's a Flying Fortress leaving Bone Airfield two hours from now, destination Prestwick in Scotland. From there, you'll fly straight on to Washington by the first available plane, Priority One. You should be there, with any luck, by early evening tomorrow. Captain Cusak will give you your documentation on the way out.'

'I'm afraid I don't understand, sir.'

'Of course you don't,' Eisenhower replied. 'You don't know what the hell I'm talking about so I'll tell you. I liked what you said about the Sicilian situation. It made sense, particularly the bit about this man Antonia Luca and the effect he could have on the campaign if he was found and brought in on our side.'

'I see, sir.'

'I've spoken on the matter to the President during our phone call earlier this evening. He agrees that anything that can help save the lives of our boys is worth trying. To that end, I want you to proceed to this penitentiary at Great Meadow to discuss further with Luciano the whole question of Mafia involvement in the invasion.' He passed a buff envelope across. 'There's your authority, in my name, to act in any way you see fit in this matter. It makes you answerable only to me and requires all personnel, military or civil, without distinction of rank, to assist you in any way you see fit. There will be a similar document waiting for you in Washington countersigned by the President.'

Carter stared down at the envelope, bewildered. 'To do what, General?'

'How in the hell do I know?' Eisenhower said. 'Talk to the man. See what he has to say. Yank him right out of that damn prison if you have to. You've got the power. Now, are you going to use it or aren't you?'

Carter, filled with an excitement he had not known in years, slipped the envelope into one of his tunic pockets and buttoned it carefully.

'Oh, yes, sir.'

'Good.' Eisenhower nodded. 'Another thing. I've arranged a promotion to full colonel for you. Only temporary, of course, but it should give you some extra muscle along the way.'

He turned before Carter could reply and switched on a lamp that illuminated the map of Sicily. He stood looking at it for a while and spoke without turning round. 'Are you surprised that I'm willing to have dealings with people like Luciano?'

'Frankly, sir, I think I've got well past being surprised at anything.'

'The Nazis have plundered and raped Europe, murdered millions of people. The stories that are beginning to emerge about their treatment of the Jews are past belief and I'm of German stock myself. Have you any idea how that feels?'

'I think so, sir,' Carter said.

'Oh, no, you haven't,' Eisenhower shook his head. 'To beat these people, Major, finish them once and for all, root and branch, I'd shake hands with the Devil himself if it were necessary.'

5

On his twentieth lap of the exercise yard at Great Meadow, Luciano increased his speed, running fast and free, the best moment of the day when there was an infinite possibility to things. Then, as usual, the north wall got in the way and he had to slow down.

He walked back through a scattering of other prisoners, acknowledging a greeting here and there, to his usual spot in a corner by the landing where Franco waited with a towel.

'You're getting better each day, Mr Luciano,' Franco said.

He had the look of a professional wrestler and the build to go with it, a New York Sicilian who had killed many times on behalf of the Mafia and was serving a double life sentence for murder.

Luciano caught the towel as Franco threw it. 'You reach my age, you got to keep in shape. Did you get that book from the library?'

'I sure did, Mr Luciano.'

He passed it across, an English translation of *The City of God* by St Augustine. Luciano sat on the step and examined it with a conscious pleasure.

He was forty-six, a dark, handsome, saturnine man of medium height. The lid drooped slightly over the left eye, relic of an old wound. In spite of the drab prison uniform he was a man to be looked at twice, and not just because of the authority and self-sufficiency that were plainly indicated in the face. There was also that perpetual slight smile of contempt directed at the world in general.

Franco said, 'Excuse me, Mr Luciano, but there's a kid here called Walton from D block. He needs a favour.'

Luciano looked up. Walton was a tall, gangling young man of

twenty-one or two with flat brown hair and arms that were too long for his shirt.

'What's he in for?' Luciano asked softly.

'One to three. Liquor store hold up. No previous.'

'Okay, let's see what he wants.'

Franco nodded to the boy, gave Luciano a cigarette and lit it for him. 'Okay, speak your piece.'

Walton stood there, twisting his cap in his hand nervously. 'Mr Luciano, they say you can do anything.'

'Except sprout wings and fly out of this place.' Luciano smiled softly. 'What's to do, boy?'

'It's like this, Mr Luciano. I've only been here two months and my wife, Carrie ... well, she's on her own now and she's only a kid. Eighteen is all.'

'So?'

'There's a detective from the eighth precinct called O'Hara. He was one of the guys who pulled me in. He knows she's on her own and he's been pressuring her. You know what I mean?'

Luciano looked him over calmly for a long moment then nodded. 'Okay. Detective O'Hara, eighth precinct. It's taken care of.' He returned to his book.

The boy said, 'Maybe I can do you a favour some time, Mr Luciano.'

Franco said, 'You will, kid. Now get out of here.'

As the boy turned away, Luciano looked up. 'Is it true that liquor store heist was your first job?'

Walton nodded. 'That's right, Mr Luciano.'

'And one to three was the best your lawyer could do? He should have got you probation.'

'I didn't really have no lawyer, not a real one,' Walton said. 'Just a man the court appointed. He only spoke to me the once. Said the thing to do was plead guilty and throw myself on the court's mercy. I didn't see ...'

'All right!' Luciano put up a hand defensively. 'I'll speak to my lawyer when he comes up Wednesday. Maybe he can do something.'

The boy walked away and Franco said, 'Keep that up and you'll have them standing in line at the bottom of the stairs every morning.'

One of the guards approached, an ageing Irishman named O'Toole, with the weary, bitter look of one who had long since faced up to defeat.

For Luciano, he managed a smile. 'The warder would like to see you in his office, Mr Luciano.'

'Now?' Luciano said.

'That's what he told me.'

Luciano got up, still holding his book, and nodded to Franco. 'See you later, Johnny.'

They moved across the yard, O'Toole in the lead. He said, 'They're waxing the entrance hall so we can't use the main door. We'll go through the showers and up the back stairs.'

His forehead was damp with sweat and his hand shook a little as he unlocked the door to the shower block.

Luciano smiled easily, every sense sharpened. 'Something bothering you, O'Toole?'

O'Toole gave him a sudden quick push inside and slammed the door and Franco, halfway across the yard, started to run, already too late as O'Toole turned, back to the door, the club ready in his hand.

*   *   *

Walton moved out of the first shower stall. He stood there, no expression on his face at all, no light in the dark eyes.

Luciano said easily, 'I thought that story of yours was strictly from the corn belt. They send you up here specially?'

'That's right.' Walton's right hand came up holding an ivory Madonna. When he pressed her feet, six inches of blue steel appeared, sharp as a razor on both edges. 'Nothing personal, Mr Luciano. With me, this is strictly business.'

'Who sent you?'

'Fiorelli. He sent you his regards and gave me strict instructions to leave you with your prick in your mouth. He said being Sicilian, you'd know what that meant.'

'Oh, I do,' Luciano said and kicked Walton under the left kneecap.

Walton shouted in agony as bone splintered, and slashed out

wildly. Luciano seized the right wrist with both hands, twisting it so cruelly that the knife dropped to the floor.

'You're going to cut someone up, kid, do it, don't talk about it.'

He twisted round and up, locking the arm as in a vice. Walton screamed as muscle started to tear and Luciano ran him face-first into the wall of the nearest stall. The boy slid down the wall, leaving a smear of blood on the tiles.

Luciano picked up the knife and closed the blade. The Madonna was about eight inches long and obviously extremely old, carved by some master of ivory and chased with silver. He slipped it into his belt against the small of his back and picked up his book.

Walton crouched at the base of the stall, moaning. Luciano turned on the shower and the boy clutched at the wall.

'So long, kid,' Luciano said softly and he opened the door and went out.

O'Toole swung to face him, instant dismay on his face. Franco dodged past him. 'You all right, Mr Luciano?'

'Oh, sure,' Luciano said, 'But that Walton kid looks as if he's slipped in the shower in there. I'd say he needs a doctor bad.'

Franco moved inside without a word and Luciano turned to O'Toole. 'I'd better get moving or the warden will wonder what's happened to me. You did say he wanted to see me, didn't you?'

O'Toole licked dry lips. 'Oh, sure, Mr Luciano,' he said feebly. 'Right away.'

Luciano smiled and moved off across the yard and Franco came out of the showers and leaned against the door, lighting a cigarette.

'Heh, O'Toole,' he said softly, a terrible smile on his face. 'I don't know what they paid you, but I think maybe you just made the biggest mistake of your life.'

*   *   *

Harry Carter, wearing a dark blue suit in place of his uniform, stood at the window of the Warden's office and looked down into the yard.

The Warden said, 'He doesn't like to be called Lucky. He's supposed to have got the name because of an incident in 1929 when rival mobsters kidnapped him, took him to a deserted wood in Staten Island, hung him up by his thumbs and tortured him. Left him for dead.'

'I wonder how he paid them off?' Carter said.

'I can imagine.' The Warden went round his desk and opened a file. 'Charles Luciano, born Salvatore Lucania in the village of Lercara Friddi near Palermo, 24 November 1897. Arrived in New York in 1907 with his family, who, I might add, are all honest people. You know how Mafia works, Colonel Carter?'

'Only the Sicilian variety.'

'It's pretty much the same in New York. They start them young. First there are the boys, the *picciotti*, gaining advancement, what they call respect, by acting as executioners when required. Some of them graduate pretty quickly to the next rank. *Sicario*, the professional assassin who's a specialist in that line of work.'

'I know,' Carter said. 'In Sicily they prefer the *lupara*, the sawn-off shotgun, for that kind of thing. You have to get close, but then, that's really the point.'

'They say Luciano's killed at least twenty men himself and that isn't those he's put a contract out on.'

'Just how powerful a figure is he?' Carter asked. 'I mean, he is in here, isn't he? You close a cell door on him every night.'

'Inside or out, it doesn't really matter. He's still the single most important influence in Mafia. Rose to power in the liquor business during Prohibition. What made him different from the others was his brain. He's a hugely intelligent man with a genius for organization. When Prohibition ended, he diversified into every possible racket that would make a dollar. Even invented a few. In 1936 Governor Dewey, who was then Special Prosecutor, brought him to trial for offences concerned with organized prostitution and succeeded in obtaining a conviction.'

'Strange,' Carter said. 'It's the one thing that doesn't seem to fit.'

The Warden smiled. 'That's what a lot of people say, but don't expect any comment from me. This is a state appointment. I know one thing. He can always be relied upon to do the unexpected thing. He was at Dannemora in 1941 just after Pearl Harbor. That was a bad time with Christmas coming up. People's minds were on other things, so there were no packages for the cons until Luciano put the word out. Christmas Day, three truckloads of gifts turned up from New York.'

There was a knock on the door. He called, 'Come in!' and Luciano entered.

He glanced at Carter casually, then turned to the Warden. 'You sent for me.'

The Warden stood up. 'This is Colonel Carter. He's from the Government and he has full authority to speak with you on a matter of national importance, so I'm going to leave you to it.'

He went out and Carter took out his silver case. 'Cigarette, Mr Luciano?'

'Heh, you're English.'

'So are the cigarettes.'

Carter gave him a light and Luciano sat down by the window. 'What the hell are you doing here?'

'I believe you've had some visitors in recent months,' Carter said. 'From Naval Intelligence. To discuss the Sicilian invasion.'

Luciano said, 'Not again, for Christ's sake. Look, I gave them all the information I could. All the right names.'

'I know,' Carter said. 'I hear they're going to drop flags with an L for Luciano on every village in the Cammarata. Was that your idea?'

Luciano moved to the window and looked down into the Yard. 'You got an ace in your hand, you play it.'

'I don't think that's going to be enough.'

'You don't think!' Luciano laughed. 'What the hell has it got to do with a limey like you, anyway?'

Carter replied in good Sicilian, 'Sure, in the Cammarata they still talk about the great Luciano. Salvatore the saviour. But turning out to fight Nazi tanks with shotguns, just because someone drops his flag on their village ... I don't think so.'

Luciano frowned, immediately wary. 'How come you speak such good Sicilian?'

'Before the war I was a university professor, ancient history, archaeology. That kind of thing. I used to spend a lot of time in Sicily excavating.'

'Excavating?'

'Digging up old ruins.'

'You mean you're only a part-time soldier? Just for the duration? A professor, eh? Now that I can respect.' He passed across his copy of *The City of God*. 'Have you ever read this?'

Carter examined it. 'St Augustine. Oh, yes. You read a lot, do you?'

Luciano nodded. 'He knew what he was talking about. God and the Devil, they both exist, only these days God's outnumbered.'

'I see,' Carter said. 'So you've settled for reigning in hell?'

'It's a point of view. Milton knew what he was talking about.' Luciano smiled softly. 'I've read him, too.'

'You know, Mr Luciano, you interest me – both of you.'

'Both of me?'

'But of course. There's Luciano number one, a streetwise hoodlum, who leaves out verbs when he speaks and manages to sound as if he's had the same script writer as James Cagney.'

'I'm complimented.' Luciano was smiling. 'A great little guy.'

'And then there's Luciano number two, who reads Augustine and Milton, speaks discreetly, sounds remarkably upper-class ...'

'So a good actor changes his performance according to his audience.' Luciano shrugged. 'I mean, who are *you* playing today, *Professore?*'

Carter smiled. 'Point taken. You're a remarkable man, Mr Luciano.'

'And you, Professor, are a remarkable judge of character. Tell me, does Tom Dewey know you're here? When he was special prosecutor he pulled enough strings to get me put away. Look at him now. Governor of New York State. The White House next stop.'

'You think Dewey was unfair to you?'

'What's fair? What's unfair? There's only life. Some kid's born with twisted legs or half a brain. Is that fair?' He got up and walked to the window. 'Look, Professor, I don't give a damn what you think, but this is the way it was. I was boss of the rackets. I had an interest in most things, but never girls. Tom Dewey tried every damn way he could to get me and failed. Finally, they brought me to trial with nine other guys and some of them were in the prostitution business. At the end of the day, the jury couldn't tell the difference between us. It's called guilt by association.'

'A nice turn of phrase,' Carter said.

Luciano turned to face him. 'If I needed girls, I rang up Polly Adler. She kept the best house in New York.'

Carter held out his silver case. 'Have another cigarette.'

'Okay.' Luciano took one. 'Now, what do you want with me?'

Carter sat down in the Warden's chair. 'When the invasion starts, General Patton's Seventh Army is going to have the task of hacking its way through some of the worst mountains in Sicily to reach Palermo. If Mafia can be persuaded to organize a popular uprising and make the Italian Army in the Cammarata surrender without firing a shot, then thousands of American lives could be saved. If not . . .'

'Look, I've done everything they asked me to do,' Luciano said.

'I know, but as I said, I don't think it's enough. I was in Sicily myself only a matter of weeks ago and I can tell you this. There's only one man with the muscle to achieve what we're asking and that's Antonio Luca. And he isn't coming out of hiding for anyone.'

Luciano had stopped smiling. 'Don Antonio? You know him?'

'Not personally. Do you?'

'Sure I do.' Luciano shook his head. 'I still get the word in here. I know about him getting out of that prison in Naples and going back to Sicily. But you're wasting your time. Even if you could find him, he hates Americans. His brother went to the chair during Prohibition.'

'I know about that but wasn't there something special about his daughter?'

'That's right, Sophia. During the First World War while she was supposed to be at school in Rome, she joined the Red Cross as a nurse. Met an Englishman called Vaughan, an infantry lieutenant serving on the Italian front, and married him. He was

killed in the last month of the war and she went back home to live
with her father in Palermo. Had a daughter called Maria the
following year. She was the light of Don Antonio's life.'

'What happened?' Carter said.

'July 1936. The kid must have been about seventeen. Her
mother borrowed her father's Ferrari one day so they could go
shopping. When she put her finger on the starter, the car blew
up. I guess whoever was responsible was after Don Antonio.'

'So the mother was killed?'

'That's right. Maria was in hospital for a while then one day
she just walked out. I think maybe she'd had time to think, lying
there on her back for so long.'

'That if her grandfather hadn't been the kind of man he was,
the whole thing would never have happened ...' Carter said
'Did she ever turn up again?'

'She wrote to him once from London to say she was well, but
never wanted to see him again. She'd British nationality because
of her old man. Don Antonio put people on to it, but they never
managed to find her. After that, he grew more and more into
himself.'

'Would he see you?'

'See me?' Luciano frowned. 'I don't get you.'

'If you were in Sicily,' Carter said. 'If he knew you were there.
If the word was out, would he see you?'

Luciano was genuinely astonished and it showed. 'You're
crazy. You've got to be.'

'You're right,' Carter said. 'After all, look what you'd be
giving up. Another twenty laps round the exercise yard tomorrow and the day after that. Thirty to fifty years, isn't that your
sentence? I should say you'll be able to apply for parole around
1956 but I wouldn't count on it.'

'Fuck you!' Luciano said. 'I shouldn't even be in here in the
first place.'

'All right,' Carter said. 'So maybe this could be a way out.'

'Go to hell!'

Carter sat there staring at him for a moment, then he got up
and went into the outer office where the Warden was sitting
talking to a secretary.

Carter took a card from his wallet and passed it across. 'Would you mind getting that number for me? It's priority one. The code word is Scorpion. That gets you through right away.'

The Warden's eyes widened as he read the card and he whistled softly. 'I certainly will.'

Carter stood at the window, coughing over a cigarette. In spite of Luciano's attitude, every instinct told him he was on the edge of something hugely important. When the Warden finally called him, he came to the phone at once.

'Is that you, Carter?' the voice at the other end of the line said. 'How goes it?'

'Problems, Mr President,' Carter said and started to explain.

*   *   *

Luciano was standing at the window looking down into the exercise yard when the door opened and Carter and the Warden entered.

Luciano said, 'Can I go now?'

The Warden moved round the desk and sat down. 'I'm afraid not, Mr Luciano. Colonel Carter's got a car waiting. You're being transferred to Washington under his care.'

'Transferred?' Luciano cried. 'To Washington? What for?'

'Let's just say for the good of your health,' the Warden said. 'They've got one of the best chest clinics in the country in Washington and we've been worried about that cough of yours for some time now.'

Luciano turned to Carter. 'You'll have to do better than this, Professor.'

Carter smiled. 'Oh, I intend to, Mr Luciano. You can count on it.'

*   *   *

It was late evening as the Packard turned along Constitution Avenue and moved towards the White House. Carter and Luciano were seated together in the rear and Luciano wound down the window and looked out at the lights of Washington.

'I hear it's impossible to get a hotel bed in this town these days, is that true?'

'Not if you know the right people.'

The Packard turned in at the White House and delivered them to the West Basement entrance where Carter presented his pass to the Secret Service agents on duty.

Luciano wore a dark felt slouch hat and a trenchcoat over a grey tweed suit, clothes he had selected for himself from the prisoners' stock at Great Meadow. He stood there, a cigarette dangling from the corner of his mouth, obviously amused by the proceedings.

'Is this for real, Professor? I mean, you wouldn't kid a guy,' he asked as they waited.

'No, Mr Luciano,' Carter told him. 'It's real enough.'

An aide appeared, a young Marine lieutenant in razor-sharp uniform. 'Colonel Carter? If you'd come this way the President will see you now.'

*   *   *

When they entered the Oval Office, the room was in half-darkness, the only light the table lamp on the massive desk, an array of service flags behind it. President Roosevelt was seated in his wheelchair at the desk working on some papers, the inevitable long cigarette-holder jutting from his mouth.

He looked up at Carter and smiled. 'Colonel Carter, how are you?'

'Fine, Mr President.'

The President nodded to the young Marine. 'If I need you, I'll call.'

The door closed quietly. There was silence for a moment while the President fitted a fresh cigarette into the holder. He lit it carefully, then finally acknowledged Luciano's existence.

'So you're Luciano?'

'That's what they tell me.'

'I hear from Colonel Carter you've been giving him trouble.'

'Now that, Mr President, depends entirely on your point of view,' Luciano said. 'I'm sitting in my cell last year when your people come and ask to see me about doing something about Nazi saboteurs on the docks after they burned the *Normandie*, so I arrange things with the unions. Then they come again the other month asking for help in Sicily. Again, I do what I can. And for what? I mean, what in the hell is there in it for me except another thirty years in the Pen? And then this guy turns up with some crazy idea I'm going to Sicily with him and put my head on the block, and you think *I'm* giving *him* trouble?'

The President leaned back and said softly, 'I'll tell you what I'm going to do, Luciano. I'm going to give you a chance to be an American again.'

'By going to Sicily with the Professor here?' Luciano said. 'Why should I? What's in it for me?'

The President said, 'A bullet in the head if the Nazis catch you.'

'And if they don't? I mean, if his whole crazy idea works, what happens then?'

'Oh, I suppose you could take to those Sicilian mountains and be a fugitive for the rest of your life. On the other hand, you could go back to that cell of yours and take your chances. I'm sure the parole board would be suitably impressed.'

'You wouldn't care to guarantee that?'

Roosevelt said, 'You can go now, I've got work to do.'

Luciano stood there, staring at him, glanced at Carter, then spread his hands wide in a very Italian gesture, turned and walked out.

The President said, 'Anything more I can do, Colonel?'

Carter took a folded piece of paper from his wallet and passed it across. 'If you could ask Intelligence to trace that person for me, Mr President, preferably before I leave, it would be helpful.'

'I'll see to it,' the President said.

'Mr President.'

Carter turned and followed Luciano, who was already on his way out. The Marine lieutenant said, 'I'll only be a moment, Colonel,' and went into the Oval office.

Luciano was smiling again. Carter said, 'Well?'

'Well, what?' Luciano said. 'He didn't exactly leave me any choice, did he?' He grinned. 'I'll say one thing for that old man. He's got balls.'

'It's been said before.'

'But he didn't promise me a thing.'

'Not on paper. On the other hand, if you can't trust Franklyn
Delano Roosevelt, who can you trust?'

'All right. You've made your point. So what happens now?'

'We're flying out just after midnight. Scotland first stop. A
place called Prestwick. Direct flight to Algeria from there.'

'That gives us five hours to kill.'

'No problem,' Carter said. 'I've booked a hotel room.'

The Marine lieutenant returned and led the way back along
the corridor to the West Basement entrance.

Luciano said, 'Yes, I can believe that, Professor. With your
kind of influence I can believe anything.'

*   *   *

As the Flying Fortress gained height, climbing out over the
Atlantic, the New England coastline falling away, Carter made
himself as comfortabe as possible in the sleeping bag the
Quartermaster had given him. Beside him, Luciano was having
the same problem.

'One thing's for sure, they didn't intend these things to carry
passengers.'

Carter took an envelope from his pocket and passed it across.
'Your name is now Frank Orsini. You're a field operative in the
Office of Strategic Services with the rank of captain. Everything
you need to back that up is in the envelope.'

'Christmas in June,' Luciano said.

He took the Madonna from one of his pockets, jumped the
blade and sliced open the envelope.

Carter said, 'Where on earth did that come from?'

'With the clothes, from good old Great Meadow.' Luciano
smiled. 'You can get most things in there, Professor. Let's just
say it was a parting gift from a friend.'

A sergeant radio-operator appeared and crouched down
beside Carter, holding a signal. 'Colonel Carter, this came
through for you just as we were leaving. Plain language. I hope it
makes sense, sir.'

Carter glanced at it and smiled. 'Perfect sense, sergeant.'

The boy moved away and Luciano said, 'You seem pleased.'

'You could say that. An interesting fact about this war, Mr

Luciano, is that the British are actually more thoroughly documented than the Germans. Every man, woman and child has to have a National Identity Card. Remember the piece of paper I gave the President? It was a request for our Intelligence people in London to see if they could run down Maria Vaughan. It didn't take them long.'

He passed the signal and Luciano's eyes widened. 'Sister Maria Vaughan. Convent of the Little Sisters of Pity, Liverpool. Holy Mother of God.'

'Careful,' Carter told him as he took the signal back. 'You almost crossed yourself.'

'Little Sisters of Pity. That's a new one on me.'

'It's a nursing order.'

'Liverpool. Isn't that a port?'

'On the north west coast of England. Lancashire.'

'You intend to go see her?'

'Yes, I would say that's a distinct possibility.'

'Everything's click-click with you,' Luciano said. 'I bet you're one hell of a chess player. But no emotion. You ever love anybody, Professor? I mean really love?'

Carter nodded. 'Oh, yes, very definitely.'

'When was this?'

'About a thousand years ago – when I was sixteen. Farmer's daughter in Norfolk where we used to go for family holidays. I can see her now, running over the sand dunes in a cotton frock.'

'What happened?'

'She died during the influenza epidemic just after the war. Now me, I ran away from school and joined an infantry battalion just before my seventeenth birthday. I thought it was a romantic thing to do.'

'That figures,' Luciano said, but he was no longer smiling.

'We started the big push in 1918 with a battalion of 752 men. Within three months, we were down to seventy-three. I couldn't get killed and she had to die of bloody influenza.'

Luciano said calmly, 'So you never married?'

'Yes, my second cousin, Olive, in 1923.'

'You loved her?'

'She was a childhood friend and she loved me.'

'You got children?'

'No, she had the worst kind of miscarriage very early on.'

'You going to see her when we get in?'

Carter shook his head. 'Not possible. She died of cancer in thirty-eight.'

Luciano nodded. 'So, the war came just in time for you.'

Carter gazed at him blankly. 'You think so?'

'Don't you?' Luciano tipped the slouch hat over his eyes, folded his arms and slept.

6

It was raining hard in Liverpool the following night when JU88 pathfinders made their first strike on the Liverpool Docks. At the General Infirmary, Sister Maria Vaughan had been due to go off duty at seven, but there was a severe shortage of experienced theatre nurses and at the last moment, she had been asked to assist Professor Tankerley with a post mortem in the mortuary. It was not a duty she cared for, but it had to be done.

In the preparation room, she quickly pulled a fresh white gown over her habit and adjusted her cowl, checking herself in the mirror. She was twenty-three and slightly built with a grave, steady face. One of those plain faces that, for some reason, most people found themselves looking at twice. Only the eyes betrayed her, full of a kind of restless searching that showed that any visible repose had to be fought for.

When she went into surgery, Tankerley was already there, a small intense man in a white gown that, from its condition, had already seen considerable service. There was no one else there except for the corpse under a sheet.

Tankerley pulled on rubber gloves impatiently. 'Do get a move on, Sister. I've got a ward round in an hour.'

He was three years past the retirement age, had only stayed on because of the war; a fine surgeon and convinced atheist who had little time for nuns at the best of times and certainly not in hospital.

An assortment of surgical instruments was laid out on a trolley beside the operating table. Sister Maria pulled the sheet away and folded it neatly. The body was that of a middle-aged man who had obviously been in remarkably good condition, with powerful shoulders and strong, muscular arms. The eyes were closed, the face peaceful.

'The general staff shortage being as bad as ever and no shorthand writer available, I'm going to have to do the report from memory later,' Tankerley told her. 'He was found on the pavement near a bus stop in Lime Street at five-thirty. Age around fifty, good physical condition, no evidence of external bruising, so obviously not the victim of an assault. What would your diagnosis be, Sister?'

'Coronary?' she said.

'Yes, I'd go along with that. Everything fits, including the age, so in the circumstances, we'll dispense with the whole works and go straight for the heart.'

He held out his hand. She passed him a large scalpel and he opened the body from throat to belly with one practised stroke. A living patient was different but this was something she had always found difficult to take. She swallowed hard as Tankerley started to break the ribs with a pair of large cutters.

'Raw meat, Sister.' He was, as usual, unable to resist taunting her. 'That's all there is to a man at the end of the day. Where's your God now?'

She passed him a small scalpel. 'A superior piece of engineering. Totally functional. There seems to be no task a human being is not capable of, wouldn't you agree?'

'Except learning how to live for ever.'

'No, but it is people at their most extraordinary I am interested in,' she said. 'Is that all that's left, a body on a mortuary slab? I don't think so. Christ, Professor, was once only a man dying on a cross. Two thousand years later he is a visible presence to millions.'

He glanced up and half-smiled in grudging admiration. 'Oh, you have a way with the words, I'll say that for you.'

And then, as the first stick of bombs fell across the docks, there was an explosion close at hand. The whole building shook, there was the crash of breaking glass. The lights dimmed for a moment and, somewhere, a woman screamed in fear.

'They certainly pick their time,' Tankerley said. 'On your way, Sister. They'll be needing you in Casualty. I'll finish up here on my own.'

As she reached the door, another stick of bombs dropped across the docks. The steel instruments rattled on the tray as the building shook again. Tankerley reached for another scalpel and continued with his task while Sister Maria wrenched open the door and hurried out.

*　　　*　　　*

There was a tremendous hubbub in Casualty, people running up and down the corridor and a smell of burning. The bombing had stopped and Maria could hear fire engines in the distance.

The hospital was working at full stretch now and she was on her own, patiently inserting twenty-five stitches into the left leg of a young seaman who had been brought in from the docks half an hour previously.

He watched her carefully, an unlit cigarette dangling from the corner of his mouth. 'You're doing a good job there, Sister. How about giving me a little kiss for being a brave boy?'

'Not part of the service, I'm afraid.'

'What a waste,' he said. 'I mean, a good-looking girl like you. It must be hell.'

Behind her, Tankerley moved into the room. He produced a cigarette lighter and flicked it on. 'Here, light your cigarette and shut up.' He leaned down to examine the leg. 'Very nice, Sister. You can go now. I'll finish here.'

She moved out through the curtain and started awkwardly to unfasten the ties at the back of her gown. Tankerley appeared behind her. 'Let me.' He pulled the bows one by one and she was aware that he was angry. 'Young swine,' he muttered.

She turned, shaking her head. 'He doesn't understand, that's all. So many people want everyone else to be as they are. And he's right. It can be hell. St Chrysostom called celibacy the little crucifixion.'

'And is it?' he asked.

'Not really, Professor. A very fair exchange in return for what is gained.'

He scowled and gave her a push. 'Go on, get out of here before you seduce me entirely. Go home.'

For once, she did as she was told, too tired, too spent to argue.

*　　*　　*

The Convent of the Little Sisters of Pity was in Huby Road, a large red-brick building behind high walls which had once been a college for the training of elementary school teachers. The teachers had long since moved out and the Little Sisters, with a considerable amount of faith and a large mortgage, had taken over. For twenty years this had been the base for all their work in the city.

The chapel was cold and smelled of damp, which was hardly surprising as no heating of any kind was possible because of fuel rationing. It was a place of shadows, candlelight and darkness alternating.

Maria Vaughan genuflected at the altar rail and lit a candle to the Virgin. She knelt in prayer for a moment, then rose, picked up her mop and bucket, moved to the central aisle and started to clean the floor. In spite of the tiredness she did not mind, for it was a simple enough task and gave her time to think.

High up in the gallery, Sister Katherine Markham, the Mother Superior of the convent, stood with Harry Carter and Luciano watching her.

'I thought you said she'd been working all day at the hospital?' Carter said.

'That's so. She's a theatre sister there.'

'Then why this?'

'However hard the day has gone, each member of the Order has an allotted task to perform each evening. However menial, Colonel, it is a symbol of the love that binds us all together. We'll go down now and I'll introduce you.'

She started along the gallery to the stairs. Luciano grinned and said softly, 'Ask a stupid question, Professor, and see what you get.'

*　　*　　*

Maria looked up as they approached and paused in her work. 'Sister?' she said.

Sister Katherine smiled. 'You have visitors, Maria. This is Colonel Carter and this is Mr Orsini.'

Maria stood there, transfixed, staring at Luciano. He smiled easily and said in Sicilian, 'Hello, pretty one. It's been a long time.'

Sister Katherine gently took the mop from Maria. 'I'll finish here. You can take these gentlemen to my office.'

Maria looked again at Luciano, turned and walked away. As Carter and Luciano started after her, Sister Katherine said, 'We use the lodge as a guest house, Colonel. You're welcome to spend the night with us.'

She dipped the mop in the bucket and started to work on the floor as they went out.

*　　*　　*

The office was small and cluttered, barely room for the desk and filing cabinets. Luciano leaned against the door, smoking, while Carter and Maria faced each other across the desk.

'So there you are,' Carter said. 'It's really very simple. All it requires is a yes or a no. Mr Orsini and I ...'

'The subterfuge in not necessary, Colonel,' she said calmly. 'I am familiar with Mr Luciano. He is a part of a past which I no longer wish to acknowledge. Which no longer forms a part of my life.'

'Can you cut off a leg, an arm and be the same person?' Luciano asked in Sicilian.

She answered in the same language. 'Good husbandry, Mr Luciano, to lop off the rotten branch to save the tree.'

Carter said patiently, 'Sister, to save thousands of lives it's necessary to persuade your grandfather to come over to our side publicly. You could just be the one to do it.'

'You're wasting your time, Colonel. I have had no dealings with my grandfather for years. This entire affair is preposterous and nothing to do with me. And now you must excuse me. I have work to do.'

She brushed past Luciano and went out. Carter picked up the

telephone and gave the long distance operator the number of SOE's headquarters in Baker Street in London.

Luciano said, 'So, what happens now?'

'She'll go,' Carter assured him.

'How can you be so sure?'

'Oh, the thought of all those dead men should do it. She's a *good* woman, after all. Can't you tell?'

The phone rang and he picked it up. 'Give me Control Two. Carter here. The code word is Scorpion.'

He reached for a cigarette and Luciano lit it for him as a voice echoed faintly in Carter's ear.

He said, 'Hello, Jack, Harry here. Yes, all systems go. This is what I'm going to need. A safe house for a few days near Manchester. Is Bransby Abbey still on the list?'

Luciano said, 'Heh, wait a minute.'

Carter ignored him. 'Two heavies as part of the back-up team. Good Italian essential plus all the usual skills, but I must have them within forty-eight hours. And signals to 138 Squadron at Maison Blanche and our friends in Bellona to make ready for a drop seven to ten days from now.'

He listened for a while then smiled. 'No, no problem.'

He replaced the receiver. Luciano said, 'Like I said, no emotion. Everything click, click, click. Only you're wrong about one thing, Professor.'

'Tell me,' Harry Carter said.

'If Maria goes, it won't be because of the thought of all those lives she might save.'

'So what's your theory?'

'Simple. She's so eaten up with guilt that it's impossible for her to say no.'

*   *   *

Sister Angela's one vice was cigarettes. Maria knew where they were kept. Behind the flour bin in the kitchen pantry. She lit one with trembling fingers and stood there in the dark, smoking furiously, like a defiant child.

The Sicilian half came to the surface rather easily on occasion, something to be fought against but not now. The sight of

Luciano's face, the old sardonic smile, had opened wounds and things walked out of dark corners to confront her again.

She could smell the burning, see again the blood on her mother's face as she crawled towards her. And afterwards, the pain. The long weeks in hospital, the skin grafts for the burns and her grandfather, sitting there day by day beside the bed, in spite of the fact that she would not speak to him.

The hate in her, the rage, was so strong now that, in a kind of panic, she dropped the cigarette in the sink, turned on the tap and bathed her face with cold water.

After a while, she felt better. The past was over and done with. She had buried her dead and that included her grand-father. Sicily and all that it stood for was a matter of total indifference to her now. She had her work, her daily routine, the hospital. There was no place for anything else. Luciano and Carter would have to understand that. She smoothed her robe, took a deep breath and went out.

*   *   *

The Refuge in what had been the old stables at the back of the convent wasn't much of a place, but the stone walls had been neatly whitewashed, there was a coke fire in the stove, benches and blankets for those who queued there each night.

They were a strangely assorted group. Whole families, mother, father, children, who had been bombed out, service-men on leave or between trains and needing a bed. And then there were flotsam and jetsam to be found in any great city, the unwashed, the destitute, the drunks who could no longer cope.

Maria and two other nuns stood together behind a trestle table doling out bread and hot broth to the slowly moving line of people.

Two young soldiers in khaki battledress were arguing at the end of the line. There was a sudden cry, a flurry of blows. Maria went round the table like a strong wind and flung herself between them. The one she was nearest to, a young, red-headed Scot, hit out wildly, still trying to reach his opponent, and struck her in the face.

Suddenly Luciano was there, looking like the Devil himself. His right hand slapped across the boy's face very fast, his left seized him by the throat.

Maria had him by the arm now with both hands, exerting all her strength. 'No, please. This isn't the way.'

And Luciano was smiling now and released his grip so that the boy fell to his knees. 'Okay, pretty one. Whatever you say,' he said in Sicilian.

There was a sudden buzz of conversation as the crowd came back to life. The soldier stood up and gingerly touched his throat.

'I'm sorry, miss,' he said to Maria. 'I don't know how it happened.'

'I know,' she said. 'Get your soup and sit down,' and she turned and went after Luciano.

*   *   *

'It's been a long time,' he said. 'The summer of thirty-five. How old were you, sixteen?'

'And you,' she said. 'You don't change.'

'So you've kept up with what happened to me?'

'Oh, yes, I know all about the great Lucky Luciano whose answer to everything is still violence. And where did it get you? Thirty years in prison.'

'On a bum rap and I'm out now, aren't I?'

'You were my hero that summer when you visited my grandfather, you know that? Robin Hood and Richard the Lionheart rolled into one. When we walked in Palermo and people stopped to kiss your hand, I thought it was a mark of respect. But I was wrong. It was only that they were afraid.'

'What about Don Antonio. You ever hear from him?'

'No.'

It seemed colder than ever in the chapel and Luciano leaned against the end of a pew as he looked down at her. 'You still love him, don't you, and that tears you apart because you should hate him.'

'Very clever,' she said.

'Listen, when I was in Sing-Sing, a psychiatrist gave me all those fancy tests and told me I was below average intelligence. Wrote it on the report. Said I should learn a trade.'

She was unable to stop the slightest of smiles from touching her lips. 'That's better,' he said. 'You laughed a lot that summer. That's what I remember best. Your smile.'

She shook her head. 'Oh, Mr Luciano, what's to become of you?'

'Look,' he said. 'I'm not making any excuses. I could say Tenth Street was no place for any kid to grow up, but I won't. I made a conscious choice. When people talk to me about the war, I say what war? I've been at war all my life, but I engage in a combat that's nothing to do with civilians.'

'Gangsters,' she said. 'Dope-peddlars, thieves, murderers.'

'I know,' he said. 'It sounds more like the Old Testament every minute.'

'You don't need to tell me,' she said. 'The world can't be innocent with Man in it.'

'And what the hell is that pearl of wisdom supposed to mean?' he demanded. 'What do you want me to do, drain the cup? All right, I'll tell you how it is.'

He walked to the altar rail and turned. 'We're fundamentally alone. Nothing lasts.'

'God,' she said. 'There is always God.'

'Well, if he exists, your God, I wish to hell he'd make up his mind. He's big on how and when. Not so hot on why.'

'Have you learned nothing?' she said. 'Has life taught you nothing?'

'Oh, yes,' he said. 'I've learned to kill with a smile. I'll probably die with one. But those soldiers who are going to die in the Cammarata, will they be smiling, do you think?'

She stood staring at him for a long moment then turned and walked out.

*　　*　　*

Sister Katherine was at her desk in the office when there was a knock at the door. Maria entered. She stood there, hands folded, obviously deeply troubled.

'Sit down, my child,' Sister Katherine told her.

Maria said, 'Sister, has Colonel Carter told you why he has come here?'

'Yes,' Sister Katherine said. 'As much as he needed to.'

Maria went round the desk and dropped on her knees. 'Sister, you know my story, you know why I came here.'

'Of course,' Katherine said. 'You came seeking refuge. Instead you found God, is that not true?'

'Sister, my bible tells me that we must love one another, but when I think of my grandfather, I know only hate.' She gripped the older woman's hands tightly. 'I am afraid of the violence I feel in myself. They would return me to everything I renounced, turned my back on. I will not do it,' she added forcibly.

Sister Katherine smiled. 'Such arrogance. You did not choose God, Maria. He chose you. For you, as his servant, there is no such thing as choice. You must do what is right. You may do no other.'

Maria stayed there for a long moment, head bowed, then she looked up. 'Which means I must go to Sicily.'

Sister Katherine nodded. 'Having no choice means there is no choice in the matter. A paradox, but true. What Colonel Carter has asked you to consider, this mission to Sicily, is one thing. The question of your hatred for your grandfather is another, hardly relevant to the greater issue. Is that not so?'

Maria took a deep, shuddering breath. 'Help me, Sister.'

Sister Katherine's hands tightened on hers, they bowed their heads together in prayer.

*   *   *

It was very quiet in the chapel when Carter and Luciano went in. The door banged, echoed in the silence. She was at the altar rail on her knees, and they paused halfway down the aisle and waited. She knew they were there, of course, the head coming up slowly. She stayed like that for a long moment, then got to her feet and turned. Her face was pale, but quite calm.

'Sister Katherine said you wanted to see me,' Carter said.

'You've made your choice, I presume?'

'Did I ever really have one, Colonel?'

Carter, suddenly desperately sorry, said, 'Put like that, I don't suppose you did.'

'When do we leave?'

'The morning would be fine.' He hesitated and said, 'Look, there's something we'd better get over with now. The only way we can get into Sicily at the moment is by parachute.'

'That's all we need,' Luciano said.

Carter ignored him. 'I've known agents going into the field for the first time drop cold, as we call it. In other words, their jump over the target is the first jump they've ever made. I'm not too keen on that. I'd like you to think you had some idea of what you're doing.'

'What would you suggest?'

'We'll be staying at a house in Cheshire for a while not far from Manchester. There's a parachute school there. Most SOE agents pass through it. A six hour course of instruction and one jump is usually enough.'

'With any luck, I could break a leg,' Luciano said.

Maria seemed totally indifferent. 'Fine, Colonel, whatever you say.' She looked around her as if taking everything in for the last time, then put a hand on the altar rail. 'I've been happy here. Truly and deeply content for the only time in my life. Perhaps that was wrong.'

Luciano said softly in Sicilian. 'Now you go out into the world again. Maybe there are answers waiting.'

'Yes, Mr Luciano,' she said. 'That could be true.' She smiled slightly. 'I will hang on to that thought, believe me. Till the morning then, gentlemen.'

She walked away along the aisle, the door closed behind her. Luciano said, 'Well, Professor, you got what you wanted. Keep this up and maybe they'll give you another medal.' He turned into the shadows, his footsteps echoing.

*　　*　　*

In Maison Blanche in Algeria just after dawn Harvey Grant walked across to the operations building. He was in a thoroughly bad temper. His mouth tasted like a sewer and his eyes were gritty from lack of sleep.

When he went into the Operations Room, he knew they were in trouble straight away, because it was deserted except for Joe Collinson, the squadron senior navigator who was night duty officer.

'Anything?' Grant asked him.

Collinson shook his head. 'I'm sorry, sir, but I'm afraid they must have bought it. Way past their fuel time now. It's just not on.'

'Four in a row,' Grant said. 'That's bad news, Joe.'

Collinson turned to the map of Sicily on the wall behind him. 'Jerry knows something's building up over Sicily, sir. Too much traffic over the past few weeks. Those Junkers 88s are out hunting every night and they're good, sir. Too damned good for a Halifax.'

'You don't have to tell me,' Grant said. 'I've seen the faces in the mess. It's reaching the stage that when you brief a crew for a Sicilian drop, you might as well give them their death certificates while you're at it.'

'So what do we do, sir?'

'What can we do except inform the AOC of the situation. If they say go, we go, you know that.'

He lit a cigarette and helped himself to coffee. Collinson said, 'There's something for you, sir, just come in.'

He pushed the envelope across the map table and Grant ripped it open. He stood there for a moment, reading Harry Carter's signal.

'Jesus,' he whispered, and slumped down into a chair.

'Is anything wrong, sir?' Collinson asked, concerned.

'Oh, yes, I think you could say that,' Grant told him heavily and passed the signal across.

★   ★   ★

It was raining in Sicily that morning as the 21st Paratroop Battalion, or what was left of it, moved along a forest road towards the village of Vilalba. Max Koenig's 35 Fallschirmjäger fitted comfortably into three armoured troop carriers. He himself was at the rear of the column in a fieldcar with a driver and machine gunner. Rudi Brandt was riding point in another fieldcar way out in front.

There was a ragged volley of rifle fire, flattened by the rain, and Koenig nodded to his driver who pulled out to overtake the column. Koenig signalled them to halt.

Brandt's fieldcar had halted in pine trees on the ridge and the sergeant major stood beside it, a pair of Zeiss field-glasses raised, examining Vilalba below. It was a miserable place, typical of the mountain villages. A small church, a square, forty or fifty houses. There were two military trucks drawn up in the square and what seemed to be the entire population of the village watched as a firing squad went to work. There were already half a dozen bodies face down, or sprawled on their backs in the unnatural postures of death. Another half dozen were being hustled forward to take their place against the church wall.

Koenig got out of his fieldcar and Brandt handed him the glasses. *'Einsatzgruppen, Obersturmbannführer.'*

Einsatzgruppen were units of the SS which had been formed by Himmler prior to the invasion of Russia. They were extermination squads, recruited from the jails of Germany, officered by the SD and Gestapo. Occasionally soldiers of the Waffen SS, convicted of some serious crime, were transferred to them as a punishment and a number of Russian prisoners of war, mainly Ukrainians, were also employed by them.

Koenig handed Brandt his glasses back, his face grim. 'All right, we'll go down. I'll lead.'

As his field car led the convoy into the square, the small crowd was already beginning to disperse, herded away by half a dozen SS armed with rifles. Fifteen or twenty women were crowded into one of the trucks, some of them very young girls, most of them sobbing bitterly.

Koenig got out of his fieldcar and walked forward to examine the dead. Three of them were teenage boys and there was another who could not have been more than ten years of age.

There was a cry behind him and someone called, 'Signor Colonel, please!'

As Koenig turned, an old man ducked past the guards and ran

before them. One of them raised his rifle and Koenig called, 'Leave him.'

The man was very old with patched clothes and a heavy white moustache and there were tears in his eyes.

'Please, Colonel, I am Angeli, the Mayor here, and you are a just man, everyone knows this.'

'What happened here?'

'They came an hour ago saying that a German sentry was murdered in the next valley yesterday. That someone from here was responsible. They took every fifth man for the firing squad and every fifth woman . . .' He appealed to Koenig passionately now, hands raised. 'In the name of God, Colonel. In the name of justice, tell your people not to do this thing.'

Koenig said calmly, 'These are not my people.'

The old man was totally distraught now. He gestured towards the truck. 'Colonel, please, my grand-daughter. The Russian, he took her inside.'

Before Koenig could reply, Brandt approached, his face grave. 'There is a difficulty here, I think, Colonel. These are Major Meyer's men.'

'Indeed,' Koenig said. 'He's inside, presumably?'

'No, he's not here personally, Colonel.'

The Fallschirmjäger waited for orders by their vehicles, weapons ready. Koenig looked them over, then adjusted his gloves.

'Release the women, *Sturmscharführer*,' he said clearly so that everyone could hear. 'If anyone tries to stop you, shoot them.'

Brandt responded instantly. '*Zu befehl, Obersturmbannführer.*' He swung to face his men. 'All right, you heard the Colonel.'

There was a burst of laughter and singing from the inn as Koenig approached. He paused at the bottom of the steps, selected a cigarette from an old leather case, lit it and passed inside.

There were half a dozen men drinking at the bar, rifles stacked. A burly *Untersturmführer* was seated at one end of a long table by the fire. He was more Eastern than European with narrow eyes and high cheekbones. The girl on his knee was small and dark, no more than fifteen, her face swollen from weeping.

There was a sudden silence as conversation died at the sight of Koenig standing there.

He said, 'You are in charge here?'

The *Untersturmführer* pushed the girl away and stood up. 'That's right. Suslov.'

Koenig smiled down at the girl. 'Go now, your grandfather is waiting for you outside.'

She stared up at him for one brief moment then, as she turned to run, Suslov grabbed at her. Koenig stepped in his path and behind him, the girl ran for the door.

Suslov said angrily, 'Here, who in the hell might you be?'

'Your superior officer,' Koenig said calmly. 'And from now on, you will speak only when I invite you to speak. You will also stand to attention in my presence.'

'*Sturmbannführer* Meyer is my commanding officer, not you.'

Koenig raised his voice and called, 'Sergeant-major!'

The rear door was kicked open and Brandt appeared, flanked by two paratroopers. All three of them carried machine pistols and looked perfectly willing to use them.

Koenig said softly, 'In future, when I give you an order, you get those heels together and shout, *Zu Befehl, Obersturmbannführer*. Do you understand me?'

There was murder in Suslov's eyes, but he did as he was told and stood to attention. '*Jawohl, Obersturmbannführer.*'

'Good. Now answer some questions. The executed – who were they?'

'Every fifth male.'

'And the women?'

'For the army brothel in Palermo. Every fifth female.' He hesitated. '*Sturmbannführer* Meyer's orders.'

Koenig nodded. 'You'll be interested to know that I've had them released. All that remains is for you and your men to remove yourselves. You have exactly two minutes in which to do that, otherwise I might be tempted to start operating in fifths myself.'

Suslov, by that stage, knew better than to argue. He turned to his men, gave a sudden command in Russian and made for the door and they followed.

Koenig selected another cigarette and Brandt offered him a light. 'This could mean trouble, Colonel.'

'Good,' Koenig said, as engines roared into life outside.

He moved to the door and stood at the top of the steps as the trucks moved out of the village. At the same moment, a Mercedes staff car came over the ridge. The leading truck stopped and Koenig saw Suslov get out and lean down to the Mercedes window. After a while, the Russian got back into the truck, it moved off and the Mercedes came down towards the village.

Koenig stood watching the villagers moving the bodies of the dead. The Mercedes pulled up and Meyer got out.

'I was under the impression that I was in command here.'

'Of this butcher's shop? You should be pleased.'

An old woman and two girls came by, pulling a handcart behind them containing the body of the ten year old boy.

'One of our men was murdered last night. I had good reason to believe the culprits came from this village.'

Koenig said, 'Amongst the women selected on your orders, were twelve and thirteen year old girls. I've had them all released, by the way. I presume Suslov told you.'

'Naturally I shall make a full report of this entire affair to Reichsführer Himmler and also to Field Marshal Kesselring.'

Koenig said, 'You know what your problem is, Meyer? You believe yourself to be a soldier of the German Reich, a natural assumption in view of the uniform you wear, but you are mistaken. Now, would you like me to tell you what you are, in simple terms so you fully understand?'

Meyer showed no emotion whatsoever, but stood there looking at him and Brandt came across and saluted. 'Ready to leave, Colonel.'

'Good,' Koenig said. 'We move out now.'

He walked across to his fieldcar and got in. He nodded to the driver and, as they drove away, the troop carriers formed up in line to follow them. The convoy disappeared over the hill and the sounds of the engines faded into the distance.

Meyer, standing beside the Mercedes, became conscious of the silence. He was suddenly aware that everyone in the square had stopped what they were doing. The old men, the women, the children working on the bodies, all stood perfectly still, looking at him.

There was infinite menace there, as someone bent down to pick up a stone, he realized that, except for the corporal driving the Mercedes, he was entirely alone.

Braun, his driver, jumped out of the Mercedes and opened the rear door. 'Please, Major,' he said urgently.

Meyer ignored him. He walked a few paces towards the villagers, hands behind his back, stopped and stood there, waiting. There was a long moment and then the youth who had picked up the stone dropped it. Meyer took out his case, selected a cigarette and lit it, taking his time, then he turned and went back to the car.

Braun was only eighteen and there was terror in his eyes now, his skin damp with sweat. Meyer took out his handkerchief, keeping his back to the villagers.

'Wipe your face. Did you know I used to be a police inspector in Hamburg?'

'No, *Sturmbannführer*.'

'Well, I did. St Pauli was my beat. The red light district. The worst bars in town. Pimps, cut-throats, murderers. I dealt with them all and you know what I learned, boy? You never turn back and you never show fear.'

'Yes, *Sturmbannführer*.'

'Remember that. Now let's get out of here.'

He settled back against the seat as they drove away and considered the problem of Koenig and with no particular rancour. There was no need, for Koenig was so vulnerable both in his actions and the things he said, that it was really only a matter of time before he did something totally unforgiveable. And when he did ...

7

The old Dakota lifted off the main runway at Ringway and climbed quickly to two thousand feet. Carter slid back the door and saw Manchester in the distance, shrouded in rain.

Besides the RAF sergeant-instructor, there were only the three of them, Carter, Luciano and Maria, all wearing British paratroopers camouflaged smocks and helmets and X-type parachutes.

Maria seemed smaller than ever under all the equipment. As he clipped her static line to the anchor line, Carter felt that she was totally vulnerable, a child playing at some grown-up game that was beyond her.

'If possible on the real target, we'll jump from four hundred feet,' he told her, 'because that way you'll hit the ground in twenty seconds which has its points; but today, we'll do it from a thousand. All right.'

She nodded. 'Fine.'

The Dakota was banking back towards the airport now. Carter said to Luciano, 'You first, Maria second and I'll bring up the rear.'

Luciano grinned as he moved towards the door. 'I hope you're getting a picture of this for my parole board.'

The sergeant-instructor moved into position as the red light blinked above the door. Luciano turned and called, 'With my luck, I'll probably break that leg. Then what happens?'

The green light flared and the Sergeant yelled, 'Go!' and slapped him on the back.

Luciano went head first into space and Maria, terrified, heart pounding, throat dry, went after him without hesitation. Carter clipped on to the anchor line and followed.

There wasn't much time to think. Luciano was aware of himself turning over a couple of times, the sudden slap of the parachute opening, a jerk and then he was swinging beneath a khaki umbrella.

The airport was laid out like a child's plaything beneath him, the hangars, the aircraft standing outside in neat rows and there were faces, lots of them, turned up to watch. He looked up and saw Maria above and to one side, Carter perhaps sixty or seventy yards further away. Then suddenly, the airport was much larger and he seemed to be going in very fast.

He hit the tarmac hard, rolled and miraculously found himself on his feet, the parachute itself giving him no problem because of the almost total lack of wind. As he turned and unclipped the harness, he saw that Maria was down forty or fifty yards away.

Carter was just hitting the ground on the far side of her. He rolled expertly, for this was his fifteenth drop, and came to his feet. As he disengaged from his harness, he saw Luciano running towards Maria who was still on the ground, crouched over her chute.

Carter hurried towards them anxiously, but before he reached them, Luciano had turned and was coming to meet him, a smile on his face.

'Is she all right?' Carter called.

'Oh, sure.' Luciano fished out a crumpled pack of cigarettes and lit one.

'What's wrong then?'

'Nothing. Two Hail Marys and three Our Father's for a safe deliverance or something like that.' He offered Carter a cigarette. 'That was great. We must do it again some time.'

'You will, Mr Luciano,' Carter said. 'Soon.'

★   ★   ★

Bransby Abbey was close to Alderley Edge, one of the most beautiful parts of Cheshire and about ten miles from Ringway Airport. Parts of it dated from the fourteenth century, but it had been heavily restored in the eighteen-fifties. It was constructed in mellow grey stone surrounded by a high wall. Bransby was one of a number of safe houses operated by SOE; a place where agents could be prepared for specific missions or receive last minute training.

On the afternoon of the following day, Luciano and Carter went for a run through the grounds. There was a trail through the woods, an assault course with commando nets, ropes stretched between trees and similar hazards. Luciano was enjoying himself in spite of the rain. He wore a commando stocking cap, and army fatigues and was soon soaked with rain and mud.

He crawled through a line of barbed wire, aware that he had lost Carter somewhere back there in the woods. As he got up, a voice called, 'Heh, you down there.'

Luciano glanced up and saw a United States Army Officer standing on the hill, wearing a fieldcap, captain's bars on his military trenchcoat.

'I want a word with you.'

It wasn't so much a request as an order and delivered in fine Bostonian tones of the kind you usually got in New England and nowhere else in America. Luciano didn't like that kind of voice, never had, so he didn't bother to reply.

'I'm talking to you, soldier.'

'Great,' Luciano said. 'I'm very happy for you.'

Then a hand had him by the shoulder and a voice that was straight out of New York's Eastside said, 'When the Captain speaks, you answer, you bum, hear me?'

Luciano glanced over his shoulder and found himself in the grip of an army sergeant who was considerably larger than he was, with a raw, bony face swollen by the scar tissue of a professional prizefighter.

'Heh, you got real medals,' Luciano said. He dipped one shoulder in under the big man's arm and twisted and the sergeant went headfirst down into the hollow.

Luciano looked up at the other officer. 'He made a mistake. Don't let him make another.'

The captain was tall with very fair hair and a handsome, arrogant face. Something moved in the blue eyes, and then the sergeant was up out of the hollow, arms reaching to destroy. When he was about six feet away, Luciano's hand came out of his hip pocket holding the ivory madonna. There was a nasty click and the blade jumped into view. The sergeant stopped dead, then crouched to move close.

He frowned suddenly and stood very still, his jaw slack with amazement. 'Heh, I know you.'

The captain called, 'Detweiler, stay where you are! That's an order.'

And then Carter joined in, appearing from the trees on the run. 'What's going on here?'

'Colonel Carter?'

'That's right.'

The Captain saluted and produced a buff envelope from inside his trenchcoat. 'Jack Savage, Captain, Ranger Division and this is Sergeant Detweiler. My orders were to report to you here as soon as possible.' He glanced at Luciano. 'I'm sorry for any apparent misunderstanding, but this soldier ...'

'Captain Orsini, OSS,' Carter said.

As Luciano started to grin, Detweiler said angrily, 'Orsini, my ass, sir. I was raised in New York, lived most of my life on Tenth Street and I've seen this guy a hundred times or more. He's a gangster named Lucky Luciano.'

*   *   *

Jack Savage was twenty four, the younger son of a career diplomat who had spent his time in places like Paris and Rome. As a result, the boy had been raised to be fluent in both languages. The Savage family was one of the wealthiest in Boston with huge interests in oil and steel, none of which interested Savage in the slightest.

The fact was that, from an early age, he had shown quite an extraordinary talent for drawing. Out of deference to his parents, he had gone to Yale to study Economics, but enough was enough and after taking his first degree he had moved on to London to study painting at the Slade.

He was in Paris living in the artists' colony in Montmartre when the Germans took the city, had stayed for another six months before moving on to Madrid. He had finally returned home to join the army just before America entered the war.

The Americans had no equivalent to the British SOE until
June 1942, when Wild Bill Donovan, who had firsthand knowledge of British methods, set up the Office of Strategic Services,
the OSS. Jack Savage, by then a very bored Intelligence
lieutenant at the Pentagon, had been one of the first re-
cruits.

                    *   *   *

He made a brave show standing in front of Carter's desk in the
library at the Abbey, a tall, handsome young man in olive drab
battledress, his pants tucked into jump boots. On his right
sleeve he carried a double set of parachutist's wings, a rare
distinction for that handful of members of American Special
Forces who had completed jump training with the British.

Detweiler was still letting his views be known forcibly.
'Orsini nothing, Captain. That guy is Luciano!'

Harry Carter held up the orders Savage had given him. 'You
have read these, Captain. You do appreciate that they place you
and the sergeant entirely under my command?'

'Of course, sir.'

'Good, I thought there might be some misunderstanding.' He
turned on Detweiler coldly. 'Which means that in future, when
I want your opinion, I ask for it.'

Detweiler was badly shocked and it showed. He turned in a
kind of appeal to Savage, 'For Christ's sake, Captain ...'

Carter cut in fast. 'Get your feet together and stay that way
until I tell you different. Come on, man! Move!'

Detweiler, red in the face, did as he was told.

Carter took the envelope from the inside pocket of his
battledress tunic, extracted the letter of authorization General
Eisenhower had given him in Algeria and the similar one he had
obtained from President Roosevelt.

'Read those.'

Savage did as he was told and looked up in astonishment.
'Good God!' he whispered.

'Exactly,' Carter said. 'I'm not going to mince matters. I don't
like your sergeant's attitude. If there was time to dump him, I
would, but there isn't.'

'Colonel, Detweiler's a good soldier. We've been through a lot together. I know.'

'Good, then show him those letters and see if you can talk some sense into him. I'll be back in five minutes to explain exactly what's going on here.'

* * *

Luciano was sitting against one of the stone lions on the terrace. He had changed into black sweater and pants, but still needed a shave.

He looked up at Carter, shaking his head. 'Where the hell did you find them?'

'His uncle's a three star general.'

'And I used to know Al Capone very well indeed. What in the hell does that have to do with the price of tomatoes? Listen, Professor, I know the type. Boston, the first four hundred. The kind of people who fell over each other in their scramble to be first off the Mayflower. Who needs him?'

'We do.'

'Would you mind telling me why?'

'Because, strictly speaking, the whole thing is an American operation, so it seemed like a good idea to the powers that be to have somebody like Savage and Detweiler along.'

'Oh, I see. You mean I didn't count?'

'Something like that.'

Carter smiled, aware that there was no strain with Luciano at all. That for some reason it was like old friends talking. No need to pretend or pull punches.

'Great,' Luciano said. 'That really makes me feel wanted.'

'He's a good man. Two DSCs, a Silver Star. Even the French have decorated him. When he operated in France as an OSS agent, the Gestapo had him and he got away. Since then he's raided across the Channel into France with Special Forces on a number of occasions.'

'France isn't Sicily. What's he doing here?'

'His father was a diplomat at the American Embassy in Rome before the war for four years. Savage went to school there. Speaks good Italian.'

Luciano said. 'Rome Italian. Professor, there are villages in the Cammarata where that will sound like Greek. Anyway, what's Detweiler's story?'

'He was born and raised in New York, but his mother is Italian. I've already given them a brief run down on the whole affair. I've arranged to meet in the library for a full briefing. Do you know where Sister Maria is?'

There was a rumble of thunder overhead as if rain threatened. Luciano said, 'I think she went for a walk in the grounds. I'll find her.'

'Good. The library in half an hour then,' Carter said and went inside.

*   *   *

Maria sat on a stone bench by the fountain in the rose garden. She wore slacks, an olive green army sweater that was at least two sizes too large for her and a scarf twisted around her head like a turban.

It was very calm, peaceful, the only sounds rooks calling to each other in the beech trees at the end of the rose garden. The fact that she was here and in the open instead of inside the house, was in itself significant.

She was trying to come to terms with freedom for the first time in years. It was nothing as simple as being away from the convent on her own. That happened every day of her life because of her hospital work. This was different. Now she was once again responsible for herself in a way that she had not been since her entry into the Order. She had not only pledged herself to God, but to a community and a way of life which had sustained her totally during that dark night of the soul she had gone through for so long. Now, she was responsible once again for her own destiny.

As thunder rumbled again, she glanced towards the sky and turned to move towards the house. Luciano came into the walled garden through the arched entrance carrying a spare trench-coat.

'Now you see why they baptized me Salvatore,' he said cheerfully.

'Thank you, Mr Luciano.'

'Carter wants us in the library in twenty minutes, just to tie up all the loose ends. The rest of the team has turned up. A Captain Savage and a Sergeant Detweiler.'

'We'd better get moving then.'

'No hurry.' He lit a cigarette and carried on in Sicilian. 'Poor Maria, I worry you, don't I? Disturb the calm order of your life. The serpent in Eden.'

'Is that how you see yourself? As some romantic outsider?'

As they went out through the arch the rain increased in force and he pulled her under the pergola to avoid the worst of it.

'And you?' he said. 'How do you see me? No, don't answer that.' He put a finger to his lips. 'Because whatever you think I am, that's what I'm not.'

'True for all of us.'

'Tell me something,' he asked her. 'The religious thing. How did that happen?'

'Oh, when I first reached London I had very little money. I worked in a shop for a while and then I became ill – very ill. For a while, I was in a charity ward in a hospital where some of the nurses were Sisters of Pity.'

'So you decided that was for you? A blinding flash, God sending someone down off the mountain to tell you or what?'

She remembered so clearly that final day during Special Mass on her knees, asking Mother Superior for permission to make her perpetual profession in the Society of the Little Sisters of Pity, resolving to undertake a life of perfect chastity, obedience, poverty and service. It still made her uneasy to discuss it and yet it could not be avoided.

'No, I think it's obvious enough now why I joined the Order. I sought refuge. I should add that I found God, Mr Luciano, but only in His own good time.'

'And Carter turns up like something out of a bad movie, saying I've to come to take you away from all that.'

'I suppose you're right,' she smiled.

'With the Devil trailing behind?'

'Is that supposed to be you? If so, where are the horns?'

'Oh, I don't know. We all end up the same way,' he said,

suddenly sombre. 'The one absolute certainty, Death.' He took her arm before she could reply. 'Come on, let's get out of here.'

*   *   *

Carter was waiting in the library with Savage and Detweiler when they went in. 'Ah, there you are,' he said and started to make the introductions. 'Sister Maria Vaughan, Captain Savage.'

She put up a hand. 'Plain Maria will be better in the circumstances.'

She took Savage's hand briefly and sat down, pulling off her turban as she did so, revealing dark hair cropped very closely to her skull, giving her a boyish look.

'Christ Almighty!' Detweiler said in a whisper.

Carter said, 'Mr Luciano, you've already met.'

Savage nodded, Detweiler glared, and Luciano, indifferent to both of them, lounged in the window seat.

Carter said, 'May I make one thing clear? I've been concerned with this kind of intelligence operation for some time now and as far as most of them go, the truth is that, succeed or fail, it isn't going to make a scrap of difference to the war as a whole.'

Savage frowned, as he was bound to do at a suggestion which so put down his own war career. 'Don't you think that's going a little far, Colonel?'

'No I don't, but one thing is for sure. It isn't true of this present venture. If we can get into Sicily in one piece, if Mr Luciano and Maria between them make the contact we hope for, then many lives will be saved. If we fail, Patton's army will sustain thousands of needless casualties. It's as simple as that.'

There was silence. It was Savage who finally said, 'When do we go, sir?'

'Tomorrow night from RAF Hovington in a Lancaster bomber, straight across France and the Mediterranean to Algiers.'

'And then?'

'Sicily any time within four or five days after that, depending on the best conditions for the drop. One more thing, Captain Savage. You and Detweiler will be operating in civilian clothes.

You understand what that means if you fall into enemy hands?'

'They've been shooting Ranger and Commando prisoners in uniform under the terms of Hitler's *Kommandobefehl* for two years now, sir. I can't see that it makes much difference.'

'As long as you understand that. Now gather round the map, all of you, and I'll go over the whole thing in detail.'

*   *   *

In Bellona, at the same moment, Vito Barbera was climbing a short wooden ladder to the coffin room above the mortuary. He opened the cupboard at the far end and felt for a hidden catch inside. The entire back, shelves and all, swung open to reveal a cubbyhole, containing a radio receiver and transmitter. He switched on the light, sat down, put on the earphones then waited patiently for the allotted hour as he did three times a week.

He straightened, suddenly excited as he started to receive a signal. He reached for a pencil and made notes. Behind him, the secret door opened and Rosa entered with coffee on a tray.

He motioned her to silence and continued to write. After a while, he took off the headphones and sat there, reading what he had written, a look of astonishment on his face.

'Is it something important?' she asked.

'Carter is returning.'

'On his own?' she said.

He shook his head. 'No, Rosa, not on his own.'

*   *   *

Looking for Carter after supper, Luciano was directed to the firing range in the basement where he discovered Carter and Savage on the firing line. Detweiler was helping the armourer, an Ordnance Corps sergeant-major named Smith, to load.

As Luciano stood watching, Carter took careful aim with both hands and squeezed one off, chipping the right arm of one of the replicas of a charging German at the other end.

'Very good, sir,' Savage told him.

'Not if you consider that I was aiming for the heart,' Carter said. He fired another five rounds and hit the target twice more, once in the neck and again in the arm. 'Oh, well, I never was much good with handguns.'

'It's a knack, sir, like anything else,' Savage said cheerfully and fired, like Carter, double-handed, but much more rapidly, hitting the general area of the chest in a solid group.

Detweiler said, 'I don't recall anyone being much better at it than you, Captain.'

Carter turned to Luciano, 'What about you?'

Luciano hefted one of the Brownings in his hand and shook his head. 'The trouble with automatics is they can jam.' He turned to the armourer. 'What else you got?'

'Webley ·38, sir?' Smith suggested.

'Too clumsy.'

'The only other revolver I have here at the moment is a Smith and Wesson ·32 with a three inch barrel.'

Luciano tried it in his right hand, then the left. 'That's more like it. You got a silencer for this?'

'Sure – over here.'

Smith got one from the cupboard and screwed it into place. As he handed the weapon to Luciano, Detweiler said, 'A popgun. You'd need to get damn close to do any good with that. But then, that's your style, isn't it?'

Luciano turned and fired twice very fast, right arm extended, both rounds hitting the heart.

There was a respectful silence. Savage said, 'I'd say the second round was rather superfluous, Mr Luciano.'

'I like to cover my bets,' Luciano told him, 'And a wounded man can always shoot back.'

Savage said to Detweiler, 'I think we could do with a couple of fresh targets down there.'

As Detweiler obediently moved down the range, Luciano laid down the Smith and Wesson, following normal safety precautions. Detweiler replaced two of the targets and turned.

Luciano called, 'Heh, Detweiler! Like you said, I always do my best work in close.' He picked up the Smith and Wesson, fired twice without apparently taking aim, and shot out the eyes of the target next to Detweiler.

Detweiler cried out in alarm and ducked and Luciano started to laugh, was still laughing as he walked out.

'They say he's killed at least twenty men personally,' Carter observed.

'Well all I can say, Colonel, is that I'm damn glad he's on my side,' Savage told him.

* * *

Maria awakened early on the following morning from a deep sleep. Pale sunshine filtered in through the curtains. She lay there for a few moments, remembering that this was the last day. Tonight, she would be on a plane for Algeria, set on a course from which there would be no turning back.

It was not that she was afraid. It was simply that nothing fitted. It was as if this was all a dream. A few days before, her world had consisted of the convent and hospital, a daily round that filled her time and life, work for the mind and for the body. Nothing that ever needed to be questioned. But now?

She got up and stood beside the bed for a moment. She had slept in the nude, something she had not done for years, always wearing the nun's linen shift of modesty.

'A crack in the fabric already, Maria,' she said softly, and pulled on a towelling robe.

Her room was on the ground floor and she opened the French window, looked out into the garden and moved on to the terrace. It was incredibly beautiful in the early morning sun, the trees touched with a kind of nimbus, the rooks cawing lazily to each other.

And yet she felt detached, not part of any of this at all, not really aware. It was as if she was looking at things under water in slow motion. She went down the steps without thinking about it, bare-footed in the damp grass.

* * *

Luciano had also awakened early. He was sitting at the window of his bedroom in pyjamas, smoking the first cigarette of the day as she crossed the lawn and entered the wood. He stood up, frowning slightly, watching her go, then tossed his cigarette out of the window, turned and started to dress quickly.

* * *

She advanced through the wood, still caught in that dream-like state and the sound of the rooks seemed to fade and there was the most profound silence she had ever known. She came out on to a long jetty beside an ornamental lake and stood there looking across the water.

Suddenly, a voice said quite distinctly: *Having nothing, yet possessing everything.*

It was her voice which had spoken, she broke through to reality again, aware of the rooks in the beech trees above her head, the smell of the damp grass, the golden glory of the morning.

'So this is what it's like!' she thought. 'Total certainty.'

She had never felt so much at one with everything so much a part of the whole. It seemed the most natural thing in the world to slip out of her robe and wade into the cold water of the lake. She turned on her back and floated there in the lily pads, face up to the sun, eyes closed.

* * *

Luciano, walking along the path through the wood, paused, aware of Detweiler crouched behind a tree where the path dipped down towards the lake. He went forward quietly until he was close enough to see the object of the sergeant's attention, Maria Vaughan floating in the water-lilies below.

'Heh, Detweiler!' Luciano whispered softly, and when the sergeant turned, lifted a knee into his face, sending him over on to his back.

Detweiler rolled over once, then was on his feet and moving in fast. Luciano's hand came up clutching the ivory Madonna, there was a click and the needlepoint drew blood under Detweiler's chin.

Luciano said, 'Now hear this and hear good because I only say it once. If I catch you anywhere near her again, they'll find you in a ditch with a very personal part of your anatomy stuffed into your mouth. An old Sicilian custom.'

Detweiler glared, an expression that was a compound of fear and hatred on his face. 'Damn you to hell, you Guinea bastard!' he said hoarsely, took a step back, turned and walked away.

Luciano folded the knife and replaced it in his hip pocket. 'Heh, pretty one!' he called in Sicilian. 'You decent?'

'Mr Luciano,' she called back. 'Please stay where you are.'

He took his time over lighting a cigarette and finally went down the path to find her on the jetty, tying her robe.

'You're crazy,' he said. 'You know that?'

Her smile was enchanting. 'I've never felt so hungry.'

'Then we'll get back and have some breakfast.'

She shook her head. 'Not possible just yet. There's a little Catholic church in the village. I'm going to early morning mass. What about you?'

'Do I look as if I would?'

'It's possible for anyone to end up on their knees, even Lucky Luciano.'

He laughed, 'Okay, I'll tell you what I'll do. I'll walk you down to the church, wait for you outside. How about that?'

'It's a start.'

They went up the path together. A small wind blowing across the lake brought with it the dark wet smell of rotting leaves. She paused, smiling.

'Isn't it wonderful? Doesn't a day like this make you feel good to be alive?'

She ran up the path, lifting the skirts of her robe and Luciano watched her go, cold in spite of the sun as if someone somewhere had stepped on his grave. Reverting to his Sicilian childhood, he instinctively formed two fingers and a thumb into the ancient sign to ward off the Evil One and went after her.

8

The Avro Lancaster was the most successful Allied bomber of the Second World War. Its exploits included the sinking of the German pocket battleship, *Tirpitz*. Only three weeks previously, Lancasters of 617 Squadron had carried out one of the most daring raids of the war, breaching the Ruhr Dams and flooding the most important industrial area in Germany.

It was shortly after nine o'clock that evening when Lancaster *S-Sugar* lifted off the main runway at RAF Hovingham and joined on the tail end of a stream of heavy bombers from stations all over the Midlands and East England.

By the time they converged over the North Sea, they comprised a force of over six hundred in a tail back a hundred miles long. The target was the docks at Genoa, all the way across France and the Alps, except for *S-Sugar* which, at an appropriate point, would leave the mainstream and change course for North Africa.

It was bitterly cold in the cramped interior and the noise from the four great piston engines was almost intolerable. Carter's party had been issued with heavy flying suits and sleeping bags and they huddled together in the body of the plane.

Luciano looked up at the gunner in the mid-upper turret above his head, then glanced across at Maria who was sitting opposite him, apparently asleep. Her eyes flickered open and he leaned across.

'You okay?'

'Fine,' she smiled.

Which was a lie, of course, for she was afraid again. Not only of the danger that lay ahead, but desperately afraid of the prospect of meeting her grandfather. At the thought of what that might unleash inside her, her stomach cramped in panic.

Luciano leaned back and burrowed into the sleeping bag, aware of the vibrations of the fuselage, the roar of the engine, the fierce cold. *What in the name of God am I doing here?* he asked himself, and closed his eyes and tried to sleep.

From further along the plane, Detweiler watched him, eyes filled with hate.

★   ★   ★

The Franciscan monastery of the Crown of Thorns lay five miles outside Bellona. Centuries earlier it had been a Saracen castle sited on a ridge a thousand feet above the valley with views across the surrounding countryside for twenty miles in every direction. And a castle was what it still most resembled, with smooth stone walls over a hundred feet high.

It took Vito Barbera an hour and a half to get there by mule from Bellona, following the dirt road which zig-zagged up the side of the mountain. The defensive ditch from the old days was still there at the base of the walls, choked with weeds and rubbish now. He crossed the wooden bridge that gave access to the only entrance and reined in at the oaken gates.

There was a bellchain to one side and he leaned over and pulled it, staying in the saddle. The sound was remote, unreal in the heat of the afternoon, and he waited, tired, gazing out across the valley.

After a while, a small shutter opened and a young bearded monk peered out. He said nothing, simply closed the shutter. A moment later, the great gates creaked open and Barbera rode inside.

★   ★   ★

Padre Giovanni, the Prior of the monastery, was a tall, frail old man of seventy, full-bearded as indeed were all the Franciscans at Crown of Thorns, although in his case it was almost pure white except for the nicotine staining around his mouth.

He wore a brown beretta on his head, a plain brown habit with knotted cord at his waist from which hung a large crucifix. His face was full of strength, firm, aesthetic, and yet shrewd good humour was never far from his eyes.

The red-pantiled roofs of the monastery extended like a series of giant uneven steps to the highest point on the ramparts where he kept his pigeons, the great love of his life. He was working on them now when young Brother Lucio brought Vito Barbera to him.

'Ah, Vito,' the old prior said. 'How good to see you.'

Barbera pulled off his cap and kissed the extended hand; not for religious reasons only for Padre Giovanni's connections with Mafia were a matter of public knowledge. Mori, Mussolini's notorious Chief of Police, had expended considerable time in attempting to prove the fact. He had even succeeded in bringing Giovanni to court, a trial which had descended to low farce and had ended with the jury finding Padre Giovanni and other members of his order not guilty of even feeding pigeons in the park.

He helped himself to a cigarette from the tin on the parapet. 'How are things in the village?'

'Bad,' Barbera told him. 'The man from the Gestapo, Meyer, and those Russians of his ...' He shook his head.

'And the other, this Colonel Koenig?'

'A good man in the wrong uniform.' Barbera shrugged. 'A holy fool, Padre. He thinks you can still fight wars according to rules, like a game of cards.'

'So.' The old man nodded. 'What can I do for you?'

'I have a message for Don Antonio.'

The old man smiled. 'My dear Vito, who knows where Don Antonio is?'

Barbera moved to the pigeon loft and scratched the wire, cooing at the birds inside. 'I'm sure he has a friend or two in here who could find him, and not too far away.'

Padre Giovanni sat down in the old wicker chair by the low parapet. 'Vito, if you have heard from your friends in Algeria again, if this is to do with Mafia and the American invasion, I tell you now you are wasting your time. Don Antonio's dislike of the Germans is followed closely by his hatred of all things American. No, in this case he stays in the mountains. He does not wish to be involved.'

'But it's all different now, Padre,' Barbera told him. 'Don Antonio's grand-daughter is coming, Maria.'

The old man looked up, astonishment on his face. 'You mean to the Cammarata? But how can this be?'

'I've had word on the radio. Carter returns, very soon now.'

Padre Giovanni stubbed out his cigarette angrily. 'The fool. I told him when he was last here that enough was enough. He seeks death, that one. But tell me more about the girl? Carter brings her with him, does he? They hope she will influence Don Antonio in a way no one else has been able to.' He shrugged. 'I'm not too sure that they are right.'

Barbera said, 'There's more, Padre, a great deal more Luciano comes with them.'

The old man stared at him. 'Lucania?' he whispered, using Luciano's Sicilian name. 'Salvatore Lucania comes here? But he is in prison.' Then comprehension dawned. 'Ah, I see now – the whole strategy. Lucky Luciano and the old Don's grand-daughter. Harry Carter must think the game is his.'

'And you, padre? What is your opinion?'

'How could that be of the slightest importance? I will see that one of my little friends here,' he touched the pigeon loft, 'takes news of this to Don Antonio. He will act as he sees fit. When do they come?'

'Within the next few days. I'll be getting a further radio communication.'

'When you have the exact date, let me know. Have you spoken of this to the district committee.'

'No,' Barbera said.

District committees had been set up during the previous summer to co-ordinate the activities of the various groups which made up the resistance movement.

Padre Giovanni put a hand on Barbera's shoulder. 'And now, my friend, you will join me at the table. Something to sustain you on the journey back to Bellona.'

* * *

Harry Carter was waiting on the terrace of the villa at dar el Ouad when Eisenhower rode into the courtyard. The General dismounted, gave his reins to a groom and went up the steps to the entrance, acknowledging the salute of the sentries. As he moved into .the hall, Cusak stood up at his desk.

'Colonel Carter's waiting, General.'

Eisenhower turned as Carter came in from the terrace. He looked at him fixedly for a moment, then said, 'Come in, Colonel,' and led the way into his office.

He dropped his riding crop on the table. 'I've read your report, Colonel. You've been busy.'

'A fair description, General.'

'Where are you staying?'

'A small villa near the airfield at Maison Blanche, sir.'

'Comfortable?'

'Adequate, sir.'

'Luciano and this man, Luca's, grand-daughter. That's like aces back-to-back. Sit down.'

Carter did as he was told. 'The invasion's still on, sir?'

'Oh, yes. Of course, they know about our preparations, we know that. They're expecting us any day now. Our deception plan is that any attack on Sicily will only be a feint; that the real targets are Sardinia and Greece.'

Carter said, 'When, sir?'

'Privileged information, Colonel, for your ears only. You don't tell the rest of your party except in circumstances of some extraordinary nature.'

'Very well, sir.'

'The ninth.' Eisenhower flipped the date pages of the desk calendar and smiled. 'It says here: A good day to sit back and take stock of your life.'

Carter was astonished. 'But that only gives us four days.'

'I know, but the weather boys have guaranteed us storms on that day. The Italians won't be expecting any attack in that kind of weather.'

'Then if we go, it would have to be tomorrow night at the latest and that would only give us three days to work in.'

'How much time do you need?' Eisenhower said. 'One meeting with this man Luca is all it takes. If he decides to join us, the rest is simply his people spreading the word, isn't that so?'

'In theory, Sir.'

'Well, theory is all we've got.' Eisenhower stood up, went to the map and jabbed his finger at the Cammarata. 'Here, overlooking the two main roads we'll be using to reach Palermo. Mainly Italian troops with artillery of every description, including 88s, and you know what they do to our tanks. They've even got a few Tigers up there as well. If they decide to fight, they could hold us for weeks. If they surrender, then the few German units in the area will have to get out fast leaving the road to Palermo clear for George Patton.'

'Yes, sir, I'm well aware of the situation.'

'What you don't know is that since we last talked, information's reached us from Rome that the whole house of cards is ready to fall. Mussolini's on the verge of being kicked out. One more push is all it takes and Marshal Badoglio takes over and that means a negotiated peace with Italy.'

Carter said, 'There is another aspect to consider. I called in at Maison Blanche before coming here to make arrangements for the drop with Wing Commander Grant. He tells me the AOC has suspended any further operations. It seems they've lost the last four Halifaxes they sent to Sicily.'

'Yes, I know about that,' Eisenhower said calmly. 'But the written authority you hold allows you to countermand that order.'

'The point is that, in Grant's opinion, the odds are heavily against one of their Halifaxes being able to reach the target.'

'You mean he says it's impossible?'

Carter remembered Grant's exact words and rephrased them. 'Let's just say that he didn't rate our chances very highly.'

Eisenhower said, 'Are you saying it's not on?'

'No, sir, I'm simply being realistic.'

Eisenhower stood up and walked to the window. He spoke, gazing out into the garden at the same time. 'You know something I've discovered about command, Colonel? That even Napoleon was only as good as his worst soldier. No matter how well you plan, the success of an entire battle can come down to half-a-dozen brave men denying a bridge to the enemy. My personal theory is that every battle is like that. Somewhere in the middle of all the action, although we may never know it, a single

incident can be the balance point that decides which way victory
will go.'

'Yes, I think I'd go along with that, General,' Carter said.
Eisenhower turned. 'Whatever happens, we go into Sicily.
We take our chances. We may win with heavy casualties, but for
all I know, this man Luca could be the kind of balance point I'm
talking about. The difference between winning and losing.'

'So we go, sir?'

This time the smile was touched with sadness. 'Difficult
decisions have always been the privilege of rank, Colonel. I say
you go and take your chances.' He held out his hand. 'I can
only wish you luck.'

*   *   *

Harvey Grant, seated at his office desk at Maison Blanche,
finished reading the two letters of authorization from General
Eisenhower and President Roosevelt. He passed them back to
Carter.

'As good a way of committing suicide as I can imagine. Like
I told you, I can't even offer you a fifty-fifty chance. Another
thing, we've not been grounded just because of losses. I know
the invasion's coming any day now. They'll tell you that in
every bazaar in Algiers plus the fact that it's just a part of a
mammoth deception to fool the enemy. For Sicily, read
Sardinia. What the eye doesn't see.'

'I can't comment on that,' Carter started to say, and Grant
suddenly slammed a hand against the window-sill.

'Christ, Harry, I think I've got it. What the eye doesn't see.
Correction, what the eye expects to see, it ignores.'

'I don't follow you.'

'You will. Come on, I'll show you.'

They went down the steps and walked towards the hangars.
'How many did you say there'll be?'

'Five. Four men and a woman.'

'A woman?' Grant said. 'My God. Still, I think it should do.'

'What exactly.'

'This.'

Grant waved a hand and led the way into the end hangar

where the black-painted JU88S night fighter crouched in the gloom.

*   *   *

'You really think it would work?' Carter said.

'We'll need a quick paint job. Replace those RAF rondels with Luftwaffe markings again. The point is, this baby has an engine boosting system that takes it up to around four hundred. That means we can hit your drop zone in just under an hour from here. In and out, Harry, and to anyone around, we're just another night fighter.'

Carter nodded slowly. 'You could be right.'

Grant said impatiently. 'The krauts used the thing for the same purposes themselves, so it has the right modification, that special door they've fitted for a fast exit. More than coincidence, Harry. The Gods are smiling.'

'All right,' Carter said. 'Let's say it works, but how about coming back? This thing will have every RAF fighter in the area on its back the moment it crosses the coast.'

'No problem,' Grant said. 'Naturally, I'll have to tell the AOC, Air Marshall Sloane that I'm going, but there won't be any problem there, not when he sees your authorization. He'll arrange the right kind of reception for me when I get back.'

Carter said, 'You're grounded, Harvey, remember?'

'Not on this one, old son.' Grant patted the side of the Junkers. 'I'm not saying I'm the only pilot in the squadron who can fly this plane, but I'm the only one who can give this operation half a chance. I'll take Joe Collinson with me, the squadron's senior navigator. He's flown as many hours as I have in her so he's familiar with the equipment.'

Carter, no choice in the matter now, nodded. 'All right, Harvey.'

'When do we go?'

'Tomorrow night, if that suits you.'

'The same drop zone as you used last time outside Bellona?'

'Yes.'

'If you come with me now to the met. office we'll check on the weather, but all things being equal, I'd say you could send a message to your people in Bellona telling them to expect you around eleven.'

'Fine by me.'

'Good, then let's get moving. There's work to be done.'

*   *   *

In Palermo, at his temporary headquarters in the Grand Hotel, General Alfred Guzzoni, commanding the Italian Sixth Army, was holding a staff conference. It was attended mainly by Italian officers although there were a handful of Germans present, among them Meyer and Koenig.

Guzzoni, a first-rate soldier and veteran of numerous campaigns, had spent an hour explaining the strategic situation in the Mediterranean.

'So, gentlemen,' he ended. 'They come soon, we know that. A feint at some point on the Sicilian coast and the main attack probably Sardinia. One thing seems certain. We can expect no activity for at least a week. Any questions? The meterological report indicates some very stormy weather.'

There were a few and after a while, Meyer raised his hand. 'General, I'd like to discuss the question of partisan activity in the mountains.'

Guzzoni said, 'In what respect, Major?'

'A question of co-operation, General,' Meyer said. 'I expect none from these damn peasants in the mountains, but when I experience what I can only describe as a total lack of assistance from units of the Italian Army ...

There was an angry murmur from the Italian officers present and it was Koenig who defused the situation by standing up and saying, 'You must excuse Major Meyer, General. He is perhaps not familiar with the fact that Italian dead lie as far east as the outskirts of Moscow and in considerable numbers in Stalingrad. I have been lucky enough to have them on my flank on more than one occasion and have been grateful for it.'

A number of Italian officers around him broke into spontaneous applause. Meyer glanced at him calmly, picked up his briefcase and walked out.

Guzzoni walked through the crowd and held out his hand.
'You've made an enemy there, I think.'

'Then I'll just have to live with it, sir.'

Guzzoni put a hand around his shoulder. 'I had the pleasure
of meeting your father in Berlin when I attended the OKW
conference last month. Come and have lunch with me and I'll
tell you how he was.'

*   *   *

The villa Carter's party was using was five miles along the coast
from Maison Blanche. It wasn't much of a place, being run
down and badly in need of a coat of whitewash, but the area
behind it was astonishingly beautiful. Sand dunes separated the
overgrown garden from the sea. Beyond them, a white beach ran
as far as the eye could see.

Carter had assembled the whole party in the living room of
the villa for a general briefing. There was a map of Sicily on the
wall and several large envelopes on the table.

Most of what he said was simply a re-working of what had
already been discussed before. When he was finished, he said,
'Any questions?'

Detweiler asked, 'When is the invasion to take place,
Colonel?'

'No need for you to know that yet,' Carter said. 'I believe it's a
sound principle to keep knowledge of dates, facts, identities of
sympathizers to a minimum when going into the field. The less
you know, the less you can disclose under pressure. False papers
have, of course, been prepared for each of you.'

Savage said, 'But if anything goes wrong with the landing? If
one of us becomes separated from the others, where do we make
for?'

'Here, at the head of the valley. The Franciscan monastery of
the Crown of Thorns. That will be our general headquarters.
Any further questions?'

There was silence.

*   *   *

Maria was sitting in a hollow in the dunes when Luciano found her. He flung himself down beside her and lit a cigarette.

'Carter's back. He wants to see us all together in thirty minutes.'

'Is it on?' she said.

'Apparently.' She turned away, gazing out to sea, hugging her knees and he said, 'What are you trying to see – Sicily?'

'It's been a long time.'

'And your grandfather. That's been a long time, too.'

'Yes,' she said. 'Maybe too long for both of us. Have you considered that?'

'I have, but I don't think the Professor has.'

She shook her head. 'The omnipotent Luciano. Is nothing impossible to you?'

'Some things. Even the Devil has his off days.' He held out a hand and pulled her to her feet. 'Come on, time to eat.'

They walked away side-by-side and disappeared over the sand dunes. There was a stirring in a patch of long grass near by and Detweiler stood up. He brushed sand from his fatigues for a moment, a strange, dazed look in his eyes, and then went after them.

9

In the living room of his house at the back of the mortuary, Vito Barbera presided over a meeting of the district committee. There was Pietro Mori, the schoolmaster, a thin, intense man of forty-six with steel-rimmed glasses, who had fought with the International Brigade in Spain. So had Ettore Russo, the one thing they had in common for the fact that Russo had inherited his father's sheep farm made him suspect in the minds of many of the comrades.

The Christian Democrats were represented by Father Collura, the parish priest for the Bellona district, and the Separatists by Berga, the innkeeper. And although it was not stated, had never needed to be, Vito Barbera stood there for the Honoured Society – for Mafia.

When he finished talking, there was a long pause. It was Mori who spoke first. 'So, what do you want us to do? Genuflect because this Mafia cut-throat comes amongst us?'

'Salvatore comes as a saviour,' Ettore Russo mocked. 'Who from?'

'The Germans,' Barbera suggested.

'Yes, but not from Mafia.' It was Verga, the innkeeper speaking now. 'We of the Separatist movement, want a Sicily that is genuinely free, not just separated from Italy, but with the same old Mafia gang running things as before.'

Father Collura said mildly, 'Shouldn't our primary task be to aid the American invasion as much as possible? The question of who is going to run the country can come afterwards. A matter of free democratic election.'

'Marvellous,' Mori said. 'Free democratic election with a Mafia hand on every throat.'

Barbera said, 'Whatever else may be said, Mafia has always stood outside politics. I think no one here can deny that.'

'And behind whoever was in power,' Russo replied.

Barbera sighed. 'I may take it, then, that no one is in favour of any concerted action at the moment?'

'When the Americans come, we will rise in the mountains,' Mori said. 'But as for Luciano. To hell with him.'

'And Don Antonio Luca's grandaughter? To hell with her also?'

There was silence at the mention of that name. Mori glanced at Russo and forced a smile. 'Now look, Vito, old friend, we certainly meant no offence to Don Antonio.'

'No, that's what I thought.' Barbera looked at his watch and stood up. 'My friends will be dropping in approximately three hours, so you must excuse me. I know, of course, that this information is safe with you. If anything did go wrong, one would so obviously know where to start looking.' He shrugged, smiling. 'But what am I saying.'

They moved out into the darkness of the side street and went their separate ways except for Mori and Russo who walked together for a while.

Mori said, 'I know we don't always see eye to eye but in this present affair, I sense a considerable agreement.'

'If you mean something should be done about Luciano, then I'm with you,' Russo told him.

Mori put an arm around his shoulders. 'Come back to my house for supper. We can talk things over in peace there and I have an excellent bottle of Chianti.'

★   ★   ★

At Maison Blanche, a heavy damp fog rolling in off the Mediterranean reduced visibility to no more than two hundred yards. The Junkers, once more with Luftwaffe markings, squatted on the runway, had been there for something like half-an-hour. Carter and the rest of his party were crowded together into the narrow fuselage, their bodies swollen with parachutes and equipment.

Flight Lieutenant Collinson, the navigator, was already on

board, familiarizing his eyes with the Lichtenstein radar set that, in effect, enabled the Junkers to see in the dark.

Harvey Grant stood outside the crew room with Air Marshal Sloane who had come down to see them off personally.

'It's not good, Harvey,' he said. 'About as bad as I've seen. If you go, you might not be able to land, even if you get back.'

A young pilot officer appeared and handed Grant a weather report. 'Rain and thunderstorms predicted,' Grant said cheerfully. 'That's good enough for me, sir. See you in a couple of hours. This soup will all be washed away by then.'

He turned and walked towards the Junkers, pulling on his flying helmet. Sloan watched him go up the ladder and pull it up behind him. A moment later, the engines, which had already been warmed up, rumbled into life.

As Grant boosted power, the Junkers moved forward with increasing speed, following the line of flares. The fog swallowed it from sight and Sloane and the others standing outside the crew room, waited, holding breath.

Not that there was any need, for at precisely the right moment, Grant hauled back the column, and the Junkers lifted, climbing up out of the fog into clear air. Grant put pressure on the right rudder and turned out to sea.

After a while he spoke to Carter over the intercom which had been specially set up. 'How are things back there?'

'Fine,' Carter said.

'Good. Estimated time of arrival in the target area, fifty minutes. The weather isn't too good there. Raining, but visibility should be okay. Thunderstorms forecast so it may get bumpy.'

He settled the Junkers at a thousand feet exactly and sat back, barely touching the controls, thoroughly enjoying himself as they skimmed the surface of the fog.

*   *   *

Twenty minutes from target and sixty miles southwest of Cape Granitola in Sicily, Collinson, leaning over the Lichtenstein set, gave a sudden cry.

'I've got something, sir, probably a night fighter.'

Grant said over the intercom, 'Red alert, Harry, we've got company.'

In their cramped quarters in the body of the Junkers, Carter, Luciano and the others couldn't see a thing. Carter said, 'Are you sure?'

'Now I am,' Grant told him as a Junkers, twin to his own, burst out of the fog to starboard and took up station. Grant raised a hand and could see the pilot of the other plane return the gesture. It stayed with them for a while, then peeled off to starboard and vanished into the night.

'Worked perfectly,' Grant said cheerfully over the intercom to Carter. 'He's just pissed off. We've got exactly fifteen minutes so better make sure you're ready.'

★   ★   ★

In a meadow at the head of the valley beyond the Contessa di Bellona's villa, Vito Barbera and Rosa waited. It was raining steadily and they sheltered under the trees at the edge of the meadow. Rosa wore a tweed cap and an old belted rain-coat.

'Are you all right?' Barbera asked. 'This stinking weather is something I hadn't counted on.'

'Why don't you worry about something important like those Communist bastards, Mori and Russo? They could bring the Germans down on us any time they liked.'

'No,' he said. 'I don't think so. Mori is no fool. He wouldn't put his head on the block so stupidly.'

She grabbed his arm. 'Listen, they come.'

In the distance, there was the rumble of engines. He said, 'You know what to do.'

She ran across to the far side of the field and Barbera tossed a match to the petrol-soaked bonfire they had prepared an hour earlier. It roared into life and on the other side of the meadow flame blossomed also as Rosa performed her part.

Barbera looked up into the night and waited.

★   ★   ★

The Junkers was down to a thousand feet when Harvey Grant saw the two fires marking the north and south edges of the meadow.

'Did you see that, Joe?' he said to Collinson.

'Got it, sir.'

Grant banked to starboard, lifting over a ridge, turned and started his run.

'You've got two minutes, Harry,' he called over the intercom.

Carter said, 'Fine, Harvey, all we need.'

He nodded to the rest of the group and they all stood, crouching awkwardly in the confined space and clipped their static lines which opened the parachute automatically when they jumped to the anchor cable. Carter moved down the line, checking each of them personally, first Maria, then Savage followed by Luciano, Detweiler bringing up the rear.

He went back to the head of the line, clipped his own static line in place, then slid back the exit door. Rain and cold air rushed in and a moment later, the green light flashed above his head.

Carter, already aware of the fire blossoming in the night below, jumped without hesitation. Maria froze for the briefest of moments only and Savage shoved her out bodily and went after her.

What happened next was not by any design. It was a kind of reflex gesture, a reflection of the hate Detweiler had come to bear Luciano. He pulled the razor-sharp gravity knife from its scabbard on his right knee. Luciano, poised in the entrance clutching his supply bag, was aware of the knife slicing through the static line above his head before the sergeant shoved him out into space.

Collinson, looking back through the open door of the cockpit, saw nothing of this action; in the half-light knew only that Detweiler was still with them for the sergeant had paused in the doorway, frozen, his mind numb, stunned by the enormity of what he had done.

Grant, already way beyond the target, was pulling back the column to take the Junkers over the ridge ahead and Collinson clapped him on the shoulder.

'We've still got company.'

And then, as the line of the ridge lifted to meet them, Grant boosted power and banked to port and Detweiler lost his balance and pitched headfirst into darkness.

*   *   *

At four hundred feet, it takes twenty seconds to hit the ground. Luciano falling, already past the half-way mark, remembered Carter's words in the Dakota at Ringway. He turned over once, twice, then released the supply bag he had been clutching and his fingers tore at the cover of the emergency chute, strapped across his belly, found the handle of the ripcord and pulled.

There was a sudden jerk, the crack of the chute catching air no more than a hundred feet to go and then he was swinging beneath that dark khaki umbrella, the supply bag below on the end of a line clipped to his waist.

And he was right on target, dropping fast towards the fire at the north end of the meadow, aware of Carter and Maria already down. He glanced up, but there was no sign of Detweiler's parachute. He drifted in over Savage as the captain hit the grass and then the fire seemed to be rushing towards him and he was aware of someone standing there looking up at him, a boy in an old raincoat and cloth cap.

The supply bag hit the ground with a solid thump, warning him to get ready. He followed it a split second later, rolling into wet grass, the breath going out of him. Then the boy in the raincoat and tweed cap was moving in to help, clutching the billowing waves of silk, and Luciano saw that it was a young girl.

He stood up, unlocking the quick release on his harness and she paused, examining him in the firelight.

'You are Luciano?'

'That's right. And you?'

'Rosa Barbera – Vito's niece.'

She started to bundle up the parachute and Harry Carter arrived on the run, Savage not far behind.

'Where's Detweiler? Vito says you were the last to jump, then the plane passed over into the next valley.'

Luciano divested himself of the main chute, the one which

hadn't opened, and held up the static line, the clean knife-cut
evident to all. 'I knew the bastard didn't like me. I just didn't
realize how much.'

*   *   *

Detweiler, drifting down into the next valley, landed in a
pinewood, his parachute snagging in branches, leaving him
suspended ten feet above the ground. He snapped the release
buckle, fell to the turf and lay there for a moment.

What in the hell was he going to do now? He hadn't intended
it, not any of it. It had been a moment of pure madness which
had left him on the wrong side of the mountain and miles off
target, alone and totally vulnerable.

One thing was certain. He had to get moving fast and try to
reach Bellona on his own. He unzipped the flying suit in which
he had jumped. Underneath he wore a patched tweed suit and
shirt without collar. There was a cap in one pocket. He pulled it
on, crouched down and opened the supply bag. He took out a
Colt ·45 automatic pistol and an M1, slipped the Colt in
one pocket and slung the M1 over his shoulder.

He threw the supply bag into the bushes and pulled on the
parachute to bring it down. It refused to budge so he abandoned
it and started to work his way cautiously down through the
wood. It had stopped raining for the moment and a pale moon
showed through a gap in the clouds. In its light, he saw a dirt
road on the far side of a low stone wall and scrambled over. He
could smell woodsmoke, saw a farmhouse down below, a light in
the window.

He paused, slipping a hand inside his jacket to make sure the
wallet was there containing the false papers Carter had given
him at Maison Blanche. Reassured, he carried on down the track
and turned in at the farmyard, leaving the M1 still slung from
his shoulder, but with a hand in his pocket on the butt of the
Colt.

A dog barked excitedly inside the house as he walked through
the mud of the farmyard to the door. He knocked. There was a
certain amount of movement and then the top half of the door
opened.

Smoke drifted out into the cold air and in the dim light of an oil lamp, Detweiler was aware of a man standing there, holding a shotgun. He was perhaps sixty, with hollow cheeks and unshaven face and wore incredibly patched clothes. A small, ragged boy of about twelve stood beside him. Beyond them by the open fire, an old woman, face as wizened as an Egyptian mummy's, lay back in a wooden rocking chair, swaddled in blankets.

'What do you want?' the man asked hoarsely.

'I'm a shepherd,' Detweiler said. 'I was walking over the top of the next valley and lost my way, then it got dark. Can you put me up for the night?'

The man nodded, 'Sure, why not. You can sleep in the barn. Giorgio here can put you on your way in the morning.' He patted the boy on the head, who drew a sleeve across his nose, but said nothing.

The man eyed Detweiler speculatively. 'Tell me the truth now. Aren't you with the boys in the mountains?'

Detweiler was uncertain what to say, but decided to take a chance. 'Perhaps.'

'I knew it.' The old man smiled suddenly, revealing blackened teeth. 'You've come to the right place, son, believe me. We're all patriots here,' and he opened the lower half of the door and drew Detweiler in.

*　　*　　*

The atmosphere inside the Junkers was of tremendous excitement as they roared through the night to the Sicilian coast line. Collinson said over the intercom, 'Cape Granitola coming up fast. We did it, sir. We did it! A perfect drop.'

'Except for that stupid sod cocking things up at the end,' Grant replied. 'God knows where he's ended up. We were miles off target by the time he jumped. What in the hell was he playing at?'

And then Collinson, staring into the Lichtenstein set, said, 'We've got company. Big trouble.'

A Junkers emerged from the cloud to starboard. A second later another took up station to port.

Collinson said, 'Better check your tail. There's another bastard there. Now what?'

'I suspect the clever thing to do would be to switch to their air-to-air frequency,' Grant said and did just that.

There was a little static and a voice said in fair English, 'Big black bird, we've been lonely without you. Last seen over Algeria a month ago. You've taken your time coming home. Now let's all go down nice and friendly, land at Otranto base and sort things out.'

'Go and fuck yourself!' Grant said and dropped his flaps as on that memorable occasion in the Dakota on his way back from Malta.

The pilot of the Junkers on his tail, shoved his column forward desperately and went into a steep dive, passing underneath and Grant went after him, switching to his G2 system to boost power, holding his fire like all great pilots until he was close. His thumb pressed on the button, cannon shell and tracer ripped into the other plane, tearing great chunks out of the fuselage. There was a sudden tongue of flame in the night that mushroomed into fireball as the Junkers disintegrated.

In the same moment, Grant's own aircraft staggered under the impact of cannon shell as one of the other planes came in on his tail. He went into a corkscrew instantly, the reflex of several years of combat flying coming to his aid, and a moment later was engulfed in cloud.

'Everything okay?' he called.

'We're in a mess back here,' Collinson told him. 'Hole in the fuselage you could drive a Morris Ten through.'

They lurched again under the impact of more cannon shell and Grant said, 'I'm going to go right down to sea level. Hang on, Joe, and we'll see if these bastards know how to fly.'

He emerged from broken cloud at a thousand feet and kept on going, levelling out at the last possible moment. It was probably the most hazardous piece of flying he had ever attempted, for the only light was the moon occasionally through a gap in the cloud and the wind was such that the sea was already lifting into forty foot swells.

The two Junkers hung on grimly, even at that suicidal level, firing whenever they could get on his tail. Again and again,

Grant's aircraft shuddered under the impact of cannon shell.

Half-an-hour at four hundred miles an hour. Engines overheating and the nitrous oxide tanks which fuelled his booster system almost empty. They couldn't take much more of this, he knew that and then, as the aircraft bucked again, this time under a burst of machine gun fire, his windscreen shattered and he received a violent blow in the left arm, another in the right leg.

His fingers came up covered in blood and the port engine started to smoke. He feathered it at once and switched to the extinguishers. The Junkers started to slow, the needle falling rapidly.

And then that voice spoke again over the radio, 'Good luck, whoever you are. You've earned it.'

Collinson cried, 'They're going, Skip. They've turned back. Why?'

'We're a hundred and fifty miles from the coast, the limit of their radius for a sea chase. See if you can find a field dressing in the box. I think I've got a bullet in the leg.'

Collinson found the first aid box and scrambled across. 'You all right, sir?'

Grant said. 'A bullet in the arm, another in the leg, the port engine burned out? Who could ask for anything more.' He grinned through the pain. 'Now cross your fingers, say a prayer, and let's see if I can still fly this thing.'

10

Vito opened the oven door of the boiler in the basement at the Contessa di Bellona's villa. He had lit the fire earlier and it glowed red hot. He turned to Luciano and Carter.

'Okay, everything inside.'

They tossed in the jump suits, the bundled parachutes, the equipment bags and Barbera closed the door. 'Harry, it's good to see you.'

'And you, Vito. When do we see Luca?'

'I don't know, Harry, don't even know where he is. Padre Giovanni is my only contact with him.'

'Who's he?' Luciano demanded.

'Prior of the Franciscans at Crown of Thorns.'

'The Mafia connection?'

'Oh, sure,' Barbera said. 'We got God on our side, too.'

'Actually, that's more accurate than you know, Vito,' Carter told him. 'Do you know where we found Luca's grand-daughter?'

'Not until you tell me.'

'A convent in Liverpool in England. Little Sisters of Pity.'

Barbera's mouth gaped in surprise. 'You're kidding?'

Luciano said. 'The old man should be pleased. Isn't it everyone's ambition to have a priest in the family? Maria's just the female equivalent.'

They went upstairs and Barbera led the way through the back passageway to the enormous kitchen at the rear of the house. There was a fire on the wide hearth which Savage was replenishing with logs.

Maria stood at the table slicing bread and salami. She wore a headscarf, a woollen jacket and a black cotton dress and looked perfectly at home in her surroundings. Rosa had taken off her raincoat and cap and crouched at the fire, stirring soup in a pot.

Savage got to his feet as the other three men entered. Like them, he wore cloth cap, patched, shabby clothes and leather leggings, the typical attire of the mountain shepherd or hunter.

Luciano shook his head. 'It's no good, kid. Even in that outfit you still look like a whisky advert.'

Savage found it difficult to raise a smile, for the knowledge of what Detweiler had done weighed heavily on him.

He said to Carter, 'Look Colonel, about Detweiler.'

'Nothing to be said,' Carter told them. 'Not until we hear the full facts.'

'When I get back to my place in Bellona, I'll radio Maison Blanche,' Barbera said. 'They'll know if he returned with the plane.' He put an arm around Luciano's shoulder. 'And now, Don Salvatore. A drink to celebrate your safe delivery.'

Double doors stood open to the terrace overlooking the rear garden. Savage moved out and Carter went after him.

'It wasn't your fault.'

Savage shook his head. 'Not good enough, sir. Poor judgement on my part. I thought I knew him.'

Carter gave him a cigarette and Savage turned and looked across the kitchen at Rosa crouched by the fire.

'The girl – how old is she?'

'Rosa? Sixteen or seventeen. She's Barbera's niece.'

'Rather young to be involved in this sort of game.'

'On the contrary, she manages very well, and that's hardly surprising. She was left to fend for herself at the age of thirteen. When Vito found her, she'd been on the streets in Palermo for three years.'

Savage, a product of the most conventional of upbringings, was shocked. 'You mean she was a prostitute?'

'So it would appear.'

Savage went and sat by the fire, watching her. She was aware of his presence, but scratched her backside, totally unconcerned. When she reached up for a ladle he saw that her dress was split under the arm so that a tuft of dark hair poked through.

'You hungry?' she said without looking at him.

'I could eat a horse.'

'Heh, I like the way you speak.' She turned. 'Rome Italian, like a real gentleman.'

'I lved in Rome for a few years before the war.'

'But you're American? Truly American?' She spooned soup into a bowl and handed it to him.

'I think you could say that.'

'From New York?'

'Boston.'

She wrinkled her nose in disappointment. 'That's a pity. New York's the place. Statue of Liberty, the Empire State building. Uncle Vito's told me all about it. I'm going to live there one day.'

'Truly?'

'Maybe after the war.'

The soup was excellent, but very hot and he burned his mouth a little.

'Good?' she said.

'Very good.'

'Have some more.'

She emptied the ladle again into his plate, then went to the table to serve the others. She walked with a kind of total movement of the body that he found disturbing. The black cotton dress was a size too small and moulded her buttocks as she leaned across the table. He was aware of Luciano watching him sardonically and hurriedly returned to his soup. The other three men sat down and Maria brought coffee from the stove.

Barbera said, 'Let's get down to business. You'll be safe here for a day or two until I get word from Padre Giovanni at Crown of Thorns. As I said before, any news from Don Antonio will come through him.'

'Time is of the essence, Vito,' Carter said. 'How long will we have to wait?'

'I don't know, Harry, it all depends on Luca. I'll keep in close touch, I promise, and I'll leave Rosa to look after you.'

'A couple of days,' Carter said. 'That's all we've got.'

Maria bowed her head and murmured a grace before eating. When she looked up, Barbera said awkwardly, 'Sister, Harry has been telling me about your situation. I'm sorry, I didn't know.'

'It doesn't signify, Mr Barbera.'

Rosa said, 'Is what he said true? Are you a nun?'

'Yes, Rosa,' Maria told her. 'A nurse in a hospital.'

'Oh, that kind of nun. Like the General Infirmary in Palermo. I was in there once. The nurses were all nuns.'

'You were in hospital?'

'Sure, when I lost my baby,' she said and continued round the table, serving the soup.

*   *   *

At Maison Blanche, the fog had lifted and it had stopped raining. Air Marshal Sloane was sitting at the desk in the Crew Room, working his way through some of the papers he had brought in his briefcase. Paperwork of the most stupefying kind, the sort one put to the bottom of the pile, hoping it would go away.

The door opened and the duty officer looked in. 'He made it, sir. Coming in now.'

Sloane went out of the Crew Room on the run, crossed to the control tower and mounted the stairs. He snapped his finger and one of the sergeants passed him a pair of Zeiss night glasses. In the pale moonlight, he could see the Junkers about two miles away.

Harvey Grant's voice sounded over the radio, totally washed out. 'No time for procedure. I'm bringing one very tired baby straight home to bed.'

Sloane lowered the glasses. 'Not good. Full emergency.'

The Junkers came in over the sea at five hundred feet. The wind whistled through the shattered screen. Collinson's face was blue with cold as he crouched behind Grant, hands on his shoulders as if to support him.

Grant sat there, hands frozen to the control column, a slight fixed smile on his face. According to the gauge, their fuel had run out fifteen minutes earlier.

As the airfield came into view, the runway clearly marked by twin lines of glittering flares, the starboard engine spluttered and started to die, the prop feathering.

'That's it,' Grant said. 'Hang on and pray, Joe.'

He brushed across the line of palms at the north end of the

runway, aware of the trail of vehicles moving from the control buildings on his right. The Junkers almost stalled. He gave a final burst of power to straighten her and miraculously, the engine roared into life briefly.

The worst landing of his career, bouncing back up again twice, before they slewed to a halt, sand spraying in a great cloud as the tail spun round and they turned full circle. But they were down.

That engine had very definitely stopped now. Grant was aware of the screech of brakes as the emergency people arrived and of Collinson shaking his shoulder anxiously. There were voices, lots of them, a confused shouting, and then he opened his eyes again and found Sloane leaning over him.

Grant smiled. 'Don't scold me, sir, not this time. Just for once, I'm rather proud of myself.'

*   *   *

Luciano moved out on the terrace, followed by Barbera. He could hear water gurgling in the conduits, splashing from numerous fountains. In the old days it was said that whoever held the meagre water supplies of the island held Sicily, and Mafia had done just that.

In the light from the rear windows, he was aware of the lush, semi-tropical vegetation pressing in on the house. Although he couldn't see it, he could smell an orange grove, almond trees. Palms swayed in a slight breeze and rain dripped from the eaves of the verandah.

He took a deep breath. 'I'd forgotten how it could be.'

'The real Sicily?' Barbera said.

'That depends on your point of view.'

Below the verandah and five yards on the other side of the path, leaves trembled and a gun barrel poked through. Luciano sent Barbera sprawling with a stiff left arm and reached under his jacket for the revolver he carried there, pushed into his belt against the small of his back. He drew and fired twice in the same fluid motion. A machine pistol jumped into the air, there was a choking cough and a man fell out of the bushes and rolled on his back.

Luciano crouched. 'There will be another,' Barbera whispered.

Savage came out through the open door in a hurry holding an M1. A shotgun blasted from the bushes over to the right, too far away to do any damage.

Luciano took a running jump into the greenery, landed badly, rolled over and came up about six feet away from the other gunman. He was clutching a sawed-off shotgun in both hands.

Luciano fired, catching him in the left arm. The man screamed, dropping the *lupara*, and Savage emptied his M1 into the man, driving him back into the bushes.

*   *   *

Luciano said, 'The idea was to keep him alive so he could tell us what this is all about.'

Savage stared at him, a dazed look in his eyes, and Barbera and Carter hurried past him to Luciano who was looking down at the body of a boy of about seventeen.

Barbera picked up the shotgun. The *lupara*, traditional weapon used in a Mafia ritual killing. He turned to Luciano. 'It was you they were after.'

'Me?' Luciano was astounded. Mafia? It doesn't make sense.'

'Not Mafia. See, over here.' He crossed to the other gunman who lay on his face. Barbera turned him over with his foot.

Carter said, 'I know him. That's Ettore Russo.'

'Who is he?' Luciano demanded.

'A Communist,' Barbera said, 'and no friend to Mafia. A member of the district committee which co-ordinates the work of the various factions which go to make up the resistance movement. I met them earlier tonight to discuss your arrival and what we hoped to achieve. He was less than pleased.'

'So decided to knock me off?'

'Not really,' Barbera said. 'I think he was used by someone much cleverer than himself. Look at it this way. If he and his boy kill you, it looks as if it's done by the Mafia. You're out of the way and everyone's confused.'

'And with this result?' Carter said.

'Lucky Luciano and his friends have butchered one of the

most important Communists in the district, which won't go down well with his friends, so we'd better bury these two as soon as possible.'

Maria moved past them, dropped to her knees beside Russo and started to pray. Barbera looked down at her, embarrassed. Luciano inclined his head and they all moved back up on the verandah.

'You think you know who's behind this?'

'Sure I do. Don't worry. He'll be taken care of,' Barbera said.

'So what happens now?' Luciano asked.

Barbera turned to Carter. 'I think you and I had better go down to Bellona and see what the situation is.'

'While the rest of us stay here?'

'No.' Barbera shook his head. 'I can't be sure someone else won't try the same thing, not until I've fixed that bastard, Mori. I think maybe Rosa better take you up to the Franciscans. Padre Giovanni will look after you. No one dare touch you up there.' He turned to Carter. 'Okay, Harry?'

Carter looked at the others, the nodded. 'It doesn't seem as if we've got much choice.'

'Good,' Barbera said. 'Then let's dispose of those bodies and get moving.'

*　　*　　*

Luciano sat at the table reloading the revolver. It was the short-barrelled Smith and Wesson ·32 he had used at the firing range at the Abbey.

Carter moved up behind him. 'Where did you get that?'

'Did a deal with that armourer.' Luciano took the silencer from his pocket. 'He was very accommodating.' He slipped the Smith and Wesson back in its place in his waistband at the small of his back.

Savage slid his arms through the straps of his rucksack and picked up his M1. Rosa came in from the bedroom, once more dressed in her old raincoat and cloth cap. Maria wore a waterproof poncho and was tying a scarf around her head.

Barbera said, 'Good, we go now. You'll be at the monastery in three hours. No problems. We'll see you up there some time tomorrow.'

He turned out the light and they all moved out on the verandah. He and Carter stood there and waited until the others had disappeared into the darkness, Rosa leading the way. When they were out of sight, Barbera turned to Carter.

'Okay, Harry, now for Mori,' he said and went down the steps.

11

Peitro Mori had sent his wife to bed early and waited for Russo's return, sitting in the old easy chair by the fire with a bottle of brandy. Not that he was particularly worried. Russo, after all, was taking the risks and it couldn't go wrong, whatever happened. That was the essential cleverness of the whole scheme.

He dozed off and was awakened by a tapping at the window. He got up and opened the casement an inch or two.

'Who is it?'

'It's me, Vito,' Barbera said. 'I must speak with you.'

'Just a minute. I'll open the door,' Mori said.

He pulled back the bolt and Barbera slipped inside.

'What is it?' Mori demanded.

'I've just come from Russo, you bastard,' Barbera told him. 'He says he's waiting for you in hell.'

His left hand went around Mori's neck, pulling him close and he kissed him full on the lips, the Mafia kiss of death. At the same time he drove the needle point of the stiletto he held in his other hand up under the ribs, probing for the heart.

Pietro Mori groaned once and died and Barbera eased him back into the chair and left him there by the fire, head back, eyes staring into eternity.

★   ★   ★

At that same moment, the others were moving down a sloping meadow in the side of the valley towards trees below, Rosa leading the way. Luciano, like Savage, carried a rucksack on his back and an M1 slung over one shoulder.

It was raining again. As they reached the trees he said to Maria, 'You okay?'

'Fine.'

Rosa motioned them to halt and they crouched down: Luciano could just make out a low wall and a road on the other side, more trees beyond.

'We cross over here,' the girl said, 'then climb the mountain on the far side. The monastery is on the ridge at the other end of the valley from here, beyond Bellona.'

'Okay,' Luciano said. 'Let's get moving.'

Rosa scrambled over the wall, followed by Savage who turned to assist Maria. They started across the road when suddenly a spotlight was turned on and vehicle headlamps.

A voice called harshly in bad Italian, 'Stay where you are.'

Rosa was already running, scrambling over the other wall, dropping out of sight followed by Savage. Luciano pulled his Smith and Wesson, fired twice in the direction of the lights, shattering one of them, then followed Maria who was running for the wall.

As he went over after her, a burst of machine gun fire chipped the stonework. He grabbed her hand and they ran together, through the darkness, towards the trees.

Even when they were into their shelter, a machine gun chattered again, slicing branches above their heads.

They could hear voices calling as their pursuers came over the wall and started to follow, firing their weapons blindly.

Luciano ducked as a bullet plucked at his cap and pulled Maria down. He could hear Rosa and Savage still moving ahead somewhere, then the voices of the soldiers seemed very close and he dragged Maria to her feet.

'This way!' he said and ran to one side, moving fast through a plantation of young pine trees, an arm raised to protect his face.

After a while, the sounds of the pursuers faded and he paused.

Maria said, 'What about Rosa and Captain Savage?'

'They'll have to make out the best way they can.'

'And what about us?'

'We climb. She said the monastery was on the ridge at the far end of the valley, didn't she?'

He took her hand. As they waded across a small stream and up the other side, it started to rain heavily.

*   *   *

Detweiler had dined well on boiled mutton and goats' cheese, washed down with a bottle of red wine and the wine particularly helped him to see things in a much more hopeful light. Now, he was deperately tired. The old man gave him a couple of blankets and took him out to the barn. Detweiler lay down, rifle close to hand, and was almost instantly asleep.

Five minutes later, as he lay snoring gently, the barn door creaked open and the old man appeared with the boy. He held up a lantern, peering down at Detweiler, then withdrew, closing the door behind him.

He gave the boy a push. 'Go now. You know what to do.'

The boy turned and walked across the farmyard and out of the gate. When he reached the track, he started to run. The old man watched him go for a while, then turned and went back to the house.

*   *   *

In the second cubby hole on the other side of the coffin room above the mortuary, Vito Barbera sat at the radio. Carter walked up and down impatiently, smoking a cigarette.

Finally Barbera took off the headphones and turned. 'He got back in one piece.'

'And Detweiler?'

'You aren't going to like this. Apparently he did jump, but far too late. Probably came down in the next valley.'

Carter exploded. 'That's all we need. Detweiler wandering around the countryside totally at sea. The man must have blown his top. I mean, what if he's picked up?'

'It'll be all right, Harry, you'll see,' Barbera said. 'I'll put the word out. We'll pull him in soon enough.' He grinned and put a hand on Carter's shoulder. 'I've told you before, all you have to do is live right.'

*   *   *

The previous year, operating as an OSS courier in occupied France, Jack Savage had called at a cafe in Tours, a staging post on the route to Spain. He had promptly been arrested and hauled off to SD headquarters where he had been interrogated with considerable brutality for three days before being put on a train for Paris under guard, his final destination, Gestapo Headquarters on the Rue des Saussaies. He had killed a guard stupid enough to turn his back on him and managed to jump from the train just outside Orleans, the start of five active days that had ended with him crossing the Pyrenees into Spain on foot.

It was a strange sensation to be hunted again, nothing quite like it, and he was conscious of the familiar nervous excitement, sharpening all the senses, as he paused on the rim of a small plateau and looked back.

There was nothing to be seen, but he could hear the soldiers calling to each other, faint and far away now.

Rosa said, 'They can't catch us, not in these hills.'

'What about Maria?' he asked. 'And Luciano?'

'There's nothing we can do,' she said flatly. 'They must take their chances. Now we must go.'

The rain had slackened again, but a strong wind began to lift through the pine trees and the clouds above them were storm-tossed, the moon showing through occasionally.

Instead of working her way across the steep hillside she went straight up. The slope lifted until it was almost perpendicular, with rough tussocks of grass sticking out of the bare rock. They came to the foot of an apron of loose stones and shale and she started to climb and Savage went after her.

Once he heaved strongly on a boulder and it tore itself free and bounced and crashed its way down the mountainside. The sound of it echoed away into the night.

She looked down at him. 'All right?'

'Sure. Just keep going.'

A moment later, the ground sloped away and he found himself standing on the edge of a broad plateau. He turned to peer down into the darkness of the valley, but could see nothing, was aware only of space and the increasingly strong wind cold on his face.

Rosa moved beside him. He said, 'Now what?'

She pointed across the plateau and in the dim light he saw that a great rock wall faced them. He said softly. 'Are you sure it can be done?'

'Oh, yes. You will see.'

She led the way across the plateau, picking her way between boulders. When they reached the base of the rock, Savage saw that it wasn't perpendicular at all, but lifted back in great slabs, most of which were split and fissured.

She said. 'Boys herd goats up here.'

Savage ran a hand over his mouth, his throat dry, fear churning his guts. His one secret was a fear of heights. He was a brave man who had placed himself in maximum danger on several occasions, had killed men in hand-to-hand combat, and yet he had never jumped from a plane with his eyes open, had gone through a private hell abseiling down the rock faces on the commando course at Achnacarry in Scotland.

Rosa started to climb. He swallowed hard and forced himself to follow her. The wind cut through his old tweed jacket. Lightning flickered on the mountain tops and it started to rain again.

At least when he looked down he could see nothing. He paused, breathed deeply to steady himself, eyes closed. When he opened them, the girl was crouched beside him.

'Are you all right?'

He nodded. 'Fine.'

But she knew, he could sense it, reaching out to touch his face briefly with the fingers of one hand. She turned, starting to climb again and Savage took another deep, shuddering breath and went after her.

★   ★   ★

Suslov the Ukrainian *Einsatzgruppen* lieutenant, crossed the farmyard cautiously followed by a corporal and two men carrying machine pistols. The old man and Giorgio, the boy who had brought the message, waited at the barn door.

The old man opened the door. From inside came the sound of Detweiler's heavy breathing. Suslov nodded to the corporal who moved in with the two SS.

There was a sudden muffled cry, the sound of blows and they reappeared dragging Detweiler between them. They dropped him in the mud and he lay there groaning.

Suslov knelt down and searched him, finding the Colt automatic and the false identity papers Carter had given Detweiler at Maison Blanche. He examined them briefly then took a silver whistle from his pocket and blew a single long blast. There was the sound of engines starting up and a few moments later, five *kubelwagens* drove into the farmyard. The first two had drivers only, but the other three had heavy machine guns mounted and carried three-man crews.

The corporal came out of the barn with Detweiler's rucksack and the M1 rifle. Suslov examined it with interest, then stirred Detweiler with his toe.

'American rifle, brand-new.' He held up the Colt. 'American handgun. You must have some interesting friends. Major Meyer's going to enjoy meeting you.' He nodded to the corporal. 'Get him in the car.'

'*Zu befehl, Untersturmbannführer,*' the corporal replied, for it was a strict regulation of Meyer's that all members of his *Einsatzgruppe* spoke German, however badly.

They handcuffed Detweiler's wrists behind his back and bundled him into the rear of one of the front *kubelwagens*. The corporal and two guards got in with him. Suslov moved over to the three rear vehicles and addressed the crews.

'From the looks of things we've got ourselves a nice one here. A partisan armed with brand-new American weapons. That means they've had a supply drop in this district recently. Patrol the villages on the heights. Anyone in the slightest bit suspicious, haul them in.'

He stood back and they drove away in echelon. As he returned to the front car, the old man pulled off his cap.

'We did well, Lieutenant, Giorgio and me, eh?'

Suslov lit a cigarette and looked him over contemptuously. 'You really are a disgusting old bastard, aren't you, but then I suppose every dog must have its bone.'

He took a roll of banknotes from his pocket and threw them in the mud at the old man's feet, then got into the *kubelwagen* and nodded to the driver who drove away at once.

The old man picked up the money and stood there, an arm around Giorgio's shoulders, listening until their sound had faded into the distance. Then he patted the boy on the head and they turned and went inside.

*   *   *

Savage was soaked to the skin and bitterly cold as he hauled himself up over the last slab. The girl reached out and took his hand.

'Over here,' she said. 'Not far.'

He followed her, head down in the howling gale which at that height threatened to blow them off their feet. They scrambled over rough grass and he was aware of another rock face looming out of the night. Then the wind seemed to drop away.

'Head down,' Rosa said. He put out a hand in pitch darkness and felt rough stone.

A match flared and he saw Rosa standing a few feet away. She held the match above her head and looked around her, searching. They were in a low roofed cave with every evidence of habitation. There was wood laid ready to burn on a crude stone hearth, a wooden table, sheepskins, blankets and an assortment of cooking pots. The match went out and she struck another and lit an old oil lamp which stood on the table.

'What is this place?' Savage asked.

'The shepherds use it during the lambing season. They stay up here for weeks.'

He put down his M1 and took off his rucksack. He was shaking with cold and folded his arms as if to hold himself together. She turned and put a hand to his cheek and there was the concern on her face that a mother might show for a child.

'Too cold, Savage. This is not your country, not your way.' She picked up one of the blankets and unfolded it. 'Undress and dry yourself with this. I'll light a fire.'

She crouched at the hearth, striking another match, and the dry twigs flared. She took off her raincoat and knelt there, putting logs on the fire. The rain had soaked through to the cotton dress so that it moulded her like a second skin.

Savage struggled to get his wet jacket off. 'What about you?'

'I'm used to it.' She filled a pan with water from a rivulet that trickled down one of the stone walls and set it on the fire.

'I thought you came from Palermo?'

She paused, turning from the fire. 'Who told you that?'

'Colonel Carter. He said ...' Savage hesitated. 'He said your Uncle Vito brought you last year from Palermo to live with him.'

There was a calculating look in her eyes as if she was trying to assess how much he knew about her. Savage was confused and embarrassed. She was instantly aware of it, smiled slightly and turned back to feed more logs on the fire.

'I've lived in Bellona with Uncle Vito for nine months now.'

He peeled off his shirt with difficulty. 'You like it better?'

'Than Palermo? Oh, sure. I help Vito with the funeral business. And when he needs a runner, I handle that too.'

'A runner?'

She picked up a blanket and started to dry his back and shoulders vigorously. 'Runners carry messages between the various resistance groups. They usually use boys, but Vito prefers me.'

'Why?'

'I'm smarter, for one thing. Anyway, it's my choice. I like the mountains. I like the air up here and I like being alone.' She started to unbuckle his belt. 'Better get your pants off.'

Her breasts were strong and firm, thrusting against the damp linen of her dress, perfectly outlined and he could see her nipples. He panicked slightly, acutely embarrassed like some gangling boy.

His hands went to the belt, pushing her away. 'That's okay, I'll do it.'

She smiled, went across to a rock shelf and rummaged amongst various utensils and other items there. She held up a tin. 'Coffee. Old, but it will do.'

She crouched down at the fire again, spooning coffee into the pan of simmering water. Savage, divested of his boots, managed the wet trousers with difficulty and quickly wrapped the blanket around him.

Rosa piled a sheepskin beside the fire. 'You come over here and get warm,' she ordered.

He hesitated, then did as he was told. She covered him with a blanket, piled another couple of sheepskins on top. They were old, certainly dirty and very possibly flea-ridden, but Savage suddenly realized that he didn't give a damn. They were soft and warm and smelled of wood smoke.

She took a cigarette from an old tobacco tin, lit it with a splinter from the fire and passed it to him without a word. He held it with shaking fingers, grateful for the comfort from the cheap, strong tobacco as he inhaled deeply.

For some reason, he remembered the dinner party his mother had given for him during his last leave in Boston. Dinner jackets, handsome men in uniform, pretty women, the Savage silver gleaming in the candlelight, discreet servants. And there was Joanna, of course, Joanna Van der Boegart who had been somewhere around since his earliest memories. Joanna whom he would marry one day, much to everyone's satisfaction.

He remembered her that last time in his arms on the terrace, up from Vassar for the weekend specially for the party. Cool, elegant, her lips firm and full, but never opening for him, not even on an occasion with the possibility of such finality to it.

Not like this – not anything like this. He watched Rosa, leaning over the fire pouring coffee carefully into an old tin cup. The damp cotton dress was so tight that he could see the shape of her pants underneath.

There was an immediate sexual stirring of a kind he had not known for some considerable time and he moved uncomfortably. Whatever a soldier monk might be, Jack Savage was a strong contender for the title. He had been celibate for over a year now. The kind of life he had led, the lengthy periods of training interspersed with brief forays into Europe, left little time for any kind of relationship with a woman. He had long since decided to cut that side of things out of his life altogether, at least for the duration.

In any case, he had never thought of himself as being any great shakes with women. The kind of upper-class girl he had been raised with, girls like Joanna, used their virginity as a bargaining factor. Episodes with the other type of girl at college had been unsatisfactory to say the least.

Even Montmarte had failed to work its magic on him during

his painting days. There were girls in plenty interested in the handsome American painter with money, but whatever it took to keep them happy, he didn't have. He had long since come to that regrettable conclusion.

Rosa passed him coffee in the old tin mug, hot and black, and Savage swallowed it greedily, burning his mouth, his hand shaking. She stood looking down at him, a hand on her hips, the steam rising from her damp dress. God, but he was cold, shaking so badly that coffee slipped down his chin and she took the cup from him.

'I think you have a fever,' she said. 'And for that, you must sweat.'

She piled more sheepskins on him, then started to unbutton the dress. As she peeled it down, firm breasts gleamed in the firelight. He closed his eyes, aware of the pants sliding down, the dark hair between her thighs, and then she was coming in under the sheepskin beside him.

There was an incredible unreality to it all, like one of those fantasies born in the mind when half-asleep.

Her lips nibbled at his ear and then her tongue was probing his mouth. Her hand slid down the blanket across the flat muscular belly and touched him.

She laughed and breathed in his ear. 'You take me to New York, eh? You take me to New York, Savage, and I make you a little bit crazy.'

And then she moved, rolling on top of him, spreading her thighs, guiding him into her.

★　　★　　★

Later, lying there, half asleep, still in a fever, his arm around her, he was aware of her whispering.

'Savage, are you awake?'

He made no reply but lay there, thinking about what had happened. He had never known anything like it or like her. The warmth, the primitiveness, the total lack of shame.

Her head went down and he was aware of her tongue tracing a course across his belly. Then she had him in her mouth. He groaned and started to move.

She pulled away and looked up at him. 'So, you are awake?'

'Yes,' he said, pushing her over on her back. 'I'm awake, damn you!'

She laughed and kissed him as he thrust into her, still half in a delirium, mounting to a climax that seemed to be without end. One thing he was aware of. The way her body moved, the sudden gasp, the hands tightening into his flesh, her smothered cries.

Then afterwards, he stayed on top of her and finally drifted into sleep as she gently stroked his face.

12

Luciano and Maria followed the same rough track for almost two hours. For most of the time its path lay through pine forest and they avoided the worst of the weather. When it emerged from the trees to climb a steep and rocky hillside, the wind drove rain into their faces so that they could only walk head down and she had to hold on to him for support.

They stopped in the shelter of an outcrop of rock and Luciano shouted. 'This is no good.'

She put a hand to his face. 'Just a moment. I think I smell wood smoke.'

She was right. He moved out of the shelter into the full force of the wind, aware instantly of the strong, pungent aroma, and they struggled on.

They came over a rise and saw a light in a hollow amongst trees. Dogs started to bark and they came to a fence and beyond, on the other side of a mud yard, was a cottage. Luciano unslung his MI and cocked it and they went across the yard. The top half of the door opened, light flooding through, and a man appeared holding a shotgun.

'Who goes?' he called.

'Travellers, caught by the night,' Luciano replied. 'We need shelter.'

'None for you here. We have trouble enough.'

He was perhaps thirty, a typical mountain man with a heavy black moustache and long unkempt hair under the cap.

He started to close the door and Luciano said, 'I got a woman with me. What kind of man are you, anyway?'

He took a step towards the door and the man raised the

shotgun to his shoulder. 'I said no. Another step and I blow your head off.'

'And answer to Mafia,' Luciano said. 'To Luca himself.'

The man froze, lowered the shotgun slowly. 'What has Don Antonio to do with this?'

Luciano pulled Maria forward. 'His grand-daughter. We're on our way to the Franciscans at Crown of Thorns.'

The shotgun came all the way down. The man hesitated; then a woman cried out in agony inside and he turned quickly.

Luciano and Maria paused at the door. The scene was incredibly primitive: bare stone walls, mud floor, an open fire on the hearth with the most rudimentary of chimneys so that the room was half-filled with smoke. There were two goats tethered beside a couple of young children wrapped in a blanket who watched what was happening at the other end of the room with great round eyes.

A young woman lay on a crude wooden bed, her face running with sweat and racked with agony. An old crone sat on a stool beside the fire stirring something in an iron pot. She had a face like wrinkled leather and wore a black scarf around her head, black dress and broken boots.

The young woman moaned again, her knees sprawling apart under the blanket, her belly swollen. Maria unlatched the lower half of the door and went in and Luciano followed her.

She leaned over the girl, placing a hand on her brow and the young man said. 'She's been in childbirth since yesterday. That's why I sent for the *strega*.'

Stregas were witches more than anything else. There was usually one in most villages who sold potions and spells that were really only herbal medicine. In the back country, they were the peasant's substitute for a doctor.

Maria started to pull back the blanket to examine the girl and the old woman reacted angrily, turning on the stool.

'*Infamita!*'

The man got hold of Maria by the wrist and twisted it. 'What are you doing? You think I want my wife shamed before strangers?'

Luciano took a handful of hair, dragged back his head and rammed the muzzle of the M1 up under his chin.

'What's your name?'

The man gasped in pain. 'Solazzo.'

'Well, listen to me. God has smiled on you tonight because the good sister here is a nurse. A real nurse from a real hospital, so stand back and leave her to it or she'll have two patients.'

The old woman at the fire started to protest. Solazzo silenced her with his hand, gazed at Luciano searchingly, then turned to Maria.

'This is true, what he says?'

'Yes,' she said.

He took off his cap, wiped his face with the back of one hand. Maria turned back to the girl on the bed who was crying now, moving her head from side to side. Maria pulled down the blanket and raised the stained shift, exposing the swollen belly.

'How long did you say she has been in labour?'

'Since yesterday afternoon.'

She leaned over the girl, examining her quickly and finally turned, her face grave. 'Mr Solazzo, we have a serious problem here. The reason for your wife's long labour is plain. A child is normally delivered head first. This one is the wrong way round.'

'God in heaven!' Solazzo said wildly and crossed himself.

'Isn't that what they call a breach?' Luciano asked.

'That's right.'

The woman cried out sharply, pushing her body up from the bed and Solazzo said, 'Help her, Sister, for the love of God.'

She raised a hand to still him. 'Exactly,' she said. 'For His sake and for hers. Now you will bring me hot water and cloths. Tear up a sheet, a shirt, anything. And as clean as possible.'

Solazzo hurried to the fire. Luciano said, 'You've got to be joking. Clean? In a hovel like this?'

'We will do the best we can, all of us,' she said. 'Including you, Mr Luciano. Now listen to me closely and I will tell you what I want you to do.'

*   *   *

Maria leaned over the young woman. 'Elena, isn't that it? I want you to trust me. Do you trust me?'

Elena Solazzo nodded wearily and Maria wiped sweat from

her face. 'When I tell you to push, use all your strength. You understand?'

Luciano was at the other end of the bed with a bowl of hot water and torn strips of linen ready. Solazzo and the old woman stood by the fire. One of the children at the other end of the room started to cry and Solazzo whispered to the old woman who went to comfort them.

Maria went to work, probing gently inside Elena for the first problem was to deliver the legs. She felt for the back of the baby's knee and prodded. The leg flexed instantly and so did the other when she repeated the trick.

'And now, Elena, push,' she said. 'Push hard!'

She held out her hands and Luciano wiped them clean and dried them. She grasped the baby firmly by the legs and pulled down until the shoulders were clear, but the arms were still inside, extended.

As Luciano watched she probed again gently, twisting to the left, hooking a finger into the left elbow and delivering the arm. A moment later, the other arm was also free.

Elena was gasping for breath like an animal, staring up at the ceiling, face contorted with pain.

'How's it going?' Luciano asked softly.

'Fine so far, but this is the most dangerous part, delivery of the head. If it's not done just right ...'

She paused and he completed the sentence for her. 'She could have an imbecile on her hands.'

Maria took a deep breath, trying to remember every aspect of her training. The essential thing was to bring the head out slowly and steadily. She put her right arm underneath the infant and got a finger into its mouth, which meant she was now supporting it.

Her other hand was on the neck, fingers spread and she started to pull. It was amazing how much strength it took; then suddenly it was clear and safe in her hands.

The baby was not breathing, was a deep shade of purple all over. She cleansed the nostrils and the mouth of mucus with strips of linen and placed a hand over the chest.

'Is it okay?' Luciano demanded.

'Oh, yes, a strong heartbeat.'

She blew into the tiny mouth, very, very gently. Quite suddenly the chest heaved and the baby started to cry. Solazzo cried out as if responding to it.

Maria tied the cord, then cut that last essential link between mother and child. 'A daughter, Mr Solazzo, in case you hadn't noticed.'

Elena was crying now, tears mingling with the sweat, and as Maria wrapped the child in strips of linen, Solazzo leaned over.

'What a little beauty. We name her after you, Sister.' He laughed out loud, tension pouring out of him.

Even the old woman was smiling and she came forward, the two children shuffling beside her, wrapped in their blanket, and the goats bleating in the shadows.

Maria washed blood from her hands in the basin. Luciano said, 'You did all right.'

'Why thank you, Mr Luciano.' She smiled back at him. 'Could I have more hot water?'

She turned and started to clean Elena's belly and thighs. Luciano went to the door and emptied the bowl into the yard. He lit a cigarette and leaned on the door, staring out into the rain. He hadn't felt so alive in years.

Solazzo appeared beside him with a bottle. 'A drink, Signor?'

Luciano took a pull. It was cheap Sicilian brandy and it burned all the way down. He choked and handed the bottle back.

Solazzo took a swig himself. 'What you said earlier about the good sister is true, Signor? She is Don Antonio's granddaughter?'

'You are of the Society?' Luciano asked.

'Since I was seventeen years. And you also Signor.' He shrugged. 'I do not need to ask. May I have the pleasure of your name?'

'Luciano.'

Solazzo's mouth gaped in astonishment. 'You – you are Luciano, Signor?'

'That's right.'

Solazzo grabbed for his right hand and kissed it. 'Don Salvatore – the Saviour. God sent you to us out of the storm tonight.'

'Very possibly,' Luciano said and glanced up.

Maria was smiling sadly at him from across the room.

*   *   *

Fifteen miles north in a small lost valley high in the Cammarata, Don Antonio Luca ate his evening meal alone, the windows to the terrace of the old rambling farmhouse open to the night. The long living room, though primitive in some respects with whitewashed walls and a stone floor, was comfortable enough with a log fire burning in the open hearth in one corner.

He sat at one end of a long dark oak table and ate sparingly of the dishes which were laid before him. *Narbe di San Paolo*, ravioli filled with sugar and richotta cheese and fried, and *cannolo*, that most famous of all Sicilian sweets. He reached for the wine bottle and, finding it empty, rang a hand bell.

The woman who entered was no more than thirty, a shapely, fleshy peasant with wide hips that stretched the conventional black cotton dress to its extremity. Her hair was night-black and fastened into a tight bun at the nape of her neck. Her skin was olive, the lines just beginning to show, and she had kind eyes.

'Another bottle, Katerina,' he said.

She went out without a word and he lit a cigar, got up and went and stirred the fire. He was sixty-five, the hair and carefully trimmed beard iron grey, a tall man still, the shoulders only slightly stooped with age.

The face was the most remarkable feature. Ruthlessness, pride, arrogance, but also a blazing intelligence. He wore the rough clothes of a mountain farmer, corduroy trousers, waist-coat, red flannel shirt, and yet there was a curious impression of elegance to him still, a suggestion of the aristocrat in gamekeeper's clothing that was strange in a man who had started life as a share-cropper's son.

Katerina came back with a fresh bottle of wine. 'Mario's here.'

'Good. Send him in and bring coffee.'

He stirred the logs with a foot and turned as the door opened again.

The man who entered was in his mid-fifties and had the face of a confident gladiator who had survived the arena. A small, greying man with an engaging presence; he could still smile as he killed, and he had killed many times on the orders of his Capo. Mario Sciara, Antonio Luca's strong right arm.

Luca said, 'Well?'

The door opened again and Katerina came in with the coffee. Sciara said, 'They are here, Don Antonio.'

'Luciano?'

'Yes.'

'And my grand-daughter? Where are they now?'

'I don't know exactly. They were at the villa of the Contessa di Bellona but there was trouble.'

'What kind of trouble?'

Katerina paused in the act of pouring coffee, waiting. Sciara said, 'You know how much the Communists have worried about increasing Mafia involvement in the resistance movement. When they heard Luciano was coming, they didn't like it. They tried to give him the business.'

'Who was it?'

'That sheepfarmer from Bellona, Russo and some boy or other. Luciano took care of it, as I understand it. They're both dead.'

'So, his hand hasn't lost its cunning. And my grand-daughter? She was there?'

'Yes, Capo.'

Luca's eyes flared and when he picked the bottle of Marsala up from the table, his hand shook. '*Infamita*. To do such a thing. Luciano can take his chances, but to place my grand-daughter's life in jeopardy.' He emptied the glass in one quick swallow. 'There were others involved?'

'Mori, the schoolmaster.'

'That bastard. Another Red. He pays, Mario, in full.'

'Already taken care of, Capo. Vito Barbera has seen to it on your behalf.'

'Good.' Luca nodded. 'One can always rely on Vito. Now, to the other business. Is the Englishman, Carter, with them?'

'Yes, Capo.'

'Excellent – I like Carter.' He turned to Katerina 'When he comes we can play bridge again with a dummy hand, but better than nothing.'

'You will see them?'

'Of course. They can come here. Make the necessary arrangements with Padre Giovanni. Now, have your coffee and tell me how the war goes.'

*   *   *

Later, standing in the darkness of his bedroom with the window open to the terrace, he watched lightning flicker over the mountain. Katerina moved in from the other room and stood beside him. She wore a robe of heavy silk and when his arm went around her, his hand cupped her left breast, his fingers stroking the nipple erect.

'You are unhappy, Antonio?'

'Can you always be so certain?'

'Of course. It is Maria, I think. You do not wish her to come? Why not? She is of your own flesh. Your only surviving blood kin. It is not natural.'

He sighed. 'How can I explain to you? As a child, I adored her and she loved me totally. She never knew her father, God rest him. I was the only man in her life. Then that day, that terrible day when she and her mother got in the car ...' his voice faded.

'My poor Antonio.' She rested a hand on his shoulder.

'She turned from me, with words of hatred on her lips.' He shook his head. 'No, my love, when she comes now, it is as if we turn over an old stone and expose the corruption that lies underneath.'

'No, Antonio. She comes with love I am sure.'

He laughed harshly. 'Is Antonio Luca a fool? Is this how he has survived all these years? She comes because I have refused to help the Americans in this coming invasion. She comes because they hope she will be able to change my mind. If it were not for that, she would not have come at all.'

There was a terrible desolation in his voice and she turned into him, holding him tight. 'Come to bed, Antonio.'

'Soon, *caro*, very soon.' He kissed her hair and pushed her gently away.

When he moved out on the terrace he could smell the mimosa, heavy and clinging on the damp air. The whole electric world waited for a sign. It came. The heavens opened and it started to rain.

13

Koenig was standing at the window of his office at the police barracks in Agrigento shortly after dawn, when Suslov and his Ukrainians drove into the courtyard below. As Koenig watched, the door opened behind him and Rudi Brandt came in with a cup of coffee.

Koenig nodded down into the courtyard as Detweiler was dragged from the *kubelwagen*. He fell to his knees and one of the Ukrainians kicked him. Then two of them ran him across the yard towards the entrance of the old police captain's house which Meyer was using as his headquarters.

'More work for the undertaker,' Koenig said.

'So it would appear, Colonel.'

'Find out who he is and report back to me.'

Brandt went out at once and Koenig opened the window. The storm of the previous night seemed to have blown itself out, but rain drifted against the window in a fine spray. He felt old beyond his years, unaccountably depressed, as he sipped his coffee and watched Rudi Brandt cross the courtyard below.

★　　★　　★

Detweiler, his wits sharpened considerably by fear, stood in front of Meyer's desk and waited. The Major ignored him, watching while Suslov took various items from the rucksack: ammunition clips, several grenades, chocolate K-rations. He laid them down beside the MI and the Colt automatic.

'So?' Meyer said.

'The weapons would appear to be brand-new, Major.'

Meyer picked up Detweiler's false papers. 'Who have we

here?' He spoke without looking up. 'Mario Brazzi, born Palermo, 1917. It says here you are a shepherd by profession?'

'Yes, sir,' Detweiler said, keeping his head down.

'Employed by whom?'

Detweiler stayed with the story Carter had outlined for him at Maison Blanche. 'Times are hard. I move from place to place. A few days here, a few days there.'

'Discharged from the Fifteenth Infantry Brigade in February as a result of a chest wound received in North Africa.'

'That's right, sir.'

Meyer nodded and Suslov put down the M1, reached across and tore open his shirt. The great raised scar of a gunshot wound was clearly visible on the left side of Detweiler's chest, souvenir of the ill-fated Dieppe landings.

Meyer sat back. 'We would appear to have a paradox. Mario Brazzi, wounded veteran and honest shepherd, found wandering the hills with brand new American weapons, American chocolate and K-rations.' He turned to Suslov. 'What would that suggest to you, *Obersturmführer*?'

'A supply drop to partisans in the area, probably very recent, Major, judging by the carbine and the other items.'

Detweiler pulled out all the stops to stay in character. 'I'm an honest man, I swear it. I stayed the night in a shepherd's hut on the other side of Viterba, high in the mountains. I found all this stuff hidden under the straw.'

Meyer grimaced and Suslov picked up the M1 and drove the butt into the pit of Detweiler's stomach with all his strength. Detweiler lay on his face, retching.

Meyer said. 'Let's try again.'

They hauled him to his feet, and at that moment the door opened and Koenig entered. He wore a camouflaged jump jacket over his uniform, his old NCO's fieldcap slanted over one eye.

'Ah, there you are, Meyer,' he said. 'I'm just off.' He paused, suitably surprised. 'What's all this?'

Meyer had long since learned to control his anger in Koenig's presence.

He jumped to his feet. 'A partisan, or so we think, Colonel. Suslov picked him up in the mountains with various items of

American equipment. It would appear some sort of drop's taken place in that area recently.'

Koenig picked up the Colt, hefted it and put it back on the desk. 'And what does he have to say?'

'That he found all this hidden under the straw in a shepherd's hut.'

Koenig looked Detweiler over and the sergeant, supported by the two Ukrainians, kept his head down, trying to catch his breath.

Koenig said, 'It's possible, I suppose.'

Meyer was astonished. 'Colonel?'

'Put him in a cell, give him something to eat and twenty four hours to think about his situation. I'm going up to command headquarters in Palermo, but I'll be back some time tomorrow. I'll see him then.'

Meyer smiled slightly. 'As you say, Colonel.'

Koenig walked to the door and opened it. He turned, 'And I'd like to find him still in one piece. Do impress that on your men. They have a tendency to get a trifle over-enthusiastic on these occasions and that would not please me at all.'

'Certainly, Colonel, that goes without saying.'

The door closed and Suslov said, 'This is crazy, Major. Just let me have my way with this bastard.'

Meyer shook his head. 'When the right moment comes I intend to have Koenig's head, believe me, but I'm not going to jeopardize the situation by a conflict over something like this. It isn't important enough.'

'So what do we do with this one?'

As Detweiler couldn't speak German he had been unable to follow what was going on. He waited fearfully, trying to play the cringing peasant, with only the expression on Meyer's face giving him a clue as to what was going on.

Meyer said thoughtfully, 'Twenty-four hours to think things over, the Colonel said. Very well, let's give him just that. Take him down to twenty-two.'

'*Zu befehl, Sturmbannführer.*' Suslov nodded to his men and they dragged Detweiler out.

*　　*　　*

They descended stone steps, Suslov leading the way followed by the two Ukrainians holding Detweiler between them.

Detweiler's mind worked furiously, assessing the possibilities. He'd been prepared for this sort of situation in training, of course. Solitary confinement that's what they usually started with, and in total darkness. He remembered what the psychiatrist lecturing to them had said. Sensory deprivation leading to total alienation of the individual. Okay, but all he had to do was hang on because he knew something these bastards didn't. That the invasion was due any day now.

They paused outside a cell door and Suslov unlocked it. The stench was appalling. When Detweiler was pushed forward he saw, as the light flooded in, that there were twelve or more filthy and ragged creatures huddled together on the floor in that confined space.

Suslov nodded and the two Ukrainians started to rip off Detweiler's clothes. When he was naked, they handcuffed his hands behind him. Detweiler had never felt so vulnerable in his life as Meyer came down the stairs and walked along the passage. He looked Detweiler over calmly, then moved into the entrance of the cell.

'Now listen to me,' he said in his bad Italian. 'This man doesn't lie down, doesn't sit, gets no rest whatsoever. And he isn't to sleep when standing. You take turns to make sure my orders are carried out. If you fail me, no water, no food for one week. Just each other.'

He nodded to Suslov who shoved Detweiler down into the cell and slammed the door. Detweiler fell over a prostrate body, aware of the stench of the place and kicked out frantically.

There were hands everywhere, crawling all over him, pulling him to his feet. Someone said hoarsely, 'I don't know who you are, friend, and we couldn't care less. It's dog eat dog in here. That means we do what that Gestapo bastard wants and you do what we want.'

Detweiler stood there in the darkness, suddenly terribly afraid. 'Listen to me, for God's sake,' he began.

The same hoarse voice said, 'God has nothing to do with it, so be a good boy and do exactly as you're told.'

*   *   *

In late spring and early summer, when the first real heat begins, violent thunderstorms are common in the Sicilian high country. It started to rain again as Savage and Rosa followed a track along a ridge between two mountain peaks.

He said, 'Does it always rain this much in Sicily?'

She laughed. 'No, this is not usual.'

Not that Savage minded. Some people were rainwalkers by nature. It gave them a lift just to be out in the stuff. The rainstorm which broke over the Cammarata that morning worked its usual magic on him. The earth came alive and there was a freshness to everything.

She took his arm. 'One thing I don't understand. Last night when you were making love to me.'

'Which time was that.' He tried to keep his face straight. 'The third or fourth?'

'No, early this morning, when you woke from sleep. You kept apologizing for being no good. You said you were much better at shooting people.'

'I don't remember,' he lied

'But you are a wonderful lover. You pleased me many times.'

He was thoroughly embarrassed. 'You shouldn't talk like that.'

'Like what?' she demanded. 'What did I say that was so terrible?'

'Let it go,' he said. 'Just let it go.'

She pulled him round and looked up at his face, grave beneath the peak of the old tweed cap. 'I don't know what they've been telling you all these years, but you are not the man they think you are.' She reached up and touched his face gently. 'Or the man they have told you to be.'

He put an arm around her and pulled her close. 'How come all this wisdom in one so young?'

'Because I was a whore,' she said harshly. 'In Palermo. But you knew this about me, I think?'

He was filled with a sense of overwhelming affection, leaned down and kissed her gently.

'Come on,' he said. 'We'd better make tracks for the monastery and find out what's happened to the others.'

*   *   *

Luciano and Maria walked quietly together through the morning rain. She said, 'I wish I hadn't had to leave that child.'

'You've provided one miracle to start with,' he said. 'It'll survive. Bound to after such a start. Anyway, I thought you were in the faith business?'

'And you're not?'

'I deal in facts.'

'You don't hate the Germans?'

'Do you?'

'I hate some of the things they've done.'

'Life's a whole lot simpler than that for me.'

'You reject any kind of personal commitment.'

Luciano shrugged. 'I know what I am. That tells me who I am. I like you, so I'm on your side.'

'And the Germans?'

'I haven't even seen one yet.'

'It's a game to you, all of it, isn't it, Mr Luciano, just like Mafia?' She shook her head. 'With your rules like some game for schoolboys. Your *omerta*. Manliness, honour, solve your own problems and kill your enemy face-to-face.'

'Everyone plays games,' he said. 'It helps you get by in life, haven't you noticed that? Flickering candles, medieval robes, plainsong, a man dressed in a woman's robe to wash your spirit clean at frequent intervals? Now what in the hell am I supposed to make of that?'

Before she could reply they emerged from the trees and saw a small village in the valley below.

'The place Solazzo mentioned,' she said. 'Viterba.'

Luciano nodded. 'Okay, let's go down and take a look. See if I can find this guy, Verda, that Solazzo spoke of.'

It was a poor sort of place. Several streets slanted down to a square, mainly open sewers if the stench was anything to go by. Thin children played listlessly in the dirt, stopping to gaze apathetically as Luciano and Maria went by. There was a wine shop, an awning stretched over a few tables outside, rain pouring over the edge.

Luciano said to Maria, 'Wait here, I'll see if he's inside.'

She sat at one of the tables and he went in. It was very dark, a few tables only and a cracked marble bar with bottles behind.

There were no customers, only a short, thick-set man in open-necked shirt and soiled white apron, who leaned on the bar reading a magazine.

He looked up warily. 'Yes?'

'Mario Solazzo sent me.'

'So?'

'I'm trying to get to the Franciscans at Crown of Thorns. He said you'd put us on the way.'

'Us?'

'I have a woman with me.' There was a long pause and Luciano said patiently, 'You are Verda, aren't you? I was told you were of the Society.'

Verda stared at him blankly and his hand was under the bar now. 'So?'

Luciano said, 'I'm going to take something out of my right hand pocket so don't shoot me. It isn't a gun.'

He produced a yellow silk handkerchief and unfolded it. Verda looked down at the black L and his eyes widened. His hand emerged, holding a Beretta automatic of the type issued to Italian officers, and he placed it carefully on the bar.

'L for Luciano.' He looked up slowly. Luciano stood there, head back, a hand on his right hip. Verda whispered. 'You've come, just like they said you would.'

He went round the bar and raised Luciano's hand to his lips and at the same moment, Maria cried out in pain. Luciano turned and ran for the door.

*   *   *

She was pressed back against one of the tables. The two men crowding her were typical of the young men of the region: Shabby clothes, broken boots, features brutalized and coarse from a life of toil.

One of them had his arms around her, hands moving over her buttocks, a cruel smile on his face. He whispered some obscenity in her ear, and she slapped his face. To a Sicilian, a woman is there to be used, to do as she is told. To be publicly humiliated by one is unthinkable. The young man raised his hand to strike.

Luciano grabbed him by the wrist and spun him round. They stared at each other, face to face. Already, the other man's expression was changing, first to dismay, then fear. It was not that he recognized Luciano, but what he saw clearly in that implacable face was the self-sufficiency, the quiet arrogance, the power of the *mafioso*.

Luciano slapped him. The man didn't say a word; simply stood there. His friend touched his arm and they walked backwards, faces blank, turned and hurried away.

Verda said, 'Don Salvatore, what can I say? And you, Signorina.'

'This good lady is one of the sisters of Pity,' Luciano informed him. 'There are reasons for her being dressed like this. She is also Don Antonio Luca's granddaughter.'

Verda turned in astonishment to look at her then caught her hand and kissed it before she could prevent him. 'Please come in. Eat with me and then I'll see you on the road to the monastery.'

*   *   *

Savage and Rosa went over a rise and paused. There was a village about half a mile to the right and below them, in the side of the valley.

'What's that place?' he demanded.

'Viterba, but we keep going this way, where the track climbs up beyond the church to the ridge. The monastery is five miles on the other side.'

As they started down the track he said, 'A strange place to have a church, out here on its own.'

'Not really. The villages in the high country are not large enough to have their own church and priest. People walk from many places to this one. It is served by the Franciscan.'

As they approached, Savage was aware of the sound of an engine close at hand and turned to see a *kubelwagen* emerge from the trees in the valley below. It carried three men, one of them sitting behind a heavy machine gun.

He raised his fieldglasses and examined them quickly. 'Germans.'

'No,' she said. 'Ukrainians – members of the SS Special
Group run by a man called Meyer. He's a Gestapo major
operating out of Agrigento.'

She grabbed his arm and hurried him along. 'Heh,' he said,
'What is this?'

'The church – we'll hide in the church.'

She was right, of course. They had really no other choice, for
the track carried on for hundreds of yards across bare mountainside. Before they could get anywhere, they were certain to be
spotted.

There was a donkey tethered outside. They moved past it and
Rosa opened the door and led the way in. It was very quiet, only
the candles, incense heavy on the damp morning air. Down by
the altar, the Virgin seemed to float out of darkness, a slight fixed
smile on her face.

Three people waited by a confessional box, a boy, an old man
an even older woman who wore the usual black headscarf and a
decaying sheepskin coat against the cold. She looked at Rosa and
Savage curiously.

Savage peered through the partially open door as the *kubelwagen* braked to a halt. The Ukrainians got out and stood beside
the fieldcar lighting cigarettes and talking, then all three of them
started up the path to the church.

They were casual enough, obviously expecting no trouble.
The corporal who led the way carried a sidearm at his belt and
the other two had Schmeissers. Savage unslung his M1,
evaluating his chances of taking all three before they knew what
was happening.

Rosa said softly, 'You might get the corporal, but not the
other two.'

'So what do we do?'

'Give me that.' She pulled the M1 from his hands. 'And now
the pack.' He did as he was told and she quickly stowed them
away behind the confessional box. The two old people and the
boy watched impassively.

'We're here to see the priest to discuss our marriage plans.'
She pulled him over to a pew in the shadows behind the others.
'No trouble, I can handle it.'

'Like you have before?'

'Sure,' she said. 'They're men, aren't they? German, Russian – what's the difference?'

'I'm the difference, damn you! I'm the difference!'

He took off his cap and slipped a Browning automatic out of his right hand pocket. He held it in his lap, covered by the cap, without Rosa being aware of the fact and waited.

There was silence, the murmur of the priest's voice in the confessional mingling with the suppliant's. The door opened and steps approached, boots ringing on the flagstones.

'So, what have we got here?' the corporal said in bad Italian.

He paused at the old people before moving on to Rosa and Savage. He stood looking down at them and the other two moved up beside him. Tough, brutal men who looked as if they'd seen everything and experienced most things.

'What are you doing here?' he demanded.

'Waiting to see the priest,' Rosa said.

'What for? To confess your sins.' Their laughter had an ugly ring to it.

She smiled ingratiatingly. 'We're getting married next week and need to see the good father to make the arrangements.'

'Married, eh?' He moved round behind her.

'Nice?' the corporal appealed to the other two and slipped a hand inside the bodice of her dress, cupping the left breast. 'Virgin, are you?'

'Yes.'

'We'll have to do something about that.' He yanked her to her feet and pulled Savage's head back by the hair at the same time. 'I'm doing you a favour, son, you do realize that?'

He took her by the arm and she twisted, pleading with Savage. 'Please, no trouble. It's nothing. I can handle it.'

As the corporal propelled her up the aisle one of the others called, 'Don't forget your friends.' He turned, grinning. 'If I know him, he'll have her on the altar.'

The other put one foot on the pew beside Savage and leaned over him. 'You don't mind, do you? Like he says, he's doing you a favour. In fact, we're in such a generous mood today, we've all decided to do you a favour.'

Savage fired through the cap, shooting him in the heart at point-blank range, killing him instantly. He shoved the body away, the Browning arching towards the other man who was frantically trying to unsling his Schmeisser. Savage's second bullet caught him in the left shoulder, spinning him round. The third shattered his spine, driving him headfirst across the back of one of the pews.

As Savage turned, the corporal already had Rosa in front of him and was jerking the Walther from his holster. He rammed it into her side.

'Drop it or she dies now.'

But exactly this kind of situation had been a feature of OSS training. Savage's arm swung up and he shot him through the head instantly, the top of the corporal's skull fragmenting as he was hurled back against the altar rail.

Savage rushed for Rosa's hand. He pulled her away and, turning, found the old couple and the boy already making for the door fast followed by another old woman who had just emerged from the confessional box with the priest.

He was about fifty, bearded and wore the brown robes of the Franciscans. He came forward, his face strangely calm considering the circumstances. Without a word he proceeded to check the three Ukrainians.

'All dead. Who are you?'

'We were on our way to Crown of Thorns to see Padre Giovanni,' Rosa said. 'I am Vito Barbera's niece and this is an American officer, Captain Savage.'

'I am Brother Lucio,' the Franciscan said.

Savage retrieved his rucksack and M1 and moved to the door quickly. 'The donkey is still there.'

'Mine,' said Lucio.

'Those people? What about them?'

'All they want to do is get home and forget this ever happened. They're too old and frightened to want to be involved.' He turned to survey the carnage. 'But we'll have to do something about this.'

'What do you mean?' Savage asked.

'If the corpses are found here, it would mean heavy reprisals for Viterba. Much better they disappear all together. Help me and we'll take them out to the fieldcar.'

'I'll clean up in here,' Rosa said.

She found a bucket in the vestry, filled it with water from the spring outside the door, went back inside and started to mop the blood from the stone floor with a rag as Savage and Lucio returned for another body. When they came back for the corporal, she was cleaning the altar beside his body.

Savage said, 'Are you okay?'

'You think I'm worried about a pig like that?'

She stirred the corpse with her toe and Savage said, 'Okay, you needn't act so tough. We'll be back in a little while.'

He and Lucio put the corporal in the rear of the *kubelwagen* with the other two, then Savage and the Franciscan got into the front and Savage drove away, following his instructions.

They left the track further down the slope towards the village and turned into the forest, bumping over rough ground between trees. Finally, Lucio tapped Savage on the shoulder and he braked to a halt at the top of a short slope above a dark and stagnant pond.

'Here, I think.'

They got out and together, put their shoulders to the fieldcar. It ran forward, gathering momentum, ploughed through a screen of young firs and plunged into the pond. One of the bodies was pitched out and the fieldcar turned over on top of him, the other two still inside. It didn't take long to disappear.

'Right,' Savage said.

'A moment, Captain, please.'

Lucio folded his hands and recited in a firm voice the prayers for the dying. *Go, Christian Soul, from this world, in the name of God the Father Almighty who created thee.* By the time he was finished, the surface mud had settled.

He crossed himself and said gravely, 'And now we go, I think.'

They hurried back up the slope through the trees and along the track to the church. Rosa was waiting outside by the donkey.

Brother Lucio said, 'You've cleaned up thoroughly?'

'Of course.'

He swung a leg over the donkey, adjusted his robe and set off. Savage and Rosa followed behind.

'Are you all right?' he asked her.

'Sure.' She took out her old tobacco tin and lit a cigarette, inhaled a couple of times and passed it to him. 'There was no need. I could have handled it.'

'No,' he said violently. 'Never again. You understand me?'

'Sure I do. I think maybe you like me Savage.'

'I think maybe you're right.'

'Good,' she said calmly. 'Perhaps I make you a little bit crazy again tonight.'

Savage, hopelessly and genuinely in love for the first time in his life, pulled her into his arms and kissed her, then they hurried after Brother Lucio.

*   *   *

Maria knelt in prayer in front of the altar of the chapel at Crown of Thorns, at peace again for the first time in days, once more a part of a calm and ordered world that she understood. Luciano and Padre Giovanni stood in the shadows by the door.

'Have you heard from Don Antonio yet?' Luciano asked.

'Not a word.'

'What do you think he'll make of her?' Luciano nodded down towards Maria.

The old man smiled faintly. 'A very remarkable young woman. A whiff of holiness would not come amiss in Don Antonio's life, but frankly, I think the fact that Maria is a nun will have little effect on him. He is a strange, stubborn man. Quite unique. Himself alone.'

The door opened, a young brother entered and whispered in his ear. Padre Giovanni said to Luciano, 'It appears that your friends have arrived.'

He turned and led the way out to the terraced cloisters.

Luciano looked over the rail and saw Savage and Rosa crossing the courtyard.

'Heh, you two,' he called. 'What kept you?'

14

Padre Giovanni led the way down the winding stone stair to the crypt of the monastery. He was preceded by a young monk carrying a couple of lanterns on a pole. Savage and Luciano followed behind.

'These cellars, more than anything else, have made Crown of Thorns famous all over Sicily,' Padre Giovanni told them.

The young monk raised the pole high and Savage saw that the place was a charnel house, the bones of the dead visible on every hand. Ribs, pelvises, hands, feet, femurs, tibulas, all cemented into the architecture. There were skulls piled everywhere.

The most horrifying aspect was the bodies, some lying down, some seated, others hanging from pegs. Many were total skeletons, but others retained skin and hair, even eyes and tattered vestiges of clothing.

'What in the hell goes on here?' Savage asked in horror. 'Who were these people?'

'Only the best, Captain Savage, I assure you,' Padre Giovanni told him. 'Sicilian aristocrats over the ages have taken it as a privilege to make this their final resting place. You will find much the same thing in the catacombs of Cappuchin Zita Church in Palermo.'

The remains of a child in a tattered velvet suit hung from a peg nearby and Savage shuddered and turned away.

Luciano said, 'To the Sicilian, death is ever present and always important. In some villages on All Souls Day, families make pilgrimages to the graves of the departed, taking their favourite food. They sit around the graves at midnight by candlelight. They leave presents for the dead in church.'

'And why not?' Padre Giovanni said. 'It reminds us that we all come to the same end. But I didn't bring you down here to find a suitable setting for a sermon. Over here, gentlemen.'

In one corner of the crypt was an ancient wooden throne in black oak, shaped as a Norman arch and set into the stone. A decaying figure was enthroned in the seat, attired in a Franciscan robe, the hood drawn over the skull.

'Padre Leonardo, prior of the monastery at the end of the last century.'

He turned a carved wooden rose in the top right hand corner and pushed and the throne swung back with its macabre burden, revealing a dark tunnel.

'This dates from Saracen times,' Padre Giovanni said. 'A way of retreat if things become too hopeless. For you also, I think, which is why it seemed sensible I show it to you.'

'Have the Germans given you much trouble here at the monastery, Father?' Savage asked.

'On occasion. Colonel Koenig and his paratroopers were here three weeks ago. They searched the monastery most thoroughly.'

'Were they looking for somebody?'

'No, I think Koenig merely wished to familiarize himself with the situation here. A strange young man. Courteous and decent in the extreme. Not like those Ukrainians of Major Meyer. We've had them here too.'

Luciano said, 'So this tunnel emerges somewhere outside the walls?'

'About a quarter of a mile down the slope. Too far for my old legs to walk, but Filippo will show you the way.' He reached up and took one of the lanterns from the pole. 'I'll see you later.'

He turned and walked back through the crypt. Brother Filippo started into the tunnel. Savage glanced sideways at the ghoul in the hooded robe on the wooden throne and hesitated, unwilling to pass him.

Luciano said cheerfully, 'He reminds me of a judge I once knew, but that's another story. Come on, let's get moving.'

He gave Savage a push and they moved on into the tunnel, following Brother Fillipo.

*   *   *

Detweiler leaned against the wall in a daze. He had never been so tired in his life and every limb, every muscle in his body seemed to ache. Conditions in the cell were appalling. The place stank like a sewer and he was weak and light-headed.

He had no idea how long he had been there just as he had lost count of the number of times he had attempted to slump down to the ground and had been kicked and beaten back on to his feet. A man could only take so much, training or no training, that was apparent. There was a rattle of bolts, the door opened and a shaft of yellow light flooded in.

*   *   *

He stood under a warm shower washing himself, watched by one of the Ukrainian guards. Standing in the passage outside, Meyer and Suslov peered in through the small glass window in the door.

Meyer said, 'I've just received word that Koenig's been detained in Palermo by General Guzzoni. He won't be returning until tomorrow.'

'An interesting situation,' Suslov said. 'Fraught with possibilities, especially where our friend in there is concerned.'

'Exactly.'

Meyer opened the door and went in followed by Suslov. Detweiler turned, instinctively covering his private parts with his hands.

Meyer said, 'I've considered your case and I've now decided you can go.'

Detweiler said stupidly, 'Go?'

Meyer ignored him and said to Suslov 'Give him his clothes, see he gets something to eat, then kick him out.'

He walked out. Suslov said, 'You're bloody lucky, my friend. If I had my way. Still ...' He nodded to the guard. 'Get him dressed, then take him to the canteen.'

He went out and the guard threw Detweiler a towel. Detweiler dried himself quickly, then dressed in his clothes which had been piled neatly on the bench. It was incredible. His story had actually worked. The bastards were going to let him go.

In the canteen, he worked his way through a large plateful of some kind of spaghetti. There was black bread, cheese in plenty, real coffee. He was beginning to feel almost human again.

There was no one else in the canteen. The guard said, 'Had enough?'

'Sure,' Detweiler told him.

'Okay, follow me.'

They went out and along the corridor and the guard opened a door leading into a small whitewashed cell with a bunk bed with a mattress on it. He gave Detweiler a cigarette and lit it for him.

'Wait here. I'll tell Lieutenant Suslov you're ready to go.'

He went out, closing the door behind him and Detweiler relaxed, inhaling deeply on the cigarette. The next stage was the important one now. How to make contact with Carter and the others. And with Suslov out of the way ...

There was a sudden hideous clamour. He looked up and saw that an electric bell jangled above the door. Then the door burst open and they rushed in, four of them, and flung themselves on him.

He was kicked and beaten all the way along the passage, dragged by the ankles down a flight of stone steps, ending up in a corner, arms raised against the flailing truncheons. When they finally stopped he looked up fearfully and found Meyer and Suslov looking down at him.

Meyer said, 'Now you know exactly where you stand. Have you anything to say to me?'

To Detweiler, in spite of his weakened state, one thing was obvious. The slightest hint of his true identity and God alone knew what they might do to him. So, he stayed in character.

'Please, Major, I'm a poor man,' he whined. 'I know nothing.'

Meyer turned to Suslov. 'He's all yours.'

As he walked away, Suslov nodded to his men. They pulled Detweiler to his feet and made him stand against the wall braced on his fingertips, legs apart. One of them placed a bag of some black material over his head leaving him in total darkness. The pain in his fingers was already intense. He groaned, moving slightly and a truncheon flailed across his kidneys.

*   *   *

Maria leaned on the battlements, staring out across the mountains to the Cammarata rising almost six thousand feet into the sky. The side of the valley was carpeted with flowers, fresh because of the rain. Red poppies, anemones, blue iris, spreading in the distance.

Padre Giovanni came up the steps to join her. 'So, here you are.' He nodded out over the land. 'Well, what do you think?'

'Nothing changes,' she said.

He nodded. 'There are caves up there that used to hide Roman slaves two thousand years ago.' He sat down. 'Are you glad to be home?'

'Home?' she said. 'This isn't home, Father. Not to me. We are taught that to hate is a mortal sin and yet I believe, with all my heart, that I hate this place.'

'And your grandfather?'

'Antonio Luca,' she said. 'Capo mafia in all Sicily. Lord of Life and Death. Does the church permit me to love such a man?'

'My child,' Giovanni said, 'it was not your grandfather who killed your mother. It was evil men who plotted his death.'

'He was responsible,' she said, 'because of what he was. If you defend him, you defend Mafia. How can you, a priest, defend that?'

'I don't,' he said tranquilly. 'I defend no one. I deal in human souls as instructed by our Lord Jesus Christ in the Gospels.'

The gate opened and before she could reply Carter and Barbera entered the courtyard below, riding on mules.

*　　*　　*

Barbera said, 'As far as we know Detweiler was arrested and taken to the barracks at Agrigento.'

'How did they find him?' Savage demanded.

'An informer. He'll be taken care of.'

They were seated at one of the refectory tables where meals were eaten; Savage and Rosa and Barbera on one side, Luciano, Carter and Maria on the other. Padre Giovanni was at the head of the table. He poured red wine into his glass and passed the bottle to Luciano.

'Even if Major Meyer is unaware of Sergeant Detweiler's true identity, he will still, I fear, be subjected to considerable brutality.' He turned to Savage. 'How strong would you say he is, Captain?'

'Oh, he's tough enough,' Savage said. 'Once during a commando raid on the French coast, he walked twenty miles to our rendezvous with a bullet in the foot.'

Barbera said, 'Most men have their breaking point. Once Detweiler opens his mouth, they'll be looking for us.'

'Which means we must see Luca as soon as possible,' Carter said.

Brother Fillipo entered, holding a pigeon in his hand. He stroked it soothingly while Padre Giovanni unfastened the tiny capsule from its left leg. He prised it open with a finger nail, took out the paper it contained and unrolled it. He examined it, looked up and smiled.

'In the morning, my friends. He will see you in the morning.'

*   *   *

There were two additional members of the district committee replacing Mori and Russo. They were waiting in the living room at the back of the mortuary when Barbera entered with Harry Carter and Luciano. Barbera made the introductions.

'Father Collura, you know, Harry, representing the Christian Democrats. Mario Verga who runs the inn here speaks for the Separatist movement.'

'Father.' Carter shook hands. 'Signor Verga. Good to see you again.' He turned to the other two men. 'And these gentlemen?'

'Zizzo and Valachi,' Barbera said, 'Of the Communist Party. There have been changes in that respect.'

Zizzo, a small, dark man in gamekeeper's leggings and corduroy suit said angrily, 'Stuff the pretty talk, Barbera. Pietro Mori murdered in his own home and Ettore Russo, our leader, vanished off the face of the earth. A direct attack on the whole Communist movement and we know who is responsible.'

'You make me sick,' Carter said. 'All of you. Nearly two years since I first came to Sicily and you haven't changed a bit, like boys, stoning each other on the way home from school for no good reason. I couldn't care less who rules Sicily after the war.

You can sort that out amongst yourselves. For the moment, the question isn't, do you want rid of Mussolini and the Fascist Party. It's, do you want rid of the Germans?'

Father Collura said mildly, 'I agree with Colonel Carter. First, we get rid of our enemies. Afterwards, when Sicily is free again, we discuss our future democratically amongst ourselves.'

The two Communists reacted angrily. Valachi said, 'Fine words which mean nothing. Why should we listen to Carter anyway? Is he one of us? No – a stranger, interested only in the needs of his own people. The English and Americans don't give a damn for Sicily or its people. We're just another pawn in the Capitalist imperialist struggle.'

Carter was tired. There was that pain in his lung again. When he breathed it hurt. More than that, he was weary. Tired of the scheming, the feuds, the personal vendettas. He was about to turn away in disgust when suddenly, Luciano was beside him.

'Why should you listen? I'll tell you why, you stupid bastards.' He tore open Carter's shirt with one quick movement, exposing the livid, raised scars left by his chest wounds. 'He's made his bones, the Professor. Two months ago, they carried him out of here in a coffin with a bullet in the lung. How much has that taken off his life at the other end? Why do you think he's come back – for the good of his health?'

Carter said, 'You're talking into the wind, my friend, and the words blow back unheard.'

He went out. There was a heavy silence. Zizzo said, 'What in the hell has it got to do with you, anyway.' He turned on Barbera. 'Who is this guy?'

Luciano took his time over lighting a cigarette. 'An interesting point,' he said. 'To the priest who baptized me I'm Salvatore Lucania, but to most people I'm simply Luciano.' His smile was terrible to see. 'Lucky Luciano. Would you like me to tell you why?'

Both Zizzo and Valachi recoiled in horror and Father Collura moved in quickly. 'Please, Don Salvatore, no harm was intended, no offence, I'm sure.'

There was a wooden, hand-painted icon of Our Lady and the Holy Infant on the far wall. Luciano's hand came out of his pocket holding the ivory Madonna, there was a click, he swung underhand and the point of the stiletto buried itself in the icon.

'You see, Father, the knife in the heart of the Virgin, something we Sicilians understand.'

There was a dreadful silence. He dominated the room now. 'Cards on the table. Come with me, all of you.'

He nodded to Barbera, who led the way through the waiting mortuary into the preparation room. Two bodies lay side by side covered by sheets. Barbera pulled back the first one to disclose the thin aesthetic features of Pietro Mori. The face had been carefully made up, the lips touched with carmine. He even wore his glasses.

'And here?' Barbera uncovered the other corpse and exposed Ettore Russo.

'We came at great personal risk to help the cause,' Luciano said. 'But these two used the occasion to work off some personal grudge against Mafia. Russo was the instrument. He and the misguided youth with him paid the price, but it was Mori who stood behind the deed. He made the worst mistake of his life, not in attacking me, but in exposing to danger of her life the granddaughter of Don Antonio Luca who was with me at the Villa Bellona at the time.'

'Holy Mother of God!' Zizzo whispered.

'Please, Don Salvatore,' Valachi had his cap off now. 'Such a thing was *infamita* and never intended. You must believe this.' He turned to Barbera. 'Vito, you can surely make plain to the good Don Antonio that this was none of our doing.'

'Of course,' Barbera said. 'Although in Don Antonio's eyes, deeds speak louder than words. The fact that the district committee speaks with one voice in future; that we work together against the common enemy in the coming invasion, would impress him as an earnest of your good faith.'

Zizzo said eagerly, 'You may rely on us of the Communist Party.'

'Politics are politics,' Valachi said. 'But we're all Sicilians first.'

Luciano moved to the window and lit another cigarette. Barbera said, 'So, the invasion will come and very soon now. You and your people must hold yourselves ready with all weapons at your command and when the time comes, you

take your orders from Colonel Carter. You understand this?'
'Yes,' Zizzo said.

Father Collura said, 'The co-operation of we of the Christian
Democrats Party goes without saying.'

Luciano turned. 'All in order now?'

Barbera nodded. 'So it would appear.'

'Good. So long as we understand each other.'

He stood there waiting, left hand on hip, head thrown back.
Zizzo and Valachi shuffled forward in turn and kissed his right
hand.

*   *   *

Savage couldn't sleep. There wasn't much room in the small bed
with Rosa squeezed in beside him. The old shirt she wore
instead of a night shift had rucked up so that her breasts were
warm against him and her hand had fallen across his stomach. In
sleep she looked not so much young as vulnerable.

Lying there with an arm about her seemed the most natural
thing in the world. He felt warm, secure and content. He
managed to turn up the lamp with one hand, lit a cigarette and
reached for a small tattered volume on the bedside locker. It was
the poetry anthology his grandfather had given him on his
thirteenth birthday. He had read it a thousand times and the
contents never bored him.

Rosa stirred and opened her eyes. She said sleepily, 'What are
you doing?'

'Reading.'

'But what?'

'Poetry.'

She touched his ear with her tongue and her hand slid down
his stomach to hold him. 'Is it better than me, this poetry?'

'You can't compare the two things.'

'So?' she pouted. 'This is how much you love me?'

'No,' he said. 'Sometimes the poetry can say how much, far
better than I can.'

'I don't believe you. Show me what you're reading now.'

'I don't need to. I know it by heart. It was written a long time
ago by a very great Englishman. Sir Walter Raleigh. He was just

about everything a man could be. A gentleman in the true sense of the word, a fine soldier, musician, writer, poet.'

'What happened to him?'

'They chopped off his head. The king was jealous of him.'

She said, 'The poem? What about this poem?'

He said aloud in English, quietly and softly,

> 'But true love is a durable fire
> In the mind ever burning:
> Never sick, never old, never dead,
> From itself never turning.'

She hardly understood the meaning of the words, but the poignancy was there. She started to weep, deeply and bitterly, as if mourning that lost innocence and everything that had ever happened to her. Savage, out of some strange perception, knew exactly what was taking place here.

He held her close, thinking about Boston and his mother and the whole Savage clan and Rosa. Suddenly he felt unaccountably cheerful. If they don't like it, he thought, they can do the other thing. She was asleep again now and he held her close, listening to the rain outside the open window.

*   *   *

In the cubbyhole at the back of the coffin room, Barbera sat at the radio while Carter and Luciano drank coffee and waited. Finally, Barbera took off his headphones and turned, his face suffused with excitement.

'They come,' he said. 'The day after tomorrow.'

Carter got to his feet and paced nervously across the room. 'It doesn't give us much time.'

'Come on, Harry,' Luciano said. 'We see Luca tomorrow. One meeting is all it takes. Afterwards, he sends messages all over Western Sicily and how long does that take? A few hours only.'

Barbera had already taken a bottle and three glasses from a cupboard. He filled them quickly.

'A drink, I think, would be in order.' He turned and twiddled the dial on the receiver. 'Let's see what the British Forces radio has to offer from Cairo.'

The music was distant and far away and the voice of the man singing was strangely compelling, something of the night in it.

'I like that,' Luciano said. 'Who is it?'

'Al Bowlly,' Carter told him. 'One of my weaknesses. Did I ever tell you I play a very fair jazz piano? He was an English crooner, South African originally. Number One in the hit parade for years. He was killed in the Blitz in forty-one. That's "Moonlight on the Highway", probably the best thing he ever did. Recorded with the Lew Stone orchestra in March, 1938.

The haunting melody filled the room. Luciano said, 'What a way to go.'

'His own choice. He was walking down Brewer Street when a bomb fell and the blast went the other way. From then on he believed in his luck, so when the siren sounded and other people went to the shelters, he stayed in bed.'

'And paid for it with his life?' Barbera said.

'Exactly.' Carter smiled. 'But this is getting morbid. A toast, gentlemen. Now, what shall we drink to?'

'Why, to all three of us,' Luciano smiled. 'And to Luciano's luck. May it hold.'

15

They left just after nine the following morning in Barbera's old truck; Luciano, Carter and Savage in the rear while Maria sat up front with Barbera.

It had stopped raining and it was already apparent that it was going to be a hot day. The truck climbed the dusty road into the mountains, passing through a medieval landscape, one wretched village after another, most of the houses windowless, the doors opening into dark caverns which in most cases housed livestock as well as people.

Luciano said, 'What a bloody country. 1907, when my people took us to America to get away from this and thirty-six years later, nothing's changed.'

'Was the east side of New York any better?' Carter asked.

They passed a long line of gaunt women, baskets on their heads, dressed in black as if mourning their daily existence, shoulders bowed as they struggled up the steep road.

'Professor,' Luciano said with deep conviction. 'Anything would be better than this, even the backside of hell.'

After an hour and a half of travelling they came into a small decaying village and Barbera pulled up outside the wine shop. He climbed down and a small, fat man came out, wiping his hands on a soiled white apron.

'Heh, Rafael,' Vito hailed him. 'How goes it?'

'Fine – everything's ready for you. Leave the truck here. I'll take care of it.'

'Okay,' Barbera called, 'All out!'

He followed Rafael round to the rear of the wine shop. Half-a-dozen mules waited in a small corral, saddled and bridled and a dark haired youth with a shotgun slung across his back, leaned against the rail.

'This is Nino. He'll take you the rest of the way. A couple of hours ride up into the mountains, that's all.'

Luciano turned to Carter. 'You really think of everything, don't you, Professor?'

'Better than walking,' Carter said.

Luciano moved across to Maria and helped her up on to the broad wooden saddle of the lead mule. She sat side-saddle and he took his time over adusting her stirrup.

'Are you worried?' he said. 'About meeting your grand-father?'

'Should I be?'

His enquiry had been one of genuine concern and the coldness of her reply angered him.

'What is it with you?' he said. 'What happened to the Christian charity bit, the human concern? Did you peel it off along with the robes?'

Nino, the young muleteer, had passed her a riding switch and in a sudden reflex action, she raised it as if to cut Luciano across the face.

'Now you're talking,' he said. 'Now I know there's some Luca blood in those veins.'

'Damn you!' she said in a low voice.

'Harsh words,' he said. 'Three Hail Marys and two Our Fathers.'

She slashed the mule across the rump and it cantered away.

                    *   *   *

Detweiler was almost completely disorientated. The pain in his fingers and arms was not so terrible any more because he had passed through some sort of pain threshold, but every so often the Ukrainians took turns to belabour the bucket they had placed over his head with truncheons. It was a technique Suslov had picked up during a spell of duty at Auschwitz concentration camp. The constant clangour had such an effect on the brain and ear drums that it usually produced total alienation within a matter of hours.

Detweiler had lost control of his bladder and his trousers were soaked with urine. Suslov, standing there watching, calmly said, 'Hose him down, then throw him in a cell. I'll deal with him when I've eaten.'

They took Detweiler out between them, feet trailing, and Suslov walked after them.

* * *

Maria guided her mule through a stream following Nino. As she started up the slope on the other side, Luciano rode up alongside her. They were moving through trees now, cork-oak and holly-oak, and above them the ridge was scattered with pines.

Luciano said, 'I've decided to forgive you.'

She smiled in spite of herself. 'You have the Devil's insolence, Mr Luciano.'

'Oh, there's a lot to be said for the Devil,' he said. 'He was, after all, a fallen angel.'

'A debatable point.'

'True, but if the Bible is to be believed, still a force to be reckoned with. Has it ever occurred to you that perhaps people turn to God when the Devil no longer has a use for them?'

'No,' she said, pain on her face. 'I can't accept that. I could never accept such a thing.'

They came through the pine trees and Nino reined in on the ridge. On the slope below was an old and rambling farmhouse amongst olive trees. There was a man seated at a table on the terrace and when Nino whistled, he stood and looked up towards them, tall with broad shoulders, grey hair.

'Don Antonio,' the boy said simply.

Luciano waited, but she said nothing, simply sat there for a moment, her face very calm, then urged her mule forward and down the slope.

Luciano turned to Carter and Savage who crowded up behind him. 'Professor,' he said. 'You know how Luciano's survived all these years?'

'No, but I'm sure you'll tell me,' Carter said.

'It's simple.' Luciano patted his stomach. 'I get this feeling in my gut and it's never wrong.'

'And what does it tell you now?'

'That this is all one hell of a waste of time. Five gets you ten that old buzzard down there isn't going to play.'

*   *   *

In Palermo at command headquarters, General Guzzoni was in conference with his staff officers when Koenig knocked on the door and entered.

Guzzoni said, 'Ah, there you are.'

The weather forecast couldn't be worse, but reconnaissance planes have located a considerable armada of allied ships south of Pantellaria.'

'The feint which Intelligence has been expecting?' Koenig said.

'So it would appear. One would expect the bulk of the force to move on to Sardinia.' He nodded to the Italian staff officers. 'That will be all for now, gentlemen. I'll call you if I need you.'

He waited until the last one had gone before offering Koenig a cigarette, then poured cognac into two glasses.

'Suddenly we have the allied airforces back in strength. Messina bombed twice in twenty-four hours. Harbour installations, airbases, all under attack once more. I don't like it and neither does Field Marshal Kesselring. I've just spoken to him in Rome.'

'General?' Koenig was guarded.

'The Field Marshal never did really buy this idea that Sicily would be only a sideshow and Sardinia the main target. And then there's the weather.'

'I must confess I was wondering about that myself. A strange time to choose.'

'The forecast for tomorrow is terrible and for the day after. Storms, gales, rain. The only reason for coming in such weather would be because it was not expected.'

'And why go to all that trouble if the attack on the Sicilian shore is only a feint, is that what you're thinking, General?'

'Exactly.'

Koenig sipped his cognac thoughtfully. 'If it wasn't a feint . . .

If it was the real thing after all, then coming in the weather which has been forecast would make excellent sense.'

Guzzoni put down his glass. 'You intend to return to Agrigento this afternoon?'

'Yes, General.'

'I think I'll come with you. See for myself what the situation is on the coast.'

*　　*　　*

Luca sat at the table on the terrace, leaning on his stick something regal about him, a true Don, Katerina at his side, and waited as they dismounted and came up the steps to the terrace. He had eyes for no one, but Maria. Katerina, with both hands resting lightly on his shoulders, could feel that he was trembling slightly.

Barbera kissed his hand. 'Don Antonio. This is Colonel Carter whom I've spoken of before and Captain Savage, an American officer. Don Salvatore, you know.'

Luca ignored him, ignored all of them.

'Leave us,' he said hoarsely. 'All of you. Katerina, see they get fed.'

She squeezed his shoulders, then smiled at the others. 'Gentlemen, if you'd come this way.'

Carter was reluctant to go, but Barbera pulled at his sleeve and they followed Katerina inside.

Maria stood there, very tired, her hands folded in front of her. Her black dress was covered with dust and she took off her headscarf and ran her fingers through the cropped hair.

'So, it is true,' Luca said. 'You are a nun.'

'For four years now.'

'Wandering the mountain like a lost soul delivering babies that by all the laws should have died. To Solazzo and his friends you are a saint already.'

'Is there nothing you don't know?'

'Nothing that happens in these mountains,' he said flatly.

There was lemonade in a jug on the table and she helped herself and sat down. 'Nothing changes. Antonio Luca is still Lord of Life and Death in all Sicily.'

'I am of the Society,' he said. 'I have no shame in that. Mafia made me. It is what I am.'

'It also killed my mother.'

'It was meant for me, that day. Those responsible paid the bill.'

'Does that make the dead walk?'

He sat there, frowning, hands on the handle of his walking stick. 'For a servant of God, you are singularly lacking in charity. I know what I am, but what are you, Maria? The nun in white robes, struggling with the sick in hospital or on your knees in the candlelight praying to the Virgin to save the soul of Antonio Luca?'

Her face was pale, her hands gripping the arms of the chair so tightly that the knuckles gleamed white.

He said softly, 'Or could it be that your prayer is to the Devil to take me straight to hell?'

She jumped to her feet, upsetting the jug of lemonade, turned and hurried down the steps into the garden. Katerina came out through the open window and joined him.

'Does it give you satisfaction, this thing? Are you happy now?'

'No,' Luca said. 'But then I never expected to be.'

He went down the steps and walked along a path that finally brought him out on one of the terraces of olive trees above the valley, where he found her sitting on a stone wall.

He sat down beside her and took a cigar from his pocket. 'Remember the summer house at Trevese? What times we had there. How old were you when I bought your first pony? Nine?'

'I broke my left arm in two places trying to jump the boundary wall,' she said.

'And we had to shoot the pony.' He sighed. 'Life walks towards death. The human condition.' There was silence for a while and then he said. 'You're happy? As a nun, I mean?'

'Perfectly. I'm a trained nurse. I spend most of my time in hospitals.'

'A strange life,' he said. 'Celibacy, for example. I could never understand that.'

She laughed, unable to help herself. 'The vow of chastity is a contract with God entered into voluntarily. Because I gave up any thoughts of a sexual life doesn't mean I don't feel any desire for it. We are human beings, flesh and blood like anyone else.'

'True enough if you're my grand-daughter,' he said. 'So, the line ends here. No more Lucas when I'm dead and gone.'

'So it would appear.'

And then he saw it or thought he did. 'Was that it, girl? Was that the intention? To cut off the flow of tainted blood?'

'Perhaps. I don't know.' She was confused and struggled against it. 'The woman?'

'Katerina? What about her?'

'Is she your wife?'

'No.'

There was another awkward silence. He said, 'Spit it out, whatever it is they wanted you to say. You didn't come all this way for love of your grandfather.'

She folded her hands in her lap. 'It's simple enough. The invasion will come soon now and the Americans need your help. One word from you and all over Sicily ...'

'No,' he said. 'I will not do it.'

'Because you hate Americans?'

'I will not do it because you have asked me.' He got to his feet. 'Even Christ only had to carry his cross so far,' and he turned and walked back along the terrace through the olive trees.

*   *   *

Meyer was working over some papers in his office when there was a knock and Suslov entered.

'Well, what is it?' Meyer demanded impatiently 'I'm busy.'

'Several interesting new developments as regards this present case,' Suslov said.

Meyer sat back. 'Go on.'

'Well, the old villain who sold him out to us was discovered on a dung heap outside the local village this morning.'

'Dead?'

'And his tongue had been cut out.'

'The traditional way the Mafia deal with an informer,' Meyer said.

'And one of our patrols has found a parachute caught in a tree not a mile from the farm where we picked up our friend yesterday.'

'A supply chute?'

Suslov shook his head. 'No, very definitely the other variety. British. The kind their paratroopers use.'

Meyer's eyes glittered. 'This could be important. He must be made to talk. He must.'

'What would the Major suggest?'

'I give you one more chance your way. If that doesn't work, then we'll try scopalomine.'

'Very well.' Suslov turned to the door and opened it. 'One other thing. We've a patrol very much overdue.'

'The same area?'

'Yes.'

Meyer nodded. 'Then get to work. It would appear there are a great many questions to be answered and our friend may provide the key to all of them.'

*   *   *

Luca sat at the table on the terrace drinking Zibibbo, an anis-flavoured wine from the island of Pantellaria which was a particular favourite of his. Carter sat opposite him and Luciano and Savage watched from the other end of the terrace.

Carter said. 'The invasion comes tomorrow or the day after, depending on the weather. I make no secret of this. I trust you as a man of honour.'

'Colonel, I salute you as a soldier and as a scholar, but you're a rotten salesman.'

'Don Antonio, if you give the word, the whole of the Cammarata will rise as one man. There's a fair chance that most Italian troops in the mountains will surrender without firing a shot. They're brave men, but they've had enough of Mussolini.'

'I'm not interested in Italy, only in Sicily,' Luca said.

'Then help us kick the Germans out.'

'Colonel – Professor – whatever you are. The Nazis have lost the war. They lost it in 1940 when Hitler stood back and let the British Army escape at Dunkirk. All we need to do is sit back and wait.'

'And see thousands of young Americans die needlessly fighting their way through the Cammarata?'

'Not my affair.'

'Why, because they sent your brother to the electric chair? Must all Americans suffer?'

Luciano said to Savage, 'There's no percentage in this and you can tell Carter I said so. He's wasting his time. I'm going to take a walk.'

He moved through the garden and found Maria walking along the terrace between the olive trees towards him.

'What's happening?' she asked.

'Carter's ramming his head against a stone wall called Antonio Luca.'

'He won't help?'

'Wouldn't lift a finger. Obviously, you didn't get anywhere either.'

'Why should I?' There was a curious edge of bitterness to her voice. 'I came here for one reason only and it certainly wasn't for love.'

'How stupid, when you think about it. I've avoided him for years, made my feelings absolutely plain. And now, to turn up in such circumstances, expecting him to come running, like snapping one's fingers to a dog.'

She walked up through the trees towards the house, head bowed, and Luciano turned and moved down towards the valley.

*   *   *

It was shortly after noon when they dragged Detweiler out into the courtyard at the rear of the police barracks. There were two posts in the centre and a thin, hollow-faced man in ragged clothes was strapped to one of them. He had obviously been terribly beaten, Detweiler was aware of that as they strapped him to the next pillar.

Suslov said, 'Right, this is it, then. No last cigarette. They're in short supply.'

Detweiler was aware of the firing squad on the other side of the square as the Ukrainian pulled a black bag over his head. His brain refused to function and his mouth was so dry that he couldn't cry out. There was a pause that seemed to go on for ever, a shouted command, a sudden volley.

Detweiler hadn't even braced himself for death, simply hung there in the straps, aware of steps moving towards him.

The bag was wrenched from his head and Suslov said, 'Still with us, I see.'

Detweiler turned and saw that the man next to him hung there, saturated in blood, head lolling to one side.

'Always like to make sure,' Suslov said.

He took his Walther from his pocket and fired at point blank range. Pieces of bone and blood sprayed, the body sagged and Detweiler cried out.

Suslov nodded to the guards. 'Bring him along.'

Detweiler was half-conscious as they took him upstairs between them. He was aware of being dumped in a chair and opened his eyes to find himself in Meyer's office.

The Major came round the desk. 'Still nothing to say. Well, we'll soon remedy that.' He picked up a hypodermic. 'Scopalomine, otherwise known as the truth drug.'

Detweiler tried to struggle, but Suslov and the guards held him firmly and Meyer moved in close and rolled up his sleeve.

★   ★   ★

It was very hot, very still on the olive terraces and thunder rumbled on the horizon, as Luciano produced a pack of cards he had found up at the house. He took out six and lined them up in a crack in a large rock. Then he walked way.

There had been a time when he could draw, turn and hit a playing card six times at that distance inside a second, but that had been long ago. His hand went under his jacket, found the butt of the Smith and Wesson. He drew, turned, crouched, arm extended and fired very fast.

He went forward to examine the cards, reloading as he did so. *Three out of six*. Not bad, considering.

Luca said, 'So the hand *has* lost its cunning.'

Luciano turned and found him standing a few yards away leaning on his stick.

'You want to try?'

Luciano offered him the gun. Luca balanced it in his hand, then emptied it very deliberately, taking his time, hitting four of the cards.

'Not bad,' he said. 'A tendency to pull to the right. Maybe you could lighten the trigger.'

Luciano took the gun back and reloaded. 'It's good to see you again.'

'And you, Salvatore, even on a fool's errand like this. What possessed you to do such a thing? The promise of a pardon?'

'Only a possibility,' Luciano said. 'Nothing on paper.'

Luca was astonished. 'Then why did you come?'

'You've been to prison. You know how it is. Can you imagine how a thirty-to-fifty year sentence feels for something you didn't do?'

Luca nodded. 'Yes, I can see that almost anything would be preferable to that.'

Luciano said, 'Anyway, what about Maria?'

'Maria and I have nothing to say to each other.'

'So, you will not do as Carter asks?'

Luca said, 'Salvatore, what has this nonsense to do with us? Whatever happens, Mafia will survive. Mussolini couldn't crush us. Neither could the Germans. The wise man keeps his own council and lives a hundred years. You know the saying.'

Luciano hesitated, then bowed his head formally. 'If that is your decision, then I accept it, naturally, Don Antonio.'

Luca put a hand on his shoulder. 'Then you will stay here with us. We can talk of old times, old friends ... Stay, Salvatore.' He reached for Luciano's arm. 'Together, there is nothing we can't accomplish. Eventually, you would take my place, that goes without saying.'

'*Capo di Tutti Capi* in all Sicily.' Luciano smiled, remembering Maria's words. 'Lord of Life and Death.'

'Look what's happened to Mafia in New York,' Luca said urgently. 'For some of the families, whores have become big business. They tell me there are even those who deal in children. I ask you. Can you believe that of a true Sicilian. And this drug thing. *Infamita*. And not for a man like you. Stay here in Sicily, where you belong. Where you have respect.'

His fingers had hooked into Luciano's arm and there was a strange kind of pleading on his face. Luciano detached himself gently.

'I'm sorry, old friend,' he said. 'But I can't be the son you never had. I go back with Carter and take my chances with that parole board. If it works, I'd be free again – really free – for the rest of my life.'

'And if it doesn't?'

Luciano shrugged. 'I'll deal with that when it happens. And there's Maria to consider. She certainly won't stay here, you must see that.'

He turned and fired left-handed so fast that it sounded like one continuous roll and knew what he would find even before he reached the cards. Six hits, each card drilled cleanly.

'Remarkable,' Luca said.

'I know,' Luciano smiled. 'It's this weather, you see.' He looked up into the sky as heavy drops of rain spotted the dry earth.

$\star \quad \star \quad \star$

General Eisenhower was due to go to Malta with Field Marshal Alexander and Admiral Cunningham. Waiting for his staff car he had a final cup of coffee, standing in front of the map of Sicily on the wall of his office at dar el Ouad. There was a knock at the door and Cusak entered.

'A signal from Admiral Ramsay with the fleet, General.'

'Anything important?'

'Everything is going well except for the deteriorating weather. Force four to five winds over the sea.'

Eisenhower nodded. 'Any word from Colonel Carter?'

'I'm afraid not.'

Eisenhower put down his cup and reached for his cap, 'There are 2,500 ships out there. Air Chief Marshal Tedder's promised us blanket air cover of five thousand planes when the right moment comes, the sole aim being to put 115,000 British and Canadians at one end of the island and 66,000 of our boys at the other to drive the enemy out of Sicily.'

Cusak helped him on with his fieldcoat. 'Quite a responsibility, General.'

'One hell of a job of organizing,' Eisenhower said. 'Months of research, planning, arguments, sleepless nights, and the irony is that the whole damn thing could quite easily stand or fall on Carter's negotiations with this – this mountain brigand or whatever he is.'

'Carter could still bring it off, General.'

'Well, all I can say is he's running it damn close,' Eisenhower said and he picked up his briefcase and went out.

* * *

At the farm it had started to rain. Katerina sat at the table at the end of the terrace with a pack of cards, laying them before her one by one. Maria came out of the living room and stood watching her.

Katerina said, 'You have wasted your time, I think.'

'So it would appear.' Maria sat down opposite her. 'I should never have allowed them to persuade me to come. He is the same man I ran from so long ago.'

'Not true,' Katerina said. 'Everything changes.'

'Even Antonio Luca?'

'He is not the man today that he was yesterday. Are you the same woman you were when they came to you back there in your convent? Has nothing changed?'

Maria smiled sadly. 'You're right, of course. There I had certainty, the days had a pattern. Now, there is only doubt.' She hesitated and when she spoke it was from the depths of her being. 'I even doubt my vocation now. I thought I sought God, now it would appear I was only fleeing Antonio Luca.'

'You hate him so much?'

Maria touched her breast. 'It is like a stone in here, a constant pain that won't go away!' She sat back. 'But for you it is different, I think. You love him.'

'Oh, yes, for me that is the only certainty.'

They sat there in silence. Behind them Luciano and Savage appeared in the doorway. Katerina shuffled the cards and laid them out again.

Maria said, 'The Tarot?'

'Yes.'

'I haven't seen that done since I was a child. My mother constantly sought news of the future.'

'It is there for those who would see.'

'Irrevocably?'

'I'm not certain. Perhaps a warning only. An opportunity to take another road.'

Maria watched her for a while and then said, 'Let's see what the cards have to say for me.'

Katerina shrugged. 'If you like. Your future on one card, although I don't think the Vatican would approve.'

She counted quickly and flipped over the seventh card. It was an ornate brightly coloured picture of a young man hanging by his ankles from a tree.

'The Hanged Man,' she said. 'Interesting. No such symbol exists in orthodox Christianity. Equal for man or woman. The individual is torn between two selves, the same and yet not the same. Symbol of a sacrificial victim since pagan times. You suffer for others, that is your destiny.'

Maria stood up. 'Goodbye, Katerina Scorza. I don't think we shall see each other again.'

She went inside and Luciano and Savage moved to the table. Luciano took the cards from her and said to Savage, 'A very superstitious people, we Sicilians.'

He counted out seven cards and turned the last one over. It was a six spoked wooden wheel, a crudely drawn dragon above it.

'The Wheel of Fortune,' she said. 'The symbol of inner order. You have cast yourself free from the bonds of society.'

'Seen through the bars of a prison cell, of course.' Luciano turned to Savage. 'If I was paying Gypsy Rose in a tent at Coney Island, I'd really think I'd had my money's worth.'

Savage said, 'What about me?'

Looking up at him, Katerina's eyes clouded and there was an unwillingness that Luciano sensed, if Savage did not.

'I'm tired,' she said. 'One can give only so much.'

'Just tell me whether I'm lucky in love,' he said. 'That will do.'

She hesitated, then took the pack and counted, turning over

the seventh card long enough to glance at it. She put it back on top of the pack.

'Great happiness results from a marriage or birth. The Three of Cups in an upright position.'

'Here, let me look.'

He reached for the card and turned it over. Two ornate birds perched on the rim of a golden goblet, each holding a smaller cup in a claw.

He laughed excitedly. 'Well, what do you know? Can I keep this? There's someone I'd very much like to show it to.' He slipped it into his breast pocket and said to Luciano, 'If it's in the cards, it's in the cards, isn't that so?'

He was smiling excitedly as he went back inside. Katerina reached for the pack and Luciano grabbed her wrist, twisting until she opened her hand disclosing the card she had palmed. It fell to the table between them.

Death stared up, crudely depicted, a skeleton, scything no field of corn, but a crop of human bodies.

*　　*　　*

In the living room, Carter stood by the fire confronting Luca.

'Is there no way I can persuade you, Don Antonio?'

'Those friends of yours in Cairo or wherever it is, must be very stupid. Did they really think that the sight of my granddaughter coming in through the door would make me change my opinion in this matter?' He poured himself a glass of Zibibbo with great care. 'Why, that in itself would be enough to make me say no, even if I had not intended to in the first place.'

'Don Antonio, men will die,' Carter said urgently.

'A habit they have,' Luca told him.

Carter turned angrily to Luciano, who lounged in the window. 'A waste of bloody time, the whole thing, just like you said. We might as well get going. The sooner we return to Bellona, the better.'

He went out and Luciano helped himself to wine. He sniffed the bouquet approvingly. 'Hate and love – it's a thin line. You should remember that.'

'Not for her.'

'A remarkable girl. I thought that when I first met her in that convent in Liverpool. Since then, she's parachuted into enemy territory by night, faced death many times, been hunted through the mountains . . .'

Don Antonio said. 'So she's my grand-daughter. Half a Luca, whether she likes it or not. Blood of my blood and she can't escape that, whatever she thinks of me, but I will not do what Carter's people want. This war is not my war. It will pass as the wind passes. Sicily will be free again and things will be as they were.'

Maria said from the doorway, 'We're ready to move, Mr Luciano.'

Luca sat there, no expression on his face, no emotion. Luciano put down his glass and moved to the door. She started to turn and he said softly, 'He's an old man. He may think otherwise, but without you, there is nothing.'

She stared up at him for a moment, then something moved in the eyes. She turned and crossed to Luca and knelt in front of him. Her words, when they came, were pure Sicilian, a ritual as old as time itself.

'I go on a long journey, grandfather. I seek your blessing.'

Luca was transfixed, his iron features dissolving. Almost as a reflex, he placed a hand on her head and replied with the same ritual words. 'Go with God, go in peace, go with my love and return in safety.'

She stood up, leaned forward and kissed him gently on both cheeks, then turned and walked out, brushing past Luciano. Luca sat there, staring blindly into space, tears in his eyes.

Luciano went forward and kissed his right hand as a mark of respect. Luca whispered, 'Can it be that she still loves me in spite of everything?'

Luciano put a hand on his shoulder. 'Old friend, she never stopped.'

16

Detweiler's body was racked by convulsions as he bucked and twisted, heaving against the chair to which he was tied. It took three of the Ukrainians to hold him still.

Meyer said, 'I'll ask you again. Where did you get the American weapons from?'

Detweiler's eyes bulged and there was froth on his lips. He tried to speak, wanted to tell them everything, but the words wouldn't come.

Meyer said, 'Give him another ten cc's.'

'I'm not sure if he can take it, Major,' Suslov said. 'I've seen them like this before. It's like a dam building up. The heart ...'

'Get on with it,' Meyer said impatiently.

Suslov jabbed in the needle. Detweiler went into another convulsion, lost his balance and fell over, still strapped to the chair.

'For Christ's sake!' Suslov said angrily and kicked him in the body.

And the dam finally burst inside Detweiler in a great aching scream and he cried out in English, 'No more! No more!'

Meyer turned from the window, thunderstruck. 'He's American.'

Suslov and his men had Detweiler upright in the chair again and Meyer leaned over him, shaking him by the shoulders. 'Who are you?' he asked in English.

Detweiler sat there, eyes glazed and Meyer turned to the desk and quickly refilled the hypodermic.

Suslov said, 'Another shot will kill him, Major. I've never known anyone survive such a massive dosage.'

Detweiler seemed to calm down after the final injection. He sat there in the chair, head slumped on his chest and Meyer waited. Finally, he leaned forward and tilted Detweiler's chin up.

'Now then, who are you?' he said again in English.

Detweiler tried hard, something moving in the eyes. The mouth parted and he said hoarsely, 'Sergeant Joseph Detweiler, Ranger Division, on detachment from the Twenty-first Specialist Raiding Force.'

Meyer pulled up a chair and sat in front of him. His voice, when he next spoke, was soft and gentle.

'I see, Sergeant. That's very interesting. Tell me more.'

*   *   *

Twice on the way to Agrigento, Koenig and Guzzoni, travelling in the general's staff car, had to take shelter in trees at the side of the road when military convoys, en route for the coast, were strafed by RAF Hawker Typhoons, whose cannon inflicted severe damage.

Before reaching Agrigento, they called at the coastal defence command post for the section of the coast bordering the Sicilian Channel. Koenig waited in the car. When Guzzoni returned, he looked glum.

'Not good,' he said as they drove on into Agrigento. 'They're hitting harbours and airports hard and Messina has taken a real pasting. They estimate five thousand tons of bombs at least. Something's up, that's obvious.'

They were driving along the coast road and Koenig looked out to sea. The waves were already lifting into white caps.

'Well, if they're coming, I don't envy them. Hell in those landing craft in this weather.'

'On the other hand, how far would you say you could see out to sea at the moment?' Guzzoni asked. 'Six or seven hundred yards? There could be an armada out there now ready to pounce.'

Koenig said delicately, 'Do we assume that the enemy must succeed with his landing?'

Guzzoni said, 'That is quite impossible, I assure you.

Mussolini has ordered us to wipe out the invader before he can break through inland.'

'Indeed?' Koenig said drily.

'Yes, I believe the phrase was, as he takes off his bathrobe and before he has time to get dressed.'

'The enemy or the Duce?' Koenig enquired.

Guzzoni laughed heartily. 'That's really very good. Have a cigarette,' and he offered his carved ivory case.

*   *   *

It was long after lunch and the officers' mess at the Agrigento barracks was empty when General Guzzoni and Koenig went in. The barman hurried to serve them and they took a corner table and waited while he opened a bottle of Chianti.

Rudi Brandt came in, glanced around quickly, then approached and saluted smartly.

'My apologies, Colonel, but might I have a word?'

Guzzoni waved his hand. 'Carry on, by all means.'

Koenig walked to the window with Brandt. 'I saw you come in, Colonel and came straight over. There's something going on to do with that prisoner. The suspected partisan.'

'I gave orders that he was to be left alone until I returned,' Koenig said.

'I don't know what happened but he's dead. I was tipped off by one of the attendants from the infirmary mortuary. But more than that, Major Meyer's left instructions that I notify him the moment you arrive.'

There was a quick step in the doorway and Meyer appeared. He carried a folder in one hand.

Koenig said, 'I told you that the prisoner brought in the other day would be dealt with by me on my return. I now find he's lying in the infirmary, dead.'

Meyer offered Guzzoni the folder. 'Read that, Herr General, and see who has behaved in the most responsible manner. Me or the Colonel.'

Guzzoni, frowning, opened the file. He scanned the first page and his eyes widened. He looked up. 'Is this true?'

'Most certainly.' Meyer turned to Koenig. 'This ragged

peasant who you treated with such consideration, Colonel. Do you know who he was? A sergeant in the American Ranger Division.'

Koenig turned to Guzzoni, who nodded. 'According to this, he parachuted in with a party two nights ago. He became separated from the others and landed in the wrong valley.'

'Read it, why don't you?' Meyer said. 'Your old friend Carter, a Colonel now, it seems, who you let slip through your fingers last time, and some interesting companions.'

Guzzoni passed the file to Koenig who moved to the window to read it. After a while, he turned.

'How did you obtain this information?'

Meyer shrugged. 'Does it matter?'

'To me it does. I'd be interested to see the condition of the body.'

Guzzoni said, 'Colonel, the morality of what has occurred here is one thing, but the facts are something else again. To speak plainly, there is considerable merit in this plan to enlist Mafia aid on the side of the Americans in the coming invasion. From what Detweiler admitted in his interrogation, the man, Luciano, is dead, but Colonel Carter still has the daughter of Antonio Luca in his charge. Luca holds immense power in Sicily, believe me. If he falls in with their wishes, then anything is possible.'

'Perhaps he already has,' Koenig said.

Guzzoni spread his hands. 'On the other hand, they have not had a great deal of time to operate. I suggest we proceed on the assumption that they haven't. This monastery they are using as a base, Crown of Thorns near Bellona. Do you know it?'

'Yes,' Koenig told him.

'The Franciscans of Crown of Thorns,' Guzzoni said. 'Now I remember. There was a considerable scandal several years ago. A trial in Palermo. The Mafia monks, the newspapers called them. You could have trouble there.'

'With respect, Herr General, I don't really think so,' Meyer said. 'I can be up there in four hours. We'll be through the front gate before they know what's hit them. If Carter and his people are still here, we'll root them out, believe me.'

Koenig laughed harshly. 'You wouldn't get within ten miles of the place before they knew you were coming. Every shepherd on the mountain, every goatherd, is in some way involved with the resistance movement. They have a signalling system from crag to crag. A normal approach would be quite impossible.'

Meyer started to protest and Guzzoni cut him off impatiently. 'Colonel Koenig, in this kind of soldiering you are second to none, that is a known fact. Is there any way at all, in your opinion, in which Colonel Carter and his party might be apprehended, particularly the lady in question, Luca's grand-daughter, this sister Maria Vaughan. Her capture is of primary importance.' He smiled gently. 'I need also, I trust, hardly stress the necessity for delicate treatment in her case. We don't wish to offend the Vatican if it can be avoided.'

'But General,' Meyer protested, 'the woman is a spy and as such liable to be shot under the rules of the Geneva Convention.'

'A question of attitude, I suppose,' Guzzoni said. 'We Italians perhaps take a different view of these matters, but then, we are an old race.' He selected a cigarette from his ivory case. 'Well, Colonel?'

Brandt, who had stood by silently all this time, stepped smartly forward and gave him a light. Koenig said, 'There is a way, General. A parachute drop.'

'Could it be done?'

'I'm not sure. I'd need some advice on that. With your permission?' Guzzoni nodded and Koenig said to Brandt. 'Get a message through to Colonel Kubel at Otranto Luftwaffe base. Present General Guzzoni's compliments and ask him to get here as quickly as he can.'

Brandt turned smartly on heel and went out on the double.

'Excellent,' Guzzoni said. 'Now, as we last ate in Palermo, I suggest some late lunch.' He turned to Meyer. 'And you, Major, must be about your duties, I'm sure.'

'Herr General – Colonel.' Meyer turned and marched out stiffly.

*   *   *

Wolf Kubel was twenty-five, and already a full colonel, *Gruppenkommandeur* at Otranto and responsible for three *Stafflen*. He had seen combat service in Poland and Norway, had shot down sixty-nine enemy aircraft over the Channel and England by the end of 1941. In Russia, he had achieved even greater distinction, adding another eighty-four to his total until a bad crash had necessitated the amputation of his left leg. Not that this had deterred him; he had returned to combat flying within six weeks until he had been relegated to a desk job on Goering's personal order.

He had very fair hair, a handsome, rather dashing young man in an old black leather Luftwaffe flying jacket who wore the Knight's Cross with Oak Leaves, Swords and Diamonds at his throat.

He leaned over the large scale map in Koenig's office, a frown on his face. 'Lousy flying country.'

'Could it be done?' Guzzoni demanded.

'Getting there is no problem – no more than fifteen minutes flying time from Otranto – but it's getting this madman and his men on target worries me. I mean, you want someone to fly up that valley at four hundred feet and drop your men inside the walls of this damn monastery.' He shook his head. 'As good a way of committing suicide as I've heard of.'

Koenig said to Guzzoni. 'General, my men are a special breed. Six jumps earns the paratroopers' qualification badge and after that, never less than six a year if he wishes to keep it. We make a speciality of jumping from under four hundred feet. Is this not so, Sergeant?' he said to Brandt.

Guzzoni said to Kubel, 'Are you saying that it can't be done?'

'Not at all, Herr General. A Junkers 52, doing no more than a hundred miles an hour, would be the thing, but they'd have to get out damn fast.'

'A dawn drop to catch them wholly by surprise,' Koenig said. 'Not the best time for flying in the mountains.'

Kubel rubbed his chin. 'Which means you're going to need the best pilot I've got.' He grinned. 'Not that I mind. I could do with a little action.'

'Twenty men including myself,' Koenig said. 'No time for

more than that number to jump over the target, but it should suffice.'

'And what of my command?' Meyer, who had been standing silently by, asked.

'Leave here in the early hours of the morning, approach under cover of darkness. No more than twenty men. You wait here at the head of the valley.' He indicated the place with his finger. 'Make your move when you see the Junkers pass overhead. By the time you reach the monastery, we should be in control and the gates open!'

'An excellent plan,' Guzzoni said. 'Which seems to cover all contingencies. Wouldn't you agree, Major?'

'So it would appear, General,' Meyer said.

'Good.' Guzzoni slapped his thigh. 'Well, I've got things to attend to. I'll try and see you off in the morning, Koenig. Until then.'

Meyer moved to the door. Koenig said, 'A moment Major.' Meyer turned. 'Well?'

'I am in command of this operation. I use you and your men with considerable reluctance, but for good or ill, they will follow my orders. Is that clear?'

'Perfectly, Colonel,' Meyer said calmly. 'May I go now?'

'Of course.'

Meyer went out and Rudi Brandt said, 'You've got trouble there.'

'Never mind that now,' Koenig said. 'We've more important things to consider. You and me, Rudi, which means selecting another eighteen. You can handle that dirty job for me. You won't be popular with the men who stay behind.'

'That's what sergeant-majors are for, Colonel.'

Brandt saluted and went out.

*   *   *

In the cubbyhole behind the coffin room at the mortuary, Harry Carter sat at the radio. He finished transmitting and waited for a reply. After a while, he took off the headphones. As he lit a cigarette, the secret door opened and Vito Barbera came in.

'Well?' he asked.

'They're on their way.'

'In this weather? It's blowing up a real storm out there.'

'All the better when they hit the coast.'

'What did you tell them?'

'About Luca? Mission a failure.' He started to cough over the cigarette and there was that sudden sharp pain in his lung again.

Vito said, 'Half a loaf's better than none, Harry. I'll call a meeting of the district committee for tonight. Father Collura, Verga, those two Reds. Warn every man to oil his gun and be ready to move tomorrow.'

'And Mafia?'

'In the Bellona valley, I speak for Mafia,' Vito said simply. 'Luciano and Captain Savage have taken Maria up to Crown of Thorns. Better you spend the night up there, too, Harry. You're not looking too good. I'll come up in the morning.'

'All right.' Carter got up and Vito Barbera led the way out through the coffin room. They passed through the waiting mortuary and Barbera opened the door to the street. It was pouring with rain, everything out of focus, the houses, the mountain beyond. He went and untethered Carter's mule and led it to the door.

Carter was seized with a violent paroxysm of coughing. He leaned against the doorpost, holding a grimy handkerchief to his mouth. When he examined it, he saw that it was stained with blood.

He held it out to Barbera and tried to smile. 'Ain't life grand?'

'Come on, Harry,' Barbera said gently. 'The sooner you're up there, the better. Maria will know what to do.'

Carter clambered up, sitting sideways on the wooden saddle. He reached for the reins and managed a smile.

'Suddenly I feel tired, Vito, really tired. You know what I mean?'

'I know, old friend, I know,' Barbera said sadly.

Carter kicked his heel against the mule's belly and moved away across the square.

★   ★   ★

Padre Giovanni, a large black umbrella protecting him from the rain, was feeding the pigeons on the battlements when Luciano came up the steps.

'How is Colonel Carter?' the old man asked.

Luciano stood under the overhanging leaves of the hut to avoid the worst of the rain and offered him a cigarette.

'Not good. High fever, something close to pneumonia. Maria says he probably needs surgery and he certainly isn't going to get that here.'

'Remember the Americans will get here soon. He'll have the best of treatment then. The finest doctors.'

'If he lives that long.' Luciano looked out at the mountains, shrouded in rain. 'Crazy when you think of it. It's only a few weeks since the guy took a bullet in the lung. He should have been invalided out, back to that university of his.'

'He is an exceptional man, I think.' Padre Giovanni said. 'For some people, moral decisions come out of a personal evaluation of what is right against what is wrong. Frequently, circumstances modify their actions.'

'What you mean, Father, is they won't do what's right if it looks as if it might prove unhealthy for them.'

Padre Giovanni nodded. 'Colonel Carter, on the other hand, does what he does because he can do no other.'

'Here I stand,' Luciano said. 'Isn't that what Martin Luther said? People like that can make life damned uncomfortable for the rest of us.'

The door opened in the small courtyard below and Maria came out. She had on an old raincoat over her shoulders and looked tired as she came up the steps.

'How is he?' Luciano asked.

'Not good. Medical supplies in the emergency kits we carried are limited. I've given him morphine for the pain and the monastery clinic was able to supply me with quinine. I've given him a heavy dose of that. It should help to reduce the fever.'

'Will that be enough?'

'No. In my opinion, the lung is ulcerated. I suspect the original wound didn't get a chance to heal properly, mainly because of a lack of any kind of convalescence.'

'I'll go and sit with him for a while,' Padre Giovanni said.

'That would be a kindness, Father.'

The old man went down the steps and Maria and Luciano stood there under the eaves, looking out across the valley as evening fell.

'So here we are,' Luciano said. 'A hell of a lot of effort that seems to have added up to a considerable waste of time.'

'Perhaps,' she said.

The wind dashed rain across the pantiled roofs. Luciano said, 'A long way from Liverpool and that convent of yours.'

'Oh, yes,' she said. 'Too far to go back.' There was an expression of infinite sadness on her face when she looked up at him. 'I know that now.'

Luciano couldn't think of a thing to say. He stood there, watching her go back down the steps to the courtyard and disappear through the door.

*   *   *

By four o'clock in the morning, under cover of darkness, Meyer and his men in an armoured troop carrier and three *kubelwagens* had taken up position in the pine forest at the south end of the valley some five miles from Crown of Thorns.

Suslov joined Meyer beside the front vehicle, glancing at his watch. 'They should be taking off in one hour exactly at five o'clock.'

There was a paleness in the sky beyond the mountains and Meyer looked up at the monastery through Zeiss nightglasses.

'Is this going to work?' Major Suslov asked.

'Of course it is,' Meyer said. 'I don't like Koenig, I make no secret of the fact. I don't think he's a good German and I have heard him make remarks which indicate a certain contempt for the Führer, but he is also a soldier of genius. If anyone can pull this off, he can.'

'And afterwards?'

Meyer turned and smiled coldly. 'Oh, that, of course, is quite another matter.'

*   *   *

At the Otranto Luftwaffe base, rain swept across the tarmac in solid sheets, but the three engines of the Junkers 52 were already ticking over. Kubel leaned out of the cockpit window and raised a thumb.

The men, in Brandt's charge, were already on board and Koenig stood beside the open hatch with Guzzoni. He wore a paratrooper's camouflage smock in the SS pattern. A machine pistol was suspended across his chest.

Guzzoni said, 'It would appear he thinks it's still on in spite of this wretched weather. You really think you can jump in conditions like this?'

'They jumped at Maleme, they dropped into Stalingrad. They'd jump into hell if I told them to.' Koenig saluted. 'And now, I think, Kubel is getting impatient.'

Guzzoni grasped his hand warmly. 'What can I say?'

'Nothing, I suspect, would be perfectly adequate in the circumstances.' Koenig placed the end of his static line between his teeth and climbed into the Junkers. The hatch was closed and Guzzoni stepped back.

Kubel increased engine revs and the Junkers moved away into the rain and darkness. The flare path had not been lit due to the ever-present chance of an Allied airstrike. The lights switched on now for the final run only. The roaring of the engines filled the morning as Kubel boosted power and the Junkers skimmed along the runway, rain spraying up in great waves on either side.

Guzzoni watched it lift above the trees and fade into the grey morning. He shivered, pulling his cloak around him, and turned away.

*   *   *

At the monastery, Carter slept fitfully, his hands clutching sheets that were drenched in his own sweat. Maria, on the chair beside him, slept the sleep of total exhaustion. The blanket she had wrapped around herself had slipped to the floor. Luciano, sitting in the window seat, crossed to her side, picked up the blanket and covered her. The wind moaned eerily around the

battlements. He lit a cigarette and stood, peering out through
the window, suddenly uneasy.

*   *   *

Savage was so tired he hadn't bothered to undress, simply lay on
the small bed in one of the monks' cells and was instantly asleep.

He couldn't remember when Rosa joined him, but when he
awakened, just before dawn, he found her lying in the crook of
his arm.

She stirred sleepily, 'Savage, is that you?'

'Who else would it be?'

She smiled, still half-asleep, then raised her head. 'What's
that? I thought I heard something.'

'The wind,' he said. 'Just the wind. Go back to sleep.'

She closed her eyes again and turned her face into his
shoulder, smiling.

17

Flying at one thousand feet the view was spectacular in the dawn light in spite of the heavy rain. Chains of mountains, peaks and ridges on every hand, the valleys dark with shadow.

Sitting beside the hatch, Koenig looked down the line of his men, anonymous in the dim light in helmets and camouflaged jump jackets and parachutes. No bulky equipment this time, no supply bags. Each man carried a Schmeisser across his chest, ammunition pouches, grenades.

'How many times have we done this, Rudi?' he asked Brandt, who sat next to him.

'God knows,' Brandt said. 'Narvik was the first, I know that, but in between is a blur. Too many good men gone.'

'Yes,' Koenig said. 'Sometimes I think that's all we have, our dead.'

'No, Colonel,' Brandt said firmly. 'We have each other. We have the Regiment. We have you.'

My God, Koenig thought. Is that all we're left with after so much suffering? Is that what it was really all about? He looked out of the window and saw the jagged peak of Monte Cammarata, the western slope. They started to descend rapidly. A jagged ridge seemed to bar their way, the Junkers lifted as Kubel eased back the stick, the spine of rock no more than fifty feet beneath them as they slipped over it.

And there was the Bellona valley below them, the river running through pine trees, the rain and mist so heavy that it was impossible to see Bellona itself or Crown of Thorns at the other end of the valley.

Kubel swung into the wind, the tip of his starboard wing

breathtakingly close to the rock face. Koenig got up, moved along the fuselage and leaned in the cockpit.

'What do you think?'

'I think it stinks. If you want to go through with it, I'll play along, but you only get one chance, remember that and when you go, go together and very fast or you'll miss the target altogether.'

'Understood.'

'Right – you've got approximately two minutes.'

Koenig moved back along the line. 'On your feet and let's get ready.'

Brandt opened the hatch as they stood and clipped on their static lines, each man checking his neighbour. The Junkers descended even further and then everything happened at once.

As the light flared above the hatch, they roared across the village and Wolf Kubel banked to starboard.

There was Crown of Thorns, the road snaking up the side of the valley to the great gate.

'Now!' Koenig cried, even before they'd reached the outer wall, and Brandt went out through the door, the others following him so fast that they seemed to be falling on top of each other.

Then it was Koenig's turn. He plunged out, aware of the courtyard directly below him, the red pantiles of the roofs and then his parachute cracked open. He glanced up to see the Junkers fading into the rain, looked the other way and saw his men to the left and beneath him, drifting in over the wall.

The essential difference between the parachutes used by the Germans and the English and Americans was that the German variety carried no shroud lines, which made any kind of manoeuvring by the parachutist impossible. This explained the popularity of drops at a very low level by German forces. But the system had its disadvantages, especially in a case like this. Koenig saw two of his men vanish on the other side of the wall, a third land badly on the battlements above the gate, then fall headfirst to the courtyard below.

Others had already landed in the courtyard itself, parachutes billowing, and then the red pantiles at one of the higher levels were rushing up to meet him. He braced himself for the shock, folding his arms and landed hard, smashing right through the roof.

*   *   *

From the pine trees, Meyer watched through fieldglasses as the parachutes drifted down.

'He's done it!'

'Fifteen, by my count,' Suslov said. 'The rest are somewhere outside.'

But Meyer didn't seem to hear him. 'Mount up,' he cried. 'And let's get out of here.'

He nodded to the driver of his *kubelwagen* and they drove away rapidly.

*   *   *

Luciano, unable to sleep, went out on the battlements just after dawn and found Padre Giovanni standing there under his old black umbrella, enjoying the first cigarette of the day.

'So, you couldn't sleep either?' he said.

'No, I guess not,' Luciano replied.

'Holy Mother of God!' Padre Giovanni said, the smile wiped clean from his face.

Luciano swung round as the Junkers appeared from the rain like a grey ghost and roared down the valley towards them at four hundred feet. And as the first paratrooper plunged into space, all became horrifyingly clear.

Padre Giovanni pushed him towards the door. 'You must leave, you and the others, as quickly as possible and take Carter with you. There is nothing to be gained by trying to stand and fight here.'

Carter, half-dazed, was struggling to sit up in bed and Maria was on her feet as they entered the room.

'We're in trouble,' Luciano said. 'Paratroopers. We've got to get out of here.'

The door opened and Savage appeared, pulling on his rucksack. Rosa was behind him holding his M1 and she passed it to him.

'What's happening?'

'Detweiler, or I miss my guess,' Luciano said.

They moved to the window in time to see Koenig crash through the red pantile roof to the left of them and disappear. The men in the courtyard under Brandt's direction, were already discarding their parachutes.

Savage raised his rifle to fire and Luciano knocked it up. 'No need for that. We're getting out of here. That way we leave it clean for the Franciscans.'

'How?'

'The catacombs,' Padre Giovanni said. 'Follow me, please, but we must hurry. There isn't much time.'

Luciano said to Savage. 'Sling Carter over your shoulder and you bring his clothes, Maria. We'll dress him later.'

They hurried along the passage outside. Padre Giovanni produced a key and opened an oak door at the far end disclosing a stone spiral staircase.

'This goes all the way down to the chapel. The entrance to the crypt, I showed you the other day. I can only wish you luck, my friends. Now hurry, I beg you.'

Luciano led the way and Savage followed, Carter over his shoulder, Rosa and Maria behind. Padre Giovanni closed the door and locked it. As he turned, one of the SS paratroopers appeared from the stairhead at the other end of the passageway and covered him with his Schmeisser.

*   *   *

Koenig's left arm was badly broken and he sat on one of the benches in the monastery refrectory while a young Brother bandaged it. There was also a gash in his left cheek and Koenig held a handkerchief against it to stem the flow of blood.

Padre Giovanni said, 'It will need stitches, I fear, Colonel and the arm is not good. Broken in two places. You will need a skilful surgeon if you are not to be left with permanent injury.'

There was a quick step and Brandt came in. 'We've searched the place thoroughly, Colonel. Not a sign of anyone except the Fathers.'

'Should there be?' Padre Giovanni enquired.

'My information was that there were enemy agents here, Father, led by a British Officer – a Colonel Carter.'

'Then I can only say you have gone to considerable trouble to no good purpose. There is no one of that description here.' He raised the crucifix around his neck to his lips and kissed it. 'I give you my word.'

Koenig stood up wearily, grimacing with pain. 'What about the men?'

'Three dead, Colonel. Two in the ravine outside. Vogel broke his neck falling off the wall. Hartman has a broken leg.'

'And all to no purpose,' Koenig turned to Padre Giovanni. 'You were right, Father.'

There was a sudden burst of firing from outside. Koenig hurried out followed by Brandt and Padre Giovanni and stood at the top of the steps. There was a young paratrooper on the battlement above the gate and Koenig called up to him.

'What is it?'

'It looks as if there are people down there in the forest, Colonel, moving towards Bellona. Major Meyer and his column have turned off the road to go after them.'

There was a renewed burst of heavy firing. Koenig turned to Padre Giovanni. 'I see now, Father. You told the truth because they'd already gone.' He didn't wait for a reply, simply turned to Brandt and said, 'Right, Sergeant-Major, round up the men and follow me at the double.'

For the first time in their long association, Brandt queried an order. 'Look, sir, I don't think in your present state that you're fit to go anywhere.'

'Your opinion is duly noted,' Koenig said. 'Now let's get moving,' and he went down the steps and hurried across the courtyard.

Padre Giovanni watched the last paratrooper double through the gate after him, then turned, hurried to the chapel and started to toll the bell, one deep solemn stroke after another. The sound echoed all the way down the valley to Bellona to where Vito Barbera, already alerted by the gunfire from the forest, stood listening.

Verga and Father Collura hurried across the square to join him. 'What does it mean?' Verga demanded.

'I don't know, but I've just been on the radio and the Americans have landed. Spread the word. Tell everyone to have what weapons they have ready.'

'It will take time,' Verga said.

'Do the best you can.'

They hurried away and Barbera went back inside, climbed up to the coffin room and entered the cubby-hole through the secret entrance. He got down on his knees, prized up a floor-board in one corner and took out a machine pistol and several clips of ammunition, then he went back downstairs.

*   *   *

On emerging from the tunnel on the hillside, Luciano and the others had stopped to dress Carter. They got him into pants and a jacket and Maria and Rosa hurriedly forced his feet into boots. Carter was still in a high fever, but reasonably articulate.

'What's happening?'

'We've been rumbled,' Luciano said. 'We're going to try to make our way down to the village to see what Barbera can do for us. Don't try to talk. Just save your strength and let's get going.'

Savage passed his MI to Rosa and his rucksack. Then he hoisted Carter on his back and they started down the slope. There was a small clearing to cross where the olive terraces ended and the pine trees began. It was when they were half way across that the firing started.

*   *   *

It was Meyer in the lead fieldcar as his column raced up the zig-zag road to the monastery, who saw them first and cried to his driver to halt.

Suslov in the *kubelwagen* at the rear of the small column, stood up, reaching for the heavy machine gun mounted on its swivel and started to fire. The bullets kicked up fountains of dirt, chasing the fugitives into the trees and Maria stumbled and fell.

Luciano reached down, dragging her to her feet and they staggered into the shelter of the trees.

'After them,' Meyer cried, urging his driver on, and the *kubelwagen* left the road and hurtled over the rough ground between the olive terraces.

*   *   *

Miraculously, it was only the heel of Maria's shoe which had been hit and they hurried along the track through the pine trees, following Savage and Rosa.

The trees at that part grew closely together, making it impossible terrain for the vehicles to operate in. After a while, Luciano, pausing to listen, heard voices.

'They're coming on foot,' he said and a burst of machine gun fire cut through the branches overhead.

He fired back quickly, emptying his M1, then rammed in another clip as he ran after the others. There was a crashing in the bushes to the right and one of the Ukrainians appeared, running very fast, his rifle held waist high. He fired twice, kicking up dirt to one side of Savage. Luciano went headlong down the hill and jumped, giving him both feet in the back. The Ukrainian rolled over twice. As he tried to scramble to his feet, Luciano shot him through the head.

Savage was gasping for breath now, lurching from side to side as he ran on, borne down by Carter's weight. He lost his balance and went headlong, Carter sprawling on top of him.

He managed to get to his feet. Carter said weakly, 'Leave me. Save yourselves.'

Luciano passed his M1 to Maria and pulled Carter to his feet. 'Lean on me, Professor. One step in front of the other, that's all it takes. Aren't you the guy who went four miles with a bullet in the lung?'

'Keep moving,' Savage said. 'I'll guard your back.'

He took a couple of hand grenades from the rucksack Rosa was holding and put one in each pocket. Then he reloaded his M1.

'Okay,' he said. 'Get going. They may need you. I'll follow on.'

She shook her head stubbornly. 'No, Savage, I won't leave you.'

There was a rustle in the bushes behind, he turned and fired from the hip and a Ukrainian pitched forward on to his face. Savage gave her a push.

'Get out of it!'

He rammed in another clip, ducking as someone fired over to his left. He fired in reply and there was a cry of pain.

She crouched beside him. 'Please, Savage, we go now.'

He slapped her backhanded across the face. 'Get out of here, you stupid little bitch!'

She recoiled in dismay, genuine hurt on her face then turned and started to crawl away. He reached out, catching her left hand.

'Heh, I love you, don't forget that. Honeymoon in New York, that's a promise.'

He turned, raising the M1 and received a burst of machine gun fire full in the chest that lifted him back off his feet.

There was blood in his mouth and he was choking on it, aware of Rosa screaming; then she was crouching over him, her face the last thing he saw as he died.

She knelt there, holding him in her arms, his blood staining her clothes and they came out of the bushes, four of them, and stood watching her.

One of them laughed harshly. 'Let's see if you know your manners.'

They were all laughing now as they lowered their weapons and moved in on her and Rosa was laughing too as she laid Savage gently on the ground. She reached in his pockets and turned, still laughing, a grenade in each hand. The Ukrainians recoiled in horror, turned to run, already too late.

*   *   *

Luciano and Maria, Carter supported between them, emerged from the pine trees and started across the patch of broken ground leading up to the village. Vito Barbera, from the upper window of the mortuary, saw the Russians moving down through the trees, higher up the slope.

There was sporadic firing and to his dismay, he heard Luciano cry out and saw him go down. Carter reeled against Maria and Barbera leaned out of the window and fired a long burst from his Schmeisser across the open ground. Miraculously, Luciano was on his feet and helping Maria with Carter again. As they reached the edge of the village, two or three Ukrainians ran out of the forest and started across the open ground.

The streets were deserted, everyone indoors, as Luciano and Maria staggered across the square with their burden. They could hear vehicles coming along the road, very close now. Luciano was bleeding profusely from the right leg, limping badly as they turned into the side street leading to the mortuary. Barbera opened the door and hastened to meet them.

*   *   *

Meyer stood in one of the troop carriers in the middle of the square and watched as the Ukrainians went from house-to-house turning everyone out. It was Suslov pausing casually on the corner of the street leading to Barbera's premises to light a cigarette, who noticed blood on the cobbles, a clearly defined trail. He followed it to the steps leading up to the mortuary door. The door was unlocked. He pushed it open, drew the Walther from his holster and moved inside cautiously.

There was more blood on the stone flags of the passage leading to the door at the end. He opened that and found himself in the waiting mortuary. It was totally silent and very still in the dim light and he recoiled at the sight of the corpse of a gnarled old woman in the first coffin on his left.

There was a spot of blood on the floor, another. He carried on, passing several open coffins containing corpses, each one holding the end of the bell pull in stiff fingers.

There was another patch of blood beside an ornate black coffin. He crouched down to examine it and then the hair lifted on the back of his neck as a bell tinkled faintly.

He stood up and peered over the edge of the coffin. The corpse of the man inside seemed peaceful enough, hands folded around an ivory Madonna. It was really very beautiful. Suslov leaned closer to examine it and the corpse's eyes opened. There was a click as the Madonna swung upward in the right hand.

*   *   *

Father Collura stood against the wall of the church facing half a dozen Ukrainians forming a firing squad while the people of Bellona watched. Meyer, standing in one of the *kubelwagens*, nodded, there was a sharp volley and the old priest fell to the ground.

'That's just to show you I mean business,' Meyer called. 'You all know who I'm looking for. I'll give you five minutes to come up with some answers. If you haven't, I'll select two more. Then four and so on. It's your choice.'

Watching from the upper window of the mortuary, Maria said, 'We must do something.'

Barbera said, 'There isn't much we can do. Most of the young men are in the hills. We didn't have time to organise. The whole thing caught us by surprise.'

'What about the American troops?' Luciano said. 'How long before they get here?'

'I don't know what's happening.'

'Then let's try the radio.'

They went out, Luciano limping badly, his left leg bandaged and Maria opened the window in time to hear Meyer say, 'The Englishman, Carter and the woman, Maria Vaughan.'

The people stood there, quiet in the steady rain. He gave an order and two of the Ukrainians moved into the crowd and grabbed a couple of old men.

She didn't really think about it, simply went downstairs, opened the front door and went along the side street into the square. There was a murmur in the crowd as she appeared. She stopped and looked up at Meyer standing there in the *kubelwagen*.

'I am Maria Vaughan, Major,' she said simply. 'You may release these people.'

Meyer gazed down at her. 'And your friends?'

'I cannot help you there. I speak only for myself.'

He looked around him. 'Where is Lieutenant Suslov?'

'I don't know, Major,' one of the sergeants told him. 'Still searching house to house, I think.'

'Very well,' Meyer said. 'Put this woman against the wall.' He looked down at her again. 'Unless, of course, you have changed your mind.'

'I have nothing to say,' she said tranquilly.

Two of the Ukrainians seized her and hustled her across to the wall. They left her there beside the body of Father Collura and another firing squad was hastily formed. She crossed herself, closing her eyes to pray and was not aware of Koenig appearing on the other side of the square, a handful of his paratroopers behind him.

'No!' he called.

They had come from the monastery on foot and he was tired. The pain in his arm was almost unbearable and his face was coated with dried blood. He moved forward, the paratroopers strung out behind him led by Brandt, and halted beside the troop carrier.

'Who is this lady?'

'The Vaughan woman. She refused to tell me where the rest of her people are.'

Koenig called, 'Fraulein Vaughan, would you come here, please.'

'No!' Meyer said violently. 'I will not have it.'

Koenig didn't even bother to look at him. 'I command here, Meyer. What you wish is of little importance.'

'Damn you, Koenig!' Meyer cried, all the pent-up hatred finally overflowing. He pulled out his Walther and shot him twice in the back.

Koenig staggered forward and Maria tried to catch him, half twisting round in an attempt to hold him up. Meyer kept firing in a kind of insane rage, bullets smashing into her, driving her and Koenig down together to lie like lovers, limbs entwined.

*   *   *

The people scattered, running for their homes in panic. Brandt dropped on his knee beside Koenig and gently turned him over. He looked up at Meyer, his face hard, and Meyer reached for the handles of the heavy machine gun on its swivel and swung it to cover Brandt and the paratroopers.

'He was a traitor to the Reich and to the Führer,' he said. 'You hear me? Now stand back, all of you!' He called to his men, 'Mount up and let's get out of here.'

The rest of them scrambled into the other *kubelwagen* and drove quickly away.

18

Luciano and Vito Barbera came out of the mortuary and ran across the square. Luciano dropped on his knees beside Maria. Brandt said, 'She's dead. They're both dead.'

Her face was peaceful, her wounds in the chest and heart. He knelt there for a long moment looking down at her, then gently touched her breast. The blood stained his fingers and he raised them to his mouth.

He stood up, wholly Sicilian now and whispered the ancient formula. 'In this way may I drink the blood of the one who killed you.'

Men had appeared in the square, old and young, armed with everything from shotguns to automatic weapons and Brandt and the remaining paratroopers moved in on each other, faces grim, ready for anything.

A teenage boy came running across the square and stopped before Barbera. 'They've taken the north road.'

'Then that means the monastery. It leads nowhere else.'

Two old women knelt beside Maria to straighten her limbs and one of them took off her shawl to cover the pale face. Luciano was filled with a sense of total despair.

He turned. 'Let's go and get him.' He nodded to the troop carrier. 'Can anyone drive this thing?'

'I can,' Rudi Brandt said.

There was a moment's silence. Luciano said, 'I thought we were supposed to be at war?'

'This is personal.'

Luciano looked at Barbera, who nodded. 'I'll get my truck.'

'Fine.' Luciano turned to Brandt. 'I'll go with you boys. Now let's get moving.'

* * *

They braked to a halt just before the crest of the hill below the main gate. Barbera, who was carrying more than twenty armed men in his old truck, got out and hurried to the troop carrier.

'How are we going to handle it?'

'The troop carrier goes first,' Luciano told him. 'The only way we'll get through those gates. If it works, you come straight in after us and remember Padre Giovanni and the Franciscans are on our side.'

'Okay.' Barbera grinned. 'Do I wish you luck?'

'When did I ever need it?' Luciano slapped Brandt on the shoulder and they drove away.

* * *

When Meyer got out of his fieldcar in the courtyard at Crown of Thorns, there was no one in sight, the whole place unnaturally quiet in the heavy rain. The only visible signs of the action which had taken place were the parachutes draped untidily on the walls or in the courtyard, lifting uneasily in the slight breeze.

* * *

At that moment in the catacombs below, Father Giovanni was supervising the departure of the last of the Franciscans into the tunnel, taking with them the young paratrooper with the broken leg. He gave one last glance around, then followed them in. The wooden throne swung back into its place with its macabre burden.

* * *

Meyer was unable to think clearly. It had all happened so quickly, the rage in him, something that could not be denied. Now he was faced with the appalling consequences.

A sergeant came out of the entrance, ran down the steps and

hurried towards him. 'Not a soul in the place. Quiet as the grave Major.'

'Impossible,' Meyer said.

One of the men on the gate called out, 'Someone's coming, Major.'

Meyer ran out and paused on the bridge over the ditch. From that vantage point the approach road could be seen in its entirety. The half-track troop carrier was coming up fast followed by an old truck. Way behind, a considerable crowd of people were following on foot.

The Ukrainians crowded around him and one of them held a pair of fieldglasses to his eyes. He lowered them and turned to Meyer, bewildered.

'I don't understand. Koenig's paratroopers in the troop carrier and the truck's crammed full of peasants.'

Meyer took the glasses from him and raised them and the troop carrier jumped into focus. Brandt, who he recognized instantly, the rest of his men and Luciano. Barbera was at the wheel of the truck behind and the men with him were armed.

'They've joined forces,' Meyer said. 'They're coming up together. Inside quickly and get the gates closed.' He turned and ran for the courtyard.

*　　*　　*

Meyer was no soldier, never had been, and the Ukrainians ignored him now. Someone closed the gates and slid the retaining bar through its sockets and the rest of them took the two heavy machine guns from the *kublewagen* and carried them up to the battlements above the gate.

They were all up there now and Meyer stood in the centre of the courtyard amongst the billowing parachutes quite alone. There was a Schmeisser in one of the *kubelwagens*. He picked it up, turned, walked away from the gate and mounted the stone steps to the east rampart.

*　　*　　*

Brandt, peering out through the open visor of the troop carrier, said to Luciano, 'Get down here. This could be a hot one.'

Luciano did as he was told. Above them, two of the para-troopers crouched over the heavy machine gun, hanging on as Brandt increased speed, turning into the last stretch, the half-tracks kicking up mud and filth from the road.

The machine guns above the gate started to fire when they had still a hundred yards to go. The armoured plating of the troop carrier took most of the brunt and their own machine gun was returning the fire now, raking the battlements above the gate.

One of the Ukrainians was hit and came over the parapet, dragging a machine gun with him, falling on to the bridge as Brandt roared on, bouncing over the body, the machine gun, hitting the gates at close to sixty miles an hour, tearing them from their hinges.

The troop carrier kept on going, smashing into one of the *kubelwagens*, drifting broadside past another. One of the para-troopers tossed a stick grenade, there was a tremendous ex-plosion as the *kubelwagen*'s petrol tank exploded.

The Ukrainians up on the wall were firing down into the yard, working their Schmeissers furiously and two of them tried to turn the heavy machine gun round. Rudi Brandt ran forward, hurling another stick grenade. It curled lazily through the air exploding above the gate. Two of the Ukrainians fell into the yard and the machine gun followed them.

The second *kubelwagen* exploded, showering burning fuel over a wide area. A dense pall of black smoke drifted across the courtyard.

Luciano, crouched at the side of the troop carrier, snatched up a Schmeisser from a fallen paratrooper. Bullets bounced from the armour plating and he turned and fired instinctively at the battlements on the other side of the courtyard, at the figure crouched up there beside the wall.

Meyer. He emptied the Schmeisser in another long burst, pulled out his Smith and Wesson and ran for the steps leading to the east rampart. He paused at the bottom, peering up through the smoke, fired three times very fast at what might have been a shadow and went up the steps on the run.

★   ★   ★

Below in the courtyard, Barbera and his friends had arrived in strength and there was a confused mêlée of hand to hand fighting in the smoke and rain.

Up there on the ramparts, it was quiet. Smoke drifted eerily and the noise of the battle in the courtyard seemed far away, as if it were happening in another time, another place.

Luciano removed his shoes and went forward cautiously on silent feet, the Smith and Wesson ready. He was at the highest point in the monastery, he knew that, smoke billowing around him. He was aware of the pigeons in their loft, fluttering in alarm, and paused. Then, quite suddenly, a gust of wind lifted across the battlements, dissolving the pall of smoke.

Meyer was standing only a few feet away, covering him with the Schmeisser. 'Drop it!' he said. 'Now!'

'Whatever you say.' Luciano put the Smith and Wesson down carefully on the battlements.

Meyer was surprisingly calm. 'Who are you?'

'Salvatore Lucania but most people call me Luciano.'

Meyer was shocked, it showed in his eyes and his finger slackened on the trigger. The ivory Madonna was ready in Luciano's left hand. As he swung, the blade jumped, catching Meyer under the chin, shearing through the roof of the mouth into the brain.

It took all Luciano's strength to pull the knife free. Meyer staggered back, still alive, a look of astonishment on his face, then he fell backwards over the low parapet.

The pigeons in the loft threshed around in panic. Luciano lifted the latch and opened the screen door and they flocked out, launching into space, climbing above the smoke into the clear rain.

He watched them go, then realized that he was still holding the ivory Madonna. For a moment, he was tempted to throw it out into space, but that would not have been Salvatore Lucania's way, nor Lucky Luciano's.

He kissed the blade, still wet with Meyer's blood, the ritual completion of the oath he had taken in the square, then wiped it clean, closed it and slipped the Madonna into his pocket.

Life for life, blood for blood and no satisfaction in it at all, but then Maria could have told him that, and he turned and went down the steps to the courtyard.

* * *

Maria Vaughan lay in a coffin before the altar of the little church at Bellona, her features relaxed and at peace in death, her wounds covered by a shroud.

Candles flared around her, placed there by the villagers, but now, the place was empty, except for Katerina sitting in the front pew and Don Antonio Luca beside the coffin.

Luciano and Mario Sciara standing in the shadows at the back of the church watched as Luca leaned down to kiss the pale face. Katerina stood up and put an arm around him. They started up the aisle. Sciara opened the door and he and Luciano waited. When he reached them, Luca paused.

'You know what to do, Mario,' he said to Sciara.

'Yes, Capo.'

'Good.'

He turned and looked at Luciano, eyes dark.

Luciano waited, but there was, after all, nothing to say. Katerina tightened her arm around him and they went out and Sciara followed them.

It was very quiet in the church and his footsteps echoed between the walls as Luciano walked down the aisle to the coffin. He stood there looking down at her, suddenly tired. He touched her hand gently. It was cold, hard, no life there at all.

Maybe people come to God when the Devil has no further use for them.

His words to her echoed in his mind and her reply: *No, Mr Luciano. I could never accept that. Never.*

He turned and walked away quickly.

* * *

Harry Carter lay in Vito Barbera's bed at the mortuary, propped up against pillows, still very weak as he sipped the brandy Barbera held for him.

'So, in the end, we got exactly what we wanted.'

Luciano, standing at the window looking down into the square, nodded. 'All over the Cammarata, in every village, every town in Western Sicily, all the way to Palermo, the word is already passing. That Don Antonio Luca is for the Americans.'

'Because a German killed his grand-daughter?'

'Exactly,' Luciano said. 'Blood for blood, an old Sicilian custom. I'd have thought you'd have realized that by now.'

Carter nodded. 'And the paratroopers?'

'We let them clear off in the troop carrier, what's left of them, to take their chances. They took Koenig with them.'

Carter frowned, 'I don't understand.'

'It turned out he was still alive. Badly wounded, but in there with a chance if they can get him to a decent surgeon in time. I should imagine that sergeant major of his will ride over the Devil himself to get him to Palermo.'

Barbera said to Carter, 'You need to eat now. I'll get you some soup.'

He went out. There was a small silence. Carter said to Luciano, 'You could take to the mountains. We could say you were killed in the fighting.'

Luciano grinned. 'Heh, don't tell me I've succeeded in corrupting you completely?' He shook his head. 'No, I'll go back.'

'Why, because the President said that was the way it had to be? He made no promises remember. You could be back inside for years.'

'Well, you take a chance every day of your life.'

Luciano walked to the window, opened it and leaned out into the rain, breathing in its freshness.

Across the valley from Crown of Thorns high up on its crag, the bells started to peal.

19

And so, the Mafia card was played and played to the full. In a single night, two thirds of the Italian soldiers defending the vital positions overlooking the main road through the Cammarata to Palermo, deserted. Even their commander was detained by Mafia trickery and handed over to Allied forces.

German units in the area, left in a hopelessly vulnerable position, had no other choice but to pull out. American forces raced north, reached Palermo in only seven days from the initial landing in what General George Patton was to describe as the fastest *blitzkreig* in history.

Mussolini was toppled from power by a war-weary nation on July 24, and in spite of spirited resistance by German forces, the whole of Sicily was in Allied hands by August 17.

Charles Lucky Luciano returned to Great Meadow Penitentiary and appeared before a State Parole Board in 1946. The circumstances of the proceedings are still shrouded in controversy, but in February of that year, Governor Dewey commuted his sentence and Luciano was sent to Ellis Island and deported.

Nearly sixteen years later, on January 25, 1962, he died of a heart attack at Capodichino airport near Naples. The body was held at the chapel of the English Cemetery until arrangements could be made to have it transported to America.

For a while, there was considerable interest and many visitors. By the third day it had slackened off a little and the young reporter and photographer from Associated Press were beginning to think about packing it in when a small tour bus appeared. Fourteen or fifteen people got out, and went to the

entrance of the chapel, mainly American women chattering amongst themselves.

'More tourists,' the young reporter said sourly. 'Five hundred lira a time to gaze at a corpse. I reckon that's about it. Put your gear in the car and let's get out of here.'

He went to the porch where the door stood open and looked inside. The women were gathered at the rail peering over at the coffin and the reporter noticed a grey-haired man in his sixties wearing a black overcoat, standing at the back of them.

They turned and came down the aisle. The grey-haired man paused, raising his collar against the cold, suddenly breaking into a paroxysm of coughing.

'Are you all right?' the reporter asked, concerned.

'Smoker's cough, that's all. Been trying to stop for years.'

'You didn't know him?'

'Who, Luciano?' Professor Harry Carter smiled. 'Did anybody?' and he turned and went down the path to where the rest of the tourists were boarding the coach.

THE END